Gotthard Vi

Clark's Foreign Theological Library

Vol. XXIV

SALZWASSER
VERLAG

Gotthard Victor Lechler, Karl Gerok

Clark's Foreign Theological Library

Vol. XXIV

Reprint of the original, first published in 1864.

1st Edition 2022 | ISBN: 978-3-75259-184-2

Verlag (Publisher): Salzwasser Verlag GmbH, Zeilweg 44, 60439 Frankfurt, Deutschland
Vertretungsberechtigt (Authorized to represent): E. Roepke, Zeilweg 44, 60439 Frankfurt, Deutschland
Druck (Print): Books on Demand GmbH, In de Tarpen 42, 22848 Norderstedt, Deutschland

CLARK'S

FOREIGN

THEOLOGICAL LIBRARY.

THIRD SERIES.
VOL. XXIV.

Lechler and Gerok's Theological and Homiletical Commentary on the Acts of the Apostles.

VOL. II.

EDINBURGH

MDCCCLXIV.

THEOLOGICAL AND HOMILETICAL COMMENTARY

ON THE

ACTS OF THE APOSTLES,

SPECIALLY DESIGNED AND ADAPTED FOR THE USE OF MINISTERS AND STUDENTS.

FROM THE GERMAN OF

G. V. LECHLER, D.D., AND K. GEROK.

EDITED BY

J. P. LANGE, D.D.

TRANSLATED BY

REV. PATON J. GLOAG,
MINISTER OF BLANTYRE.

VOLUME II.

EDINBURGH:

1

MDCCCLXIV.

THE ACTS OF THE APOSTLES.

PART FOURTH.

PROPAGATION OF THE CHURCH OF CHRIST AMONG THE GENTILES BY PAUL, THE APOSTLE OF THE GENTILES, IN THREE MISSIONARY JOURNEYS, FROM EACH OF WHICH HE RETURNS TO JERUSALEM, AND FOSTERS AND PRESERVES THE UNION BETWEEN THE GENTILE CHRISTIANS AND THE ORIGINAL JEWISH CHRISTIAN CHURCH (CHAP. XIII.–XXI. 16).

SECTION I.

THE FIRST MISSIONARY JOURNEY OF PAUL, IN COMPANY WITH BARNABAS, TO THE ISLAND OF CYPRUS AND THE ASIATIC PROVINCES OF PAMPHYLIA AND PISIDIA (CHAP. XIII. AND XIV.).

A.

Delegation of Paul and Barnabas to the Missionary Work from the Church of Antioch, in consequence of an intimation by the Holy Ghost.

Chap. xiii. 1–3.

1 But there were at Antioch, in the Church there, prophets and teachers;
as Barnabas, and Symeon called Niger, and Lucius of Cyrene, and Manaen
who had been brought up with Herod the tetrarch, and Saul. 2 And as
they performed divine worship to the Lord and fasted, the Holy Ghost said,

Separate to Me Barnabas and Saul to the work to which I have called them.
3 Then they fasted, and prayed, and laid their hands on them, and sent them away.

Ver. 1. After ἦσαν δὲ the textus receptus has τινες, which is wanting in the Codd. A.B.D., in several cursive MSS. and old versions, and is doubtless a spurious addition, designed to intimate that those named were only a portion of the prophets and teachers of the Church of Antioch.

EXEGETICAL EXPLANATIONS.

1. We now lose sight for a time of the Church of Jerusalem and the apostles, and in place of Jerusalem, Antioch, comparatively speaking, becomes the centre of Church history. Indeed the two chapters (xiii. and xiv.) which compose the first section of the Fourth Part form an independent and self-contained memoir from an Antiochean point of view. And it has, not without plausibility, been supposed that Luke has here made use of an original document and inserted it in his book, which document may have proceeded from the Church of Antioch (Meyer, Bleek, Studien und Kritiken, 1836, p. 1043), or may have belonged to a biography of Barnabas (Schwanbeck), or may have been a missionary narrative of their journey which Barnabas and Saul had made (Olshausen).

2. *But there were at Antioch.*—Ver. 1 in particular reads as if it belonged to a special history of the Church at Antioch. Its prophets and teachers are mentioned by name: προφῆται, those who, as the direct organs of the Holy Ghost, and in a state of inspiration, gave declarations and utterances to the Church; διδάσκαλοι, those who voluntarily and deliberately devoted themselves to the instruction of others. We are unable to distinguish who of the five persons mentioned were prophets, and who were teachers. The corresponding particles τε—καί—καί and τε—καί (Meyer) afford no sufficient ground of distinction. Neither does the circumstance that Barnabas received his name from the apostles on account of his prophetic gifts prove anything, for he was placed first on the list because he was at that time the most important and distinguished person at Antioch; whilst Saul, as the last who had come in connection with the Church, and as still in retirement, is mentioned last. Of the three intervening persons, except what is here said, nothing is known. Symeon called Niger. Lucius, whose identity with the Lucius mentioned in Rom. xvi. 21 is wholly uncertain: from

the circumstance that he is mentioned as a native of Cyrene, it has been supposed that he might have been among the first preachers of the Gospel at Antioch, for Luke has described them as men of Cyprus and Cyrene (chap. xi. 19). Also nothing more is known about Manaen. The Herod with whom he had been brought up was not Herod Agrippa II., who at the death of his father, Herod Agrippa I., was only seventeen (Jos. Ant. xix. 9, 1); because a companion of his would be much too young to be at this time a teacher of the Church. From this it follows that Herod Antipas, the ruler in the time of Jesus, and who beheaded John the Baptist, must have been intended. In that case, we must suppose Manaen to have been a man from forty-five to fifty years of age. Σύντροφος may signify *cum aliquo nutritus*, a foster-brother, according to which Manaen's mother would have been the nurse of Herod Antipas (Vulgate, Kuinoel, Olshausen); but usually the word has only the signification of a play-fellow or comrade. Be this as it may, it is remarkable that a man who had been brought up at a royal court, and that court the court of Herod the Great, should have become a Christian pastor and teacher.

3. *As they worshipped the Lord.*—Luke now relates how the intimation of the Spirit to appoint Barnabas and Saul to the missionary work was communicated to the Church. It was while the Church was engaged in divine worship, and fasted, that the Holy Ghost gave the order to that effect. Λειτουργεῖν is in classical writers used to express the performance of civil offices and duties; in the Septuagint, and in Heb. x. 11, the priestly ministrations in the temple of Jehovah; and here evidently it expresses the performance of divine worship. The subject αὐτῶν is not to be limited to the five prophets and teachers mentioned in ver. 1, but is to be extended to the whole Christian congregation at Antioch, because the command ἀφορίσατε (according to the whole section, see chap. xiv. 26–28) is addressed not simply to the teachers, but to the whole congregation, and therefore αὐτῶν must also be referred to the congregation. The Holy Ghost spoke, namely, by one of the prophets, "Separate to Me Barnabas and Saul," namely, to a holy service. 'Αφορίζειν contains in itself the idea of sanctity and consecration, as קָדַשׁ always includes the idea of separation from a common and daily use. The work to which the Holy

Ghost called them is not expressly named. It was doubtless already known that Saul was called to preach the Gospel to the heathen (chap. ix. 15).

4. *They fasted.*—That the Church well understood this revelation of the Spirit, is proved by the immediate ordination and mission of Barnabas and Saul. With fasting and prayer they laid their hands on them, commended them—their journey and business—to the protection and grace of God, and sent them away.

DOGMATICAL AND ETHICAL THOUGHTS.

1. The Redeemer, only as the Crucified, has become also Lord and King, the Exalted. Even so, His Church always exists under the sign of the cross, *hoc signo vincet.* The first severe onset on the Church, when Stephen was stoned, served to the spread of the Gospel in Palestine, and, indeed, directly brought about its transition to the Gentiles. So now, in consequence of the second severe persecution, whose victim was the Apostle James, and which Peter escaped only by a miracle, the mission to the Gentiles comes into full operation. "To conquer by yielding."

2. The apostleship of Paul, in point of fact, begins with this mission. Here, for the first time, he was sent forth (*ἀπόστολος*). He did not offer himself, nor resolve to go of his own accord, but he was called, *rite vocatur*, chosen and sent, and that by divine authority. Jesus Himself, during His earthly life, chose and sent the twelve provisionally (Matt. x.), but after His resurrection, He fully and ultimately empowered and sent them; yet they must wait for their preparation by the Holy Ghost, before they betake themselves to action. Even so, Saul was called by Jesus Christ in His state of exaltation, after His ascension; and the Lord Himself had declared to him that He would send him to the Gentiles, and to Israel. But now, only after a sufficient time of internal growth and faithful exercise, of humble activity in quiet seclusion, he is sent, and his great course as the Apostle of the Gentiles discloses itself. It is the Holy Ghost who calls him and Barnabas to the work. But He does this by means of human instrumentality. It was one or other of the Christian prophets at Antioch, in whose soul the Spirit was, and by whose mouth He declared that Barnabas and Saul should be separated to the work. And it was the Church to

whom this command was addressed, and who, in the obedience of faith, with prayer and fasting, ordained these two with the imposition of hands, and forthwith sent them away. Considered in a human point of view, Barnabas and Saul were missionaries of the Church of Antioch; that Church was the association or authority by whom they were commissioned and sent. But, in point of fact, the Church of Antioch was only the instrument in carrying into effect, and in accomplishing the previous internal call of the Redeemer and Lord of the Church. The caller and the sender was the Lord Himself, who by His Spirit made known His will to the Church, and then by the Church sent forth the missionaries. And only this certainty of a divine call and mission by the Lord could confer on them the joyfulness and the confidence requisite for their work. The work of Christ proceeds gradually, in the ordinary course of congregational and ecclesiastical development. This was remarkably the case with regard to Saul. As he was arrested and awakened directly by the Redeemer, but his conversion completed by a disciple of Jesus, a simple member of the Church at Damascus; so he originally received his call to be the Apostle of the Gentiles from the Lord Himself, but it was realized and carried into effect by the Church at Antioch. This concurrence and interpenetration of the divine and human, this interposition of the divine will by means of human instruments, takes place at the call and ordination to the ordinary ministerial office, as well as to the missionary work; and only this *rite vocari*, inside of ecclesiastical ordinances, is a support to true ministerial joyfulness, and an incentive to true ministerial fidelity.

HOMILETICAL HINTS.

But there were at Antioch, prophets and teachers (ver. 1). A Church is now regarded as well provided, if it has many buildings of stone, temples, endowments, and beautiful vestments. The Church of Antioch had none of all these, but it had prophets and teachers, who are now commonly wanting (Gossner).—*Manaen, who had been brought up with Herod the tetrarch.* Two are often brought up together, nourished at the same breast, of whom the one is taken and the other left (Starke).

And as they fasted, the Holy Ghost said (ver. 2). The Holy Ghost comes not into a full belly and a distracted spirit. A full belly is no diligent student and no spiritual worshipper (Gossner).—*Separate to me Barnabas and Saul to the work to which I have called them.* The divine choice, the supply of gifts, preparation by manifold providential dealings, awakened willingness, precede and constitute the internal call. The call of the Church, separation and confirmation, follow: these constitute the external call (Rieger).—*Separate them to Me*, that they may live, labour, think, and strive entirely for My service, will, and pleasure. Teachers ought to be God's peculiar people, chosen and separated only to please Him (Apost. Past.).—*Wherefore Barnabas and Saul?* All God's servants must be ready, when the Lord will use them. But the divine call and command alone is the hint which they follow. Whoever is called, let him not despise him who remains; and whoever must wait, let him not envy him who receives an office (Apost. Past.).—The meanest office, imposed on one according to the divine call, is worthy to be received: the greatest dignity is not worth running after (Rieger).

Then they fasted (ver. 3). Thus no feast at their going away, but a fast. Now-a-days we are commonly accustomed, even in the concerns of the kingdom of God, to observe beforehand a feast of joy, therefore mourning feasts come afterwards. (Williger, who adds the charming narrative of the ordination and mission of John Williams, the Apostle of the South Sea Islands.)

On the whole section (vers 1–3).—*The Lord sends labourers to His harvest.* 1. The harvest which He has in view. 2. The labourers whom He chooses. 3. The mission, how it is to be conducted (Lisco).—How the messengers of the Gospel should be sent to the heathen. 1. On the call and intimation of the Lord: *a.* Those who send must be moved, not by their own spirit, but by the Holy Ghost. *b.* Those who are to be sent must be chosen, not according to the dictates of human prudence, but according to the evident marks of divine grace in them. 2. With holy behaviour: *a.* Those who send should fast—abstain from all superfluities, in order to have enough for the wants of the heathen. *b.* They should pray: the prayer of the sender co-operates mightily with the word of the preachers. *c.* The messengers should depart with the imposition of hands; regularly ordained, if they are to have an orderly ministry for the salvation of the heathen and the advancement of the

Church (Lisco).—*The first missionary ordination at Antioch.* 1. Why did the first missionaries proceed from Antioch? *a.* On account of the peculiarly flourishing condition of that Church. *b.* According to the peculiar will of Divine Wisdom. 2. The appointment of the first missionaries: *a.* What men were appointed. *b.* How their ordination took place (Lisco).—*An internal and an external call pertain to the ministerial office.* 1. The internal call. 2. The external call (Lisco).—*Christianity has a missionary power in itself.* 1. Where the Church is living, missions must be flourishing. 2. Where missions are living, the Church must be flourishing (Lisco).—*The best travelling attendance for a missionary on his departure.* 1. The divine call concerning him. 2. The impulse of the Spirit within him. 3. The prayers of the Church behind him. 4. The sighing of the heathen world before him.—*The blessed bond of union between the Church at home and its missionaries abroad.* 1. The blessing which the missionaries receive from home in spiritual and bodily gifts, ordination, prayer. 2. The blessing which flows back to home from the missionaries abroad: by exhortation to supplication, call to praise God, invigoration of faith, and vivification of love.—*Wherein consists the strength of the missionary work?* 1. In the call of God which it follows. 2. In the fidelity of the labourers, whom it sends. 3. In the prayers of the Church, on which it relies.—*How the Church* must begin its enterprises, in order that they may be blessed. 1. Not with worldly computation, but from the impulse of the Spirit. 2. Not with a precipitous shout of triumph, but with humble prayer. 3. Not trusting to human names, be they even called Barnabas and Saul, but in the name of the living God, on whose blessing all things depend.

B.

Journey to Cyprus. Results of the Labours of Barnabas and Saul in that Island.

Chap. xiii. 4–12.

4 Now they, having been sent forth by the Holy Ghost, went down to
Seleucia; and from that they sailed to Cyprus. 5 And when they arrived
at Salamis, they preached the word of God in the synagogues of the Jews;
and they had also John as an attendant. 6 But when they had traversed

the whole island unto Paphos, they found a man, who was a sorcerer and
false prophet, a Jew, named Barjesus, 7 Who was with the proconsul,
Sergius Paulus, an intelligent man. The same called for Barnabas and
Saul, and desired to hear the word of God. 8 Then Elymas, the sorcerer
(for so is his name interpreted), withstood them, and sought to turn the
proconsul from the faith. 9 But Saul (who also is called Paul), filled with
the Holy Ghost, looked sharply on him, and said, 10 "O thou, who art
full of all subtilty and all levity, thou child of the devil and enemy of all
righteousness, wilt thou not cease to pervert the right ways of the Lord?
11 And now, behold, the hand of the Lord is upon thee, and thou wilt be
blind, and not see the sun for a certain time." And immediately there fell
upon him a mist and a darkness, and he went about seeking some to lead
him by the hand. 12 When the proconsul saw what was done, he believed,
being astonished at the doctrine of the Lord.

Ver. 4. οὗτοι is not so well attested as αὐτοί.

Ver. 6. ὅλην before τὴν νῆσον is omitted in the textus receptus, but is sufficiently attested: it might have appeared superfluous.—Ἄνδρα before τινά also appeared superfluous, on which account it was omitted in the textus receptus on the authority of some MSS.: it is, however, to be retained as genuine.

EXEGETICAL EXPLANATIONS.

1. *Now having been sent forth.*—We are not informed by Luke what induced Barnabas and Saul to select the island of Cyprus and the Asiatic provinces of Pamphylia and Pisidia, as the aim of their journey. Without doubt they allowed themselves to be led by circumstances as they occurred, in connection with the principle that they would first think on what was nearest. Now Cyprus was not only geographically near, but also near to them, in so far as it was the native country of Barnabas (chap. iv. 36); besides, an opportunity of journeying there might soonest present itself. Their way led them from Antioch, down the Orontes to the convenient port of Seleucia, distant about three or four geographical (German) miles, and not far from the mouth of the river. Here they embarked and sailed to the island of Cyprus, on whose eastern shore was the city of Salamis, with its convenient haven. Here the two messengers of the Gospel landed, accompanied by a third in a subordinate position (ὑπηρέτης), John named Mark, whom they had taken with them from Jerusalem to Antioch (chap. xii. 12, 25). From Salamis they traversed the whole island, which has a considerable area (about 300 German square miles), and at that time possessed a number of populous and wealthy cities. At length

they stopped at Paphos (New Paphos), a sea-port on the west side of the island, and at that time the residence of the Roman proconsul. From Paphos, they again left the island.

2. *And when they arrived at Salamis.*—Luke describes the labours of Barnabas and Saul by three traits: 1. Preaching the Gospel in the Jewish synagogues. 2. The encounter with the sorcerer Barjesus. 3. The conversion of the Roman proconsul, Sergius Paulus.

Luke mentions very summarily that they preached the Gospel in the synagogues of the Jews. Where? We must, first of all, think of Salamis; but we may not limit this notice exclusively to that city, because, although it was of considerable size, it would hardly have more than one synagogue. And as Barnabas was a native of Cyprus, so it is highly probable that he and Saul would preach the Gospel of the Messiah and Redeemer who had already appeared, first of all to the Jews, who resided in great numbers in that island.

The encounter with the sorcerer Barjesus took place at Paphos. This man, as it appears, gave himself the name of Elymas,—an Arabic word from the same root as the Turkish title Ulema,—and thus gave himself out to be a wise man, that is, an oriental magian. The opinion concerning him is contained in the epithet, a false prophet. This man had acquired influence with the proconsul, and was in his company; and when Sergius Paulus had sent for Barnabas and Saul in order to hear them, Elymas, fearing lest he should lose the confidence of the proconsul, withstood their words, and sought to perplex (*διαστρέψαι*) the Roman, and draw him from the faith. Then was Saul filled with the Holy Ghost: the Spirit gave him a sudden insight into the man, enabled him to discern the innermost state of his soul, and filled him with a holy indignation, which at first showed itself by a penetrating and steady look (*ἀτενίσας εἰς αὐτόν*), and forthwith in the words of reproof. These words unveil, first of all, the spiritual condition of the sorcerer (*Ὦ—δικαιοσύνης*): full of all subtilty and wickedness, and hostile to all righteousness, that is, to everything that is right and pleasing to God, a child of the devil (*υἱὲ διαβόλου* in contrast to the name Barjesus, and by which also is expressed that such a disposition proceeded from the sworn enemy of all that is divine and good). Secondly, the reproof censures the opposition to God of his present conduct, *οὐ παύσῃ—εὐθείας*: the ways of God lead straight to salvation and blessedness; but he thwarts them as much as he can, and seeks to divert them from this end, in order that the proconsul should give no credit to the word of God, and should not attain to salvation. Thirdly, he announces in ver. 11 the divine punishment of temporal blindness: *χεὶρ κυρίου*, the punitive power of God. Saul expressly declares that he shall be blind only for a certain season, and thus not for ever. This declaration was fulfilled on the spot: immediately there fell upon him a mist, and soon complete darkness.

3. The conversion of the proconsul, Sergius Paulus. Barnabas and Saul met with this man in Paphos. Under Augustus, the island of Cyprus was for a time an imperial province, when it would be governed by a prætor; but Augustus restored it to the people (Strabo, xvii. 810; Dio. Cass. liii. 12, liv. 4), and from that time it was governed, as all senatorial provinces were, by proconsuls. The entirely incidental notice of Luke, that the highest authority in the island was an *ἀνθύπατος*, thus strikingly agrees with history, and with the coins of the reign of Claudius; whilst, before these proofs were taken notice of, it was for a long time supposed that Luke, in using the title proconsul, had committed a mistake, or that he did not know the exact import of that appellation (see Hackett's Commentary). The proconsul at this time, Sergius Paulus, unknown in classical writings, is described as *ἀνὴρ συνετός*: this he may have been, notwithstanding that for a time he lent an ear to the Jewish sorcerer. He showed at least his sagacity in desiring, of his own accord, the acquaintance of Barnabas and Saul. Finally, he attained to the faith, partly because he was an eye-witness of the actual and sudden judgment on Elymas, and partly by the positive impression of the doctrine of Christ, which filled him with astonishment.

4. *But Saul, who also is called Paul.*—For the first time the name Paul along with Saul occurs, and henceforth the name Saul is no more mentioned. Even as from chap. vii. 57 to chap. xiii. 7 he is constantly called by his Hebrew name Saul, so from this onwards he is only called by his Roman name Paul. This cannot be accidental, as Heinrichs thinks (on the mention of Sergius Paulus, it occurred to Luke that Saul also was called Paul); but it must be designed and intentional. There are various suppositions as to what that intention was.

The oldest, and also the latest most approved supposition, is that Luke here introduces the name, because the apostle from this event, and in memory of the conversion of Sergius Paulus, received his name Paul. So Jerome: *a primo ecclesiæ spolio, proconsule Sergio Paulo, victoriæ suæ trophæa retulit, erexitque vexillum, ut Paulus diceretur e Saulo.* So also Laurentius Valla, Bengel, Olshausen, Meyer, Baumgarten, Ewald. Whether it be supposed, with Jerome, that the apostle adopted this name himself, or, as Meyer thinks, that other Christians called him so in memory of the remarkable conversion of his first convert. But were this so, we would have expected that Luke would have informed us: he does not do this, and indeed introduces the name, not in direct connection with the conversion of the proconsul, but in connection with the severe rebuke pronounced on the sorcerer; and indeed (which is not usually considered) in connection with the significant precedence of the apostle before Barnabas. Hitherto Luke has represented Barnabas as the chief person; but here, not Barnabas, but Saul steps forward, taking the lead in word and action; as also in ver. 16 and the following verses: in ver. 13, the whole company is named after Paul as the principal person (*οἱ περὶ Παῦλον*); and henceforth, as a rule, it is said "Paul and Barnabas" (chap. xiii. 46, 50, etc.), and it occurs as an exception, when Barnabas is placed before Paul. It therefore appears that the name Paul stands in connection with the independent prominence and work of the apostle; and certainly it is not unintentionally and accidentally that Luke, at the same time when he first introduces the new name, observes that Paul was filled with the Holy Ghost. Accordingly, at this critical moment an internal progress and a decided elevation by the Spirit of Christ occurred to him, by means of which, Paul, who hitherto had remained passive, stepped forward, working independently and taking precedence of Barnabas; and thus in connection with this, and not precisely in connection with the conversion of the proconsul, stands the constant use by Luke of this name, which the Apostle of the Gentiles also uses personally of himself. By this certainly it is not explained when and where the apostle received his Roman name. Possibly he had it at his birth in the capacity of a Roman citizen; but in his pharisaical period, and also in the first years after his conversion, he used only the Hebrew name Saul; whereas during his career as the Apostle of the Gentiles, he preferred the Roman name Paul.

DOGMATICAL AND ETHICAL THOUGHTS.

The encounter of the Apostle Paul with the sorcerer Barjesus took place from the fulness of the Holy Ghost. 1. The penetrating look into the inmost soul of the sorcerer was, in point of fact, a gift of the Spirit of God. Paul had not at an earlier period discerned him. How could he, in consequence of a short meeting, see into the bottom of his disposition without divine illumination? And he accused him justly. If the man had been a heathen magian, his spiritual condition and guilt might not have been so bad as the apostle asserted. But the more the knowledge of the true God and His ways, of His counsel and commands, was in his power as a Jew, the more decidedly must his character have been averted from all truth and righteousness, the more must he have been an enemy of the kingdom of God, when with such craft and sophistry he sought to pervert the ways of God. 2. Further, the Spirit of God and of Christ displays itself in the announcement of the punishment. Here is not the spirit of an Elias, who commanded fire to fall from heaven, and who slew the prophets of Baal. Here is not carnal zeal, which so easily mingles itself with righteous indignation. There is moderation, forbearance, and compassion in the procedure. The apostle reveals to the perverted spirit that he will be blind, but not for ever,—on the contrary, only for a season. Thus the prospect is indirectly opened up to him of a termination of the punishment, provided he would cease to pervert the ways of God (οὐ παύσῃ, ver. 10). This is the Spirit of Christ, who came not to destroy men's lives, but to save them.

HOMILETICAL HINTS.

They being sent forth by the Holy Ghost (ver. 4). This is here emphatically repeated, because in this consists the ground of all the blessed providences, labours, and miracles, which are mentioned in what follows (Apost. Past.).—*They repaired to Seleucia, and from that sailed to Cyprus.* With the true servants of God, all the steps of their lives are not only important, but also blessed. The eyes of God watch over them, and direct their goings from place to place in the right way. It is not forgotten by the Spirit of God, where they wander. It is not the fame of the place, nor the importance of their stations; but their conduct in following the call of God as faithful and obedient servants, remaining in the guidance of the Holy Ghost, and honestly performing their daily work,—these are the things which preserve all the steps of their lives in blessed remembrance. A blessing also attends the footsteps of the faithful servants of Christ, even where they only preach as sojourners and as strangers: even so was it with Jesus, who in all His journeys and on every opportunity left a blessing behind (Apost. Past.).

They preached the word in the synagogues of the Jews (ver. 6). Salvation was to proceed from the Jews. The public schools of the Jews gave the most inoffensive opportunity of delivering a discourse. When we find before us an open door, we must use it and work while it is day (Rieger).

They journeyed through the whole island unto Paphos (ver. 6), with its wanton and vicious worship of Venus. In such a stronghold of Satan, did the ambassadors of Christ break ground. The prince of this world certainly defies the ambassadors with this taunt: I am here before you! Thus here in the person of the sorcerer Barjesus (Rieger).

Who was with Sergius Paulus, an intelligent man (ver. 7). To be prudent and to be a Christian agree well together. The truth of God in the Gospel may be looked at straight in the face by men of understanding (Rieger).—This is intelligence, when one is eager to learn the word of God (Starke).—Sergius Paulus was an intelligent man, and yet he could allow himself to be bewitched by Barjesus. Not only has reason weak eyes, but the peculiar witchcraft of a deceiver consists in this, that it blinds the eyes of reason; therefore we see so many great minds so greatly ensnared by the love of the darkness (Apost. Past.).

And sought to turn the proconsul from the faith (ver. 8). The great have always people about them who seek to turn them from good, and suggest evil to them; but they have not always apostles who guard them against the evil, 1 Sam. x. 3 (Quesnel).

But Saul, who is also called Paul, filled with the Holy Ghost, looked on him (ver. 9). Whoever is in his own eyes a Paul, that is to say, weak and little, is to others a Saul, that is, desired and beloved (Starke).—As generals receive honourable titles from the places of their victories, so has Saul received the name, which as an apostle he bears, from the first trophy which he has won for Christ. But he himself has still more pleasure in this exchange of his name, because Paul signifies "little" (Eph. iii. 8; 2 Cor. xii. 9). He had his Hebrew name in common with the king from the same tribe, who was taller by a head than all the people; and as the same persecuted David, the man according to God's own heart, so had Saul, when he towered above all others in pharisaical pride, persecuted Jesus, the Son of David (Besser).—*And said, O full of all subtilty.* This is something else than that mere scolding which the heat of passion produces. A teacher, though he has, by reason of his office and conscience, to rebuke, should examine well whether he is in proper composure of mind, and whether he can speak and act as in the sight of God, and from the fulness of the Holy Ghost (Apost. Past.).

Thou child of the devil, and enemy of all righteousness (ver. 10). Word for word, and blow for blow, Paul tears the mask from his countenance and discovers to him his spiritual condition. "Child of the devil," in contrast to "Bar (son) Jesus." "Full of all subtilty and mischief," in contrast to "Elymas" (a wise man). "Thou enemy of all righteousness and perverter of the ways of God," because he called himself a prophet of God, and thus a revealer of the true way of salvation (Williger).

Behold, the hand of the Lord is upon thee (ver. 11). Not as with the true servants of God to enlighten and strengthen, but to blind and paralyze, though only for a season; for in the spirit of the Gospel it was to be a chastisement to lead to righteousness, not a condemnation and rejection.—The punishment was, 1. in correspondence with the transgression—he who blinded others is himself blinded; 2. striking and convincing for the spectators; 3. with all its severity, conducive to amendment by an intimation of the divine mercy. Paul himself had at his conversion been blind for a season, and knew from his own experience how profitable this darkness was for internal collection and composure of mind (Apost. Past.).

When the proconsul saw what was done (ver. 12). The fall of one must serve for the elevation of another (Starke).—The judgment upon Elymas placed Sergius Paulus at liberty from his seductive powers, but the doctrine of the Lord must convey the appropriate seed and root for faith (Rieger).—The soul of the meanest slave in Paphos was certainly not less valuable than the soul of the governor; yet it signified something to the apostle, that the first of those called by his preaching was one of those few noble who hear the word of God, 1 Cor. i. 26. His commission was to bear the name of Christ before kings (chap. ix. 15), and Sergius Paulus represented the royal government in the country (Apost. Past.).

On the whole section (vers. 4–12).—*The first missionary ship.* 1. Its bold crew: the great Paul, the noble Barnabas, the youthful Mark. 2. Its fresh wind: the east wind filled the sails, the Holy Ghost inspired the teachers. 3. Its favourable anchorage: the renowned Cyprus, with its natural beauties and sinful abominations. 4. Its great prizes: the sorcerer vanquished, the governor converted.—*The first missionary intelligence, an emblem of all succeeding;* representing the missionary work,—1. In its manifold courses: externally, Seleucia and Cyprus, by sea and by land; internally, to Jews and Gentiles. 2. In its severe contests: with heathen vices—the worship of Venus at Paphos; with heathen superstition—the sorcerer Elymas. 3. In its blessed victories: the powers of darkness are overthrown (Elymas); souls are gained (Sergius Paulus).—*Paul in Paphos, or the preaching of the cross in its power to conquer the world.* It conquers: 1. The sinful lusts of the world: in the lascivious myrtle and rose groves of Venus, the apostle plants the cross of Christ, as the symbol of repentance and of the crucifixion of the flesh. 2. The false wisdom of the world: the deceits of Elymas, the sorcerer, dissolve before the light of evangelical grace and truth. 3. The power and weapons of the world: the Roman proconsul surrenders as a prisoner to the word of God.—*How before the heavenly light of the Gospel all the delusive and seductive arts of the world dissolve.* 1. The enchantment of the world's lusts (Cyprus with its vineyards and altars to Venus). 2. The enchantment of the world's wisdom (Elymas with his deceits). 3. The enchantment of the world's power (Sergius Paulus, the Roman proconsul).—*Sergius Paulus, the first great trophy of the great Apostle of the Gentiles.* 1. Taken from the midst of the hostile camp: a Roman, a man of power, a man of education. 2. Wrested from a crafty possessor: Elymas the sorcerer, as the representative of the falsely praised art of human sophistry. 3. As a permanent ornament to the apostle, prefixed to his now prevailing name Paul, whether he adopted it on this occasion for the first time, or whether he only then rightly merited it.—The Gospel, the savour of life unto life to the one (Sergius Paulus), and of death unto death to the other (Elymas).—*How a true servant of God uses his office of reproof.* 1. Not in carnal passion, but in the Holy Ghost (ver. 9). 2. Not with worldly weapons, but with the sword of the word, by which he discloses the evil state of the heart (ver. 10), and announces the judgment of God (ver. 11). 3. Not for death and condemnation, but for warning and for the salvation of souls (ver. 11).

C.

Continuation of the Journey. Labours and Sufferings at Antioch in Pisidia.

Chap. xiii. 13–52.

1. *Journey through Pamphylia to Antioch in Pisidia* (vers. 13, 14).

13 But after Paul and they who were with him had sailed from Paphos,
they came to Perga in Pamphylia. But John separated from them, and
returned to Jerusalem. 14 But they proceeded from Perga, and came to
Antioch in Pisidia.

2. *The Missionary Discourse of Paul at Antioch* (vers. 15–44).

Here they went on the Sabbath into the synagogue, and sat down.
15 And after the reading of the law and the prophets, the rulers of the synagogue sent to them, saying, Brethren, if ye have a word of exhortation
to this people, say on. 16 Then Paul stood up, and beckoning with his
hand, said, Men of Israel, and ye who fear God, hearken. 17 The God of
this people chose our fathers, and exalted the people when they were sojourners in Egypt, and with a high arm led them out of it. 18 And about
forty years He bore them, nourishing them in the wilderness. 19 And He
destroyed seven nations in the land of Canaan, and divided their land among
them as an inheritance. 20 And after that He gave them judges, about the
space of four hundred and fifty years, until Samuel the prophet. 21 And
afterward they desired a king; and God gave them Saul, the son of Cis, a
man of the tribe of Benjamin, for the space of forty years. 22 And when
He had removed him, He raised up to them David for a king; to whom also
He bare witness, and said, I have found David, the son of Jesse, a man after
My own heart, who will do all My will. 23 Of this man's seed has God,

according to the promise, brought to the people of Israel, Jesus to be a Saviour; 24 John having preached before His entrance the baptism of repentance to all the people of Israel. 25 And as John fulfilled his course, he said, For whom do you take me? I am not He: but, behold, after me He cometh, whose sandals I am not worthy to loose.

26 Men and brethren, sons of the race of Abraham, and those among you who fear God, to you has the word of this salvation been sent. 27 For the inhabitants of Jerusalem, and their rulers, have not known Him, and have fulfilled by their sentence the voices of the prophets, which are read every Sabbath; 28 And without finding any cause of death in Him, they desired Pilate that He should be slain. 29 And when they had fulfilled all that was written of Him, they took Him down from the tree, and laid Him in a grave. 30 But God raised Him from the dead: 31 And He was seen many days of them who came up with Him from Galilee to Jerusalem, who now are His witnesses to the people. 32 And we declare unto you the message of the promise, made unto our fathers, 33 That God has fulfilled the same to us their children, having raised up Jesus, as it is written in the first Psalm, "Thou art My Son, to-day have I begotten Thee." 34 And as concerning that He raised Him from the dead, so that He will never return to corruption, He thus spoke: "I will give to you the sure holy things of David." 35 Therefore he says also in another place, "Thou wilt not suffer Thy Holy One to see corruption:" 36 For David, after he had in his time served the counsel of God, fell asleep and was gathered to his fathers, and saw corruption; 37 But He whom God raised saw no corruption. 38 Be it known unto you then, men and brethren, that through this man is preached unto you the forgiveness of sins; 39 And that in Him every one who believes is justified from all things, from which ye could not be justified by the law of Moses. 40 Beware lest that come upon you which is spoken in the prophets; 41 "Behold, ye despisers, and wonder, and come to naught: for I do a work in your days which you will not believe, though one should declare it unto you."

Ver. 17. Τοῦ λαοῦ τούτου, omitting Ἰσραήλ, is the original reading.

Ver. 18. Ἐτροφοφόρησεν is decidedly more strongly attested than ἐτροποφόρησεν, for which also Deut. i. 31, the passage apparently referred to by the apostle, speaks, where also the probable reading of the Septuagint is ἐτροφοφόρησεν.

Ver. 23. Ἤγαγεν is far better attested than ἤγειρε, which has only a few authorities for it, and which appeared the simpler reading.

Ver. 26. Modern critics, on account of external testimonies, have preferred ἐξαπεστάλη to the simple and also more familiar ἀπεστάλη.

Ver. 31. Νῦν is indeed wanting in the greater number of the uncial MSS., but appears to have been omitted, because the apostles had been for a long time witnesses, and not only now for the first time: it is to be retained as genuine.

Ver. 33. Αὐτῶν ἡμῖν was not understood by many transcribers, and therefore ἡμῶν was made out of it, and αὐτῶν omitted. Both words are genuine. —Griesbach, Lachmann, and Tischendorf have justly preferred πρώτῳ, which is attested chiefly by MS. D., and also by the fathers, as Origen, Tertullian,

Hilary, and others, who express their opinions on this surprising numeration.

Ver. 41. Ἔργον ὅ, on the authority of numerous testimonies, is to be preferred to ᾧ, which has no uncial MS., and to the omission of this second ἔργον.

EXEGETICAL EXPLANATIONS.

1. From Paphos, the journey proceeded again by sea, and that in a north-western direction, to the Asiatic province of Pamphylia, situated on the Mediterranean. They there visited the city of Perga, not far from the coast, lying a good (German) mile above the mouth of the river Cestrus. There it appears that John Mark separated from Paul and Barnabas to return to Jerusalem. That this did not take place from good reasons, but from a morally blameable motive, is evident from chap. xv. 37–39, where Paul at a later period so blamed this departure of Mark, as that even Barnabas, who was related to Mark (Col. iv. 10), separated from Paul in consequence. We cannot, however, determine the reason of this departure. Baumgarten thinks that Mark was incapable of the self-renunciation necessary to found an independent church among the Gentiles, and that therefore he returned to Jerusalem. But a weakness, which would no longer submit to the privations and fatigues of the missionary journey, may have been his fault. *Οἱ περὶ Παῦλον*, according to the classical *usus loquendi*, clearly makes us recognise Paul as the chief person, as the centre and soul of the company.

2. *But they proceeded from Perga.*—Paul and Barnabas by themselves journeyed farther inland from Perga,—at first to Antioch, a populous city, about twenty-five (German) miles to the north, in the interior of Asia Minor, and which, according to the change of governments, was reckoned as belonging at one time to Phrygia, at another time to Pamphylia, and at another time to Pisidia. Here it is called *Ἀντιοχεία τῆς Πισιδίας*; and so also Strabo mentions it as *Ἀντιοχεία ἡ πρὸς τῇ Πισιδίᾳ* (Strabo, xii. 12). From this city Luke relates the labours and experiences of the missionaries in detail.

3. *But they went on the Sabbath into the synagogue.*—As in the island of Cyprus, so here they met with many Jews, who possessed a synagogue in the city. Paul and Barnabas visited this synagogue on the Sabbath; and after the usual reading of a section from the Thora (Parash) and from the prophets (Haphthara), the rulers of the synagogue (the רָאשׁ הַכְּנֶסֶת, toge-

ther with the elders present) requested them to give an address, if they intended a word of exhortation (ἐν ὑμῖν). Wetstein and Kuinoel have supposed that this request arose from the fact that Paul and Barnabas had sat down on the rabbinical benches (ἐκάθισαν). But this word does not import so much, but only that they sat down in order to listen. As, however, we are hardly to suppose that this was the first day of their residence in the city, so it is probable that they had already shown themselves in several private discourses to be men of religious intelligence and knowledge of the Scriptures, and that this gave occasion to the request. Bengel, from the circumstance that in the discourse of Paul (vers. 17–19) the words ὕψωσεν, ἐτροφοφόρησεν, κατεκληρονόμησεν, rarely used in Scripture, occur (of which the first is in Isa. i., and the other two in Deut. i.), has inferred that on that Sabbath these two chapters (which are even at present the Parash and the Haphthara on the same Sabbath) were read, and that in the Greek translation, so that Paul added his discourse to this section of Scripture. But the contents of these chapters present too little analogy to the discourse, as to warrant such a conclusion.

4. *Then Paul stood up.*—Paul, after requesting silence by a movement of his hand, commenced with an address, partly to the Israelites themselves, and partly to the numerous proselytes then present. The apostle in ver. 26 addresses the latter—that is, such Gentiles as were not yet incorporated into the people of Israel by circumcision, but had learned to know the true God and worshipped with the Jews—along with the posterity of Abraham. The discourse itself, after a short but important retrospect of the history of Israel from the patriarchs to David, passes to the history of Jesus Christ, and to the doctrine of forgiveness through Him. Ὁ Θεὸς τοῦ λαοῦ τούτου, referring to the Israelites then present, is evidently primarily spoken to those who were not Jews. The chief point apparently is, that God has chosen the progenitors of this people (Abraham, etc.); so that the people have to thank not themselves, but the free election of God (to be His people) for what they are. In like manner, the exaltation of the people during their residence as sojourners in Egypt (ὕψωσε), *i.e.*, their increase to be a numerous and powerful people, and His leading them forth out of Egypt with a high and uplifted arm, *i.e.*, with irresistible power, are to be

ascribed wholly and entirely to the grace of God. To refer ὕψωσε to the exaltation by leading out the people from Egypt (Meyer), is not suitable, because ὑψοῦν is restricted entirely to the residence in Egypt, and the history of their deliverance from Egypt is separated from it.

5. *And about forty years.*—Further Paul brings prominently forward the fact, that Israel has to thank God, and Him only, for His nourishing and cherishing care and support in the wilderness for forty years (compare Deut. i. 31, "As a man doth bear his son"), and for the possession of the land of Canaan; for He destroyed and rooted out the seven nations of Canaan, Deut. vii. 1.

6. *And after that He gave them judges.*—Proceeding further, Paul mentions the rulers of the people until David, and in such a manner that he causes his hearers to recognise throughout, how these were raised and in turn deposed by God. After the possession and division of the land, God gave them judges for the space of 450 years, until Samuel. Here Paul gives the duration of the government by judges according to a mode of reckoning which does not agree with 1 Kings vi. 1 (480 years from the departure out of Egypt to the fourth year of Solomon, that is to say, 331 years for the time of the Judges), but which approximates to the reckoning of Josephus, Ant. viii. 3, 1 (from the departure out of Egypt to the building of the temple 592 years, *i.e.*, 443 years for the time of the Judges). See Meyer's Commentary. We are thus obliged to suppose that Paul here follows a chronology in use among the learned Jews of his time. After this, that is, from the time of Samuel, the Israelites requested a king, and it was God who gave them Saul for a king, for the space of forty years. The words ἔτη τεσσαράκοντα evidently denote the duration of Saul's government, and not the duration of the governments of Samuel and Saul together (Beza, Bengel). In the Old Testament, the duration of Saul's government is nowhere determined; but Josephus mentions that he reigned 18 years during the life of Samuel, and 22 years after his death: another proof that Paul, in his chronological reference, conforms to an extra-biblical tradition. In ver. 22 Paul uses expressions, in reference both to the rejection of Saul and to the elevation of David to the throne, which strikingly illustrate the absolute and free government of God. Μεταστήσας,

having removed him, which refers not to the death of Saul (Meyer), but to his deposition by the sentence of God: his actual continuing to reign (the duration of which is reckoned at 40 years, ver. 21) is thus left out of consideration;—ᾧ is without doubt to be connected with *μαρτυρήσας*, not with *εἶπε*. In this testimony of God, Paul has changed and fused into one saying of God to David, what Samuel said to Saul, 1 Sam. xiii. 14, and what is said in Ps. lxxxix. 21 of David. The chief point of this testimony is, that David, on account of his disposition, has the divine approval, and that he will fulfil the divine commands, whatever they may be.

7. *Of this man's seed.*—After the comprehensive retrospect of the history of Israel to David, Paul passes to Christ (vers. 23–25), as the descendant of David, according to the promise. God has brought Jesus as a Saviour to the people of Israel (*ἤγαγε* as הֵבִיא Isa. xlviii. 15): to *ἄγειν* corresponds *ἡ εἴσοδος αὐτοῦ*, His solemn entrance as *σωτήρ*, as well as the *προκηρύσσειν* of John, as a herald going before and announcing who is to come. The course which John was fulfilling (Impf. *ἐπλήρου*) was that of a herald. *Τίνα* is not equivalent to *ὅντινα*, but is an interrogative word, so that the point of interrogation stands after *εἶναι*. The discourse is arousing and lively, and therefore is divided into short sentences. *Οὐκ εἰμὶ ἐγώ*, according to the context, I am not the Messiah.

8. *Men and brethren.*—Paul approaches his hearers with a personal offer of grace in Jesus Christ made to them, and with a more precise and objective confirmation of the truth, that salvation is in Christ, the Crucified and the Risen One. Addressing his hearers anew, and saluting the Israelites as brethren in a more endearing manner than in the beginning of the discourse (ver. 16), he impresses strongly upon them the word of salvation, as sent especially to them from God by means of himself and Barnabas. This *applicatio* is repeated in a still more urgent manner, vers. 32, 38, 40. In the first place, Paul unfolds the *λόγος τῆς σωτηρίας ταύτης*, prosecuting it in vers. 27–29. The inhabitants of Jerusalem have not known Jesus, have condemned, crucified, and buried Him,—by which actions the prophecies were fulfilled. Then in ver. 30, and the following verses, he goes further, and says, But God has raised Him from the dead, and His disciples have seen Him after His resurrection.

In ver. 27, Meyer refers γάρ to the contrast between the hearers (ὑμῖν, ver. 26) and the dwellers and rulers in Jerusalem; as if the apostle would say, These have rejected the Saviour; therefore, instead of to them, the message of salvation now comes to the Jews of the dispersion, such as you. But Paul does not certainly intend to affirm that they in Jerusalem were to forfeit the message of salvation; and yet this idea is the only point of contrast. A distinction is indeed made between the dwellers at Jerusalem and the hearers at Antioch, but only this, that the former were personally concerned in the sufferings of Jesus, the latter were not so in the same way: but by no means that salvation was now to be brought to the latter, but no more to the former. *Γὰρ* is rather to be referred to *ὁ λόγος τῆς σωτηρίας ταύτης*, which is now explained and developed: thus *γὰρ* is explanatory, not causal. Those in Jerusalem and their rulers have not known Jesus, and therefore have also (*καὶ*) pronounced sentence against Him, by which they have unconsciously fulfilled the voices of the prophets, although these are read every Sabbath. In ver. 28, *εὑρόντες* intimates, that they took all pains to find out cause of death in Him, but in vain. Ver. 29 ascribes also the taking down from the cross and the laying in the grave to the inhabitants of Jerusalem and their rulers; and although both were done, not, as the sentence and crucifixion, by the enemies of Jesus, but by His friends, yet with good reason, because both Joseph of Arimathea and Nicodemus belonged to the *ἄρχοντες*, and Nicodemus also to the inhabitants of the city. In ver. 30, in contrast to what man has done, Paul places what God has done: He has raised Jesus from the dead, of which His disciples from Galilee, who saw Him after His resurrection, are witnesses. By this, Paul evidently excepts himself and Barnabas from the number of original disciples and witnesses.

9. *And we announce unto you.*—In vers. 32–37, the apostle intimates that in the appearance of Jesus, and in His resurrection, the promises made to David were fulfilled. *Ἡμεῖς εὐαγγελιζόμεθα* distinguishes the two missionaries from *μάρτυρες αὐτοῦ*, and places them, as contrasted with the eye-witnesses, in the class of evangelists. De Wette, Meyer, and Baumgarten, after the example of Luther and other ancients, explain *ἀναστήσας Ἰησοῦν* of the resurrection. But incorrectly; for vers.

32–37 are, according to the connection, not to be restricted to the resurrection of Jesus, but place both the mission of Christ in general as well as His resurrection in the light of prophecy and fulfilment. Further, it is evident that by δὲ something else is spoken of in ver. 34 than in ver. 33. In ver. 34 ἀνέστησεν—ἐκ νεκρῶν undeniably refers to the resurrection, whilst in ver. 33 ἀναστήσας without that addition might indeed be understood of the resurrection, but from the context can only signify *præsentem exhibere*. Calvin, Beza, Grotius, Bengel (whom Meyer in his third edition rightly places in this class), and among the moderns Kuinoel, Olshausen, and Hoffmann, have with good reason preferred this interpretation. The quotation from the Psalms (Ps. ii. 7), relating to the theocratic ruler whom God has made His Son, is referred to the divine Sonship of Jesus, as the perfect King: by this only is that declaration of God fulfilled. This also appears more natural than to refer it to the resurrection of Jesus. And now for the first time (vers. 34–37) Paul comes to the fulfilment of the divine promises in Christ's resurrection, which henceforth excludes all power of death and corruption in reference to Him. Here he appeals to two prophecies. 1. Isa. lv. 3, τὰ ὅσια Δαυὶδ, according to the Septuagint, instead of חַסְדֵי דָוִד. The meaning is, God has promised sure mercies to David—gracious gifts of a permanent nature. The unending life, which is the condition of this eternal state of grace, is the resurrection-life of Christ. 2. Ps. xvi. 10, where David in prayer expresses his confident hopes of life. Λέγει may very well be referred to David, who was last named, but cannot possibly be referred to God (Meyer), to whom the confident address is directed. In proof that this prophecy has only been completely fulfilled in Jesus, Paul reminds them that David, after he had in his own generation been serviceable according to the counsel of God, died. Τῇ ἰδίᾳ γενεᾷ cannot be taken as the *dat. commodi* (Meyer), because Θεοῦ βουλῇ is already in the dative. It is by no means flat and superfluous, if the sense be thus understood: David was not appointed to be the eternal servant of God, he has only served God in his time, and has done so honestly. David's death is described as a falling asleep, in consequence of which he was gathered to his fathers and saw corruption. This last quotation (vers. 34–37) strikingly reminds us of the proof brought forward by Peter (Acts ii. 24–31), when he employs the same words as a prophecy of the resurrection of Jesus; only the points of view are different. Peter intends to indicate that Jesus, on account of the prophecy, could not be holden of death, in other words, that Jesus must necessarily rise again. Paul proceeds further, and asserts, that in Jesus the promises of God are actually fulfilled, especially the promise of life and of immoveable and permanent grace.

10. *Be it known unto you.*—From what goes before, Paul draws the inference in vers. 38–41, and presses the point in question on the heart of his hearers. In vers. 38, 39, he makes known to them that in Christ, the Crucified and the Risen One, forgiveness of sins is offered (*ἄφεσις ἁμαρτιῶν διὰ τούτου*), and that every one who believes in Him is justified from all things, from which ye could not be justified in the law of Moses. See Dogmatical and Ethical Thoughts, No. 4. The conclusion admonishes the hearers lest the prophetic warning of God (*ἐν τοῖς προφήταις*, in the book of the prophets, Hab. i. 5 according to the Septuagint) befall them, namely, an astonishing and destructive confusion of the despisers of God by the experience of a work of God which one, on the hearing of it, will hold to be incredible.

11. This discourse, the first express speech of the Apostle Paul which Luke communicates, has had very unfavourable judgments passed upon it. That it does not bear the impress of Paul's mind, but is rather an echo of the speeches of Stephen and Peter; that it is unhistorical, and only a free production of the author himself (Schneckenburger, Baur, Paulus). In particular, it has not been known what to make of the historical part of the speech, especially vers. 17–22; and hence it is supposed, either that Paul only wishes to show his acquaintance with the Old Testament (Roos), or that he wishes to win the attention and confidence of his hearers (Neander), if there is not even found in it an entirely flat enumeration of Jewish history (Schrader). But Paul manifestly intends by it to bring into view the free grace of God and His unmerited choice, by which Israel became the people of God, and David became the servant of God and king, in contrast to the rejection of those who resisted God. Also, what Paul says of Jesus carries in itself a peculiar impress of truth, inasmuch as he brings everything in

connection with David: he introduces Christ as the descendant of David; he represents King David as the significant type, whose fulfilment has appeared in Christ. Lastly, the doctrinal declaration of justification through Christ for those who believe on Him, in contrast to the inadequacy of the law, is decidedly Pauline, and has nothing similar to it in any earlier speech. Moreover, in comparing this speech with the epistles of Paul, it must not be overlooked that this is a missionary discourse, and not a treatise going deeper into the subject, and addressed to those already converted. All things then being considered, we find no reason to doubt the genuineness and historical authenticity of this discourse.

DOGMATICAL AND ETHICAL THOUGHTS.

1. The choice of the patriarchs, the exaltation of their descendants to be the people of God, their deliverance from Egypt and settlement in Canaan, the appointment of their judges and kings, were all entirely acts of God, emanating purely from His own free determination and gracious choice, and not conditioned by human merit and works. And, indeed, it is especially the beginnings, the groundwork of fellowship and worthiness, that are conditioned by the absolute act and work of God. Here the doctrine of the free grace of God, further developed and asserted with precise reference to Israel by the Apostle Paul, emerges in its first outlines, and that principally in reference to the Israelites among his hearers. Human pride, and the notion of evident worthiness, engender a claim of merit which, with reference to God, is in all circumstances false and wrong, and renders the soul unsusceptible for the reception of grace. The Mosaic law, with its promises and threats, as an economy of retribution, easily gave rise to such a feeling. But, besides, every human heart has a side, according to which it may attain to such a feeling of merit with reference to God. On the other hand, the grace of God in Christ demands another soil for its reception, and for the growth of a plant of righteousness to the praise of the Lord. Humility is the soil in which the grace of redemption can take root and bear fruit. Thereon the apostle, whose self-righteousness the Redeemer Himself has thrown to the ground, labours; and only now has he, in the light of grace, obtained the disposition with which he recognised the

grace of God in the old economy: *in novo Testamento vetus patet.* "In Thy light we shall see light," Ps. xxxvi. 9.

2. Moral worthiness, freedom of the will, and personal responsibility, are in no wise denied by the acknowledgment of the absolute and prevenient election of God. Saul was rejected and set aside (*μεταστήσας*, ver. 22), after he had been placed on the throne, not in consequence of the arbitrary will of God, but simply in consequence of his disobedience, as is evident from the passage in 1 Sam. xiii. 14, which Paul changes by an application to David. And David himself is described as a man according to God's own heart, who does all His will. The ideas are not identical; but there is first the good tree, then the good fruit; first the right disposition of heart, and then the good act in the obedience of faith. Accordingly, the apostle in his discourse impresses it with all earnestness upon the hearts of his hearers, that they should immediately turn their wills to the obedient reception of the word, and to earnest conversion.

3. The more comprehensive our view of the history of revelation, the more clearly does Christ step before us, as the centre of all divine revelation. And the more the heart has learned to know Jesus as its Saviour, the clearer is the view of sacred history and its continuity.

4. Justification by faith in Christ (vers. 38, 39). A proposition precedes which is not peculiar to Paul: "Through Christ is preached to you the forgiveness of sins." Peter also (chap. ii. 38, iii. 19) held out *ἄφεσις ἁμαρτιῶν* to those who were converted and baptized. But the direct and close reference to the person of Jesus Christ, as the medium of forgiveness, is more prominently brought forward in this discourse of Paul than by Peter. But it is not expressly asserted how and wherefore Christ is the organ and medium of forgiveness (*διὰ τούτου*), as the discourse is only a summary testimony, and not a development of doctrine. The proximate idea is, that the resurrection is the chief fact on which this mediation rests, for directly before this the resurrection of Jesus is explained. The crucifixion of Jesus, as the foundation of reconciliation and forgiveness, is at least not more immediately indicated. However, from this discourse we have no reason to understand the resurrection exclusively, and not also the crucifixion, as the ground of forgiveness through Christ. On the other hand, what follows, *καὶ ἀπὸ*

πάντων—δικαιοῦται, is, as has been stated in the Exegetical Explanations, entirely new in thought and expression. It contains a negative and a positive assertion: negatively, the law is inadequate to δικαιωθῆναι; positively, in Christ, all who believe are justified. In both assertions the chief idea is δικαιωθῆναι. This, on account of its connection with the above proposition, διὰ τούτου ἄφεσις ἁμαρτιῶν, and in virtue of ἀπὸ πάντων, must include the remission of sins, exemption from guilt and punishment; but also, on account of the root of the word (δίκαιος), it includes the idea of righteousness—of the approval of God. Forgiveness, remission of sins, freedom from guilt and punishment, is the need of all. This is what the Israelite seeks by the law of Moses. This is what the apostle offers in Christ. But he asserts that this blessing is sought for in vain in the law of Moses: it is not possible (οὐκ ἠδυνήθητε) to receive forgiveness and justification by the law. 'Ἀπὸ πάντων ὧν, etc., does not import that even for those sins for which there was no justification through the law, forgiveness might be obtained through Christ (Schwegler); *i.e.*, that in the law an actual, but only a partial, justification was possible; in Christ, on the contrary, a complete justification. Neither the context, nor the doctrine of Paul elsewhere, nor the scriptural doctrine generally, gives any countenance to that idea, but the reverse. Indirectly indeed, but yet unmistakeably, Paul gives us to understand that the Mosaic law and its observance cannot possibly procure actual forgiveness and justification.—By this assertion, the following truths are attested: 1. Justification is not only a negative, but a positive blessing. 2. Jesus Christ is the only medium of justification. 3. The universality of Christianity, especially the universal accessibility of the justifying grace of Christ (πᾶς ὁ πιστεύων). 4. Faith is the only condition of justification on the part of man (πιστεύων). 5. The contrary proposition is asserted, that the law is not able to assist in obtaining justification. All these truths are truths which the Apostle Paul, in consequence of the peculiar manner in which he was led to Christ, has developed, and which are here stated for the first time.

HOMILETICAL HINTS.

And John departed from them (ver. 13). Whosoever puts his hand to the plough, and looks back, is not fit for the kingdom of God.—Scripture does not conceal the failings of the saints. It is comforting to know that none of them has passed through life without the confession, "My foot slipped, but Thy mercy, Lord, upheld me," Ps. xciv. 18 (Besser).

But they proceeded (ver. 14). It should not make us averse to proceed in the work of the Lord, when some fall from it (Quesnel).

If ye have a word of exhortation to this people, say on (ver. 15). To preach a sermon, as a stranger, in another community, when an opportunity occurs, is apostolical, and serves as a testimony of unity in doctrine, and as an encouragement to the hearers, who listen more eagerly to such sermons: it enables them to trace the various gifts of the Spirit. But no teacher should thrust himself forward, but wait until he is requested to preach (Starke).—The apostles might certainly speak extemporally, for they had the fulness of the Holy Ghost, and their hearts lived in the element of the Gospel (Apost. Past.).

Then Paul stood up (ver. 16). This is the first discourse which the Acts of the Apostles gives us from the mouth of a learned man, and is an example how true grace knows to consecrate to the service of Jesus Christ all gifts and powers of nature, all insights and judgments, so that thus one may arrange his discourse in an orderly and edifying manner, or, better still, for conviction to reach the heart (Apost. Past.).

The God of this people chose our fathers (ver. 17). The apostle labours so to represent the course of the Old Testament, that he might impress upon the Israelites the unmerited kindness of God, the free choice of His grace, and His long-suffering patience amid their manifold disobedience. Thus, before he threatens them with punishment, he lays a truly evangelical foundation, in order to melt their hard hearts by the persevering love of God (Apost. Past.).—Paul places before the Jews the set years and seasons into which God divided the history of their fathers, in order to show that the wisdom of God was displayed in the whole course of their history, and that everything happened as He determined it, and also that now the time of the new covenant was fulfilled, as the appointed years had expired (Apost. Past.).

After that He gave them judges (ver. 20). All kinds of government are of God, both aristocracy and monarchy (Starke).

When He had removed Saul (ver. 22). It is possible that God may choose a man for His service and work, and afterwards set him aside. It is sad when a man is at first one of God's instruments and servants, and is afterwards as Judas and Demas, having again loved the world (Apost. Past.).—*I have found David, a man after My own heart.* It is a rare thing, when God finds a man whom He can rightly employ in His service. The more does He make of him (Apost. Past.).—*Who will do all My will.* There is no other way to the heart of God than to do His will in all things (Quesnel).

John preached the baptism of repentance (ver. 24). John's preaching, according to its entire character, was a preaching of repentance and in the wilderness. He, by his whole appearance, represented, as it were, his people once more at their entrance to Canaan: he showed them how they hitherto, with all their kings and prophets, yet stood in the wilderness, outside of the promised land. Now for the first time they were to be led out of the wilderness (Williger).

I am not He, but there cometh one after me (ver. 25). The office of a teacher is to testify of Christ, to point from himself to Him (Starke).—When Paul would magnify Jesus to the people, he leads them away from all the celebrated men of former times, in order to fix their eyes upon the only Saviour: therefore he has pointed them away from the patriarchs, from David, from John to Jesus. All these holy men were only the servants of God in their day and generation. Jesus is the eternal Saviour, to whom all eyes and hearts should be directed. How blessedly does a teacher act, when he rightly uses this gift to hold up Jesus only before souls! (Apost. Past.)

Men and brethren (ver. 26). A new solemn address. They are called together who are appointed to inherit the true Canaan. Joshua's time returns, has only now thoroughly come. Only now comes the right time of salvation.—*And whosoever among you feareth God.* The Gentiles who feared God are particularly mentioned. They belong to the covenant which God made with Abraham (Williger).—*The word of this salvation.* Take a firm hold only of this word in thy heart, that Christ has sent to thee a sermon of salvation, that is, redemption from and victory over sin, death, the grave, corruption, hell, and the devil. Therefore is this glory of the sermon concerning Christ, which Paul here calls "a word of salvation," much more and greater than if he had told them about all the kingdoms, riches, and glory of the world, yea, of heaven and earth. For what could all these avail me, if I had not this word of salvation and eternal life? For when it comes to the need and danger of sin or of death, then am I obliged to say, Away with all the world's blessings and joys, that I may hear and have only this sermon of salvation sent by Christ (Luther).

For the inhabitants of Jerusalem—laid Him in a grave (vers. 27–29). Paul knew well how great the offence of the Jews was to the cross of Christ. Therefore he seeks to obviate their prejudices, and refers them partly to the evident and authentically established innocence of Jesus, and partly to the fulfilment by His death of all that was written of Him. Both reasons are sufficient to remove the offence of the death of Jesus (Apost. Past.).—There is a higher council than the chief council of the rulers in Jerusalem, namely, the company of the holy prophets; and to them Paul appeals, while he is obliged to acknowledge to his brethren at Antioch, that Jerusalem has not recognised the Saviour of Israel. Thus he throws the shield of the prophetic word over the shame of Jesus. Let no one be offended at a Saviour, for whom Jerusalem had nothing but a cross and a guarded sepulchre. Thus it is written, and thus it must take place (Besser).

But God raised Him from the dead—saw no corruption (vers. 30–37). Paul preaches not only the cross, but also the resurrection of Jesus. Both must be combined, so that we may have a complete justification in Christ. The testimony of the apostles and the predictions of the prophets are the proofs of the resurrection. The apostle here appeals to both.—Paul joins his own testimony to the testimony of the apostles. How good is it to have the happiness to be able to join ourselves, from our own experience, to the cloud of the witnesses of Jesus!—Paul selects three passages, to prove the resurrection of Christ, from the prophets. The first establishes the eternal birth and the appointment of the Son for the salvation of the world; the second maintains the inviolable fulfilment of all promised grace; and the third clearly determines the incorruptibility of the Messiah. Thus, then, the certainty of the resurrection of Jesus rests on God's eternal decrees, infallible covenant of grace, and express promise (Apost. Past.).—*David, in his time, served the will of God.* David's time was certainly a very evil time; yet this servant of the Lord continued in the obedience of the divine will. To all of us our time is determined, and our task prescribed. Let the time be what it will, and men as wicked as they will, yet the will of God must continue to be the aim of our daily work (Apost. Past.).—A fair renown and the best epitaph is, when it can be said with truth of one after his death: This man, although his life was short and the times were evil, has done the will of God to the best of his ability (Starke).

Be it known unto you—declare it unto you (vers. 38–41). Paul, in his discourse, taught in a thorough manner, and now he begins to stir them up powerfully: both methods must be conjoined.—The severe law of Moses had this important design, to awaken and preserve the longing after a Saviour. It is therefore good when a teacher of the new covenant often makes the comparison between free grace in Jesus Christ and that old yoke of bondage. Jesus will thus become more delightful to souls.—In order to extol the exceeding riches of the grace of God in Christ Jesus, a teacher must show that the blood and merits of Jesus go farther than nature, morality, and law; that Jesus delivers sinners from impurities and miseries, from which they could not be delivered by any other means.—To the Jews who, attracted by Paul's discourse, sought his company (ver. 43), he has further explained this chief point of all Christian doctrine—justification by faith; but we possess this explanation in his epistles, which are nothing else than a development of the sketch which the apostle has given of his doctrine in the concluding sentence of his first discourse (Besser).—The apostle finds it good to attach to his evangelical sermon a legal *pondus*, and to put the despisers of the grace of Jesus in a holy fear by a severe threat. The free Gospel, in its widest extent, does not abolish the use of the law (Apost. Past.).—Thus Paul had fulfilled his task: he had shown that to receive Jesus as Christ, as David, and as King, and to be God's people, are one and the same (Williger).

On the whole section (vers. 13–25).—*I will make you fishers of men.* The apostles, in obedience to this saying, have, 1. cast their net in many places (ver. 13); 2. suffered not themselves to be hindered in their work, though many went back (ver. 13); 3. regarded every time of work as opportune (ver. 14); 4. taken advantage of every place (ver. 14); 5. disregarded no request in order to testify of the grace of God in Christ Jesus (ver. 16), (Lisco).—*The work of God advances, even although some sharers in that work draw back.* 1. Statement of this truth. 2. What conduct we ought to observe in consequence (Lisco).—*The providence of God in the history of Israel, an encouraging type of the divine government over mankind.* 1. Wherein this providence is recognised: *a.* in the history of Israel; *b.* in the history of the kingdom of God in general. 2. What influence the certainty of this divine government ought to have upon us: *a.* We should be comforted with the sure confidence that the issue of things will be the best; *b.* we should do our part, in order that the divine plan of salvation may be more and more realized (Lisco).—*How the history of the world is transfigured in the light of the Gospel into the history of the kingdom of God.* 1. Its place is sketched out before in the eternal councils of divine power, wisdom, and love. 2. Its sections of time are stations on the progress of humanity to its destination. 3. Its heroes are the vassals of Christ, and, willingly or unwillingly, the servants of His kingdom. 4. Its end is the glorification of God in humanity.—*The hours on the world's clock.* 1. Moving slowly forward as the hours of the eternal God, with whom a thousand years are as one day, and of the long-suffering God, whose patience has borne with this perverse world, as it did with Israel for forty years in the wilderness. 2. But unceasingly progressing to the end appointed by God: of the world's redemption; of the world's judgment.

Vers. 26–41. *Jesus Christ, the end of all prophecy.* 1. As crucified. 2. As risen (Lisco).—*Only in Jesus Christ is eternal salvation.* 1. In Him, salvation; forgiveness of sins, justification by faith (vers. 38, 39). 2. Out of Him, no salvation, but judgment (vers. 40, 41), (Lisco).—*Christ, the world's Saviour.* 1. Foretold in the Old Testament (vers. 16–25). 2. Rejected by His people (vers. 26–29). 3. Preached as the salvation of believers (vers. 30–41), (Lisco).—*The goodness of God should lead thee to repentance.* 1. Think what the Lord has done for thee (the gracious dealings of the Lord toward His chosen people from the time of the patriarchs to the mission of Christ, vers. 17–25: application to His gracious manifestations toward us). 2. Consider how thou hast repaid Him (Israel's ingratitude, vers. 24–29; our ingratitude). 3. Embrace the grace which He even now offers thee. (Still it is time; the Crucified is risen; God has taken even sin into the plan of salvation; the murderers of Christ must minister to the work of redemption; but delay not; judgment will at length break forth upon unbelievers), (Lisco).—*To you is the word of this salvation sent*, an admonition also to us: 1. To contemplate attentively the wonderful ways of God in the preparation of this salvation from of old (vers. 17–26). 2. To embrace believingly the salvation in Jesus Christ, the Crucified and the Risen (vers. 27–39). 3. To guard scrupulously against ingratitude, which thrusts grace from it (vers. 40, 41).

The triumph of the divine government, that even those who fight against God must fulfil His counsel (vers. 27–29). 1. Seen in the cross of Christ. 2. Established in the history of the world. 3. Applied to our heart and life.—*Saul the chosen, and yet the lost:* an admonitory example not to end in the flesh what is begun in the spirit.—*Christ the Son of David, more than David.* 1. According to His spiritual disposition: David, a man according to God's own heart, to do all His will (ver. 22); Christ, God's own Son, fulfilling in perfect obedience His Father's work. 2. According to His career: David ascended the throne through lowliness and hardship; Christ, humbled to death on the cross, exalted to the Father's right hand (vers. 27–37). 3. According to the sphere of His work: David, as king over Israel, a shepherd of his people and a terror to his enemies; Christ, as the Saviour of the world, an eternal Prince of Peace to His people, and a terrible Judge to the despisers (vers. 38–41).—*The way of salvation.* 1. Long and laboriously prepared: long, by the times of preparation of the old covenant (vers. 17–21); laborious, by the bitter sufferings and death of Jesus (vers. 27–29). 2. And yet now short and smooth: short, merely to embrace the cross of Jesus by faith (ver. 39): smooth, for therein we find forgiveness of sins, life, and salvation (vers. 38, 39).—*Paul, in his introductory discourse at Antioch, already a complete Paul.* 1. The profound interpreter of Scripture (vers. 17, 33). 2. The large-hearted Apostle of the Gentiles (vers. 16, 26). 3. The truly evangelical preacher of faith (vers. 38, 39). 4. The undaunted witness of the truth (vers. 40, 41).

D.

In consequence of the joyful reception of the Gospel by the Gentiles, Paul and Barnabas are expelled the city through the jealousy of the Jews.

Chap. xiii. 42–52.

42 But as they went out, they requested that these words might be spoken
to them on the next Sabbath. 43 Now when the synagogue was dispersed,
many of the Jews and of the devout proselytes followed Paul and Barna-
bas; who spoke to them, and exhorted them to continue in the grace of God.
44 But on the next Sabbath, almost the whole city assembled to hear the
word of God. 45 But when the Jews saw the multitudes, they were filled
with envy, and contradicted what Paul said, contradicting and blaspheming.
46 Then Paul and Barnabas spoke boldly, and said, The word of God must
first be spoken to you; but as ye thrust it from you, and judge yourselves
unworthy of eternal life, lo, we turn to the Gentiles. 47 For so has the Lord
commanded us: I have set Thee for a light of the Gentiles, that Thou mightest
be for salvation even to the end of the earth. 48 But when the Gentiles
heard that, they were glad, and glorified the word of the Lord; and all who
were ordained to eternal life believed. 49 And the word of God was spread
throughout the whole region. 50 But the Jews stirred up the devout and
honourable women, and the chief men of the city, and raised a persecution
against Paul and Barnabas, and expelled them out of their territories.
51 But they shook off the dust of their feet against them, and came to
Iconium. 52 And the disciples were full of joy and of the Holy Ghost.

Ver. 42. Instead of αὐτῶν, the textus receptus has ἐκ τῆς συναγωγῆς τῶν Ἰουδαίων, probably inserted because a church lesson commenced here; but the simple αὐτῶν is sufficiently attested by MSS. and versions, and also by the text of Chrysostom.—Τὰ ἔθνη after παρεκάλουν is undoubtedly spurious, and erroneous as a matter of fact.

Ver. 44. Ἐρχομένῳ, instead of ἐχομένῳ, is a correction and spurious.

Ver. 45. Ἀντιλέγοντες is omitted by Lachmann after A.B.C.G.; but is, however, genuine, for it was left out as being considered tautological.

EXEGETICAL EXPLANATIONS.

1. *But as they went out*, namely, not the Jews (according to the other reading, and as Bengel following it judges), who would not hear Paul to the end; but Paul and Barnabas, who went away immediately after they had finished their discourse, because they were strangers, whilst the members of the synagogue remained together until the formal dismissal (λυθείσης τῆς συναγωγῆς). But before Paul and Barnabas left the place of meeting, a request was made to them for another discourse next

Sabbath (μεταξὺ, the Sabbath lying between the other days, but not σάββατον = week, the week lying between, for ver. 44, τῷ ἐχομένῳ σαββάτῳ, supposes that the request was made in the first sense). Who were the παρακαλοῦντες? Without doubt those assembled in the synagogue, perhaps the rulers (ver. 15). After the congregation was dispersed and dismissed in the usual manner, a considerable number of Jews and proselytes followed Paul and Barnabas to their dwelling, and received a yet more familiar exhortation, that they should continue faithful and stedfast in the grace of God, by which they had been drawn.

2. *But on the next Sabbath*, matters were brought to a crisis. On the one hand, the extraordinary susceptibility of the Gentile inhabitants of the city, and the strength of the impression which Paul's discourse and the private communications of himself and Barnabas had made, were displayed. This time the whole city came together, partly in and partly before the synagogue, to hear the Gospel. On the other hand, at the sight of this multitude, the Jews were stirred up to envy and jealousy. They envied Paul the extraordinary concourse which he had found, and their Jewish egotism might also be wounded and aroused by the presentiment that these Gentiles, no less than Israel, were permitted to be partakers of the offered salvation. Exasperated in consequence, they interrupted and contradicted the apostle in his discourse; and these contradictions increased in vehemence and in violence (Hebrew repetition ἀντέλεγον—ἀντέλεγοντες), so that they were hurried along to blasphemies, probably against Jesus, His missionaries, and those who believed on Him.

3. *Then Paul and Barnabas spoke boldly.*—They, on their part, were not stirred up to passion and abusive language; but they openly declared that henceforth they would turn from them, and offer the saving word of God to the Gentiles. It was certainly necessary that the word should first be preached to them, the Jews (ἀναγκαῖον). This necessity is founded on the command of Christ (Acts i. 8, iii. 26; Rom. i. 16), and on the plan of the divine economy. But now the apostle acts upon this, that these fanatical Jews had thrust the Gospel from them, and thus in fact passed judgment on themselves, that they were not worthy of the eternal life offered in Christ Jesus. On the ground of this fact, and without attempting a reply to the contradictions and blasphemies, and so casting their pearls before

swine, they declare, "Behold, we turn to the Gentiles." This also was done, not from mere temper, but in obedience to the will of God (ἐντέταλται). What in Isa. xlix. 6 is spoken of the Messiah, that He was appointed not only for Israel, but also to be a light and salvation to the Gentiles, these messengers of Christ apply to Him, and thus ground their exhortations, now directed exclusively to the Gentiles, on Scripture itself. Without doubt, Paul and Barnabas immediately after this declaration left the synagogue.

4. *But when the Gentiles heard this*, they received the Gospel with so much greater joy and respect, and as many as were appointed to salvation by God believed (τεταγμένοι; Chrysostom, ἀφωρισμένοι τῷ Θεῷ). By this Luke does not intend to say that the whole multitude of the Gentile inhabitants who were assembled were actually converted, but only a portion of them, and that portion which was marked out and ordained to eternal life by God. See Dogmatical Thoughts, No. 3. The short observation in ver. 49 shows us that Antioch in Pisidia was a centre, from which the Gospel spread into the neighbourhood.

5. *But the Jews* in Antioch, chiefly by aid of some honourable female proselytes (who remained unsusceptible to the Gospel, and therefore so much the more easily excited on behalf of Judaism, which they favoured) and of the chief men of the city, raised a persecution against Paul and Barnabas. The διωγμός, however, did not consist in the infliction of personal injury, but only in the expulsion by the authorities from the city and its territory (ἐξέβαλον), mentioned immediately afterwards. But they, in conformity with the command of Jesus (Matt. x. 14), shook off the dust from their feet, not as a sign of contempt (Meyer), but of renunciation of all and every fellowship with such people and with their merited fate. They repaired to Iconium, south-east of Antioch, a populous city at the foot of Taurus, which belonged at one time to Pisidia, at another time to Lycaonia or Phrygia, and is now called Coniah. The disciples, that is, the Christians at Antioch, were, by the departure of their teachers, not cast down or dispirited: on the contrary, they were filled with joy and with the Holy Ghost.

DOGMATICAL AND ETHICAL THOUGHTS.

1. The exhortation to continue faithful and stedfast in the

grace of God is in so far worthy of remark, as the special idea of χάρις τοῦ Θεοῦ occurs for the first time in the Acts of the Apostles, and, indeed, in the mouth of Paul and Barnabas. In chap. iv. 33, the grace of God is mentioned which rested on all the members of the Church; but by this was meant the continued fellowship of love between souls and God. But here by χάρις Θεοῦ is evidently meant the grace of reconciliation and redemption in Christ directed toward sinners—the grace of God in contrast to sin. In this sense χάρις occurs in the Acts for the first time, but henceforth frequently, as, for example, chap. xiv. 3, λόγος τῆς χάριτος; chap. xv. 11, χάρις κυρίου Ἰ. Χ. And this circumstance is not to be regarded as accidental, because the foregoing missionary discourse of Paul has already shown traces of that deeper knowledge of the truth in Christ, which was granted to the Apostle Paul, and through him to the Church of Christ.

2. The indwelling divine power of the Gospel shows itself not only in this, that it conferred on those who believe, conversion, holy joy, and salvation (vers. 48, 52); but also that it did not leave those who refused it as they were, but stirred them up to ungodly zeal, passion, and blasphemy (ver. 45). The Gospel was to the one the savour of life, and to the other the savour of death, 2 Cor. ii. 15.

3. Ver. 48: *Ἐπίστευσαν, ὅσοι ἦσαν τεταγμένοι εἰς ζωὴν αἰώνιον.* What does this, attentively considered, import? According to Calvin, it means that those became believers, whom God, in virtue of His absolute decree, had ordained to salvation, whom He had resolved to convert and not to harden. But the free self-determination of the human will is here as little denied as affirmed; a *decretum absolutum* is by no means contained in *τεταγμένοι*. But, on the other hand, it is equally inadmissible when *ἦσαν τεταγμένοι* is understood in the middle voice: *quotquot se ordinaverant ad vitam æternam* (Grotius), which is ungrammatical, or puts the meaning into the word; or is explained thus: *apti facti (oratione Pauli) ad vitam æternam adipiscendam* (Bretschneider); or what is allied to it, *qui juxta ordinem a Deo institutum dispositi erant* (Bengel), so that *τάσσειν* is made to denote the plan of salvation. The words import nothing else than that all those, and only those, were actually converted who were ordained by God to eternal life. It is not left either to accident, or to the arbitrary caprice and fancy of man, whether

any one, and who, shall attain to eternal life; but this result is under the government of divine Providence, ordering everything before the decisive moment. For, in matters of salvation and of eternal life, not the very least thing happens, unless the will and power of God ordain and determine it: a truth which humbles as well as elevates and comforts. But, on the other hand, nothing takes place in the matter of salvation except what man determines and resolves of his own free will: thus in the context (ver. 46) this is recognised as regards unbelievers; and elsewhere the Scripture bears testimony, in a thousand instances, to the freedom and independent action of man. Only this is not expressed in ver. 48, because Luke's design is to teach us to recognise the work of conversion, as a work dependent on the divine government.

4. The joyfulness which filled the Christians at Antioch, even after the forced departure of Paul and Barnabas, is a clear attestation of the gracious operations of the Holy Ghost. Only the communion of the Spirit of the Father and of the Son could be a sufficient compensation to them for the intercourse with the missionaries and teachers which they lost. They were not converted to these men, but to the Lord; and the Lord remained with them as He remains with His people, even to the end of the world. Even suffering and persecution cannot diminish their joy, for these are the badges of the Crucified One, and were foretold by Him to His disciples.

HOMILETICAL HINTS.

But when they were gone out, they requested (ver. 42). The Gospel never departs fruitless: although many despise it, yet there are always some, whose hearts are touched by it (Starke).—Many Christians would rather not go to hear sermons, far less request to hear one (Starke).

Followed Paul and Barnabas (ver. 43). As the lamb follows the shepherd, and children their mother, because they had received so much good in their souls from them (Starke).—*Who exhorted them to continue in the grace of God.* Beginners have most need of exhortation to continue in grace, for they are yet tender grafts which the storm of opposition may easily break off from Christ (Starke).—"Continue in the grace of God:" a text for all the awakened (Williger).

But on the next Sabbath, almost the whole city assembled to hear the word of God (ver. 44). Blessed Sabbath which is spent with the word of God, instead of with worldly pleasure! Blessed city which comes together to the house of God, instead of to the place of amusement! Blessed preacher who can preach before a congregation desirous of salvation, instead of to empty benches! How many Christian cities must be ashamed of their Sabbaths before this Sabbath observance in heathen Antioch!

But when the Jews saw the multitudes, they were filled with envy (ver. 45). The envy of the Jews, proud of their privileges, who were offended at the intercourse of Jesus with publicans and sinners, grudges alike to the apostles the following of the people, and to the Gentiles participation in the kingdom of God. They will hear nothing of mercy for the lost son, by which their worship and their fulfilment of the law would lose all preference. Every contradiction to the word of truth proceeds from this troubled fountain of envious pride, which will not bend to the mysteries of the Gospel (Leonh. and Spieg.).—*Contradicting and blaspheming.* Contradiction might take place with some show of reason, but the blasphemy, soon added to it, proves what sort of kindlings from hell were at the bottom of it (Rieger).

Then Paul and Barnabas spoke boldly (ver. 46). How much is such boldness now wanting!—*The word of God must first be preached to you.* Not on account of your worthiness, but on account of the promises of God, who cannot deny Himself, and remains faithful, notwithstanding our unfaithfulness (Leonh. and Spieg.).—*But as ye thrust it from you.* It is very proper to represent to the despisers of grace, how they unmercifully injure, not God, not Jesus, not their teachers, but themselves (Apost. Past.).—All despisers of the divine word judge themselves unworthy of eternal life, not that they think so, but that they make themselves so (Starke).—*Lo, we turn to the Gentiles.* Buy, because the market is before the door; gather, because the sun shines and it is good weather; use the grace and word of God, while they are present. For this you are to know, that God's grace and word is as a passing shower, which comes not again where it has been. It has been with the Jews; but it is thence, they have it no more. Paul brought it to Greece; it is thence also, now they have the Turks. Rome and Italy also have had it; but it is gone, they have now the Pope. And, ye Germans, do not think that ye will have the Gospel always. Therefore embrace and hold it, ye who can embrace and hold: lazy hands have a bad year (Luther).

But when the Gentiles heard this, they were glad (ver. 48). Blessed be God! The grace announced in the Gospel is universal! And we will, as those Gentiles, be glad and rejoice in it with our whole hearts to the praise of God, and to our eternal honour and joy.—*And all who were ordained to eternal life believed.* Whilst Israel, as the elder son (Luke xv. 26), in his self-righteous envy excludes himself from the gracious feast of the Father, the Gentile world rejoices at the revelation of commiserating love, which has remembered them for hundreds of years with gracious promises, and has now entrusted them with all the rights and privileges of sonship. Whilst it is evening with Israel, the Gentiles rejoice in the morning dawn which has risen upon them. The Gospel dove of peace, when it is driven from one place, soon finds again a house where she may bring forth her young. Yet all did not become believers, but only so many of them as were ordained to eternal life, who therefore thus placed themselves in the divine plan of salvation by faith and repentance. God's electing and calling grace is indeed the only ground of all conversion and salvation of men; but yet our text shows in the case of Israel, who deprived themselves of salvation by their own fault, that the condemnation of men, as well as their appointment to salvation, does not rest on any absolute decree of God (Leonhardi and Spiegelhauer).

And the word of the Lord was spread throughout the whole region (ver. 49). The word of the Lord has free course throughout the whole world, and no human barriers can set bounds to it (Apost. Past.).

But the Jews stirred up the devout and honourable women (ver. 50). These were bigots who depended on their devotions, and imagined they were pious before these new teachers came. Thus an honourable and a devout nature becomes a barrier to Christianity. Such people are certainly easy to stir up, and they say, What better do they pretend to have than we possess? We are pious and honest already (Gossner).—The mockers of Christianity have often calumniated our holy religion, that it has been propagated chiefly by the help of women. But here one sees the contrary (Apost. Past.).—*Per mulieres multa sæpe impedimenta vel adjumenta adferuntur regno Dei* (Bengel).

And they shook off the dust from their feet (ver. 51). The world must see proofs, that we speak the truth only for the salvation of men, and not for our own benefit. If it will not have heaven, let it keep the earth and its dust (Starke).

And the disciples were filled with joy and with the Holy Ghost (ver. 52). Whether indeed everywhere the experience of the awakened turns out well? There are many awakened congregations in the world which fall asunder, as soon as the instruments of their awakening are taken from them. And although everything does not entirely cease, yet they become more lukewarm. Believers say, It is not with us as it once was; and unbelievers, The excitement has ceased (Williger).

On the whole section (vers. 42–52).—*Who is fit for eternal life?* 1. He who judges himself worthy of eternal life, ver. 46. 2. He who opens his ears to the word of God. 3. He who silences the opposition of his natural understanding. 4. He who continues stedfast in the grace of God (Langbein).—*How may we attain to eternal life?* 1. If we recognise it as the chief good, and hold it to be worthy of our most earnest endeavours. 2. If we reckon ourselves to be by nature unworthy of such a blessing. 3. But yet if we do not doubt that God by His grace has deigned to honour us with it. 4. And if we willingly conform to the Lord's plan of grace (Langbein).—*The call of the Gentiles to eternal life.*—*The course of the Gospel.* 1. Information concerning it: from the text; from the history of God's kingdom in general. 2. Earnest exhortation contained therein for us (Leonh. and Spieg.).—*Various states of the heart toward the preaching of the Gospel.* 1. Open enmity against the word. 2. Lukewarm indecision toward the word. 3. Believing submission to the word (Leonh. and Spieg.).

The wrath and the grace which rule in God's kingdom. 1. Man's choice excludes from it (ver. 46). 2. God's choice leads to it (ver. 48), (Beck).—*On Thy word, comfort and salvation belong to me as my peculiar portion.*[1] 1. Be anew convinced that the will of God to save is as earnest as it is loving (vers. 46, 48). 2. Be earnestly warned against the obstinacy which thrusts salvation from it (vers. 45, 46). 3. Be established in the resolu-

[1] From a German hymn.

tion ever more carefully to yield to the gracious leadings of thy God (ver. 43). 4. Let nothing deprive thee of the joy to be permitted to enter into fellowship, ever more and more complete, with the Saviour (vers. 48, 52). 5. Employ thyself to lead others to the Lord (vers. 45, 49). 6. Particularly let thy sufferings serve to make thy calling and election sure (ver. 50), (Schmidt).—*By the word of God, the thoughts of many hearts are revealed.* 1. Of the Gentiles; that is, those who were hitherto at a distance and strangers to the word of God (vers. 48, 49). *a.* They rejoice in its contents. *b.* They praise the grace of God. *c.* They embrace it by faith. *d.* They taste the blessedness of believing. 2. Of the Jews; that is, the self-righteous, who will not be saved by grace (ver. 50). *a.* They are inflamed with hatred against the evangelical message. *b.* They interest others against it. *c.* They persecute the messengers of salvation. 3. Of believers, who experience in themselves the power of the word. *a.* Their faith is not perplexed by calamity (ver. 51). *b.* They experience holy joy (ver. 52). *c.* They grow in the grace of God through the Holy Ghost (ver. 52), (Lisco).—*The first shall be last, and the last first.* 1. The first shall be last. *a.* Who are the first? Those who have earliest experienced the divine love, and are considered most richly endowed with gifts. *b.* Why do they become the last? Because they did not use to their salvation the love of God experienced by them, and became proud of their gifts. *c.* How do they become the last? By receiving, according to the measure of their small fidelity, only an inferior position in the kingdom of God (Matt. xx. 10), or, as the reward of their complete unfaithfulness, by being entirely excluded from the blessings of the kingdom of God (ver. 46). 2. The last shall be first. *a.* Who are the last? Those who are called at a later period, and who possess inferior gifts. *b.* Why do they become the first? Because the knowledge of their defects makes them desirous of salvation. *c.* How do they become the first? By being themselves received into the kingdom of God, and assisting in its wider extension (vers. 49, 52), (Lisco).—*The opponents of the Gospel injure only themselves.* 1. They disclose their evil hearts (ver. 45). 2. They judge and make themselves unworthy of eternal life (ver. 46). 3. They disgrace themselves by the bad weapons they employ (ver. 50). 4. They do not arrest the victorious course of divine truth (vers. 48-52).—*Envy at the success of the Gospel*, a witness, 1. Against the envious: their secret pride, their evil conscience, their internal unhappiness. 2. For the envied: there must be something in it, a truth which cannot be entirely denied, a goad against which we cannot contend, a blessedness which cannot be mocked away.—*The severe farewell, "We turn ourselves," in the mouth of the faithful witnesses of the truth* (ver. 46). 1. Not the language of cowardly fear of men, but of resolute obedience to the intimations of the Lord. 2. Not an expression of proud contempt, but of commiserating pity toward those who thrust salvation from them. 3. Not a signal to a lazy retreat, but to a new work in a new field of labour.—*When is it time for a servant of Christ to shake off the dust from his feet?* 1. When he has not only knocked in a friendly manner, but also boldly kept his ground. 2. When he has been called on to proceed, not only by men, but also by the Lord. 3. When not only the door here is closed, but when he also sees it opened elsewhere for successful work.—*Israel's temporary rejection.* 1. Wickedly caused by themselves, through pride and ingratitude. 2. Righteously ordained by the Lord, in virtue of His holiness and truth. 3. Converted into a blessing to the world by the spread of the Gospel. 4. An admonitory example to Christianity, and also an impressive call to go after the lost sheep of Israel.

E.

Events in Iconium and Lystra: Return and Conclusion of the Journey.

CHAP. XIV. 1-28.

1. *Successful Labours in Iconium, until they are obliged to flee from the city before ill-usage; whereupon they repair to Lycaonia* (vers. 1-7).

1 And it came to pass at Iconium, that they entered together into the synagogue of the Jews, and so spoke that a great multitude of Jews and Greeks believed. 2 But the unbelieving Jews stirred up and irritated the souls of the Gentiles against the brethren. 3 They continued there a long time, speaking boldly in reliance upon the Lord, who gave testimony to the word of His grace, and granted signs and wonders to be done by their hands. 4 But the multitude of the city were divided, and some held with the Jews, and others with the apostles. 5 But when there was a movement

on the part of the Gentiles and of the Jews, with their rulers, to maltreat and to stone them, 6 They became aware of it, and fled to the cities of Lycaonia, Derbe and Lystra, and to the neighbourhood. 7 And there they preached the Gospel.

Ver. 2. Ἀπειθήσαντες is far better attested than ἀπειθοῦντες.

EXEGETICAL EXPLANATIONS.

1. *But it came to pass.*—*Κατὰ τὸ αὐτό* = *simul.* They spoke thus (*οὕτως*), *i.e.*, in such a manner, and with such a result, that a multitude of Jews and of Greeks (who are also to be considered as present in the synagogue, and thus proselytes in the wider sense) believed. But those Jews who continued unbelieving, and were disobedient to God's will of salvation (*ἀπειθήσαντες*), sought to enrage the Gentiles against the brethren, *i.e.*, not only against Paul and Barnabas, but also against the newly converted Christians in the city. This, however, did not immediately succeed; on the contrary, Paul and Barnabas could for some time longer quietly labour at Iconium, and preach the Gospel unhindered and boldly, by reason of the Lord (*ἐπὶ τῷ κυρίῳ*), that is, of the protection and blessing of Christ, inasmuch as He bore witness with deeds to the word of His grace which they preached, and enabled them to perform miracles of healing and other signs.

2. *But the multitude of the city were divided.*—Meanwhile, however, the seeds of distrust and wickedness were silently growing: in consequence of this, there was a division among the inhabitants of this populous city, and some were on the side of the embittered and hostile Jews, and others on the side of the apostles. At last it went so far, that the Jewish party with their rulers, together with those Gentiles who were stirred up by them, formed some secret design against the strange preachers (*ὁρμή* cannot signify an "assault," for those threatened escaped before it broke out; the meaning "plot" is not in accordance with the *usus loquendi;* on the other hand, an *impetus* to something is very frequently denoted by the word). *Ἄρχοντες αὐτῶν* cannot be the rulers of the city (Ewald), for they would not lend themselves to a tumultuary demonstration (*ὑβρίσαι καὶ λιθοβολῆσαι*), but would have prepared some lawful measure, as expulsion from the city and the like. *Λιθοβολῆσαι*, however, agrees perfectly with the ideas of the Jews, and thus with the ideas of the rulers and elders of the synagogue. The apostles

fortunately received information of the design, and considered it advisable to escape before the outbreak of the storm. They made their escape to the cities of Lycaonia, a district which forms a whole, not politically, but ethnographically. These cities were Lystra, south-east of Iconium, and Derbe (a small city at the side of the Isaurian range), south-east of Lystra: both cities lying to the north of Taurus. To these cities they repaired, in order to preach the Gospel there and in the neighbourhood.

DOGMATICAL AND ETHICAL THOUGHTS.

1. Although Paul and Barnabas had been expelled from Antioch by the wickedness and intrigues of the Jews, this did not prevent them, in another place, from going first into the synagogue and preaching the Gospel to the children of Israel. The divine necessity is not abolished by the opposition of individuals: God remains true; He cannot deny Himself (Rom. iii. 3, xi. 29; 2 Tim. ii. 13).

2. Here also the exalted Redeemer is the proper Agent. Paul and Barnabas are His messengers and organs; they bring His Gospel, and speak the word of His grace (ὁ λόγος τῆς χάριτος αὐτοῦ, *præclara definitio evangelii*, Bengel); and He it is who, as the faithful Witness, bears testimony to what they say, and that with deeds. As Jesus Himself lived what He taught, so He grants to His servants to produce powers of life, to perform miracles of healing, for a sign and testimony that it is the Lord—that the word is the word of the Lord. Such miracles take place διὰ τῶν χειρῶν αὐτῶν, by means of their hands; they lay their hands on them, and the sick become whole. But it is not they who work, and in whom the saving and miraculous power of life resides: it is He who works; they are merely His instruments.

HOMILETICAL HINTS.

And it came to pass at Iconium, that they entered into the synagogue of the Jews, and spoke (ver. 1). The persecution at Antioch had effected no other change on the apostles than a change of place. When they left Antioch, they commenced again at Iconium. They continued unmoved in the same mind, and in the same business which had occasioned them so many sufferings at Antioch (Apost. Past.).—Also, they did not desert the synagogues of the Jews: neither their love to their people nor their courage was broken by their bitter experiences of the Jews.

But the unbelieving Jews, etc. (ver. 2). Whoever is disobedient to the truth, is easily induced to turn others from it. "Ye neither go in yourselves, and ye prevent those who would," was fulfilled in those envious Jews (Rieger).—Pilate and Herod, Jews and Gentiles, are soon united, when it is against Jesus and His truth (Starke).—*Against the brethren.* Luke has here used the endearing name of "brethren" for Christians, because it was peculiarly hateful to the unbelieving Jews, that believing Jews and believing Gentiles should become one holy brotherhood in Christ (Besser).

They continued there, speaking boldly, in reliance on the Lord, who gave testimony to the word of His grace, and granted signs and wonders to be done by their hands (ver. 3). He who honours God by a courageous deliverance of the testimony of His truth, him God often honours by an extraordinary testimony of His protection and blessing, 1 Sam. ii. 30 (Starke).—The Lord has means enough to stop the mouths of His enemies. If the Jews had succeeded in making the words of the apostles suspected, so now signs and miracles were granted to them, which took place before the whole world, and were a matter-of-fact preaching to the excited Gentiles (Williger).—How little the apostles depended on miracles is evident from this, that they effected their ministerial success at Iconium only by the preaching of the Gospel, and had already converted a great number before any miracle took place. They continued to preach, and God performed the miracles, in order to set His seal upon the word of His grace. (Apost. Past.).—The Acts of the Apostles is no chronicle of miracles, but a mirror of grace (Besser).

But the multitude were divided (ver. 4). Such a division is not entirely unpleasant to a faithful teacher, because the Lord Jesus says that He came into the world to cause such divisions. The Lord fulfils this saying as often as He by His servants shakes the kingdom of darkness, awakens a holy disquietude, and teaches men to turn from their unrighteousness. He will, in the future, complete the division with terrible authority on the great day of judgment (Apost. Past.).

But when there was a movement (when a storm arose), (ver. 5). After the apostles had spent a sufficient time in the dissemination of the seed at Iconium, God caused the persecution to break out into a storm, without doubt on purpose that the seed might be driven farther, and be blown to Lystra and Derbe (Apost. Past.).—The wonderful ways of God are seen not only in the victory, but also in the yielding of His people. Yet this yielding is no yielding. The apostles regard the information of the design of their enemies only as a divine passport for a farther journey (Williger).

And they fled (ver. 6). We ought not always to submit to shame and injury; we must learn to consider what is most or least conducive to God's honour (Quesnel).

And there they preached the Gospel (ver. 7). The apostles did not waste their time in complaining of the injustice they suffered; on the contrary, they set themselves again to the joyful undertaking of the work which God had assigned to them (Rieger).

On the whole section (vers. 1–7).—*God's word does not return void.* 1. It is always embraced in faith by many, when it is freely and purely preached, and is accompanied with signs of holy conduct and self-denying love in its ministers; 2. although it does not gain all, because the wickedness of many keeps back others from the faith, and all wickedly disposed hearts are united in enmity against the Gospel; 3. but the enmity against the Gospel aids its farther extension (Lisco).—*When they persecute you in one city, flee ye to another.* 1. The preachers among the heathen are not obstinately to remain where their preaching is persecuted (where, namely, remaining may be said to tempt God). 2. Persecution ought not to discourage them from new efforts (Lisco).—*Concerning proper witness-bearing* (martyrdom). 1. Wherein it consists: *a.* Not in the degree of the external sufferings which the man has suffered on account of his faith, but in the measure of fidelity which he has displayed for the sake of Christ. *b.* The apostles waited on their ministry with perseverance and joyful courage, and therein lay their fidelity. *c.* The apostles forsook the places which had become dear to them, as soon as they were made aware that the Lord had no more use of them in those quarters. 2. Why is it so difficult? *a.* Because there is nothing in it to flatter our refined selfishness. There is wanting the "halo before the world," for fidelity is clothed in homely garments. *b.* Because it destroys to the foundation self-will. Perhaps death was easier than flight to the apostles, as formerly the Baptist had found self-sacrificing activity for Christ easier than inactively languishing in a prison. 3. Wherein consists its blessing? *a.* It brings about that God's will is done, and not man's. *b.* Therefore it is rich in fruits of all kinds. The apostles' preaching produces faith (ver. 1). The Lord manifests Himself to them (ver. 3). Their flight is converted into a blessing; they are enabled to carry the word farther (ver. 7), (Lisco).—*The blessed divisions in the Church.* 1. Their cause: the resolute preaching of the divine word, which is quick and powerful, and sharper than a two-edged sword. 2. Their fruit: the sifting of the Church; the state of the heart is disclosed, the truth proves itself in conflict, faith is tested, love established, and the Church edified.—*The permitted flight of a servant of God,*—how it takes place. 1. After the conflict, as with Paul and Barnabas, and not before, as with Jonah. 2. In obedience to the Lord, and not from fear of man or carnal tenderness. 3. With weapons in their hands, as the apostles continue to preach with unbroken courage, not after having cast their weapons away. 4. To a new field of conflict (Derbe and Lystra), not to rest.—*How the servants of God conquer in yielding.* 1. Internally: their courageous faith remains unbroken in external trouble and shame. 2. Externally: the true cause cannot perish; here chased away, it finds room elsewhere; now crushed, it will raise itself anew at a later period. 3. Eternally: to the faithful soldier, the heavenly crown of victory is promised.

2. *The Cure of a Lame Man at Lystra gives occasion to an idolatrous adoration which Paul and Barnabas with difficulty avert; notwithstanding Paul is afterwards, at the instigation of those from Antioch and Iconium, nearly murdered* (vers. 8–20).

8 But a man at Lystra, powerless in his feet, being lame from his
mother's womb, who never had walked, sat there. 9 The same heard Paul
speak; who looked stedfastly on him, and perceived that he had faith to be
healed; 10 And said with a loud voice, Stand upright on thy feet. And he
sprang up and walked. 11 And when the multitude saw what Paul had
done, they lifted up their voice, saying in the Lycaonic dialect, "The gods
have become like to men, and are come down to us." 12 And they called
Barnabas Jupiter, and Paul Mercury, because it was he who led the discourse.
13 But the priest of Jupiter, who was before the city, brought
oxen and garlands before the gate, and would offer sacrifice with the people.

14 When the apostles, Barnabas and Paul, heard that, they rent their
clothes, and rushed out among the people, crying out, 15 And saying, Sirs,
why do ye this thing? We also are men of like destiny as ye are, and
preach to you, that ye should turn from these vanities to the living God,
who has made heaven, and earth, and the sea, and all things that are there-
in; 16 Who in time past suffered all nations to walk in their own ways;
17 Although He left not Himself unwitnessed, in that He did good, and gave
us rain from heaven and fruitful seasons, filling our hearts with food and
gladness. 18 And with these words, they were scarcely able to restrain the
people from offering sacrifices to them. 19 But there came thither Jews
from Antioch and Iconium, who persuaded the multitude; and they stoned
Paul, and dragged him out of the city, supposing that he was dead. 20 But
as the disciples stood round him, he arose and went into the city; and on the
day after, he departed with Barnabas to Derbe.

Ver. 8. The pluperfect περιπεπατήκει has been preferred by Lachmann and Tischendorf to the aorist περιεπάτησεν: the latter corresponds to the usual mode of expression in relative sentences, and was therefore inserted instead of the pluperfect by the transcribers.

Ver 9. Ἤκουε is only in the MSS. B. and C.; therefore Lachmann and Tischendorf prefer the aorist ἤκουσε, which is in most MSS. But as the other verbs are in the aorist, the imperfect would be sooner altered into the aorist, than the aorist, if the original reading, would be altered into the imperfect; therefore the imperfect is to be preferred.

Ver. 14. Ἐξεπήδησαν is decidedly to be preferred to εἰσεπήδησαν, which has only a few later MSS. for it.

Ver. 17. Καίτοιγε is to be considered the genuine reading; the other readings omit either τοι or γε.

Ver. 19. Νομίζοντες, present participle, is better attested than νομίσαντες.

EXEGETICAL EXPLANATIONS.

1. *A man at Lystra.*—Luke relates several particulars. 1. The cure of a lame man by Paul (vers. 8–10). 2. The attempt of the multitude, occasioned by the miracle, to honour Paul and Barnabas with sacrifices as gods, which they were only able to prevent by the most determined interference (vers. 11–18). 3. The later ill-treatment of Paul, caused by the instigation of foreign Jews, which almost cost him his life (vers. 19, 20).—The cure of the lame man resembles the miracle performed by Peter at Jerusalem (Acts iii.). The unfortunate man at Lystra, as well as the one at Jerusalem, was lame from his birth, never had walked, and was obliged to sit (ἐκάθητο sat there, not dwelt in Lystra: Kuinoel). He constantly listened to Paul when he preached (the critically preferable reading ἤκουε, imperfect, expressing long duration, and thus here constant and earnest listen-

ing). Paul, struck by this, looked stedfastly on him (ἀτενίσας), in order if possible to discover his spiritual condition; and he recognised by this look that the man had faith to be healed (τοῦ σωθῆναι is the supplement to πίστις, and indicates the object of his believing confidence). Probably the discourse of Paul, in connection with his whole appearance, excited the confidence of the cripple toward the apostle, that he could and would aid him. And this disposition the apostle recognised from his appearance. The lame man reasoned from what was internal to what was external, so that he hoped with confidence for a cure of his bodily weakness: the apostle reasoned from what was external in the lame man to what was internal, so that he was convinced that his soul was full of faith. Here lies a distinction between this occurrence and that at the gate of the temple at Jerusalem. That lame man at Jerusalem desired and expected nothing except to receive alms, even when Peter exhorted him to look on him and John (chap. iii. 3–5). But this lame man, who was an attentive and earnest hearer of Paul, already possessed the believing confidence that Paul would help him. Then the apostle called aloud to him to stand up, and to walk erect on his feet. He does not, as Peter did (chap. iii. 6), invoke the name of Jesus, on whose authority the call was issued, and in whose strength it could be obeyed; because the lame man had already learned from the preaching of Paul to recognise Jesus as the Saviour. Here again another distinction. At this call the lame man leaped up at once (ἥλατο, aor.), and walked up and down (περιεπάτει, imperfect). Here there is a third distinction; inasmuch as Peter took the lame man by the hand and lifted him up: whereas here this lame man, entirely without help, is able to leap up of himself.

2. *When the multitude saw what Paul had done.*—The impression which this miracle produced upon the Gentile multitude, who, as it appears, were collected in numbers, is very remarkable and singular in its kind. The cure of the lame man appeared to them so wonderful and so purely divine, that the thought struck them, that the men who have come with such heavenly doctrine and superhuman power are nothing less than gods in human form. They then, after some had given expression to the conjecture, cried out together with a loud voice, as if it were a demonstrated truth, " The gods have become like to men, and are

come down to us;" and they called Barnabas Jupiter, and Paul Mercury, because he was the leading speaker (ὁ ἡγούμενος τοῦ λογοῦ); Mercury being the diligent messenger of the gods, and their eloquent herald and interpreter. Luke does not inform us why they took Barnabas for Jupiter: doubtless he conducted himself with dignified composure, and appeared on that account (perhaps also as the elder, and on account of his imposing exterior, ἀπὸ τῆς ὄψεως ἀξιοπρεπής, Chrysostom) as the more distinguished god. But why they were taken for Jupiter and Mercury in particular, is explained from the local worship of these two gods, of whom Jupiter had a temple before the city (ver. 13). In this very Phrygian territory, the myth of the appearance of Jupiter and Mercury in human form, when they were entertained by Philemon and Baucis, was current (Ovid, Metamorph. viii.). Ewald advances the striking supposition, that this might have been yearly repeated at the festival of Jupiter, and that therefore the people arrived so much the more readily at that conjecture concerning Paul and Barnabas. Luke observes (ver. 11) that the multitude, in their idolatrous jubilee, cried out λυκαονιστί, that is, in their native Lycaonic dialect. This notice was designed to explain why the apostles did not interfere on the spot, and why they permitted it to proceed nearly to the act of sacrifice. They did not understand what the people intended to do, because they spoke not in the Greek, but in a provincial dialect, unknown to them. To what class of languages this belonged, cannot be determined: that it was a corrupt Greek, or a branch of the Assyrian language, are groundless suppositions. It has been lately asserted that this notice of the language was invented (Zeller); but, on the contrary, the thing is in itself very natural, because, psychologically and according to experience, it is precisely in excitement that the native tongue is wont to come uppermost in preference to an acquired language. But when the priest of Jupiter, who had his temple and image before the city, brought sacrificial animals and garlands to adorn the sacrifice and the altar before the gate, and was in the act along with the multitude of offering sacrifices to the supposed gods who had honoured the city with their appearance, then the apostles understood it, rent their clothes from pity and indignation at the sin of idolatry which was about to be committed, rushed out in full haste without the gate (ἐξεπήδησαν) among the multitude assembled for the sacrifice, and, hindering them, cried out in passion and zeal:

3. *Sirs, why do ye this thing?* The call, at first abrupt and hasty, immediately took the form of an address (λέγοντες), *ἡμεῖς ὁμοιοπαθεῖς ἐσμεν ὑμῖν ἄνθρωποι.* The gods are even to the heathen *ἀπαθεῖς*, blessed, immortal, free from want; we, as well as you, are men subject to suffering, sickness, death. *Εὐαγγελιζόμενοι ὑμᾶς* denotes the object of their arrival: not to receive divine honour, but to bring to you good tidings, that ye turn from these vain idols (*τούτων*, not neuter, but masculine, referring to the temple of Jupiter with his image) to the living God; which was at the same time a permission, a friendly invitation (*εὐαγγελιζόμενοι*). The living God, in contrast to the lifeless idols and the fanciful images, is likewise the Creator of heaven, and earth, and the sea, the threefold territory of the world, each of which, according to the heathen, had its peculiar gods.

4. The call to conversion (*ἐπιστρέφειν*) to the living God supposes that the way hitherto taken was a wrong way. Paul says in an apologetic manner: God has hitherto suffered all nations to walk in their own way. That these ways were wrong ways is not expressly said, but is sufficiently indicated for him who will understand. Nevertheless, God has not even in this period left Himself without a witness. The witnesses for Him were His pure acts of kindness (*ἀγαθοποιῶν*) in the territory of nature and of corporeal life (*ὑετούς, καιροὺς καρποφόρους*): all these He has given from heaven (*οὐρανόθεν*), in order to draw men to heaven, which is God's dwelling. Thither should joy draw the heart by means of gratitude. But when it is said, "God has filled the heart with food," the interpenetration of the corporeal and the spiritual is supposed: the heart, as the seat of spiritual feelings, is certainly by the enjoyment of food and by the feeling of satisfaction filled with gladness.

5. *But there came thither Jews from Antioch and Iconium.*—The arrival of certain Jews from Antioch of Pisidia and from Iconium (*ἐπῆλθον* to the inhabitants of the place) was certainly not accidental, but occasioned by the news received of the success of the apostles at Lystra: they wished to thwart their work there also. And it is a genuine example of the fickle disposition of the multitude (vers. 18 and 19, both times *οἱ ὄχλοι*), that they, so excessively unstable, were induced by suggestions and represen-

tations to stone him half-dead, to whom a little before they had destined divine honour and sacrifices. It is to be supposed that the stoning proceeded from the Jews, and is to be ascribed to the usages of that nation; although the sense evidently is, that the inhabitants of Lystra were stirred up by them, and joined with them. The disciples, that is, the converts at Lystra, stood round Paul, supposed to be dead, not in order to bury him (Bengel), or to watch him (Ewald), but to see whether he was alive, and was yet to be aided. Then Paul rose up and went to the city, but departed from it the following day, and came to Derbe.

DOGMATICAL AND ETHICAL THOUGHTS.

1. Paul regarded the faith of the lame man that it might be helpful to him. His spiritual condition was the centre and turning-point of the whole transaction. Faith proceeds from the word: as here faith, the confident expectation of deliverance and help, proceeded from hearing the word, so faith, where it is excited, proceeds from the preaching of the Gospel, Rom. x. 14, 17. And even though faith does not at first lay hold on the centre of redemption—the spiritual and moral cure of the soul—but cleaves to the periphery, or only to the cure of the body, yet if it be only founded on the Saviour, it is an apprehension of salvation pleasing to God. *Σωτηρία* itself is not something wholly spiritual, but embraces body, soul, and spirit; and as the redemption of the spirit can penetrate to the body, sanctifying, glorifying, and redeeming it, so may also the *σωθῆναι* (ver. 9) begin with the body, and proceed to the soul and spirit.

2. The adoration of the apostles arose from a mixture of heathen superstition with truth. The truth was the impress of divine power and grace which penetrated life. This was, indeed, the kernel in the cure of the lame man; for that was a miraculous and gracious act of God. But with this truth they immediately blended their superstitious and polytheistical fancies concerning Jupiter and Mercury, and of the appearances of these gods in human forms (in a docetic manner). The wish to offer sacrifices on the spot to these supposed gods was the natural result of this notion. How could they otherwise express gratitude, divine honour, and worship? We have an insight by the help of this incident into the origin of idolatry. We are not justified in seeing in it only mere fancy, and falsehood, and sin. The error

of the heathen ever cleaves to a truth. A genuine and true feeling—a just observation or presentiment of the divine—lies at the foundation. But a rash inference is drawn from this. The natural and the created, in which the divine power, goodness, and justice are manifested, are forthwith deified: and hence arises the religion of nature, polytheism, heathenism.

3. The character of the apostles is tested in this history. In a position similar to that of Herod Agrippa, they act in a directly opposite manner. He had no word of opposition or protest, when the people deified him (Acts xii. 22). The apostles protested on the spot with painful indignation, as quickly and as energetically as they could, in order to avert the sin of idolatry from themselves, to whom divine honour was about to be rendered, and from those who wished to pay such honour. And yet there was no small temptation in this matter. They might think, This idolatrous prejudice must be excused; there is a spark of truth in it; the esteem for our persons may be serviceable for the spread of the Gospel; the idea of the appearance of gods on earth may lead to the doctrine of Christ, the Son of God. But that would be nothing else than to suppose that the end sanctifies the means. How often do we thus act? And always to the detriment of the truth and honour of God, which we thought to promote. The apostles took vigorous measures: they tore asunder the web of this delusion when it was yet forming itself, instead of helping to complete it; and God permits them to succeed.

4. The apostles averted the practical design, the sinful idolatry, by an admonition full of instruction. Because an error cannot otherwise be successfully combated than by establishing the positive truth, so the Apostle Paul (for we will not err if we ascribe the thoughts indicated by Luke specially to him) does not long remain with the negation, but passes quickly over to the development of those truths which the occasion suggested. 1. The idea of the living God in contrast to *μάταια*. And here, without doubt, the chief points are the attributes of reality or real existence, of absolute power and of self-determination; whilst the singular *ὁ Θεός*, in contrast to the plural *τὰ μάταια ταῦτα*, attests the unity of God, monotheism. 2. The idea of creation, as a free independent act of God, by which everything that is, is established and called into being. This proposition

(ver. 15) is an indirect protest against all creature-adoration. 3. The self-manifestation of God: how it is promulgated to all men, and was so from of old, and that by benefits on the territory of nature. 4. The division of time in the history of the human race into chief parts—the time before Christ and the Christian era: to the latter period the preaching of the Gospel belongs, which requires conversion (εὐαγγελιζόμενοι); the period before Christ, on the other hand, is distinguished by the freedom which God has left to all nations to walk in their own ways (ver. 16). Evidently εἴασε πορεύεσθαι cannot be made to agree with the predestinarian idea, as if the error of the Gentiles was of divine and absolute enactment. On the contrary, the liberty of self-determination and development is clearly asserted which God has permitted and granted, in order that they may experience how far they can go.

It is apparent that these thoughts are decidedly Pauline. In particular, the contemplation of the world as it is divided by the appearance of Christ into the periods of antiquity and of the Christian revelation, as well as the intimation of the self-attestation and manifestation of God by means of nature, are peculiar to the Apostle Paul. And the declarations of the one living God, and of the creation of all things by Him, which were occasioned by the circumstances of the case and the practical design in view, do not indeed belong to that class of truths by which Paul is distinguished from the other apostles, but certainly to those which he holds as the inalienable fundamental truths of the Gospel.

HOMILETICAL HINTS.

Lame from his mother's womb (ver 8). The third cure of a lame man recorded in the Acts of the Apostles (chap. iii. and ix. 33). The cures of such diseased persons are peculiarly significant: a sign of what must take place spiritually. It is not sufficient when the eyes and ears are opened to the Gospel, and when hearts are impressed. The impressed must learn to walk in the light (1 John i. 7), and make sure steps for their feet (Heb. xii. 12), (Williger).

He looked stedfastly upon him, and perceived that he had faith to be healed (ver. 9). If the apostle looked so narrowly at the feeble spark of faith in the heart of this poor man, how may not the all-seeing eyes of God look at the same in us! "Lord, Thine eyes have regard to faith" (Apost. Past.).—The essence of true faith is a desire and confidence that He is willing and able to help us. By this it is distinguished from dead knowledge and extravagant feeling (Apost. Past.).—This is one of those scriptural examples, from which can be explained the reciprocal action which the word of one often has upon the faith of another, and, on the other hand, which the faith of one has upon the heart of another; and how also, on the contrary, the unbelief of others can place, as it were, a bolt and bar upon a man, so that he is able neither to speak nor to act (Rieger).

And said, Stand up on thy feet. And he leaped and walked (ver. 10). The apostle required only to say, Stand up on thy feet; it was not necessary here to add, In the name of Christ (chap. iii. 36). Christ (by the preceding discourse of the apostle and the faith of the lame man) was already present, and had manifested His power in the soul and body of the lame man. The exhortation was only necessary, that by leaping up he should give proof of what the Lord had done in him (Williger).

The gods have become like to men, and are come down to us (ver. 11). If the heathen, from extraordinary benefits and operations, recognised God as the Author, what is to be said of Christians who nevertheless blaspheme what they neither know nor understand? (Starke.)—There appears in all these heathen fables of the appearances of the gods a presentiment of the truth: backwards, an unconscious recollection of the happiness of Paradise, when God held intercourse in human form with man; and forwards, an unintelligent pointing to the restoration of the fallen and desolate creation by the incarnation of God in Christ (Langbein).—The people observed something divine in the apostles; but instead of recognising the divinity of their doctrine and office, they fall to the adoration of their persons, in order to reconcile the miraculous powers of the apostles with their superstition. Thus it is with the blind world, when it has to judge of divine things (Apost. Past.).—Carnal reason, perhaps, might have thought to be able to make use of this prejudice as a means to effect an entrance for the Gospel, and to build on it the doctrine of the incarnation of the Son of God. But in what a godly manner do the apostles despise these false means and foolish artifices! The Gospel requires no crooked ways for its propagation. The apostles preached not only in divine strength, but also in divine purity (Apost. Past.).—The apostles might easily have come in the place of those gods whom they overthrew. But they rather love to show in what earthen vessels God has placed His treasure. There is even now-a-days danger that many may be converted to their pastor, as to a new god. The world can now bring its marks of honour, as these people with their oxen and garlands, but its incense of praise is the more poisonous, when it intends to ensnare one therewith (Rieger).—The idolatry of the creature and of men is the characteristic of all heathenism both of ancient and modern times. For this is the disgraceful curse which befalls all despisers of the incarnation of the Son of God, that in their thoughts and actions they sell themselves to human guides, as if they were gods from heaven; that they with great spirits, mighty warriors, and imaginative poets practise such an unchristian worship of genius, as if these were the saviours and the divine authors of the human race (Leonh. and Spieg.).

But the apostles, when they heard that, rent their clothes (ver. 14). In suffering and persecution, the apostles submit in silence, as sheep led to the slaughter; but when carnal superstition will heap upon them undue honour, then they resist with all their might, as against the dangerous snares of Satan. "This is holy anger, wherewith the servants of God must be inflamed, as often as they see His glory profaned. And assuredly no man shall be able otherwise to serve God sincerely and faithfully, unless he put on that feeling of jealousy, of which St Paul speaks in 2 Cor. xi. 2, that he be no less courageous and active to defend the glory of his Lord, than a husband is vigilant to defend his wife's chastity" (Calvin).—But what would these apostles have done, if they saw the adoration of their pretended bones, the worship of their images, and the idolatry which is now practised with them? (Leonh. and Spieg.)

We also are men of like destiny with you (ver. 15). It has its peculiar blessing when teachers, whom men regard in an idolatrous manner, place themselves in the same class with the lowest sinners, and testify: We are such poor and lost men as ye are, and it is only by the grace of God that we are made better. This gives to the unconverted pleasure and hope of deliverance; and the awakened, when they perceive human infirmity in their teacher, are thereby preserved from directly falling into error (Apost. Past.).—Praise is of no service to the Christian. It displeased Paul, when a certain damsel everywhere followed him, crying, These men are the servants of the Most High God, who show to you the way of salvation. The Christian does not forget that he is a flower, a shadow, a nothing without the grace of God. When one will praise his qualities, his alms, his works, his merits, then he says, I am also a mortal man (Leupold).—*We declare unto you that you should turn from these vanities unto the living God.* With this address the apostles stepped into the most decided opposition to heathenism, whose false gods are nothing else than the powers of nature, and whose worship is an ever increasing deviation from the truth. But, even in Christianity, the Gospel is not yet released from the old contest with the worship of nature. Sometimes more openly, sometimes more covertly, the idolatry of nature meets us. One hears of nature, of creation, of heaven, a thousand times, ere the personal thrice holy God is named once. If the second article of the creed is set aside, then the first article can be held no longer; for, as St John says, "Whosoever hath not the Son, hath not the Father also" (Langbein).

Who in times past suffered all nations to walk in their own ways. Nevertheless He hath not left Himself without a witness (vers. 16, 17). That God should suffer the Gentiles to walk in their own ways—the ways of pride and disobedience, and on that account of death and destruction—shows, in the first place, His punitive righteousness; but also His love is concealed therein, which by the bitter fruits of sin designs to make hearts anxious after salvation, and susceptible for grace. And also this "suffering them to walk in their own ways" does not exclude a control of these ways on the part of God. Whilst the Jews received the vocation to try whether they might not attain to the will of God by their own will, so the heathen were to see whether they might not know God in His wisdom by their own wisdom. But as God so often assisted the weak will of the Jews by severity and kindness, so He has not left the darkness of heathenism altogether without light. Even the natural blessings of God were voices sufficient to stir up, at least among the more earnest heathens, the dormant thought of the one true God (Williger).—*Filling our hearts with food and gladness.* God gives rain and fruitful seasons, not only for the satisfaction of the body, but also hearts are to be refreshed with earthly blessings, that they may praise the Lord with grateful joy and trust in His goodness (Leonh. and Spieg.).

And with these words scarce restrained they the people (ver. 18). How do men toil in the service of false gods, whilst they grudge to the true and living God one hour in the week! And how difficult is it to bring them off from the evident foolishness of their superstition, whilst the silly talk of a loose perverter is able to tear the faith from their heart! This shows that our natural heart loves the darkness rather than the light (Leonh. and Spieg.).

And they stoned Paul (ver. 19). How fickle is the world! First it brings garlands, then stones (Starke).—Every race subsequently stones its own gods; only each period has its own method of stoning (Ahlfeld).—Those who most bravely encounter the kingdom of darkness have the most enemies: Paul was stoned, and not Barnabas (Ahlfeld).—God must have had His own reasons why He preserved Paul from stoning at Iconium, whilst He subjected him to it at Lystra. Might not His design in this have been the more impressively to repel that adoration which men would render to the apostles? Thus God has often known how to humble with greater sufferings those teachers, who have acquired too much regard and an extravagant popularity. For the Lord will form of His servants not idols, but followers of His cross (Apost. Past.).

But as the disciples stood round him, he rose up (ver. 20). The world is often deceived in its views of the kingdom of Jesus and of the fate of its members. The enemies often shout, Raze it, raze it even to the foundation; it shall never rise, and the memory of its name shall be blotted out from the earth. But the soul of the oppressed exults: Rejoice not over me, O mine enemy; when I fall, I shall arise (Mic. vii. 8). For they that wait upon the Lord shall renew their strength; they shall mount up with wings, like eagles; they shall run and not be weary (Leonh. and Spieg.).—In a similar manner the Lord rescued the martyr Numidicus at Carthage, in the time of Cyprian. Half-burned, and heaped over with stones, he lay as one dead. His daughter came to bury him; then he arose and went with her into the city.—*And he went into the city.* Thus into the city, where they had almost murdered him. Was not that to venture too much? Formerly they fled; but this may not always be. There might be reasons, why he should come again to the place, from which he had been forcibly expelled. The poor converted Gentiles must see that he still lives (Gossner).

On the whole section (vers. 8–20).—*How the Christian should meet those who give to him the honour which is due to God.* 1. With the sorrowful expression of pity for their blindness. 2. With humble acknowledgment of his own weakness. 3. With courageous confession of God's majesty (Leupold).—*The idolatry of our days.* 1. To whom it is directed. 2. Whence it springs. 3. Whither it leads (Leonh. and Spieg.).—*The cure of the lame man at Lystra, a representation of the way in which the new man in us learns to walk* (vers. 8–10). 1. The natural lameness. 2. The learning to walk (Lisco).—*The horror of Paul and Barnabas at the adoration rendered to them at Lystra, a testimony against the idolatrous tendency of our age.* 1. The nature of such idolatrous tendency, from what it arises, and how it expresses itself (vers. 8–13). 2. Why a healthy disposition cannot refrain from horror and disgust on account of the falsehood of such adoration, and the ingratitude to God contained in it (vers. 14–20), (Lisco).—*The reprehensibleness of the adoration of the saints in the Romish Church.* 1. Its nature. 2. Its reprehensibleness. —*The contest of Christianity with heathenism.* 1. A contest with the idolizing of men, while it proclaims the incarnation of God. 2. A contest with the worship of nature, while it proclaims the living God as the Lord of creation. 3. A contest with walking in our own ways (Acts xiv. 16), while it requires us to walk in God's commandments (Langbein).—*The gods have become like to men, and are come down to us.* 1. A statement of a foolish delusion in the mouth of the heathen; attesting the vague longing of the human heart after the condescension of a gracious and merciful God, but denying the unapproachable majesty of the Invisible and All-holy. 2. A statement of a blessed truth in the kingdom of Christ; pointing to the mystery of the divine incarnation in Christ; evidencing the blessedness of mankind reconciled with God.—*We also are men of like destiny as you*, a reproof against all idolizing of men in our day. 1. The heathen idolatry, as it rules in the midst of Christianity, from the worship of genius in heroes, thinkers, and poets, down to the worship of singers and dancers. 2. The Romish idolatry, from the adoration of saints down to the kissing of the Pope's toe. 3. The Evangelical Lutheran idolatry, partly as confessional idolatry of the reformers and confessions, and partly as pietistic idolatry of preachers and conversion to men.—*That ye turn from these vain idols to the living God, an earnest call to all idolaters among us.* 1. Who are your idols? Mammon? The belly? Mortal men? Your own self? Nature? Art? etc. 2. How are they able to assist you? Can they save you here and hereafter? Therefore to-day, whilst you hear His voice, harden not your hearts. Turn from these vain idols to the living God, who, indeed, even in the visible and transient, shows to us the gifts of His love, the reflection of His glory; but only in the Gospel of Jesus Christ manifests Himself in His fulness —in His holy majesty, as well as in His condescending grace.—*God in nature* (vers. 15–17). 1. As the almighty Creator, ver. 15. 2. As the gracious Preserver, ver. 17. 3. As the holy Governor, ver. 16.—*The book of the world (nature and history), introductory to the book of books.* 1. By its revelations, all of which lead to the living God of the Bible. 2. By its problems (sin and death), which find their solution only in the Gospel.—*The sacrifice which is pleasing to God* (vers. 14–18). 1. Presented not to dead idols or to mortal men, but to the living God, the Giver of all good things. 2. Consisting not in the fruits of the fields or in wreathed sacrifices, that is to say, not in any external gifts and works, but in living hearts full of repentance, faith, and new obedience.—*Paul at Lystra, or the stedfast walk of a servant of God through this changeable and easily excited world.* 1. Its garlands do not ensnare him (worldly success and popular favour do not inflate him, but he humbly gives God at all times the glory). 2. Its stones do not overwhelm him (popular hatred and worldly shame do not crush him, but he walks upright through trouble in the strength of his Lord).

3. *The Journey back to Antioch, on which they are mindful to strengthen and to put in order the youthful Churches in Lystra, Iconium, and Antioch in Pisidia* (vers. 21–28).

21 And after they had preached the Gospel in that city, and had gained
numerous disciples, they returned to Lystra, Iconium, and Antioch, 22
Strengthening the souls of the disciples, and exhorting them to continue in
the faith, and teaching them that we must through many troubles enter

into the kingdom of God. 23 And they elected them elders in every church,
and commended them by prayer and fasting to the Lord, on whom they had
believed. 24 And they journeyed through Pisidia, and came to Pamphylia.
25 And they spoke the word in Perga, and went down to Attalia. 26 And
thence they sailed to Antioch, from which they had been recommended to
the grace of God for the work which they had now accomplished. 27 But
when they were come, they assembled the church, and declared how much
God had done with them, and had opened to the Gentiles the door of faith.
28 And they abode there, not a short time, in company with the disciples.

EXEGETICAL EXPLANATIONS.

1. *After they had preached the Gospel in that city.*—In Derbe the preaching of the Gospel appears to have been accompanied with great success; at least the expression that they made *ἱκανούς* disciples leads us to suppose a considerable number of converts. Also they did not stay on sufferance merely in this city of Lycaonia, where nothing opposed their work. From this they commenced their return to Syria, yet not by the geographically nearest route through the province of Cilicia, bounding Lycaonia on the south-east; but they left the direct course to Syria, and journeyed back to the same cities which they had visited on their way out. And, indeed, in doing so, no other motive is to be thought on, than that they considered it as their nearest duty to visit once more all the churches founded on this missionary journey, and to confirm them both internally and externally. Accordingly they returned from Derbe to Lystra, Iconium, and Antioch of Pisidia, the three cities in which they had succeeded in founding churches.

2. What is related in vers. 21–23 refers summarily to all the three cities, or rather to all the four; for they would have done the same in Derbe before they left it, what certainly grammatically is related of Lystra, Iconium, and Antioch only. The work which they performed was partly direct by word and action, and partly indirect by prayer to God. Directly and personally, they endeavoured to strengthen the souls of individuals by the word of doctrine and of exhortation that they should continue firm, and cleave stedfastly to the faith which they had received. To this they added the declaration (*ὅτι* supposes *λαλεῖν* or *διδάσκειν* included in *παρακαλεῖν*), that the way to the kingdom of God leads necessarily (*δεῖ*) through many troubles. This declaration was necessary to strengthen their minds, because opposition and suffering might easily have made them err and have

caused them to apostatize from the faith. Moreover, Paul and Barnabas endeavoured to strengthen the churches by practical measures: they gave them elders to be rulers and overseers of the church (*πρεσβυτέρους κατ' ἐκκλησίαν*); *i.e.*, not perhaps an elder to each church, but several elders, otherwise we cannot represent the appointment as after the model of the elders among the Jews. But the mode of appointment expressed in *χειροτονήσαντες αὐτοῖς* is doubtful: whether Paul and Barnabas named suitable men entirely according to their own judgment, and from their personal authority; or whether the church engaged in the choice of those who were to be invested with office. *Χειροτονεῖν* is used to signify "to hold up the hands," "to elect by a majority of hands;" and, according to this, the expression leads rather to the idea, that the apostles appointed and conducted a congregational election. And to this also points the precedent in chap. vi., the election of the seven deacons in Jerusalem conducted by the apostles. And, indeed, it consisted with the nature of the transaction, that the apostles would give the most decided weight to the public opinion and confidence of the members of the church. The distance of these Asiatic churches from Antioch in Syria, which was their mother church, taken in connection with the circumstances of time and place,—by reason of which, they being at the commencement detached from the synagogue, were in want of a social footing, and were obliged to find such footing in themselves; and also opposed as they were to the hostile Jewish multitude, they were necessarily obliged to exist compact and united among themselves,—all this made an independent church government, and therefore overseers, indispensably necessary. (Against Schrader, who calls in question this notice, and supposes that here a later arrangement is without reason removed to so early a period, and referred to the apostles; see Lechler's "Apostolic Times.") A solemn religious service preceded the departure from each church, in which, with prayer and fasting, Paul and Barnabas recommended the newly converted to the Lord in whom they had believed; that is, to Jesus Christ,—to His gracious presence, His internal grace, and mighty protection. *Παρατίθεμαι* is used when one entrusts something to be preserved in order to be returned in due time by him with whom it is deposited; *fidei alicujus committere, servandum et custodiendum tradere.*

3. *They journeyed through Pisidia.*—From this their course proceeded again to the coast. They arrived again at Perga (chap. xiii. 13), in the province of Pamphylia. Here they preached the Gospel, but with what success we are not informed. They then went down to the coast (κατέβησαν), to Attalia, a city to the south-east of Perga, and bordering upon Lycia (built by Attalus Philadelphus, king of Pergamus, and named after him), from which they embarked. They then sailed in an easterly direction to Seleucia and the Orontes, and thence to Antioch. Here Luke unites the end of this self-contained narrative with the beginning—the now successful completion of the missionary work (ἐπλήρωσαν τὸ ἔργον, ver. 26) with the prayer of the church of Antioch for the protecting grace of God (παραδεδομέναι τῇ χάριτι τοῦ Θεοῦ, compare chap. xiii. 2–4). Paul and Barnabas, on this journey, which may have lasted two or three years (46–48 after Christ), had traversed, besides the island of Cyprus, a considerable district of Asia Minor, the south-eastern quarter of it; and, not to mention individual conversions, they had founded at least four Christian churches, consisting for the most part of Gentiles, and which promised well.

4. *And thence they sailed to Antioch.*—Arrived there, Paul and Barnabas assembled the church, in order, not only to render an account to it (by which they had been sent forth, and recommended to the grace of God) of what they had done, but also, and indeed chiefly, to give information of what the Lord had done with them. *Μετ' αὐτῶν*, not equivalent to δι' αὐτῶν, but equivalent to "being with them," "assisting them." The θύρα πίστεως, which God had opened to the Gentiles, refers not only to the external opportunity and call to believe, which God had granted to them by this missionary journey of Paul and Barnabas, but likewise to the internal opening by the gracious operations of the Holy Ghost—to the awakened willingness to believe which God had given them. The χρόνος οὐκ ὀλίγος which Paul and Barnabas remained with the disciples, that is, with the church of Antioch, may be supposed to be some years; and this residence might be of the greatest importance both for the missionaries and for the church itself.

DOGMATICAL AND ETHICAL THOUGHTS.

1. The idea of the kingdom of God, as it is represented in

ver. 22, evidently includes something of the other world, and cannot be understood entirely of this world; for only through many θλίψεις can we enter into the βασιλεία τοῦ Θεοῦ. The θλίψεις are the way, not the end; the gate, not the house itself. And yet those who suffer the tribulations are pious and believing persons, who stand fast in the faith (ἐμμένοντες τῇ πίστει). As long as they go through tribulations, they have not yet entered into the kingdom of God. Thus, then, the kingdom of God evidently lies on the other side of the tribulations, and is a kingdom of blessedness. Those who go through tribulations, already walk in the faith, and are already members of the Church of Christ; but they belong to the Church militant: not until they die, do they find themselves in the Church triumphant, in the βασιλεία τοῦ Θεοῦ. The Church and the kingdom of God, then, are not precisely the same: the one is the outer court, and the other is the sanctuary, or rather the holy of holies.

2. In the conduct of the apostles of the Gentiles (vers. 22, 23) the proper degree and mode of acting in the doctrine and government of the Church, dictated by the Holy Ghost, is represented to us modally and typically. It is the proper union and interpenetration of doctrine and order, of human action and divine gracious operation. That the churches recently planted can only be preserved by the presence and grace of Christ, is certain to the apostles. Therefore they earnestly recommend them, with prayer and fasting, to the Lord, who is the strong fortress and rock of all believers. But, far removed from fanatical trust in God, the apostles also do their part by word and action, in order to strengthen the young plants of the Church, and to give them stability to the utmost of their power. They do so not primarily and chiefly by regular ordinances and directions, as if the guarantee of continuance and favour lay chiefly in these things; but, in the first instance, by the word of exhortation and doctrine, of comfort and promise (παρακαλοῦντες),—all this resting on the word of God. Nevertheless, the apostles do not agree with those who would allow the word to work exclusively, and who put no value whatever upon ecclesiastical forms, rights, and ordinances, and entirely dispense with them. On the contrary, they have, in order to give to the churches the necessary social independence, appointed elders in every church, and, as it seems, by the election of the churches. And yet these

were youthful communities, in which as yet no long Christian experience, no stedfastness of Christian character, no deep insight could be sought. But that these elders were to have been exclusively, or even chiefly, preachers and teachers, may safely be denied, because the Jewish elders were not invested with the office of teaching, and because the πρεσβύτεροι, mentioned in chap. xi. 30, are only brought forward as rulers, not as teachers.

3. At the close of this section (chap. xiii. and xiv.), the impression is again brought prominently forward, that all the mighty acts of the apostles—all the deeply founded, illustrious, and victorious actions of believers—are to be regarded as the actions of God and of the Lord Jesus Christ Himself. It is God who has done all those things which Paul and Barnabas have all this time performed. He was with them (μετ' αὐτῶν, ver. 27); He has opened the door of faith to the Gentiles. They have certainly completed the work (ἐπλήρωσαν), but they have only been successful in virtue of the grace of God, to which they had been commended. The blessing and progress, the fruit and success, the honour and glory, are His. This is not only the Redeemer's mind and view (John xiv. 12-14), but was also the Apostle Paul's own conviction (1 Cor. xv. 10). This is, and is still and ever will remain, the truth.

HOMILETICAL HINTS.

After they had preached the Gospel in that city, they returned to Lystra, Iconium, and Antioch (ver. 21). As heat makes brick only the stronger and the more enduring, so does the fire of trouble make a believing servant of God (Starke).—What a pressure of love must have filled the heart of this apostle, that he immediately returns to this same city after having suffered stoning, and, without bitterness against his enemies, with gentleness and commiserating love, continues to preach the Gospel, with the determination not to leave off, though it cost him his life! Ought not this earnestness to put us to a holy shame? (Apost. Past.)—The wounds of the apostle and the marks of the stoning still bleed; and yet he preaches again the Gospel of the cross, and his wounds also preach concerning the power of faith (Leonh. and Spieg.).

Strengthening the souls of the disciples (ver. 22). See here the work of a teacher in its entire compass. 1. εὐαγγελίζειν, to preach Christ, ver. 21. 2. μαθητεύειν, to instruct individuals and to make disciples, ver. 21. 3. ἐπιστηρίζειν, to strengthen and confirm them in the faith, ver. 22. 4. παρακαλεῖν, to exhort and comfort them in suffering, ver. 22 (Apost. Past.).—*That we must through much tribulation enter into the kingdom of God.* This lesson must be preached to all Christians. In laughter, the Church decays: the more it sows in tears, the more beautifully it flourishes; the more God's vine is pruned, the better it grows (Starke).—"Trouble will entirely cease," was not the comfort which the apostles left to the disciples on their departure; but, "It will come, it must come, it must be seen in you, that you are of the order of the cross" (Williger).—Very sad sounds this "must;" but it rests not on the will of a cold and unbending fate, but on the appointment of God, that believers are to be conformed to Christ (Rom. viii. 17); on the enmity that was established from the beginning between Christ and Satan (Gen. iii. 15); and, in short, on the necessary crucifixion of our own corrupt flesh (2 Cor. iv. 16), (Starke).—Thinkest thou that thou wilt come into the kingdom of heaven without the cross and tribulation, which Christ neither would nor could permit even to one of His dearest friends and saints? Ask the triumphant citizens of heaven, whom thou wilt: all will answer thee, Through the cross and chastisement have we reached the glory of God. Well, then, take the yoke of the Lord upon thee, which, for those who love Him, is easy and light. Remain at the sacred cross, which blossoms with virtues, and drops with the oil of grace. What wilt thou otherwise? This is the true, the holy, the perfect way, the way of Christ, the way of the just and the elect. Carry it willingly, so will it carry thee, and conduct thee to that place where there is an end of all thy sorrows and the goal of thy longings (Thomas Aquinas).—The Head was crowned with thorns, and the members must not expect chaplets of roses (Scriver).—O what happy men are we Christians! We have the best pledge of our Father's love in the heart, the cup of suffering in the hand which brings us into the fellowship of the Saviour's cross, and the crown in the eye which follows on the fellowship of the cross: who then will tremble or be sad? (Tholuck.)

Elected them elders, and commended them by prayer and fasting to the Lord (ver. 23). The apostles thought the ministerial office necessary for believers, and therefore ordained elders to their new congregations; but they did not bind the people to their teachers, but commended them to the Lord in whom they had believed. This is the proper medium between immoderate exaltation and complete rejection of the ministerial office (Apost. Past.).—When we can no more see and personally care for those whom we love, we must by believing prayer recommend them to God, and thus be calm (Starke).—To establish order in churches already founded, is no less important than to found them by the Gospel (Williger).

But when they were come, they gathered the Church together, and declared how much God had done with them, and had opened the door of faith to the Gentiles (ver. 27). He who has the keys of David can open all doors. Only no preacher must assume the keys to himself, and imagine that he can open hearts, but must pray that the Lord may do it, and give the glory to Him alone (Gossner).—God must open three doors, if something is to be effected for the salvation of souls: the door of the mouth of the teachers, and the doors of the ear and heart of the hearers (Starke); and, finally, a fourth and last door—the door of heaven.—We must not conceal God's works and wonders, but in humility of heart proclaim them, in order that others along with us may be stirred up to praise God's goodness and power (Starke).—This was also the glory of Jesus when He returned to His Father: "I have finished the work which Thou gavest Me to do." And nothing else than this faithful performance of the task enjoined upon us, will redound to our honour at our departure (Apost. Past.).

And they abode there in company with the disciples (ver. 28). The relaxation of the faithful servants of God is only a change of work (Quesnel).

On the whole section (vers. 21–28).—*A picture of apostolic efficiency.* 1. They do not suffer themselves to be disconcerted by severe sufferings. 2. They carry the word to those who do not know it. 3. They nourish the faith implanted. 4. They arrange the ordinances of the Church. 5. They render an account (Lisco).—*The blessing which the preaching of the Gospel among the heathen brings.* 1. To the preachers: confirmation by suffering, and by the experience of the divine aid, vers. 20–22. 2. To the converted: instead of heathen disorder, Christian order of life; instead of loose fables, the divine word, vers. 23–25. 3. To the senders: refreshment in the faith and increase in love (After Lisco).—*The return of Paul and Barnabas, a representation of our return to our home above.* 1. A representation of the incidents of the journey, vers. 20–22. 2. A representation of the business of the journey, vers. 23–25. 3. A representation of the arrival home, vers. 26–28 (Lisco).—*The comfort of the discourse, that we must through much tribulation enter into the kingdom of God.* 1. As Christ's prophecy, it deprives tribulation of its strangeness. 2. It discovers to us the nature of our hearts and the importance of tribulation. 3. It makes clear to us the position of the kingdom of Christ and our own position with reference to the world (Harless).—*The way of tribulation.* 1. Its travellers: all true Christians; "we;" therefore do not wonder at it. 2. Its necessity: "we must;" therefore do not shun it. 3. Its nature: rugged and long; "through much tribulation;" therefore do not despond on account of it. 4. Its end: blessedness; "must enter into the kingdom of God;" therefore do not neglect it.—*The blessing of the cross.* 1. While it shows us the vanity of earthly prosperity, it excites us to strive after heavenly treasures. 2. While it shows us the uncertainty of human love, it excites us to seek assistance in God alone. 3. While it shows us our own weakness, it stirs us up to be strong in the Lord (Leonh. and Spieg.).—*How are we qualified as soldiers of Christ to fight the good fight?* 1. When we early reconcile ourselves in patience to trouble. 2. When we exhort and strengthen one another to stedfastness in the faith. 3. When with all fidelity we rely upon the Lord in prayer (Langbein).—*By the cross to the crown.* The way of Christ, of the apostles, and of every true Christian.—*The evangelical pastorate,* with its sufferings and dangers, its works and labours, its joys and victories.—*The comfort of a pastor on his departure from his congregation.* 1. The good seed which he sees germinating, vers. 21, 22. 2. The faithful fellow-servants, to whom he hands over the field, ver. 23. 3. The chief Shepherd, to whom he recommends souls, ver. 23.—*The best gain of a servant of God, returning home.* 1. Wounds received in the service of his Lord, vers. 19, 20. Souls gained for the kingdom of Christ, vers. 21–23. 3. Psalms sung by the assistance of God, vers. 26, 27.—"The word gone out of My mouth shall not return unto

Me void," proved by the success of the first mission to the Gentiles.—"*The Lord has done great things for us:*" the hymn of praise of all God's faithful servants on the retrospect of their pilgrimage. It expresses great joy, for what the Lord has done in them and through them; and deep humility, that to the Lord alone is the honour due.

SECTION II.

MISSION OF THE GENTILE APOSTLES, PAUL AND BARNABAS, ON THE AFFAIRS OF THE GENTILE CHRISTIANS, FROM ANTIOCH TO JERUSALEM. TRANSACTIONS THERE, AND THEIR RESULTS (CHAP. XV. 1–34).

A.

The requirement of Circumcision by the Judaizers excites dissensions in Antioch; on which account, Paul and Barnabas are sent to Jerusalem. Their Journey, and the first events which happened at Jerusalem.

CHAP. XV. 1–5.

1 And certain came down from Judea, and taught the brethren: If ye
be not circumcised according to the manner of Moses, ye cannot be saved.
2 As then no small dissension and dispute arose between Paul and Barnabas
and them, they arranged that Paul and Barnabas, and certain others of them,
should go up to Jerusalem to the apostles and elders, about this controversy.
3 So they then were accompanied by the Church, and journeyed through
Phenicia and Samaria, declaring the conversion of the Gentiles, and caused
great joy to all the brethren. 4 But when they arrived at Jerusalem, they
were received by the Church, and by the apostles and elders; and they
declared to them how much God had done with them. 5 Then arose cer-
tain of the sect of the Pharisees, who believed, and said, It is necessary to
circumcise them, and to command them to keep the law of Moses.

Ver. 1. Περιτμηθῆτε instead of περιτέμνησθε is strongly attested, and is preferred by all the modern critics.

Ver. 2. Ζητήσεως, which, along with καί, is wanting in MS. E., is far more strongly attested than συζητήσεως, which is to be found in no uncial MS.

Ver. 4. Παρεδέχθησαν is indeed in fewer MSS., but yet it might have been exchanged for ἀπεδέχθησαν, because it is an unusual word.

EXEGETICAL EXPLANATIONS.

1. *And certain came down.*—The appearance of certain from Judea, and what they proposed at Antioch, reveals to us at once a deep fermentation in the Church, and an important question which must be solved and debated. Luke describes those who cast the stone into the water, which caused ever-widening circles, as τινές ἀπὸ τῆς Ἰουδαίας, certain who were from Judea, who came from it. This is undoubtedly not to be understood merely geographically, but it likewise points to the engrained Jewish disposition and mode of thought. The Syrian version and Cod. 8 have after Ἰουδαίας: τῶν πεπιστευκότων ἀπὸ τῆς αἱρέσεως τῶν Φαρισαίων, an insertion for the sake of explanation borrowed from ver. 5, but which without doubt correctly represents the matter. Some such Christians from Judea, and probably from Jerusalem, came to Antioch. It is to be supposed that they did not come accidentally, but that they journeyed there on purpose, and indeed on an understanding with those who held the same opinion. And from the circumstance that the apostles sent their official letter not only to the Gentile Christians at Antioch, but to the converted Gentiles in Syria and Cilicia, it is inferred, with some appearance of truth, that these Judaizers did not confine themselves to Antioch, but sought to work upon the Gentile Christians in Syria and Cilicia.

2. *If ye be not circumcised.*—The intruders came forward with a formal doctrine; ἐδίδασκον, *data opera* (Bengel): they advanced confidently a certain definite proposition in a categorical form, as universally applicable, and with a claim to acknowledgment and observance. It is evident that they did not express themselves only in the form of scruples, doubts, suppositions, or misgivings, although they may have done so at first and by way of trial. Their fundamental proposition consisted in this: that the Gentile Christians could not possibly receive deliverance from destruction and salvation in Christ, unless they submitted to circumcision according to the custom of Moses, *i.e.* according to the custom legally sanctioned by Moses.

3. *No small dispute arose between Paul and Barnabas and them.*—It is easy to conceive that, in consequence of this, there was

excited in the Church of Antioch (which consisted for the most part of Gentile Christians, who were hitherto free from the law of Moses) a great disturbance, a στάσις, a division; from which it may be inferred that the whole Church did not rise up as one man against the new teachers, but that a part may have gone over to their side, while their representations were not without influence upon individuals. Also there arose a great ζήτησις, a disputation, in which Paul and Barnabas took the side of Christian freedom against the legalists. However, at Antioch no final decision was come to. Neither did the Judaizers give way and permit themselves to be convinced of the Gentile Christians' divine right of freedom from the law, nor would Paul and Barnabas sacrifice evangelical freedom and give up the field to the Judaizers; besides, the Church of Antioch was itself interested in the matter, and could not be a judge of its own business. The right expedient was taken to transfer the decision to Jerusalem. The new teachers with their disturbing views had come from Judea, and they likewise appeared, as we may suppose, in the name of others, perhaps ostensibly in the name of the original Church and of the apostles. Accordingly the matter must be decided in Jerusalem. Therefore the Church resolved (*ἔταξαν, sc. οἱ ἀδελφοί,* the Christians at Antioch) that Paul and Barnabas, and certain others from among them (the former, as the Gentile missionaries, in an independent capacity; the latter, as the representatives of the Church of Antioch), should journey to the apostles and elders at Jerusalem, in order to dispose of this question, and if possible to bring it to a definite decision. Antioch was, it is true, the mother Church of more newly formed Christian congregations; but Jerusalem continued the metropolis of Christianity, chiefly because the apostles in part still resided there, than whom there was no higher authority for Christians in the world. If we compare Gal. ii. with vers. 1 and 2, neither the ἀποκάλυψις, in consequence of which Paul journeyed to Jerusalem, excludes the τάσσειν on the part of the Church of Antioch, nor the reverse. The objection which was made by the legally minded Jews is the same in both narratives. And whilst Paul relates that he and Barnabas took Titus with them, this notice perfectly agrees with this, that καί τινες ἄλλοι ἐξ αὐτῶν accompanied them.

4. *They were accompanied by the Church.*—Προπέμπω is either

to send forward, or to accompany: here the latter must be meant. The Church escorted them from Antioch a part of the way; a proof what general sympathy prevailed, and what importance was attached to the journey. During their journey by land, which they took through Phenicia and Samaria, they visited the Christians, and caused great joy among them, both by their visit and by the communications which they made of the *ἐπιστροφὴ τῶν ἐθνῶν*, *i.e.*, not of the conduct of the Gentiles (Luther), which is never the meaning of the word, but of their conversion. Compare chap. xiv. 15, and xv. 19, *ἐπιστρέφειν*. The missionary journey in Asia Minor, with its success, was evidently the chief subject of the *ἐκδιηγήσεις*: compare *διήγησις*, Luke i. 1.

5. *But when they arrived at Jerusalem.*—Here the reception was official. *Ἀπεδέχθησαν*, they were publicly and honourably received as the ambassadors of the Church of Antioch, by the Church as well as by the apostles and elders in a solemn assembly, after they had, as is evident, imparted the occasion of their mission to individuals. In this assembly of the Church, Paul and Barnabas detailed what God had done through them, and in connection with them (*μετ' αὐτῶν*, as in chap. xiv. 27) to the Gentiles. With this the subject of dispute was expressly introduced, but at first without argument or disputation. Immediately, however, certain Jewish Christians, who before their conversion had belonged to the sect of the Pharisees, protested against the reception of so many Gentiles into the Church of Christ without any regard to the law of Moses. *Ἐξανέστησαν*, namely, in that assembly; so that the narrative of Luke is continuous: not however that *ἐξανέστησαν*, etc., were words spoken by the ambassadors from Antioch (Beza, Heinrichs). What these pharisaically minded Christians maintained, differs essentially from what their associates in opinion proposed at Antioch. 1. Those in Jerusalem demanded the circumcision of the Gentiles, as something to be forced upon them, *δεῖ περιτέμνειν αὐτούς*, as something to which the Gentiles must be compelled. 2. In Antioch, the Mosaic law was only asserted in so far as it sanctioned circumcision, and that as a custom or usage (*τῷ ἔθει Μωϋσέως*, ver. 1); here, at Jerusalem, they went further, and demanded that the observance of the Mosaic law in general should be imposed upon the Gentile Christians as a duty (*παραγγέλλειν τε τηρεῖν τὸν νόμον Μωϋσέως*).

The faction found themselves upon their own ground at Jerusalem, and there felt the stronger; they brought forward their ultimate conclusions; whereas the speakers of the same faction had found the atmosphere at Antioch such that they found themselves obliged to proceed with prudence and reserve.

DOGMATICAL AND ETHICAL THOUGHTS.

1. The difference here presented to us is a deeply comprehensive and fundamental one. The question discussed is this: Law or Gospel? evangelical freedom or legal bondage? The opponents did not indeed think that they had rejected Jesus; for then they would not have been Christians at all, whereas they were πεπιστευκότες, ver. 5. And there is no reason to suppose that they were not truly in earnest in their belief on Jesus as their Saviour, and in their entire Christianity. But yet the whole tendency of their views went absolutely to assert circumcision, this sign of the old covenant, and along with it the old covenant itself and the law of Moses, as essential to salvation. And whenever we substitute something else for Jesus Christ and living communion with Him as the ground of salvation, then is the Redeemer and His work injured and disregarded. At first the two are united and put on the same footing: Christ's redemption and the law of Moses; Christ's grace and our own works; or thus, Christ and the saints; or, perhaps thus, Christ personally and the true doctrine. But then, involuntarily, a step further is taken, and what was only co-ordinate with the chief matter is placed in the first rank, and thus the truth is entirely deranged. What is here not indeed expressly discussed, but yet at the root of the discussion, is the fulness and sufficiency of Christ—the exclusiveness of His divine-human person.

2. This is one side of the question. The other side is, that evangelical freedom was threatened. And this Paul brings prominently forward in Gal. ii. The grace of God in Christ conditions the evangelical freedom of the redeemed. The more grace is restricted in its all-sufficiency, so much the more is freedom of conscience also restrained by the yoke of the law. Thus, then, as the peculiar dignity and all-sufficient merit of Christ is here discussed, so also are the dignity and internal freedom of redeemed souls, and the slavish, or, on the other

hand, the childlike, joyful condition of the conscience toward God.

3. Moreover, the universality of Christianity is here called in question. The pharisaical Jewish Christians would indeed have consented that the Gentiles should be received into the Church of Christ; they would not certainly have opposed the conversion of the Gentiles, provided they submitted to circumcision and the law of Moses. Thus they might liberally enough admit and affirm, that the destination of the Gospel to be the religion of the world was not to be interfered with. But, in point of fact, they erected a mighty barrier in the way of the human destination and of the all-comprehensive significance of the salvation of Christ. To adhere to the Mosaic law as absolutely binding, and its observance as necessary to salvation, is, in fact, to perpetuate the old covenant, and to hinder the new covenant from gaining ground; to maintain the separation between Jews and Gentiles, and to perpetuate segregation.

4. For these reasons, Paul durst not be silent, nor yield. Peace is a valuable blessing, and the unity of the Church is an important end. Yet it would be wrong to seek and to preserve peace at any price, and unity as absolutely the highest blessing. Truth is higher. The pure Gospel of the grace of God must be preserved or restored, even at the cost of concord. Thus did the apostles, and thus did the reformers in their time act. But the matter must concern the kernel, and not the mere husk,—the faith itself, and not the mere scientific and learned comprehension of it,—the glory of God and Christ, and not mere human and party interests.

For Homiletical Hints, see below.

B.

Course of Transactions at the deciding Assembly at Jerusalem.

Chap. xv. 6–21.

6 But the apostles and elders assembled to consider this matter. 7 And
when there had been much disputation, Peter arose and said to them: Men
and brethren, ye know that, a long time ago, God made choice among you,
that by my mouth the Gentiles should hear the word of the Gospel, and
believe. 8 And God, who knoweth the hearts, bore them witness, giving
them the Holy Ghost, even as to us; 9 And made no distinction between

**us and them, purifying their hearts by the faith. 10 Wherefore now tempt
ye God by placing a yoke upon the neck of the disciples, which neither our
fathers nor we were able to bear? 11 But we believe that, through the
grace of our Lord Jesus, we shall be saved in the same manner as they.
12 Then the whole multitude were silent and listened, as Paul and Barnabas
related what great signs and wonders God had done among the Gentiles
through them. 13 And after they were silent, James answered and said:
Men and brethren, hearken to me; 14 Simon has declared how God at the
first has chosen a people from among the Gentiles, in order to take them to
Himself for His name. 15 And with this agree the words of the prophets,
as it is written: 16 Afterwards will I return, and build up the fallen taber-
nacle of David, and will build again its ruins, and raise it up, 17 In order
that the residue of men may seek the Lord, and all the nations upon whom
My name is called, saith the Lord, who does these things. 18 These things
are known from of old. 19 Therefore I judge that we trouble not those
who are converted to God from the Gentiles; 20 But enjoin them to abstain
from the pollutions of idolatry and fornication, from things strangled and
from blood. 21 For Moses has from ancient times in every city those who
preach him, being read in the synagogues every Sabbath.**

Ver. 7. *Ἐν ὑμῖν* in MSS. A.B.C. has justly been preferred by Lachmann and Tischendorf. *Ἐν ἡμῖν* is, at all events, the simpler reading.

Ver. 11. *Τοῦ κυρίου Ἰησοῦ* is decidedly better attested than *κυρίου Ἰησοῦ Χριστοῦ.*

Ver. 14. The dative *τῷ ὀνόματι* is without doubt correct, whilst *ἐπὶ* before these words is a spurious addition.

Ver. 17. *Ταῦτα* after *πάντα* is, according to the best MSS., spurious.

Ver. 18. *Γνωστὰ ἀπ' αἰῶνας*: only these three words are in the MSS. B. and C., in 13 cursive MSS. and several Oriental versions. To these original words, some MSS. have added *αὐτῷ* or *τῷ κυρίῳ*, or *τῷ Θεῷ πάντα τὰ ἔργα αὐτοῦ*, E.G.H. Instead of the plural A.D. and some versions have the singular: *γνωστὸν ἀπ' αἰῶνος τῷ κυρίῳ τὸ ἔργον αὐτοῦ*, a reading which Lachmann has preferred.

EXEGETICAL EXPLANATIONS.

1. *But they assembled.*—*Συνήχθησαν*: this assembly was expressly called for this one object, to take this matter, *ὁ λόγος οὗτος*, *i.e.*, the present controversy, into consideration. Luke names only the apostles and elders; but that the whole Church was also present, and indeed that they were present not only to listen but to determine, is undoubtedly evident from vers. 21 and 22 (*πᾶν τὸ πλῆθος, ὅλη ἡ ἐκκλησία, οἱ ἀδελφοί*).

2. *But when there had been much disputation.*—At first there arose a lively debate, much disputation (*πολλὴ συζήτησις*, ver. 7), whilst the conflicting and exclusive views were openly

strongly, and firmly expressed and opposed to each other. We may suppose that the pharisaical Jewish Christians on the one side, and the Gentile Christians of Antioch on the other side, opposed one another. But now Peter arose, in order, in the confusion of contending views and feelings, to give a clue which might help to a solution. He directs himself, as the interrogative reproach (ver. 10) evidently shows, to the pharisaically and legally disposed, in order not only to satisfy them, but to convince them of their error, indeed of their injustice and sin. For this purpose he reminds them of a fact well known to them (*ὑμεῖς ἐπίστασθε*), namely, the conversion of Cornelius and the Gentiles who were with him. He describes this event as one that happened a long time ago (*ἀφ' ἡμερῶν ἀρχαίων*); at all events, a period of at least ten years had elapsed since then.

3. *Then Peter arose and said.*—He first characterizes the conversion of Cornelius and the Gentiles according to its essential importance (vers. 7–9), and then makes an application of it to the present question. The importance of that event consists in the following particulars. 1. God was there the Agent (*Θεὸς ἐξελέξατο*, etc., *ὁ καρδιογνώστης Θεὸς ἐμαρτύρησεν αὐτοῖς*, etc., *καὶ οὐδὲν διέκρινε*, etc.). 2. The preaching of the Gospel, by which these Gentiles believed, was not exclusively an affair of Peter, but it belonged as well to the whole Church; God only selected him (*ἐν ὑμῖν ἐξελέξατο*). 3. The omniscient God has, by the communication of the Holy Ghost, borne witness to these Gentiles of His satisfaction (*αὐτοῖς, dat. comm.*). By this it is taken for granted that God imparts the Holy Ghost only to those who are pleasing to Him. But that He could not be deceived in these persons, *καρδιογνώστης* gives us to understand. 4. God, after He had purified the hearts of the Gentiles through faith, made no difference between them and the believing Jews. *Οὐδὲν διέκρινε—καθαρίσας* is unmistakeably an allusion to the words of the vision, chap. x. 15. What God has cleansed are the hearts of the Gentiles: their uncleanness cleaves not, as the pharisaical view supposes, to the body; the instrument of purification, therefore, is not circumcision, but faith.

4. *Wherefore tempt ye God?*—Ver. 10 makes the application to the present controversy in the form of a reproachful question. As the matter stands thus (*οὖν*), wherefore then tempt ye God, whilst ye would put a yoke upon them? This is a tempting of

God, *i.e.*, an action in which a man runs the risk of God's showing and carrying out His will to that man's hurt and destruction. By the yoke which these men would put on the necks of the disciples is to be understood, not circumcision in and by itself, but along with it the whole Mosaic law. When now Peter maintains that neither the fathers, nor he himself, nor all the converted Israelites, the pharisaically disposed included (ἡμεῖς), have been able to bear this legal yoke, he certainly gives up the Mosaic law as a law binding in itself, and declares, first, that no man was able perfectly to fulfil it, and, secondly, that the law on that account cannot be the means of salvation.

5. *But we believe.*—To the proposition which denies the way of salvation by the law, Peter with ἀλλά opposes the way of salvation through the grace of Jesus Christ. As they (ἐκεῖνοι, the Gentile Christians), so we also are assured of salvation by the grace of Christ. In both propositions—in the negative (ver. 10) and in the positive (ver. 11)—the Gentile Christians are placed in juxtaposition with the Jewish Christians. There, the thought is, These can as little bear the law as we: here, the meaning is, We can be saved by the grace of Christ as well as they.

6. *Then the multitude were silent.*—This silence of the multitude gives us to understand that the πολλὴ συζήτησις was allayed by the speech of Peter, and that the minds of the disciples were quieted by the truth explained. Barnabas and Paul now address the assembly. Here Barnabas is again mentioned, as at an earlier period, before Paul. Without doubt he spoke first, as having been longer and better known to those present. The purport of their addresses had reference to the incidents of their recent missionary journey to the Gentiles. They related the wonderful works of God among the Gentiles, which He had done through them as His servants; *i.e.*, the wonderful conversions and operations of the new divine life which had been manifested among so many Gentiles. These accounts agreed with, confirmed, and carried further what Peter had imparted from his earlier experience. And thus the impression must have been strengthened, that the conversion of the Gentiles is a work of God, and that the Christianity of the believing Gentiles, even without the observance of the law, must be pleasing to God.

7. After Barnabas and Paul had finished their communications (here σιγᾷν is employed in a different sense than in ver.

12), James addressed the meeting. This is without doubt "the brother of the Lord" (see chap. xii. 17) who stood at the head of the Church in Jerusalem, and who on account of his legal strictness had received the honourable appellation of "the Just." His address was connected with the speech of Peter, which he resumed, and the main thought of which he confirmed by reference to the prophecies of the Old Testament. James, as a Hebrew speaking to the Hebrews, calls the Apostle Peter by his Hebrew name Συμεών instead of Σίμων (being only a difference of the Greek manner of writing שִׁמְעוֹן). Ἐπεσκέψατο λαβεῖν, God has looked round to take to Himself a people, or God has resolved, as the middle with the classics frequently signifies *considerare.* The phrase ἐξ ἐθνῶν λαόν is expressive, for elsewhere ἔθνη always forms a contrast to λαός (Israel); but here, out of the Gentiles, God has taken a people. *Τῷ ὀνόματι αὐτοῦ*, for the acknowledgment and veneration, for the confession of His name. What Peter related and characterized as a matter of fact, James now illustrates by the prophetical word as a fulfilment of the promises of God. *Οἱ λόγοι* many prophecies, of which, however, he only mentions one.

8. *And build again the fallen tabernacle of David* (Amos ix. 11, 12).—In the original Hebrew text, the restoration of the fallen house of David is promised (אֹהֶל, σκηνή, because it was decayed); and it is also added, that the Israelites should inherit (יִירְשׁוּ), that is, subject to their authority Edom and all the heathen on whom Jehovah's name is called, who are consecrated to Him. The Messianic restoration is here so described that it will result in good to the heathen nations who embrace the worship of Jehovah; and accordingly the conversion of the Gentiles to Christ is a fulfilment of this prediction. The Septuagint, which the text follows, deviates somewhat from the original, and supposes another reading than the Masoretic text; for example, instead of יִירְשׁוּ אֶת־שְׁאֵרִית אֱדוֹם the words יִדְרְשׁוּ שְׁאֵרִית אָדָם; and James in this passage adds a few words of his own, as ἀναστρέψω, and then the words γνωστὰ ἀπ' αἰῶνος, *scil.* αὐτῷ or τῷ Θεῷ (which some MSS. have inserted), which he mixes up with the original words. James by this addition intends to say, What has happened to-day, God has from the beginning known and determined to do; what we live to see, is only the fulfilment of an eternal counsel of God.

9. *Therefore I judge.*—From the fact which Peter had brought to their recollection, and from the promises of the prophetic word concerning the reception of the Gentiles into the kingdom of God, James now draws the practical conclusion (διὸ ἐγὼ κρίνω), that those Gentiles who were converted unto God should not be burdened (παρενοχλεῖν). This is a conclusion which recognises the evangelical liberty of the Gentile Christians, rejects the demands of the pharisaically disposed, and agrees perfectly with Paul.

10. *That they abstain.*—But at the same time James proposes to require certain abstinences from the Gentiles. Ἐπιστεῖλαι, *mandare;* it is not always *literas mittere,* though that meaning is very frequent, and suits well here. James means that something must be required from the Gentiles. Yet what he proposes differs widely from what was the aim of the Judaizers. They declared the positive submission to circumcision and to the whole Mosaic law to be the indispensable condition of salvation. But James only requires an ἀπέχεσθαι, an avoidance of ἀλισγήματα. Ἀλίσγημα, a word which is entirely unknown in classic Greek, derived from ἀλισγέω, which occurs in the Septuagint and the later Hellenistic writers in the sense of "to pollute," "to defile;" consequently ἀλίσγημα signifies a pollution. The four following genitives mention the things by which they may be polluted.—*Εἴδωλα,* idols, and what is connected with their worship. *Πορνεία,* used without any defining mark, can, as little as εἴδωλα, be taken in a limited and metaphorical sense (*e.g.,* idolatry, incest, marriage within forbidden degrees), but must be understood in its usual sense, unchastity, fornication. The two other points have reference to food. They must abstain from partaking of τοῦ πνικτοῦ, that is, of the flesh of animals which have been strangled. According to Lev. xvii. 13, before animals could be eaten, both by the Israelites and by the stranger that sojourned among them, their blood had first to be poured out. So also the Gentile Christians had to abstain from blood (τοῦ αἵματος), because in the blood is the life of every living creature, Lev. xvii. 14; Gen. ix. 4. The laws with reference to food are in the old covenant of a higher nature than the Levitical; every one who transgressed them was to be cut off (Lev. xvii. 14), and they are expressly extended to the גֵּרִים. James thus intends that the Gentile Christians should avoid

whatever is entirely inconsistent with the true religion of the holy God, according to their ancient tradition, and what would make on every Israelite the deepest impression of heathen abomination and of extreme offensiveness.

11. *For Moses has.*—The logical connection of the concluding words is very doubtful. James observes, that from of old, in every city, Moses is preached, inasmuch as the Thora is read in the synagogues every Sabbath-day. But by this he does not intend to say that Moses was read in the Christian assemblies as well as in the Jewish (Grotius); but he supposes that the Christians still adhere to the synagogue. *Γάρ* gives us undeniably to understand, that this fact contains a reason. But it is not clear what idea is to be confirmed by it. Either the adduced fact is given as a reason for the required abstinences, ver. 20 (it is indispensable to ordain abstinence from these four things, because otherwise the reading of the law every Sabbath will preserve alive the offence of the Jewish Christians to the Gentile Christians, Meyer); or it gives the reason for the proposed emancipation of the Gentile Christians from the law, ver. 19 (notwithstanding that the Mosaic law has been so long read, still few submit to its observance; the ceremonial law, therefore, must be set aside as a barrier to the general propagation of the true religion, Gieseler); or James intends by this to support and confirm his whole proposal, chiefly the exemption of the Gentile Christians from the legal requirements, by the removal of a scruple (we may well agree to this, for the fear that the Mosaic law will come into disuse is entirely unfounded, because in every city the law is still weekly read). So, approximately, Erasmus, Wetstein, Schneckenburger, Thiersch, and Ewald. This last interpretation appears to be most suited both to the whole state of matters, and to the peculiar Jewish disposition and position of James.

DOGMATICAL AND ETHICAL THOUGHTS.

1. Peter, before all things, puts experience in the scale for the solution of this question, important and decisive for all times, Whether the law of Moses is binding upon the Gentiles; the experience acquired in the transaction at Cæsarea, that the Gentiles as well as the Jews received the Holy Ghost. This fact he understands as a significant and doctrinal decision of God. God has

by this placed the Gentiles on entirely the same footing as the Jews (οὐδὲν διέκρινε)—has shown no preference to the latter above the believing Gentiles. God has, by the communication of the Holy Ghost, borne witness to the Gentiles (ἐμαρτύρησε). He has, by word and deed, made known His favour to them. This experience accordingly proves the perfect equality of Jews and Gentiles before God, provided only they believe on Jesus Christ. This demonstration is convincing and conclusive. And the manner in which the Apostle Peter employs the history of the Church as a source of doctrinal knowledge, is also, in its general application, a pattern. The whole revelation of God in both Testaments rests on history, and consists essentially in history. And as the life of Jesus Christ is rich in doctrine, whilst He not only lived His own doctrine, but preached His own life; so also is the life and experience of the apostles a rich source of doctrine. The doctrine of the Apostle Paul is his own life wrought out in consciousness and knowledge. And the doctrine of the Apostle Peter is also his own life formed into opinions and ideas. The manner in which God governs His Church in the course of time and events,—in other words, the history of the Church,—forms the doctrine, not only in the article of the Church itself, but also in other matters. Thus here not only the idea of the Church, but also the insight into the significance of grace, of the *usus legis*, etc., is obtained.

2. The knowledge of the nature of faith has also by these facts been advanced and further developed. What is not included in that proposition which Peter expressed in reference to the signification of the transaction at Cæsarea: "God has purified their hearts by faith?" First, it implies that faith is not entirely and exclusively dependent on men, but on God: it is a work and gift of God, a gracious operation by Him. Secondly, the apostle here asserts that faith possesses a purifying power: faith is accordingly something full of life and strength: as Luther says, "a living, active, and working thing;" and it operates in a purifying manner, so that the heart, which was before ungodly and impure, is changed, sanctified by God, morally purified. Thirdly, in this proposition the truth is also contained, that faith has its seat in the heart, not simply in the memory or in the thoughts, but in the centre of the receptive and active life of the soul, comprehending in itself the feelings and motives.

3. The opposition between law and grace is here, for the first time, made clear to the disciples. Even Paul himself, who, by the manner of his conversion and guidance, was personally led to the knowledge of the grace of God in Christ, has only, by the opposition which he encountered on the soil of the Gentile churches, clearly seen evangelical freedom in a state of grace as opposed to legal bondage. And so, in a similar manner, with Peter. Only by the experience of the grace of Christ has he become aware that the law is a yoke, heavy, and indeed impossible, to bear. Grace makes everything easy which the law makes difficult for man. For, under the law, personal performance depends on our own strength, on the perfect purity of the will; whereas, in a state of grace, God purifies the heart, and causes it to delight in goodness.

4. James illustrates, by the word of promise, the question which Peter, along with Paul and Barnabas, had explained by their experiences, acquired in the service of the Gospel. The prophecies of Scripture have been chiefly employed by the apostles for the purpose of understanding the signs of the present, and of knowing what was right to do in the sight of God. They have not used the prophetic word in order to know the future, to discover in it times and seasons, circumstances and persons, as in a magical mirror. The will of God, His counsel in respect of the course which His kingdom takes, and the statutes of the kingdom, are so much the more surely to be known from prophecy, when we reflect on the enduring, eternal and firm ideas of God (*γνωστὰ ἀπ' αἰῶνος*, ver. 18).

5. The prophecy of Amos, which James adduces, has the house of David as its chief object. David's royal house is decayed, converted into a tent, fallen into ruins. God will raise again that which is fallen, anew re-establish it, even enlarge it; and the kingdom, which is God's kingdom, will extend over the Gentiles on whom His name is called,—that is, who resolve upon the acknowledgment and service of Jehovah. And God will do all this Himself, and bring it to pass, as He has resolved from of old. This prophecy casts light upon the question. The circumstance is already significant, that the theocratic kingdom—the kingdom of God—is the centre of the prophecy, and not the law as such. Also it is of importance that nothing but the invocation of the name of God, or the imposition of His name, is made

the condition of incorporation into the kingdom of God. And this condition has already been fulfilled by the converted Gentiles (*ἐπιστρέφουσιν ἐπὶ τὸν Θεόν*, ver. 19). Finally, *κύριος ὁ ποιῶν ταῦτα* is decisive; *i.e.*, not, we have to effect the business, and to add the chief matter, according to our judgment; but God, the Lord, has promised that He will do it; He has already done the chief matter; He has already taken a people from among the Gentiles (ver. 14). Consequently, we durst not, and should not, make that a condition to the Gentile Christians, which would suppose that the chief matter was not already completed.

6. It is worthy of remark that James, who, according to all the descriptions which have come down to us, was a man of the strictest legal piety, and was therefore called *ὁ δίκαιος*; that this very man advocates the freedom of the Gentiles from the law of Moses, and only expressly demands from them the abstinence from certain offensive things, partly moral and partly social. This would be incomprehensible and incredible, if it were impossible that one and the same person could be severe toward himself and mild toward others. But we must consider James entirely as a person of this description—a character which is worthy of the highest respect. The slight intimation given us in ver. 21, shows that Moses was not a matter of indifference to him; and it is also evident that he hopes for regard for the Mosaic religion more from its gradual extension and from voluntarily joining it, than from a compulsion put upon the consciences of men to their disquietude. That, in the character of James, the mildest and tenderest love toward others was combined with an habitual severity toward himself, is seen from the anecdote preserved by Hegesippus in Eusebius, that he prayed incessantly in the temple for the forgiveness of his nation. If he thus, with such compassionate love, prayed for his unbelieving countrymen; he was certainly also capable of meeting, with loving forbearance and mildness, the Gentiles who had been converted to the Redeemer. In this latter trait, we see the image of Jesus Himself shining forth from the soul of His brother, both according to the flesh and according to the spirit.

HOMILETICAL HINTS.

And certain came down and taught the brethren (ver. 1). Paul had come from disturbance for repose at Antioch, and he and the brethren had begun to be edified in their common faith, when this new commotion arose. But how fortunate was it, that the blessed proofs of God among the Jews had preceded; and from them the reasons for a decision might be taken. That which is disagreeable enters after the blessing (Rieger).—These were for the Gospel new-birth pangs; as a check which the enemy wished to put to it. His object was to destroy the joy which the conversion of the Gentiles had caused. We must beware of such diversions in the militant Church, for by means of them we may lose our crown (Starke).—The Acts of the Apostles exhibits the Church to us under two opposite aspects. Under the one, she appears at her birth as the reconciliation of all earthly contradictions, in the harmonious choir praising God with the tongues of all nations under heaven, as the happy bride resting on the bosom of her Beloved; and while the world desponds before the signs of the last days, she, in singleness of heart, looks forward to the day of her espousals. Under the other aspect, the Church is represented in labour and conflict; she can call nothing her own; she has yet everything to win, to labour for, and to gain by a hard struggle. And just as that sense of bliss pervaded her whole being, so did this feeling of want and destitution pervade her whole frame, and we see her trembling in anguish and sorrow. It is the same contrast which the Gospels display to us in the life of the Lord; here too, on the one hand, the heavenly light of the glory of the only-begotten Son of God, and on the other hand the abysmal, deadly darkness of abandonment by God (Baumgarten).

When there was no small disputation between Paul and Barnabas and them (ver. 2). Better dissension with possession of the truth than peace with the loss of it (Starke).—*That Paul and Barnabas should journey to Jerusalem.* They might have maintained their own authority, and refused to take their orders from Jerusalem. Others might say, These two ought not to be sent, but those whose judgment was more unbiassed. But on both sides all things were done in a moderate and candid spirit (Bengel).

They were accompanied by the Church (ver. 3). By this all expressed their sympathy in the journey. "Bring to me that little word *sola* (alone, namely, by faith alone), or come not back again." Thus the Elector of Brandenburg dismissed his ambassadors to a conference with the Papists. The ambassadors of the Church of Antioch did not require this exhortation; yet the love and intercession of the Church was comforting and refreshing to its pastors and teachers (Besser).—*Declaring the conduct of the Gentiles, and caused great joy to all the brethren.* We must, with a zeal for orthodoxy, not forget or slight the building of the kingdom of God.

They declared how much God had done through them (ver. 4). Before they state the existing variances, they first relate what God had done with them, as a proof that they neither carried on the controversy in heat and passion, nor yet forgot by reason of it the remaining condition of the Church of Jesus. On the contrary, they commence first to proclaim the good of the kingdom of God, and then to show the errors and failings for the purpose of having them remedied. This teaches us, with all the faults of the Church of God, never to banish from our thoughts what an amount of good God nevertheless exhibits in all places.

Then rose up certain of the sect of the Pharisees (ver. 5). How difficult is it to lay aside the pharisaical leaven, and to keep to the pure grace of God! Faith does not remove from us all darkness and weakness: this is only the result of experience and conflict (Starke).—*Who believed.* Thus it is not always wicked people, but also upright men who may excite divisions, when they give way too much to their fancies and prejudices (Apost. Past.).

But the apostles and elders assembled (ver. 6). Neither a consultation with one another nor an examination of the divine word is abolished, by reason of the divine inspiration with which the apostles wrote and spoke (Starke).—How ought this apostolic simplicity to put to shame the pride of later times! (Apost. Past.)—In this assembly we have a representation of the Church, as is elsewhere only once represented to us in the pentecostal Church. The Church stands in the presence of her righteous Lord and Head. She feels herself in great perplexity and ignorance with regard to her mission: no experience, no principle, no scripture comes in to supply her need. But she knows that her Lord has promised to her, in her totality, sufficient strength and aid. Therefore she exhibits true humility in inquiring, but also joyful courage in the confession of the truth (Leonh. and Spieg.).

When there had been a long disputation (ver. 7). This was no quarrel, but a long conference, in which reasons for and against were weighed. Such a procedure was praiseworthy in the apostles, and showed both their long-suffering in listening to the opinion of their meanest brethren, and also their care to consider divine truth not superficially, but maturely (Apost. Past.).—*Peter rose up*. We hear him speak for the last time in the history of the apostles. In his words we recognise the brotherly hand which he extended to Paul concerning the mystery of grace, the actual revelation of which constitutes the sense of the Acts of the Apostles (Besser).—*God made choice that the Gentiles*. Because neither the written word of the Old Testament nor the judgment of the brethren led to any sure result, Peter takes the ground of decision from the experience of what God Himself had done under their own eyes.—Thus it is seen how necessary it is to attend to the economy of God in His Church, and to acquire from experience a conscience exercised to discern good and evil (Apost. Past.).—*Men and brethren*. This was likewise a superscription on the whole transaction. It was to be conducted in a brotherly manner. "Ye know," says Peter; not, "Know ye:" he speaks not as a dictator, but as a brother; he does not lord over the brethren *ex cathedra*, but places himself with them before the throne of the only Lord of the Church (Besser).

And God, who knows the hearts, bore them witness, giving them the Holy Ghost, even as to us (ver. 8). The gracious counsel of God concerning the heathen was converted into a visible gracious act in the Spirit bestowed on Cornelius.

Purifying their hearts by faith (ver. 9). Faith is the real New Testament circumcision, the true and only instrument of evangelical purification; for it purifies from all filthiness of the flesh and of the spirit, whilst it pervades the soul with the power of the blood of Christ. "We obtain another, new and pure heart by faith, as St Peter says; and God, for the sake of Christ our Mediator, will reckon, and does reckon us as entirely righteous and holy" (Smalk. Art. iii. 13).

Wherefore now tempt ye God? (ver. 10.) Different times have different customs and ordinances of God in His Church. The greater illumination and faith, the less the burden of the slavish yoke of the law. Mark it well: The greatest imposers of burdens are not the best teachers (Starke).— *Which neither our fathers nor we were able to bear.* Just as oxen in the yoke must proceed with great difficulty and labour, and yet do not merit their daily fodder; for, however long they have served, at length they are smitten on the head and slain: so is it also with those who wish to be justified by the law; they must be taken and tormented under the yoke, and when they have long laboured and toiled with the works of the law, their final reward is, that they must throughout eternity be poor and unblessed servants (Luther).—*Nor we were able to bear.* Peter would say, Men and brethren, can you honestly say that you have kept the law? (Besser.)

But we believe that, by the grace of the Lord Jesus Christ, we shall be saved (ver. 11). This is a precious summary of the Gospel which Peter here, in the first Christian synod, expresses for all times. It already includes the confession of the Council of Nice,—the confession of Christ, as the true God; for Christ can only confer saving grace, if He is the Lord to whom all power is committed in heaven and in earth. We believe to be saved by the grace of our Lord Jesus Christ: this is even now the holy symbol and shibboleth of all true believers. By the words "by grace alone" the children of the house recognise each other. Therefore Melancthon, in his Apology, declares the article of justification by grace to be "the highest and most important of all Christian doctrines, the key to the understanding of the whole Bible, and without which no conscience can attain to a true, and stedfast, and sure peace." And Luther says, "We must not yield or give up this article, though heaven and earth, and whatever will not endure, perish" (Leonh. and Spieg.).—What glory, what comfort, what joy for the members of the Evangelical Church! Ye are one with the original Apostolic Church in your faith and in your confession.—*In the same manner as they.* As the fathers and prophets preceded the triumphal chariot of Christ, so we follow after. Their faith and ours are one: they believed that as future, which we believe as having taken place (Lindhammer).

Then the whole multitude were silent (ver. 12). Verily a real council of the Holy Ghost, when one speaks only so long as he does not yet hear the voice of the Lord, but then is silent and humbled under God's word. Where the Spirit of truth obtains entrance into the hearts, and vain pride and egotistical desire of strife do not contend, there the unity of the Spirit reconciles all dissensions by the bond of peace, and the truth is found and testified with one accord, for the counsel and the act of the Lord decide (Leonh. and Spieg.).—The two words, "yoke" and "grace," burned in their heart, and in calm consideration they sat there before the Lord (Besser).—*And hearkened to Paul and Barnabas.* Paul and Barnabas illustrated and confirmed what Peter had related of the salvation of God to the Gentiles. Thus it is right when a teacher continues where another has left off, when one has yet more to relate than another of the wonders of God; and all things are in such harmony that it is seen, that it is one Lord and one Spirit who has His work in them all. Where it thus proceeds, there the apostolic blessing rules (Apost. Past.).—Lord Jesus, do Thou Thyself notify the true counsel and preserve it, and deliver Thy people by Thy glorious advent (Luther on the Smalk. Articles).

And James answered and said—and with this agree the words of the prophets (vers. 13–15). Peter's speech had respect rather to the work of God; now James adds how with this the word of God, in the writings of the prophets, agrees (Rieger).—Although miracles and signs precede, yet it must be inquired whether the Scripture agrees with them (Apost. Past.).—By the mouth of Peter, the apostles have spoken; James, the brother of the Lord, addresses the assembly, as the elder or bishop of the Church (Besser).

Afterward will I return (ver. 16). It was not without the Holy Ghost that James was directed to this passage. For in it is contained, first, the fall of the Jewish Church, and the abolition of the temple service; secondly, the promise that God will build a new Church on its foundation, and assemble to it all the Gentiles; and, thirdly, that this Church was to receive salvation only by the name of the Lord which was to be named upon it; *i.e.*, that it would believe on Him (Apost. Past.).—*And will build again the tent of David, which is fallen in pieces* (Luther's translation). The kingdom of Christ is not of this world, therefore it is here called a tent, which appears at first fallen into pieces; and yet the Gentiles are by grace to be encamped in it. The period of the New Testament is in general a period of restoration and raising up of the fallen (chap. i. 6; Rev. xxi. 3,

5; Heb. ix. 10), (Starke).—God will build up, He will fill up the breaches thereof, and raise again that which is fallen; God will do everything. Precious comfort! Let us also be faithful servants and fellow-helpers of the grace of God (Apost. Past.).

That we trouble not them who, from among the Gentiles, are turned to God (ver. 19). We may, by the imposition of many external usages, very greatly injure the conscientious who are really turned to God, and either lead them to a false confidence or perplex their conscience. Those who are less in earnest, care the less about everything (Rieger).—The conclusion of the apostolic council, which possesses its eternal and universal validity, is the freedom of believers of the new covenant from the yoke of the old ceremonial law. An important conclusion, which the Church of Christ has thankfully to receive and practically to use, as a sweet fruit of His merits. In this is manifested the divinity, purity, and importance of this first ecclesiastical council, which in the following ages, when similar councils were assembled, partly from carnal passion and partly about trifles, has been so remarkably forgotten (Apost. Past.).

That they abstain from pollutions of idolatry (ver. 20). Obedience to God demanded abstinence from idolatry and fornication; love to the brethren demanded abstinence from things strangled and from blood.—It is the mark of a purified Christian, that he avoids not only evil, but also the appearance of evil. To a Christian, nothing is indifferent. The things which he does, must either advance the glory of the Lord or injure it. But, at that time, in the intercourse of the Jews and Gentiles, it would be injured, if one did those things which were regarded by the whole world as undeniable signs of heathenism (Williger).

On the whole section (vers. 1–21).—*The importance of the first ecclesiastical assembly.* 1. The question which was discussed: a question concerning the conditions of salvation. 2. The spirit in which it was discussed: a spirit of love and truth. 3. The rule according to which it was decided: God's testimony in word and deed. 4. The confession which lay at the foundation of the resolution determined on: "We believe to be saved through the grace of the Lord Jesus Christ."—*How the Christian fights the battles of the Lord.* 1. Bravely, in order that he may preserve his crown. 2. Fraternally, in order that love may not grow cold. 3. Humbly, in order that the Scripture may exercise the office of umpire (Ahlfeld).—*We believe to be saved through the grace of the Lord Jesus Christ.* 1. A confession of penitence which rests on a clear consciousness of sin. 2. A confession of humility which attests the demerit of good works. 3. A confession of faith which has recognised the riches of the love of God in Christ. 4. A confession of joy which is founded on the peace of a pardoned heart (Leonhardi and Spiegelhauer). —*We are saved not by the law, but by grace* (Lisco).—*That God purifies the heart through faith* (vers. 6–12). 1. The heart of man must be purified. 2. This purification takes place through faith. 3. Such purification of the heart through faith is the work of Almighty God alone (Langbein).—*The confession, We believe to be saved through the grace of the Lord Jesus Christ.* 1. Its purport. 2. Its source. 3. Its fruit (Langbein).—*How we are to distinguish between the perishable and the imperishable in Christianity.*—*How controversies among Christians ought to be managed.* 1. We should suffer ourselves to be taught by the undeniable proofs of the power of God. 2. We should search the Scriptures, and consent to them (Lisco).—*The ecclesiastical assembly at Jerusalem, a model for all times.* 1. Its occasion, a life-question of the Church (vers. 5, 11). *a.* A question not of faith, for concerning that there was no dispute, and concerning that no assembly can finally decide; but, *b.* a question of life, of the practical application of the incontestable truths of faith to ecclesiastical ordinance and Christian practice. 2. Its spirit, a truly evangelical spirit: *a.* a spirit of truth, depending on the word of God and Christian experience; *b.* a spirit of love, seeking not its own, but the good of the whole. 3. Its result, a blessing for the Church: *a.* a progress by the decisive victory over antiquated external ordinances; but, *b.* on the ground of stedfast Christian faith and love.—*The upshot of the first ecclesiastical assembly, a triumph of the Holy Ghost.* 1. As a Spirit of freedom over the yoke of external ordinances. 2. As a Spirit of faith over the illusions of our own wisdom and righteousness. 3. As a Spirit of love over proud obstinacy and a narrow-minded spirit.—*A maxim of Irenæus* (formerly ascribed to Augustine: see Herzog's Encyclopedia) *for the observance of all times.* 1. In necessariis unitas (ver. 11). 2. In dubiis libertas (ver. 19). 3. In omnibus caritas (vers. 7, 13, 20).—*The Holy Ghost, the best President of an ecclesiastical synod and of a pastoral conference.*

1. He permits every one to speak: those without name in the assembly, as well as the leaders; the scrupulous, as well as the liberal. 2. He retains all together on the common foundation of the divine word, and of living faith. 3. He brings the transaction to the happy conclusion of resolutions wisely pondered and unanimously agreed to.—*In brotherly consultation, there is a time to speak and a time to be silent*, Eccl. iii. 7. 1. To speak boldly, when it concerns conscientious scruples and decided convictions. 2. Humbly to be silent, when it concerns filial obedience to God's word and will, and pacific yielding to the brethren. —*There is a time of contention and a time of peace in the Church*, Eccl. iii. 8. 1. Brotherly contention, in order to find the right. 2. Brotherly peace, after it is found.—*There is a time to build and a time to break down in the kingdom of God*, Eccl. iii. 3. 1. To build the fence of the law of the old covenant. 2. To break down that fence in the New Testament.—*What should turn the scale in the deliberations of the Church?* 1. Not blind prejudice, but sober judgment. 2. Not the weight of human names (Paul, Barnabas, Peter, James), but the divine truth. 3. Not the majority of voices, but unity in the spirit.—*Be not again entangled in the yoke of bondage* (Gal. v. 1), an admonitory call of the apostles to modern Christianity. 1. Paul calls (vers. 2–4),—the great apostle of the Gentiles, who hazarded his life in order to break down the embankment of Jewish ordinance in the power of evangelical liberty. 2. Peter agrees (vers. 7–10),—the rock of the old Church, whom God Himself led to the knowledge that all men should be helped, and to whom the infallible church to no purpose appeals as their patron saint. 3. James sides with them (ver. 13),—the preacher of the law, for a testimony that there exists no other way of salvation than the righteousness of faith.—*We believe to be saved through the grace of the Lord Jesus Christ.* The common watchword of the evangelical Church, as well as of the apostolical.—*The confession of faith at Augsburg, no other than that at Jerusalem.* 1. The enemy with which it contends: Pharisaism, in slavery to man, and in the righteousness of works. 2. The ground on which it rests: God's word and Christian experience. 3. The spirit which it breathes: bold truth and mild love. 4. The way of salvation which it announces: free grace on the part of God, and living faith on the part of man.

C.

The Resolution and the Epistle of the Assembly.

CHAP. XV. 22–29.

22 Then the apostles and elders, together with the whole Church, re-
solved to choose men from the midst of them, and to send them to Antioch
with Paul and Barnabas, namely, Judas, surnamed Barsabas, and Silas, who
were leading men among the brethren. 23 Delivering to them the following
epistle: The apostles, and elders, and brethren salute the brethren who are
of the Gentiles in Antioch, in Syria, and Cilicia. 24 As we have heard
that certain who went out from us have troubled you with words, subvert-
ing your souls, to whom we have given no direction; 25 We have therefore
resolved, being assembled with one accord, to choose men, and to send them
to you with our beloved Barnabas and Paul, 26 Men who have hazarded
their lives for the name of our Lord Jesus Christ. 27 We have therefore
sent Judas and Silas, who themselves will also declare the same things by
word. 28 For it pleased the Holy Ghost and us to lay upon you no further
burden than these indispensable things; 29 To abstain from offerings to
idols, and from blood, and from things strangled, and from fornication.
Therefore, if ye keep this, it shall go well with you. Fare ye well.

Ver. 23. Five principal MSS., A.B.C.D. and the Sinaitic MS., omit *καὶ οἱ* before *ἀδελφοί*, as also some of the fathers and versions; and therefore Lachmann has erased *καὶ οἱ*. According to this reading, *ἀδελφοί* forms an apposition to *οἱ ἀπόστολοι καὶ οἱ πρεσβύτεροι*. But it is more probable that the omission may have been caused from an objection to the co-operation of the Church with the apostles. E.G.H. and most versions and fathers have *καὶ οἱ*, which Tischendorf retains as genuine.

Ver. 24. *Λέγοντες περιτέμνεσθαι καὶ τηρεῖν τὸν νόμον* is wanting in A.B.D., several versions and fathers, and is a gloss taken from vers. 1 and 5, and therefore is properly erased by Lachmann and Tischendorf.

Ver. 28. Tischendorf has erased *τούτων* after *τῶν ἐπάναγκες*, but on the authority only of one MS., A.: Lachmann reads according to B.C.D., *τούτων τῶν ἐπάναγκες*.

Ver. 29. Tischendorf reads, with A. (first hand) B.C., *καὶ πνικτῶν*; whilst A. (second hand) E.G. and H. have the singular *πνικτοῦ*.

EXEGETICAL EXPLANATIONS.

1. *Then the apostles resolved.*—After the explanations and transactions, there follows the resolution of the assembly. *Ἔδοξε* (vers. 22, 25, 28) is, in classical Greek, always used to express the formal resolutions of a senate, of an assembly of the people, or

of some other court, on which account the resolutions themselves are called τὰ δεδογμένα or δόγματα (compare chap. xvi. 4). The assembly, according to this account, consisted of three classes: first, the apostles; secondly, the elders of the Church of Jerusalem; thirdly, the members of the Church, who were fully assembled,—that is to say, the males (οἱ ἀδελφοί), and doubtless, also, only those who were of full age. But it is clear enough from this expression, σὺν ὅλῃ τῇ ἐκκλησίᾳ, along with οἱ ἀδελφοί, that the usual name for this assembly, the "Apostolic Council," is not strictly correct. Not to mention that at least the elders of the Church, along with the apostles of the Church of Antioch (chap. xv. 2), were present, and acted with the apostles (vers. 6, 22), the Church of Jerusalem itself was present in the assembly, not only to hear, but to participate in forming the resolution (σὺν ὅλῃ τῇ ἐκκλησίᾳ).

2. *To choose men.*—The resolution to select ambassadors from the Church of Jerusalem, and to send them to Antioch (ἐκλεξαμένους—πέμψαι = ἵνα ἐκλεξάμενοι—πέμψωσι), has not as yet been mentioned in the transaction. The idea, by whomsoever it may have been first suggested, was very proper. The Church of Antioch had sent a deputation to Jerusalem (καί τινας ἄλλους ἐξ αὐτῶν, ver. 2); and, accordingly, it was a proper return of this embassy that the Church of Jerusalem should also send a deputation to Antioch, in order to express their brotherly feeling, and to draw more closely the bond of mutual fellowship. Moreover, it was expedient that ambassadors from Jerusalem should accompany Paul and Barnabas, because by their testimony the information of those from Antioch who had returned would be confirmed; *omnibus modis cavebatur, ne Paulus sententiam concilii videretur pro suo referre arbitrio* (Bengel). Compare ver. 27, καὶ αὐτοὺς—ἀπαγγέλλοντας τὰ αὐτά.

3. The men who were selected for this purpose were Judas, surnamed Barsabas, otherwise entirely unknown to us (from his surname, certain learned men, as for example Grotius, suppose him to have been a brother of Joseph Barsabas, the candidate for the apostleship with Matthias); and Silas, afterwards the well-known companion and fellow-labourer of Paul in his missionary journeys, and called by that apostle Silvanus (1 Thess. i. 1; 2 Cor. i. 19). Luke describes both as ἄνδρες ἡγούμενοι ἐν τοῖς ἀδελφοῖς; that is, not only prominent men, but office-bearers

of the Church, who have to lead others. (Compare Heb. xiii. 7, 17, where the overseers and teachers of the Church are called by this title.) They were probably elders of the Church in Jerusalem. In ver. 32, Luke describes Judas and Silas also as prophets.

4. *Delivering to them the following epistle.*—The circumstance that a circular letter should be issued to the Gentiles has not yet been mentioned in the account of the transactions, provided that ἐπιστεῖλαι (ver. 20) does not denote *literis mandare*, but simply *mandare.* An epistle was the most suitable means for conveying the resolution and pleasure of the assembly, in its original form and authentic expression, to the distant Gentile Christians, to whom it referred. The epistle was (διὰ χειρὸς αὐτῶν, ver. 23, that is, of Judas and Silas) not delivered to Paul and Barnabas, but to the two ambassadors from Jerusalem. It is the only ecclesiastical circular epistle of apostolic times which has come down to us, and the oldest synodical letter (so to speak) that we know. Luke does not mention who composed the letter, by whom or in what language it was written. However, the genuine Greek epistolary form, beginning with χαίρειν and concluding with ἔῤῥωσθε, also containing the words εὖ πράττειν, so customary in letters, makes it extremely probable that the letter was originally composed in Greek, and that accordingly Luke has preserved the original itself. Moreover, the supposition is highly probable which Bengel suggested, and Bleek (*Studien und Kritiken*, 1836, p. 1037) has supported, that James, the brother of the Lord, composed this letter in the name and at the request of the assembly. He possessed at this time important and leading influence in the Church, and had, besides, in this very assembly brought about the decision. Moreover, the Epistle of James, which certainly was written by him, offers more than one point of analogy with this letter.

5. *The apostles and elders.*—The epistle is directed to the Gentile Christians, and to them as brethren (τοῖς—ἀδελφοῖς τοῖς ἐξ ἐθνῶν), by which their perfect equality in rights and privileges with the Jewish Christians is plainly recognised. These Gentile Christians are described as resident in Antioch, Syria, and Cilicia. The capital, whose Church had mooted the matter, is fitly put first; then the whole province of Syria is named; and, thirdly, Cilicia. From this we must suppose, both that there were

Christian churches in Cilicia, and that in these churches the disturbance by judaizing intrigues had also occurred. On the other hand, the newly formed churches in the provinces of Pamphylia and Pisidia are not named, although the resolutions at Jerusalem referred to them (chap. xvi. 4). These churches may not yet have been visited by the demands of the pharisaical Jewish Christians.

6. *As we have heard.*—The occasion of the letter is shortly but significantly stated in ver. 24. The assembly declare the conduct of those who had molested the Gentile churches with their judaizing demands to be without authority: *οἷς οὐ διεστειλάμεθα*, they have received no order or authority from us. Their conduct is described as *ταράσσειν λόγοις*, causing disturbance, doubts, and scruples. Paul, in Gal. v. 10, uses the same expression, *ὁ ταράσσων ὑμᾶς*. Further, the consequence is denoted as *ἀνασκευάζειν τὰς ψυχὰς ὑμῶν*, *evertere, destruere animas.* This verb never occurs in the Septuagint, and only here in the New Testament: it signifies to subvert or destroy a building, and hence is the exact opposite of *οἰκοδομεῖν*. The assembly, therefore, have not spared the originators of that movement, but have condemned their action, as not proceeding from them and as subverting the conscience.

7. *To choose men.*—On the other hand, the assembly in its circular epistle interests itself decidedly in favour of Paul and Barnabas. Both are advisedly named *οἱ ἀγαπητοὶ ἡμῶν*, ver. 25. The Jewish apostles and elders, and the whole Church in Jerusalem, testify their sincere love and their intimate union of spirit with Paul and Barnabas, in opposition to the hostile position which the judaizing emissaries had taken towards the Gentile apostles. Moreover, they praise their entire devotion, ready even to sacrifice their lives for the Lord Jesus,—for the confession of Him and for His honour. *Παραδοῦναι τὴν ψυχήν*, to give up, to hazard their lives. So much for the recommendation and justification of Paul and Barnabas, personally suspected no doubt by their opponents, but for whom the assembly answers. The circumstance that Barnabas is mentioned before Paul, as being longer known to the apostles and to the Church, is a proof of the genuineness of the epistle.

8. The resolution is stated as *γενομένοις ὁμοθυμαδόν* (an adverb, where we would expect an adjective), *unanimous; i.e.*,

the resolution was not adopted by a majority of voices, by a variety of sentiment, but it was unanimous. According to this, we must suppose that the Pharisees, who had so strongly advanced their opinions (vers. 5, 7), must have been completely silenced by the decided testimony of the apostles and the cordial concurrence of the whole assembly. (See Baumgarten, vol. ii. p. 65, English translation.) This will not certainly imply that the judaizing spirit was actually overcome and rooted out in them, but only that for the moment they felt themselves defeated, and that they bent before the power of the truth.

9. *We have accordingly sent.*—The two ambassadors, Judas and Silas, who were chosen to accompany Paul and Barnabas to the Gentile Christians (ver. 25), were to announce *διὰ λόγου*, *i.e.*, by word of mouth, *τὰ αὐτά*, the same things, namely, what the epistle mentions: that is to say, the same things that we announce by letter, they will tell you by word of mouth. *Τὰ αὐτὰ* therefore cannot, as Neander thinks, denote the same things as Paul and Barnabas have announced. Besides, *ἔδοξε γὰρ* shows that the object of *ἀπαγγέλλειν* is no other than the resolution concerning the Christianity of the Gentile Christians.

10. *It pleased the Holy Ghost and us.*—As regards the grammatical construction, we are permitted to deviate from the most natural meaning (according to which two subjects are placed together, to whom the decision and the resolution are referred) only in the case when no intelligible meaning can be made out of it. But the most natural meaning here is entirely suitable. See Dogmatical and Ethical Thoughts, No. 4. Therefore there is no reason to refine and to adopt a *ἓν διὰ δυοῖν*, either "the Holy Ghost in us" (Olshausen), or *nobis per Spiritum sanctum* (Grotius). Still more artificial appears to be the interpretation of Neander, who takes *τῷ ἁγίῳ πνεύματι* in the ablative: "It seemed good by the Holy Ghost to us also," *i.e.*, as well as to Paul and Barnabas. The resolution proceeds on this, that the assembly would not put any greater burden on their brethren among the Gentiles (*ἐπιτίθεσθαι* not passive—*imponi per quosvis doctores*, Bengel,—but, as it is used in most instances, in an active sense) except these necessary points.

11. *To lay upon you no greater burden.*—The assembly thus declare, that the Gentile Christians should remain exempt from every further imposition of the Mosaic law, and should only

abstain from those four necessary things which James had named. The enumeration in ver. 29 differs from that of ver. 20, only in εἰδωλόθυτα being put instead of εἴδωλα, partaking of meats offered to idols, and by the mention of πορνεία in the fourth place instead of in the second. It is evident from the concluding sentence, ἐξ ὧν—εὖ πράξετε, that ἐπάναγκες cannot mean a moral necessity; for this were too flat and weak, and, indeed, wholly unsuitable, if all the prohibitions were indispensably required. Accordingly, the last sentence is rather a faithful and earnest advice. Ἐξ ὧν is not to be directly connected with διατηρεῖν, *abstinere a re;* for διατηρεῖν is always constructed with the accusative, seldom with μή, and never with ἐκ: ἐξ ὧν, then, means "in consequence of," "accordingly." Εὖ πράττειν is not to do morally right, but to thrive: therefore, to consider it as identical with σωθῆναι (Kuinoel) is against the *usus loquendi* of the whole of the New Testament.

12. Concerning the agreement between the narrative of the assembly and its transactions with the account of the Apostle Paul in Gal. ii., see Lechler's Apostolic Times, 2d edition, p. 393.

DOGMATICAL AND ETHICAL THOUGHTS.

1. This is the first ecclesiastical assembly or synod in the history of the Church. It is an apostolic model for all times, and was occasioned by a deeply important question for life and doctrine, which must be discussed and solved. This matter concerned the whole Church of Christ—directly the Gentile Christians, and indirectly the Jewish Christians. The solution was voluntarily referred by the Church of Antioch, who were primarily interested in it, to Jerusalem, as the mother Church, the sacred metropolis, so to speak. But the apostles did not take the decision upon themselves, much less did Peter: not even the apostles in conjunction with the elders; but the whole Church of Jerusalem was present, and essentially participated in the solution of the question proposed. The different views entertained were perfectly freely and frankly expressed in the synod. But the truth, evangelical liberty, prevailed, and that indeed purely by the power of the Spirit, of the divine word, and of the deeds and acts of God. Not a doubtful majority, not a majority tyrannizing over the minority, but an entire unanimity decided the business. The result was not certain beforehand, so that the

transaction was only for the sake of appearance, and a deceptive display; but the judgment and the practical resolution took place only by means of the transactions and the explanations. The resolution was not formed by mutual concessions, agreed upon in a prudent and calculating manner, but resulted from an honest, truth-loving, and God-fearing consideration, formed by the guidance and illumination of the Holy Ghost.

2. The assembly issued an epistle to the brethren among the Gentiles. The authenticity and correctness of the resolutions were to be warranted by writing. It was wise and kind not to entrust everything to oral communication. And although Paul and Barnabas stood so high in the love and esteem of the apostles and of the Church of Jerusalem; although Judas and Silas were such esteemed and true ἡγούμενοι: yet they were not infallible and absolutely trustworthy reporters. Writing alone gives the meaning fully, purely, and faithfully. *Verbo solo* is our evangelical motto. The word of Scripture which the Spirit has inspired, the word in which the Spirit lives, and which permits the Spirit purely and directly to work on susceptible souls, is our treasure and our sure ground of faith.

3. True Christian love is not effeminate, weak, and spiritless, so that it lets everything pass. If the Redeemer had not been able to pronounce His "Woe" on the perverted scribes and Pharisees, His "Blessed" would not have the heavenly strength of love which it possesses. If the apostles and brethren had not contradicted the Pharisees in the Church, and condemned and judged their doings with severity and sharpness, they had not displayed true love to the Gentile Christians, and to Paul and Barnabas. But they pushed the former violently from them with the left arm, in order to press the latter more cordially to their breast with the right arm. He only who frankly honours the truth, can also practise true Christian love.

4. The assertion, "It seemed good to the Holy Ghost and to us," is important: an expression which has, on the one hand, been often and greatly misunderstood and condemned, as hierarchical fancy and presumption; and, on the other hand, has been explained and softened with good intention, but rashly. In order to estimate the words properly, it is not to be lost sight of, that in the letter the resolution of the assembly is twice given, but only once in this manner. The resolution to send ambassadors

to the Gentile Christians is introduced only with these words, *ἔδοξεν ἡμῖν γενομένοις ὁμοθυμαδόν*; whereas the resolution not to impose any greater burden on them, and only to require the necessary abstinences, is thus introduced, *ἔδοξε τῷ ἁγίῳ πνεύματι καὶ ἡμῖν*. Thus, not the whole resolution of the assembly is referred to the Holy Ghost, but only the weighty decision, important for the conscience both of the brethren among the Gentiles and of the Jewish Christians themselves. And this the assembly recognises as a decision not merely humanly arrived at, but divinely inspired, communicated by the illumination and guidance of the Holy Ghost Himself. Was there anything erroneous or wrong in this consciousness—anything fanatical, or designed to dazzle others from spiritual pride or hierarchical ambition? By no means. On the contrary, it is a striking truth, soberly conceived, and piously and deliberately asserted. They acknowledge with humble gratitude, and are not ashamed of their acknowledgment before men, that they have not to thank themselves for the true reconciling principle,—a solution of the question which neither sacrifices the truth to love, nor violates love for the sake of the truth,—a solution which preserves evangelical freedom, as well as secures the unity of the Church. But they have to thank the Holy Ghost, who guides them into all truth; and thus they give God the glory. But they do not therefore deny that they also worked and took all labour of general consultation and honest inquiry; that the result was not revealed to them from heaven in a dream, but was obtained as the fruit of earnest and honest trouble, *καὶ ἡμῖν*. In this expression, both the divine operation of the Holy Ghost and human independence in inquiry and in labour are recognised; all one-sidedness of consciousness is avoided; humility and Christian dignity are united. Finally, it is to be noticed that this passage is an indirect proof of the personality of the Holy Ghost. For only under this supposition can *δοκεῖν*, as it is here intended, be referred to the Holy Ghost, *i.e.*, voluntary intention and decision.

HOMILETICAL HINTS.

Then the apostles resolved (ver. 22). Here is given a model of Christian prudence for all times: how in the management of a congregation, in the decision of a matter, in the carrying out of a regulation, we ought to proceed in such a manner, that nothing be done prejudicial to conscience, love, or free-will, and thus our procedure may be blessed for the benefit of the greatest number (Rieger).—*To select men from the midst of them.* The selection of ambassadors from the Church of Jerusalem was expedient both for the churches and for Paul and Barnabas themselves. The churches thus received the conviction that their ambassadors did not, as it often happens, insensibly and without intending it, give their meaning as that of the assembly. And, on the other hand, Paul and Barnabas could wish for nothing more than to have the lawfulness and unblameableness of their apostolic office confirmed by Jerusalem (Williger).

Delivering to them the following epistle (ver. 23). Oral communication even by honest brethren did not appear to the apostles sufficient, in order to make known points of faith and ecclesiastical ordinances. They considered it necessary to add a written explanation of their meaning. So little among the apostles was the absolute infallibility of one, even of the most considerable of their brethren, established. We have to thank the wisdom of God, that He has not suffered His word to rest on oral testimony, but that He has given us a sure prophetic word in writing. Now have we a sure ground of faith, since we can say, Thus is it written (Apost. Past.).

Forasmuch as we have heard that certain who went out from us have troubled you, subverting your souls (ver. 24). Mark that the Holy Ghost does not send teachers of works and of the law, but names them, perverters and troublers of souls (Luther).—The Holy Spirit does not send false teachers, but they come of themselves; they do not edify, but perplex and disturb. As wholesome doctrine makes the heart joyful and strong in God, so false doctrine unsettles the soul, and does not permit it to attain to true peace (Starke).

With our beloved Barnabas and Paul, men who have exposed their lives (vers. 25, 26). As decidedly as they had thrown off the pharisaical Christians in Jerusalem, so decidedly did they acknowledge Paul and Barnabas. They call them dear friends; and wherefore? They have sacrificed their lives for the name of the Lord Jesus, not only while they exposed themselves to danger, but also while they dedicated all the powers of their souls to the service of Jesus. This is even now the duty and the praise of a servant of Christ. His instruction is, "To die in the work of gaining souls for the Lamb" (Williger).

Who will announce the same things in words (ver. 27). As oral testimony should be confirmed by the written, so should written testimony be confirmed by the oral. The dead letter of Scripture must by the Holy Ghost, who speaks by the men of God, be made living. Thus it is, now-a-days, not enough that the word of God be read, it must also be listened to, from the mouth of divinely enlightened men (Williger).

For it seemed good to the Holy Ghost and to us (ver. 28). The judge and arbiter in religious matters is the Holy Ghost.—The decision of a matter which has been considered by believers in the light of the Holy Ghost, may fitly be regarded as a decision of the Holy Ghost.—Our approbation should not precede, but follow that of the Holy Ghost.—No one should venture to obtrude his fancies upon others, as the will of the Holy Ghost (Starke).

Therefore, if ye keep this, it will go well with you (ver. 29). Thus for these small points, recognised as necessary, they use only the moderate expression, "Ye do well," as opposed to that violent threat, "Ye cannot be saved" (Rieger).—As we see from the superscription of this letter that the command was not directed to all the churches, so from this conclusion we infer that, according to its contents, it was not to concern all times, but to subsist only until the attachment to the Mosaic ordinances had abated a little (Apost. Past. and Bengel).—*Fare ye well.* With this concluding salutation, according to the Greek custom, the Hebrews become Greeks to their Greek brethren. "Fare ye well" may well be said to brethren who in their faith on the Lord Jesus have eternal life, and in their love to the brethren possess the rule for all the business of this temporal life. "Fare ye well," that is, Abide in Jesus (Besser).

With what wisdom and love ought errors and the erring to be treated in the Church!—The Church of the Lord has the right of giving laws. 1. Because the Spirit of God works in it (ver. 28). 2. Because it is its duty to consider the changing relations on earth in reference to the salvation of man (vers. 24, 29), (Lisco).—*How the transient in Christianity is to be withdrawn.* 1. When is it time for that purpose? 2. With what consideration is it to be proceeded with? (Lisco.)—*The letter of the Church of Jerusalem to the brethren among the Gentiles, as the competent passport for mankind, emancipated from the slavery of the law.* Competent: 1. From its urgent occasion: it concerned the question, Moses or Christ? Human ordinances or God's word? 2. From its unassailable origin: it was dictated by the Holy Ghost (ver. 28). 3. From its honourable bearers: the heralds of evangelical grace and truth, accredited by God Himself (vers. 25, 26). 4. From its incontestable contents: freedom from the temporary ceremonial law, but not from the eternal moral law; deliverance from the yoke of slavish obedience, but not from the service of self-denying love to the Lord.—*The true evangelical liberty.* 1. To be indeed free from human ordinances and ceremonial service. 2. To be bound, in the love of God, to the eternal moral law.—*The written word of God and its living bearers,* the one accredited by the other. 1. The writing by the character of its bearers. 2. The bearers by the character of the writing.

D.

Return to Antioch. Operation of the Letter and of the Ambassadors from Jerusalem.

CHAP. XV. 30–35.

30 So when they were dismissed and had come to Antioch, they assembled the multitude and delivered the epistle. 31 When they had read it, they rejoiced for the consolation. 32 But Judas and Silas, who also were prophets, exhorted the brethren with many words, and confirmed them. 33 But after they had remained a long time, they were dismissed by the brethren in peace, in order to return to the apostles. 34, 35 But Paul and Barnabas tarried at Antioch, teaching and preaching the word of the Lord, in company also with many others.

Ver. 34. Ἔδοξε δὲ τῷ Σίλᾳ ἐπιμεῖναι αὐτοῦ is decidedly spurious, and is rejected by Griesbach, Lachmann, and Tischendorf, for these words are in only two uncial MSS. On the other hand, they are wanting in the five remaining uncial MSS., in 50 cursive MSS., several old versions, and in Chrysostom and Theophylact. The addition was without doubt made, because otherwise ver. 40 appeared inexplicable.

EXEGETICAL EXPLANATIONS.

1. *So when they were dismissed.*—Ἀπολυθέντες, apparently in a solemn assembly of the Church, called together at their

departure. The two ambassadors from Jerusalem are, probably, primarily to be regarded as the subjects of this dismissal; for they, according to vers. 23 and 27, had received the epistle, and they only could deliver it to the Church at Antioch. However, the whole company, including Paul and Barnabas and the others from Antioch, would be in a solemn manner and in a brotherly spirit sent away by the Church at Jerusalem.

2. *They assembled the multitude.*—At Antioch they immediately executed their commission in an assembly of the Church: the epistle was delivered and read, and in consequence the Christians heartily rejoiced at the παράκλησις contained therein,—the brotherly address, allaying all the disturbance caused by the pharisaical demands (Luther, "comfort;" similarly, De Wette, "consolation"). The two ambassadors, Judas and Silas, now followed up the words of the epistle; and as they also (καὶ αὐτοί, as well as Paul and Barnabas) were furnished with the prophetical gift of inspired and inspiring holy discourse, so now they addressed the Church, exhorting and confirming them in the faith, with the living word, in detailed discourse.

3. *But after they had remained a long time.*—After remaining a considerable time at Antioch, the two ambassadors of the Church of Jerusalem were solemnly dismissed by the brethren, *i.e.*, by the Church of Antioch, in peace (μετ' εἰρήνης, with the feeling of peace and with the wishes of peace, *i.e.*, blessings), in order to return to the apostles. It appears that both Judas and Silas at first returned to Jerusalem; while the supposition, found in Codd. Ephræmi and Cantabrig., of the 5th and 6th centuries, that Silas remained behind at Antioch, was inserted into the text.

DOGMATICAL AND ETHICAL THOUGHTS.

There occur in this narrative many different forms of discourse of Christian truth: παρακαλεῖν and ἐπιστηρίζειν, ver. 32, compare ver. 41, chap. xiv. 22; διδάσκειν, ver. 35, and εὐαγγελίζεσθαι τὸν λόγον τοῦ κυρίου in the same verse. The last, as in chap. xiv. 7, 21, is the publication of the Gospel to those to whom the message of peace was unknown—evangelizing. Accordingly, ver. 35 must refer to the labours of Paul and Barnabas partly within and partly outside of the Church, the last in the neighbourhood of Antioch. Διδάσκειν is the work of teaching, intended to produce a more thorough knowledge and a more firm conviction of the truth already known. *Παρακαλεῖν* is exhortation, a mode of discourse which takes hold of the will and disposition, and forms the character; the effect of which is *ἐπιστηρίζειν*, the actual strengthening of souls.

HOMILETICAL HINTS.

Which when they had read, they rejoiced (Luther, they were full of comfort, ver. 31). They had only received a short epistle, and yet they rejoiced. How ought we to rejoice that we can read so many epistles of the apostles! How much more ought we to be delighted with the whole Scripture, which is, in truth, an epistle of God to man! (Quesnel.)—No one can properly taste the comfort which freedom from the law inspires, except him who has formerly experienced the oppression of this heavy yoke (Apost. Past.).

But Judas and Silas exhorted the brethren (ver. 32). They would not be idle at Antioch. How the heart of a true teacher delights to be in its element, namely, engaged in leading souls to the Saviour! The idle servant, on the other hand, boasts of what he has done, when he fulfils his indispensable and official duties (Apost. Past.).—Even the apostolic time did not despise such extraordinary means of strengthening, along with the usual means of edification from the word of God. In every servant of God, the Lord's glory is reflected with a peculiar lustre, and therefore the same old evangelical truth often makes a peculiar impression, whenever it is preached to us in a manner as yet unusual (Williger).

They were dismissed by the brethren in peace (ver. 33). When one has well executed his mission, he may return in peace to him who sent him, John xvi. 5, 28 (Starke).—*But Paul and Barnabas remained* (ver. 35). Observe, O my soul, this weighty saying: If Jesus beckons, then go: if He draws, then run: if He holds, then stand.—When Jesus glorifies His grace, sometimes here and sometimes there, then rejoice in the compassion which befalls others.—When He will use thee, then rise up in strength; if Jesus will be quiet in the soul, then also undertake nothing (Zinzendorf).

The bond uniting the Christian churches. 1. We see it in the teachers who labour from church to church. 2. In the truth which is preached in unison by all (Lisco).—*The Gospel of the free grace of God in Christ Jesus, a comforting epistle for all consciences distressed by the law.*—*The blessed course of the messengers of the Gospel of peace.* 1. They bring peace to troubled hearts (ver. 31). 2. They unite in peace believing souls (ver. 32). 3. They return home in peace to the mother Church, the heavenly Jerusalem (ver. 33).

SECTION III.

SECOND MISSIONARY JOURNEY OF PAUL, IN COMPANY WITH SILAS AND TIMOTHEUS, TO ASIA MINOR AND EUROPE (CHAP. XV. 36–XVIII. 22).

A.

Commencement of the Journey. On account of John, surnamed Mark, Paul separates from Barnabas; so that Barnabas with Mark journeys to Cyprus, and Paul with Silas to Syria and Cilicia.

CHAP. XV. 36–41.

36 And after certain days, Paul said to Barnabas, Let us return and see
again our brethren in every city in which we have preached the word of
the Lord, how they do. 37 But Barnabas counselled to take with them
also John, surnamed Mark. 38 Paul, on the contrary, thought it not right
to take him with them, who had fallen away from them from Pamphylia,
and went not with them to the work. 39 Therefore it came to a hot con-
tention, so that they separated from each other; and Barnabas took Mark,
and sailed to Cyprus; 40 And Paul chose Silas for his companion, and
departed, being recommended by the brethren to the grace of the Lord.
41 And he journeyed through Syria and Cilicia, and confirmed the churches.

Ver. 37. Ἐβουλεύσατο has, it is true, only two uncial MSS. for it, whilst four uncial MSS. and almost all the versions have ἐβούλετο; but the latter would sooner be substituted for the former, than that ἐβουλεύσατο should have been the correction.

Ver. 40. Κυρίου is to be preferred to Θεοῦ, which appears formed from the parallel passage in chap. xiv. 26.

EXEGETICAL EXPLANATIONS.

1. The commencement of the second missionary journey of Paul is left chronologically undetermined. It took place "after

certain days." According to ver. 33, Silas and Judas had remained a long time in Antioch. And after their return, Paul and Barnabas remained yet longer at Antioch (in this interval, indeed, the visit of Peter to Antioch occurs, Gal. ii. 11), until it occurred to Paul to set forth again upon a journey. On the first occasion, the suggestion to the missionary journey proceeded from the Holy Ghost by the mouth of certain prophets, chap. xiii. 2. This time it was Paul who exhorted Barnabas to it. And, indeed, he appears to have had nothing further in view than a journey of visitation to those churches, established on the first missionary journey. This is contained in *ἐπιστρέψαντες*, retracing a way formerly taken; also in *ἐπισκεψώμεθα πῶς ἔχουσι*. Only those cities were at first to be visited, where Paul and Barnabas had preached the Gospel; they intended to look after the brethren: *πῶς ἔχουσι*, how they morally conducted themselves, and how they throve.

2. Barnabas appears immediately to have acquiesced in this mutual journey of visitation; but he counselled Paul (*ἐβουλεύσατο, consulere*) to take with them John, surnamed Mark, as a companion. Paul refused: he could not approve of taking him with them after his conduct on their last journey, which appeared to him as a falling away (*ἀποστάντα* in the strict sense) from them. *'Αξιοῦν* denotes a moral judgment: he has not merited that we should take him with us; he has made himself unworthy of it. Also the expression *τὸν ἀποστάντα — μὴ συμπαραλαβεῖν τοῦτον* evidently betrays the vivacity and energy of his indignation at such conduct (see chap. xiii. 13).

3. As Barnabas did not agree with this, and did not share in the severity of Paul (Mark was besides his nephew, Col. iv. 10), there took place an angry scene, a sharp contention (*παροξυσμὸς*). The consequence was a separation of the two, and of the ways they took. Barnabas remained resolved to have Mark with him, and went to the island of Cyprus, his native country. Paul chose Silas as his companion, who had returned to Jerusalem (ver. 33), but in the interval appears to have come back again to Antioch. The solemn dismissal, and the intercessory recommendation to the grace of the Lord on the part of the Church (ver. 40), appears to have referred only to Paul, and not also to Barnabas. Perhaps Barnabas, after the occurrence with Paul, went off quickly; at least his journey (ver. 39) is more directly

connected with that scene, than is the journey of Paul. At all events, Barnabas in his journey to Cyprus pursued the same object which Paul had proposed (ver. 36). Paul, with Silas, on the other hand, went by land at first through Syria and Cilicia, so that he, even as Barnabas, betook himself to his native country, and at first confined himself to the Christian churches already established, which he confirmed in the faith and in the Christian life.

DOGMATICAL AND ETHICAL THOUGHTS.

1. Paul has, as it appears at first sight, undertaken this second missionary journey—which reached a much greater extent than the first, and led him to Europe—purely from the impulse of his own mind; while he was sent forth on his first journey by the Church of Antioch, and at the suggestion of the Holy Ghost. Nevertheless, the journey, which was so much blessed, did not spring from mere human thought or individual choice. It was without doubt a feeling of duty toward the churches of Asia Minor, established on his first journey—an impulse of conscience, illuminated and guided by the Spirit of God, which induced Paul to resolve to undertake this journey, and to exhort Barnabas to it. What floated before his mind was not primarily the preaching of the Gospel to the unconverted, the external mission; but care to look after and to nourish those already converted, the internal mission. And only in the course of the journey did he aim at wider objects. The journey was to be a kind of apostolic journey of visitation; the object of it was *ἐπισκέψασθαι τοὺς ἀδελφοὺς πῶς ἔχουσι*, *quomodo se habeant in fide, amore, spe; nervus visitationis ecclesiasticæ:* Bengel. An apostolic model of church-visitation. (Compare chap. viii. 14, ix. 32.)

2. Paul has directed toward Mark the entire sharpness and severity of his moral judgment, and put it into practice. He has judged his separation from him and Barnabas, and their common work (chap. xiii. 13), not as morally indifferent, but as an unjustifiable want of fidelity and Christian constancy. Mark had not fallen from Christ Himself, but from them (ver. 28, *ἀπ' αὐτῶν*). Paul does not condemn him in an exaggerated and passionate manner, as if he had been an unbeliever and an enemy of Christ. But he refused him permission to accompany him on the new journey, regarding this as a privilege, an

honour, a distinction (ἠξίου), of which Mark had rendered himself unworthy. Barnabas does not share in this severe judgment: he suffers mildness, moderation, and forbearance to rule. Both indeed were serviceable to Mark's spiritual welfare: the severity of Paul served to lead him to repentance, to humble and to warn him; while the mildness of Barnabas served to preserve him from despondency. Paul, at a later period, did not continue his resentment to him, but must have forgiven him; otherwise he would not have saluted the Colossians in a friendly manner from Mark (Col. iv. 10), and would not have recommended him to the Church.

3. The contention between Paul and Barnabas, so far as we can see, was so passionate and hot, that it could not have ended without sin on both sides. The word of God does not conceal the sins of the most worthy servants of God, covering them with a cloak, but declares them with perfect candour on account of the truth. It is a proof that the grace of God in Christ is yet mightier than sin, when, in spite of so many temptations, in spite of so great weakness of the flesh, grace preserves, sanctifies, and improves the children of God. Indeed, even this separation, which could not have occurred without sin, must, by God's providence, causing all things to turn out for the best, serve for good. Not only was the work of Paul now developed in full independence, unchecked by a companion equal or originally superior to him; but also the division of work between Paul and Barnabas promoted the cause. Hitherto Paul and Barnabas pursued in common one course: now two missionary journeys are made at the same time, and instead of one pair of missionaries, two pairs labour in different places.

HOMILETICAL HINTS.

Let us return and visit our brethren (ver. 36). It is not enough to plant a church, it must be watered and nourished, 1 Cor. iii. 6 (Starke).—A well-organized church-visitation is necessary both for ministers and for hearers (Quesnel).

Therefore it came to a hot contention (ver. 39). Even the greatest saints are not without their failings, but these must be distinguished from ruling sins (Starke).—But why has this dissension taken place and been here recorded? Is there not here an offence for all times? By no means. Even in this very particular, scriptural history is distinguished from human biographies. Scripture describes a good man as he is, and accordingly relates many of his failings, how they are by divine grace turned to good. Human biographies confine themselves almost entirely to beautiful incidents, and thus give us only a doubtful representation of the whole man. To Mark, who afterwards was found upright (Col. iv. 10), on the one hand, Paul's severity may have served for humiliation, and, on the other hand, Barnabas' indulgent love for comfort and encouragement. The one was as necessary as the other (Rieger).—Barnabas occupied the place of a good and kind mother, who willingly excuses and overlooks the faults of her children. Paul proved himself to be a severe father who uses the rod, and thinks the spoiled child must be made to feel (Gossner).—Paul appears to have been most in the right. He had in Gideon an Old Testament model, Judg. vii. 3. But he would assuredly not have contended so sharply with Barnabas, had he thought on the example of Abraham, Gen. xiii. At all events, it was well that these two men separated. Original minds rarely suit one another: the one can with difficulty accommodate himself to the other; they are to stand each by himself alone, without prejudice to their brotherly fellowship in Christ (Williger).—Let us look from the fallible weakness of the saints, which Scripture never conceals, to the infallible hand of the Lord, turning all things for the best. The severity of Paul did not injure Mark, but excited him to greater fidelity; and Paul still considered Barnabas as a companion faithfully united to him in the work of the Lord, 1 Cor. ix. 6 (Besser).

But Paul chose Silas (ver. 40). Silas, the Jewish Christian, matured in Jerusalem, the companion of the apostle of the Gentiles! What blessed and comprehensive results has not that occurrence mentioned in ver. 1 produced! (Williger.)—*Being recommended by the brethren to the grace of God.* This peculiar attention of the Church to Paul is a token, that the brethren considered him to have been most in the right (Rieger).

Human weakness even in the most advanced Christians. 1. That it is so. 2. Comfort from it (Lisco).—*The contention of the brethren.* 1. Wherefore they contend? Both, as they imagined, for Christ; but both, unconsciously, for themselves and their own will. 2. Who was in the right? Both intended the right—the salvation of the erring and the promotion of God's kingdom. Neither was in the right, because each in a one-sided manner stood firm to his own opinion. Both did right, separating voluntarily, in order not to interrupt love any further (Lisco).—*Wherefore does Scripture disclose to us the weaknesses of God's servants?* 1. For the mortification of spiritual pride, in order that none may boast, I shall never more be overcome. 2. For the comfort of human weakness, that it may be encouraged by the thought, They are also flesh of our flesh. 3. For the glory of divine wisdom, which converts the faults of men into a blessing.—*Barnabas, Paul, and the Lord;* or, good, better, best. 1. The forbearing love of Barnabas was good. 2. The holy severity of Paul was better. 3. The wisdom of the Lord, converting all things into good, was best.—*The triumph of the Lord in the weakness of His servants.* 1. Without Him, even their virtues are converted into failings: the mildness of Barnabas is converted into a weak forbearance; and the severity of Paul into an unbending harshness. 2. By Him, their faults prove blessings: the humiliation of Mark serves for wholesome recovery of strength; and the separation of the apostles divides the stream of the Gospel into two arms, and extends it the wider.—*The contentions of the children of God carry healing in themselves:* For it is one ground of faith on which they stand, one aim which they pursue, and one Lord and Master to whom they are subject.

B.

Paul adds Timotheus as a companion, and after a visit to the recently established Churches, travels rapidly through Asia Minor to Troas.

CHAP. XVI. 1–8.

1 Then he came to Derbe and Lystra. And, behold, there was a disciple
there named Timotheus, the son of a Jewish woman who believed, but of a
Greek father; 2 Who had a good reputation of the brethren at Lystra and
Iconium. 3 Him Paul wished to go with him, and took and circumcised
him, on account of the Jews who were in those quarters; for they all knew
that his father was a Greek. 4 And as they went through the cities, they
delivered to them the decrees to observe which had been resolved upon by the
apostles and elders in Jerusalem. 5 And so were the churches confirmed
in the faith, and increased in number daily. 6 But when they had

journeyed through Phrygia and the region of Galatia, and were forbidden of the Holy Ghost to preach the word in Asia, 7 And had come to Mysia, they attempted to go to Bithynia, and the Spirit of Jesus suffered them not. 8 Then they passed by Mysia and came down to Troas.

Ver. 7. Εἰς τὴν Βιθυνίαν is overwhelmingly attested, whilst κατὰ τ. Β. has only two MSS. for it.—The textus receptus has simply τὸ πνεῦμα; on the other hand, the five oldest MSS. have τὸ πν. Ἰησοῦ, which is undeniably genuine.

EXEGETICAL EXPLANATIONS.

1. *Then came he to Derbe and Lystra.*—Timotheus was without doubt a native of Lystra and not of Derbe, for ἐκεῖ is nearest to the former name; and ver. 2, where Lystra is again named along with Iconium, but not Derbe, confirms this view. This view is adopted by De Wette, Winer, and Meyer; whilst the usual opinion (as also Neander) considers Derbe as the native city of Timotheus. He was already a disciple before Paul came on this journey into the neighbourhood; so that it is supposed that he was converted on the first missionary journey. He was sprung from a mixed marriage, inasmuch as his mother was a Jewish Christian (named Eunice, 1 Tim. i. 5) and his father a Gentile (Ἕλλην). There is no trace that his father embraced Christianity: on the contrary, from the words ὅτι Ἕλλην ὑπῆρχεν it is rather to be inferred that he was at that time still a heathen, and had neither become a proselyte to Judaism, nor was converted to Christ. "His father had been a Greek" (Luther) is an incorrect rendering of the original.

2. *Him Paul wished to go with him.*—Paul resolved (ἠθέλησεν) that Timotheus should go with him (ἐξελθεῖν) from his parents' house and from his home, on the missionary journey. Why he did so, is not expressly said. However, the connection indicates the reasons. First, the esteem in which Timotheus stood (ἐμαρτυρεῖτο) with the Christians in Lystra and Iconium influenced the apostle; and this esteem was founded both on his character—his pious, upright conduct—and on his gifts. Secondly, the circumstance also, that, according to his descent, he belonged in a manner both to Jews and Gentiles, may have determined the choice of the apostle.

3. *Paul took and circumcised him.*—Λαβὼν περιέτεμεν seems to indicate that the apostle did it himself, and not that it was done by a third party (Neander). The apostle, as well as every

Israelite, was entitled to do so. It must necessarily be supposed that Timotheus willingly submitted to circumcision. Respect to the Jews of those cities, who all knew that his father was a Gentile, was the reason of this action. Accordingly, the motive to it was not compliance with the pharisaical and judaizing Christians, far less a supposition that circumcision was necessary for salvation; but only a regard to the unconverted Jews of that district, who might have taken offence and been less susceptible, if Timotheus, as the son of a Gentile and uncircumcised, had taken an active part in the work of Paul; especially as, according to the strict Jewish ideas, a Jewess ought never to marry a Gentile, and the children of such a marriage were reckoned bastards (Ewald).

4. *And as they went through the cities.*—To the cities of Pisidia, Lycaonia, and Pamphylia, which Paul again visited in company with Silas, and now also with Timotheus, he delivered the decrees of Jerusalem to observe. And both by this and by their renewed intercourse with the apostle, the churches received internal confirmation and steady increase. Bengel makes this striking remark: *Rarum incrementum, numero simul et gradu.*

5. From Pisidia they proceeded at first northward, over the mountain range of Taurus, to the interior countries of Asia Minor: *Phrygia*, the Phrygia Major of ancient geographers; and *Galatia*, which received its name from certain Gallic or Celtic tribes, who, in the third century before Christ, broke forth from Thrace over Asia, and had settled here. Though the narrative passes over this journey very rapidly, yet it is to be assumed that Paul on this journey founded those churches in several cities of Galatia, to which he, probably in the year 55 after Christ, wrote his important epistle.

6. *And were prevented by the Holy Ghost.*—From Galatia and Phrygia Paul wished, as it appears, to proceed directly westward to Asia; that is, to *Asia proconsularis*, or to the west coast district of Asia Minor, including Mysia, Lydia, and Caria. But they were prevented from making this journey and preaching the Gospel there by the Holy Ghost (by means of some intimation or internal direction). Therefore they went northward to the eastern boundaries of that district, to Mysia, where this north-west corner of Asia Minor borders on the east upon Bithynia, a maritime district on the Bosphorus and Black Sea;

and they intended to penetrate into this country, and were again hindered by the Spirit of Jesus. As regards the grammatical construction, we consider it most natural to understand the three participles in vers. 6, 7, διελθόντες, κωλυθέντες, and ἐλθόντες, as expressing events occurring the one after the other in order of time. This suits also best from geographical considerations. Therefore they were induced to pass by Mysia, *i.e.*, along the southern border of Lesser Mysia, and to go down to the coast of the Ægean Sea, to the sea-port of Troas, which lay south of Cape Sigeum.

DOGMATICAL AND ETHICAL THOUGHTS.

1. The circumcision of Timotheus by Paul has been greatly objected to, whereas in Jerusalem, according to his own declaration, Gal. ii. 3, he would not suffer his companion Titus to be circumcised. It has been thought, that if what this passage mentions were true, the apostle must have been guilty of great inconsistency; and therefore this narrative has been regarded as entirely incredible (Baur, Zeller). But the two cases are so totally different, that they cannot be placed under the same category. In Jerusalem, Paul had to do with the judaizing Christians, to whom he would not yield; here, he had respect to the unconverted Jews of Asia Minor, whom he feared to repel by the co-operation of an uncircumcised missionary assistant, and whom he might hope, by the circumcision of that assistant, to render susceptible to the Gospel. Moreover, there circumcision was directly demanded as something absolutely indispensable for salvation: then it was a duty to the truth of the Gospel not to give way. But here the motive was entirely a regard to circumstances, and not a supposed religious necessity. Already the Formula Concordiæ, p. 792, Rech., has rightly distinguished, *Circumcisionem Paulus alias (in libertate tamen christiana et spirituali) observare aliquoties solebat,* Acts xvi. 3. *Cum autem pseudo-apostoli circumcisionem ad stabiliendum falsum suum dogma (quod opera legis ad justitiam et salutem necessaria essent) urgerent, eaque ad confirmandum suum errorem in animis hominum abuterentur, ingenue affirmat Paulus, quod ne ad horam quidem ipsis cesserit, ut veritas evangelii sarta tectaque permaneret.*

2. It was by the guidance of the Spirit of God that Paul

was led from the centre of Asia Minor to the sea-coast opposite Europe. By πνεῦμα ἅγιον (ver. 6) we cannot understand the holy spirit of prudence which judged correctly of circumstances (De Wette), but, according to the doctrine and language of the whole book, the objective Spirit of God, who within the human spirit can make Himself understood and can make known His will—His holy determination, positively or negatively, to the soul. Here the guidance of the Holy Spirit appeared, not positively commanding (as, for example, in chap. xiii. 34), but negatively hindering, preventing (κωλυθέντες—οὐκ εἴασεν αὐτούς): the latter expression seems still stronger than the former. Once (ver. 7) the Spirit is called the Spirit of Jesus (τὸ πνεῦμα Ἰησοῦ). The Spirit of the glorified Redeemer, who lives and rules, here directly interposed, when the Gospel should go beyond the boundaries of one quarter of the world and pass over to Europe, hindering by His irresistible intimation; so that, in short, only the choice remained to go to the sea-coast, and from that to Europe.

HOMILETICAL HINTS.

Then he came to Derbe and Lystra (ver. 1). This was the soil where Paul, according to chap. xiv. 19, had sown a bloody seed of suffering. But how beautiful is the harvest of joy which God permits him to see from it! When he comes again, he finds a multitude of disciples, and among them Timotheus, as a trophy of his suffering and a seal of his apostleship (Apost. Past.).—*Timotheus, the son of a Jewish woman who believed, but of a Greek father.* Who would have expected such a blessing from so unequal a marriage? Probably the father was at that time already dead, or had deserted his wife, so that the believing mother had freer hands to bring up her son in the knowledge of the holy Scriptures. On the other hand, she had not been able to circumcise him in childhood. How many orphans are there, who, watered by the tears of pious mothers, grow up to be plants of the Lord! (Rieger.)—True disciples and servants of Jesus do not always spring from learned and pious fathers.—Often it is only the prayer and blessing of a pious mother or grandmother, by which the first spark of a living knowledge of Jesus is kindled in the youthful heart (Apost. Past.).

Who was well reported of by the brethren (ver. 2). This is more than a *testimonium*, which a candidate surreptitiously obtains from worldly men (Apost. Past.).—As the child Jesus Himself grew in favour, not only with God, but also with men; so God prepares His instruments also by the good report which at first a young man obtains from others, and this often exerts a great influence on his future career (Rieger).

Him would Paul have to go with him (ver. 3). Besides the good report of others, Paul must have had an anticipation that he had no man so entirely like-minded as he, Phil. ii. 20 (Rieger).—What one refuses and appears to lose from pure motives, that God restores better in another. Paul from pure motives would not take Mark with him, but God here gave him a better qualified and a more faithful Timotheus (Starke).—*Circumcised him on account of the Jews.* This was not contrary to the apostolic resolution at Jerusalem; for according to that, circumcision was only not to be forced upon any, as necessary to salvation. Paul acted in both cases only for the sake of the Gospel: where an injury to the Gospel was to be apprehended, he resisted the compulsion; but when a furtherance of the Gospel was to be hoped from it, then he would permit one to be circumcised, and thus he could become to the Jews as a Jew. There may often be seen in every one's conduct something like carnal wisdom, or which may be blamed as an act of inconsistency, and yet it may proceed from the same principle of faith and love (Rieger).—"Paul circumcised Timotheus, in order to abolish circumcision;" that is, in order by the Gospel to obtain access to the Jews (Chrysostom).—Just as I myself in the present day, if I were to go among the Jews, and had to preach the Gospel, and saw that they were weak, should be willing to submit to circumcision, and to eat and abstain as they did. But this I would be willing to do no longer and otherwise than I could be with them, and could advance the Gospel (Luther).—Thus, in our days, the missionary Gützlaff became a Chinese among the Chinese.

Delivered to them the decrees to observe (ver. 4). Wholesome decrees and ordinances must be diligently brought into play, otherwise they are as a bell without a clapper (Starke).—He lowered himself to the Jews, until faith sprung up in them. He interested himself heartily in the believing Gentiles, that he might announce to them a perfect freedom from the Jewish law, and refer them only to the grace of the Lord Jesus, until he saw both people united in the same spirit of faith (Apost. Past.).

Then were the churches established in the faith (ver. 5). An obstacle requires often to be removed, if the blessing is to be spread in full measure.—As long as the fear of the heavy law of Moses ruled in the churches, the course of the Gospel was checked. As soon as Paul removed this, there resulted a fair increase. Let us in our congregations watch and be on our guard, lest some false opinion or fault of manner check the blessing of our discourses (Apost. Past.).—*And increased in number daily.* A rare increase: at once in numbers and in the degree of faith (Bengel).

And were prevented by the Holy Ghost (ver. 6). Although the grace of God in Christ Jesus is intended for all men, yet He has appointed to each land, and city, and individual, the set time of visitation.—We have thus to commit the periods of awakening of lands and nations humbly and believingly to the wisdom of God; and also, in our peculiar office, to imitate the conduct of God: always to consider what soul needs our assistance and exhortation most, and where we may effect the greatest blessings. Certainly not of our own choice, but the Spirit of God must be our teacher in this (Apost. Past.).—Whoever will force everything against the drawing of God and the administration of His Spirit, employs himself in an indiscreet business, which, indeed, often obtains the praise of men, but is of little value before the searching eyes of God (Rieger).—Here the apostle was hindered by the Holy Ghost; at another time, Satan hindered him, 1 Thess. ii. 18. We cannot thus always refer a certain disinclination to preach the Gospel, in some particular place, to the Holy Ghost (Apost. Past.).—It were to be wished that among preachers and candidates for the ministry, many would observe the restraints and intimations of the Holy Ghost, then the Church would receive the right men in the right places (Besser).

Then they passed by Mysia and came down to Troas (ver. 8). A new furtherance was to arise from the apparent hindrance of the cause of Christ, although at present they did not know how. This exact narrative is of peculiar importance to us Europeans. The transplantation of the Gospel to our quarter of the world was not a plan resolved upon by man and only consented to by God; on the contrary, the apostles were driven to it against their intentions: it was the will of the Lord, directly commanding them (Williger).—The name Troas (Troy) reminds us of the first famous war between Europe and Asia in hoary antiquity. From the places where formerly the heroes of Greece fought, the warriors of Christ march in their holy warfare to the conquest of Greece and of the whole world (Besser).

On the whole section (vers. 1–8).—*Timotheus, a model of a gracious youth.* 1. What grace was bestowed on him: his mother, a pious woman; his intercourse with believers; his teacher, the Apostle Paul. 2. What he became through grace: his mother's pride and comfort, as opposed to an unbelieving husband (ver. 1); the ornament and blessing of the Church (1 and 2 Tim.; 2 Cor. i. 19; Phil. ii. 22; 1 Cor. xvi. 10); the apostle's joy and support (1 Thess. iii. 3; 2 Tim. i. 4; Phil. ii. 20).—The blessing of a pious youth.—The high position of mothers in the kingdom of Christ: Hannah, the mother of Samuel; Mary, the mother of Jesus; Salome, the mother of Zebedee's children; Eunice, the mother of Timotheus; and Monica, the mother of Augustin.—A mother's prayers, a guardian angel to her children.—*The well-instructed Timotheus; or the harvest of joy from the mother's tears.* 1. The mother's tears certainly flowed at the education of her son, beside a heathen father; and at the departure of the youth to the perilous missionary service. 2. The harvest of joy did not fail in the lovely progress of the boy at home, and in the glorious ripening of the man for the service of the Lord.—*Paul and Timotheus; or the blessed bond between a noble master and a faithful disciple.* Blessed for the disciple, for the master, and for the world.—*How can we succeed in the ministry of the divine word, in becoming all things to all men, in a proper manner?* 1. When we observe the wants of our hearers for the time being; 2. but do nothing to the prejudice of divine truth from human considerations (Lisco).—*The hours of grace in the kingdom of God* (for nations, churches, individual souls, vers. 6, 7). 1. To be accelerated by no human will. 2. To be retarded by no human power.—"There is a time for everything," proved in the history of the kingdom of God on earth. —In the kingdom of the Spirit, nothing is to be forced.—The apparent hindrances in the kingdom of God are only the means of its furtherance.—"A man's heart deviseth his ways, but the Lord directeth his steps," Prov. xvi. 9, xxi. 2.

C.

Divine intimations lead the Apostle to Europe. Successful commencement, persecution, and imprisonment, but also divine deliverance at Philippi.

Chap. xvi. 9–40.

9 And during the night, a vision appeared to Paul. There stood a man of Macedonia, and entreated him, saying, Pass over to Macedonia, and help us. 10 And after he had seen the vision, we immediately sought to go to Macedonia, inferring that the Lord had called us to preach the Gospel to them. 11 We therefore sailed from Troas, and went by a straight course to Samothracia, and the day after to Neapolis; 12 And from thence to Philippi, which is the first city of the district of Macedonia, and a colony. In this city we remained some days.

13 And on the Sabbath we went out of the gate to the river, where a place of prayer was wont to be: there we sat down, and conversed with the women who were assembled. 14 And a woman, named Lydia, a dealer of purple, of the city of Thyatira, who feared God, heard us; whose heart the Lord opened, that she attended to the things which Paul spoke. 15 But when she was baptized, and her house, she besought us, saying, If ye have judged me to be a believer in the Lord, come into my house, and abide there. And she constrained us. 16 But it came to pass, as we went to the place of prayer, that a female slave, who had a soothsaying spirit, met us, who brought much gain to her masters by soothsaying. 17 The same followed Paul and us, crying, and saying, These men are servants of the Most High God, who announce to you the way of salvation. 18 And this she did many days. But Paul was grieved, and turned, and said to the spirit, I command you, in the name of Jesus Christ, to come out of her. And he came out the same hour.

19 But when her masters saw that the hope of their gains was gone, they seized on Paul and Silas, and dragged them to the market-place to the rulers; 20 And brought them before the magistrates, saying, These men create disturbance in our city; they are Jews, 21 And announce customs which we dare neither receive nor observe, being Romans. 22 And the multitude rose up together against them: and the magistrates commanded to rend off their clothes, and to beat them with rods. 23 And when they had given them many stripes, they cast them into prison, and commanded the jailor to keep them safely. 24 And he, having received such a charge, cast them into the inner prison, and put their feet in the stocks. 25 And at midnight Paul and Silas prayed and praised God; and the prisoners heard them. 26 And suddenly there was a great earthquake, so that the foundation-walls of the prison were shaken; and immediately all doors were opened, and the bands of all were loosed. 27 But when the jailor awoke and saw the prison-doors open, he drew a sword, and would have killed himself, thinking that the

prisoners had fled. 28 But Paul cried with a loud voice, Do thyself no harm; for we are all here. 29 Then he called for a light, and sprang in; and trembled, and fell at the feet of Paul and Silas, 30 And brought them out, and said, Sirs, what must I do to obtain salvation? 31 And they said, Believe on the Lord Jesus; so shalt thou and thy house be saved. 32 And they spoke to him the word of the Lord, along with all who were in his house. 33 And he took them the same hour of the night, and washed their stripes; and he and all his were forthwith baptized. 34 And he brought them to his house, and set meat before them, and rejoiced, with all his house, that he had become a believer in God.

35 But when it was day, the magistrates sent the lictors, saying, Release these men. 36 And the jailor told these words to Paul, The magistrates have sent to release you: now then depart, and go in peace. 37 But Paul said to them, They have beaten us openly without right and judgment, who yet are Romans, and have cast us into prison: and now will they thrust us out secretly? No; but they ought to come themselves, and bring us out. 38 And the lictors told these words to the magistrates; and they feared, when they heard that they were Romans; 39 And they came, and besought them, and brought them out, and entreated them to depart from the city. 40 But they, having come out of prison, went into the house of Lydia; and when they had seen the brethren, they exhorted them, and left the city.

Ver. 10. Ὁ κύριος, after D.G.H., several Oriental versions and fathers, is to be preferred to ὁ Θεός, as Θεός might easily be substituted for κύριος.

Ver. 13. The textus receptus has πόλεως; instead of which, the reading πύλης is better attested.

Ver. 16. The textus receptus has, after several MSS., πύθωνος, whilst the oldest MSS. have the accusative πύθωνα, which the transcribers do not appear to have understood.

Ver. 31. The textus receptus has Χριστόν after the majority of MSS.; nevertheless, after A. and B., the word is to be erased, as a spurious addition. So Lachmann and Tischendorf.

Ver. 32. Σύν is overwhelmingly attested, and is to be considered as genuine; it was exchanged for καί, which seemed simpler.

Ver. 34. The imperfect ἠγαλλιᾶτο is in C. (first hand), in the Codex Cantabrigiensis, and in Chrysostom, Oecumenius, and Theophylact; it is therefore to be preferred to the aorist ἠγαλλιάσατο.

EXEGETICAL EXPLANATIONS.

1. *And during the night.*—A vision in the night (ὅραμα, not a dream, of which there is no trace, and which is by no means necessarily implied by διὰ τῆς νυκτὸς) points the apostle to Macedonia. The vision consisted in this: there stood before Paul a man who by his words gave himself to be understood to be a Macedonian, and a representative of his nation (*Μακεδονίαν — ἡμῖν*). Perhaps also Paul recognised his origin from his

national dress; for although it is true that he had never as yet set foot on Europe, still in his native city, Tarsus, which carried on a flourishing trade, he might frequently have seen sailors from Macedonia. The man in the vision entreated him to come over the sea to Macedonia, to the assistance of the inhabitants. That an angel, in the form of a man of Macedonia, appeared to the apostle (Grotius), is not to be maintained. The *ὅραμα* requires, as little as the vision on the house-top at Joppa, to have been something objective.

2. *And after they had seen the vision.*—This vision directed the thoughts and plans of Paul and his companions immediately to Macedonia, so that they sought for an opportunity of sailing (*ἐζητήσαμεν*), having, by reflection on the connection of things, come to the conviction (*συμβιβάζοντες*, compare chap. ix. 22) that the Redeemer had called them to Macedonia, in order to bring the Gospel to that land. The elements which, by their concurrence, established this assurance were these: 1. The Spirit of Jesus had prevented them preaching the Gospel in the western coast of Asia Minor (*ἡ Ἀσία*, ver. 6). 2. They had likewise been hindered from labouring in Bithynia (ver. 7). 3. And now in Troas, situated on the coast of the Ægean Sea, the vision allures them over to Macedonia; and this cannot be a mere accident. Further, the assistance which is requested from Paul can certainly be nothing else than that which is contained in the word of God, and in the saving grace of Christ. Therefore it is He Himself who by the vision calls us to Macedonia, and for this reason He has prevented the preaching of the Gospel in the territories of Asia Minor.

3. *We immediately sought.*—With *ἐζητήσαμεν*, ver. 10, the pronoun "we" suddenly occurs. The historian by this discovers himself to have been an eye-witness and fellow-traveller of the apostle from Troas. Therefore it has been, from of old, inferred that Luke joined them at Troas, or rather that Paul took him with them from that place as a companion. On this point, Luke wastes no words, because the matter, as well as his personal relations, were known to Theophilus, and to his first readers in general. The objections which have been urged in modern times, for the purpose of ascribing the narrative of this journey from ver. 10 and onwards, as well as all those passages of the Acts of the Apostles where "we" occurs, to another com-

panion of the apostle (to Timotheus—so Schleiermacher, Bleek, and De Wette; or to Silas—so Schwanbeck), are by no means convincing. On the contrary, it would be in the highest degree surprising and inexplicable, that only now the inclusive form of narrative should occur, after the one and the other had journeyed for some time with Paul,—Silas even from Antioch, and Timotheus at least from Lystra. And as regards the only difficulty, directly drawn from this passage, that the personal participation in the deliberations and resolutions which is contained in ἐζητήσαμεν — συμβιβάζοντες does not suit one who had so recently joined them, it is entirely without force. If Paul met Luke at Troas, and united him (who without doubt was before this a Christian) to himself as a companion, then he could and might, as well as Silas and Timotheus, deliberate and determine with him.

4. *We sailed from Troas.*—With this embarkation of the company, now increased to four, commences the second part of this missionary journey, which embraces Macedonia. In a swift and fortunate voyage, they came by a straight course to Samothracia, an island to the north-west of Troas, in the Ægean Sea, and only 38 Roman miles from the Thracian coast. From this they went on the following day to Neapolis, a haven of Thrace on the Strymonic Gulf, now called Cavalla. And knowing that they were called to Macedonia, they set out on their journey, without pausing, to the Macedonian city Philippi, about two geographical (German) miles from Neapolis, and lying to the north-west. This city was built and fortified on the Thracian territory, on the site of the village Krenides, by Philip, the father of Alexander the Great, and accordingly bore his name. Luke describes it in a twofold manner: 1. as the first city of the part of Macedonia; and 2. as a colony. The latter description is confirmed by other accounts, according to which Octavius established the partisans of Antony there, and colonized the city, to which he also granted the privileges of a colony (*jus Italicum*). But, on the other hand, the first notice has given rise to much difficulty. The words πρώτη τῆς μερίδος τῆς Μακεδονίας πόλις might at first suggest the idea that Philippi was to be reckoned as the capital of this district of Macedonia; but we know exactly from classical authors what were the capitals of the four districts, into which Macedonia was divided by

the Romans, and among these Philippi is not mentioned; on the contrary, Amphipolis was the capital of that district to which Philippi belonged (*Macedonia prima*). Therefore πρώτη cannot have this meaning; and still less can the expression be understood, with Ewald, as if Philippi were made the capital of the entire province of Macedonia, because probably the Roman governor resided there at that time. The interpretation also, that πρώτη was a title of honour, and referred to some peculiar privileges which were granted to Philippi (Hug, Kuinoel), does not recommend itself, as nothing of this kind is known: neither does the combination of πρώτη πόλις with κολωνία—the first or most distinguished colonial city of the district (Meyer)—because the position of the words shows that κολωνία is a second independent predicate: *eademque colonia* (Van Hengel). Therefore it only remains to take πρώτη τῆς μερίδος topographically—the first city belonging to the province of Macedonia. Meyer objects to this meaning, that there is no reason why Luke, contrary to his usual method, should make such a precise geographical statement. But this objection is removed, and our interpretation recommended, when the peculiarly accurate, and therefore the more careful, narrative from ver. 8 is kept in view. In Troas it was revealed to the apostle in a night vision that the Redeemer called him to Macedonia, in order to preach the Gospel there. From that moment, Macedonia stood before him and his companions as the nearest aim of their distant missionary journey. They sought immediately the quickest opportunity of journeying to it. After they had found a ship and sailed from Troas, the voyage proceeded quickly by a favourable wind (εὐθυδρομήσαντες) past Samothracia to Neapolis. But Neapolis was a city of Thrace, and they were bound for Macedonia. Therefore they journeyed without a pause from this to Philippi, "which is the first city of the district of Macedonia." Thus ἥτις retains its assigned signification, and this so much the more since Rettig (Quæst. Philippenses) has proved that Neapolis belonged at that time to Thrace, and that it was not joined to Macedonia until the reign of Vespasian. Thus already Erasmus explains it: *ea civitas colonia, prima occurrit a Neapoli petentibus Macedoniam;* so also, of moderns, Olshausen and De Wette.

5. *Philippi was the first city* of Europe, at which the ambas-

sadors of Jesus Christ halted and preached the Gospel. And this happened, at first, on a Sabbath (ver. 13), and in a place appointed and consecrated by custom (ἐνομίζετο) for assembling for prayer (προσευχή, a place of prayer, as a substitute for a synagogue), on the bank of a river. This river has been supposed to be the Strymon (Neander, De Wette, and Meyer), but erroneously; for the Strymon was more than a day's journey to the west of Philippi: the wide plain on which the celebrated battle was fought, when the republican army was defeated by Octavius and Antony, stretches between them. Another river, then, must be meant, which flowed at a distance of not more than five or six furlongs, *i.e.*, a Sabbath-day's journey, from the city. Probably it was that river which Appian calls the Gangas or Gangites. Hackett, the same American divine who wrote a commentary on the Acts of the Apostles, found, on a visit to the place, in winter certainly (13th Dec. 1858), a considerable river flowing past the east side of the ruins of Philippi. It was on the banks of rivers, or on the sea-coast, that they preferred to perform their religious worship, as they had water for their sacred washings.

6. *And on the Sabbath.*—The day and place show that, primarily, only Jews and proselytes are referred to. It would seem also, that at that time there were no Jewish men in the city; for Paul and his companions, at that rural place of prayer, only spoke to women who were assembled there. Even these were probably few in number, as Paul only engaged in familiar conversation with them, and did not deliver a set discourse. This is evident from καθίσαντες ἐλαλοῦμεν, in distinction from λέγειν, διαλέγεσθαι, etc., an easy, colloquial conversation. They also spoke sitting, not standing, which betokens a less formal and solemn discourse. One of the hearers was peculiarly susceptible, and evinced an earnest attention to what Paul said (διανοίγω signifies to open fully and widely): this was Lydia, a proselyte, and a dealer in purple, of the city of Thyatira. This city lay in the Asiatic province of Lydia, to the north of Sardis. It is indeed possible that she was called at Philippi, on account of her birth-place, "the Lydian," although Lydia was in ancient times a very common female name. Thyatira was celebrated for its purple dyes and fabrics; and thus the circumstance that she was a πορφυρόπωλις, a dealer in purple fabrics,

agrees with her descent. And as Thyatira was a Macedonian colony (Strabo, xiii.), so it is easy to imagine that Lydia came to Philippi in the way of business.

7. *And a woman named Lydia.*—The baptism of Lydia and her family was not performed on the spot, but soon after. Afterwards, she invited and pressed the apostle and all his companions to come to her house as guests, and to abide there. *Παρεβιάσατο*, she constrained us: the word is also used in Luke xxiv. 29 for friendly and repeated pressing and entreaty; from which, however, it is not to be supposed that the missionaries of the Gospel at first resisted (Bengel, Baumgarten). This hospitality was a proof of her love to the Redeemer arising from faith, which showed itself by unselfish and ministering love toward His messengers. Her entreaty appealed to this, that they had judged, *κεκρίκατε* (otherwise they would not have baptized her), that she was a believer in the Lord (*πιστὴν τῷ κυρίῳ*): not "faithful to the Lord," for that judgment would have been precipitate. That the messengers of the Gospel granted her request, and went as guests into the house of Lydia, is certainly to be assumed; for *παρεβιάσατο* expresses, as in Luke xxiv. 29, not only the *conatus*, but likewise the *actus*.

8. *But it came to pass.*—Some days later, but not on the same Sabbath (Heinrichs and Kuinoel, whom Meyer has refuted), occurred the expulsion of the soothsaying spirit from a female slave. She had a *πνεῦμα πύθωνα*, and practised soothsaying (*μαντευομένη*), and indeed, as it appears, as a ventriloquist; for this is inferred from *πύθων*. Python was the serpent at Delphi which Apollo killed: latterly a soothsaying *δαιμόνιον* was so called; and in particular Hesychius mentions that a *πύθων* was a ventriloquist, a soothsayer by means of ventriloquism. Plutarch also incidentally mentions, that in his time what was called *πύθων* was formerly called *ἐγγαστρίμυθος* or *εὐρυκλῆς*. Those who gave credit to her soothsaying regarded it as probable that a prophetic god resided in her; but Paul recognised her as possessed by an unclean spirit, as a demoniac (ver. 18). She was the slave of many (*οἱ κύριοι*) who turned her to profit, and drew a considerable gain, making the people pay for the soothsayings of their slave. This person met Paul and his companions as they went to the place of prayer, ran after them and cried to the passers-by, that these were the servants

of the Most High God, who announce the way of salvation. She spoke the truth by means of a clairvoyance and divination, which were conferred upon her in a supernatural manner. As she often repeated this, Paul was grieved (διαπονηθείς), because he could receive neither recommendation and support nor honour, from a spirit which was not of God. Therefore, turning suddenly round to the woman following him, he commanded the spirit, in the name of the Lord Jesus, to come out of her.

9. *But when her masters saw.*—This transaction occasioned hostility, and indeed was the cause of the scourging and imprisonment of Paul and Silas (vers. 19–24). Ἰδόντες, not on the spot, for it is not to be supposed that they were present at the occurrence; but after the masters of the slave were convinced that she had passed over into the normal mental condition, that the prophetic spirit had departed from her, and that consequently the prospect of further gains from her soothsaying was taken away: ἐξῆλθεν used designedly in an equivocal sense. Self-interest goaded them on to an attempt at revenge; and accordingly they forcibly seized on Paul and Silas (Timotheus and Luke, as subordinate companions, remained unmolested), drew them to the market-place before the rulers (*οἱ ἄρχοντες* in general), and placed them before the *στρατηγοί*, as accused. Στρατηγοί, the Roman *prætores*, was an honourable title, ordinarily given to the highest authorities in the Roman colonial cities, properly *duumviri* (Cicero de lege agrar. c. 34: *cum ceteris in coloniis duumviri appellentur, hi se prætores appellari volebant*). The complaint went on political disturbance (*ἐκταράσσειν, perturbare*); and was founded on the circumstance that these men, as Jews, wished to introduce customs which the citizens, as Roman subjects and colonists, durst neither receive nor adopt. The name Ἰουδαῖοι is here not only opposed to Ῥωμαίοις οὖσι, in order to set forth the national distinction, but it is also used in an obnoxious and contemptuous way, in order to excite the people. Ἔθη is taken in a wide sense, including both the customs of religious worship and the religious life. Moreover, Ἰουδαίοις οὖσι shows that these accusers did not as yet recognise Christianity as such, but still confounded it with Judaism.

10. *And the multitude rose up together against them.*—The multitude, quickly gathered together, made common cause with

the masters of the female slave against the Christians (συνεπέστη), probably with tumultuous outcries against them. And the duumviri, without doubt intimidated, and thinking only to appease the excited crowd, immediately ordered, without trial or judicial proceedings, corporeal punishment with numerous blows of the rod upon the naked body. *Περιῤῥήξαντες τὰ ἱμάτια*: compare Livy ii. 5, 8, *lacerantibus vestem lictoribus.* The magistrates certainly did not tear off the clothes themselves (Bengel), but through the officers of justice (*ῥαβδοῦχοι*, see vers. 35, 38, lictors), who also inflicted the scourging with rods (*virgis cædere*). Probably the scourging was so quickly and passionately ordered and done, that no protest was allowed to be advanced. After this infliction of scourging, which took place without any trial, Paul and Silas were committed to prison with the charge of strict custody; in consequence of which, the jailor, as if they were dangerous criminals, placed them in a cell situated in the interior of the prison (*ἐσωτέραν*), and moreover, according to the Roman custom, put their feet in the stocks (*τὸ ξύλον, nervus*). This was a heavy piece of wood with holes, into which the feet were put, and stretched apart from one another; it was thus also an instrument of torture.

11. *And at midnight.*—The miraculous aid (vers. 25–28). Whilst Paul and Silas, in so shameful and painful a position, nevertheless prayed and praised God with a loud voice, so that the other prisoners, astonished, heard them, the foundation-walls of the prison were shaken by a great earthquake, all the doors of the building were thrown open, and not only their fetters, but also the fetters of all the prisoners (*πάντων*), were loosened. The jailor, suddenly awaking, thought at first, when he found the doors open, that his prisoners had escaped, and intended, with loud cries of desperation, to kill himself. Then Paul called to him, and calmed him with the assurance that they were all there. The other prisoners had heard the prayers of Paul and Silas; and, as the earthquake which opened the doors and loosened their fetters occurred immediately, they felt the power of God, and, struck with the miracle, remained motionless in their cells.

12. *Then he called for a light.*—Consequence of the miracle as regards the jailor (vers. 29–34). He came quickly with a light into the inner prison (*εἰσεπήδησε*), and cast himself down

with fear and trembling, from anguish of conscience (ἔντρομος), at the feet of Paul and Silas, because he was obliged to recognise them as the protected by God. Then he brought them out of the ἐσωτέρα φυλακή (ver. 24), and led them to the inner space of the court of the prison (προαγαγὼν ἔξω), and here asked them in a respectful manner (κύριοι) what he must do to obtain the salvation which they announced (ver. 17). They required faith in Jesus as the Lord, and so would he and his house be saved. And accordingly they commenced to announce summarily to him, and to all belonging to his house, the word of Jesus Christ. The effect of this was, that he, along with all his household (πανοικί, almost only among the later classics), believed on God (πεπιστευκὼς τῷ Θεῷ, so expressed because he had been a heathen and polytheist), and could, even on the same night, be baptized with all his, and that certainly within the space belonging to the prison, in a well or pond. This took place, as may be supposed from ver. 33, directly in connection with his washing the bloody stripes of Paul and Silas: they repaid him this service with another, baptizing him and his family in the same water. Hereupon he prepared for them, exhausted by deeds of violence, scourging, and severe imprisonment, a refreshment in his house. Ἀναγαγὼν εἰς τὸν οἶκον does not suppose that his official dwelling was a storey higher than the prison (Meyer), but only that it was a storey higher than the court of the prison, in which the ablution of Paul and Silas and the baptism took place. Παρέθηκε τράπεζαν is both a Hebrew and a Roman form of expression: Ps. xxiii. 5, תַּעֲרֹךְ לְפָנַי שֻׁלְחָן *apposuit mensam:* so also used in the Greek by Homer (Od. E. 93).

13. *But when it was day.*—Honourable dismissal of the prisoners (vers. 35–40). On the morning, the duumviri, after deliberate consideration, finding that they had acted rashly, perhaps also having received information of what had occurred in the prison that night, wished to settle the affair speedily by the dismissal of the prisoners. Accordingly they sent an order by the lictors to the jailor to release these men (designedly spoken contemptuously). The jailor informed Paul, supposing that they would now be pleased to be set at liberty (ἐξελθόντες), and to be permitted to pursue their journey unmolested (ἐν εἰρήνῃ), when Paul objected. He represented to the officials (πρὸς αὐτούς, sc. the jailor and the lictors) that this procedure was

contrary to all justice. They had, against all justice, punished them without trial and sentence (ἀκατακρίτους); moreover, contrary to the Roman law, they had beaten them with rods, who, as Roman citizens, ought not to be subjected to such punishment; and that publicly (δημοσίᾳ), which was an aggravation of the punishment. Hereupon they had been imprisoned: and now they would wish to dismiss the affair in all secrecy (λάθρα, contrast to δημοσίᾳ) by thrusting them out of the prison (ἐκβάλλουσιν), which they have already done, as far as depended on them. This is injustice, Paul will say, and hence his peremptory refusal (οὐ γάρ; the γάρ indicates that the refusal, οὐ, is the reason of the preceding exclamation of indignation), and his decided demand that the duumviri should come themselves (αὐτοί, not merely by means of their lictors), in order to bring them out of the prison. It would have cast the appearance of guilt on the prisoners, and might at a later period have been regarded as an escape, if they had permitted themselves to have been dismissed from prison without forms and ceremonies. Paul here declares, that both he and Silas were Roman citizens (ἄνθρωποι Ῥωμαῖοι). Of Silas, this is not elsewhere mentioned; but in Acts xxii. 25–28 we are informed that Paul possessed the privilege of Roman citizenship from his birth. This was not because he was born in Tarsus, as has been hastily inferred from the character of this city as *urbs libera* (Bengel); but the father, or some earlier ancestor of the apostle, must have received the Roman citizenship as a reward for some service to the State, or have acquired it by purchase.

13. *And they feared.*—The magistrates of the city were struck with fear (φοβηθέντες) at the information brought back, and especially by the circumstance that their prisoners possessed the privilege of Roman citizenship, inasmuch as injustice toward Roman citizens might bring upon them an accusation and punishment. Accordingly they were constrained to repair in person to the prison, and to beseech their prisoners (παρακαλεῖν in this connection includes apology and request that they might be satisfied), and to bring them with honour out of the prison (ἐξαγαγόντες), to which they added a friendly request (ἠρώτων) that they would voluntarily depart from the city. They yielded, but yet in no pressing haste; on the contrary, only after they had made a visit to the house of Lydia (ἐξελθόντες—εἰσῆλθον),

and had there seen, exhorted, and strengthened the brethren, that is, both their fellow-travellers, Luke and Timotheus, and the newly converted. *'Εξῆλθον* refers only to Paul and Silas, and supposes, taken in connection with the earlier inclusive form of narrative, that Luke at least, and perhaps also Timotheus, remained behind.

DOGMATICAL AND ETHICAL THOUGHTS.

1. The grain of mustard-seed, the work and kingdom of Christ, increasing from small beginnings, progresses in a striking manner with the establishment of the Gospel in Europe. Arrived in the first city of Macedonia, whither he knew himself called, the apostle, with his companions, finds at first no other listeners to the truth of salvation which they bring than some women. And this is not too trifling for the servants of Christ. Jesus Himself at a well conversed with a Samaritan woman, and the disciples were surprised that He talked with her (John iv. 27). So here also, the apostles of the Gentiles. They could not speak with many, and therefore they were content to speak to a few. Their communication could not be a sermon or a set discourse, and therefore they were delighted to be able to speak in simple conversation of Jesus. And from this inconspicuous mustard-seed, there sprang a rich and precious harvest—the flourishing Church of Philippi.

2. One individual among the few female hearers took to heart the things which were spoken by Paul, and listened with devout attention. Her susceptibility was itself the effect of grace. The Lord Jesus Christ had called His ambassadors to Macedonia, and it was He who opened her heart. Christ has the keys of David; He can open, and no man can shut. The human heart is barred and closed by sin, so that the divine truth cannot penetrate, illuminate the spirit, seize upon the will, and renew the man. Grace opens the heart, and converts it into good ground, where the seed can remain, and take root, and grow. The word is the same, but the hearing is twofold: if the Lord open the heart, so may the man be converted; but only when the man himself also willingly attends to the word, is conversion effected. Chrysostom: *τὸ μὲν οὖν ἀνοῖξαι τοῦ Θεοῦ, τὸ δὲ προσέχειν αὐτῆς ὥστε καὶ θεῖον καὶ ἀνθρώπινον ἦν.*

3. Baptism occurs twice in this chapter, and both times a whole

family is baptized: Lydia and her household, ver. 15; and the jailor and his household, ver. 33. For the first time, since Luke records the missionary acts of Paul, does he mention the baptism of the converted; and it is of significance, that in both instances in our chapter, all belonging to the parties concerned are baptized along with them. Both passages, vers. 15 and 33, have been quoted in favour of infant baptism, as an apostolic custom, on the supposition that the family certainly numbered little children: as Bengel asks, *Quis credat, in tot familiis nullum fuisse infantem?* But certainly this cannot be so surely maintained, as that an argument can be founded on it. The chief importance of the transaction does not rest on this, whether there were children in the family, and how young they may have been; but on the indisputable fact, that, in both instances, the whole house, all belonging to the families, were baptized along with the head of the house. There is contained in this the idea of a Christian family—of a Christian household. Personal decision is a great matter, but the isolation of individuals is not the truth. The unity of the family in Christ, the consecration of the household by grace, all belonging to one Lord, is here represented to us as something well-pleasing to God. And it is a remarkable fact, that this side of salvation in the apostolic history is first prominently brought before us on European ground.

4. On Macedonian-Hellenic ground, the apostle of the Redeemer comes into conflict with heathen nature. Soothsaying was much in vogue, after the period of the Peloponnesian war. There was a polytheistic foundation for it: the Pythian oracles stood in close connection with the worship of Apollo. But the relatively more pure culture, in course of time, degenerated into superstitious mantology; and calculating selfishness, together with base and crafty deceit, went alongside of superstition. All this—truly heathenish—was amalgamated in an unearthly manner in the incident with this soothsaying female slave. What caused the worst injuries to the apostle, were the injured interests. But we ought not therefore to regard the whole affair as purely an imposition; for in that view, the outcry of the female slave, "These men are the servants of the Most High God, who show to you the way of salvation," would be completely inexplicable. There must have been included in it a kind of clairvoyance. And in this the apostle recognises a demoniacal power,

and expels the spirit by a powerful command in the name of Jesus. Bengel remarks, *Erat Spiritus non e pessimis—sed tamen expelli dignus.* A toleration of such expressions, or rather an association with such spirits, would only have resulted in the dishonour of the Gospel—in the injury of the exclusive grace and truth of God in Christ.

5. But the expulsion of the spirit, in the power of Christ, brought upon the apostle a political accusation. In Jerusalem, the ostensible ground of persecution against the apostles (chap. iv. 2, 7, v. 28) and against Stephen (chap. vi. 11–14) was always religious. They were accused of encroachments on the hierarchical priesthood, of blasphemies against God and Moses, against the temple and the law. In Philippi, the persecution takes a political colour: Paul and Silas are accused as disturbers, because they ostensibly propagated customs contrary to the Roman polity. Here, for the first time, a persecution, originating not only on heathen ground (this was also the case in Antioch of Pisidia, in Iconium, and in Lystra), but, in fact, from purely heathen motives. And here the Roman authorities, in consequence of the injured avarice of individuals, and of the blind excited passions of the multitude, permitted themselves rashly to follow proceedings undeniably unjust—a prelude to all those bloody persecutions which the Roman imperial government, in the course of two centuries, inflicted on the Christians (Baumgarten, vol. ii. pp. 122–124, English translation). Moreover, the passion of Christ itself is the essential emblem of all the persecutions which have befallen His Church; in particular, inasmuch as He Himself was placed both before Jewish and Gentile tribunals, and was condemned by the Jewish hierarchy for irreligion, and by the Roman governor for political offences. These are at first separated in His disciples, so that first hierarchical-religious, and afterwards political accusations are brought against them.

6. "To conquer by yielding" is here also the motto. In deep distress, with their feet in the stocks, with their backs all bleeding, among common criminals, these two imprisoned witnesses of Jesus, in the middle of the night, pray to God, so joyfully and cheerfully that they sing praises with loud voices. Thus the spirit overcomes the flesh: thus faith and patience overcome the tribulation. The divine miracle, by which their bands were burst asunder and the prison-doors were thrown

open, is the answer to their prayers and praises. The prison is converted into a church and chapel for baptism—into a place of quiet and ministering care for the sick (ver. 33), and of joyful agapæ (ver. 34).

7. The question and the answer are both, so to speak, classical. Both strike directly the very point—that is, the centre of the heart and the centre of salvation. The question proceeds from the heart, and the answer goes to the heart. At Pentecost, those Israelites, who were pierced to the heart by the words of Peter, inquired, "Men and brethren, what shall we do?" Here, at Philippi, the jailor, agitated by the event and troubled in his conscience, asks, full of respect, "Sirs, what must I do to be saved?" Anguish of conscience, fear of divine punishment, the eager desire of salvation, constrained him to a question in which, along with a desire for practical instruction, there is also expressed the inward longing after the end (σωθῆναι). The latter is wanting in chap. ii. 37; but the Gentile, whose natural way was closed in the darkness of total absence and denial, is precisely by this negatively prepared to inquire and to seek from the depths of a heart, empty, yet thirsting after God and after the salvation in God. But he not only desires to receive and to take, he is also willing and resolved to do (ποιεῖν) what is requisite in order to reach the end. Thus in this soul the feeling of need, the desire of salvation, thirst for the truth, and willingness to do good, are combined. And where the heart is full, there the mouth speaks. This is the disposition of a soul truly awakened, near to the kingdom of God, happily apprehended by divine grace, inquiring and seeking.—The answer of the two servants of Christ is worthy of the question. To the inquiry after the means and the way, they answer shortly and well, pointing simply to the chief thing, "Believe on the Lord Jesus." They place the person of Christ, in whom alone is salvation, directly and without circumlocution, before the inquiring soul. They name and demand faith in His divine person: nothing more than faith, but also nothing less. *Fide sola* is the motto of the Apostle Paul, as it was the motto of the Reformers, after his example. They do not require from the jailor, who was ready and willing to do anything, various performances and works, but simply faith, *i.e.*, cordial acceptance and appropriation of the personal Saviour, along with absolute

confidence. But the faith, to which the jailor attained, also constrained him to all possible services and works of love and gratitude, so that he compassionately washes the stripes of Paul and Silas, and cheerfully strengthens them with food in their exhausted state.—The jailor had desired salvation. On this point also the messengers of Christ reply to him. They do not remain stationary in the way, but point him to the end. But as God does above all that we can ask or think, and as His grace is transcendently greater than the desires of men, so was it the case here. The jailor had thought only on himself (σωθῶ); the answer says, *σωθήσῃ σὺ καὶ ὁ οἶκός σου*. Not only to him, but likewise to his whole house, will salvation happen. God's love in Christ Jesus is great and large enough to bestow at once on many forgiveness, salvation, and peace, to receive the father along with his family into His grace. Accordingly, Paul and Silas speak the word of the Lord to him and to all that were in his house, and baptize him along with all his.

8. The alteration in the sentiments of the authorities, the deliverance, and the honourable and respectful bringing out of the prison, is a prophetic emblem of the victories and honourable termination, in which all the humiliations and persecutions of Christianity by the Roman empire will result. The glorious resurrection of Christ followed His passion and crucifixion. And the Church of Christ, which is under the sign of the cross, has, in her times of depression—which seem to lead to death and destruction—always to expect again an Easter morning and a glorious victory, if only she follows in His footsteps and does not deny Him.

HOMILETICAL HINTS.

And during the night a vision appeared to Paul (ver. 9). The faithful servants of Jesus must walk day and night before God, and even in the hours of the night, whether they sleep or wake, inquire after the will of God (Apost. Past.).—*Come over and help us.* When a teacher vividly represents to himself the melancholy situation of unconverted sinners, or the eager desire of awakened souls, should not his heart be ready to break, and his bowels move him to hasten to the aid of such miserable persons? The Lord Jesus had compassion on the multitude, when He saw them as sheep without a shepherd (Apost. Past.).—*The great missionary call, Come over and help us.* 1. How it sounds from the heathen world to Christianity: (*a*) to display to us its wretchedness; (*b*) to stir up our helping love. 2. How it again sounds from Christianity upwards to heaven, calling upon the Lord for help: (*a*) that He might direct us in the right path (ver. 10); (*b*) that He might open the hearts of the heathen (ver. 14).—*Come over and help us.* 1. Once this call for help sounded from the heathen West to the Christian East. 2. Now it sounds from the East, sunk again into the old night, to western Christianity. 3. And the time may come when this cry of want will sound from our lands now blessed with Christianity, because the candlestick of the Gospel, on account of our ingratitude, may be removed out of its place; because God's word, as Luther calls it, "the passing rain," will have passed by. 4. Therefore, to-day, whilst ye hear His voice, harden not your hearts.

And immediately we endeavoured to go (ver. 10). So modestly, without any parade, and almost by stealth, does Luke introduce himself into the narrative. He steps entirely behind the great apostle, and all persons in his view step behind the Lord and His cause.—*Inferring that the Lord had called us.* Thus the Lord was already before them in Macedonia, and this vision represented to them His presence already preceding them (Bengel).—So soon as we are assured of the divine will, we are to think how we might put it in practice without delay (Quesnel).

We came with a straight course (ver. 11). When a man's ways are pleasing to the Lord, the wind and the weather also must be helpful to him (Starke).—The favourable voyage increased their confidence. All hail to you! said Europe (Bengel).

To Philippi, which is the first city (ver. 12). Great cities have also often great sins; but it is there that good may soonest be done (Starke).

And on the Sabbath-day we went out of the gate to the river (ver. 13). Paul and his companions were divinely called in an extraordinary manner to Macedonia, but we may see how artlessly and simply they commence their labours. They remain some days by themselves; then they go, as others, to the usual place of devotion, content themselves to speak there with some women; and, full of believing calmness, are ready to follow in all things the leadings of God. They force nothing; they do not betake themselves to great and special matters. May the Lord lead us also on such a middle path, between an extravagant natural zeal and an inactive negligence: He knows how to bestow the blessing at the proper time (Apost. Past.).—To true prayer all places are suitable: the field (Gen. xxiv. 63), the shore (Acts xxi. 5), the prison (Acts xvi. 25), the belly of a fish (Jonah ii. 2), the fiery furnace (the prayer of the three children), (Starke).

A woman, named Lydia, who feared God (ver. 14). The apostles did not gain over by their discourse whole crowds, but a single woman only. The kingdom of God commences like a grain of mustard-seed. From a converted Lydia, afterwards sprang that glorious Church of Philippi, to which the apostle wrote such an excellent epistle, and which he called his crown (Apost. Past.).—Lydia was in such a state of mind, as the man of Macedonia in the vision which was represented to Paul (Apost. Past.).—*A dealer in purple.* Thus a merchant in easy circumstances. We may fear the Lord and love His word in all stations, and thus in the station of a merchant; and therefore Paul did not advise her to give up her trade. But unbelief, avarice, and the care of the body, must not regulate the trade and the accounts; and the word of God must be dearer to us than all temporary gain (Bogatsky).—She learned from Paul to know the most precious purple, of which Gerherd sings, "When at length I shall enter into the joys of Thy kingdom, my purple shall be this blood, I will clothe myself therein."—*The Lord opened her heart.* Teachers strike the ears in vain, if the Lord does not open the heart (Starke).—God opens the heart, but man must permit it to be opened (Rev. iii. 20).—If the Gospel seizes on a heart, this does not prove that one is an excellent preacher, but it proves that the Lord Himself stands in person at the door, and has opened the internal ear (Gossner).

She exhorted us, saying, If ye have judged that I am a believer in the Lord (ver. 15). Pure marks of a genuine faith. 1. It is humble, submits itself to the judgment of advanced Christians: "If ye have judged me." 2. It is desirous of learning, longing after further progress. 3. It is grateful to God. 4. It works by love: all this is indicated in the words, "Come to my house and abide there." 5. It is fruitful by example: "She and all her house were baptized."—*And her house.* What would Lydia have said, if the preachers of the Lord Jesus had refused to baptize the little children of her house? She must have become doubtful of her own faith—the free gift of God (Besser).

On the section, vers. 9–15.—*The first planting of the divine word in our part of the world.* 1. How it took place (vers. 11–13). 2. How it prospered (vers. 14, 15), (Lisco).—*Blessed are they that hear the word of God and keep it.* 1. How ought we to hear it? *a.* Collectedly, away from the distractions of the world: Lydia went out of the city. *b.* With a heart consecrated by prayer: Lydia went to prayer. *c.* With an eager expectation of what the Lord will give: the Lord opened the heart of Lydia. 2. How ought we to keep it? *a.* Not resting satisfied with a mere temporary impression, but walking with the Lord in true fellowship of life: Lydia was baptized. *b.* Endeavouring to convey to others our newly acquired faith: with Lydia, her house is baptized. *c.* Labouring to pay our debt of gratitude to the Lord by self-sacrificing love to our neighbour: Lydia constrained her benefactors to come to her house (Lisco).—*The first Gospel sermon in our part of the world.* 1. Who sends the preacher? 2. Who is the preacher? 3. Who is the hearer? (Beck.)—*How, in the history of the propagation of the kingdom of God on earth, heavenly guidance and human circumspection must be united.* 1. God sends the vision to Paul, and opens the heart of Lydia. 2. Paul follows intelligently the guidance of the Lord, and chooses with circumspection the time and place for his first discourse at Philippi (Lisco).—*Lydia, the first Christian of Europe, a lively example how the Lord imparts to His word an open door.* 1. By sea and by land. Paul's passage to Europe: the necessity of the world calls him; the love of Christ constrains him; the hand of the Lord leads him. 2. In the ear and the heart. Paul's first sermon at Philippi: the Lord gives the opportunity to preach the Gospel, causes ears to hear it, ánd opens a heart to receive it. 3. In the house and the congregation. The fruits of Lydia's conversion: the Lord opens her mouth to public confession, her household to pious imitation, and her hand to the service of grateful love.—*The decisive victory at Philippi.* By the bloody battle of Philippi, a hundred years before, the foundation of the empire of Augustus was laid; by the bloodless victory of Paul, the foundation of the kingdom of Christ on earth is laid.—*The messengers of Christ in Lydia's house:* or the bird has found a house, and the swallow a nest, where she may bring forth her young, Ps. lxxxiv. 3. 1. The bold flight of the swallow across the sea. 2. The dear nest in the strange city. 3. The charming brood which there thrives. (Compare the Epistle to the Philippians.)

Had brought her masters much gain by soothsaying (ver. 16). It is a common practice of men, that they, liberal in curious matters, bestow not one mite on the true worship of God, and on useful institutions (Starke).

She cried and said, These men are the servants of the Most High God (ver. 17). When a wicked man pretends to be pious, he is most wicked.—The devil often preaches the article of faith concerning God, but he reserves to himself for what purpose he will employ it (Starke).—When the devil cannot entirely arrest the kingdom of God, he would fain, at least, make common cause with it, and thus introduce by this something of his stain. But this the Lord Jesus, with His servants, always carefully guards against. Luther, on his part, also experienced how one endeavours to ensnare us with fair promises (Rieger).—Three arts of the devil are involved in this. 1. He sought to excite the self-complacency of the apostles, and to weaken by worldly praise their zeal for Jesus. By this art, he has already made many honest teachers fall. 2. He sought to flatter them, that they might let him alone in the matter of the female slave, and not disturb his dishonest trade. 3. He thought to persuade the people that the apostles were his good friends, in order that thus the power of Christianity might be hindered (Apost. Past.).

But Paul was grieved (ver. 18). Christ does not require the devil's praise either for Himself or for His servants. The praise of the ungodly should be suspected by true Christians, indeed be hateful to them (Starke).—Thus that heathen philosopher, "What evil have I done, that every one praises me?"—*I command thee to come out of her.* The powers of falsehood, until now spread abroad, the miserable condition of the damsel who might yet be rescued, and also a reasonable fear lest Christianity should be taken for a magic art, working in the dark, thus stirred up Paul (Rieger).—Follow not, O Zion! follow not the world that seeks to make thee great; esteem not her wealth and gold;

occupy not the throne of the dragon. O Zion, though it promises thee much pleasure, follow not (Schmidt, in the hymn "Proceed").

On vers. 16–18.—*The servants of the Most High God teach the way of salvation:* a true testimony, though proceeding from a lying mouth. 1. Who are the servants of God? Those who serve not the false spirit of the world—not selfishness and proud nature, but only God and His word, vers. 16, 18. 2. What way of salvation do they teach? Answer contained in ver. 31 (Lisco).—*What ought to be the Christian's conduct in reference to the miraculous, which does not proceed from the power of faith, and is not connected with it?* 1. The apostle's mode of acting. 2. The rule derived from that for us (Schleiermacher).—*No fellowship between the kingdom of truth and falsehood.* 1. The kingdom of truth does not require it. 2. It has never profited by it.—*Mistrust, O Christian, the praise of the world.* 1. It will stir up thy vanity concerning what is not thy merit, but the work of grace. 2. It will cripple thy zeal against ungodliness. 3. It will allure thee from the service of God to the servitude of man.

But when her masters saw that the hope of their gain was gone (ver. 19). The Gospel certainly prevents much gain, because it forbids and condemns many arts and trades, and because it brings along with it trials and hardships.

These men create disturbance in our city (ver. 20). In general, they who disturb the false peace of sinners are cried out against as disturbers of the common peace, 1 Kings xviii. 17; Amos vii. 10 (Starke).—*Lupus in fabula!* The sheep troubled the water to the wolf, and yet the wolf drank higher up in the brook.

They are Jews, and teach customs which it is not lawful for us to receive, neither to observe, being Romans (ver. 21). Very craftily was this accusation framed against the disciples of Christ: they appeal, on the one hand, to the Roman name, the highest recommendation which there was; and, on the other hand, they stir up hatred against the apostles by calling them Jews, which name was at that time ignominious (Calvin).—The devil at first bore witness that they announced the way of salvation; but now he calls their doctrine a custom which it is not lawful to observe. The perverse world (Apost. Past.).—Two well-founded complaints, before the court of the world, against the ambassadors of Christ. 1. They create disturbance in the city: they frighten sinners out of their false peace. 2. They are Jews, and announce what was not the custom of the Romans: they humble the pride of the natural man.

Commanded to rend off their clothes, and to beat them with rods (ver. 22). Better to suffer for the sake of Jesus than to be praised by the devil (Apost. Past.).

They cast them into prison (ver. 23). After Christ Himself was numbered among transgressors, it has been an honour to His servants to be punished with imprisonment for His sake (Starke).—The writings of the apostle are to us so much the more precious, on account of the *honorarium* which he received (Besser).

And he, having received such a charge, put their feet in the stocks (ver. 24). To be faithful in office, though with want of understanding, is no hindrance, but is often an occasion, to conversion (Starke).—The limbs feel nothing in the stocks, when the heart is in heaven (Tertullian).—The feet of those who publish peace are never more beautiful than when bound in fetters and iron (Gossner).

But at midnight, Paul and Silas prayed and praised God (ver. 25). True Christians may convert even a porch of death and a gate of hell, by prayer and praise, into a sanctuary and a gate of heaven (Starke).—Places do not sanctify persons, but persons sanctify places (Quenstädt).—It is certainly no difficult matter, in the external, tolerated, and protected church, to sing praises, when one is paid for it; but to sing praises in prison and in bonds, after being scourged, this can only a true disciple of Jesus, who has grace, do (Gossner).—*The wonderful nocturnal service in the prison at Philippi.* 1. The unusual hour of prayer: midnight. 2. The singular temple: a prison. 3. The remarkable conductors of the service: Paul and Silas in the stocks. 4. The strange congregation: the prisoners in their cells.—The nocturnal hymn of praise of Paul and Silas; or, our faith is the victory which has overcome the world.—The nocturnal prayer in prison, and the Amen from heaven added to it (the earthquake).

And suddenly there was a great earthquake (ver. 26). This was the answer to their song of praise (Gossner).—The prayer of the saints moves heaven and earth (Starke).—A great miracle, that, by the earthquake, all doors were opened and all bands loosed; but a greater miracle still, that the hearts of the jailor and of his household were opened (Starke).—Every preliminary deliverance of God's servants bears a resemblance to their final deliverance, when, at the hour of the last trumpet, the prisons of the grave will be opened, and the bands of corruption will be loosened, and yet men's souls, as if rooted to the spot, will remain in eager expectation of the things which shall then occur (Williger).—*The earthquake at Philippi, a miraculous act of the breaker of all bonds.* 1. He breaks the bonds of tribulation, when His elect call to Him day and night (Paul and Silas). 2. He tears asunder the fetters of sin, when bound souls sigh after Him (the jailor). 3. He makes a path for His word and kingdom, even when the world puts fetters on it (God's word is not bound). 4. He bursts open the prison of the grave, when the hour of eternal redemption strikes (that hour is said to be midnight).—*The midnight hour in the prison of Philippi, an image of the great hour of the Lord.* 1. The world sleeps, but believers wait for it with watchfulness and prayer. 2. The earth quakes, but the Lord is near. 3. The servants of sin tremble before the judgment, but the children of the kingdom lift up their heads with joy, because their redemption draweth nigh.

But the jailor, when he saw the doors open, drew a sword, and would have killed himself (ver. 27). God permitted it to take place that the jailor, who was to be converted at that hour, should be cast into extreme fury and desperation, as a true brand plucked out of the burning, in order to commend the power of the Gospel, which is able to remove sinners from the brink of hell into heavenly life. Such examples encourage us not to spare the Gospel to the wildest and most barbarously disposed men, and in the most desperate circumstances. Even a self-murderer, who has already the sword at his breast, may yet be saved (Apost. Past.).

But Paul cried with a loud voice (ver. 28). The jailor, in his fright and in the darkness of the night, cannot see Paul; but Paul saw him, and rescued him from his danger. When a sinner is imprisoned in the deepest night of sin and fear, then the gracious eyes of Jesus look compassionately upon him.—*Do thyself no harm, for we are all here.* God's command and will bind His own more firmly than iron shackles and the stocks.—*We are all here*, a comforting word of the messengers of the Gospel to despairing men. Not only Paul and Silas call this, but Peter and John, and all the apostles and prophets unite with them. We are all here with the testimony of our word, with the example of our conduct, and with the intercession of our love.

And came trembling (ver. 29). This was no longer trembling for office and honour, for the body and life, because the danger was over, the prisoners were all there; but the anguish of an awakened sinner, the trembling before the unknown yet ever near God.—*And fell down before Paul and Silas.* The jailor on his knees before his prisoners: what a wonderful change! A powerful attestation of the majesty of God's genuine servants, and of the nothingness of worldly powers.

And said, Sirs, what must I do to be saved? (ver. 30.) Before, it is said that he called for a light, in order to see after his prisoners in the prison. Now he calls for the true light, in order to come out of his own prison.—Now the call, "Come over and help us," bursts forth from the heart of the jailor, to his great advantage. When we have to do with such awakened consciences, then we may come far in a short time, and with few words; but how difficult it often is, and how long does it take, until the question is asked in earnest, What must I do to be saved? (Rieger.)

And they said, Believe on the Lord Jesus Christ, and thou and thy house shall be saved (ver. 31). Here many might think: This is short and quick work; thus would I also like that all might be settled with a few words. But these few words contain many thousand words. We willingly allow this to all poor sinners, but rough men must not abuse it. A single little word of the Lord Jesus may certainly help us. Nevertheless much would afterwards take place in the soul of this jailor (Starke).—The apostate Julian cast it as a reproach on Christians, "Faith is all your wisdom." Let us continue stedfast in this single wisdom (Besser).—The most important question, and the most correct answer (Lisco).—*Believe on the Lord Jesus Christ, and thou and thy house shall be saved* (a wedding sermon). For, with this faith, thou obtainest a divine family friend, a holy family rule, a delightful family peace, a secure family condition, an infallible family remedy, and a heavenly family portion.

And they spake the word of the Lord to him, and to all who were in his house (ver. 32). The apostles not only promised salvation to him and to his house, but they also brought it to them by the preaching of the Gospel (Williger).

And he took them and washed their stripes (ver. 33). Where faith comes into the heart, it makes entirely other men: of a stern jailor, a tender physician and host (Starke).—*And he was baptized, he and all his.* First, he purified them from bodily defilement—from the blood of their wounds, for it was impossible for him to see any longer the ill-treatment of God's servants; then he requested of them in baptism the purification of his own and of his household's spiritual defilement (Williger).—Now the jailor himself has become a prisoner of Jesus Christ: but these are blessed bonds.

And set food before them, and rejoiced, with all his house (ver. 34). Here now were certainly true festive days, when the whole house rejoiced (Bogatsky).—The circumstantial narration of all this is to make apparent to us the joyful, Martha-like service of the now believing jailor; which is then only in place when the Mary-like quietness has preceded, and it is right with the one thing needful (Williger).—In Philippi, first a shop and then a prison are converted into a missionary station. Two families become the hearth and the lodging of the Church: the Christian family in the Gentile world must be converted into the maternal nursery of the congregational life—every household a small congregation, and every congregation a large family (Besser).

On vers. 25–34.—The conversion of the Philippian jailor. 1. By what means it was prepared: externally, by the earthquake; internally, by the change of opposite feelings—despairing anguish and joyful calmness. 2. How it took place: by the question, inquiring after salvation; by the answer, proclaiming salvation. 3. What followed: active gratitude toward the apostles; abiding blessing for the jailor and his house (After Lisco).—*The miracle in the prison.* 1. The prayer, ver. 25. It is night. All are buried in slumber. A dark building; a lodging for the night, a prison. But light is in one of the prison-cells; internal light, the light of faith. Therefore prayer and praise. 2. The shock, vers. 26–28. The earthquake. Not only were the walls of the prison shaken, but also the heart of the jailor. Certainly, at first, a shock of anguish and despair.

But eternal love watches and prevails. The comforting word, We are all here. Hope returns; but he wishes to see his fortune and to grasp it with his hands, ver. 29. 3. The great question, vers. 30–32. It is not entirely unpremeditated. Already the praying apostles have caused the presentiment of something higher to rise up in him. Perhaps also earlier experiences in his dismal employment. The earthquake has ripened the slumbering seed. The apostles have not fled. How secure and happy must they be! What must I do, that I also may be the same? The great life-question finds also a great life-answer. There is only one answer: Without Christ, no one is saved; through Him, all may be saved: "Thou and thy house." 4. The first love, vers. 33, 34. What is it? The attempt to make a return for what has been received: to do good to Christ in His servants, in His brethren. The internal blessedness has not sufficient room in the heart. It is a fire kindled in the house, by which all the members are affected (After Lisco).—*How the Lord causes His gracious light to arise in the middle of the night.* 1. To His friends: Paul and Silas. 2. To His enemies: the jailor and his house.—*The gracious miracle of the Lord in the prison of Philippi.* 1. He frees those who are bound: internally free, in the interior of the prison—they pray and sing; externally free—their chains fall off, and the doors spring open. 2. He binds those who are free: terribly bound in anguish and fear—the fear and trembling of the jailor; blessedly bound in faith and love—the conversion and rejoicing of the jailor.—*What the Lord is able and desirous to make of a prison* (for a jail sermon). 1. A quiet chapel of prayer (ver. 25). 2. An alarming place of judgment (vers. 26–29). 3. A wholesome school of repentance and faith (vers. 30, 31). 4. A brotherly house of Christian love and compassion (vers. 32, 33). 5. A blessed birth-place of the new life (ver. 34).

And when it was day, the magistrates sent (ver. 35). The apostles had not vindicated themselves to the rulers; but the Lord had smitten their conscience. When His servants are silent and suffer, the Lord undertakes their cause (Apost. Past.).—*Let these men go* (release these men). Jesus acquired this order for His servants on the Mount of Olives, when He said to His enemies, "If therefore ye seek Me, let these go their way." By means of the power of Christ, must the world, and death, and the devil let the children and servants of Jesus go (Apost. Past.).—The unexpected command to release Paul was also a tender forbearance which God showed for the good of the jailor, as a beginner in the faith. It had been a hard trial for him, if he had been commanded to torment these servants of Jesus yet more. On the other hand, it was to him true joy to announce their innocence and deliverance. We must always deal somewhat gently and indulgently with beginners and young persons, until they become strong (Apost. Past.).

Now then depart in peace (ver. 36). The jailor considered it a wonder that the rulers of themselves should be induced to this. But they are to be still more deeply humbled. There are times coming for proud sinners, when they will one day be obliged to sue for pardon, not only from the Lord, but also from His servants; for the saints will be their judges, 1 Cor. vi. 2 (Williger).

But Paul said to them (ver. 37). It is prudence and love, at times to speak a little boldly to those who cannot otherwise be restrained from evil than by fear (Quesnel).—We must yield nothing to wickedness, yet not from revenge, but in order that its shame may be manifested to the glory of the name of Christ; otherwise it will always assert itself to be in the right, 1 Kings xviii. 18 (Starke).—The world would willingly enough bury and conceal all its perpetrated acts of unrighteousness, but we must not always suffer it to do so. The Holy Ghost teaches us that we are not to be submissive out of season; but each time so to conduct ourselves as it agrees with the leadings of God. It is necessary that, in the course of the Gospel, something of a superior power be always made known to those occupying worldly offices (Rieger).—*Who are Romans.* Our citizenship and our conversation are in heaven. By this the apostle knew himself better than by his Roman citizenship, Phil. iii. 8, 20 (Starke).

And they feared, when they heard that they were Romans (ver. 38). They feared, because they were Romans; but it did not startle them, that they had maltreated Christians. Thus God often attaches something to the pilgrim garb of His servants, which may not indeed convert others to sincere love, but yet may terrify them from further acts of violence (Rieger).

And besought them to leave the city (ver. 39). Unchristian rulers, when they see that the Gospel makes a noise, wish Christ and His word at India and Turkey, because they then hope for more peace in the usual state of things. Thus the Gergesenes, Matt. viii. 34 (Starke).

And when they had seen the brethren, they departed (ver. 40). An honourable departure of these faithful witnesses of Jesus. They had performed the purposes for which they had been sent: they had made and comforted brethren. Now they went their ways. May God grant that our course of life be so spent, that we at our end may take with us out of the world a like testimony from God (Apost. Past.).

Vers. 35–40.—*The unexpected upshot.* 1. The sudden deliverance. 2. The strong protest. 3. The honourable apology. 4. The peaceful departure (Lisco).—*The honourable retreat of the servants of God from Philippi.* 1. The power of the Lord is displayed. 2. The shame of His servants is wiped away. 3. Proud enemies are humbled. 4. True friends are gained.—*When and how a Christian may set a value on his honour, and stand to his rights?* 1. When his motive is not injured self-love, but the feeling of violated right and zeal for God's honour. 2. When his method of doing so is not rough self-help, but the way of law and of calm vindication. 3. When his object is not the overthrow of the injurer, but his conviction and improvement.—*Depart in peace* (ver. 36), *the most beautiful farewell for the servants of God.* 1. From friends, to whom they have brought salvation and peace (the jailor). 2. From enemies, who dare not touch God's anointed (the rulers). 3. From the Lord, who gives them this testimony: They have done what they could, Mark xiv. 6.

D.

Labours and Experiences in Thessalonica and Berea.

Chap. xvii. 1–15.

1 And they travelled through Amphipolis and Apollonia, and came to Thessalonica, where was a synagogue of the Jews. 2 And Paul, according to his custom, went in unto them, and discoursed with them for three Sabbaths out of the Scriptures, 3 Opening and showing that the Messiah must suffer, and rise from the dead; and that this is the Messiah, even

Jesus whom I preach to you. 4 And some of them were convinced, and
were added to Paul and Silas, and a great number of devout Greeks, and
not a few of the chief women. 5 But the Jews associated with themselves
certain wicked men from the market rabble, and collected them together,
and made an uproar in the city; and they beset the house of Jason, and
sought to bring them out to the people. 6 But when they did not find
them, they drew out Jason and certain brethren before the rulers of the city,
crying, These who have disturbed the world are come here also; 7 Whom
Jason has received as guests; and these all do contrary to the commands of
Cæsar, maintaining that there is another king, namely, Jesus. 8 And they
troubled the people and the authorities of the city who heard these things.
9 And they took security of Jason, and of the rest, and let them go.

10 But the brethren immediately sent away Paul and Silas by night to
Berea. And when they had arrived there, they went into the synagogue of
the Jews. 11 These were of a better sort than those of Thessalonica; and
received the word with all readiness, searching the Scriptures daily to see
whether these things were so. 12 Therefore many of them believed, and of
honourable Greek women and men not a few. 13 But when the Jews of
Thessalonica learned that the word of God was also preached of Paul at
Berea, they came and sought to stir up the people there also. 14 Then im-
mediately the brethren sent forth Paul, that he should journey by sea; but
Silas and Timotheus remained there. 15 And they who conducted Paul
brought him as far as Athens, and received a commandment to Silas and
Timotheus, that they should come to him as quickly as possible, and they
departed.

Ver. 2. Διελέγετο is to be preferred to the other readings, διελέξατο and διελέχθη, because the aorist might easily have been inserted instead of the imperfect, as the other verbs in the narrative are in the aorist.

Ver. 5. Προσλαβόμενοι δὲ οἱ Ἰουδ. τ. ἀγ. This is the shortest, and probably the original reading, with the omission of ζηλώσαντες δὲ οἱ ἀπειθοῦντες, which was placed before Ἰουδαῖοι προσλαβ. for the sake of limiting the opposition and describing it. There are a great variety of readings of this passage.

EXEGETICAL EXPLANATIONS.

1. *And they travelled.*—Paul, with Silas and Timotheus, travelled from Philippi, without staying at Amphipolis (situated on the Strymon, and surrounded by it) or at Apollonia (about thirty miles farther south), to Thessalonica, where Paul halted, and remained about four weeks. This city was situated on the Thermaic Gulf, and under the Romans grew to be a very populous and rich commercial town. It was also the capital of the second district of the province of Macedonia, and the residence of a Roman prætor. Numerous Jews also must have settled here: their synagogue appears to have been the only one in

northern Macedonia. The definite article attached to *συναγωγὴ τῶν Ἰουδαίων*, which, not being understood, some MSS. have omitted, indicates that there was no synagogue in Philippi, Amphipolis, or Apollonia; that the Jews who lived in these cities had only a place of prayer (*προσευχή*), and were, so to speak, attached to the synagogue in Thessalonica.

2. *According to his custom.*—Luke intentionally lays stress upon it, as if it had struck him for the first time (hence the unusual expression *κατὰ τὸ εἰωθὸς τῷ Παύλῳ εἰσῆλθε*), that Paul here also remained faithful to his custom of preaching the Gospel first in the synagogue, where there was one. He discoursed for three successive Sabbaths with the Jews. The word *διελέγετο* (imperfect, because it occurred frequently) signifies usually a dialogue, more seldom a self-contained discourse; *ἀπὸ τῶν γραφῶν*, proving from the Scriptures. His communication consisted in this, that he from the Old Testament "opened and showed" to his hearers (Bengel: *ut si quis nucleum fracto cortice, et recludat et exemtum ponat in medio*), first, that, according to the prophecies, the Messiah must suffer and rise again; and secondly, that this person, namely, Jesus, is the Messiah. The most natural connection is (Luther and Bengel), that *οὗτος* is the subject, and *Χριστός* the predicate; and that *Ἰησοῦς—ὑμῖν* is only a more exact explanation of *οὗτος*. It is forced to consider *οὗτος ὁ Χριστός* as a predicate (this Messiah, who, according to the Scriptures, must suffer and rise again: Meyer); and to consider *Χριστὸς Ἰησοῦς* combined as a predicate (this is the Christ Jesus whom I preach: De Wette, Baumgarten), recommends itself no better.

3. *And some of them were convinced.*—This reasoning had a partial success: some (a few, as it appears) of the Jews, but a great number of the Greek proselytes, who visited the synagogue, and not a few honourable women of Greek origin, who were also proselytes, were convinced by these proofs from the Old Testament of the Messianic dignity of Jesus, and were added to Paul and Silas. *Προσκληροῦν* is to add by lot, *sorte lectum adjungere*, usually to associate. It must here be taken in a passive sense, so that God is to be considered as the agent. See Dogmatical and Ethical Thoughts, No. 2. On the contrary, the majority of the Jews did not submit to the faith. The readings *ἀπειθήσαντες* and *ἀπειθοῦντες* have correctly represented their unbelief; whilst *οἱ Ἰου-*

δαῖοι, in contrast to τινες ἐξ αὐτῶν (ver. 4), makes us see that the believers formed an exception and a small minority. The undoubtedly spurious reading ζηλώσαντες expresses, according to the analogy of chap. viii. 45, ἐπλήσθησαν ζήλου, the passion which was the motive for their conduct. The unbelieving Jews excited a persecution against the messengers of the faith, whilst they first gained over the unprincipled and venal idlers and loungers about the market (ἀγοραῖος, a common word in the classics), and with their aid made an assault; in particular, the threatening crowd collected before the house of one Jason, with whom the missionaries dwelt. Jason is not otherwise known to us. That he was a resident in Thessalonica, had attached himself to the youthful Church, and lodged Paul and his two companions, is obvious from the narrative. Whether he was a Jew who had changed his Hebrew name Joshua or Jesus into the Greek form Jason (Ewald), or whether he was originally a Greek, cannot be determined. The design of this onset before the house of Jason was to seize the two strangers, and to bring them out to the people: ἀγαγεῖν εἰς τὸν δῆμον, *i.e.*, to expose them to the excited rabble.

4. *But when they did not find them.*—As the principal persons were perhaps warned in time, and had gone away from the house which was threatened, they seized, instead of them, the host himself and some Christians, and dragged them before the authorities of the city (it is remarkable that this otherwise rare word πολιτάρχης has been found by Böckh on a Greek inscription in Thessalonica), with passionate outcries against them, and a denunciation of them as political disturbers, who had already put the whole world into a ferment. The exaggeration which is contained in τὴν οἰκουμένην strikingly agrees with the passion which gave rise to the word. Οὗτοι πάντες is designed to stigmatize all the Christians, both their absent chiefs and their present followers, as alike answerable for the transgression of the positive decrees of Cæsar, which, by the acknowledgment of another king, namely, Jesus, they had committed. By δόγματα Καίσαρος we are to understand such decrees as interdicted high treason (Meyer). Βασιλεύς is the superior idea, including both the imperial majesty and the royal dignity of the Messiah.

5. *These, who have disturbed the world.*—This false representation was not without effect. Both the people and the autho-

rities were troubled. The authorities, therefore, took security of Jason and of the other Christians before they liberated them. *Τὸ ἱκανόν*, as also *satisdatio, satis accipere*, in Latin, is the proper technical expression for surety, whether it be a money pledge or personal bail. Undoubtedly the first is here meant. Chrysostom supposes that Jason himself became surety in person; but this is contradicted by *ἀπέλυσαν αὐτούς*. But for what must Jason and the others give security? Without doubt for this, that they would not pursue any treasonable plans; but hardly for this, that they would no longer harbour Paul and his companions. The sending away of Paul and Silas immediately, ver. 10 (whilst Timotheus, not named in ver. 10, probably remained behind for the present in Thessalonica, in order some time later to repair to Berea), appears to have been only because they did not trust their opponents, and feared that they might indulge in further designs against the missionaries.

6. *Berea* was situated in the third district of Macedonia, the capital of which was Pella, to the south-west of Thessalonica, at the south corner of the whole provice of Macedonia. Here the preachers of the Gospel found a reception from the numerous Jews, entirely different from their reception at Thessalonica. The resident Jews here were *εὐγενέστεροι* than those of Thessalonica, *i.e.*, of a nobler disposition, not according to descent, *generosiores*, but *magis ingenui*. This they proved both by their complete willingness (*πᾶσα προθυμία*) to receive the Gospel, and by the earnest and persevering zeal with which they daily (*τὸ καθ' ἡμέραν*, compare Luke xix. 47) searched the Scriptures, in order to prove for themselves whether these things were so (*οὕτως*, as it was represented to them). In consequence of this (*οὖν*), many of the Jews believed (*πολλοὶ ἐξ αὐτῶν*, not only *τινες ἐξ αὐτῶν* as in Thessalonica); besides numerous proselytes, men and women of station (*εὐσχήμων*, as in chap. xiii. 50, not in a moral sense, as the word is usually employed in classical language, but in a social sense, exactly as the English word "respectable") were converted.

7. *But when the Jews.*—The Jews of Thessalonica sought to disturb the work at Berea also. *Κἀκεῖ σαλεύοντες*, stirring up the multitude here also, as before in Thessalonica; *τοὺς ὄχλους*, the rabble, designedly, not *τὸν δῆμον*. In order to anticipate the outbreak, the Christians of Berea immediately sent

away Paul, whilst Silas and Timotheus (who had in the interval joined them) remained for the present at Berea. Ὡς ἐπὶ τὴν θάλασσαν: ὡς is not to be understood as an appearance on purpose to deceive, "as if he would go by sea" (Bengel, Neander), for Paul actually did make the journey by sea, otherwise something would be mentioned of the way which he took, and of the cities which he visited; but ὡς expresses only the definite purpose to take the direction to the sea. *Καθιστάνειν*, to bring one thither; *ἐξήεσαν*, to depart away from Athens.

DOGMATICAL AND ETHICAL THOUGHTS.

1. The representation of the truth, which Paul made to the Israelites, always took the holy Scriptures as the starting point. "Thus it is written" is the principle of the apostle, as well as of the Redeemer Himself. The method which he took is nowhere so distinctly marked as here. He proceeds from the Messiah of the old covenant, from the prophecies and types, and proves that the Messiah is essentially a suffering Messiah, but also that He must rise again. So far only the understanding of the prophetic word—only the Christology of the old covenant—is the point in question. This part was eminently a *διανοίγειν*. But, secondly, Paul shows that "Jesus of Nazareth whom I announce is the Messiah:" He is indeed crucified and risen again: the essential idea of the Anointed of God and the facts of His appearance are fulfilled in Jesus, and in Him only. This is *παρατίθεσθαι*.

2. The conviction to which many were led, and their entrance into intimate fellowship of faith and life with Paul and Silas, is not a human work by them, but the work of God. The passive *προσεκληρώθησαν* undeniably points to God as the essential agent. Moreover, a leading idea is contained therein, that of *κλῆρος*. "Added by the lot to Paul and Silas," cannot be its meaning. "They were added to them as a lot, as a portion, possession, and gain," is a representation which is elsewhere favoured by nothing. On the other hand, the idea may consist in this, that to them, the newly converted, the lot has fallen pleasantly, that whilst they were associated with Paul and Silas, God Himself was to them their portion and His grace their lot. (See Ps. xvi. 5.)

3. As in Philippi, so also in Thessalonica, the messengers of Jesus Christ were suspected as political disturbers, and accused

of treason. On both occasions, we perceive the influence of the Roman empire, as a barrier to the conquest of the world by Christianity. The distinction between them is, first, that in Philippi, only the public customs and the life of a Roman colony and of Roman citizens stand ostensibly in the way of the introduction of new customs; in Thessalonica, on the other hand, the majesty of Cæsar and the imperial legislature are urged against Christianity. Secondly, in Thessalonica, the person of Jesus was opposed to that of Cæsar, the kingdom of Jesus as the Messiah was represented as an outrage and as treason against the emperor, which was not the case in Philippi. It is possible that the explanation of Paul (ver. 3), which brought prominently forward the idea of the Messiah, the kingdom of Jesus, afforded a handle to this suspicious view. Thirdly, there is also this difference, that in Philippi the political accusation was purely of heathen origin; whereas in Thessalonica it was caused by the Jews, who used the Roman imperial interests only as a means and a pretext in order to oppose the Gospel. In doing so they denied the Messianic hope of Israel, and said of Him who is yet our and their King, "We will not have this man to reign over us." This conduct is typical of all the hostile and political aspersions raised to the disadvantage of the Gospel and of living Christianity, by which Christianity is represented as a kingdom of this world, and the political and religious are confounded together,—an old stratagem of the enemy of Christ.

4. Christian nobility of soul (*εὐγενέστεροι*) consists in genuine willingness of mind to receive the word of God, and in sincere and earnest love of the truth. Both are here united: receptivity and spontaneity (*ἐδέξαντο—ἀνακρίνοντες*), humble devotedness and independent searching and testing. Faith is not implicit belief, blind credulity, the renunciation of the understanding, of proof, and of conviction. On the contrary, it is a Christian virtue, honestly and earnestly to prove, to search, and to go to the bottom. The authority of a teacher and pastor must not be urged in such a manner, that the renunciation of self-examination and personal conviction is demanded as soon as the teacher has spoken. Here even an apostle has taught; nevertheless those in Berea did not blindly believe on his word, but first searched whether he was in the right and taught the truth. And this was not reckoned to them as a fault; on the contrary,

it is praised as a noble virtue. This is liberty of conscience, evangelical searching of the Scriptures, the exercise of the universal priesthood.

HOMILETICAL HINTS.

They came to Thessalonica (ver. 1). Paul has himself informed us with what courage he came to Thessalonica (1 Thess. ii. 2). Although he had been shamefully entreated at Philippi, yet he had come to Thessalonica, "bold in his God." This is the true composure of mind, with which a servant of God is to proceed from one work to another, from one suffering to another, and from one victory to another (Apost. Past.).

Discoursing with them for three Sabbaths out of the Scriptures (ver. 2). Paul always commenced the preaching of the Gospel from the Scriptures. His apostolic character did not free him from the bonds of the Scripture. He had already often borne witness with miracles and powers; nevertheless he continued with the Scriptures, and drew his testimony of Jesus from the prophets. The Lord still in our days binds the heart and mouth of all witnesses very closely to the Scriptures. All deviation from them brings irreparable damage in doctrine or in conduct (Apost. Past.).—For three whole Sabbaths, he discoursed with them, unwearied by their contradictions. What Luke has here related reads as a light matter; but it cost Paul more grief than the scourging at Philippi. The Jewish schools were schools of patience (Besser).

That the Messiah must suffer and rise again (ver. 3). Paul had no other theme than that of the cross and of the resurrection of Jesus. To us, after several thousand years, there must appear no matter more important and more effectual than this preaching on the sufferings and resurrection of Jesus. However, in this comprehensive matter, wisdom must direct us to urge the points which are the most important for our hearers. With the Jews, this was the necessity of the personal sufferings of the Messiah (Apost. Past.).

And some of them were convinced (ver. 4). The best teachers succeed gradually. First one, then some, and then a great multitude. But nothing must be forced (Apost. Past.).—*And of the chief women not a few.* Grace gives no preference to persons in high station, but yet it does not thrust them away, 1 Cor. i. 26–28 (Starke).

Associated with themselves from the market rabble certain wicked men (ver. 5). The world uses the rabble, as it suits its views. If the rabble side with the Gospel, it is despised: thus it is said, Only the ignorant multitude are drawn after Him (John vii. 47–49). But if the world succeeds in exciting the rabble against the Gospel, then the rabble is to it very respectable (Rieger).

These, who have disturbed the world (ver. 6). How afraid the world still is of the kingdom of God! How, with its clay-like nature, it always dreads its own overthrow! It has thousands ready to stand up for its protection; but if ten Christians will keep together, it fears from them injury and disturbance (Rieger).—The apostles have, in truth, disturbed the whole world, not to tumult but to conversion, not to destruction but to salvation (Starke).—When the Gospel makes a noise, as water in lime, and the flesh can and will not endure it, it must be a perversion and disturbance of the state! (Starke.)—Although these raging enemies sought to blacken the apostles with pure calumnies, yet in the midst of their rage they are obliged to bear an honourable testimony to the extension and power of the Gospel. It is a blessed testimony to the witnesses of Jesus, when their preaching creates a powerful awakening and a wholesome disturbance (Apost. Past.).—*Christ came not to send peaçe, but a sword.* 1. The Gospel certainly brings discord; internal, in the heart (Rom. vii.); external, in the social relations (Matt. x. 34). 2. But from this discord, true peace proceeds: peace of heart; peace of the world.—"*These are they who disturb the world," the best founded complaint against the apostles, and yet the most honourable testimony in their favour.* 1. The best founded complaint, for the whole internal and external world is transformed by the Gospel: heart and conduct, family and state, arts and sciences. 2. The most honourable testimony, for not subversion and destruction, but regeneration and transfiguration are the objects aimed at in all those fields. —*The appearance of Christianity the greatest, but also the most lawful, revolution in the world's history.* 1. The greatest: by its breadth, it aims at the whole world; by its depth, on the territory of the spirit is its proper soil. 2. The most legitimate: by its aim, the salvation of the world; by the means employed, the weapons of the Spirit.—*It is yet a little while, and I will shake the heavens and the earth, the sea and the dry land.* This ancient prophecy of the great shaking of the world (Hag. ii. 6, Heb. xii. 26; compare the "Götterdämmerung" in the northern mythology) finds its reality in Christianity. 1. In the internal commotions of the heart. 2. In the historical transformation of the world. 3. In the eschatological renewal of heaven and earth.

Maintaining that there is another king, namely, Jesus (ver. 7). To mix the *statum politicum* with the cause of Christ, and by the jealousy of the authorities of the world to hinder the kingdom of Christ, is an old stratagem of the enemy of Christ (Apost. Past.).—It is true that faithful teachers preach another King, but one who rules by humility and the cross. By Him the kings of the earth reign, and He makes kings of all His true servants, but in heaven, Rev. i. 5, 6 (Quesnel).

And they took security of Jason (ver. 9). What a friend to Paul had the Gospel in a few days made Jason! (Williger.)—It will import much to be surety for the persecuted Christians, for the whole world was ashamed of them (Gossner).

On vers. 1–9.—*Paul in Thessalonica.* His labours, vers. 1–4. Their termination, vers. 5–9 (Lisco).—*On evangelical preaching.* 1. Its nature is the same for all ages: founded on Scripture, culminating in the person of Jesus. 2. And also its issue: favourable to some, unfavourable to most (Lisco).—*How the enemies of the Gospel conform themselves to circumstances.* 1. They pervert the truth, in order to be able to accuse the disciples; they convert Christ and His apostles into disturbers of the peace. 2. They themselves commit the very sin of which they accuse the disciples: they create disturbances (Lisco).—*Paul and Jason, a model of a noble guest-friendship.* 1. The dangerous, and yet beloved guest. 2. The threatened, and yet blessed host, Heb. xiii. 2.

And when they arrived, they went into the synagogue (ver. 10). The flight of a servant of God is only a change of place, not of work, of mind, of zeal, of love for the cross (Apost. Past.).

Searching the Scriptures daily, to see whether these things were so (ver. 11). The holy Scripture is the true touchstone, according to which we are to try our faith; and the true rule, according to which we are to regulate our lives (Starke).—In the sea of the holy Scriptures there are not wanting pearls.

May God always give more divers who will search for them (Starke).—O man, thou takest not a ducat untested! wherefore then a belief, the injury arising from which, when found false, is irreparable in time?—This is a truly noble disposition, which does not build its faith on man, but on the word of God (Starke).—The apostles have thus sought no blind conversions, and demanded no implicit faith: they restrained no man, but sought to lead souls to examine their doctrine and compare it with Scripture (Apost. Past.).—The genuine spirit of an inquirer is always in keeping with the Gospel. Earnest inquirers will not at once rashly condemn the word of God. With true inquirers, those objections at least cease which the superficial understanding has always at hand against the Gospel (Williger).

Women and men (ver. 12). That the women here precede the men may have its ground in this, that they, as it often happens, first come to the faith, and draw the men after them. The kingdom of God increases outwardly from houses and families, where, at all events, the woman has her sphere (Rieger, Starke, Williger).

The Jews of Thessalonica came, and stirred up the people there also (ver. 13). Believers seldom do as much for the truth, as the ungodly do against it. For the former effort is up-hill, the latter down-hill (Quesnel).

And received a commandment to Silas and Timotheus, that they should come to him as quickly as possible (ver. 15). Paul did not wish to be alone: he did not consider himself sufficient alone. He desired fellow-workers to pray, to witness, to strive, and to suffer with him (Gossner).

On vers. 10–15.—*On Christian nobleness of soul* (*εὐγενέστεροι*, ver. 11). It shows itself in willing and candid reception, and in free and independent digestion of the divine word and the divine salvation.—Searching the Scriptures, the blessed right, the holy duty, and the rare art of the evangelical Christian.—True belief of the Scriptures and genuine searching of the Scriptures go hand in hand. 1. Faith, which condemns searching, is blind. 2. Searching, which despises faith, is useless.—*The stages of a true use of the Scriptures.* 1. Willing reception, as opposed to frivolous contempt, ver. 11. 2. Diligent searching, as opposed to blind imitation, ver. 11. 3. Living faith, as opposed to dead knowledge, ver. 12.—*How the Gospel and how fanaticism stir up the people.* 1. Here it avails to build (vers. 3, 4); there to pull down (ver. 13). 2. Here noble spirits are stirred up (ver. 11); there the rabble (ver. 5). 3. Here one fights with the sword of the Spirit (ver. 11); there with the weapons of the flesh (ver. 6).

E.

Paul at Athens; his Observations and Discourses there; and, lastly, his Missionary Address on Mars-hill, and the effect of it.

CHAP. XVII. 16–34.

16 But while Paul waited for them at Athens, his spirit was roused
within him, when he saw the city full of idols. 17 Therefore he spoke in
the synagogue to the Jews and proselytes, and in the market-place daily to
those who happened to be present. 18 But some of the Epicurean and
Stoic philosophers encountered him. And some said, What will this babbler
say? But others, He appears to be an announcer of strange divinities; be-
cause he preached to them the Gospel of Jesus, and the resurrection. 19 And
they took him, and led him to the Areopagus, and said, Can we know what
is this new doctrine which thou speakest? 20 For thou bringest certain
strange things to our ears. We would gladly know what these things may
be. 21 For all the Athenians and the strangers in the city were disposed
for nothing else than to tell or to hear something new.
22 Then Paul stood in the midst of the Areopagus, and said, Ye men of
Athens, I perceive that ye are on all points very God-fearing. 23 For as I
went through the city, and observed your sacred things, I found an altar
which had the inscription, "To an unknown God." What therefore ye
without knowing it worship, that announce I to you. 24 God, who made
the world, and all things therein, as he is Lord of heaven and earth, dwelleth
not in temples made with hands; 25 Neither is He ministered to by human
hands, as if He needed anything, whilst He Himself gives to all life, and
breath, and all things; 26 And has made that of one blood every nation
of men should dwell on the whole face of the earth, having fixed their deter-
mined times, and the boundaries of their habitations; 27 To seek God, if
perhaps they might feel after Him and find Him, although He is not far off
from any one of us: 28 For in Him we live, and move, and are; as also
some of your poets have said, "For we are also His offspring." 29 Because
then we are the offspring of God, we ought not to think that the Godhead
is like to gold, or silver, or stone, to an image of art and device of a man.
30 And the times of ignorance God has overlooked: and now He commands
all men everywhere to change their disposition; 31 Because He has ap-
pointed a day, in which He will judge the world in righteousness by a man
whom He has ordained, having offered faith to all men, in that He raised
Him from the dead.

32 But when they heard of the resurrection of the dead, some mocked; but others said, We will hear thee another time concerning this. 33 So Paul departed from the midst of them. 34 But some men joined themselves to him, and believed; among whom was Dionysius the Areopagite, and a woman named Damaris, and others with them.

Ver. 23. Ὃ—τοῦτο is the original reading—A. (first hand) B.D.; whilst the reading ὃν—τοῦτον is a correction to suit what follows.

Ver. 25. Ἀνθρωπίνων is more strongly attested than ἀνθρώπων.

Ver. 26. Προστεταγμένους is decidedly attested, whilst προτεταγμένους has only the uncial MS. D. (first hand) for it.

Ver. 27. Τὸν Θεόν is decidedly better attested than τὸν κύριον.

Ver. 31. Καθότι is, on the grounds of extrinsic evidence, to be preferred to διότι, which is more current.

EXEGETICAL EXPLANATIONS.

1. *But Paul.*—The first part of the second missionary journey of Paul referred to Asia Minor: the second and third parts referred to Europe; the second part embracing Macedonia—Philippi, Thessalonica and Berea; and now the third part commences, which referred to Greece proper, at that period called Achaia, limited, however, to the two capitals, Athens and Corinth. In Athens, Paul waited until Silas and Timotheus, whom he had called hither, joined him; and whereas Luke is here entirely silent as to this, and only in chap. xviii. 5 makes them rejoin Paul at Corinth, we must (according to 1 Thess. ii. 17–iii. 2) suppose that Timotheus soon came to him to Athens, but was again sent back with instructions to Thessalonica. Luke meanwhile was still in Philippi; and this circumstance the more easily explains why he passes over in silence the arrival of Timotheus at Athens.

2. *Παρωξύνετο τὸ πνεῦμα αὐτοῦ ἐν αὐτῷ*, his spirit was filled with indignation, morally stirred up; and this feeling (by means of the imperfect tense) is indicated not as a sudden and passing emotion, but as an abiding state of mind. The cause of this was, that looking for a long time, and attentively (*θεωρεῖν*, not merely *ἰδεῖν*), he found the city full of idols. ***Κατείδωλος***, otherwise unknown, but according to analogies properly formed, is not subjective *idolis dedita*, but objective *idolis abundans*. As, for example, *κατάδενδρος*, *κατάμπελος*, *arboribus plenus*, *vitibus abundans*. This characteristic, as one by which Athens was distinguished above all other Greek cities, is abundantly confirmed by Greek and Roman testimonies: as, for example, Xeno-

phon calls Athens, Ὅλη βωμός, ὅλη θῦμα θεοῖς καὶ ἀνάθημα; and Livy, xlv. 27, says, *Athenas—multa visenda habentes—simulacra Deorum hominumque omni genere et materiæ et artium insignia.*—In consequence of his indignation, and in order to oppose this idolatry, he engaged in conversation, both in the synagogue with the Jews and proselytes, and in the market-place with all who happened to be present; the object of his διαλέγεσθαι being religious truth. In the market-place, he could find a daily (κατὰ πᾶσαν ἡμέραν) opportunity. Nothing of this kind is said concerning the synagogue, as an opportunity would only occur on the Sabbath. Ἡ ἀγορά would seem to indicate that there was only one market-place. This has been long called in question; and it has been supposed that Paul discoursed in the so-called Eretrian-place. This last name, however, rests on a mistake; and, in general, the more recent topographers of Athens are convinced that there was never more than one market-place in Athens, and thus the correctness and fidelity of the narrative, even in a point so entirely insignificant (ἡ ἀγορά), is established.

3. Certainly such discourses were delivered in public places, whereby certain philosophers, partly Epicureans and partly Stoics, came in contact with Paul. Συμβάλλω signifies, chap. iv. 15, simply to discourse in friendly conference; it does not exactly imply a disputation. In consequence of such conversations, the Athenians were divided in their opinions. Some thought, disparagingly, that Paul was a hollow babbler (σπερμολόγος, originally a rook, then an inflated and empty babbler) who had nothing to say. The question τί ἂν θέλοι—λέγειν primarily signifies, We do not rightly know what he really means; but here it implies a disparaging judgment on the subject. Others were rendered at least inquisitive: "He seems to announce strange divinities" (ξένα δαιμόνια, as in the accusation against Socrates it was said καινὰ δαιμόνια εἰσάγει). Luke explains this notion from the fact, that Paul preached to them the Gospel of Jesus, and the resurrection. It is, however, improbable that the Athenians should have taken the ἀνάστασις for a goddess (Chrysostom, Baur, Baumgarten); it rather appears that Luke only named the resurrection along with the person of Jesus, because this subject appeared to the Greek philosophers most surprising and strange (ξένος).

4. In consequence of this latter opinion of Paul's discourse, and of the curiosity excited, the apostle was conducted (ἐπιλαβόμενοι αὐτοῦ, *leniter prehensum*, Grotius) to the Areopagus, that is, to Mars-hill, north of the western corner of the Acropolis, where the supreme court of the republic usually held its sittings. Not, however, as the Netherland divine Adami, Observatt., 1710, supposes, and as recently Baur and Zeller have maintained, that Paul was led before the Areopagus, as a court of justice, to vindicate himself, and that consequently his discourse was a legal defence. The entire connection of the passage disproves this opinion; particularly the polite question (ver. 19) and wish (ver. 20); the observation of the author, which points only to curiosity, and not to fanaticism and intolerance, as the motive to the whole affair (ver. 21); the entire tone of the discourse, which never takes up a defensive and apologetic position; and, lastly, the concluding scene, when Paul departs unmolested and without any trace of a judicial procedure.—The request for a speech (ver. 19) is, in particular, extremely polite—Attically courteous (δυνάμεθα γνῶναι); but also in some measure ironical, the questioners being convinced that they knew all things already, and all things better. Also in ξενίζοντα τινα (ver. 20), some strange things, there is a tinge of Greek pride toward the barbarians. As an explanation, Luke adds, that all the Athenians, strangers who resided there as well as natives, liked nothing better (εὐκαίρουν, *vacabant*, had always plenty of time for that) than to tell or to hear some new thing. Bengel strikingly explains the comparative καινότερον: *nova statim sordebant, noviora quærebantur.* They not only sought enjoyment in hearing something new, but also the honour and distinction of telling something new (λέγειν, ἀκούειν). The imperfect εὐκαίρουν describes the characteristic custom, as it was at the time when this occurrence happened, without affirming that it was still the case.

5. The apostle, so pointedly asked, even though not from the pure love of truth, and in an ironical tone, does not shrink from addressing the most refined audience in the Gentile world. He was called to bear the name of Jesus among the Gentiles. With the sure confidence of faith, he takes his position (σταθείς) in the middle of the plateau which the hillock, about 60 feet high, forms. He had before him the more lofty Acropolis, with its

famous works of art; beneath him the magnificent temple of Theseus; and around him a multitude of temples, altars, and statues of the gods.

6. With conciliating kindness and mildness, willingly recognising all that was good, he commences to bear his testimony to the Athenians, on the ground of his observations, that they were very God-fearing. Ὡς before δεισιδαιμονεστέρους imports, I recognise you as such, you appear as such. Δεισιδαίμων is certainly used by classical writers in a blameable sense,—superstitious: so the Vulgate, Erasmus, Luther, and others;—but it is *vox media*, and not unfrequently occurs in the sense of actual fear of God. And so it is here undoubtedly to be understood, although the word appears designedly chosen, in order mildly to indicate the idea of fear which prevailed in their religion and led to superstition. The comparative δεισιδαιμονεστέρους does not contain the additional idea of excess, but compares the Athenians with other Greeks; and in this there was no flattery, but a recognised fact among the ancients. Isocrates calls the Athenians τοὺς πρὸς τὰ τῶν θεῶν εὐσεβέστατα διακειμένους. Similar testimonies are given by Wetstein from Sophocles, Plato, Xenophon, and Josephus. Γάρ (ver. 23) gives us to understand that Paul's opinion (ver. 22) concerning the well-known fear of God of the Athenians was founded on the circumstance, that among many other sacred things (the afore-mentioned idols), he observed an altar dedicated to an unknown God. Σέβασμα is *res sacra*, or *quod religionis causa homines venerantur*, and may thus comprehend holy places, temples, groves, altars, images, etc.; ἀναθεωρῶ means to contemplate successively.

7. *An altar with an inscription, To an unknown God.*—It has been frequently supposed, even in Christian antiquity, that Paul here took the liberty of giving in the singular what there stood in the plural. Thus Jerome on Tit. i. 12: *Inscriptio autem aræ non ita erat, ut Paulus asseruit, "Ignoto Deo;" sed ita, "Diis Asiæ et Europæ et Africæ, Diis ignotis et peregrinis." Verum quia Paulus non pluribus Diis ignotis indigebat, sed uno tantum ignoto Deo, singulari verbo usus est.* Whilst this father of the Church here supposes a rhetorical liberty of the apostle, the change has most recently been laid to the account of the historian: the singular is unhistorical, but the plural ἀγνώστοις θεοῖς may possibly have been the inscription; so Baur and Paulus.

But wherefore? If the article stood before ἀγνώστῳ θεῷ, such an inscription in Athens cannot be thought of; but what is there impossible in the dedication, "To an unknown God"? Moreover Pausanias tells us that at Phaleros there were βωμοὶ θεῶν τῶν ὀνομαζομένων ἀγνώστων καὶ ἡρώων; and Philostratus, Vita Apollon. vi. 2, says, It is wiser to speak respectfully of all gods, especially at Athens οὗ καὶ ἀγνώστων θεῶν βωμοὶ ἵδρυνται. Both expressions may certainly be so understood, as if each of the altars in question was dedicated to unknown gods; however, it is at least equally possible, indeed according to the expressions more probable, that each altar of this kind was dedicated to an unknown god, and bore that inscription. And indeed there appears to have been at Athens, in different places, altars with that inscription. But how the origin and determination of such altars is to be explained, concerning which there is a variety of opinions, we may here omit, as all these opinions are mere suppositions.

8. Connected with these observations, and thereby applied to the conscience of the hearers as something not entirely strange, follows the theme of the discourse: "What therefore ye ignorantly worship, that declare I unto you." The neuter ὃ—τοῦτο designedly denotes the object of worship (εὐσεβεῖτε, *religiose colitis*) in an abstract indefiniteness, corresponding to ἀγνοοῦντες: the apostle gives the concrete, the personal, ὁ Θεὸς ὁ ποιήσας, etc., only in his positive announcement. The Athenians expected to hear something entirely strange (ver. 18, ξένων δαιμονίων καταγγελεύς; ver. 20, ξενίζοντά τινα εἰσφέρεις); but Paul builds upon this feeling, and proceeds from something expressed in the inscription on the altar in the sense, *ignotum, non tamen peregrinum, prædico vobis.*

9. In the first place, Paul announces the true God as the one, free, and absolute Creator and Lord of the world, raised above the need of a dwelling in temples, or of care by human hands, that is, by the priests. Θεραπεύειν is frequently used of the worship of the gods; also the expression προσδεῖσθαι, equivalent to τὸ ἔχειν μὲν μέρος, ἔτι δὲ δεῖσθαι πρὸς τὸ τέλειον (Ulpian), is appropriate. In sight of glorious temples adorned with all the wonders of art, of which the Athenians were so proud, the apostle announces, "God does not dwell in temples made with hands." In the midst of numerous idols he declares,

"God is not ministered unto by human hands." *Αὐτὸς διδούς*, confirming his remarks, or rather refuting the error; on the contrary, it is He Himself who gives to all life, and breath (*πνοιή*, as necessary for the continuance of life), and all things (*καὶ τὰ πάντα*, all that is necessary).

10. In the second place, in connection with these fundamental truths concerning God, Paul explains the true idea of man,—that the human race collectively is one, by means of the divinely appointed propagation from a term, one blood. *Αἷμα* is not only in the Scriptures used with reference to the idea of the connection of life and procreation with the blood, John i. 23, but also according to classical usage; even in Homer, Il. *Z* 211, Od. *Π* 300, and also in Sophocles, Euripides, and Aristotle, it is used of procreation and blood-relationship, and here consequently is so much the more suitably employed. As regards the construction of the sentence, *πᾶν ἔθνος* is not, as the object, dependent on *ἐποίησε*, but the entire sentence *πᾶν ἔθνος—κατοικεῖν* is governed by *ἐποίησε*: *instituit, ut ex uno sanguine orta omnis hominum gens —habitaret.* With this proposition, Paul combats not so much the special notion of the autochthonism (*αὐτόχθονες*) of the Athenians, but rather the common notion of all natural religions which derives nations from different origins.—A second thought is, that the division of mankind into nations rests on divine ordinance: "God has caused men to spread over the face of the earth, having appointed and limited the set times and boundaries of the nations." *Καιροί*, in consequence of *κατοικεῖν* preceding and *κατοικίας* following, refers to the dwelling-places of the nations, how long each should reside in the land they possess, and when they should be removed. It is also here plainly indicated that God regulates the history of the nations.

11. Paul, turning from national to individual life, indicates, thirdly, the highest aim of man—to seek God, to whom man is near and related. According to the structure of the sentence, *ζητεῖν* refers to *πᾶν ἔθνος ἀνθρώπων*, to the nations: the design of the divine division and boundaries of the nations was that they might seek the Lord, *τὸν κύριον*; compare ver. 25, "the Lord of heaven and earth." *Ζητεῖν* refers not only to the bare knowledge of God (Meyer), but to living and internal fellowship with God. *Εἰ ἄρα γε*, constructed with the optative, indicates the result as doubtful, by which Paul tenderly points out that man-

kind collectively have mistaken their end. The consequence of the search, if successful, would be ψηλαφεῖν and εὑρίσκειν: when one obtains the object sought, he has touched it, and thus has found it. *Καίτουγε*, although He requires not to be long sought after, inasmuch as He is not far from any one (so much the more inexcusable is the failure of the search). Ver. 28 is a confirmation (γάρ) of the last sentence, and shows why God is not far from any: because we are ἐν αὐτῷ, in God, as in encompassing space, or as in the atmosphere which surrounds us on all sides, and on which the functions of life depend. *'Εν αὐτῷ* is not "through Him" (Grotius, Kuinoel), or "on Him," depending upon Him: the most grammatical explanation is also logically the most suitable. *Ζῶμεν, κινούμεθα, ἐσμὲν*, is, as regards the objective relation of the idea, a descending series; but understood subjectively in accordance with the connection, an ascending series. Life is itself more than motion, and motion is more than bare being. But it is a climax when it is said, Without God, isolated and apart from Him, we should have no life, not even motion, and accordingly no existence. In confirmation of and in agreement with his proposition (ἐν ἀυτῷ—ἐσμέν), Paul quotes the expressions of some Greek poets (οἱ καθ' ὑμᾶς), "We are also His offspring." The words cited form the commencement of a hexameter and stand *verbatim* in Aratus, a poet of the third century before Christ, born in Solœ of Cilicia, who, in the introduction to his astronomical poem *Φαινόμενα*, has the words—

—— πάντη δὲ Διὸς κεχρήμεθα πάντες
τοῦ γὰρ καὶ γένος ἐσμέν.——

Τοῦ, poetical for τούτου, refers there to Jupiter, and is applied by Paul to the true God. When, however, Paul attributes this thought to several poets (τινες—εἰρήκασι), he probably has also Cleanthes of Lycia in view, who, in his hymn to Jupiter, has these words: ἐκ σοῦ γὰρ γένος ἐσμέν. Paul might quote such passages without having had a regular Greek education, or a special acquaintance with Greek literature. Such passages might have come to his knowledge and been impressed upon his memory, by reason of his education in a city of Grecian culture like Tarsus; and this so much the more readily, as Aratus belonged by birth to the same country as the apostle.

12. From this poetical saying, as a proposition known to his hearers and conceded by them, Paul draws a further conclusion

(*οὖν*) against the worship of images, and the idolatrous idea at the foundation of this practice (*νομίζειν*). This refutation, though severe in principle, is in the form of expression extremely mild and forbearing, particularly in the inclusive form of expression, *οὐκ ὀφείλομεν*; whereas he might have said, It is foolish and irrational of you to fancy this. The inference is, If we are thus related to God, if we are homogeneous with Him, then the Godhead (*τὸ θεῖον*, as in the philosophical language of the ancients) cannot be homogeneous with that which is, as regards its matter, only metal and stone, and thus heterogeneous to man, and as regards its form, is represented by art. This the apostle says, notwithstanding, or rather precisely because the most precious statues of the gods of silver and gold, of marble and ivory, the most splendid masterpieces of antiquity, stood on the Acropolis and other places, as well as in the temples of Athens. *Χάραγμα*, an image, a sculpture (from *χαράσσω*), which is the production of the art and deliberation of a man. *Ἐνθύμησις* is, according to the *usus loquendi*, not desire—the motive of the artistic inclination (Meyer), but thought, deliberation. According to this, the apostle, in order to show the unreasonableness of image-worship, directs attention both to the material out of which the images are made—and to the art and wisdom of their formation and completion, partly by the hand of the artificer (*τέχνης*), and partly by means of thought and reflection as to what is to be made. The striking contrasts *ἀνθρώπου* and *τὸ θεῖον* are designedly placed near each other.

13. In vers. 30 and 31, Paul comes to the third head of his discourse: concerning salvation and the Saviour, repentance, and faith. Thus far it was evidently to be understood that man had hitherto mistaken the truth—had erred. On account of this (*οὖν*) the apostle now testifies that God has overlooked the times of ignorance (*ὑπεριδών*, has allowed them to pass by without any positive manifestation of His grace, but also without severe censure); but now, as in a turning point of the times (*ταvῦν*), He demands of all men change of disposition (*τοῖς ἀνθρώποις πᾶσι πανταχοῦ* expresses universality in the most definite manner). This demand is proclaimed, and this proclamation, which concerns all men, is in course of being published, with reference to this, that (*καθότι*) God has appointed a day for the righteous judgment of the world, which He will accom-

plish by a man whom He has ordained for that purpose (ᾧ ὥρισε, the usual construction), having by His resurrection from the dead offered faith to all men. *Πίστιν παρέχειν*, that is to say, made faith possible, brought it near, namely, by means of the actual testimony in favour of Him and His dignity which lay in the resurrection.

14. At this point, but not having come to the conclusion of his discourse, the speaker is interrupted by loud mockery of the resurrection. *'Ανάστασις νεκρῶν*, with the intentional omission of the definite article before the genitive, which would denote the resurrection of all the dead, whereas the discourse is only about the resurrection of one, namely, Jesus. The other hearers, who did not exactly mock, at least in a polite manner gave Paul to understand that they would hear him again another time, but that they had had enough of it for the present. And thus, *οὕτως*, *i.e.*, after so unpromising a reception of his words, Paul left the assembly. Nevertheless some men joined him, and were converted; among whom Luke mentions only Dionysius, a member of the Areopagus, that most ancient and far and widely esteemed court of Athens. That Dionysius was a distinguished man, is to be inferred from the circumstance, that that court of judges was composed of the noblest, the most independent, and the most upright men. The legends of the Church have converted him into bishop of Athens and a martyr; and, later still, many writings and the notorious system of the mystic art have been ascribed to him. Damaris is entirely unknown; and from the manner in which she is mentioned, it has been asserted, without reason, that she was the wife of Dionysius (Chrysostom).

15. The unity of the speech is striking. The inscription of that altar, *ἀγνώστῳ θεῷ*, is the theme of discourse. The apostle gladly admits to the Athenians a certain degree of religious feeling, but he asserts, on the ground of that inscription, that they failed in the true knowledge of God. Therefore he proclaims to them the truth, 1. concerning God (vers. 24, 25); 2. concerning man, as appointed to seek and to find God, and as related to God (vers. 26–28). After the intervening remark (ver. 29) which censured the worship of images as wrong, Paul announces, 3. that the times of ignorance are at an end, and that God requires conversion and faith in the Risen One who is the Saviour and Judge of the world (vers. 30, 31). See Lange's

Church History, vol. ii. p. 222. The whole speech is in the highest degree appropriate to the time and place, of a wisdom and ripeness so considerate and yet at the same time so frank, so forbearing and yet at the same time so penetrating, so great in contemplation and purely Pauline in the fundamental principles of the unity of the revelation of God in creation, in conscience and in the work of redemption, and of the separation of history into the pre-Christian and the Christian periods,—that we cannot consider the doubt well-founded as to the credibility of the narrative of Paul's appearance and of his speech at Athens.

DOGMATICAL AND ETHICAL THOUGHTS.

1. The number of the master-works of ancient art, the beauty of the productions of architecture and statuary, awakened in Paul no æsthetic pleasure, far less amazement and inspiration, but, on the contrary, moral indignation. When, for the first time, the Spirit of Christ in one of His disciples and apostles comes in contact with the perfection of ancient art, He passes upon it a sentence of condemnation. Are then, as many fancy, Christianity and art in themselves opposite powers which mutually repel each other? No; it is only so far true, that the Spirit of Christ does not recognise or admit an exclusively æsthetic and purely artistic impression of works of art, but apprehends and judges art only in and with the religious and moral thoughts on which it is founded. And in this the Spirit of Christ agrees with classical antiquity, inasmuch as both value nothing that is one-sided, but always apprehend the whole man in a harmonious manner. The Apostle Paul, whilst he views the works of art in Athens, cannot separate the artistic designs from the thoughts which are expressed by them, and from the purposes for which they were made. The beautiful temples, the glorious statues, etc., are essentially the creations of the heathen spirit, and the instruments of polytheistical worship; the city, adorned with works of art, is a *κατείδωλος πόλις*. And therefore the sight of this world of art awakens in him a moral indignation at the error and sin against the living God which is contained therein. The Spirit of Christ never permits a judgment entirely apart from morality and religion.

2. As with art, so also with philosophy, Christianity comes in contact for the first time. Here also this contact is not

friendly. Only with this difference, that in the former case the apostle, in the name of Christianity, was the assailing party, but in the latter the philosophers. Neither in the narrative (vers. 16–18), nor in the whole speech before the Areopagus, is a thought to be recognised which may be regarded as a direct attack upon philosophy. The Epicurean and Stoic philosophers, however, express themselves, both before and after the speech of the apostle, partly disdainfully and partly coldly concerning his doctrine. This is comprehensible, because it was precisely the schools of Epicurus and Zeno who came in contact with Paul. The former, by their doctrine of the Godhead and of pleasure as the chief good, and the latter, by their moral self-satisfaction, were farthest removed from the Christian doctrine. But that Christianity in itself is hostile to philosophy, is by no means to be inferred from this first encounter. On the contrary, we may, from the fruitful germs of thought which are scattered in this speech at Athens, readily predict that the truth in Christ Jesus will give rise to a Christian philosophy.

3. The primary thought of this missionary discourse is *ὃ ἀγνοοῦντες εὐσεβεῖτε—καταγγέλλω ὑμῖν.* Paul proceeds from an inscription on that altar, "To an unknown God." What is there inscribed, he apprehends more widely and more deeply. In the worship of an unknown God is contained the confession both of ignorance and of a pressing necessity of worshipping the unknown. The gods who are known, and named, and worshipped as known, do not satisfy the religious need; this feels itself constrained to aspire beyond the existing worship. But what is worshipped along with them is admittedly a being unknown and unnamed (*ὃ ἀγνοοῦντες εὐσεβεῖτε*, ver. 23; *ἡ ἄγνοια*, ver. 30). And in the worship of an unknown divinity lies the dim idea of the unknown God. Thus even under the mass of heathen myths, and worship, and superstition, religious truth lies concealed, only dim and unknown. And what the religious feeling, blindly groping around, seeks after (*ζητεῖν, ψηλαφεῖν*, ver. 27), that revelation has clearly announced (*τοῦτο—καταγγέλλω ὑμῖν*). This is the germ both of a philosophy of mythology and of a philosophy of revelation.

4. Paul proclaims the one personal God as the Creator and the Lord of the world, exalted above all creatures. By this he advances the truth affirmatively, without controversy or reason-

ing. By this, however, he contradicts all that mixture of God and nature which lies at the foundation of natural religion, is expressed in their myths, and also cleaves to the ancient philosophy. The Greek gods came into being: no theology is without a theogony: even philosophy does not attain on classical ground to a true distinction between God and the world, and still less to the idea of creation. See Baumgarten, vol. ii. p. 166, English translation; and as regards Plato, see Zeller on the philosophy of the Greeks. The fact of creation, and the idea of the supernaturalness of God, as the Lord of the world, remains for all times, and for all stages of thought, as fundamental principles of truth which cannot be denied or set aside without danger.

5. We owe to revelation the true idea of man and humanity. The unity of the human race is foreign to all polytheistic religions. Corresponding to the plurality of gods, they proceed from an original plurality and an unequal dignity of nations and of their progenitors. And as the origin, so the progress. An idea of the unity of the history of the human race is entirely foreign to heathenism. Even the educated nations, the Greeks and the Romans, have only a conspicuous centre for the history of the world in their own nation; but they have not a united universal history of mankind. See Baumgarten, vol. ii. English translation, pp. 174–177. Only the revelation both of the Old and of the New Testament presents a unity, and that by means of the reference of human history to the one and true God. The history of the world, proceeding from God and pointing to God, is the biblical truth, revealed in the Old Testament by significant histories, and realized and fulfilled in the New Testament in the person of the Redeemer, who is at once the second Adam and the Son of God.

6. The apostle asserts the indwelling of man in God: *ἐν αὐτῷ ζῶμεν—ἐσμέν*. This proposition has often been misunderstood and abused. Even pantheism has been found in it; but with perfect injustice. For, first, the discourse is not here of the world, of the creature in general, but only of man, and that in connection with the proposition that man may find God, and is near to Him. Secondly, it is only said that we are and live in God; but this is something far removed from asserting that God is identified with the world, or that the world is substantially one and the same with God. Thirdly, the superiority of

God to the world is clearly enough asserted by the idea of creation and of *κύριος οὐρανοῦ καὶ γῆς*, in order to protest against all mixture and identification of God with the world, and conversely. As has been well said, the indwelling of God in the world is not contained in these words of Paul, but the reverse, the indwelling of man in God; *i.e.*, not merely the conditional dependence on God and His life, His power and His being, but also the intimate nearness to Him, the All-present, who everywhere surrounds and sustains us, as space, or as the atmosphere.

7. Christ, as the turning point of the world's history, is prominently brought before us in the close of this speech. Before Him, the times of *ἄγνοια*; with Him and after Him, light. Before Him, indulgent forbearance; now and henceforth, the prospect of the righteous judgment of the world—of the appointed great day. Change of mind is everywhere preached to all men, in order that they may not fall a prey to the judgment. The person of Jesus Christ is only denoted by two marks: as man, a member of the human race, a partaker of human nature, subject to death (*ἐκ νεκρῶν*); and as the Judge of the world, to which office He was appointed by God (*ὥρισε*), and by means of the resurrection from the dead is held forth by God to man as the object of confident faith. But if God will judge the world in the person of Jesus Christ, then Christ is not merely man, but also the suitable and perfect instrument of the holy and righteous, the omniscient and almighty God, and therefore Himself a partaker of the divine nature and dignity.

HOMILETICAL HINTS.

His spirit was stirred within him (ver. 16). Thus in the first contact, into which the Spirit of Christ came with the sublimest works of human art, the judgment of the Holy Ghost is set up as the narrow gate, through which all have to pass. But He has not therefore taken the axe, and destroyed the images and altars, as the iconoclastic Puritans, who condemn art in and by itself as something unchristian and ungodly.—It concerned Paul, not so much to throw down the idols from their altars, as especially to thrust them out of their hearts (Leonh. and Spieg.).—" When I first came to Athens," writes Lucian, " I was astonished and enraptured in contemplating the glory of the city." But Paul viewed the city, which was called " the altar and town-house of the Greeks, and the inventress of the sciences," with other eyes (Besser).

And in the market daily to those who happened to be present (ver. 17). For there were always many idle loungers, who stood idle in the market-place, Matt. xx. 3 (Starke).—Because the Gospel rests on a true foundation, it is not to be concealed, Luke xii. 3 (Starke).

Some of the Epicurean and Stoic philosophers encountered him (ver. 18). In Jerusalem the Sadducees and Pharisees, in Athens the Epicureans and Stoics, now-a-days on the one hand worldliness and pleasure, and on the other hand pride of reason and self-righteousness—these are always the two chief enemies, between which the preaching of the cross must force its way.—*The preaching of the cross to the Greeks foolishness, now as formerly.* 1. To Epicurean frivolity; inasmuch as that is unbelief and the service of the flesh. 2. To Stoical pride; because of its pride of reason and self-righteonsness.

What is this new doctrine which thou teachest? (ver. 19.) Whilst the world finds in the Gospel something new, an unexpected and unheard-of doctrine, this preaching is older than all human wisdom, and survives all rising and falling systems of philosophy, as a power of God for ever (Leonh. and Spieg.).—*They brought him to the Areopagus.* The Lord knows how to honour His servants. Here He gives to the poor and abased Paul an opportunity to bear an honourable and public testimony to the truth before the world-famed Areopagus at Athens, and before a great assembly. Thus the Lord knows to choose the base things, in order to confound the wise in their foolishness (Apost. Past.).

For all the Athenians were disposed for nothing else than to tell or to hear something new (ver. 21). The spirit of curiosity is in general a hindrance to the truth; but sometimes God employs it to bring the truth to the heart (Quesnel).—Desire after something new is to be praised, when we desire a new heart, the new man, and the new Jerusalem (Starke).—*Worldly curiosity and Christian desire of knowledge.* The former seeks pleasure, the latter instruction. The former seeks the new, the latter the true. The former is dissipated in the many, the latter finds peace in the one.

But Paul stood in the midst of the Areopagus, and said

(ver. 22). Neither the peculiar audience of philosophers, nor the solemnity of the place, nor the curiosity of the hearers, entices the apostle to deviate in the least degree from his Gospel, and to enter upon the fancies of the Athenians. But it may easily be perceived that he adjusts his discourse to the peculiar state of their hearts, and seeks with wise mildness to make an impression on them (Apost. Past.).—*That ye are in all points very God-fearing.* Wherefore the Athenians will rise up in the judgment, as accusers against the heathens among Christians. 1. The former were God-fearing; the pious fear of an unknown God lay at the bottom of their superstition. 2. The latter are estranged from God, and in their unbelief reject a revealed God.—How the heathen were prepared for the Christian faith (Nitzsch).

To the unknown God (ver. 23).—How many altars of the heart have this inscription! The Godhead is naturally inscribed on the heart of all men, and who is there that does not think that he serves God? But, alas! this light of knowledge is with most darkened by carnal curiosity, prejudice, and evil example, so that the true God is to them still an unknown God (Starke). —How necessary were it that a Paul should rise up in all our Christian churches and houses, and preach to modern Christians, that they, with all their show of knowledge and adoration, serve and build altars to an unknown God! (Gossner.)—The preachers of the Gospel are those who announce the unknown God (Starke).—There are many whose heart is as the market-place of Athens, or as the Pantheon, a temple of all gods. One idol stands there beside another: anger, pride, lust, covetousness, indolence, worldly honour. Search into thy heart, whether these images are not there. Most of us must answer, Yes; and say, My God is my life, science, art, gold, joy, my lover, my bride, my wife, my children, and the other blessings of this world. And behind, in a little corner, in the uneasy agitations of conscience, there is an altar with the inscription, "To the unknown God;" that is to say, to the God in whose name I am baptized and confirmed, to whom I have dedicated myself, who preserves and sustains me with His loving-kindness, but with whom I stand in no living intercourse, and whose commands I at pleasure transgress (Ahlfeld).—He is an unknown God also to those who do not live in Him, but in the world and its pleasures. These are they who carry the maxims of the Epicureans into practice, these ordinary men to whom the sum of existence consists in enjoyment, who know nothing, and wish to know nothing, of their immortal souls, but whose language is, Let us eat and drink, for to-morrow we die. These also are that great multitude who have no altar in their houses, not even with a faded inscription, not even in the most secret corner, but revile the altar in the house of the Lord, or internally despise it, because they have not God in their hearts. They have forgotten that they are of divine origin; their life is torn away from the maternal soil of the Church, and is starved in the soured soil of worldly pleasure; the living God has become for them a strange and unknown God, after whom they do not inquire (Langbein).—*To whom is the living God an unknown God?* 1. To those who think themselves wise. 2. To those who perform the external acts of worship without seeking God Himself. 3. To those who do not live in Him, but in the world and its lusts. 4. To those who do not desire to find God in Christ (Langbein).—*The believing heart, an altar to the well-known God.* 1. In him, the presentiment of His being is converted into undoubted certainty by the word of God. 2. In him, the uneasy fear of His holiness is changed into holy peace by the redemption of Christ. 3. In him, the inclination to sin is overcome by the Holy Ghost (Florey).

God, who made the world (ver. 24). He wishes to show them that this is the one God who called from nothing into existence the globe, with its apparatus of elements, bodies, and spirits, by the word which gave the command, by the wisdom with which He arranged it, and by the power with which He effected it (Tertullian).—But with this Paul also breaks in pieces the idols of the Athenians; for in testifying of the glory of God, whose throne is heaven and whose footstool is the earth, he smites the idols who dwell in temples made with hands. God can only dwell in Himself, where He was before He made the world. He is Himself His temple. But yet He has built to Himself as many temples as there are living hearts who love Him. There He will dwell, be recognised and worshipped.—Without, we have lost our way; to within, we are directed. Within, in thyself, do thy work; and if perhaps thou seekest an elevated sanctuary, give thyself internally to God for a temple. If in a temple thou wilt pray, pray in thyself; for the temple of God is holy, which temple ye are (Augustin).—*Where is the temple, where I may seek, find, and worship God?* 1. Heaven, where the spirits made perfect stand before His throne. 2. The visible creation, in which He has never left Himself without a witness of His power, wisdom, and goodness. 3. The Church, in which the unknown God is a revealed God in the Gospel of His Son. 4. My heart, in which He desires to dwell by His Holy Spirit.

He is not ministered unto by human hands, as if He needed anything (ver. 25). God has no need of us, but we have need of God (Starke).—The idols certainly require the care of human hands. There are still in the cities of India and China workshops with this inscription on their sign-boards, Here old gods are repaired and renovated (Leonh. and Spieg.).

And has made of one blood every nation of men (ver. 26). The unity of the human race from one progenitor is a necessary consequence of the unity of the Creator, and of the formation of man after His image.—The one Adam, in whom everything is finished (ver. 31), points, as the second Adam, back to a first (Stier).—We men are all one people. This is the great new view which the Gospel has cast upon the Greek and Roman nationalities, and upon all the other nationalities of the ancient nations (Stier).—*And has appointed the time, how long and how widely, they should dwell.* What think ye, ye mighty warriors and devourers of land? Hearken, God has yet something to say when ye distribute kingdoms, Num. xxxiv. 2; Ps. x. 5 (Starke).—As in the creation so in the government of the world, as in nature so in human life, God's holy and almighty hand is seen.—The change or the permanence of national boundaries is regulated not according to soil, climate, and nationalities, but according to a divine plan of government and the internal development of the human race. Israel is scattered into all lands, when the time of its obduracy has arrived. Athens is no eternal city, and Rome no immortal Rome. The glories of both fall, when their time is fulfilled; for the earth in its present form is only a provisional dwelling of men for the higher end (ver. 27), that they may be led back to their God (Stier).—*God in history.* He manifests therein, 1. His creative power, causing the human spirit to be unfolded in the multiplicity of national spirits; 2. His gracious goodness, giving to each nation time and space to develop its peculiarity; 3. His judicial righteousness, appointed to each nation, whether it be Greece, or Rome, or Israel, the apple of His eye, the end and limit of its power and prosperity; 4. His holy love, the whole history of the world aiming at this, that the kingdom of God may come, and that men may seek and find Him.

That they may seek God, if perhaps they might feel after Him and find Him (ver. 27). Paul here preaches natural truths: he speaks of the perfections of God, and of His providence over the human race. But do we find here empty definitions and distinctions, dry propositions and proofs? Not in the least: the truths are living in his mouth; and his heart, living in God, directs all things to this, to induce souls to seek God, who is so near to them. All philosophy, which stirs us up to this, is evangelical and divine (Apost. Past.).—O that this saying were inscribed in all our hearts, that we are on earth only for the purpose of seeking God in the creatures and in ourselves! (Quesnel.)—To this seeking, the finding will not fail, for He is not far from any one of us. The whole universe with eloquent silence proclaims the Lord as the great Original, that all might feel after Him, not with the bodily, but with the spiritual senses (Calov).—Therefore thou need'st not say, Who will ascend to heaven, and bring Him down from above? or, Who will descend into the abyss, and bring Him up from the dead? He is as near to thee as the law of the Holy One in thy conscience, as the longing after salvation in thy soul, as the involuntary cry for help, and the ceaseless sighing after peace in thy heart and mouth (Menken).—This seeking indicates our great loss—the erroneousness of our own ways. Nothing can be done without seeking, or rather without feeling and laying hold of, which also indicates two things: first, that darkness has covered the nations; and secondly, that, notwithstanding this, God, being still and always near, may be certainly and easily laid hold of (Stier).—Paul represents the final purpose of all the great arrangements of God in the world, that men should seek Him, and the feeling and finding of Him as the highest end of our perfection. Let us attend to the end and the way (Schleiermacher).

For in Him we live, and move, and are (ver. 28). All men have God thus near to them, if they would but believe. But the human race has loved to wander far from Him. It yet imitates the old method in paradise, when our first parents hid themselves from the presence of the Lord (Gossner).—God alone is such a Being, that He is necessary of Himself: our being and existence is only borrowed (Isa. xliv. 6; 1 Cor. viii. 6), (Starke). —In the Father, of whom are all things, we are; in the Son, who is the Life, we live; in the Holy Ghost, who is the Breath of all flesh, we move (Cyprian).—*We are His offspring.* 1. By creation, after the image of God. 2. By redemption, through the incarnate Son of God.—*We are of divine origin.* 1. Truth of this statement: from Scripture, from the human heart, from history. 2. Effect of this statement: holy humility; holy courage (Tholuck).

Because we are the offspring of God, we ought not to think, etc. (ver. 29). The heathen had wickedly misunderstood their own words. They argued: If we are of divine extraction, then the gods must be of human extraction, so that we may and should make human images of them. Paul presents to them another inference. Those who are of divine extraction dishonour themselves, if they do not refer their religious worship to their great progenitor, the Lord Himself—if they bow down to any being, inferior to Him, who is the Lord of all. With the same argument, he might attack those children of our age, who do not indeed render superhuman honour to invented images, but to the inventive spirit of man, the so-called genius; for thus they worship nothing else than their human thoughts. Indeed, all dead Christians, with their external acts of worship, are rebuked by this word; for their god is a distant and a dead god, not the living and the all-present, in whom we live, and move, and are (Williger).

The times of ignorance God has overlooked (ver. 30). That indeed was something strange, that Paul should speak of ignorance to one at a university; yet it was the truth. There were whole centuries of ignorance, in the midst of the most polished heathenism.—Leniently, Paul brings forward the side of ignorance in heathenism. But that this ignorance was blameable, is likewise indicated in the expression of indulgent forbearance, in the call to repentance, and in the threat of judgment (Stier).—*But now He has commanded all men everywhere to repent.* The greater the tenderness to the hearers, the more urgent must the call to repentance become. Every word lays hold on us, and shows how Paul will suffer nothing, no ignorance, no philosophy, no dignity, to avoid the common medium of repentance, commanded by God Himself (Apost. Past.).—*The narrow way of repentance, the one way for all.* Nothing releases from it. 1. No ignorance and no knowledge. 2. No depth of sin and no height of virtue. 3. No heathenism and no belief in Christianity.

A day in which He will judge the world (ver. 31). Popular paraphrase of vers. 30 and 31. God will graciously not punish former sins; but henceforth, He above all things demands repentance, whilst He, in a warning manner, announces the impending judgment by Jesus; and will then produce, in every one who penitently recognises the appointed Judge, confidence in the self-same man, whom God has appointed to be the Saviour also; and, since His resurrection, offers the new life through Him to all believers (Stier).—Whoever regards the earth with spiritual eyes, can form no other opinion than that there is a future judgment (Starke).—*By a man.* This is the man, without form and comeliness, before whose cross all the gods and demigods of Athens—Theseus and Hercules, Jupiter and Apollo—with all their glory, sink into the dust; before whose foolishness of preaching, all the wise men of Greece—Thales and Pythagoras, Socrates and Plato—are struck dumb; and whose invisible and inconspicuous kingdom shall outlast the laws of Solon and Lycurgus, and the empire of Alexander.

Some mocked; but others said, We will hear thee again concerning this (ver. 32). The world is almost entirely divided into these two classes of sinners. The one mock at saving truths, the other postpone from one time to another to turn them to advantage (Quesnel).

Thus Paul went from the midst of them (ver. 33). And came not again. The Lord Himself forbade to give His sanctuary to the heathen, and to cast pearls before swine, and did not reply to the inquisitive questions of Herod. When a man has gone such a length, as not any more to be even offended at the Gospel, but either to mock or carp at it, as a passing phenomenon among many others; then the servants of God have nothing more to hope, but only to be silent (Williger).—Thus opportunities pass by, whilst we deliberate. We neglect to take along with us the good counsel and the presence of a man of God. He is taken from us; he comes not again; and we die, before we have put our conscience in a position to appear before God (John viii. 21), (Quesnel).

But some believed, among whom was Dionysius (ver. 34). A single individual among such a numerous company of wise men! What a miracle of power was necessary, in order that a wise man of this world should bend to the cross of Christ! (Quesnel.)—A great number is no sign of a true church. Common stones are much more numerous than jewels, but which are the most valuable? (Starke.)—Thus a victory of the truth. And there was afterwards, according to the testimony of the ancients, a very flourishing Christian Church at Athens. Thus, even under suffering, the Christian religion prevails over all academical eminence (Bogatsky).

On the whole section (vers. 16–34).—*The wisdom of the world and the divine wisdom.* 1. The former inquires indeed, but only to excite a pleasant play of the spirits; the latter strives clearly to understand and surely to attain to the aim and import of life. 2. The former, indeed, surmises something of the being and nature of the living God, but directs its full adoration to imaginary gods; the latter, in the light of revelation, dives into the innermost depths of the Godhead. 3. The former has, indeed, a presentiment of the original glory of man, but of the redemption of the fallen it can know nothing; the latter finds its perfection in the redemption of the world through Christ (Leonh. and Spiegel.).—*The apostle's Gentile discourse also addressed to Christian hearts.* 1. God's power in the creation of the world. 2. God's love in the government of the world. 3. God's holiness in the redemption of the world (Beck).—*The loftiness of the divine nature, and the dignity of the human nature* (Beck).—*The messenger of the Gospel in the heathen world.* 1. His feelings: he feels himself repelled by the abominations of the heathen nature; he is full of holy grief at the heathen idolatry. 2. His conduct: he avails himself of every opportunity to work for God and Christ; every kind of hearer—Jews, proselytes, and Gentiles,—and every place where he can testify the truth, are welcome to him. 3. His audience consists of educated philosophers, people of the most perverted opinions, and the inquisitive (Lisco).—*The drawing of men to God.* 1. The departure from God (vers. 16–26). God becomes to man an unknown God, and in vain does he seek his happiness in sensual pleasure, in human wisdom, or in external works of piety. 2. The communing with his own heart (vers. 26–29).

What hadst thou from sin? Nothing. After what does thine heart long? After the Highest. Where is He, thy God? Not far off (ver. 27). He who has appointed to all men their aim, thought also on thy weal and woe. What is thy soul? His breath. What is thy body? His temple. And wilt thou serve sin? Wilt thou seek the Eternal in temporal things? No: He dwelleth not in temples made with hands. Thou wilt find Him, if thou becomest as He is; and He has made that possible for thee. 3. The return to the Father (vers. 30, 31). He who is invisibly near to thee in thy conscience, and in the leadings of thy life, has drawn visibly near to thee in His Son Jesus Christ. In Christ only, thou recognisest how thou art of divine origin, and canst atone for thy apostasy from God. God will graciously overlook the old. But now thou must come to Him through faith and repentance. Whoever believes on Him, is not condemned (Lisco).—*The conduct of Paul's hearers at Athens, a picture of the conduct of hearers in the present day* (vers. 32–34). 1. Some mocked. 2. Some said, We will hear thee again of this matter. 3. Some clave to Paul, and believed (Lisco).—Luther in Rome, and Calvin in Paris, are exciting pictures in history. But there is more here: Paul at Athens! Let us contemplate the picture, and attend, first, to the sensations with which the apostle tarried in the city of the Athenians. The herald of the mystery of the bloody cross never yet trod on such a soil as this. He does not shut his eyes to the monuments of the most ingenious art: he discerns in them something of the nobleness of the human spirit. But he does not permit himself to be captivated with that sensuous charm of beauty, or to be dragged down from his high stand-point on which the divine grace in Christ placed him; and a deep feeling of compassion for the error of the human spirit remains as the key-note of his innermost feelings. Secondly, attend to the testimony which he there bears. There are three great truths, which the apostle places in clear contrast to the three great falsehoods which at that time governed philosophy, and from which we are not yet freed: the creation out of nothing, as opposed to naturalism; the personality of God, as opposed to pantheism; the nature of sin, as opposed to antinomianism and rationalism. Thirdly, attend to the result. This is at first not very consolatory: prejudices too deeply rooted thwarted the apostolic word; but his calm expectation did not deceive him. A single convert already weighs heavily in the balance of the kingdom of God. No one succeeds in remaining neutral (Krummacher).—This was, in every respect, an extraordinary appearance. A remarkable contrast between a speech so spiritual and powerful and those sophistical declamations with which such matters as those on which Paul here discourses are often darkened, and which declamations even Socrates has complained of and mocked. What would a Socrates (there was none such then at Athens) have said to such a discourse as that of Paul? Probably, he would have recognised in it the kingdom of God from which he was not far, and been among the number of those who wished to hear more of the divinely appointed Judge of mankind and of the resurrection. In the person of the Redeemer of the world, he would have found more than that ideal of the just man whom Plato describes. He would have liked to hear rather of the unknown God than to have listened to the most eloquent sophists on gods, the creations of the imagination. He would have agreed neither with the Epicurean nor with the Stoic philosophers, when these called Paul a babbler (Hess).—Lavater gives a poetical paraphrase of this sermon of Paul at Athens in his "Jesus Messias, or the Gospels and the Acts of the Apostles in verse," 1786.—*Three books of the knowledge of God.* 1. The book of the world with its two parts—nature and history, vers. 24–26. 2. The book of the heart with its two parts—reason and conscience, vers. 27, 28. 3. The book of Scripture with its two parts—the law and the Gospel, vers. 30, 31.—*Paul at Athens;* or, "God has chosen the foolish things of the world to confound the wise, and God has chosen the weak things of the world to confound the things which are mighty" (1 Cor. i. 27). 1. The discourse of Paul at Athens was to the world foolishness; yet with its contents it confounded all the wise men of Greece. 2. The success of Paul at Athens was to the world weakness; yet it was the commencement of the end of heathenism.—*The Christian in relation to worldly art and science.* 1. He does not despise them, but recognises in their masterpieces a gift and a presentiment of God, who is not far from any one of us (vers. 26–28); and sees, even in their errors, the striving of the human spirit after God (vers. 29, 30). 2. But also he does not fear them: he boldly measures their praised works by the holy standard of God's word (vers. 24, 25, 29); and, even with their strongest errors, confidently expects the victory of Christian truth (vers. 30, 31).—*Paul at Athens, a true university preacher.* 1. He grants to every noble art and science its human right: *a.* by the contents of his discourse, in which every academical discipline is referred to: philosophy, vers. 24, 27; natural science, vers. 25, 26; history and law, ver. 26; art and poetry, vers. 28, 29;—*b.* by the form of his discourse, which, refined and suited to the audience, shows the striving of the apostle to become a Greek to the Greeks. 2. But he judges all by divine truth: *a.* pointing to sin and error, as the foul stain in all merely human effort, vers. 29, 30; *b.* and with the light of revelation pointing to God, as the source and the aim of all spiritual life.—*Paul at the tribunal of Athens.* 1. Apparently, indeed, judged and condemned by the superficial wisdom of man, which in frivolity mocks, or with an air of superiority turns aside (ver. 32). 2. In reality judging and bringing to naught, in the name of the living God,—*a.* heathen error, with the discourse on the Creator of heaven and earth (vers. 24–29); and *b.* human sin, with the sermon on repentance and faith (vers. 30, 31).

F.

Activity, Persecution, and Successes of the Apostle at Corinth.

CHAP. XVIII. 1–17.

1 After these things, he departed from Athens, and came to Corinth.
2 And he found there a Jew, named Aquila, born in Pontus, who had lately
come from Italy, with his wife Priscilla, because Claudius had commanded
all Jews to depart from Rome. 3 And he went to them, and because he
was of the same trade, he abode with them and wrought; for according to
their trade, they were tent-makers. 4 And he discoursed every Sabbath in
the synagogue, and sought to convince both Jews and Greeks. 5 But when
Silas and Timotheus came from Macedonia, Paul was pressed by the word to
testify to the Jews, Jesus as the Christ. 6 But when they opposed and
blasphemed, he shook his garments, and said to them: Your blood be upon
your own head. I, pure, will from henceforth go to the Gentiles. 7 And
he departed thence to the house of a man named Justus, who was God-
fearing, and whose house adjoined to the synagogue. 8 But Crispus, the
ruler of the synagogue, believed in the Lord, with all his house: and many
of the Corinthians hearing believed, and were baptized. 9 And the Lord

spoke to Paul through a vision by night: Fear not, but speak, and be not
silent: 10 For I am with thee, and no one will assault thee to injure thee;
for I have much people in this city. 11 And he continued there a year and
six months, teaching among them the word of God. 12 But when Gallio
was proconsul of Achaia, the Jews made insurrection with one accord against
Paul, and brought him to the judgment-seat, saying, 13 This person per-
suadeth men to worship God contrary to the law. 14 But when Paul was
about to open his mouth, Gallio said to the Jews: If it were a wrong or a
wicked crime, O ye Jews, I would then with reason bear with you; 15 But
if it be a question concerning doctrine, and names, and your law, look ye
to it yourselves; for I am unwilling to be a judge of such matters. 16 And he
sent them away from the judgment-seat. 17 Then all seized on Sosthenes,
the ruler of the synagogue, and beat him before the judgment-seat; and
Gallio concerned not himself on that account.

Ver. 1. 'Ο Παῦλος after χωρισθεὶς is indeed wanting only in a minority of authorities, but is undoubtedly spurious: it was added because a Church lesson commenced here.

Ver. 2. Ἀπὸ is far better attested than ἐκ, and has lately been with justice preferred.

Ver. 3. Τῇ τέχνῃ is on the ground of MSS. to be preferred to the accusative τὴν τέχνην, which is the more usual form.

Ver. 5. Τῷ πνεύματι is only in one uncial MS., whilst the rest have τῷ λόγῳ, which besides, as the more difficult reading, merits the preference.

Ver. 7. The reading Τίτου instead of Ἰούστου has only one MS. E. for it, and deserves no consideration.

Ver. 15. Ζητήματα is in three MSS., and has been received by Tischendorf; yet the singular ζήτημα is to be considered as the genuine reading, because it would have occurred to none to insert the singular, if the plural originally stood there, especially as three points of inquiry are mentioned.

Ver. 17. After πάντες four uncial MSS. have οἱ Ἕλληνες, whilst some MSS. of a later period read Ἰουδαῖοι; but both are to be considered as spurious additions, as three of the oldest MSS., among which also is the Sinaitic, together with some versions and fathers, have simply πάντες.

EXEGETICAL EXPLANATIONS.

1. *Paul departed from Athens.*—Corinth, the well-known rich commercial city, situated on the isthmus between the Ægean and Ionian seas, was at that time the political capital of Greece, and the residence of the Roman proconsul. Here Paul met with Aquila. He was a native of the Asiatic province of Pontus. The supposition that *Ποντικὸν τῷ γένει* might be an error, arising from a misunderstanding of the name Pontius Aquila (Cicero Ad Fam. x. 33; Suet. Cæs. 78), whilst he may have been a freeman of a Pontius Aquila (Reiche on Rom. xvi. 3), rests only on a coincidence, and has no support from the statement

of Luke. His wife Priscilla is called, in Rom. xvi. 3, Prisca. Meyer has shown that this married couple are not to be considered, with Neander, Ewald, and others, as converted before this. *Τινα Ἰουδαῖον* without *πεπιστευκότα* or *μαθητήν*; also *πάντας τοὺς Ἰουδαίους*, among whom Aquila is reckoned; finally, the motive which induced Paul to join them (ver. 3), because they were of the same trade, not because they were of the same faith in Jesus: all these things taken together prove that the married couple were not Christians, before Paul knew them at Corinth. Accordingly, it is to be supposed, that they, by their intercourse with Paul, were soon after converted; for in ver. 26 we see both already engaged in the work of teaching and instruction.

2. *And found there.*—Aquila and Priscilla had only shortly before (*προσφάτως*) arrived from Italy at Corinth. Without doubt they had resided in Rome, for their departure from Italy is explained by the expulsion of the Jews from Rome. According to our passage, Claudius had by an edict banished all the Jews from Rome. And with this agrees the well-known account of Suetonius, Claud. 25: *Judæos impulsore Chresto assidue tumultuantes Roma expulit.* On the other hand, the narrative of Dio Cassius, 60, 6, appears to conflict with this. He affirms that Claudius did not expel (*οὐκ ἐξήλασε*) the Jews, because that measure appeared hazardous on account of their great number; but only forbade the arrival of new-comers. But there is no reason to suppose that our passage and Suetonius, and, on the other hand, Dio Cassius, speak of the same period of time. We have at least one confirmatory testimony. However, Acts xxviii. shows that soon afterwards Jews and Christians were resident in Rome.

3. *He went to them.*—Paul visited this married couple lately come from Italy, and abode in their house, because he carried on the same trade as Aquila, and wrought with him at the occupation of a *σκηνοποιός*, a tent-maker. It has been often supposed that this must be understood of the fabrication of tent-cloth, particularly of Cilician cloth from goats' hair (*cilicium*), which was then much admired. However, *σκηνοποιός* does not indicate the preparation of the stuff itself, but the making of it into tents (Chrysostom, *σκηνοῤῥάφος*). At all events, we are indebted to this passage for the interesting notice concerning the

branch of trade which Paul knew; as from his own letters (1 Cor. iv. 12; 1 Thess. ii. 9; 2 Thess. iii. 8), we only know that he was accustomed to live by his own handiwork.

4. *But he discoursed in the synagogue.*—Even at the commencement, the apostle did not neglect to preach the Gospel; but he restricted himself to the Sabbaths and to the synagogue, in which he had still an opportunity to bear the truth in Christ not only before the Jews, but also before the Greeks who attended divine worship. This he did with an honest desire to convince them (ἔπειθεν). Here there is no mention of the result, but only for the first time in ver. 6.—But after Silas and Timotheus had come from Macedonia (compare chap. xvii. 14, 15, and 1 Thess. iii. 6, i. 1), a crisis took place. Συνείχετο τῷ λόγῳ may be understood either in the middle voice or in the passive; the former in the sense *instabat verbo* (Vulgate), *totus occupabatur*, he laboured strenuously in the doctrine (Kuinoel, De Wette, Baumgarten, Lange, and Ewald); the latter in the meaning, he was pressed in respect of the doctrine (Meyer, 2d edition), and certainly the New Testament *usus loquendi* is strongly in favour of the passive signification of συνέχεσθαι. Moreover it is also passive, if συνείχετο be thus understood, he was wholly apprehended and seized by the doctrine (Meyer, 3d edition); so that here we are not to think of his adversaries, but of an internal pressure of spirit.—Now, however, opposition and blasphemy arose on the part of the Jews, and this induced the apostle to break with the synagogue. Ἐκτιναξάμενος τὰ ἱμάτια, shaking the dust from his garments (as in chap. xiii. 51 shaking the dust from his feet), as a sign of renunciation, by which not even the least particle should remain cleaving to him. The imprecation expressed with energetic brevity, τὸ αἷμα—ὑμῶν, imports, May the bloody consequence, the inevitable judgment of God, befall your persons (κεφαλήν) and no others. Καθαρός, which stands first as a principal idea, refers primarily to τὸ αἷμα ὑμῶν, pure of the guilt and responsibility of your destruction.

5. *And he departed from them.*—Μεταβάς, departed from the synagogue to another house adjoining, which belonged to a Gentile proselyte, named Justus. This breach with the synagogue led to an internal decision on the part of Crispus, the ruler of the synagogue. From this time also many Gentile inhabitants of the city (for with Κορινθίων we can only think of

such), who now heard the word at this new place of meeting, believed and were baptized.

6. *But the Lord spoke through a vision.*—This nocturnal appearance of Jesus, who encouraged the apostle, and commanded him to speak without reserve, was designed to beget joyfulness for the work at this post, partly by the promise of divine protection against all opposition and ill-treatment (ἐπιθέσθαι, *invadere, impetum facere*), and partly by the revelation that Christ has a numerous people in this city (λαός, the Lord's people, in contrast to ἔθνη). This must, even as οὐδείς—σε, be a revelation of a fact not yet discernible, and thus cannot refer to the already converted, but only to those who were to be converted, and whom the Redeemer already names and knows as His own.

7. *And he continued there.*—In consequence of this revelation, Paul remained at Corinth a year and a half (ἐκάθισε, compare Luke xxiv. 49), teaching among them (ἐν αὐτοῖς, *i.e.*, the Corinthians) the word of God. With a play upon the word ἐκάθισε, Bengel remarks, *Cathedra Pauli Corinthia, Petri Romanâ testatior.* The common opinion is, that the chronological statement in ver. 11 embraces the whole period of the apostle's residence at Corinth, until his departure. Rückert and Meyer, however, restrict it to the time before the accusation in ver. 12; first, because ver. 12 forms a contrast to ver. 11; and secondly, because ἔτι in ver. 18 denotes a new section of time. But ver. 12 does not in point of fact form any contrast to ver. 11. On the contrary, everything after ver. 10 to ἱκανάς in ver. 18 is the consequence and the fulfilment of the divine revelation mentioned in vers. 9, 10. In consequence of that intimation and promise, Paul remains at Corinth. The promise of Christ, that no one would injure the apostle, is fulfilled in vers. 12–17; and after this episode, Paul could still remain "a good while" in Corinth. Accordingly, the statement of time in ver. 11 denotes the entire residence of Paul at Corinth.

8. Gallio, the proconsul of Achaia, *i.e.*, of the Roman province which since the conquest (B.C. 146) embraced Greece and the Peloponnesus, was the brother of the philosopher L. Annæus Seneca. He was originally called M. Annæus Novatus, and received the name M. Annæus Gallio in consequence of his adoption by the rhetorician L. Junius Gallio. The emperor Tiberius had converted the originally senatorial province of

Achaia into an imperial province, and had sent a procurator to it (Tac. Ann. i. 76); but the emperor Claudius restored it to the senate (Suet. Claud. 25): accordingly the title ἀνθυπατεύοντος strikingly agrees with history.

9. *The Jews made insurrection against Paul:* κατεφίστημι, *insurgo contra.* In the procuratorship of Gallio, the Jews with one accord rose against Paul. Ὁμοθυμαδόν alone contradicts Ewald's supposition, that the Jews dragged Sosthenes, the ruler of the synagogue, along with Paul, because they reproached him with partiality to Jesus. The accusation rested on an alleged violation of the law, *i.e.*, of the Mosaic law, by persuading others to a different mode of worshipping God. Ἀναπείθειν is to shake and to root out a conviction by other thoughts and reasons. Τοὺς ἀνθρώπους is stated generally, intentionally, in order to stigmatize Paul as one who seeks to proselytize in general.

10. *But when Paul would have opened his mouth.*—Gallio puts a stop to the trial, even before the apostle could begin to make his defence, because it was no legal offence, but only a question about the Jewish religion. Οὖν, a consequence arising from the accusation. Ἀδίκημα, an act of injustice, an infraction of private rights, which might be the ground of a civil complaint. Ῥᾳδιούργημα πονηρόν, wicked audacity, a real transgression, which it would be criminal to commit. Εἰ constructed with the imperfect, distinctly enough expresses that this was in point of fact not the case in the present instance. Κατὰ λόγον, reasonably, *i.e.*, here, justly, bound in duty. Ἀνέχεσθαι is designedly chosen to express partly the declaration of the court of justice, but partly also to indicate to the Jews that the whole information was troublesome to the proconsul, unbearable in the full sense of the term. The other alternative, which, according to the opinion of the proconsul, was actually the case, is also hypothetically expressed, εἰ—ἐστι, ver. 15. Ζήτημα, a scholastic question, disputation, which belongs not to the judicial sphere, but to the theoretical and scientific, gives us to understand that the matter did not belong to a court of justice. Still more, the objects about which the question treats also show that it was not a judicial matter: doctrine (λόγος), names (ὀνόματα puts the matter in the category of words; without doubt the accusers had mentioned the names of Messiah and of Jesus of Nazareth), and your law (νόμος ὁ καθ' ὑμᾶς, *i.e.*, the special law of the

Jews, not the law of the Romans or of the State). *Ὄψεσθε αὐτοί*, ye may yourselves search into it and settle it. *Κριτής* placed foremost by way of emphasis: the judicial decision of such matters, I wish not to usurp.—This conduct of Gallio harmonizes with his character as given by his brother Seneca, Quæst. Nat. iv. Præf. He praises not only his talents, but also his disinterestedness, amiability, and mildness: as, for example, *cœpisti mirari comitatem, et incompositam suavitatem.—Nemo enim mortalium uni tam dulcis est quam hic omnibus.* Thus by the self-restraint of the Roman in his judicial department, and by the personal kindness and philanthropy of Gallio himself, the promise of the Redeemer, that no harm should befall the apostle, is fulfilled.

11. *And he sent them away from the judgment-seat.*—In consequence of the negative answer, the proconsul sent away the accusers from his tribunal. It is probable that this "driving away," in consequence of the obstinately continued representations of the Jewish leaders, who would not immediately depart, was caused and completed by the officers of justice. The occurrence also immediately mentioned in ver. 17 might be brought about by this obstinacy. *Πάντες*, *i.e.*, all present; but certainly neither the Jews, as Ewald thinks, nor the Christians, but the Gentiles, stirred up by the importunity and ceaseless enmity of the Jews, and encouraged by the refusal of the judge, seized on Sosthenes, the ruler of the synagogue, and beat him. He was either the successor of Crispus, mentioned in ver. 8, or his companion in office (thus, in chap. xiii. 15, several rulers of the synagogue are mentioned); but it is very unlikely that he was, as Theodoret and Ewald think, identical with the helper of the Apostle Paul mentioned in 1 Cor. i. 1. This man was beaten publicly before the judgment-seat, without Gallio troubling himself about it. This was indeed impartiality carried too far, or rather indolence, for here was an *ἀδίκημα* (ver. 14), a personal injury. But Luke mentions it as a proof how completely the promise (ver. 10) was fulfilled: so little happened to the apostle, that the accusers themselves were beaten.

DOGMATICAL AND ETHICAL THOUGHTS.

1. The scene at the departure from the synagogue is an affair of conscience. The apostle lays the entire burden of their

crime upon the conscience of his opponents; his own conscience, he testifies, is pure. With this twofold declaration, the word of God to Ezekiel (chap. xxxiii. 8, 9) probably occurred to the apostle. The wicked man, if he refuses to be warned, shall die in his iniquity, but his blood will not be required at the hand of the watchman. His blood—that is to say, his bloody death, his punishment, his eternal destruction—is entirely his own fault. There is a common life in humanity, not only in a natural manner, but also by means of divine intimation and revelation. He to whom office, and power, and a message to others are entrusted, will be a partaker of their guilt, defiled by their sins, if he does not bear witness according to his ability. Indeed, even such a judicial announcement as that in ver. 6 may serve for conviction, and may produce change of mind and conversion, as appears to have been the case with Crispus.

2. Christ has much people in the city where the apostle knows and can name, although many, yet proportionally only a small number of converts. Man sees what is before his eyes; but the Lord looks at the heart. Man sees only what is present; but the Lord, to whom the future and the past are a continuous present, sees what is to come. The Redeemer has said, "I have other sheep;" and these had not as yet heard His voice: they did not know Him, but He knew them. So Christ knows His people of every place, whom He has chosen, and who will do homage to Him. "The Lord knows them who are His," 2 Tim. ii. 19.

3. The conduct of Gallio is not worthy of such unrestricted praise, as has often been bestowed on him. He certainly did not aid an act of injustice against Paul; but he looked quietly on an act of clamant injustice, without, in virtue of his authority, preventing or punishing it. And thus, on account of the indolence obviously displayed on this occasion, it is doubtful whether his refusal to the Jews proceeded from a pure disposition and a noble character. Possibly ease and pleasure greatly contributed to make him get rid of a matter repugnant to him by a declaration of its incompetency. But apart from personal motives, the principle expressed by Gallio, to resent judicially only legal offences, and to hand over questions of doctrine and internal matters of religion to their proper sphere, is certainly correct, and is a rule for the relation even of Christian authorities to

ecclesiastical matters—of a Christian State to religious opinions. But the principle must be practically carried out with more consistency and conscientiousness than here.

HOMILETICAL HINTS.

After these things, Paul departed from Athens and came to Corinth (ver. 1). How great is the mercy of God! No Nineveh, Sodom, or Corinth is so wicked, that He does not send to them preachers of righteousness (Starke).—Christ is sometimes more readily embraced by open sinners than by the learned and the apparently righteous. Paul effected more in vicious Corinth than in learned Athens (Starke).—Paul had the joy of forming a pure bride out of those impure sinners whom he brought to Christ; so that he could afterwards say, "Ye were thieves, and robbers, and fornicators, and such like; but ye are washed, ye are sanctified, ye are justified, in the name of the Lord Jesus, and by the Spirit of our God." What a support of faith and incitement to fidelity is contained therein, not to become weary, even when we have to deal with the most wicked sinners! (Apost. Past.)

And he found there a Jew named Aquila (ver. 2). As Paul came to Corinth according to the will of God, so His fatherly providence accompanied him, which had already, before he came to Corinth, prepared for him a house, work, fellowship, and an open door for the Gospel. In Rome, the emperor must expel the Jews, in order that Aquila may come to Corinth, and offer house and board to the apostle. Thus the all-ruling God uses the designs of princes, and the changes of the world, to provide for His children, and to advance His kingdom (Apost. Past.).—Paul found Aquila and Priscilla. This declaration indicates two things: 1. How easily God's servants and children, as it were by a secret elective affinity, learn to find and to know each other, even in a foreign country. 2. How the apostle regarded these honest souls as a costly booty, as a noble spoil, over which he rejoiced more than over the greatness and the splendour which he found in the rich commercial city of Corinth (After Apost. Past.).—Whoever has learned with Paul to be content, will easily find a host (Starke).—He who has experienced sorrow and affliction, knows how to assist the sorrowful (Starke).—Paul and Aquila at Corinth; or, "Thou leadest Thy servants, O Lord, in a most blessed, and yet wonderful manner." 1. The Lord had led these persons in a wonderful manner to Corinth. Paul, as a witness of the truth, driven with mockery from Athens, durst not expect anything better in vicious Corinth. Aquila, as a son of Abraham, forcibly expelled from Rome, sought nothing in Corinth but a temporary shelter. 2. The Lord brings them happily together at Corinth. He conducts Paul, the stranger, to Aquila, the friendly fellow-countryman and host. He conducts the upright Aquila to Paul, not only as a companion in trade and in the house, but as a preacher of righteousness and guide to eternal life.—*The entertainment of Paul by Aquila at Corinth;* or, "Be not forgetful to entertain strangers, for thereby some have entertained angels," Heb. xiii. 2. 1. The command. 2. The promise. Examples: the angel of the Lord with Abraham; Elijah at Sarepta; Jesus entertained by Zaccheus, etc.—How the Lord converts a foreign country into a home to His servants. 1. They have the Father with them. 2. They find brothers and sisters. 3. They do not long require to seek for work.

And because he was of the same trade, he abode with them and wrought (ver. 3). To sit down in a workshop, and to earn our bread and wages with hard labour, ought to shame no workman: it did not disgrace Paul (Starke).—No teacher ought to be ashamed of manual labour: Christ Himself was a carpenter's son, and the apostles were fishermen. If we cannot otherwise support ourselves, we ought not to lie at the feet of the ungrateful, or be troublesome to the refractory, who hate the Gospel and the office of the ministry because it costs them something (Starke).—*Paul in the workshop.* 1. An admonitory example to preachers. Though the apostle's manner of acting is now no longer suitable for the ministerial office, yet by the disposition manifested in it, he puts to shame spiritual ministerial pride and unspiritual luxury and sloth. 2. An encouraging example for the artisan. Be not ashamed of thy trade, for every honourable occupation is well-pleasing to God; but in thy trade be not ashamed of thy God and of thy Christianity. Thus, in trade, a man may be a servant of God, a Christian, and an apostle among his associates.—*Christian journeymen on their travels.* 1. The dangers in the foreign country (the temptations in luxurious Corinth). 2. The acquaintance by the way (Aquila). 3. The work at the trade (ver. 3). 4. The care for the soul (God's word, sanctification of the Sabbath, ver. 4).

He discoursed in the synagogue every Sabbath (ver. 4). He who is faithful in that which is least, is also faithful in much. As Paul carefully earned his bread by his own hands, so he was not the less careful diligently to perform his ministerial duties every Sabbath (Starke).—It is emphatically noticed that the apostle taught every Sabbath, and that he laboured among all men, both Jews and Greeks. So accurately does God observe the diligence and fidelity of teachers; and so precious is it in His eyes, when He finds one who will omit no opportunity, and will neglect no individual soul (Apost. Past.).—Weekly labour and Sabbath sanctification,—the one requires and promotes the other. 1. Weekly labour creates hunger and thirst after Sabbath-rest and Sabbath-fare. 2. Sabbath sanctification imparts strength and pleasure to the daily work of the week.

But when Silas and Timotheus arrived, Paul was pressed (ver. 5). A slothful servant would willingly devolve the work on others. Paul, on the contrary, when he has obtained fellow-workers, becomes the more zealous. Many evangelical workers, who are at one, encourage each other in the work, for spiritual fellowship is useful for the work of God, Phil. ii. 22 (Quesnel). —*To testify that Jesus was the Christ.* Because teaching every Sabbath is perceptibly distinguished from testifying that Jesus is the Christ, so it is to be supposed that Paul did much in the way of preparation, which was effectual to produce an awakening among Jews and Greeks. Yet he would not too long continue doing this, but the love of Christ constrained him to come forward with the principal truth of the Gospel (Rieger).—Hitherto he had indeed suffered the apostolic spirit to appear, but he had not yet ventured to discourse upon the chief matter (Williger).

Your blood be upon your own head (ver. 6). As there was here no corporeal blood-guiltiness, so this is to be understood of the guilt of spiritual self-murder. As they rejected the life in Christ, so were they spiritual suicides (Starke).—Paul owed this holy severity not only to the dignity of the preached Gospel, but also to the obstinate souls themselves, many of whom might thereby be brought to consideration. But carnal zeal must not appeal to this example. He who would gladly wish to imitate the apostle, and to say, that he is pure of the blood of the lost, must first prove whether he has done all that the apostle has done for these sinners (Apost. Past.).

And he departed thence to the house of a man named Justus (ver. 7). Paul's zeal against the stiff-necked does not lead him from his work. With the same holy earnestness with which he separates himself from the blasphemers, he turns to the little company of awakened souls, continues in his business, and does not make the whole flock suffer for the guilt of a part. Many teachers adopt this wrong course, when they follow the inclinations of the flesh (Apost. Past.).—His entering into the house close to the synagogue, proved how gladly he would have remained in the synagogue; but also, as now probably this house was the place of meeting for willing hearers, it was for the hardened Jews a loud testimony to the blessing which they had despised (Williger).

But Crispus, the chief ruler of the synagogue, believed, with all his house (ver. 8). Crispus belonged to those concerning whom Paul said, not none, but only not many, wise men after the flesh, 1 Cor. i. 26 (Williger).—A special proof of the care of God for His faithful servants. When Paul with a troubled spirit departed from the blaspheming Jews, God opened to him a door in the house of Justus, near to the synagogue, and imparted to him this joy, that the chief ruler of the synagogue, with all his house, was converted, and many of the Corinthians were thereby led to the Lord (Apost. Past.).

And the Lord spoke to Paul in a vision by night, Be not afraid, but speak, and be not silent (ver. 9). Thus the greatest saints and the strongest heroes of God have their hours of weakness and times of temptations, when they require encouragement and strength from above. For example, Abraham before Abimelech; Moses in the wilderness; David in the penitential Psalms; Elijah under the juniper-tree; John in prison; Jesus in Gethsemane; Luther in his temptations, who once said, "Many think, because I appear so joyful in my external conduct, that I walk on roses; but God knows how it is with me."

For I am with thee, and no one will attack thee to injure thee; for I have much people in this city (ver. 10). O glorious passport! Faithful pastors are comforted by this, although they are placed before judges, and a bath of suffering is prepared for them. Therefore, O teacher, be not silent; otherwise the beams will cry out, and thou wilt be dumb before the judgment-seat of God (Starke).—"Fear not," the comforting exhortation of the Lord to His servant, dismayed at his dangerous post. The Lord points His servant,—1. To His gracious presence: "I am with thee;" 2. To the weakness of all enemies: "No one will attack thee to injure thee;" 3. To the success, as yet secret, of His word: "I have much people in this city."—The declaration of the Lord to His servant, "I have much people in this city." 1. An earnest exhortation to ministerial fidelity: "Feed My sheep; feed My lambs." 2. A sweet comfort in ministerial distress: say not, "And I only am left."

And he continued there a year and six months, teaching the word of God (ver. 11). Much prayer, much patience, much trust in God, much diligence in work,—these are the means to promote the cause of God (Quesnel).—Not until now, could Paul in his Christian work sit down as on a soft cushion; whereas, before this he always held himself at Corinth as a stranger and a passer through, waiting for the intimation, Now thou must go forth. The apostle had never, as yet, remained so long in one place (Williger).

But when Gallio was proconsul of Achaia, the Jews made insurrection with one accord against Paul (ver. 12). The promises of divine protection in this life are not to be understood to the exclusion of the cross (Starke).—That the Jews remained quiet for a year and a half, and granted rest to the apostle, was not from their own inclination, but through the special providence of God, according to His promise. We dare not always trust the world. The world is and remains the world still. God has only to remove the barrier, and the suppressed bitterness of the world breaks forth anew. Let us bear this in mind, in the rest which God at present grants to us (Apost. Past.).

This person persuadeth men to worship God contrary to the law (ver. 13). We easily persuade ourselves that that is contrary to the law of God, which is contrary to our desires (Quesnel).—It is nothing new, that those who err most in religion, accuse others of heresy (Starke).

But when Paul was about to open his mouth, Gallio said (ver. 14). As the Lord had promised assistance to the apostle, so Paul did not even require to open his mouth in his defence. The surest passport is the divine promise, which the world and the bitterest enemies must respect. The Lord stops the mouth of the adversaries, as he stopped for Daniel the mouths of the lions (Apost. Past.).

But if it be a question of doctrine, see ye to it (ver. 15). It is wisdom, when magistrates will not judge on matters of religion which they do not understand. But it is not piety, when magistrates neither learn nor understand what religion is, and do not, according to their office, protect believers (Starke).—When we consider Gallio as a heathen judge, we must praise his equity and impartiality. It puts to shame that persecuting spirit, and that thirst for blood, which so many magistrates, Christians in name, have displayed under pretext of religion. But when Christian magistrates, by this example, excuse their indifference to all religion, the fallacy of the reason is easily made evident. This sinful Gallioism has, alas! in our days spread from the courts of kings to the huts of peasants (Apost. Past.).—"Fulfil your civil duty, and I do not ask about your faith;" such is the political wisdom of the present day, but is it the true wisdom?

They beat Sosthenes, the ruler of the synagogue, before the judgment-seat; and Gallio concerned not himself on that account (ver. 17). We thus see how indifference to religion makes a man negligent even in the administration of civil justice (Apost. Past.).—*The laudable and the censurable administration of justice by Gallio, a guide for all magistrates.* 1. The laudable administration of justice in Gallio's judgment concerning the point of complaint (vers. 12–15). He rejects the complaint of the Jews, because it referred to a purely religious matter. 2. The censurable administration of justice in his conduct at the violence of the Greeks (vers. 16, 17). He here shows himself indifferent and unfair. Magistrates have in ecclesiastical controversies to distinguish between what is above the law and what is against the law, and have to resent what is unlawful on whatever side it happens (Lisco).—*The heathen Gallio, no pattern for a Christian judge;* for a Christian judge should not indeed interfere in the affairs of another's conscience and religion, but he should have a conscience and religion himself: he should not indeed judge in matters of doctrine and faith, but he should protect the ill-treated, whatever their belief, against rough usage.

On the whole section, vers. 1–17.—*The task of the evangelical ministry, Compel them to come in.* 1. With noble self-denial: Paul supports himself with the labour of his own hands, vers. 1–3; see 1 Cor. ix. 2. With unwearied zeal, which employs every time for work, turns to all with the message of salvation, is ever anew kindled by the Spirit of God, and represents Jesus as the Christ to all, vers. 4, 5. 3. With stedfast courage, in opposition to the adversaries, vers. 6–11 (Lisco).—*Earnest exhortation and divine consolation for the publishers of salvation.* 1. The earnest exhortation: Speak, and be not silent, even at the risk of giving offence; but let thy actions agree with thy words (vers. 2–4). 2. The divine consolation: I am with thee, and no man shall injure thee: I have much people in this city (ver. 10). Whoever perseveres, will receive the heavenly crown, 2 Cor. ii. 14, 15 (Lisco).—*With what confidence, we ought to go and preach the Gospel to the heathen.* 1. The Lord commands: "Speak, and be not silent." 2. The Lord comforts: "I am with thee, and no man shall injure thee." 3. The Lord promises: "I have much people, even in the heathen city" (Lisco). —*The decisive word in the mouth of the preacher, that Jesus is the Christ.* By this is determined: 1. The spirit from which he speaks—whether it is the spirit of human wisdom and complaisance, or the Holy Spirit of the Lord; 2. The nature of the hearts of the hearers: some contradict and blaspheme, others believe and are baptized; Christ is the Rock, on which the one are broken in pieces, and the other are raised, vers. 5–8; 3. The result of his work: hitherto at Corinth, Paul had experienced neither the cross nor the blessing; now both come—Christ's cross (ver. 6) and Christ's blessing (vers. 9–11).—*Paul at Corinth;* or, "When I am weak, then am I strong," 2 Cor. xii. 10. 1. Paul was weak: *a.* Externally, as an unknown stranger and a poor artisan, opposing himself with the foolishness of preaching to the heathen lusts of the splendid city of Corinth, as well as to the prejudices and hatred of his Jewish countrymen. *b.* He feels himself internally weak: while perhaps still depressed by his small success at Athens, he delays to come out with the essence of his discourse, that Jesus is the Christ. 2. But Paul is strong in the power of the Lord: *a.* Internally, the Lord strengthening his apostolic courage, and awakening in him the bold spirit of a martyr, by the arrival of dearly beloved fellow-labourers, and still more by the encouragement of His Holy Spirit, and by the revelation of His gracious presence, vers. 5, 9, 10. *b.* Externally strong in his conflict with his adversaries, upon whose head the apostle, undismayed, throws back their sins, and whose mouth against His servants, the Lord stops; and also in the increase of the Church, which flocks in ever increasing numbers around the apostle, vers. 7, 8, 10, 11.

G.

Return of the Apostle by Ephesus and Jerusalem to Antioch.

CHAP. XVIII. 18–22.

18 But Paul remained there yet a considerable time; and then took his leave of the brethren, and sailed to Syria, and with him Priscilla and Aquila; having shaved his head in Cenchrea, for he had a vow. 19 And they arrived at Ephesus, and he left them there. But he went into the synagogue, and spoke with the Jews. 20 But when they desired him to remain longer with them, he consented not, 21 But took leave of them, and said, I will come again to you, if God will. And he sailed from Ephesus. 22 And he came to Cæsarea, and went up and saluted the Church, and went down to Antioch.

Ver. 19. The plural *κατήντησαν* is in four uncial MSS., whereas the singular *κατήντησε* is only in two: the singular corresponds with the preceding and succeeding form of the narrative, and therefore, if the original reading, would not have been changed into the plural.

Ver. 21. Not less than four uncial MSS. have *ἀποταξάμενος καὶ εἰπών*: only two uncial MSS. of the ninth century, G. and H., read *ἀπετάξατο*, which appeared a simpler construction.—*Δεῖ με πάντως τὴν ἑορτὴν τὴν ἐρχομένην ποιῆσαι εἰς Ἱεροσόλυμα* is entirely wanting in four important MSS., A.B.E. and the Sinaitic MS., as well as in nine cursive MSS. and several old versions; whilst D.G.H. have the words. They appear, as so many insertions in the Acts, to have been added, because *πάλιν ἀνακάμψω* seemed too cold. Mill and Bengel, and latterly Griesbach, Heinrichs, and Kuinoel, considered the words as an interpolation; Lachmann and Tischendorf have omitted them.

EXEGETICAL EXPLANATIONS.

1. *But Paul remained there yet a considerable time.*—*Ἀποτάσσεσθαι τινι, valedicere alicui.* Paul embarked at Cenchrea, the eastern port of Corinth, about a (German) mile and a half from

the city, situated on the Saronic Gulf, whilst the western port was called Lechæon.

2. *Having shaved his head in Cenchrea.*—The shaving of the head and the vow, though briefly related, and precisely on account of this brevity, have occasioned much speculation. As regards the first particular, it is asked, Who shaved his head at Cenchrea? Paul or Aquila? The latter is certainly mentioned immediately before, and, indeed, in a noticeable way after his wife, which has been thought to show that Luke had used this order, for the purpose of making the reference of κειράμενος to Aquila more pointed. But the naming of Priscilla before her husband occurs also in Rom. xvi. 3 and 2 Tim. iv. 19; and the reason of it appears to have been the superior character of the wife, who perhaps engaged in the Christian cause with a more lively spirit, and a more active zeal. Taking this into account, nothing to aid the solution of the above question can be drawn from the order in which this married couple are placed. Moreover, according to the nature of the affair and the form of the narrative, Paul being so much the principal person, and Aquila and Priscilla only subordinate persons, it is most natural to refer the words κειράμενος—εὐχήν to Paul. Besides, what would this trait mentioned of Aquila import? Accordingly κειράμενος is to be referred to Paul; as Augustine, Erasmus, the Reformers, Bengel, and, in modern times, Olshausen, Neander, De Wette, Baumgarten, and Ewald do; whereas the Vulgate, Theophylact, Grotius, Kuinoel, Schneckenburger, and Meyer understand the expression of Aquila. The chief reason for this latter interpretation, expressed or not, is that it was thought that this carnal ceremony connected with vows among the Jews was inconsistent with the mental freedom of the apostle. This reason, provided we do not represent the liberality of the apostle according to our imaginary notions, but derive it from facts, has no weight. But what the import of this shaving of the head was, can only be understood by the consideration of the nature of the vow.

3. *For he had a vow.*—The shaving of the hair was connected with a vow, and was in consequence of it (εἶχε γὰρ εὐχήν). But this expression is also indefinite. We are not told what kind of vow it was, or whether the shaving of the head was connected with the commencement or the termination of the vow. This vow has, in former times, been considered as the

vow of the Nazarites (Wetstein and others); according to which, a man, in honour of God, allowed his hair to grow for a certain definite period, and after that period his hair was shaved off in the temple, and cast into the sacrificial fire. But this is not applicable here, because the loosening of the Nazarite from his vow must take place in the temple, and consequently in Jerusalem; and the assertion, that Jews on a journey were not bound by this regulation, is a supposition incapable of proof. Also the opinion, that the Nazarite vow was here interrupted by Levitical uncleanness, and renewed by the shaving of the head, cannot be defended, because such a renewal likewise could only take place in the temple, Num. vi. 9–21. Accordingly this shaving of the head is not connected with the vow of the Nazarite; but this vow of Paul could not have been a Levitical vow, and must have been unconnected with the temple. At all events, it appears, from all that we know of such transactions elsewhere, that the shaving of the head was connected, not with taking the vow, but with the loosening from it, for then it was the custom of the Hebrews to shave their hair. According to this, εἶχε here would import "he had had." But what was the occasion of the vow, and wherein it consisted, cannot be determined, and it is useless to make suppositions about it.

4. *And they arrived at Ephesus.*—Paul now, for the first time, on his return from his second missionary journey, comes to Ephesus, the famous ancient capital of Ionia, and at that time the capital of proconsular Asia, a city which carried on a flourishing trade, and soon became the Christian metropolis of Asia Minor. Here he left Aquila and his wife. Κατέλιπεν anticipates, and indicates that they remained at Ephesus, whilst Paul proceeded on his journey. He himself sought to work upon the Jews in the synagogue, and indeed with success, so that they wished him to remain longer; but he, in order to hasten back to Antioch, did not consent. However, he promised to come to Ephesus again, which promise, according to chap. xix., he soon fulfilled.

5. *And he came to Cæsarea, and went up and saluted the Church.*—Some of the earlier interpreters—as, for example, Calovius and Kuinoel—understood ἀναβάς of Cæsarea itself, as one must go up from the shore to the city situated higher. But it is incomprehensible that Luke, who from vers. 19–22 inclu-

sive writes so briefly and summarily, after he had already said *κατελθὼν εἰς Καισάρειαν*,—which, indeed, is to be referred to the city, and not merely to the coast or haven,—should yet expressly have given prominence to the going up to the city. Further, *κατέβη εἰς 'Αντιόχειαν* is not appropriate to a journey from Cæsarea, because Antioch is three (German) miles inland, and consequently more elevated than the sea-port Cæsarea. On the other hand, this expression is entirely appropriate, and corresponds to the *usus loquendi* elsewhere in the Acts (for example, chap. xv. 2, *ἀναβαίνειν* from Antioch to Jerusalem), if we suppose Jerusalem the *terminus ad quem* for *ἀναβάς*, and the *terminus a quo* for *κατέβη*; which also *ἡ ἐκκλησία* (*κατ' ἐξοχήν* without *ἡ οὖσα*, chap. xiii. 1) appears to indicate. That, nevertheless, *ἀναβὰς* must necessarily be referred to Cæsarea, taking for granted the spuriousness of the words *δεῖ με πάντως*—*'Ιερος.*, ver. 21, is an erroneous opinion of Meyer; for, even without that sentence, the reasons above given are of weight. But the brevity of Luke's narrative here is, under all circumstances, remarkable; especially that he intimates a visit of Paul to Jerusalem so briefly, with only five words, and mentions only a salutation of the Church. The stay of Paul with the mother Church was doubtless very short.

DOGMATICAL AND ETHICAL THOUGHTS.

The vow, regarding which a certain obscurity will never be entirely cleared away, was at all events a vow taken in the spirit of evangelical freedom, and caused by some special occasion.

HOMILETICAL HINTS.

But Paul remained there yet a considerable time (ver. 18). To please the "much people" who were indicated to him in the heavenly vision, and to profit by the mild disposition of Gallio, so far as it was to be used for the kingdom of Christ, were the reasons which retained Paul so long at Corinth (Rieger).—*For he had a vow.* "Pay thy vows to the Most High." 1. What vows are we permitted to make? No unevangelical vows, by which we think to serve God by dead works and to purchase His grace; but the sincere vows of penitence, faith, and new obedience. 2. How should we pay them? With conscientious zeal to do what we can; with humble renunciation of all merit.

He arrived at Ephesus, and went into the synagogue, and spoke with the Jews (ver. 19). The fellowship of his most beloved brethren was not so pleasant to him, as that he should on that account relinquish intercourse with a people so hostile to him, and give up his efforts to convert them. This is the pattern of a servant who laboured not for himself, but for the Lord Jesus. He is always calumniated and oppressed, and he aims only at glorifying his Saviour (Apost. Past.).

They desired him to remain longer with them, but he consented not (ver. 20). An instructive example of intercourse with brethren. However tender the bond of love, yet he was not subject to them in blind obedience: he refused them their request, because he did not recognise it as the mind and the will of the Lord. This example should teach us not to concede everything to the brethren and pious souls, but to love our God and Saviour above the brethren, and to prefer His will to all human wills (Apost. Past.).—"Whoso loveth father or mother more than Me, is not worthy of Me," Matt. x. 37.

I must keep the feast at Jerusalem (ver. 21, according to the Lutheran text). May God grant us such a determined zeal on our journey to the heavenly Jerusalem, and teach us to oppose this "must" to all the allurements of the world and of the flesh (Apost. Past.).—*If God will, I will come again to you.* As courageous as he was in pursuing the path prescribed to him, as resigned was he in submitting to the leadings of God. He is a lion in the battle with the world, but a lamb under the guidance of the Lord (Apost. Past.).

He went up and saluted the Church, and came down to Antioch (ver. 22). His departure from Jerusalem, immediately connected with his saluting the Church, gives us to understand that at this time he did not find a field of labour at Jerusalem (Rieger).

On the whole section (vers. 18–22).—*I must work while it is day, the motto of the ambassadors of Christ.* 1. Where do they work? Where the Lord shows a way and opens a door. 2. How do they work? With unwearied zeal, but with humble attention to the intimations of the Lord. 3. For what, do they work? Not for their own glory and gain, but everywhere for the kingdom of God, and along with that for the salvation of man.—*The desire after Christian fellowship.* 1. How strong it was with Paul: it drew the apostle, so highly gifted in himself and so richly favoured, from a distance to Jerusalem. 2. How strong it should also be with us (Lisco).—*Paul, on his journeys, an example of a servant of God, obedient to the intimations of the Lord.* 1. No hostile hatred restrains him, where the Lord sends him, ver. 19. 2. No brotherly love retains him, when the Lords calls him away, ver. 20. 3. No place is too distant to him: he hastens, when the Spirit draws him thither, ver. 21. 4. No place is too pleasant to him: he takes his leave, when the Lord cannot use him there, ver. 22.—*I must go up to Jerusalem, the watchword of a pilgrim of God,* by which he breaks through all the temptations of the world, in love and suffering, from friend and foe.

SECTION IV.

THIRD MISSIONARY JOURNEY OF PAUL TO ASIA MINOR, MACEDONIA, AND GREECE: RETURN TO JERUSALEM (CHAP. XVIII. 23–CHAP. XXI. 16).

A.

First Part of this Journey. Labours and Experiences of the Apostle in Asia Minor, particularly at Ephesus.

CHAP. XVIII. 23–XIX. 41.

1. *Commencement of the Journey, and Visit to the Churches in the centre of Asia Minor.* (CHAP. XVIII. 23.)

23 And after he had spent some time there, he departed, and went in order through the Galatian territory and Phrygia, strengthening all the disciples.

2. *Episode concerning Apollos, and his Labours at Ephesus and Corinth.* (CHAP. XVIII. 24–28.)

24 But a Jew, named Apollos, born at Alexandria, an eloquent man and
mighty in the Scriptures, came to Ephesus. 25 This man was instructed
in the way of the Lord, and being fervent in spirit, he spoke and taught
diligently concerning Jesus, knowing only the baptism of John. 26 And

**he began to speak boldly in the synagogue. But when Aquila and Priscilla
had heard him, they took him to them, and explained to him the way of
God more thoroughly. 27 And when he wished to go to Achaia, the
brethren exhorted him to it, and wrote to the disciples to receive him. And
when he was come, he helped them much, through grace, who had believed.
28 For he publicly convinced the Jews with energy, showing by means of
the Scriptures that Jesus is the Christ.**

Ver. 25. The oldest codices, a number of cursive MSS., and versions have 'Ιησοῦ; whilst only the two youngest uncial MSS., G. and H., read *τοῦ κυρίου*, an alteration which was made, because it was not known how to reconcile 'Ιησοῦ with *ἐπιστάμενος*—'*Ιωάννου*.

Ver. 26. The transposition Πρ. *καὶ* 'Ακ. has only a portion of the authorities for it, whilst in ver. 18 all the authorities agree in this position: here the precedence of the wife appears to have been taken from ver. 18.

EXEGETICAL EXPLANATIONS.

1. *He departed.*—This third missionary journey, occurring in the year 54 or 55 after Christ, was at first, exactly as the second missionary journey, directed to the churches already established. However, Phrygia and Galatia only are here named. Pisidia, Pamphylia, and Lycaonia are not mentioned. Whether these provinces, on account of the extreme brevity of the narrative, are unintentionally passed over in silence, or whether Paul only visited the churches in Galatia and Phrygia, founded on his second missionary journey, cannot be determined. Neither are we informed who were his companions; but from chap. xix. 22, it is evident that Erastus and Timotheus must have journeyed with him.

2. *But a Jew named Apollos.*—Before Luke mentions the arrival of Paul at Ephesus, and his labours there, he inserts the narrative concerning Apollos. Baumgarten supposes that the importance of this narrative consists in Apollos being the substitute and representative of Paul at Corinth. But the place which this episode occupies, seems rather to indicate that the attention of Luke was directed to Ephesus, and he relates the appearance of Apollos there, because it occurred not long before the arrival of the apostle.

3. *Apollos* is an abbreviation of *'Απολλώνιος*, as the Codex Cantabrigienses reads. He was a Jew of Alexandria; and as he is described as a man of eloquence (λόγιος, learned and eloquent; but as scriptural learning is here specially mentioned, λόγιος here signifies chiefly eloquent), and of great knowledge

of the Scriptures (δυνατὸς ὢν ἐν ταῖς γραφαῖς, whose strength lay therein), so it is probable that, as an Alexandrian, he was indebted, both for his method of scriptural interpretation and for his eloquence, to the school of Philo.

4. *This man was instructed in the way of the Lord.*—As regards the Christian knowledge of Apollos, Luke represents him as in a measure instructed in the way of the Lord, *i.e.*, in the divine plan of salvation (κύριος here cannot be Jesus of Nazareth, but God the Father) to enlighten and redeem Israel and mankind by the Messiah: he however required a more exact explanation and instruction concerning the way of God (see ver. 26). Luke mentions wherein he was defective: he knew only the baptism of John. Ἐπίστασθαι is here to be understood, not according to its verbal sense, *expertum esse* (Grotius), but according to the common *usus loquendi*, to know —objectively and intelligently to know. Certainly we must understand from this, that he had received only the baptism of John, and perhaps had been instructed by John's disciples. Accordingly he still wanted baptism in the name of Jesus, and along with this, doubtless, both the knowledge of the crucified and risen Saviour, and the gift of the Holy Ghost. With all these defects, Apollos was full of the fervour of inspiration (ζέων), full of zeal and devotion, which constrained him to speak. Therefore he spoke and taught (ἐλάλει, in conversation and intercourse; ἐδίδασκε, in teaching proper) accurately of Jesus. (Ἀκριβῶς may mean *exacta cura et diligentia*, but also *exacte*, the former being subjective, the latter objective; but as ἀκριβῶς cannot be taken in any other sense than ἀκριβέστερον in the next verse, the objective signification is to be preferred, yet in a relative and limited sense.) In such a manner, then, Apollos spoke and taught concerning Jesus; also he commenced to speak in the synagogue, and that with boldness. When Aquila and his wife heard him speak and became interested in him, they recognised both what was good and promising in him and the defects which yet cleaved to him; and they sought to supply these defects by a more thorough, more complete, and deeper instruction (ἀκριβέστερον ἐξέθεντο) concerning the way of God. This comprehended a deeper initiation into the knowledge of the person and work of Jesus Christ.

5. *But when he wished to go into Achaia.*—This wish of

Apollos, after he was further advanced by private instruction, had a twofold reason: first, a delicate reserve might prevent him, after being fully instructed, from again coming forward in Ephesus, where he had already appeared with such unripe and defective knowledge; and secondly, what he had learned from Aquila and his wife about the Corinthian Church, would direct his attention to it. From chap. xix. 1, it appears that he went to Corinth. Here the whole province is named, whose political capital was Corinth. Meyer, after Luther and others, refers *προτρεψάμενοι* to the *μαθηταί* in Achaia: "they wrote exhorting them." This is incorrect: *προτρεψάμενοι* precedes *ἔγραψαν*, and refers to Apollos himself; it means *ad cursum incitare, instigare, ut progrediatur* (so, after Chrysostom, Erasmus, Grotius, and Bengel). There is no ground for supposing that *αὐτόν* must be expressed along with it: it is understood by itself. The writing of the Ephesian Christians to those at Corinth was the first (Christian) letter of recommendation (*ἐπιστολὴ συστατική*).

6. *And when he was come.*—Apollos was of special use to the converts at Corinth: *συμβάλλομαί τινι* is frequently used in classical language in the sense of *prosum, adjuvo. Διὰ τῆς χάριτος* is to be connected with *συνεβάλετο*, not with *πεπιστευκόσι*, as Meyer connects it; for here the attention is directed to Apollos and his labours, and not to the Corinthian Christians. The addition is designed to indicate that the improvement of the Corinthian converts by means of this new preacher was brought about by the grace of God, which was with him. The circumstance mentioned in ver. 28 is introduced by *γάρ*, as a proof of the grace which strengthened him: he confuted, with ability and perfect success, the Jews (*εὐτόνως, intentis omnibus virium nervis*). *Διακατηλέγχετο τοῖς Ἰουδαίοις* is to be understood thus: he adduced complete and striking proofs for his assertion, in opposition to the Jews. *Δημοσίᾳ* is not to be limited to the synagogue as the place of contest,—at least entirely different expressions are employed for this, *e.g.* ver. 26, chap. xix. 8; but rather points to a transaction in a public and open place. What is here related of the nature and mode of the work of Apollos, harmonizes with what Paul himself in 1 Cor. i.–iv. says. Paul planted and Apollos watered; the latter did not lay the foundation, but built thereon (1 Cor. iii. 10), that is to say, forwarded what was already begun.

DOGMATICAL AND ETHICAL THOUGHTS.

1. With an incomplete and defective knowledge, Apollos yet laboured, and after a manner taught solidly. What qualified him for this, was partly his natural gifts, and partly the pre-Christian school of Philo; but also an acquaintance with the Scriptures of the Old Testament, and a knowledge of Jesus, though certainly very defective. What, however, is especially to be taken into account, is his fervent zeal. This constrained him to discourse and to labour. A little light is still light; and whoever traffics faithfully with a few pounds, to him more will be entrusted. A heart eager for the truth and beating warmly, even although it has not the full and sacred fire of the Spirit of the Father and of the Son, is led further into all truth. There is a difference when the low stand-point of an individual rests on unblameable ignorance, and when it rests on blameable retrogression.

2. It is instructive, that a man so important and influential in the apostolic age as Apollos should have been indebted to a plain married couple, as Aquila and Priscilla, for his peculiar preparation for his ministry, and for his thorough introduction into positive Christian truth. These were the persons who first took notice of him and his promising gifts, but who also recognised what was defective in him: these were they who initiated him, certainly more highly gifted and more learned than themselves, more thoroughly in the Christian truth: these were they who assisted his coming to Corinth, and did their best to place the right man in the right place. Accordingly, here simple laity, and especially a woman of a pious disposition and of solid Christian knowledge, have performed what, according to our ideas, is the business of theological educational institutions and ecclesiastical boards,—a proof of the universal priesthood of the apostolic times. This is also a remarkable example how, in the kingdom of Christ, events are mutually connected. The Apostle Paul formed a connection with Aquila and Priscilla at Corinth, and probably was the instrument of their conversion. After longer intercourse, and certainly also after a prosperous growth in grace, they accompanied the apostle to Ephesus. They there became acquainted with Apollos, and interested themselves in him, assisting him in Christian knowledge. And now Apollos, so prepared

by this married couple, allied to the apostle, comes to Corinth, and steps into the apostle's field of labour. Thus the streams of grace flow hither and thither, and what is done to one member produces good to another. The fruitful seed-grains fly up and down, and indications of blessing may be traced here and there; but the guidance is in the hand of the Lord of the Church.

3. That Apollos was profitable to the Christians at Corinth to their spiritual growth, was the gift of grace, ver. 27. It is not to be ascribed to his natural abilities, nor to the school through which he passed, nor to the persons who imparted to him deeper Christian knowledge, nor to his own inspiration and fervour, but to the grace of God, if actual profit and blessing followed. "Neither is he that planteth anything, nor he that watereth; but God who giveth the increase:" 1 Cor. iii. 7.

HOMILETICAL HINTS.

He went through Galatia and Phrygia, strengthening the disciples (ver. 23). Many attend only to the awakening; but if, neglecting the strengthening and establishing of souls, they do not trouble themselves about the awakened, and do not fan the spark of a begun conversion, everything goes to ruin (Apost. Past.).

On Apollos (vers. 24–26). Apollos exhibits a beautiful union of natural and gracious gifts in a teacher. 1. He was naturally eloquent. 2. He was mighty in the Scriptures, by which his natural eloquence received a sterling value. 3. He was instructed in the way of the Lord, having pressed from a mere dead knowledge of the Scriptures to a Christian knowledge of the divine plan of salvation, though at first his knowledge was imperfect. 4. He was fervent in spirit, filled with a noble zeal to make his knowledge fruitful, to work for the kingdom of God. 5. And as the fairest and rarest quality along with so many gifts, he was desirous of learning and teachable, permitting himself to be led more deeply into Christianity by Aquila and Priscilla, two simple Christians.—*Apollos, a model of a Christian teacher.* He should be, 1. learned in human arts and sciences, but, above all, in the Scriptures; 2. fit to teach, to which not only natural eloquence, but, still more, holy zeal is necessary (fervent in spirit); 3. teachable, in order that he may make progress, not only by his own research, but also by humble learning from living Christians.—*An eloquent man.* Eloquence is a noble gift of God, when it is properly employed, whether in the Church or in the State; but if it is abused, it is as a sword in the hand of a madman (Starke).—*Mighty in the Scriptures.* Not mere knowledge of the literal meaning, but blessed experience of the Scriptures in the heart, makes teachers mighty in the Scriptures to edify others from them (Apost. Past.).—*Instructed in the way of the Lord.* Every Christian ought to be so, but much more every teacher, otherwise he is a blind leader of the blind (Starke). —*He spoke with a fervent spirit* (Luther's translation). When the heart of a teacher is pervaded with the love of Christ, and inflamed with the fire of the Holy Ghost, then fire proceeds from him, and kindles hearts (Apost. Past.).—But alas! if the enthusiasm and the zeal pass away with the moment. Then are teachers stocks without life, who have neither spirit nor power from Christ (Starke).—*Knowing only the baptism of John.* In the Christian Church at many periods, especially when a new great advance of the kingdom of God is at hand, there have been teachers who have been compared, not without reason, to John the Baptist. They were appointed to excite attention to the new era which was coming, to point to a new life, compared with which the present condition was dead; but they could not produce the new itself. They stood at the threshold of the new ecclesiastical era, and so far illuminated it with their bright light, that the disciples saw the entrance, through which their teachers were unable to guide them. The disciples must learn to look beyond their master to the true Master. Thus the great Schleiermacher (Williger).—*Aquila and Priscilla took him, and explained to him the way of God more thoroughly.* He who knows Jesus, can instruct in the Bible the most learned (Apost. Past.).—It is the sign of a humble spirit, that however learned a man may be, he learns from others, though it were from a tradesman (Starke).—The first Epistle to the Corinthians shows how greatly Apollos assisted the believers at Corinth. "All things are yours, whether Paul or Apollos," writes the apostle, with unenvious joy at the noble gift, which was imparted to his beloved Church in this helper of their salvation (Besser).

He helped them much, through grace, who had believed (ver. 27). With all his fair gifts and powers, yet he helped them only through grace. Grace alone makes the word fruitful and living (Apost. Past.).

He publicly convinced the Jews by the Scriptures (ver. 28). In the schools of philosophy, there is no proof more certain than a mathematical demonstration: in the Church of Christ, none is more to be depended on than that taken from the holy Scriptures (Starke).—Apollos, a proof that learning and education may be very useful in building the kingdom of God (Lisco).—*How the high cultivation of the mind may be serviceable in the kingdom of God.* 1. When it rests on the foundation of faith (ver. 25). 2. When it does not close itself against further learning (ver. 26). 3. When it is directed to the proper place (vers. 27, 28), (Lisco).—*Growth in Christian knowledge.* 1. Necessary for all, even for the gifted, ver. 24. 2. Attainable, by humble desire of learning, ver. 26. 3. Fruitful, by blessed working for God, vers. 27, 28.—*Apollos in Alexandria and Apollos in Ephesus; or, the high school of worldly knowledge and the low school of spiritual experience.* 1. What we may learn in the former school. 2. What we can only learn in the latter school.—*The blessed progress of Apollos;* or, To him that hath shall be given, and he shall have abundance. 1. What Apollos possessed. Not only a fair talent of natural gifts, but also an honest zeal to traffic with his talent by learning and teaching. 2. What was given to him, that he might have abundance. To his knowledge, the full light of the knowledge of Jesus Christ; and to his work, the all-sufficient power of divine grace.—*Paul and Apollos, two different and yet two blessed instruments of the Lord.* The material from which, the way by which, and the purpose for which, the Lord prepared them.

3. *Arrival of Paul at Ephesus. He meets with certain of John's Disciples, whom he leads to the full grace of Christ.* (CHAP. XIX. 1–7).

1 But it came to pass, that, while Apollos was at Corinth, Paul, having
passed through the upper districts, came to Ephesus, and found certain
disciples. 2 And he said to them, Have ye received the Holy Ghost since
ye believed? And they answered him, No, we have not so much as heard
whether there is a Holy Ghost. 3 And he said, To what then were ye bap-
tized? They answered, To John's baptism. 4 But Paul said, John indeed
administered the baptism to repentance, saying to the people that they

should believe on Him who should come after him, that is, on Jesus. 5 When
they heard this, they were baptized in the name of the Lord Jesus. 6 And
when Paul laid his hands on them, the Holy Ghost came on them; and they
spoke with tongues, and prophesied. 7 And all the men were about twelve.

Ver. 1. Tischendorf and Lachmann, after A.B., some cursive MSS. and the Vulgate, have received εὑρεῖν and εἶπέν τε (ver. 2); whilst the reading εὑρών—εἶπε is an evident conjecture.

Ver. 2. Εἶπον before πρὸς αὐτὸν is wanting in many important MSS., and is a spurious addition.

Ver. 3. Πρὸς αὐτούς is also a spurious addition.

Ver. 4. Only the two youngest uncial MSS. have τὸν Χριστὸν before Ἰησοῦν: it is certainly spurious.

EXEGETICAL EXPLANATIONS.

1. *But it came to pass.*—Ἀνωτερικὰ μέρη are, in comparison with the sea-coast, where Ephesus was situated, the inland and more elevated districts, as Galatia and Phrygia, chap. xviii. 23. Paul had been at an earlier period prevented by the Holy Ghost from labouring in the western coasts of Asia Minor, and on his return from his second missionary journey he had paid only a flying visit to Ephesus; but now he was permitted to reside all the longer, and with greater benefit, in that city.

2. *He found certain disciples.*—Luke calls the men, mentioned in vers. 1–6, μαθητάς, *i.e.*, Christians, certainly in a wide sense. The apostle must have been induced, by the observations which he made, to doubt whether they on their conversion had received the gift of the Holy Ghost, and to put the question expressly. But this very question, and especially the word πιστεύσαντες, rests evidently on the supposition that they are, in point of fact, Christians. Their answer with ἀλλά supposes, first of all, a negative answer. They go further, and express themselves unreservedly, that they had not learned even by hearsay, far less by personal reception, whether a Holy Ghost existed. This must evidently be taken according to the meaning of the question, *i.e.*, the Holy Ghost as a gift of God in Christ, and as a Christian spiritual communication to men. The meaning cannot be, that they had never heard whether there was a Holy Spirit of God. Men who had received the baptism of John, must necessarily have had the knowledge of God and of the Messiah, and also of the Spirit of God; especially as we must consider these disciples to be Jews by birth, for the silence of Luke on their Jewish descent proves nothing; their expressions by no means point to

a heathen origin, and there is no trace whatever that the disciples of John had spread among the Gentiles.

3. *To what then were ye baptized?*—This question can have no other meaning than, To what did the baptism ye received refer? Their answer, at all events, shows a want of clearness in their views. They do not certainly say, *εἰς τὸν Ἰωάννην*: that would be opposed to the humility and the entire character of the Baptist. But we may not therefore accept it as the evident meaning of the answer (as Meyer does), "To that which constituted the subject of John's baptism," namely, repentance and faith in the coming Messiah. This was the case in point of fact, and certainly these disciples had been baptized to the (unknown) Messiah; but it appears that the clear consciousness of this was wanting to them: otherwise Paul would not have instructed them on this point, ver. 4. The opinion of Wetstein, that these men had been instructed by Apollos, before his deeper acquaintance with Christianity, has no positive point of defence.

4. *John indeed administered the baptism of repentance.*—Paul states shortly and well the nature of the baptism of John: it signified only change of disposition; it was only a baptism of repentance, united with the duty of believing on Him who should come after. *Ἵνα* is not to be understood strictly in the sense of purpose: "he administered baptism, in order that they might believe" (Meyer); but it is to be understood, in conformity with the gradual expansion, in course of time, of concise expressions in the development of the Greek language, for the infinitive, as the object of the saying and the exhortation. When Paul adds, that is to say, on Jesus, he unites the fulfilment to the promise, and testifies that though the baptism of John was in fact not a baptism to Jesus, yet essentially it pointed to none other than to Him. In consequence of this declaration, these disciples of John were baptized to Jesus as the Lord. *Εἰς τὸ ὄνομα*, to the belief and confession of Him.

5. *They were baptized in the name of the Lord Jesus.*—Whether the baptism was administered by the apostle himself or by another, is not said. However, as the imposition of hands is expressly asserted of the apostle, it would seem that the baptism was not administered by himself. In consequence of the imposition of hands, after the complete Christian baptism, the bap-

tized received the Holy Ghost, whose operation was made apparent in speaking with tongues and in inspired effusions.

DOGMATICAL AND ETHICAL THOUGHTS.

1. The disciples of John, even before they received the proper Christian baptism, and came to the full knowledge and confession of Jesus, were regarded as disciples, that is, as Christians. Luke calls them *μαθηταί*, and the apostle presumes them to be converted and baptized. Thus, even in the apostolic time, there existed a wider as well as a narrower circle of the discipleship of Christ, that is to say, of the Church. The christianizing of nations, and still less the intertwining of ecclesiastical and political relations, did not, for the first time, cause the Church to be divided into a narrower and a wider circle; but the reason of this division lies in the spread of Christianity generally. What, however, forms the proper boundary between the narrower and the wider circle, is nothing else than the relation to the person of Jesus Christ Himself. Whoever is united to Him in heart and spirit, by faith on the one hand, and by grace on the other, belongs to the narrower circle of His people. Whereas he who stands in a merely distant and purely external relation to the personal Redeemer, is incorporated into the wider circle.

2. For the last time, John the Baptist, in the effects of his work, is mentioned in the New Testament. How widely his influence stretched itself in the world, and how long it endured, is to be measured from the fact, that in the heathen commercial city of Ephesus, about the year 55 after Christ, almost a generation later than the Baptist himself, twelve of his disciples were baptized, who indeed had joined themselves to the Church of Christ, but had not stepped beyond John and his baptism. Indeed, they had rather retrograded, as easily happens on a wider extension and longer duration of a tendency, when the originator of the tendency is withdrawn, and there is wanting a pure and living vehicle of communication (as Scripture and the Holy Ghost in the Church of Christ). However, it is still the best sign of susceptibility for progress and truth, that these twelve are baptized to Jesus, and the remainder of the disciples of John pass over to the Church of Christ, instead of closing themselves against the full truth and grace, and of becoming hardened on

their stand-point. Only, in one word, it is to be observed, that the so-called Johannic Christians (Mandeans) in Mesopotamia stand in no historical connection with John the Baptist: they never applied this name to themselves; it was only introduced by Christian travellers and theologians (see Herzog's Encyclopedia: article Mandeans).

3. The administration of baptism to John's disciples has given rise to many dogmatical doubts. The Reformers (Calvin and Beza), and the later Lutheran theologians, thought that they were obliged to defend ver. 5 partly against the notions of the Anabaptists, and partly against the dogma of Trent concerning the essential difference between the baptism of John and the Christian baptism. In opposition to the Anabaptists, Calvin adopted the unhappy evasion of interpreting ver. 5, not of the baptism of water, but of the baptism of the Spirit; so that ver. 6 only explains what is meant in ver. 5. But undeniably ver. 5 speaks of the baptism of water. This circumstance, however, is of no service to the opponents of infant baptism. The twelve were not baptized a second time because they had been baptized as infants, but because the baptism which they had received was not the full Christian baptism: a circumstance which is not in the least in favour of the repetition of the Christian baptism. And as regards the Roman canon, that the baptism of John has not the same efficacy as the baptism of Christ, there is nothing opposed to this in Scripture; and only dogmatical prejudices could lead to the opinion that the baptism of John was not essentially, but only in its accidents, different from the baptism of Christ. And because our passage contradicts this opinion, violence has been done to it, and ver. 5 has been regarded as the expression of Paul concerning John's baptism. This requires no confutation. The twelve disciples, at all events, had not been baptized to the person of Jesus, and this had to be supplied. Only in Jesus Christ, and for the sake of Christ, is the Spirit imparted. True baptism, and along with it fellowship with the Redeemer Himself, and not the imposition of hands, *i.e.*, apostolic authority (as Baumgarten supposes), is the condition of the gift of the Spirit.

HOMILETICAL HINTS.

Paul came to Ephesus, and found certain disciples (ver. 1).

Paul would not have so often found, had he not been diligent in seeking. He who seeks, finds. With Paul the blessing was always at hand, because his whole heart was directed to the cause.—Although these men were still very weak in experience and in knowledge, yet the Holy Ghost numbers them among the disciples. Thus a beginner in Christianity is worthy of this noble name, if he has only in God's eyes a heart desirous of salvation. A teacher should interest himself in such souls in an entirely peculiar manner. These are the sucklings, to whom we ought to show the fidelity of a nurse (Apost. Past.).—The fashion of some Christians of modern times, which exhibits neither great love nor great knowledge, to consider Christianity only in its highest perfection, as the true Christianity, was not the manner of the apostle (Menken).

Have ye received the Holy Ghost? (ver. 2.) This was the theme of all the apostle's inquiries. He sought by many inquiries to convince himself, according to the course of their conversion, whether the experiences had been thoroughly felt, which the Holy Ghost alone can effect by His indwelling in man. And all their answers referred to this: "We know as yet nothing of the Holy Ghost" (Williger).—And must not, in the present day, many disciples, to whom we must concede a certain degree of Christian knowledge and Christian conduct, yet honestly confess, We as yet know nothing of the Holy Ghost, of the spirit of repentance, of the new birth, of adoption, of freedom, and of love?

To what then were ye baptized? (ver. 3.) This question all Christians ought to ask themselves daily; for "every one, during his whole life, has to learn and to make use of baptism, for he has to make it his constant business to believe firmly what it promises and brings: victory over the devil and death, the forgiveness of sins, God's grace, the whole Christ, and the Holy Ghost with all His gifts" (Luther).

But Paul said, John indeed administered the baptism of repentance (ver. 4). How honourably does Paul here speak of John! He does not detract from this servant of God, but exhibits his sacred ministry which he in his days performed, and shows that it lay not with him, but with men, if they did not use it aright. So it ought to be. It is not good to despise and depreciate other teachers (Apost. Past.).—After this passage, no mention occurs of the Baptist in the New Testament. Here at last he wholly gives place to Christ (Bengel).

When they heard that, they were baptized (ver. 5). Before the completion of the work of redemption, the baptism of John as a baptism to Christ, as to Him who was to come, was the true baptism; but after Pentecost, the true baptism is a baptism pointing back to Christ as to Him who has already come, a baptism into Christ as the present One, and the mediation by means of the forerunner now ceases.—"Therefore the baptism of John is now of no more value. If one says, I baptize thee with the baptism of John the Baptist for the forgiveness of sins, that would not be rightly to be baptized; for his baptism was only a precursor of the forgiveness of sins. But we ought to say simply, All thy sins are forgiven thee through the coming of the Lord Jesus Christ; I baptize thee in the name of the Father, and of the Son, and of the Holy Ghost. That is, I take away all thy sins; I do not send thee further, as John has done. But John was obliged to say, Prepare yourselves, and receive Him who will give to you in baptism the Holy Ghost, and bring forgiveness of sins" (Luther).—Those who were baptized with the baptism of John were rebaptized, because John was not the ground of our justification and the bestower of the Holy Ghost, but only the herald of the Spirit and of saving grace, which Christ soon after acquired for us, as the only ground and Author of our justification (Justus Jonas).—Whoever clearly understood the true and complete meaning of the baptism of John, as the forerunner of Jesus, did not require, as a follower of Jesus Christ, a new baptism. But when John was regarded as the head of a sect, and his baptism as a ceremony, then it could not be counted, and could not operate as the Christian baptism (Rieger and Apost. Past.).

And when Paul laid his hands on them, the Holy Ghost came on them. And all the men were about twelve (vers. 6, 7). The twelve were furnished, by the supplicating and consecrating hands of the apostle, with the gifts of the Holy Ghost, a new company of disciples, appointed for this purpose to be a seed of the Church in Asia; in a similar manner as the twelve apostles, who were formerly in part the disciples of John, and only after the outpouring of the Holy Ghost became the true disciples of

Christ, and a living seed for the regeneration of the world (Williger).

On the whole section (vers. 1–7).—Paul, our instructor in the proper pastoral care. 1. His pastorate has the proper extent. 2. It has the proper diligence and zeal. 3. It is performed with the proper wisdom (Leupold).—*To whom were ye baptized?* 1. To God the Father, as ye have received the adoption of God. 2. To God the Son, as ye have redemption through Him by His blood. 3. To God the Holy Ghost, as ye have become the temples of God (Leonh. and Spieg.).—*Resemblance of many Christians among us to the disciples of John at Ephesus.* 1. Wherein it is seen (vers. 1–4). 2. What must on this account take place with many Christians (vers. 5–7).—*We ought to regard those as belonging to us, who yet stand on a lower step of the truth.* 1. Who these are. 2. How we ought to reckon them as belonging to us (Lisco).—*Have ye received the Holy Ghost? a testing question to all who call themselves the disciples of Jesus.* For only in the power of the Holy Ghost is our faith proved to be living (ver. 2), our baptism to be blessed (vers. 3, 4), and our tongue to be consecrated to the service of the Lord (ver. 6).—*To what were ye baptized? a powerful admonition to all baptized persons:* to remind them, 1. of the divine ground, on which baptism rests —Jesus Christ, vers. 4, 5; 2. of the holy duty, which proceeds from baptism—repentance and faith, ver. 4; 3. of the blessed fruit, which springs from baptism—the gifts of the Holy Ghost, ver. 6.—*The twelve disciples of John and the twelve disciples of Jesus; or, One is your master, even Christ.* 1. Human masters may transmit their words; Christ only can impart His Spirit. 2. Human masters may teach the elements; Christ only can conduct to the goal. 3. Human masters may establish schools; Christ only can found a church.

4. *Further Labours of the Apostle at Ephesus: his teaching and miracles.* (CHAP. XIX. 8–20.)

8 And he went into the synagogue, and stood up boldly, for the space of three months, discoursing and endeavouring to convince concerning the kingdom of God. 9 But when certain were hardened and unbelieving, and calumniated that way before the multitude, he departed from them, and separated the disciples, discoursing daily in the lecture-room of one Tyrannus.
10 And this continued for the space of two years: so that all the inhabi-

tants of Asia heard the word of the Lord, both Jews and Greeks. 11 Also
God wrought not common deeds by the hand of Paul; 12 So that even
handkerchiefs and aprons from his skin were laid on the sick; and the
sicknesses departed from them; and the evil spirits went out of them.
13 But certain of the strolling Jewish exorcists presumed to call the name
of the Lord Jesus over them who had evil spirits, saying, I adjure thee
by the Jesus whom Paul preaches. 14 And there were certain sons of
Sceva, a Jewish chief priest, seven of them, who did so. 15 But the evil
spirit answered, and said, Jesus I know, and Paul I know; but who are
ye? 16 And the man, in whom the evil spirit was, leaped upon them,
overcame both, and prevailed against them; so that they fled from that
house naked and wounded. 17 And this was known to all the Jews and
Greeks who dwelt at Ephesus; and there fell a fear upon all, and the name
of the Lord Jesus was magnified. 18 And many of them who believed
came and confessed, and announced what they had done. 19 And many
who had practised superstitious things brought together their books, and
burned them in the presence of all; and they counted the price of it, and
found it to be fifty thousand pieces. 20 So mightily grew and prevailed
the word of the Lord.

Ver. 9. Τινός after Τυράννου is indeed wanting in some MSS., but it might easily have been omitted.

Ver. 10. Ἰησοῦ after κυρίου has only one uncial MS. for it.

Ver. 12. Ἀποφέρεσθαι is as strongly attested as ἐπιφέρεσθαι; but it would sooner be altered into ἐπιφ. than the reverse, and therefore the former is to be considered as genuine.

Ver. 13. Ὁρκίζω is much more strongly attested than the plural ὁρκίζομεν, which, for the sake of sameness with ἐπεχείρησαν—λέγοντες, was put instead of the singular.

Ver. 16. Ἀμφοτέρων before ἴσχυσεν is better attested than αὐτῶν, which later transcribers substituted, as in the narrative elsewhere there is no mention of two only being concerned in the matter. If ἀμφοτέρων were not originally there, it would not have been inserted.

EXEGETICAL EXPLANATIONS.

1. *But he went into the synagogue.*—His labours in the synagogue lasted for a quarter of a year. So long there was no opposition on the part of the rulers or of individual members of the Jewish community; and the apostle was permitted to discourse boldly, and with all openness, concerning the kingdom of God, in order to win souls for it (πείθων). The supposition that Paul here discoursed with peculiar mildness (Baumgarten) is not supported by ἐπαῤῥησιάζετο.

2. *But when certain were hardened.*—A crisis now took place. Some became by degrees closed and decided against the offers of grace in Christ. The imperfect ἐσκληρύνοντο καὶ

ἠπείθουν gives us to understand that this spiritual condition was gradually developed, and then became lasting. At length it proceeded so far that they indulged in open abuse against Christianity in the synagogue. Ἡ ὁδός, the way of salvation which God has prepared and opened up for men (see chap. xviii. 26). This induced the apostle, not only himself to give up all fellowship with the synagogue, but also to separate the Christians from it (ἀφώρισε). Henceforth he chose, for the place of his discourses, the lecture-room of one Tyrannus, who is otherwise unknown. The lecture-rooms of philosophers were called by the later Greeks σχολαί; and as the place is here mentioned under a purely Greek name, nothing is more natural than to suppose that its possessor was a Greek, perhaps a rhetorician and public teacher of rhetoric. Suidas mentions a sophist of the same name, but without determining his abode and age, who wrote a work, περὶ στάσεως καὶ διαιρέσεως λόγοι. The circumstance that Luke neither intimates the going over to the Gentiles (as in chap. xiii. 46, xviii. 6, 7), nor distinguishes Tyrannus as a proselyte (compare chap. xviii. 7), does not make the opinion (of Meyer) probable, that this man was a Jewish rabbi, and the proprietor of a private synagogue (בֵּית מִדְרָשׁ). Both σχολή and the name Tyrannus—which, indeed, occurs in Josephus, Ant. xvi. 10, 3; Bell. Jud. i. 26, 3 (both times the same person), and in 2 Macc. iv. 40 (in a doubtful reading), but there also not as the name of an Israelite—point to a Greek.

3. *Discoursing daily.*—This hall stood open to the apostle, not only on the Sabbath, but at all times, and was used by him for two years (from the year 55 to 57); a space of time which is undoubtedly to be understood exclusive of the three months mentioned in ver. 8. Both on account of the importance of the city, its active commerce, and its famous temple, and in consequence of the labour of the apostle lasting for upwards of two years, it is easy to understand that Ephesus became a centre of evangelization for the whole country of Asia (in the narrow sense: proconsular Asia), so that the population of the western coast of Asia Minor, far and wide, heard the word of the Lord. Πάντες οἱ κατοικ. is evidently hyperbolical; however, ἀκοῦσαι τὸν λόγον τοῦ κυρίου is not to be understood of hearing Paul himself, but may very well also include hearsay. How many Asiatics might, in the course of two years, journey as pilgrims

to the temple of Artemis, or come to the city in the way of business, and during their stay there hear Paul, who caused a sensation, in the lecture-room open to all, and might afterwards relate it in their homes.

4. *And God wrought no common deeds.*—Besides teaching, Luke relates the practical works of the apostle, the miracles of healing which God effected through him (by means of the imposition of hands, διὰ τῶν χειρῶν). Δυνάμεις οὐ τὰς τυχούσας, *i.e.*, extraordinary works of power. Ὁ τυχών means the first whom one accidentally meets; hence common, unimportant. As proofs and examples of this general statement, Luke adduces two things: 1. That Paul cast out evil spirits, healed the possessed (this, in consequence of the narrative which follows, is mentioned in the second instance); 2. That clothes which were used for cleansing by Paul, and had come in contact with his skin, handkerchiefs and aprons (σουδάριον, from *sudor*, *sudarium*; σιμικίνθιον, from *semicinctium*), were laid upon the sick, in consequence of which they were healed. It is here, indeed, to be observed, that Paul himself by no means adopted this plan, but rather, according to ver. 11, healed by the imposition of hands. Others, however, who had confidence in him, hit upon such means. Nevertheless healing was obtained in such cases.

5. *And evil spirits went out of them.*—The cure of demoniacs by the apostle in the name of Jesus was imitated by the sons of Sceva, a Jewish chief priest (perhaps connected with the family of the high priest, or chief of one of the twenty-four priestly courses), otherwise unknown,—men of the description that then wandered about the Roman world, many of them of Jewish origin, as exorcists, wonder-workers, and conjurers. The circumstance that the name of Jesus had received an importance in Ephesus, and the fact that Paul had cured demoniacs by the invocation of this name, led these seven sons of Sceva to the attempt to use the name of Jesus for the exorcism and the expulsion of demons. This, two of the seven brethren (as is evident from the genuine reading ἀμφοτέρων, ver. 16) did in a certain instance. But they came badly off. Not only did the demon, who spoke by the possessed, answer the exorcists with contempt, as men whom he did not know, whose authority he did not recognise as he did that of Jesus and of His apostle Paul; but the possessed man, whom they thought to heal by

conjuring, rushed upon them with fury and maltreated them, so that with torn garments and wounds, and certainly also with scorn and shame, they fled from the house.

6. *And this was known.*—This event, which became known in Ephesus, created an immense sensation, and excited an indefinite fear of the mysterious power which was attached to the name of Jesus (φόβος): the name of Jesus rose in public estimation (ἐμεγαλύνετο). This occurrence caused those who were already converted to come (ἤρχοντο) to the apostle, and publicly to confess what they had done. Πεπιστευκότες are certainly not those who now for the first time, in consequence of the impression made by this last occurrence, were converted (Meyer), but, in accordance with the perfect tense, such as had already been converted and continued believers. See Dogmatical and Ethical Thoughts, No. 4. The πράξεις, which they announced, were certainly not acts of faith which they had performed (Luther); this contradicts not only the New Testament usage of ἐξομολογούμενοι, which always denotes confession of sins, but also the connection of the passage. Only πράξεις need not on that account be limited to magical deeds, but must be understood in a comprehensive sense of sinful deeds in general.

7. *And many who practised superstitious things*, had engaged in magic and such like, brought their magical books (probably directions for soothsaying and magic). Τὰ περίεργα πραξάντες, a mild expression, *res curiosæ*, which is often used for magical things. Ephesus was reckoned as the seat of pure magic, which was originally connected with the worship of Artemis. The ἐφέσια γράμματα were especially celebrated, magical sentences on paper or parchment, which, as preventives of possible dangers, were repeated to ward off impending evils or to acquire success, or were carried about as amulets. The former possessors burned their books openly, as formerly the writing of Protagoras concerning the gods was burned by the State, and as the emperor Augustus collected and burned the soothsaying books. They reckoned their value (τὰς τιμὰς, the prime cost), and summed it up (εὗρον, found as the sum) to 50,000 pieces. The coins, according to which it was here reckoned, are doubtless drachmæ, the common Greek silver coin, which was also current with the Jews after the captivity. Accordingly, as a drachma was equal to 7 new groschens or 24 kreutzers, a sum of about

from 11,000 to 12,000 thalers or about 20,000 florins would result.[1] Grotius and others, lately Tiele, Studien und Kritiken, 1858, p. 763, think that the money was reckoned according to the Hebrew shekel; according to which mode of reckoning, it would amount to four times that sum. But it is in the highest degree improbable that the possessors of these books, who were doubtless Greeks, would have estimated the price according to foreign, and not according to their own money.

DOGMATICAL AND ETHICAL THOUGHTS.

1. Christianity is not schismatic. As long as it was possible that same apostle, who had with the greatest earnestness contended for freedom from the law and for the independence of the Church of Christ, continued in the synagogue. And only in consequence of open blasphemies against the truth, against which he found no protection in the synagogue, Paul resolved to separate from it, and to constitute an entirely independent church.

2. The cure of the sick by means of clothes, which had come in contact with the body of the apostle, is certainly something in the highest degree surprising. Although, as is evident, it was not advised or encouraged by Paul, yet he must have known of it and permitted it. The occurrence indeed is not to be put in the category of the worship of relics (Baur), because it is evident that the healing and miraculous virtue were not supposed to reside in the clothes, so that they might at any time be used for healing; but the healing was conditioned by the living personality of the apostle, and these clothes were the medium of his miraculous power only when directly taken from him (ἀποφέρεσθαι ἀπὸ τοῦ χρωτὸς αὐτοῦ). And beyond all doubt, the faith of those sick persons was not only the condition of their susceptibility, but also the motive to that course of action, at which certainly also the name of Jesus would be invoked in pious prayer. Magnetic influence cannot be regarded as something analogous to that mode of healing. However, the impression remains unobliterated, that this kind of healing represented the extreme limit of Christian miracles, and that it could not have been exceeded without danger of going astray into the magical.

3. In a remarkable manner, there stands alongside of this, as a warning, an actual magical abuse of the name of Jesus. The

[1] About L.1770.

Jewish exorcists sought to employ the name of Jesus in their idolatrous superstition, but in vain. Not only did they effect nothing, but they came ignominiously off; and deservedly so, for they took the sacred name of the Redeemer in vain. They wished only to benefit themselves, and to employ the name of Jesus for that purpose. And according to their notion, the mere utterance of the name of Jesus, without sincere faith in Him and personal union with Him, was to produce the desired effect on the possessed. This is magic, when the mere dead formula is substituted for the morally determined will and the religious character. These exorcists confess that they stand in no personal relation to Jesus, calling Him, "the Jesus whom Paul preached." But Paul preached Jesus, because he believed on Him: "I believe, and therefore do I speak." Therefore he could perform works in the name of Jesus, which were impossible for the others to do. This is also contained in the answer of the evil spirit. He knows Jesus, as the Master and Conqueror of the world of fallen spirits. He knows Paul, who was furnished with the power of Jesus Christ, because he was morally united to Him by true conversion and faith. On the other hand, he asks, "But who are ye?" They wanted the intrinsic worth and the power of the inner man, only to be obtained by inward and true fellowship with the Redeemer.

4. The confession. Many believers came and confessed what they had done. It makes a difference whether these were such as were just now converted, or had been already converted. Meyer considers the latter as impossible, because change of mind was the condition of faith. But according to the words, no other view is possible than that those are here spoken of, who had already at an earlier period been converted. These still partially continued in their idolatrous superstitions: change of mind and conversion had not yet completely penetrated everything; even the insight into the sinfulness of their superstitious dealings, and of many other things, might not have been so clear to them as it had become in consequence of this late event. How tenaciously does custom cleave, and how easily after better times may an idolatrous disposition again creep in among those who yet are Christians! There can be no doubt that those who confessed, had been believers for a considerable time. But now by this remarkable occurrence the Spirit of God obtained a pene-

trating power for renewal and sanctification. He imparted to them knowledge of sin and sincere repentance (*passiva contritio*, not *activa*, not artificial repentance. Art. Smalc. iii.). Secondly, they confess their deeds (*confessio*). Thirdly, they act up to their confession: they bring their magical books, and burn them publicly. But all this is not legal, but truly evangelical. For, first, all this takes place of their own accord, on the impulse of the Spirit, who convinces them of sin; not on account of an objective ordinance, an external command, or even a social constraint. Secondly, what they do has not in the least the character of a *satisfactio operis*, in order to atone for sin, or to procure thereby forgiveness and eternal life; but it was the voluntary and indispensable result of sincere and honest repentance, which urges a man to free himself completely from all sin, and from all enticement and occasion to sin.

HOMILETICAL HINTS.

He went into the synagogue, and preached boldly for the space of three months (ver. 8). How Paul acted toward the twelve men is a model of private pastoral care; now information is given of his public labours (Rieger).—He did not creep with those twelve and with the other few disciples into a corner, in order to edify himself alone with them, when none others were present, but he also regarded the other Ephesians as his congregation. The Gospel is to be preached on the house-tops (Williger).

But when certain were hardened, he departed from them, and separated the disciples (ver. 9). Here the object was not to cast pearls before swine. Paul here created no schism; for he separated the disciples not from the true, but from the false church (Gossner).—As a watchful shepherd, he observed the mangy sheep, and separated the healthy, lest they should be infected (Apost. Past.).

And this continued for the space of two years (ver. 10). How blessed is a land, city, or village, when God makes the light of His Gospel shine! (Starke.)—But how great is the judgment on the darkness, on which the shining of the light has fallen, but which has not comprehended and retained it! (Leonh. and Spieg.).—*So that all who dwelt in Asia heard the word of the Lord.* The opportunity which a man has had of hearing the

Gospel is reckoned to him by God as if he had heard it, even although he has not actually heard it (Starke).—Not accidentally does Paul treat, in his Epistle to the Ephesians, in an especial manner, of the mystery of church-fellowship. Ephesus was the bond of union between the churches in the east and in the west, and the centre of the Church in the province of Asia. In these two successful years, when Paul taught in Ephesus, four churches were formed in the province of Asia: along with the original Church in Ephesus, the branch churches of Colosse (Col. i. 7), Laodicea (Col. iv. 15, 16), and Hierapolis (Col. iv. 13). We have thus seen flourish three times four churches of apostolic planting, twelve trees to the praise of the Lord, sprung from the root of Jesse: four in Lycaonia and Pisidia, four in Macedonia and Greece, and four in the province of Asia (Besser).

So that from his body were brought unto the sick handkerchiefs and aprons (ver. 12). These were no relics of a dead man, but the instruments of a living, wonder-working apostle, with whose death and ministry these miracles ceased. They were not preserved in order to perform by them similar miracles in the future; besides, the power was not derived from them, but from God and Christ (Starke).—As formerly, in Jerusalem, the shadow of Peter did not work miracles, so neither here at Ephesus did the handkerchiefs of Paul. If a healing efficacy actually manifested itself from them, it resulted from the living Christ, whose power was mighty in the weakness of His instruments, so that from their body, as well as from their spirit, streams of living water flowed; and this power operated on the sick, not by corporeal touch, but by the spiritual "rapport" of faith.—*Wherefore is the Romish worship of relics, a dead idolatrous worship?* 1. Because it expects salvation from dead instruments: from bones, rags, and pieces of wood, instead of from the living God and His spiritual instruments. 2. Because it receives salvation with a dead hand: with the dead works of pilgrimages and ceremonies, instead of with the spiritual instrument of a living faith.

I adjure thee by the Jesus whom Paul preaches (ver. 13). It is a just judgment of God, that the nation who had been appointed the custodiers of the true word of God, when they forsook the truth, should fall into the most wicked magical arts.—These deceivers wished to imitate the apostle, but in what? Not that they would learn the truth or convert souls; this did not please them. But they would imitate the miracles and works which had procured such honour to the apostle, and they wished to place themselves in similar credit. Thus do all false teachers. Their object is not the salvation of souls or the knowledge of the truth, but to obtain importance, to make for themselves a name; and therefore they seek to clothe themselves in the livery and feathers of the true servants of God.—These men had themselves experienced nothing of Jesus; they knew Him only from hearsay, as Him whom Paul preached. A pitiable condition of a teacher who uses the name of Jesus without the least experience of Him in his heart! When one learns the language of Canaan, imitates the powerful expressions of the servants of God, talks of a Jesus whom Paul preaches, no wonder that he comes to scorn and shame (Apost. Past.).

But there were seven sons of one Sceva, a chief priest (ver. 14). We are here reminded of many sad examples, how Satan makes use particularly of the sons of priests. Should not this excite all ministers to pray earnestly to Jesus for their children from the womb? (Apost. Past.)

Jesus I know, and Paul I know, but who are ye? (ver. 15.) Even the evil spirit is obliged to confess and to confirm it, that Christ and His servants have no fellowship with Belial. He knows well the difference between the righteous and the ungodly.—Whoever without faith and a proper calling presumes to enter into conflict with Satan, will necessarily come to shame (Starke).—Men who praise the truth and do not possess it, who set themselves up as teachers and know nothing, who proclaim the covenant of God and yet hate all discipline, who have Jesus on their tongues, whom they deny in heart and conduct, must bear that Satan opposes them in all their words and works, and dismisses them with the answer, "Jesus I know, but who are ye?" If this does not now take place so openly, yet it still takes place inwardly by means of the accusations of an evil conscience. For whoever preaches the truth, which he himself does not believe, and proclaims Jesus, whose enemy he still is, must be upbraided by his own heart with the same mockery with which the evil spirit met the pretences of these deceivers (Apost. Past.).—*Jesus I know, and Paul I know, but who are ye?* A reproving question to all false prophets and hypocritical disciples. 1. To discover to them the falsehood of their heart, by which they do not even deceive the devil and the world, far less the true God and the children of the light. 2. To show to them the weakness of their devices, by which they can effect as little as the servant Gehazi did with the borrowed staff of Elisha. 3. To point them to the true source, from which alone strength proceeds for actions done in God—the Spirit of Jesus and of His faithful witnesses.

And overcame both, and prevailed against them, so that they fled out of that house naked and wounded (ver. 16). Satan rewards his most faithful servants with ingratitude. He who serves him most zealously, will at length be most tormented by him. Flatteries at the beginning change into torments. One carries nothing away from his service, but a naked and a wounded soul (Apost. Past.).

And there fell a fear upon all, and the name of the Lord Jesus was magnified (ver. 17). Thus the devils must minister to the glory of Jesus, if God wills it. The power of the name of the Lord Jesus is made known both by the apostle's expulsion of devils, and by the exorcists' non-expulsion of devils in the name of Jesus (Starke).—The blessed name of Jesus is magnified: 1. In His servants, by their victory; 2. in His enemies, by their discomfiture.

And many confessed, and announced what they had done (ver. 18). The power of sin is its secrecy: when once silence is broken, its bands are rent asunder (Blumhardt of Möttlingen, on the awakening of his congregation, by means of the confession of sins, 1844).—A teacher can certainly neither demand nor enforce similar confessions of former abominations. But when they occur voluntarily, from the constraint of conscience and the impulse of the Spirit, they ought to be made use of by faithful pastors, in order that souls may be brought to true repentance and liberty (Apost. Past.).—Thus we now teach how excellent, and precious, and comforting a thing, confession is; and we exhort that such a precious blessing be not despised, considering our great necessities. If thou art now a Christian, thou requirest no force or command, but thou wilt be self-constrained. Therefore, when I exhort to confession, I do nothing else than exhort every one to be a Christian (Luther, "Brief Exhortation to Confession").

And many brought together their books, and burned them pub-

licly (ver. 19). The world will always be deluged with pernicious books until the judgment. We ought often to make a similar burning (Rieger).—Though many liberal Christians of our time may blame this act as being too scrupulous, and antiquarians may regret the loss of such treasure; we cast no stone at those Ephesians, who were yet fervent in their first love (Rev. ii. 4); as little as we do at those earnest Christians of our days, who do not only give up doubtful pleasures, but also doubtful gains, for the sake of the Gospel (Williger).—Christian booksellers and librarians ought to lay this text to heart (Besser).

Thus mightily grew and prevailed the word of the Lord. This "thus" is a true divine Amen, a testimony from heaven: This is My beloved Church, in which I am well pleased. O Lord, grant that Thou mayest pronounce such a "thus" on all churches which confess Thy name; that the earnestness of Thy people to free themselves from the most hidden cursed thing may be manifested, and that the world may make no other reproach than that of earnest pursuit after holiness, without which no man will see the Lord (Williger).

On vers. 8–20.—*The power of the Gospel, as it proved itself at Ephesus.* 1. In the acts of Paul (vers. 8–12). 2. In the disgrace of the false miracle-workers (vers. 13–17), (Lisco).—*How victoriously the simple word of God disenchants the enchanted world.* 1. It frustrates the magical arts of loose seducers in the hearts of believers, ver. 9. 2. It loosens the magical bonds of satanic possession by the power of salvation and life, ver. 12. 3. It discloses the magical delusion of sanctimonious hypocrites with unsparing severity, vers. 13–17. 4. It tears asunder the magical fetters of the prescriptive service of sin by the power of sincere repentance, ver. 18. 5. It burns the magical books of a deceitful wisdom in the fire of the divine truth, ver. 19.—*How Christ has come into the world to destroy the works of the devil.*—1. What are these works? 2. How Christ destroys them?—*What is the right confession?* 1. Whose root is faith. 2. Whose motive is repentance. 3. Whose fruit is new obedience.—*The evangelical Christian at the confessional.* 1. What impels him thither? No dead custom, or command of a despotic church, but the internal constraint of a heart penitent and desirous of salvation. 2. What should he take away from it? Not a load of humanly-imposed expiations, nor a licence to new sins, but the gracious comfort of the divine forgiveness, and incitement to grateful obedience.—*Whether the burning at Ephesus were not suitable for the present day?* Yes; but only for the proper books, and with the proper fire. 1. The proper books are not works of exact science, or of noble poetry, or of human law; but the pernicious fugitive pieces of a frivolous superficial knowledge, the seductive works of an impure light literature, and the arrogant decrees of an unchristian tyranny of the conscience (as Luther burned them at the gate of Wittenberg). 2. The proper fire for this burning is not the gloomy glow of a narrow puritanism, nor the sullen fire of a condemnatory fanaticism, nor the incendiary torch of a revolution; but the holy fire of a repentance, which thinks especially on its own sins and wants; of a love to the Lord, which joyfully sacrifices to Him whatever is most costly; and of a zeal for God's house, which desires nothing else than that His kingdom may come, as in churches, houses, and hearts, so also in the state, in arts, and sciences, ver. 20.—*The burning of books at Ephesus, or the word of man and the word of God.* 1. The word of man: deceitful; perishable. 2. The word of God: saving; indestructible.

5. *Whilst the Apostle is preparing to proceed on his journey to Macedonia and Achaia, a tumult breaks out in Ephesus.* (CHAP. XIX. 21–41.)

21 After these things were fulfilled, Paul purposed in the Spirit to pass
through Macedonia and Achaia, and then to go to Jerusalem, saying, After
I have been there, I must also see Rome. 22 And he sent to Macedonia
two of them who ministered to him, Timotheus and Erastus, and he tarried
for a season in Asia. 23 But there arose about this period a not inconsider-
able disturbance about that way. 24 For one named Demetrius, a silver-
smith, who made silver temples of Artemis, procured to the workers no small
gain. 25 These he collected together with those of similar occupation, and
said, Sirs, ye know that from this trade our prosperity proceeds. 26 And
ye see and hear, that not only at Ephesus, but almost throughout all Asia,
this Paul unsettles and perverts much people, saying, They are no gods
which are made with hands. 27 And not only this our portion is in danger
of being ruined, but also the temple of the great goddess Artemis of being
counted for nothing, and her greatness will be destroyed, whom all Asia
and the world worship. 28 When they heard these things, they were full
of wrath, and cried, saying, Great is Artemis of the Ephesians. 29 And
the city was filled with tumult: and they rushed with one accord into the
theatre, and caught Gaius and Aristarchus of Macedonia, Paul's companions.

30 But when Paul wished to enter among the people, the disciples did not suffer him. 31 Also certain of the Asiarchs, who befriended him, sent to him, and entreated him, not to repair to the theatre. 32 Then some cried one thing, and others another; for the assembly was confused; and the greater part knew not wherefore they were come together. 33 But they drew forth Alexander out of the multitude, the Jews pushing him forward. And Alexander beckoned with his hand, and wished to defend himself before the people. 34 But when they observed that he was a Jew, they all lifted up their voices, crying for two hours, Great is Artemis of the Ephesians. 35 But the state-scribe silenced the people, and said, Ye men of Ephesus, what man is there who does not know that the city of the Ephesians is the guardian of the great Artemis, and of the image which fell from heaven? 36 These things being incontrovertible, ye ought to be quiet, and to do nothing rashly. 37 For ye have brought these men, who are neither robbers of temples, nor blaspheme your goddess. 38 If, then, Demetrius, and the craftsmen who are with him, have any matter against any one, there are court-days and proconsuls, when they might plead against one another. 39 But if ye desire anything further, that may be settled in a lawful assembly. 40 For we are in danger of being accused concerning this day's uproar, whilst there is no ground on which we could defend ourselves, on account of this tumult. 41 And having spoken thus, he dismissed the assembly.

Ver. 25. Ἡμῖν is much more strongly attested than the genitive ἡμῶν, which is the simpler reading.

Ver. 29. Ὅλη is evidently a later addition, which some MSS. and old versions do not have.

Ver. 33. Προεβίβασαν is indeed, externally, not more strongly attested than συνεβίβασαν, but yet is to be considered as genuine, because the latter word gives no sense.

Ver. 37. Ὑμῶν is more strongly attested than ἡμῶν, and a transcriber might more easily have altered the former into the latter, than the reverse.

Ver. 39. Περαιτέρω is indeed only in one uncial MS., the Vatican, and in about 15 cursive MSS., whilst most MSS. and Church fathers have περὶ ἑτέρων. But the former is certainly genuine: it was corrected only as being the more uncommon word.

Ver. 40. Οὐ after περὶ οὗ has indeed three uncial MSS. for it; but yet it is, according to Tischendorf, to be erased as spurious.

EXEGETICAL EXPLANATIONS.

1. *Paul purposed in the Spirit.*—The plan of the apostle is here so expressed, that the journey through Macedonia and Greece appears only as an episode (and it is, in point of fact, very briefly related in the narrative itself, chap. xx. 1–6), whilst the visit to Jerusalem is represented as the true aim. We are not here informed what was the reason of this; but from the epistles of the apostle (1 Cor. xvi. 1–8; 2 Cor. viii.; Rom. xv.

25-28), we know that the collection for the Church of Jerusalem was in his mind, which Paul himself also incidentally mentions (chap. xxiv. 17). But it is remarkable that the apostle should here also, and for the first time, turn his eyes on Rome, as the end which he must yet attain.—Before he himself set off, he sent two of his assistants, Timotheus and Erastus, to Macedonia; Erastus, besides 2 Tim. iv. 20, is not known, as his identity with the Erastus of Rom. xvi. 23 is doubtful. *'Επέσχεν —εἰς τὴν 'Ασίαν*: he yet tarried—in the direction of Asia.

2. *A not inconsiderable disturbance.*—The exciter of the disturbance, Demetrius, was an *ἀργυροκόπος*, a silversmith, doubtless the proprietor of a large manufactory which was concerned only with one article, namely, with silver temples of Artemis, *i.e.*, with small models of the famous temple together with the statue. These miniature temples were placed in rooms, or carried on journeys (Ammianus Marcellinus, xxii. 13, observes of the philosopher Asclepiades, *deæ cælestis argenteum breve figmentum quocunque ibat secum solitus efferre*). Such a business might be so much the more lucrative, when carried on upon a large scale. Demetrius employed not only proper craftsmen (*τεχνῖται*, vers. 24, 28), but also a number of mechanics (*ἐργάται*, ver. 25), who obtained from it their bread, and comparatively much gain. The supposition that *ναοί* were not models, but medals with the picture of the temple (Beza and others), has little to recommend it.

3. *These he collected.*—Demetrius, a man on whom many hundreds might be dependent, and who in the diminished sale of his productions had a sensible standard of measurement of the apostle's influence in injuring the worship of Artemis, collected an assembly of workmen, both of the higher and of the lower classes (ver. 25, *οὓς* sc. *τεχνίτας, καὶ τοὺς—ἐργάτας*), engaged in his business, and artfully excited them. In his discourse, he places two facts in juxtaposition, and draws the conclusion. The first fact is the great gain and profit which this celebrated branch of trade yielded to them; and the second fact is the change of opinion among the people, occurring far and wide, through Paul (*ὁ Παῦλος οὗτος*, this Paul, spoken contemptuously, and for the purpose of exciting the passions) and his opposition to the worship of images (*οἱ διὰ χειρῶν γινόμενοι*). When Demetrius says, that in Ephesus, and indeed in all Asia (pro-

consular Asia), a great multitude had been turned, something may be deducted as intentional exaggeration, in order the more strongly to excite the people; but still a considerable influence must remain, otherwise the whole intrigue would have no foundation. The inference which he draws from these facts is twofold: our portion, our interest is threatened to come to naught (ἀπελεγμὸς from ἐλέγχω, confutation, contempt); and, what is still more (ἀλλὰ καὶ), the temple of Artemis will be less esteemed, and the majesty of the goddess herself will decay (αὐτή, the goddess herself, in distinction from her temple: μεγαλειότης refers to the usual prefix of the Ephesian Artemis, ἡ μεγάλη, *e.g.*, Xenophon, Ephes. i.). Thus this representation reckoned both on self-interest and on religious fanaticism, although the interest of the goddess was hypocritically represented as the higher and the more important.

4. *Great is Artemis of the Ephesians.*—The address took effect, and the fanatical passion of those concerned, aroused by their interest, broke out at the first in this outcry. The workers of Demetrius, with this exciting outcry, dispersed themselves in the city, which was quickly thrown into a tumult. They rushed into the theatre, which in Greek cities was often used for great assemblies, and particularly for popular assemblies. The companions of the apostle, as he himself was not at that moment to be found, who were forcibly dragged along, were Aristarchus, a native of Thessalonica (chap..xx. 4, xxvii. 2), and Gaius, a Macedonian, who is to be distinguished from Gaius of Derbe (chap. xx. 4).

5. *And certain of the Asiarchs.*—Some who, without being Christians, were friendly disposed to the apostle, warned him not to venture into the theatre. These were the elected deputies of proconsular Asia, who were required to celebrate the public games in honour of the goddess at their own expense: a patriotic honorary office.

6. *Then they cried, some one thing, and others another.*—The description of this tumultuous assembly is striking. The Alexander whom the Jews pushed forward, and then others drew out of the crowd (προεβίβασαν), in order that he might address the people, was certainly not a Christian (as Meyer and Baumgarten, after Calvin, suppose, and that the Jews pushed him forward from malice), but an unconverted Jew. His

Christianity is not to be inferred from his design to defend himself. The multitude would easily confound Christians and Jews, because the Jews were long known to be the opponents of idolatry. The Jews wished Alexander, perhaps a practised orator, to speak for them, in order to shift the blame from themselves, and to put it upon the Christians. But when he was about to speak, and was recognised as a Jew, he was not permitted to say a word: on the contrary, the excited fanaticism broke out afresh in the united and unceasing outcry which the workmen of Demetrius had already begun.

7. *But the state-scribe silenced the people.*—The γραμματεὺς (*i.e.*, the officer entrusted with the writing, publication, and custody of all the documents and decrees of the community—the secretary of state—an important office in the cities of Asia Minor) at length silenced the people, and completely allayed the excitement by his address. *Γάρ* with τίς supposes a pacifying exhortation to quietness. *Νεωκόρος* is originally a temple-servant who has to clean and to adorn the temple, then an honorary title, allied to the priesthood, a keeper and guardian of the temple, a title which was bestowed even on imperial persons, to confer honour on them. The wooden image of Artemis is here called τὸ διοπετὲς, because, according to the fable, it fell down from heaven.

8. *Ye men of Ephesus.*—The address of the state-scribe is designed to calm the excited multitude, and to restrain them from reckless conduct. 1. By reminding them of the undisputed and notorious fact of the Ephesian worship of Artemis (ver. 35). 2. By the legal remark, that the men arrested were guilty of no crime against Artemis or her temple; and therefore, if it were a private matter, they ought to be sued by Demetrius and his companions (λόγος, a discourse, a matter of complaint); or if a public matter should be made of it, a regular assembly was the competent court (vers. 37–39). *'Αγόρ. ἡμέραι, dies forenses sive judiciales habentur. 'Ανθύπατοι* is in the plural, in the sense: there is always a proconsul on the spot. By *ἡ ἔννομος ἐκκλησία* the state-scribe evidently enough, though indirectly, assumes that this concourse was not an assembly of the people, but a rabble, and that it was not competent to decide in a lawful manner. 3. He draws their attention to the account of the riot likely to be required from them (ver. 40). *Γάρ* before *κινδυνεύομεν* is designed to impress them with the dread

of the denunciation of the tumult, as ground for a judicial procedure. *Μηδενὸς αἰτίου ὑπάρχοντος* is not masculine (Vulgate), "No one being the cause;" but neuter, "There being no ground of vindication for this *συστροφή*," chosen instead of *στάσις* as a milder word.

DOGMATICAL AND ETHICAL THOUGHTS.

1. The plan of the apostle, expressed at Ephesus, embraced in the first instance Macedonia and Greece, and afterwards Jerusalem and Rome. As the Redeemer, when He had fulfilled His course, set His face stedfastly to go to Jerusalem, Luke ix. 51; so Paul also always turns back to that city where the Lord was crucified, and where He had founded His first church. But His regard and desire go beyond that to Rome; he purposed going thither in the Spirit, by means of divine direction and illumination. What Jesus had directly disclosed to him after his conversion, and to which He had appointed him, now springs forth from his own soul, by means of spontaneous resolution, as a divine necessity.

2. The threatening tumult in Ephesus, of purely heathen origin as at Philippi, was also occasioned chiefly by the vulgar motive of avarice; yet it was so far distinguished, inasmuch as the material interest of a certain trade appears to be essentially interwoven with the local worship of a heathen city. This event is an expressive image of so many outbreaks of fanaticism against Christianity and the pure Gospel, when, under the appearance of zeal for the sanctuary, nothing else than selfish motives are concealed.

3. Holy zeal and carnal heat are as different as day and night. The former springs from unselfish love to God and His honour; the latter from selfish and low motives. The former acts with warmth and persevering exertions, but always with self-possession and the clear light of consciousness; the latter blazes passionately and excitedly, causing error and indistinctness, indiscretion and unreasonableness. The former produces permanent fruit; but the latter can only operate dangerously and destructively, or, consuming itself, may be ignominiously extinguished.

4. The representations of the state-secretary suppose that the apostle and his assistants entirely abstained from all derision

and abuse of the heathen gods; otherwise, what he says would be wanting in truth, and would only have called forth contradictions and augmented passion. Also the speech of the agitator Demetrius to his associates in trade indirectly confirms this fact, inasmuch as he, if he could have acted otherwise, would certainly have employed the positive attacks of Paul on the worship of Artemis to attain his object. The prudently forbearing demeanour of the apostle at Athens entirely agrees with this. Thus the method of exposing to the heathen what is irrational and foolish in their religion, in an offensive and irritating manner, has not the precedent of the great apostle for it. That method may indeed wound, but will not illuminate and heal. The apostolic procedure is positive, not negative: the testimony of the true God and of His Christ, our Redeemer, the publication of the Gospel, is a power of God which illuminates, edifies, and saves; and it is only in connection with this that error and sin are refuted and rebuked.

HOMILETICAL HINTS.

After these things were finished, Paul purposed in the Spirit, etc. (ver. 21). Paul considered it not time to rest here, but he thirsts to extend himself yet farther, as if he had done nothing. He gains possession of Ephesus and Asia; he resolves to go to Macedonia and Achaia; he has Jerusalem in view; he meditates on Rome; thence to Spain (Rom. xv. 24). No Alexander, no Cæsar, no other hero, approaches the large-mindedness of this little Benjamite. The truth of Christ, faith in Him, love to Him, made his heart wide as the ocean (Bengel).—There are times, when, oppressed with the burden of our ministry, we can hardly restrain ourselves from praying with Elias, "It is enough, O Lord, take away my life from me." But there are other times, when we may soar in spirit, and, in the feeling of the dignity of our office, may fix similar regards and intentions on the future as Paul here has done (Rieger).—Jerusalem and Rome are two peculiar, and, in spiritual and worldly matters, very remarkable cities; from which at first much that was good, and afterwards much that was pernicious, proceeded far and wide; and in which much blood of the saints was found to be avenged, and will yet be found, Matt. xxiii. 35; Rev. xviii. 24. It is worthy of remark that Luther also, before the beginning of the

Reformation, must see Rome (Rieger).—God often grants the desires of His people, but not according to their opinion, but as He knows to be most useful for His honour and their salvation. Paul would see Rome, but he came thither in bonds (Starke).—Jerusalem and Rome, the cities of suffering and trial to this witness of Jesus, yet under all his changes remained ever in view. This was the course marked out for him by the Lord, to which he always hastened in spirit, even as Jesus to His cross and death (Apost. Past.).

But there arose at this time no small disturbance about that way (ver. 23). This "way" did not please all men, for with it they must give up their business and their own ways; therefore they make a noise, and Satan would always willingly barricade the narrow way (Gossner).—St Luke would evidently not lead us through the lands and cities of heathendom, without pointing out to us the dark abyss, out of which many a tearful and bloody affliction had occurred to the Church of Christ (Baumgarten).—As St Paul was on the point of proceeding on his journey, God suffers him to experience trouble and a snare in Ephesus, in order that he may take away with him from all places the marks of the sufferings of Jesus, and might, with the blessing which the Lord conferred on him, carry also his cross after him (Apost. Past.).

For one named Demetrius, etc. (ver. 24). The occasion of the tumult was thus covetousness under the disguise of religion. Demetrius, the silversmith, is a type of all those false religious zealots who pretend to be zealous for the true doctrine, for the glory of God, for the maintenance of truth and order, but who secretly seek to preserve nothing but their own fortune, credit, and ease (Apost. Past.).

Sirs, ye know that by this trade we have our wealth, and this Paul turns away much people (vers. 25, 26). The Gospel of Jesus cannot possibly agree with the dead gods which the world worships. It rebukes the sinful pleasures and evil works, in which the world delights. What wonder that such a discourse should excite the hatred, envy, and zeal of men who will not abandon their idols!—There are certain immoral trades, which for a long time stand in the way of the conversion of people of this kind. Many tradesmen have tacitly agreed that usury, fraud, and unjust gain shall, as it were, be privileged among them. This is the ban of Satan, by which he retains such men in his service. A wise teacher must be diligent to discover such secret snares, and labour to tear them in pieces (Apost. Past.).—Where Jesus Christ comes, the true Lord of all men, there He draws to Himself hearts, love, prayers, the external act, even external sacrifices; they are withdrawn from their former idols. If the idols of the heathen and the idols of Christians could complain and sigh, they would begin to complain and sigh in those days, when the Holy Ghost opens up a path among the nations. The heathen priests have frequently lied to the people who were impressed by the Gospel: the god in his temple has complained and sighed on account of the withdrawn offerings. But who complains and sighs? Those who are interested in the god, and who draw their wealth from him (Ahlfeld).—Tetzel, in his time, and the enlightened Pope Leo, spoke in a precisely similar manner (Besser). Even in this present day, and in the midst of Christianity, the uproar of selfishness against the divine truth is repeated in hearts, as well as in science and life. Is it not the selfishness of the proud understanding, which does not bend in obedience to Jesus Christ? Is it not the selfishness of the carnal mind, which does not break with carnal lusts and pleasures? Is it not the selfishness of the natural will, which will of itself create the righteousness which avails before God? (Leonh. and Spieg.)

And not only this our portion is in danger of being ruined, but also the temple of the great goddess Artemis to be counted for nothing (ver. 27). How finely does greed know to conceal itself under the cloak of zeal for religion! (Quesnel.)

And they cried and said, Great is Diana of the Ephesians (ver. 28). How many tradesmen make an idol of their trade! (Strade.)—True religion is not carried on with tumult (Starke). —Who is the cause of this uproar and tumult? Is it Elijah who troubleth Israel? Or is it Jezebel, and those who commit adultery with her? (Gossner.)—Do you not shudder at such blindness of a people, who were otherwise so highly cultivated? But let not the matter rest with such a momentary shudder. Let this popular commotion, from the nature of its origin, be an admonitory picture to you. Learn from the history of the immediate past, how individual wicked persons easily knew how to collect to themselves a great concourse of followers, how to employ the ignorant for their own purposes, how to allure by promises and to deter by threats; and whilst they stood up with the appearance of right, they flattered human passions, and employed reprehensible means, and so befooled whole communities and masses, that they were not ashamed blindly to follow their blind leaders (Apelt.).—For the truth, or for a portion of the truth, a certain external zeal may be stirred up, and a crowd drawn, who change holy zeal for the Lord into an unholy outcry: Great is our Diana! As, at the time of the Reformation, the controversy concerning original sin, whether it belongs to the nature of man (substance) or is something attached to him (accident), was carried into taverns, and the most ordinary peasants were divided into two parties, Substantialists and Accidentalists, who liked best to carry on the controversy with blows (Williger).

And the city was filled with tumult (ver. 29). Behold here a true picture of a riot! It usually originates in one or two base persons. Then it extends further, and, as a mighty flood, overflows town and country (Starke).

But when Paul wished to enter in among the people, the disciples suffered him not (ver. 30). Christians should indeed be stedfast, but not obstinate (Lindhammer).—Where the blind rage of the rabble roars and foams as the stormy ocean, there even the most powerful testimony dies away without leaving any trace, and even a Paul can for an instant do nothing better than be silent.

Also certain of the Asiarchs who were his friends (ver. 31). With all the hatred of the world, an honest teacher yet retains friends among the rulers and the great. Herod greatly esteemed John, although he persecuted him afterwards. The recognised purity, honesty, and truth which, if we are the servants of Christ, must shine forth from our words and conduct, meet with the approbation of intelligent worldly people, so that they highly esteem such a man, though they themselves are not converted. A servant of Jesus does not seek the favour of the world; but when God makes many high and honourable men the friends of His servants, they are the instruments of His gracious providence to bestow upon His people protection and help in various circumstances (Apost. Past.).—Man's favour and God's grace are good, when we have them together. But if man's favour is not to be, God's grace alone suffices (An old proverb).

And some cried one thing and others another, and the greater part knew not wherefore they were come together (ver. 32). Thus does it happen in the present day with the blind multitude in political and religious factions and excitements. How many honourable German burghers have in these last years joined in a cry in a popular assembly, signed a petition, or voted at an election, and hardly knew what it was about! The intelligent man and the honest Christian may sigh, smiling with the dying Huss, *O sancta simplicitas!* and immediately remember the compassionate prayer of our merciful High Priest, "Father, forgive them, for they know not what they do!"

But they drew forth Alexander out of the multitude, the Jews pushing him forward (ver. 33). The hostilely disposed among the Jews soon united themselves with the raging rabble among the Gentiles, and wished to set up Alexander as their spokesman, who had it in his mind to defend the Jews, but yet more to attack Paul. But he was not allowed to speak. We cannot read the narrative of this uproar without shuddering: whoever reflects on what Paul experienced at it, will be able to understand how he in 1 Cor. xv. 32 describes it as a fight with wild beasts (Rieger).

And they cried for the space of two hours, Great is Diana of the Ephesians (ver. 34). The Holy Spirit does not make men drunken (chap. ii.), but the evil spirit who works in the children of disobedience does so. He often gives them the intoxicating cup of pride and falsehood, full to the brim, so that they, in drunken adoration of their idols, lose all apprehension of, and sober consideration for, the truth. "Great is Diana of the Ephesians!" this outcry is still unchanged, only the name of the idol is changed. The popular ideas of the time and the heroes of the day are indebted chiefly to this outcry of the foolish multitude for their honour and consideration. And yet is this cry no proof of their internal merit. When the devil observes that his time is but short, he rages the more. The great outcry at Ephesus was a sure sign that it was at an end with the whole affair (Leonh. and Spieg.).

But the state-scribe (Luther: chancellor) *appeased the people* (ver. 35). Uproar and mutiny are often more happily extinguished by the eloquent tongue than by a strong arm and the power of the sword (Starke).—The speech of the chancellor is indeed no apostolical discourse; yet there shines from it the spirit of a wise, prudent, firm, and just man, which might serve as a model to many Christian magistrates. He appeases and wins over the people with the assurance that the renown of their city was eminent beyond all dispute. But, at the same time, he does not address the seditious multitude according to their opinion, he does not concede the point to them, he does not abandon to them the persecuted disciples (Leonh. and Spieg.).

Ye have brought these men, who are neither robbers of churches nor blasphemers (ver. 37). The Christians at Ephesus were now repaid, that they walked according to the rule of Paul to Titus: "Put them in mind to be subject to principalities and powers, to obey magistrates, to be ready for every good work, to speak evil of no man, to be no brawlers, but gentle, showing all meekness unto all men," Tit. iii. 1, 2 (Besser).—It is seen from this how prudently the apostles must have borne testimony against the heathen idols, so that it could be said of them that they were not blasphemers of Diana. Nothing good is effected for the truth with carnal weapons (Rieger).—It was not Paul's method to set the heathen against their idols. He first preached to them Jesus Christ, and erected in them a new thing, and then the old fell to the ground of itself (Ahlfeld).—To defame the idols of the world does not help us preachers, if we do not likewise know how to make Christ glorious to it.

If then Demetrius has any matter against this man, there are court-days (ver. 38). What a gracious gift of God is the power of a wise government, which upholds law and order against caprice and injustice! (Leonh. and Spieg.)—Thus Paul here experienced in reality what he said in praise of government: "It is the minister of God to thee for good," Rom. xiii. 4 (Williger).

And when he had spoken thus, he dismissed the assembly (ver. 41). Their quickly kindled rage was as quickly extinguished (Chrysostom).—Thus was the uproar quieted by the wisdom and eloquence of the chancellor as an instrument of the rescuing grace of God, and the point of the enmity against the Gospel was broken: the still power of the divine word and the captivating address of the Holy Ghost, who is the true chancellor of the people of God, alone can eradicate the roots of it. O Lord Jesus, whom wind and sea obey, do Thou still the raging of the nations and of our own flesh and blood against

Thee, and blessedly calm our hearts in the obedience of Thy truth, and in the peace of Thy life (Leonh. and Spieg.).

On vers. 21-40.—*The uproar against the Gospel of Christ.* How selfishness excited it, blindness accomplished it, and the power of divine grace victoriously overcame it (Leonh. and Spieg.).—*The teaching of experience concerning the deceptions of the spirit of sedition in ancient and modern times.* 1. One pretends to high aims, and is influenced by the grossest selfishness. 2. One thinks himself free to act, and is the involuntary instrument of crafty seducers. 3. One values himself as enlightened, and commits the most unreasonable acts of folly. 4. One prides himself that he contends for the right, and perpetrates the most unrighteous deeds of violence. 5. One is filled with extravagant expectations, and in the end has gained nothing (Bode).—*The tumult of the idolaters at Ephesus, a warning for our time.* 1. Its occasion and origin. 2. Its progress and issue (Apelt.).—*How selfishness is always hostile to the Gospel.* 1. Its instruments, vers. 25-27. 2. Its success, vers. 28-30 (Lisco).—*The enmity of idolaters against the Gospel.* 1. Their reasons, vers. 23-27. 2. Their declarations, vers. 28, 29 (Lisco).—*Rules for our conduct toward excited minds, drawn from the speech of the chancellor at Ephesus,* vers. 35-40. 1. To recognise what is right in the complaints. 2. To make evident the accompanying errors. 3. To refer to the legal remedy. 4. To represent the punishable and dangerous nature of a tumultuous conduct (Lisco).—*How the Lord knows to protect His Church even by means of its enemies.* 1. Bringing to light the impurity of the adversaries, and thereby the right of the good cause: superstition and selfishness of the rioters at Ephesus. 2. Converting the internal contradiction of the wicked into a protection for the truth: the Gentiles will not unite with the Jews against the Christians—a victory of the truth, vers. 33, 34; the uproar turns to the disadvantage of the rioters, and the good cause remains uninjured, vers. 38-40 (Lisco).—*The silversmith, Demetrius, and his companions in modern times.* These are: 1. The abject slaves of business, who in the pursuit of temporal gain have lost all regard for eternity (vers. 24, 25). 2. The blind adherents of established customs, who from every fresh movement of the Spirit fear the disturbance of their ease, indeed the destruction of the world (vers. 26, 27). 3. The self-satisfied priests of the

Beautiful, who, in idolatrous veneration for nature and art, acknowledge no consciousness of sin and no need of grace (ver. 27). (Compare Gœthe's poem, "Great is Diana of the Ephesians," and his confession in his correspondence with Jacobi: "I am even now one of the Ephesian silversmiths, who has spent his whole life in the contemplation, and admiration, and adoration of the wonderful temple of the goddess (Nature), and in imitation of her mysterious forms; and to whom it cannot possibly stir up an agreeable feeling, if any apostle will obtrude another and a formless God.") 4. The hypocritical zealots for the Church and religion, who with their apparent zeal for God's house have only their own interest in view (ver. 27).—*Great is Diana of the Ephesians, but greater is the God of the Christians.* 1. Great and glorious is the kingdom of nature; but we find our true home and our right place only in the kingdom of grace. 2. Great and beautiful are the works of the human mind in art and science; but art and science fall into the grossest error without the discipline of the Divine Spirit and the light of the Christian revelation. 3. Great and strong is the power of the human will; but with the best will we are able to render to the holy God no pure service, to build no worthy temple, if His Spirit does not cleanse our hearts into His sanctuary and perfect His strength in our weakness. 4. Great and remarkable are the histories of earthly kingdoms (as Greece and Rome),; but the cross-kingdom of Jesus Christ triumphs over all: Ephesus lies in ruins, and the temple of Diana in ashes, but the gates of hell shall not prevail against the Church of Christ.—*The uproar at Ephesus, a terrific picture of rebellion against the Gospel of God*, as it ever again repeats itself: 1. In the dark heathen world, on the part of brutal, yea, satanic heathen nature; dark pictures from the missionary field—bloody persecution in Madagascar; the Indian mutiny. 2. In unconverted Christianity: on the part of the carnal mind, which will not suffer itself to be rebuked by God's word, and of the materialistic spirit of the age, which will know nothing of heavenly things. 3. Even in the heart of true Christians: on the part of proud reason, of the self-righteous heart, and of the flesh which shuns the cross.—*Wherefore do the heathen rage, and the people imagine a vain thing? He who dwells in the heaven shall laugh; the Lord shall have them in derision.* 1. The raging of the heathen: in their wrath, vers. 23–29; in their blindness, ver. 32. 2. The laughter of the Lord, who sits enthroned in unruffled majesty above His raging enemies, and converts their plans into shame, even before the world, vers. 35–40.—*Christ, the almighty Conqueror of the storm, in the raging of unchained nations.* 1. In the hour of danger, He hides His own in the ark of safety: Paul, vers. 30, 31. 2. He places a rock in the sea, against which the raging billows break themselves: the chancellor, ver. 35. 3. He causes the storm of the passions to cease, and to sink of itself: the appeased people, ver. 40. 4. He guides in safety yet further the bark of His Church: progress of Paul in the following chapter.—*The messengers of the Gospel, opponents indeed, but not blasphemers of heathenism.* 1. Their Christian prudence, which, with all zeal for the house of the Lord, is yet not indiscreetly zealous. 2. Their evangelical love, which, with all hatred to heathen abominations, is yet filled with compassion for heathen misery. 3. Their apostolic wisdom, which, in all the darkness of heathen folly, yet finds a spark of original truth.—*The chancellor at Ephesus, a model of an able statesman.* 1. In his undaunted courage. 2. In his wise discretion. 3. In his impartial justice. 4. In his philanthropic benevolence.

B.

Second Part. Summary information concerning the Journey through Macedonia and Greece, and then back to Miletus.

Chap. xx. 1–16.

1 And after the uproar had ceased, Paul called to him the disciples,
took leave of them, and departed from the city, to go to Macedonia. 2 And
when he had gone through these regions, and had exhorted them, he came
to Greece. 3 And after he had spent three months there, and the Jews
laid wait for him, as he was about to sail to Syria, he resolved to return
through Macedonia. 4 And there accompanied him to Asia, Sopater the
son of Pyrrhus, of Berea; and of Thessalonica, Aristarchus and Secundus;
and Gaius of Derbe, and Timotheus; and of Asia, Tychicus and Trophimus.
5 These went before, and waited for us at Troas. 6 But we sailed after the
days of unleavened bread from Philippi, and came unto them at Troas in
five days: there we tarried seven days. 7 And on the first day of the
week, when we were assembled to break bread, Paul discoursed to them,
intending to depart on the following day, and continued his speech until
midnight. 8 And there were many lamps in the upper chamber, where we

were assembled. 9 But a young man, named Eutychus, who sat at a
window, sank into a deep sleep; and as Paul was long speaking, he was
overcome by sleep, and fell down from the third storey, and was taken up
dead. 10 But Paul went down and fell on him, embracing him, and said,
Trouble not yourselves, for his life is in him. 11 Then he went up, and
broke the bread, and ate something, and discoursed much with them till
daybreak; and so he departed. 12 And they brought the lad alive, and
were not a little comforted. 13 But we went before to the ship, and sailed
to Assos, intending from thence to take up Paul: for so had he appointed,
wishing himself to go by land. 14 And when he met with us at Assos, we
took him up, and came to Mitylene. 15 And we sailed thence, and came
on the following day over against Chios; and the next day, we drew near
to Samos, and tarried at Trogyllium; and on the following day we came
to Miletus. 16 For Paul had resolved to sail past Ephesus, because he
would not spend the time in Asia: for he hasted, if it were possible, to be
at Jerusalem on the day of Pentecost.

Ver. 1. Before ἀσπασάμενος, Lachmann reads, after some MSS., καὶ παρακαλέσας, which however, as there are several variations in the reading, appears to be spurious, and is erased by Tischendorf.

Ver. 4. Πύῤῥου after Σώπατρος is omitted in the textus receptus, but it has for it four important uncial MSS., thirty cursive MSS. and ancient versions, and is omitted only in the two youngest uncial MSS., G. and H. It was perhaps omitted on account of the similarity of sound with Βεροιαῖος immediately following it. Lachmann and Tischendorf have with justice retained it.

Ver. 7. The textus receptus, which also Griesbach and Scholz follow, has τῶν μαθητῶν, after G. and H.: this is, however, certainly a later alteration for the sake of αὐτοῖς: the uncial MSS. A.B.D.E., twenty cursive MSS., and most of the versions have ἡμῶν.

Ver. 8. Only a few cursive MSS. have ἦσαν, instead of ἦμεν, supported by all the uncial MSS.

Ver. 11. Τὸν ἄρτον, according to A.B.C. and D. (first hand); whilst the article is omitted in E.G.H. and D. (second hand). Ver. 7 was inconsiderately followed.

Ver. 15. Lachmann, after A.B.C.E., some cursive MSS. and versions, omits the words καὶ μείναντες ἐν Τρωγυλλίῳ. But the uncial MSS. D.G.H., most cursive MSS., and the majority of versions and fathers, have the words. They were probably omitted, because they were not from the context understood, *i.e.*, the context appeared to imply that Trogyllium was in Samos, whereas it was known that it was not there.

Ver. 16. The textus receptus has ἔκρινε, but only after the two youngest uncial MSS. and some fathers. The accredited reading, recommended by Griesbach, and adopted by Lachmann and Tischendorf, is κεκρίκει.

EXEGETICAL EXPLANATIONS.

1. *And after the uproar had ceased.*—The departure of the apostle was not (as Hug, Ewald, and others suppose) occasioned

or hastened by the disturbance which had broken out, as if he had to escape from impending danger. The first words of the chapter mark only the time, not the motive, of the departure: they indeed import that Paul waited for the disturbance being quieted; but the departure itself was already in his plan, chap. xix. 1, 2.

2. *And when he had gone through these regions.*—*Αὐτούς* indicates, according to *μέρη ἐκεῖνα* and *Μακεδονίαν*, the Christians in Macedonia. By *Ἑλλάς* is not to be understood Greece exclusive of Achaia, and particularly of the Peloponnesus (Bengel), but the whole of Greece, which Luke elsewhere calls by its then official name Achaia, but here by the old national name Hellas. The participle *ποιήσας* is an anacoluthon: in the succession of sentences is seen the haste with which Luke passes over the labours of the apostle at this period in Europe. The crafty design on the life of Paul by the Jews occurred doubtless at Corinth, from which Paul had intended to sail directly to Syria. This accordingly caused him to choose a journey by land, which led him back through Macedonia, but which also occupied so much more time, that he was at last constrained to be expeditious, if he would be at Jerusalem at the appointed time.

3. *And there accompanied him.*—Luke here mentions the companions of Paul, of whom he names no fewer than seven, whilst he himself also, according to vers. 5–7, 13–15, was along with them. Three were Macedonians by birth, and four Asiatics. Sopater of Berea, otherwise unknown, is named first, because the apostle on his return reached Berea in the south before Thessalonica, to which the two next mentioned companions belonged. Of these, Secundus is not elsewhere mentioned, whilst Aristarchus was already in the company of the apostle at Ephesus (chap. xix. 29), and at a later period accompanied him on his voyage to Rome (chap. xxvii. 2), and shared his imprisonment in that city (Col. iv. 10; Philem. 24). Gaius of Derbe is a different person from Gaius of Macedonia, mentioned in chap. xix. 29. Timotheus is named without any designation, because he was, since chap. xvi., well known. Tychicus also was, at a later period, with Paul at Rome (Col. iv. 7, 8; Eph. vi. 21), and brought over the epistles of the apostle to the Asiatic churches (compare 2 Tim. iv. 12; Tit.

iii. 12). Trophimus, we are informed in chap. xxi. 29, was a native of Ephesus: he was, as a Gentile Christian, but from no fault of his, the occasion of the tumult and of the imprisonment of the apostle at Jerusalem. The words ἄχρι τῆς Ἀσίας specify *Asia proconsularis* as the destination of the convoy; but do not indicate that it was concluded there, for some of them—as, for example, Aristarchus and Trophimus—remained in the company of the apostle even to Jerusalem. All together were in the retinue of the apostle to Asia, but not farther. The supposition of Baumgarten, that all accompanied the apostle to Jerusalem, in order to appear there as the seven representatives of the converted Gentile world, not only before believers, but also before all Israel, is destitute of sufficient foundation.

4. *But we sailed.*—The seven companions left Philippi earlier than Paul, who followed with Luke. For Luke again indicates himself by ἡμᾶς (ver. 5 and the following vers.); and to suppose Timotheus the author of all those passages where "we" occurs, is forbidden by the distinction between οὗτοι (among whom Timotheus is mentioned, ver. 4) and ἡμεῖς. Luke, on the second missionary journey of Paul, had remained at Philippi, chap. xvi. 40; now he again joins the apostle, at the same city, on his return from his third missionary journey. And here accordingly commences a very exact record of time, as if a journal of this journey were kept.

5. *After the days of unleavened bread* and of the Passover, Paul sailed with Luke from Philippi, and came in five days to Troas; whereas the voyage from Troas to Philippi required only three days (chap. xvi. 11, 12).

6. *On the first day of the week.*—Vers. 7–12 relate an incident at Troas,—the restoration of a young man to life, who had fallen down dead. This occurred on the occasion of the religious service, which Paul held on the first day of the week. According to the Hebrew idiom, which is peculiar both to the Gospels and the Acts of the Apostles, and to the epistles of Paul (1 Cor. xvi. 2), μία stands for πρώτη. The first among the days of the week was our Sunday. This is the first trace of the observance of Sunday in the history of the Church. It cannot indeed be disputed that this assembly of Christians, met for the breaking of bread,—*i.e.*, for a sacred and religious enjoyment of bread, for the Lord's Supper and the word of God,—might happen acci-

dentally on the first day of the week, because Paul was to depart on the morrow (Meyer). But according to this view, it is not explained why Luke expressly names this day. This evidently indicates, that this day of the week was a holy day which was usually solemnized with religious meetings. And with this, the circumstance strikingly agrees, that the observance of the Sunday is first mentioned in a congregation of Gentile Christians, since, from the nature of the case, this custom would be introduced earlier and more easily among Gentile Christian than among Jewish Christian congregations.

7. *When we were assembled.*—By ἡμῶν, the historian indicates that he himself was present at the assembly; but he adds διελέγετο αὐτοῖς, because the discourse of Paul was chiefly a farewell discourse (μέλλων ἐξιέναι), and was accordingly addressed to those who remained behind, not to Paul's travelling companions, among whom was the historian. This has not been generally observed, particularly by the transcribers, who, instead of ἡμῶν, thought that τῶν μαθητῶν must be placed. The lamps (not torches, according to Luther, but hand-lamps; it is the same word as in Matt. xxv. 1) were numerous, for the sake of solemnity.

8. *But a young man.*—Eutychus, in this assembly, sat at a window, that is, on the seat or bench of the window, which, according to the custom of the ancients, was not closed with glass panes, and here also was without shutters. From this he fell, in his sleep, down three storeys. The construction with the four participles is as follows: A young man, sitting at a window, falling into a deep sleep, while Paul was long preaching, being overcome by sleep, fell, etc. The definite article stands with ὕπνος the second time, because the sleep was already mentioned. Ἤρθη νεκρός is simply, he was taken up lifeless, *i.e.*, not that he was carried into the house, but that he was found dead, when they came to lift him up. There is no reason, either here or in the context, to take νεκρός for ὡς νεκρός (as De Wette, Olshausen, and others), and to consider it only as the appearance of death, a fainting fit.

9. *Paul fell upon him.*—The actions of the apostle, laying himself upon the dead (ἐπέπεσεν), and embracing him, are analogous to those of Elisha with the dead son of the Shunammite woman (2 Kings iv. 34), and of Elijah with the son of the

woman of Sarepta (1 Kings xvii. 21), reanimating the lifeless by means of corporeal touch and warmth of life. After this had taken place, Paul said to those standing around, that they should not trouble themselves or be concerned (*θορυβεῖσθαι* in the middle voice, *consternor;* not "to raise an alarm," according to Luther and De Wette, which appears less suitable to the context). "His life is in him," says St Paul: certainly not, "it is again in him," but also not "it is yet in him." Paul cannot say the latter, for the young man had fallen down dead; and he will not expressly say the former, in order not to magnify himself and his miraculous power. Nevertheless the representation is of such a nature, that we must suppose a restoration of the dead to life, by means of the miraculous operation of the apostle. Also, *ἤγαγον ζῶντα* (ver. 12), as opposed to *ἤρθη νεκρός* (ver. 9), is proof sufficient of the manner in which Luke understands it. That Paul, after this incident, breaks bread and eats, and thus now does what was contemplated at the beginning (ver. 11; compare ver. 7), and also resumes his discourse and continues it till break of day, gives the impression how little the object and the continuance of the meeting were disturbed by an interruption which might have had the most melancholy consequences. *Κλᾶν ἄρτον* is not to be understood here otherwise than in ver. 7, as Grotius and Kuinoel, who suppose here a meal before a journey, and there a religious meal. *Οὕτως* before *ἐξῆλθεν* imports that Paul departed without resting any that night.

10. *And sailed to Assos.*—The journey from Troas to Miletus is very exactly described by Luke, vers. 13–15. The companions of Paul sailed by themselves, and coasted from Troas to Assos in Mysia, opposite the northern corner of Lesbos, while Paul traversed the distance, amounting to nine (German) miles, by land. Why Paul made this arrangement (*ἦν διατεταγμένος*, middle voice) Luke does not inform us; and the suppositions concerning the possible motives, as regard to his health (Calvin), foresight of Jewish snares (Michaelis), ministerial activity in the intermediate places (Meyer), desire to be alone (Baumgarten, Ewald), have no foundation to rest on. From Assos, where the apostle embarked, the voyage proceeded in a southern direction so near the coast, that they sailed between the islands of Lesbos (on the east side of which was the charming Mitylene), Chios,

Samos, and the western coast of Asia Minor. *Παραβάλλειν* is here rather "to touch at," than "to pass," which it also certainly means. From Samos they sailed over to the opposite coast of Ionia, and landed at the promontory and city of Trogyllium, forty furlongs distant from Samos, at the foot of Mount Micale. They had, even before they touched at Samos, sailed past Ephesus. Luke informs us why Paul did not land there: he was afraid of the length of residence he would have had to make, and time pressed, if he would reach Jerusalem at Pentecost. Therefore he stopped only at Miletus, a city situated about nine (German) miles to the south, where he arrived on a Saturday.

DOGMATICAL AND ETHICAL THOUGHTS.

1. The festival of Sunday is, according to the biblical history and doctrine, not legal, but evangelical. It is here mentioned in a very unpretending manner: it may even appear to be entirely accidental that this assembly for religious worship occurred on a Sunday. The apostolic sanctification of Sunday was not a law, but only a custom, corresponding to the Spirit of Jesus as well as to the character of the Apostle Paul. Accordingly, the Augsburg Confession declares that Sunday is an ordinance to be observed for the sake of peace and love, but not as absolutely necessary for salvation.

2. In the actions of the Christians assembled at Troas, divine worship and Christian fellowship are interwoven together in a holy manner. The Apostle Paul there takes leave of the brethren; but his farewell discourse was also a discourse from the word of God; and, conversely, his teaching of divine things was also a free, social conversation (*ὁμιλεῖν διαλέγεσθαι*). They assembled together to break bread: this was a holy sacramental supper of the Lord, but also, on the other hand, a meal of brotherly fellowship. The Spirit of Christ sanctifies the natural, and imparts to the bond of union between man and man true stedfastness, a higher value, and a more friendly cordiality. And the grace of God in Christ, the God-man, communicates itself to believers in visible signs and material pledges. Thus the human and the divine, the material and the spiritual, nature and grace, join hand to hand in Christianity.

3. The restoration of the young man to life took place by means of the contact and embrace of the apostle. Paul brought

the warmth of his life directly into contact with the scarcely dead body. Certainly there was no virtue in this to impart life to the dead; that was due to the almighty power of God. But while this operated through a man full of faith and the Spirit, corporeal and natural means are employed. So with most of the miracles of Jesus; so in the healing by the imposition of hands; so here, in the restoration of the young man to life. But the unpretending manner in which the apostle speaks of it, shows that the supernatural becomes itself natural in the higher order of things, and therefore requires no great ado about it.

HOMILETICAL HINTS.

Now after the uproar had ceased, Paul called the disciples, and blessed them (Luther's translation), *and departed* (ver. 1). Not as a hireling who sees the wolf coming did Paul flee, but he took his departure after the battle had been fought and peace re-established (Rieger).—The servants of God, when they depart, leave their blessing behind them: not only the blessing of the scattered seed, but also the blessing of their prayers, the blessing of their tears numbered by God, and the blessing of their Saviour's promises to them. Verily, a beautiful legacy of the servants of God (Apost. Past.).

And when he had gone through these regions, and had exhorted them (ver. 2). As a prudent householder is not only diligent to make gains, but also to preserve what he has gained; so ought a teacher not only to win souls for Christ, but also to endeavour to preserve them for Him (Starke).—We find Paul in all circumstances one and the same. In imprisonment, in tumults, among the disciples, in the world, on journeys, in short, wherever he was, he was a servant of God, so that he did not forget, in the most difficult paths and in all places, to exhort, comfort, and strengthen believers. How does this shame those who divest themselves of their ministerial character with their pulpit-gown, and leave it behind at the church-door, and do not in the least consecrate their journeys to the service of Jesus! (Apost. Past.)

But the Jews lying in wait for him, he resolved to return through Macedonia (ver. 3). Paul knew well that he could not long escape the snares of his enemies, but he wished to avoid them, until the hour of the Lord came (John vii. 30), (Williger).

—He has said, "Fear not them who can kill the body:" but He has also said, "Beware of men" (Rieger).

And there accompanied him, etc. (ver. 4). How variously is a Christian regarded! Some lie in wait for his life: others were ready in love to lay down their lives for him (Rieger).—God must have had peculiar delight in the fellowship of those believers with the sufferings of Paul; so that He has caused all the names of those who accompanied the apostle in his exile to be carefully noted. He thus declares their trial of faith and love to be worthy of everlasting remembrance (Apost. Past.).—Six or seven pious people united together are a formidable enemy to the devil, especially when they have a Paul for their leader. O Lord, grant such missionaries to the heathen! (Quesnel.)

After the days of unleavened bread (ver. 6). Paul remained quiet during the holy Easter week. Holy days should not be spent on journeys, so far as these can be adjourned (Lindheim).

But on the first day of the week, when we were assembled to break bread, Paul preached to them (ver. 7). The bread of the divine word and of the Lord's Supper agree well together. The first must prepare us for the second, and the second must impart more pleasure to the first (Starke).—*And continued his speech until midnight.* That it is said of Paul that he exhorted them with many words (ver. 3), and here again that he continued his speech until midnight, is a delightful example of the fulness of grace and ardour of spirit with which his heart was filled, even to the end of life. No excuse, however, can be derived from this for too long preaching. Not every preacher is a Paul, whose word overflows with the Spirit, and whose heart overflows with grace. And not every sermon is a farewell sermon as this was, when Paul intended to depart the next day (Apost. Past.).

And there were many lamps in the upper chamber (ver. 8). The Gospel has sanctified all times of the day, even those of the darkness, for its service. And the evening hours in particular, sanctified by the meetings of believers, have something peculiarly affecting, because by this the victory of the Lord over all the powers of darkness becomes very perceptible. Certainly also the enemy has sought, and not without success, to foist in his darkness into these nocturnal assemblies of the children of the light (Williger).—The fact that the many lamps in the upper chamber are remembered, is a sign how carefully they endeavoured to avoid all offence (Rieger).

There sat a young man (ver. 9). If this sleep was fatal which occurred at midnight, what excuse can there be for those who sleep in the church in the day-time? And if bodily sleep is so dangerous, how much more dangerous is the spiritual sleep of false peace! (Starke.)—How can Christians be excused who never sleep in church, because they do not go there; who, lulled in the deep sleep of false security, not only fall down from the third storey, but from God and heaven, into the abyss of sin and hell, and are entirely dead? (Gossner.)—An accident, which takes place when we are engaged in a lawful and holy work, is no proof of the divine displeasure (Starke).

But Paul went down and fell upon him (ver. 10). To extend himself upon the dead, is a posture which, indeed, Elijah and Elisha employed; but our blessed Saviour never, nor Peter at the raising of Tabitha. Everything has its propriety (Rieger). —*Make no noise* (Luther). Noise ought never to be, especially at the tokens of God's presence; but it is particularly to be avoided at death, and those present are then to be referred to what is to be discerned concerning the invisible and the ministry of angels in such a place, and to what is to be conjectured on scriptural grounds (Rieger).

Then he went up and broke bread (ver. 11). Everything proceeded without interruption,—a beautiful proof of the internal composure of those assembled (Williger).

And they brought the lad alive, and were not a little comforted (ver. 12). God preaches sometimes by the dead and sometimes by the living, Sirach xxxviii. 23 (Starke).—The disciples received him again alive, a true Sunday child, and a precious farewell gift of the apostle (Besser).

He himself purposed to go by land (ver. 13). The circumstance that Paul went on foot, and was thus separated for a time from intercourse with his beloved brethren, had doubtless a very peculiar transaction with God for its reason. Probably this witness, hastening to suffering, found it necessary to pray earnestly to God, and to consecrate himself as a willing sacrifice to the good pleasure of God. In such cases we must, as Jesus did with His disciples, separate ourselves from all brethren, and deal with God alone (Apost. Past.).

For he hastened to be at Jerusalem at Pentecost (ver. 16). A teacher must be like-minded as his Lord and Master. As He, at the time of His passion, met His sufferings voluntarily; so here Paul hastened to be at Jerusalem at Pentecost, although he knew that bonds and afflictions awaited him there (Starke).

On the whole section (vers. 1–16).—*The Lord bless you* (ver. 1). By this we implore: 1. That God may preserve you in body and spirit; 2. may bestow upon you His grace in the forgiveness of sins, and in the adoption of children; 3. may give you peace in country, church, house, and heart (Lisco).—*When they persecute you in one city, flee ye to another.* 1. How Paul followed this counsel. 2. What we should learn therefrom (Lisco).—*How trouble and persecution are blessed to the servants of God.* 1. They thereby become more fit for the performance of their work. 2. They are thereby united in closer love to one another (Lisco).—*The communion of saints*, vers. 7–17. 1. How it is manifested in the love-feast, and in the preaching of the word, which is readily preached and willingly heard. 2. How it is tried by a dangerous interruption, but which by God's aid terminates in holy joy. 3. How it becomes fruitful in harmonious action and suffering (Lisco).—*Preaching and the Lord's Supper.* 1. In their nature. 2. In their connection. 3. In their blessing (Lisco).—*The resuscitation of the dead at Troas.* 1. The fulfilment of the promise of Christ. 2. The means of strengthening our faith (Lisco).—*How to the faithful servant of God, every deliverance from danger is a new incitement to redeem the time for the service of the Lord:* representing to him the impending nearness of death and the helpful nearness of his Lord.—*The last missionary ways of Paul:* or, "I must work while it is day, before the night cometh, when no man can work." The day of the apostle draws toward evening, his pilgrimage is near its close; but he continues to work unweariedly: 1. blessing the brethren, in love, vers. 1, 2; 2. suffering persecution, in patience, ver. 3; 3. preaching the Gospel, in power, ver. 7; 4. working miracles, in faith, vers. 9–12; 5. and hastening to the appointed end, in stedfast obedience.—*The peaceful campaign at Troas.* 1. The peaceful host, which marches thither: Paul with his seven companions (vers. 4–6). 2. The peaceful work, which is there completed: the preaching of the Gospel, and the resuscitation of Eutychus (vers. 9–12).

3. The peaceful return which is permitted them: departure in love (ver. 13); farther journey to Jerusalem (ver. 16).—*The memorable nocturnal service at Troas.* 1. An admonitory example of Christian zeal for God's word: on the part of the apostle, who is not weary of preaching; and on the part of the congregation, who are not weary of hearing until midnight. "O Lord Jesus, abide with us, for it is toward evening: let not Thy bright light be extinguished among us."[1] 2. A warning example of human weakness and sloth: the sleep and fall of Eutychus. "Watch and pray, that ye enter not into temptation." "The spirit is willing, but the flesh is weak." 3. A consolatory example of divine grace and faithfulness: the resuscitation of the young man, the comfort of the Church. "We have a God who helps: the Lord, He is the Lord who delivers from death."—*The young man Eutychus, an instructive example to all the unstedfast in the Church.* 1. By his dangerous sleep in the midst of the assembled congregation: during the hearing of the divine word, the heart may be overpowered by the sleep of false security. 2. By his terrible fall from the third storey to the street-pavement: an admonitory representation of the great fall from an imaginary height of faith to sin and perdition. 3. By his miraculous deliverance. In the arms of a Paul, who penetrates him with his power of life and warmth of love, even the deeply fallen, he who is thought dead, may by the wonderful grace of God again become living. But it remains a miracle, of which even the Scripture does not relate many similar. Let us not run the risk. Be sober, be vigilant. It is a precious thing, when the heart is stedfast.—*The dangerous sleep, and the blessed awakening.* 1. The sleep of one, slumbering in false security towards spiritual death. 2. The awaking of a soul, penetrated by the grace of God, from death to life.—*Paul over the dead body of Eutychus; or, the miraculous power of an apostolic personality.* 1. He went down, in compassionate tenderness. 2. He fell upon him, with quiet and earnest prayer. 3. He embraced him, with encircling and assiduous love.—*Make no noise;* a friendly exhortation in every house of mourning. 1. Desecrate not the quiet chamber of the dead: with wild complaints against God; with disconsolate mourning; with vain funereal parade; with unbrotherly contentions about

[1] From a German hymn.

the inheritance. 2. But remain still in the Lord: in patient submission under His mighty hand; in meek reception of His comforting word; in childlike trust on His gracious presence; in tender ministration of love. "When it is quiet, an angel passes through the room: thus the holy angels of God pass through the quiet house of mourning, the angel of judgment, but also the angel of comfort."—*Paul alone on his way to Assos:* or, the quiet hours of a much employed servant of God, as hours of testing intercourse with himself, of holy communion with the Lord, of blessed rest from the tumult of the world, and of earnest collectedness for new conflicts.

C.

Farewell Discourse of Paul to the Ephesian Elders.

CHAP. XX. 17–38.

17 And from Miletus he sent to Ephesus, and called the elders of the
Church. 18 And when they came to him, he said to them, Ye know, from
the first day that I came into Asia, how I have been with you during the
whole time, 19 Serving the Lord with all humility, amid tears and tempta-
tions, which befell me by the snares of the Jews: 20 How I have kept back
nothing that was profitable, but have announced to you, and taught you
publicly, and in your houses, 21 Testifying both to the Jews and to the
Greeks, change of mind toward God, and faith toward our Lord Jesus
Christ. 22 And now, behold, I go bound in the spirit to Jerusalem, not
knowing what will befall me there, 23 Except that the Holy Ghost wit-
nesses to me, from city to city, saying, that bonds and afflictions await me.
24 But I esteem my life of no account for myself, in order to finish my
course with joy, and the ministry which I have received from the Lord
Jesus, to testify the Gospel of the grace of God. 25 And now, behold, I
know that ye all, among whom I have gone with the proclamation of the
kingdom, will see my face no more. 26 Therefore I testify to you this day,
that I am pure of the blood of you all. 27 For I have not shrunk back from
declaring to you the whole counsel of God. 28 Take heed then to your-
selves, and to all the flock, among whom the Holy Ghost has set you as
overseers, to feed the Church of the Lord, which He has purchased by His
own blood. 29 I know that after my coming ravenous wolves will enter
among you, not sparing the flock; 30 And from the midst of you will men
arise, speaking perverse things, in order to draw disciples after them.
31 Therefore watch, and remember, that for the space of three years I did
not cease day and night to exhort every one of you with tears. 32 And
now I commend you to God, and to the word of His grace, who is able to

build up and to give an inheritance among all them who are sanctified.
33 I have coveted no man's silver, or gold, or apparel. 34 Ye yourselves know
that these hands have ministered to my necessities, and to my companions.
35 I have showed you all things, how that ye ought to work, and to assist
the weak, and to be mindful of the words of the Lord Jesus; for He Himself
has said, "It is more blessed to give than to receive."

36 And having spoken these things, he kneeled down and prayed with
them all. 37 And there was much weeping among all, and they fell on
Paul's neck and kissed him; 38 Sorrowing most for the word that he had
spoken, that they would see his face no more. And they accompanied him
to the ship.

Ver. 19. Πολλῶν before δακρύων is a later addition: it is wanting in the majority of uncial MSS., and in many versions.

Ver. 23. After διαμαρτύρεταί, the five oldest MSS. have μοι, which the textus receptus, after the two youngest uncial MSS. G. and H., has erroneously omitted.

Ver. 24. The most difficult reading, ἀλλ' οὐδενὸς λόγου ποιοῦμαι τὴν ψυχὴν τιμίαν ἐμαυτῷ, attested by four MSS. of the first rank, B.C.D. (second hand) and the Sinaitic Codex, and by several Oriental versions, is undoubtedly to be preferred; whereas the textus receptus has ἀλλ' οὐδενὸς λόγον ποιοῦμαι οὐδὲ ἔχω τ. ψ. μου τιμ.; and Lachmann reads οὐδενὸς λόγον ἔχω οὐδὲ ποιοῦμαι τ. ψ. τιμ. ἐμ. Both are evidently alterations for the sake of simplifying the original text.

Ver. 25. Τοῦ Θεοῦ after βασιλείαν is an explanatory addition, but is wanting in the three most important uncial MSS.; whilst it would certainly not have been omitted, if it were originally there.

Ver. 28. Here there is a dogmatically very important difference in the reading: τὴν ἐκκλησίαν τοῦ κυρίου and τὴν ἐκκλησίαν τοῦ Θεοῦ. The textus receptus has the latter reading; but the former is decidedly supported by external authorities, and is certainly the original reading. For four uncial MSS., A.C.D.E., 14 cursive MSS., several Oriental versions and fathers, have κυρίου. Only one uncial MS., the Vatican, but also, according to Tischendorf's *Notitia editionis codicis bibliorum Sinaitici* 1860, the Sinaitic Codex of the fourth century, lately discovered by him, several cursive MSS., the Vulgate, but none of the fathers before the fourth century, and before the Arian controversies, have Θεοῦ. Some MSS. unite both κυρίου and Θεοῦ, sometimes with, and sometimes without καί. As regards the internal evidence, the circumstance which Bengel adduces in favour of Θεοῦ rather decides against it, that Paul never uses in his epistles the expression ἐκκλησία τοῦ κυρίου, but eleven times the expression ἐκκλ. τ. Θεοῦ. Therefore some transcribers might adapt it to the Pauline usage, by which the combination of κυρίου and Θεοῦ, and the alteration of Θεοῦ instead of κυρίου, might have been introduced. Besides, αἷμα τοῦ Θεοῦ was congenial to the dogmatism of the fourth and fifth centuries.

Ver. 29. Οἶδα is the original reading; not γὰρ οἶδα τοῦτο, which Tischendorf, on the ground of some younger MSS., has adopted with the textus receptus. The additional words are a favourite interpolation.

Ver. 32. Ἀδελφοί after ὑμᾶς is also a later addition: it is wanting in

A.B.D. and in six old versions.—*Οἰκοδομῆσαι* is the original reading: Tischendorf has erroneously, after G. and H., adopted the compound verb *ἐποικοδ.*; whereas the simple verb has the five remaining uncial MSS. for it.

Ver. 35. The genitive plural, *τῶν λόγων*, is undoubtedly original. Both *τὸν λόγον* and *τοῦ λόγου*, which are not sufficiently supported by external authorities, arose from the fact that only a single saying of Jesus is adduced.

EXEGETICAL EXPLANATIONS.

1. *And from Miletus.*—Paul, having called the elders of the Church of Ephesus, addressed to them this memorable farewell discourse; evidently to the elders of Ephesus only, and not to those also of other neighbouring churches (Irenæus). He reminds them, first of all, of the fidelity and conscientiousness of his ministry among them. *Ἀπὸ πρώτης—Ἀσίαν* is logically to be referred to *πῶς—ἐγενόμην*, not to *ἐπίστασθε*. The manner of his conduct he describes in vers. 19–21, as that of an earnest and at all times faithful servant of the Lord Jesus Christ. *Πᾶσα ταπεινοφρ.* is a genuine Pauline expression: with every possible expression of humility. Ver. 20, *ὡς*, etc., is a further exposition of *πῶς—ἐγενόμην*. *Ὑποστέλλεσθαι* is even by classical writers, as, for example, Demosthenes, Isocrates, and Plutarch, used for reserved discourse; *οὐδὲν ὑπεστειλάμην* is to be referred to genuine boldness; *τοῦ μὴ ἀναγγεῖλαι* expresses, in virtue of the original import of the infinitive with the genitive of the article, the design, but in this, as in many other instances, it denotes merely the manner or mode: *quominus ea vobis annuntiarem*. *Διαμαρτύρεσθαι* has here the object, to which the testimony practically refers, and to which it will incite, in the accusative. *Μετάνοια εἰς τὸν Θεὸν* is change of disposition, conversion toward God, and is not, as Beza, Bengel, and others think, to be restricted to the Gentiles, as if the Jews, according to the opinion of Jesus and of the apostles, did not require conversion as well as the Gentiles, in order to be received into the kingdom of God.

2. *And now, behold, I go.*—The apostle, in ver. 22, passes from the past to the future. *Δεδεμένος τῷ πνεύματι* has given rise to many interpretations, both as regards *δεδεμ.* and as regards *πνεύματι*. The first has been often understood of bonds and fetters; *spiritu jam alligatus, vincula præsentiens* (Erasmus, Grotius, Bengel). But this by no means suits *τὰ—μὴ εἰδώς*. Accordingly *δεδεμένος* must be understood in the biblical sense,

constrained, necessitated. Many interpreters refer πνεῦμα to the Holy Spirit; so that they understand it either, "constrained by the Holy Spirit" (Beza, Calvin); or, "bound to the Holy Spirit" (Meyer, 1st edition); or, "on the impulse of the Holy Spirit, I go bound" (Oecumenius). But as in ver. 23 τὸ πνεῦμα τὸ ἅγιον is expressly named, so πνεῦμα in ver. 22 cannot be understood of the Spirit of God, but of the spirit of the apostle himself: constrained in spirit, led by an internal necessity, I go up to Jerusalem.

3. *Except that the Holy Spirit.*—Ὅτι after πλήν is still dependent on εἰδώς. The Holy Spirit, namely, by the mouth of Christian prophets (compare chap. xiii. 2, xxi. 4, 10). Paul says, that bonds and afflictions were predicted to him at Jerusalem from city to city. It is true that nothing of this kind is related until chap. xxi. 4, 11; but who will assure us that Luke, who from ver. 3 has related everything summarily, has omitted nothing of this kind? Only on this supposition can it be maintained that Luke has committed an anachronism (Schneckenburger). The predictions of the prophets caused the apostle to expect imprisonment and other troubles in Jerusalem; but it was not exactly known to him what would befall him there.

4. *But I esteem my life of no account.*—The reading οὐδενὸς λόγου ποιοῦμαι τὴν ψυχὴν τιμίαν ἐμαυτῷ is hardly to be construed, with Meyer, as if οὐδενὸς λόγου τιμίαν were connected together; for although τίμιος once occurs with the genitive of value (Plato, in the Sophists), yet in far the greatest number of instances it is used absolutely, especially as ποιοῦμαι itself contains the idea of value. Accordingly, the literal meaning is, "I esteem my life of no account, as a life valuable to myself.' The two other readings, λόγον ἔχω and λόγον ποιοῦμαι, import, "I have regard to nothing; I do not even count my life dear to myself." Bengel takes ὡς τελειῶσαι comparatively: "My life is not to me so dear an object as the finishing of my course." This might be grammatically simple, but logically it does not recommend itself, as we would then expect, "to finish my course faithfully," instead of, "with joy." The infinitive with ὡς must therefore express the design: "In order that I may finish my course with joy."

5. *And now, behold, I know.*—The apostle did not know what was to befall him at Jerusalem. But he asserts it as a definite

knowledge, that those present from Ephesus, indeed all the churches to whom he had preached the Gospel, would see his face no more. Ὑμεῖς πάντες indicates the Ephesian elders as, in a manner, the representatives of all those churches in Europe and Asia Minor, founded by the Apostle Paul. Paul here speaks very positively of his presentiment of death, but not, however, as a divine revelation. At a later period, indeed, in his epistles during his imprisonment at Rome,—as, for example, the Epistle to the Philippians,—he was not so certain whether he might not be set at liberty, and again visit the churches. But as his liberation at Rome is, historically, extremely doubtful, his foreboding here did not deceive him. To maintain that Luke put these words in the mouth of Paul *post eventum* might be defended, if the impossibility of Paul's thus speaking at that time could be made out.

6. *Therefore I testify to you this day*, namely, because I take my final departure, and may never again address you. Bengel understands μαρτύρομαι here, as it frequently occurs in the classics, *testem cito, in testimonium voco*, which would indeed give an excellent sense, only the dative ὑμῖν is opposed to it, as, according to this interpretation, the pronoun would have been in the accusative. Ver. 27 is in point of fact, and also in part verbally, identical with ver. 20. The counsel of God is His counsel of grace and redemption: πᾶσα, with all that belongs to it.

7. *Take heed then to yourselves.*—The farewell exhortation is united to the declaration of the apostle's innocence: I am not to blame; the blame will only rest on you; therefore (οὖν) do your part, in order to take heed both to yourselves and to all the flock. The Church is, as it were, a flock which must be fed and protected against ravenous wolves (ποίμνιον, ποιμαίνειν, λύκοι). For this purpose the elders are to minister; they are appointed as overseers. The word ἐπίσκοποι is here used, not as an official term, but only to express the business and the duty of the elders, to exercise watchful oversight and care. Ποιμαίνειν in itself comprehends practical guidance and government, as well as nourishment and maintenance with the wholesome food of the word, and with all the means of grace. Περιποιεῖσθαι is to purchase, to convert into our own property. See Dogmatical and Ethical Remarks, No. 7.

8. *I know that, after my coming, grievous wolves will enter in.*

—Careful pastoral oversight is the more necessary, because wolves and seducers will come, who will treat the Church in an unsparing manner. They will come μετὰ τὴν ἄφιξίν μου; that is, not, as most interpreters render it, after my going away—the departure of the apostle: ἄφιξις never signifies departure, but only arrival, coming. Accordingly the words simply mean, "after my coming, at a later period, other people will come." *Primum venit Paulus, deinde venient lupi:* Bengel. But they come εἰς τὴν ἐκκλ., not ἐπὶ τ. ἐκκλ.; they come from without, and enter into the Church. Persecutors, therefore, cannot be here meant (Grotius, *persecutio sub Nerone*); but false teachers, who will come into the Church from without. On the other hand, seducers are mentioned from the midst of the Church. Ἀποσπᾶν indicates that to join with these men would be an apostasy from the truth and from the true Church of Christ.—If we consider what conflicts the apostle, according to his epistles, had at this time with false teachers, and how he must have known exactly how matters stood at Ephesus, and in Asia Minor in general, there is nothing in the least surprising that here, looking at the future, he should foretell internal and external dangers for the Church at Ephesus, which dangers, however, he describes only in their bare outlines. There is then no reasonable ground to suspect here an anachronism, a prediction after the event, which the historian has put into the mouth of the apostle (Baur, Zeller).

9. *Therefore watch.*—Διὸ γρηγορεῖτε is the same logical connection as ἐγὼ γὰρ οἶδα, etc. (ver. 29); the impending dangers make watchful oversight a duty. Paul here reckons his residence at Ephesus at three years. According to chap. xix. 8, 10, he taught for three months in the Jewish synagogue, and afterwards for two years in the lecture-room of Tyrannus. This is not contradictory, as in such statements of time the period is not to be understood as strictly chronological, which, especially in the context, would be flat.

10. *And now I commend you.*—If the elders are to exercise inviolable fidelity, they themselves must stand firm in the grace and fellowship of God. Therefore Paul commends them to the mighty and faithful protection of God. Τῷ δυναμένῳ, etc., cannot be referred to λόγῳ (Erasmus and others), because the reference here to the personal Word (Gomarius, Witsius) is

wholly groundless, and the bestowal of the eternal inheritance cannot possibly be referred to the word, but only to the personal God. Accordingly τῷ δυναμένῳ is to be referred, with the Vulgate, Luther, Calvin, Grotius, and Bengel, to Θεῷ, so that καὶ τ. λόγῳ τ. χάριτος αὐτοῦ is passed over. God is able to build up, *i.e.*, to bestow stability of spiritual life; and He is able to bestow an inheritance, *i.e.*, to grant a lawful and secure portion in the kingdom of glory among all those (in fellowship with them) who are sanctified to God.

11. *I have coveted no man's silver or gold.*—Finally, the apostle reminds them of his own unselfishness, and exhorts the elders to similar conduct, in accordance with the word of the Redeemer. Τοῖς οὖσι μετ' ἐμοῦ are his companions and assistants in his apostolic work, for whose maintenance Paul also provided by his own labour, so that he was accustomed to require the means of support from the churches neither for himself nor for his assistants. Πάντα, placed first by way of emphasis, in all things; ὑπέδειξα, namely, by his own example. Ἀντιλαμβ. τ. ἀσθενούντων can hardly be meant literally, for then it would signify to assist the sick and the physically weak: it is a deviation from the primitive meaning to refer it to the support of the poor (Chrysostom, De Wette); for although ἀσθενής, in some passages from the classics collected by Wetstein, signifies "poor," yet the verb ἀσθενεῖν and its participle never have that meaning. Thus, then, it only remains to understand ἀσθενοῦντες of weakness in faith and in Christian disposition, and ἀντιλαμβ. of kind forbearance, inasmuch as the asking, or even the receiving of money and pay, might give to unconfirmed minds the impression of covetousness, and might obstruct the entrance of the truth, whilst the complete unselfishness of a teacher would operate powerfully upon them. Among the many sayings of Jesus referring to this (λόγων), the apostle adduces only one, and that not given in the Gospels, but which, without doubt, he learned from oral tradition. The saying of Jesus is, according to its original intention, certainly not to be limited to the superior blessedness of giving (Meyer), but is to be understood in its full sense: "It is more blessed to give than to receive," viewing it from the conduct of God toward men, in the sense of Matt. v. 48, and other passages; and so that both giving and receiving are here to be understood in the most comprehensive sense, including

spiritual and bodily, temporal and eternal blessings. The application which Paul makes of it is thus the more suitable.

12. The speech is divided into three parts.—I. The retrospect of the past, reminding them of the labours of the apostle at Ephesus, vers. 18–21. II. A glance into the future, and the announcement of his final separation, vers. 22–25. III. An exhortation to the elders concerning their duty to the Church, with reference to the apostle's faithful and unselfish activity on its behalf, vers. 26–35. It is unnecessary to observe how appropriate this discourse was to the circumstances of the case as a farewell address and an episcopal charge, how impressive and consoling, how full of love and holy earnestness. Nevertheless, it has lately been asserted to be unhistorical, and the pure composition of the author of the history (Baur, Zeller). On the other hand, Tholuck (Studien und Kritiken, 1839, p. 305) has pointed out that this speech represents to us the same spirit and heart which the epistles of Paul exhibit. Moreover, as regards the doctrine, the peculiarly Pauline nature of this address is evidently seen.—See Dogmatical and Ethical Thoughts, No. 4 and 7.

13. *And after he had spoken thus.*—At the conclusion, the apostle kneels down, all follow him, and he closes his address to men with a prayer to God. After this the farewell of each individual from Paul takes place, embracing him and with many tears, particularly because the announcement deeply affected them, that they would see his face no more (*θεωρεῖν*, significantly, while Paul, ver. 25, simply said *ὄψεσθε*, Meyer); finally, they accompanied him to the ship, and thus tore themselves from him.

DOGMATICAL AND ETHICAL THOUGHTS.

1. Paul, in this address, more than once reminds them that he had taught the whole doctrine, and had kept back nothing (vers. 20, 27). He thus puts stress not only on this, that he had taught the pure doctrine, the real and uncorrupted will and counsel of God (*βουλὴ Θεοῦ*, ver. 27), that which was profitable to souls (*τὰ συμφέροντα*, ver. 20), and nothing unprofitable or absolutely pernicious and leading to error; but, in his justification, and as proof that he was pure of the blood of all, he specially adds, that he had reserved nothing. The pure truth, and the whole truth. The word of God is an organic whole, in

which all is connected together, and no member of which can be put in the background, or be neglected, without doing injury to the other members. God's counsel of redemption is a whole, in which righteousness and grace, the realization and appropriation of salvation, conversion and holiness, the individual and the congregational, may certainly be distinguished, but cannot, without blame and injury, be separated. In God Himself, and in His work of salvation, everything is inseparably and eternally united; in the Scriptures, as a totality, everything is internally and exactly joined; in the announcement of the Gospel, as well as in systematic theology, no part ought to be put in the background and overlooked; but the pure truth and the whole truth ought to be developed, and all the parts and articles of the truth to be represented in their exact *temperamentum*, in their natural harmony.

2. The apostle describes his labours as twofold—publicly, and from house to house, ver. 20; turning himself not only to the Church, but also to individuals, ver. 31. Paul omitted neither of these, and neither ought to be neglected. Christianity certainly aims at the salvation of individuals by conversion and sanctification, entwines around man the bond, torn by sin, of living and blessed fellowship with God, and in the work of renewal draws that bond continually the closer and the firmer. The Spirit of God is imparted to individuals, and constitutes them the children of God. But the individualism of Christianity is not unhealthy and that of a recluse: on the contrary, conversion to the Lord makes individuals sociable, and the family, as well as the Church and Christendom, are pervaded by the spirit of Christianity; yet this is not a regeneration only of the man, but also of humanity (the second Adam, 1 Cor. xv. 45, 47), according to its different phases in society.

3. The apostle testified, both to the Jews and to the Gentiles, repentance and faith; change of mind or conversion toward God, and faith toward the Lord Jesus Christ: not the one without the other. Faith without repentance is superficial; the pupil of faith is a broken heart; Christ came not to call the righteous, but sinners to repentance. Repentance without faith is either inconsolable, and ends in despair; or self-righteous, and ends in making redemption superfluous.

4. Twice in this speech Paul calls the Gospel, "the word of

God's grace:" τὸ εὐαγγ. τ. χάριτος τ. Θεοῦ, ver. 24; ὁ λόγος τ. χάριτος αὐτοῦ, ver. 32. The characteristic, by which the revelation of God in Christ is properly distinguished from the old covenant, is the manifestation of grace toward sinners; redeeming, forgiving, sanctifying, and saving grace. But to represent this as the very centre of the whole counsel of God, and to call that counsel by this short name, was granted only to the Apostle Paul, inasmuch as his personal leading to Christ and his course of life among the Gentiles assisted him to this knowledge. That the Gospel is here called by this name, is a proof of the genuineness of this address.—It is likewise to be observed, how highly the word of grace was esteemed by the apostle. The ministry which he received from Christ is concerned with nothing else than with the publication of the Gospel of the grace of God, ver. 24. And in the corresponding verse (ver. 32), the word of God's grace is represented as a power. It is true τῷ δυναμένῳ οἰκοδ. καὶ δοῦναι κλη. refers to God Himself, and not to His word. But still it would have no meaning to commit the brethren not only to God, but also to His word, if the word were not in itself also powerful and efficient. Accordingly the word of God is a power "which strengthens, comforts, and helps us," a genuine means of grace.

5. Paul states the anxious presentiment of the things which await him at Jerusalem. Prophets, illuminated by the Holy Ghost, foretell to him bonds and afflictions. He himself does not value his life, and knows that all the churches he has founded will see him no more. These are certainly significant statements. But still they do not convince us that it was determined in the divine counsels, that Paul should suffer death as a martyr at Jerusalem, but that God graciously heard the supplication and mourning of the Gentile Christians for the life of the apostle, and on that account permitted Paul, already condemned to death, to be rescued by the Roman power, and granted to him a continuance of life and labour (Baumgarten, vol. ii. p. 372, English Translation). As no clear and certain text favours such a view, we are not permitted to make such a supposition.

6. The ministry and the Holy Ghost. The elders are appointed overseers by the Holy Ghost, in order to feed the Church of the Lord. We are not informed how the elders at Ephesus

were ordained to the ministry; but from analogy (chap. vi. 2–6, and xiv. 23), it is to be supposed that they were chosen under the direction of the apostle, and not without the co-operation of the Church, and were set apart by prayer and the imposition of hands. This was the human and visible side of the transaction. But the apostle draws attention to the invisible and divine side. It is the Holy Ghost who has acted; it is He, properly, who has appointed and commissioned the persons; they are bound and responsible to Him. The apostle does not deny the co-operation of man, but he brings prominently forward the decisive action of the Holy Ghost, to deny which would be at least as erroneous and wrong. As in the Redeemer, the divine and the human are one, so also is it in the Church, which is eminently the Church of the Lord (ἡ ἐκκλ. τ. κυρίου). Only there is this difference, that in the Church the Spirit of the Father and of the Son works, and that the union is not personal and inseparable. But in the true acts of the Church, which refer to the kingdom of God, and take place from a regard to God and His Anointed, according to the rule of the divine word, and with prayer, it is the Holy Ghost who there rules. And if, then, the Holy Ghost works and decides, so must He dwell in the members of the Church who act: accordingly, the appointment of elders to the pastoral office by the Holy Ghost rests on the universal priesthood of believers, as a presupposition, instead of being, as it might at first sight appear, a hierarchical idea.

7. The Church and the death of Christ. With the design of bringing before the elders their pastoral duty to the Church in its entire holiness and responsibility, Paul testifies that the Church is the property of the Lord, being purchased by His own blood. Thus the blood of Jesus Christ, shed at His violent death, is the means by which He has converted the Church into His lawful property. *Διὰ τοῦ αἵματος τοῦ ἰδίου* is hardly to be considered as the purchase-money, by a strict adherence to the image of *περιποιεῖσθαι*. But the crucifixion of Jesus is viewed as the means of appropriation, by which souls, who without His sufferings and death were not His, have become His property; objectively, inasmuch as He has procured a right of possession to them by His death for them; and subjectively, inasmuch as the love of the Redeemer which impelled Him to death fills souls with the love of gratitude, and draws them to Him. Accord-

ingly, not only in the work of redemption is the greatest stress laid upon the death of Jesus, but this is also put as the essential foundation of the Church of Christ; an idea which in itself is very profound, and also purely Pauline.

8. The false teachers. The apostle, in his prophetic warning, distinguishes two kinds of false teachers: those who come from without, and, as ravenous wolves, lay waste the Church; and those who arise from the Church itself, and seek to gain followers. The latter will *διεστραμμένα λαλεῖν*. *Διδάσκειν* is designedly not chosen; that were too great an honour for such perverted instruments. What they speak are perverted, distorted things. As a member of the body may be strained, and by violent bending put into a distorted position; so also truths may be perverted, placed in false relations to each other, distorted by exaggeration, changed into caricatures of that which they originally represented. And this is the nature of all false doctrine. Error is only a misrepresentation of truth; every false doctrine has some truth at bottom, which is misrepresented by the fault of man.

9. The inheritance among all those who are sanctified. The inheritance of the blessed consists not only in perfect communion with God, but also in communion with all the saints. The rich inheritance of the invisible Canaan is among all who are redeemed from sin by the grace of God in Christ, and who are sanctified by the Holy Spirit. It is remarkable that this idea occurs in the epistle, though not originally intended exclusively for the Ephesian Church, yet written for it: *ἡ κληρονομία αὐτοῦ ἐν τοῖς ἁγίοις*, Eph. i. 18. And certainly the comprehensive fellowship with all the saints is an exaltation of the glory of the inheritance, and of the blessedness of the future world.

10. It is more blessed to give than to receive. The natural man, led by selfishness, reverses this statement. But every morally improved and virtuous man feels its truth in some measure. Plutarch mentions of Artaxerxes that he said, *ὅτι τὸ προσθεῖναι τοῦ ἀφελεῖν βασιλικώτερόν ἐστι*. And Aristotle, Eth. Nicom. iv. 1, says, *μᾶλλόν ἐστι τοῦ ἐλευθερίου τὸ διδόναι ᾧ δεῖ, ἢ λαμβάνειν ὅθεν δεῖ*. Both of these are expressed in accordance with the aristocratic view of antiquity. In the former, with reference to the contrast between rulers and people; and in the latter, with reference to the contrast between freemen and

slaves. Whereas Seneca, De Benefic. iii. 15, starts from the gods, when he says, *Qui dat beneficia, Deos imitatur; qui recepit, fœneratores*. Still, that there is in all these classical expressions a certain aristocratic pride of disposition, is undeniable. On the contrary, the saying of Christ rests on the fact that God is love; and the use which the apostle makes of it, rests on experience of the redeeming and gracious love of God in His Son, and on the desire to extend to all the blessedness of loving and of giving.

HOMILETICAL HINTS.

And from Miletus, he sent to Ephesus, and called the elders of the Church (ver. 17). It is not merely the remembrance of the divine blessing which he experienced amid his conflicts and sufferings at Ephesus, but his earnest desire to see the brethren, and to impart to them, and through them to the whole Church, an abiding blessing, that induced Paul to call the elders to Miletus (Leonh. and Spieg.).—Superintendents and inspectors should, after the example of Paul, be interested in the pastors under their inspection, confer with, exhort, and encourage them; for what is done to a preacher, is done to a whole congregation. And the servants of the Lord ought willingly to embrace the opportunity of hearing wholesome admonitions from their superintendents, and from esteemed theologians, and to promote their good intentions (Starke).

And when they came to him, he said to them (ver. 18). The address of Paul to the Ephesian elders is a glorious compendium of practical pastoral theology, as it was practised by the apostle; a mirror in which we may see with shame our dissimilar form. It is generally used by ministers in their first and their farewell discourses, but the Lord knows how often it is abused (Apost. Past.).—*Ye know from the first day, how I have been with you during the whole time.* Ye know! Happy he who can thus begin his discourse, while the conscience of his hearers bears testimony for him (Bengel).—Paul appeals only to the conscience of his hearers, not to their empty flattery. Not a letter of commendation from men, but fruit and truth, were what he cared for (Apost. Past.).—Paul had served the Lord at Ephesus from the first day. A teacher loses this blessing who enters upon the ministry in an unconverted state. He may, it is true, be converted in the ministry, but much is lost. This should stir up all candidates for the ministry to get themselves, in due season, well qualified by God (Apost. Past.).

Serving the Lord with all humility, and with many tears and temptations (ver. 19). There are in the ministry many kinds of tears; tears of love, tears of sorrow, and tears of joy. O Lord, grant us many Pauls (Starke).—The ministry has not purely good days; for Paul is not mindful of them, but of tears. Mark this, ye candidates for the ministry: prepare yourselves for them (Starke).—The excellent qualifications of a faithful teacher: humility before God; patience under many crosses; candour and fidelity; indefatigableness in feeding the flock; thorough knowledge how and what we are to teach for edification; undaunted courage in meeting persecution; zeal and diligence in running in the way of the Lord, both in the life and in the ministry; earnest love to the Church; a confident mind and a divine boldness in speaking the truth to every one, according to his necessities; high esteem of precious, purchased souls; prudent foresight of future trials; contentment in temporal things and hatred of greed; and earnestness in prayer (Starke). —Paul places the dignity of his ministry primarily in his upright and humble conduct. In the present day, ministers appeal chiefly to the *honorem ordinis, orthodoxiæ*, etc. (Apost. Past.). —An old minister of our church requested *gratiam lacrimarum.* —A faithful servant of Jesus may also appeal to his sufferings, for these are a seed of tears, and bring him honour (Apost. Past.).—If we are without trials, we learn nothing, and do not prosper; for that is the knighthood and practice of Christians; that is our theology which we do not soon and easily learn (Luther).—Paul speaks of his tears, for he was a Christian and no Stoic. His whole office was a ministry of tears, abundantly saturated with bitterness; but also looking forward to the glorious reward, of which the psalmist speaks, "They that sow in tears shall reap in joy." By the power of his faith, he anticipates the joys of harvest. He triumphs, while he weeps; but he weeps not the less, while he triumphs. He weeps, when at midnight he sings praises in the prison of Philippi. He weeps, when he writes to the Thessalonians, "Rejoice evermore." He weeps, when he testifies at Miletus, "that I may finish my course with joy." He weeps, when at Rome he sings his dying song,

"I have fought a good fight, I have finished my course, I have kept the faith."—We need not wonder that Paul recurs so often to the narrative of his sufferings: this is no egotism, but an earnest desire to win for the truth. He had learned this method in the school of his Lord. If the sufferings of Jesus plead with the Father for mercy to sinners, so they plead with men for the reception of the doctrine of God our Saviour (Monod).

How I have kept back nothing that was profitable (ver. 20). Thus only what was useful, and all that was useful: not what was learned, what was new, what was beautiful, what was sublime, what was rare, etc.; but what might produce fruit to edification. This, and unabridged, was the contents of the apostolic preaching. Mark that, ye pulpit orators (Apost. Past.).—Not to keep back what was profitable from fear of men, and not to advance what was curious to please men, has constituted, at all times, a chief point in the fidelity of a steward of God (Rieger).—*Publicly and privately.* Thus, not only in the pulpit, but also in houses; not only in the sermon, but also in the pastoral office; not only publicly, but also privately, a faithful teacher serves the Lord and His Church. Two things must be overcome in the power of ministerial fidelity: fear of men, and carnal sloth.

Testifying repentance toward God, and faith toward the Lord Jesus Christ (ver. 21). This is the true summary of salvation, of which all sermons must treat; the general imposts which the messengers of God must demand from all men on the whole earth. They do not engage in other matters (Gossner).

And now, behold, I go bound in the Spirit to Jerusalem, not knowing the things which shall befall me there (ver. 22). Faith does not wish to know and to see everything, but follows God and the impulse of His Spirit, as with blindfolded eyes. Faithful teachers have not power over themselves; but are, by reason of their office, bound in heart and spirit to do and to suffer, not what they will, but what God wills (Starke).—The foreknowledge of what may befall us, is not of so much importance, as the strength derived from the Gospel to resist the enemy, lest he should at any time find us lovers too much of our own lives (Rieger).—Love, which has bound me to her yoke in soul and body; Love, which has overcome me and taken possession of my heart; O Love, I resign myself to thee, to be thine for ever[1] (Angelus Silesius).

Except that the Holy Ghost witnesseth in every city, that bonds and afflictions abide me (ver. 23). The Holy Ghost is a Prophet of suffering, but also a Comforter in suffering (Quesnel).

But I count not my life dear to myself, that I may finish my course with joy (ver. 24). "Fear not those who can kill the body, and are not able to kill the soul," Matt. x. 28.—The children and servants of God look not so much to danger as to duty; but the children of the world reverse it (Quesnel).—*And the ministry which I have received of the Lord Jesus.* Paul's ministry was consecrated not only by his tears, but also by his blood. And consecrated by how much more blood, sweat, and tears, have we received it! Should not the recollection of the holy band of witnesses and martyrs shame us at our indifference in the defence of the truth, which was testified by the fathers with blood? (Williger.)—No one should force himself, purchase himself, marry himself, or beg himself into the ministry, and thus run and preach without a divine mission and call; but wait until he receives it, and is sent. But an orderly call, in the fear of God, is not without the divine power and blessing. Whom God sends, him He qualifies (Starke).—*To testify the Gospel of the grace of God.* Paul announces grace, the Gospel, with the last breath of his life; not law, not morals. Millions of moral sermons, and folios of moral books, will not, in a thousand years, bring you so far as this despised little word, grace, the Gospel, will bring you, in one minute, when faith understands, and the heart embraces it (Gossner).

I know that ye will see my face no more (ver. 25). The thoughts of death make zealous preachers. He who thinks, This may perhaps be my last sermon, and my hearers will see my face no more, will entreat them the more earnestly, "Be ye reconciled unto God."—A faithful teacher may indeed let his hearers be lost from his sight, but never from his mind (Starke).

Therefore I testify to you this day, that I am pure of the blood of all men (vers. 26, 27). Many in their farewell discourses would wish to imitate the apostle in his joyfulness, in testifying that he is pure of the blood of all; but this is the fruit of long-continued humility, trials, and tears (Rieger).—

[1] From a German hymn.

Much is required in order to be pure of the blood of all men: we must have said all things, and kept back nothing of the whole counsel of God, ver. 27; we must have spoken to all publicly in the pulpit, and privately in the pastoral cure, ver. 20; we must have spoken in all ways, not only by the word in the sermon, but by the example of Christian life and suffering, vers. 18–20. How many omissions weigh on the consciences of such as we, so that instead of the joyful declaration, "I am pure of your blood," we are rather constrained penitently to pray, Purify me, O Lord, with Thy blood!

Take heed to yourselves and to all the flock (ver. 28). A preacher must be on his guard against two errors: either of attending too much to himself and neglecting the flock; or of so devoting himself to the flock, that he forgets the care of his own salvation (Quesnel).—We must be purified, and then purify others; instructed, and then instruct others; enlightened, and then enlighten others; we must first ourselves draw near to God, and then point the way to others (Gregory Nazianzen).—An evangelical preacher takes heed to himself, when he feeds his own soul with the Gospel of the grace of God; the experience of wholesome doctrine protects against the error of pernicious doctrine. Abide a sheep of the Good Shepherd; so wilt thou become no false shepherd (Besser).—Can a blind man point the way to the blind? It is a fearful thing to be an unsanctified professor, but much more to be an unsanctified minister. Does it not make you tremble, when you open the Bible, lest you should read the sentence of your own condemnation? When you pen your sermons, little do you think that you are drawing up indictments against your own souls (Baxter's Reformed Pastor).—*Among whom the Holy Ghost has set you as overseers, to feed the Church of God, which He has purchased by His own blood.* What a powerful call to fidelity, when we think that we have to feed a flock which God has purchased with His own blood! (Starke.)—Paul will not here repeat his instructions, in what manner they are to feed the flock. He wishes not to instruct, but exhort. He wishes, at this holy time, to speak an imperishable word, to leave behind him an inextinguishable impression and an indelible impulse in the souls of his hearers. When he says only one word, he says all, and supersedes all further exhortation, while he must make his hearers so deeply feel the greatness and sanctity of their work, that all human eloquence would not be able to effect so much as this one word of truth. He calls the Church, "the Church of God,"—His property in a yet higher sense than were the people of the old covenant, whom He bore on eagles' wings,—His property by the blood of His own Son (Menken).—The poorest village is a church of God, purchased by the blood of Jesus. Thus your minister is not settled among you to collect money, to be a light of learning, an antiquarian, a gardener, a sloth; He is called to be a shepherd of Jesus, the Chief Shepherd (Apost. Past.).

After my departure, will wolves come among you (ver. 29, according to Luther's translation). False teachers think, Let there be only peace while I live. But an apostolic teacher seeks also to prevent mischief from breaking out after his death (Apost. Past.).

And from the midst of you will men arise speaking perverse things (ver. 30). The enemies, of whom the apostle warns, are described partly as grievous wolves, that is, open seducers and murderers of souls, and partly as false brethren who arise from the Church itself, and under a fair appearance of words utter pernicious heresies. The apostle earnestly warns them against both. The first are easily known; the other are more concealed, and therefore more dangerous (Apost. Past.).—Then might the elders, as formerly the disciples, ask, one after another, Lord, is it I?

Therefore watch and remember, that for the space of three years, I did not cease, day and night, to exhort every one of you with tears (ver. 31). All is not vain self-praise which evil-disposed men construe to be so. Love constrained the humility of Paul to disclose to us his tears (Starke).—It is as if we could, in these tears of compassionate love, see into the heart of the faithful apostle, and discover the whole secret of his inner life. There we see the labour of fidelity in the service of Jesus Christ, which does not cease, day nor night, to exhort every one; a seed of tears which, in due time, springs up as a harvest of joy. The recollection of this apostolic fidelity is a powerful call to imitation of that great forerunner, and to the prayer, Awake, spirit of the first witnesses!—If thou couldst with the tears of a Paul, and with the tears of Him who bore our weaknesses and took upon Himself our diseases, step among the wicked generation of this time, thy word would not return to thee void. But when wilt thou be susceptible of such tears? Then only, when thou art no more weak in faith, lax in doctrine, cold in heart for God's cause, unsettled in the chief matter, jealous in subordinate matters; but hast learned from the apostle the truth in love. In short, wouldst thou learn like him to weep for others, learn first to weep truly for thyself (Monod).

And now I commend you to God (ver. 32). Behold here the heart of a faithful teacher. He recommends his flock to God and to the word of His grace, even as Christ graciously recommended His disciples to the Father, John xvii. 6, 9. When ministers have taught, confuted, rebuked, comforted, and done their part, they ought to bring everything again to God, and humbly to recommend the whole matter to Him (Starke).—We cannot be sufficiently comforted by this apostolic word. It is a greeting of the apostolic times to our distracted times, by which the Church in its misery is yet comforted by those fathers, as the true Church of God, with the assurance that it shall not be overcome by the gates of hell (Williger).

I have coveted no man's silver, or gold, or apparel (ver. 33). "I seek not yours, but you," 2 Cor. xii. 14. Although the preachers of the Gospel do not work with their own hands, as Paul, but live by the altar, 1 Cor. ix. 13, yet this word remains for them as a principle. They ought, in self-denying activity, which imports much more than necessary official duties, and in perfect freedom from avarice, to show themselves as those, of whom the world with injustice says, that they would have the least work and the greatest wages (Williger).

It is more blessed to give than to receive (ver. 35). This saying of the Lord, which the Holy Ghost has caused to be preserved to us without the Gospel, must be the motto of every true disciple of Jesus Christ, who came into the world, not to be ministered unto, but to minister, and to give His life a ransom for many; and who also on the throne of His glory imparts Himself in the fulness of divine grace to His Church on earth, and finds His blessedness in such free giving (Leonh. and Spieg.).—To give is more blessed than to receive; for the nearer we approach to God, the more blessed are we. God does not receive, but gives. God is called the "Good One," and it is the property of the Good to impart itself. The more we give, the more we have. In blessing others, we bless ourselves. Let no heart depart sad from thy door, so God will not send thee sad from Him (H. Müller).—As regards God, we should and must receive out of His fulness, grace for grace. The more we receive, the more blessed we are. The more we receive from Him, the more can we give to others. To be unwilling to receive from Him, that is in truth unhappiness (F. Arndt).

After he had thus spoken, he kneeled down, and prayed with them all (ver. 36). Kneeling down in prayer is a privilege of the children of God. Others are ashamed of it, and therefore it is to take place only in the closet or in company with those who understand it, and is not to be unnecessarily exposed to the mockery of the world (Williger).—More is often obtained by prayer than by preaching (Apost. Past.).—If Christian friends thus separate with prayer to God, they will only become the more united in God (Starke).

And they all wept much, and fell on Paul's neck and kissed him (ver. 37). Christians are no Stoics, who would free themselves from all mental emotions. Their love is a fountain, which often gives forth the water of tears.—We are also to fall on Paul's neck, that we might retain him with us; this takes place when we receive his doctrine and believe his Gospel, 1 Thess. ii. 13 (Starke).

Sorrowing most of all for the saying, that they should see his face no more (ver. 38). If the sorrow is so great to see no more here below the face of those we love, how much greater must be the sorrow to be deprived for ever of the sight of God, the angels, and the elect! Therefore our comfort and aim in all our temporary separations, is the reunion in the heavenly Jerusalem (Leonh. and Spieg.).

On vers. 17–38.—*The true relation between shepherds and the flock of Christ.* It is then true, enduring both for time and for eternity, when it is: 1. Fellowship in true doctrine. 2. Fellowship in true love. 3. Fellowship in true prayer (Harless).—*Paul's farewell to the elders of Ephesus.* 1. In reminding them of his apostolic labours, he names the chief points of evangelical preaching, vers. 17–21. 2. In his willingness to suffer, he exhibits to them the believing courage of self-denying love to Christ, vers. 22–25. 3. In pointing to the glory of the Church of God, he exhorts them to a faithful performance of their precious ministry, vers. 27–31. 4. In the prayer at separation, he leads them to the source of all strength and joyfulness in the hour of trial, ver. 32 (Leonh. and Spieg.).—*What sweetens the bitterness of separation.* 1. The consciousness of faithfully fulfilled duty. 2. Resignation to the clearly recognised will of God. 3. The assurance, strengthened by prayer, of the divine guidance and protection (Leonh. and Spieg.).—*The farewell address of Paul at Miletus.* 1. His testimony to his labours in the churches, vers. 18–21: to the performance of his ministry in general, that he performed it with humility and fidelity, and amid temptations; to the substance of his preaching, that he declared the whole counsel of God, especially faith and repentance. 2. His announcement of his final departure, vers. 22–25: of his impending fate—Jerusalem his aim, the sufferings there floating before his mind; of his resolute determination in prospect of his impending fate—readiness to give up his life, such a termination of life certain to him. 3. His last will to the elders, vers. 26–38: an exhortation to fidelity—what obliged them to it, wherefore they would particularly stand in need of it; a recommendation to divine grace—what he wishes for them, how they have consequently to conduct themselves (Lisco).—*Two things necessary for all.* 1. Repentance, vers. 20, 21: a ladder of sorrow, by which we descend into the depths of our own hearts; it has three steps—knowledge of sin, sorrow, and desire of salvation. 2. Faith, ver. 21: a heavenly ladder, on which we mount to God and eternity; it also has three steps—knowledge that the Redeemer has come, holy joy that He has taken up His abode with us, and unshaken confidence in His reconciling, sanctifying, and saving grace (Lisco).—*Glory and comfort of a Christian preacher* (a farewell discourse). 1. His glory: nothing external, neither riches nor honour, ver. 19; rather trial and misapprehension, ver. 19; but still the glory of having continued in joy and suffering with his congregation, of having concealed from it nothing of the wholesome doctrine of the Gospel, especially of having preached to it the two chief points, faith and repentance, vers. 20, 21. 2. His comfort: the hour of separation is come, duty calls him to new and greater conflicts, vers. 22, 23; the preacher does not regard that—the performance of his ministry is above all considerations, ver. 24; but although the separation is sad, he knows that he is pure of the blood of all, and he recommends his flock to faithful successors, and to the grace of the great Chief Shepherd, vers. 26, 27, 32 (Lisco).—*How should a preacher govern his congregation.* 1. He is to live with them: *a.* his life is to be devoted to their service, ver. 19; *b.* he is to enter into the circle of their life, as a friendly sympathizer in their joys and sorrows, ver. 18; *c.* he is to enlighten them by his example, and yet to continue humble, conscious of his own weakness, ver. 19. 2. He is to impart to them the whole truth: *a.* to communicate the whole counsel of God—faith and repentance, ver. 21; *b.* to do so in living application to the necessities of the times, ver. 20; *c.* to every one in particular, that so he may account to God for every soul, vers. 20, 26, 27. 3. He is to suffer for them: *a.* he looks courageously forward in faith to the threatening storms, vers. 22, 23; *b.* he joyfully gives up even his life for Him who gave Himself for us all, vers. 24, 25; *c.* he confidently commends himself and his flock, in life and death, to the grace of the Lord, ver. 32 (Lisco).—*Paul's discharge of his ministry at Ephesus, a model of an evangelical pastor.* From it we are to learn: 1. To serve the Lord with all humility. 2. To feed the flock with all love. 3. To resist the enemy with all fidelity. 4. To look forward to our departure with all joyfulness.—*The blessed seed of tears of a faithful pastor.* 1. It is sown in sorrow. Bitter to a faithful pastor are the tears of self-accusation in weakness and temptation, as those shed by David, Peter, and Paul; the tears of compassion for the sinful wretchedness of the world, as those shed by Jeremiah over the slain of his people, by Jesus over Jerusalem, and by Paul in reference to the wolves threatening his flock; the tears of love at the departure from those with whom we were united in the Lord, as those shed at the grave of Lazarus, and at the separation at Miletus. 2. But the seed of bitter tears ripens into a harvest of joy. From the bitter tears of repentance, flows the sweet assurance of forgiveness. The sad tears of compassion are changed into tears over rescued souls. The hot tears of love are quieted by the hope of reunion in the heavenly Jerusalem.—*The tears of the noble servants of God.* 1. A painful tax of human weakness, which even the best have to pay in external trials and internal temptations. 2. A precious ornament of holy souls, from which shines forth the faithfulness which follows the Lord in suffering, and the love which weeps over the misery of the world. 3. A fruitful seed for a beautiful harvest of joy, which shall ripen to those who weep, not only above in the heavenly plains, where those who sow in tears will reap in joy, but also below on the field of the heart, since their labour is not in vain in the Lord.—Ambrose's saying to Monica, the mother of Augustin, "The son of so many tears cannot be lost."—*What is our best discourse to our congregation?* 1. The discourse of our evangelical word is good. 2. The discourse of our evangelical conduct is better. 3. The discourse of our evangelical suffering is best.—*Behold, I go up to Jerusalem, the blessed watchword of the Christian on dark ways.* With this watchword he proceeds: 1. bound, it is true, by the irresistible will of his Lord, but free in the obedience of love; 2. not knowing, it is true, what will befall him, but assured of the faithful guidance of his God; 3. prepared, it is true, for trials, but comforted in looking forward to the heavenly termination.—*How can a servant of God, in this vale of tears, finish his course with joy?* 1. When he carries in his heart the peace of a good conscience, relying on the consciousness of faithful labour, and on the assurance of divine grace, vers. 18–20, 26, 27. 2. When he leaves behind him in the world the seed of the kingdom of God, which will spring up over his grave by the labour of honest successors, and by the faithfulness of the eternal God, vers. 28–32. 3. When he ventures to hope in heaven for the gracious reward of his Lord, and for the goal of his blessed consummation, ver. 24.—*When are we pure from the blood of all those souls, whom the Lord has entrusted to us?* 1. When we have preached all that the Lord has commanded us, and kept back nothing of the counsel of God, vers. 20, 27. 2. When we have interested ourselves in all to whom we have access; in public and in private; to Jews and Greeks, vers. 20, 21. 3. When we have done everything to procure an entrance to our word by the example of an evangelical conduct, in obedience, humility, love, patience, and self-denial, vers. 18, 19, 31–35. 4. When we have washed away everything, of which our conscience accuses us before God, in the blood of Jesus, which must cleanse and reconcile us as well as our hearers, vers. 24, 36.—*I know that ye will see us no more:* a solemn thought, both for ministers and for hearers.—*Take heed!* a weighty exhortation to all pastors. 1. Take heed to yourselves; your doctrine and your conduct. 2. Take heed to the flock; its divine dignity and its human weakness. 3. Take heed to the wolves, who in a dreadful form come from without, as well as to those who steal into the Church, clothed in sheep's clothing.—*And now, brethren, I commend you to God:* the best conclusion of all evangelical pastoral work. 1. An expression of evangelical love, which cares even beyond its own period of labour. 2. An expression of evangelical humility, which feels, even after the faithfully completed labours of the day, that of ourselves we can do nothing. 3. An expression of evangelical faith, which trusts to the power and faithfulness of the great Shepherd of souls and Preserver of men.—*The farewell discourse of the apostle at Miletus.* 1. A sermon of apostolic fidelity of love and of apostolic power of faith, for our example. 2. A sermon of comfort, under the pains of separation and the fears of love. 3. A sermon of repentance, for our ministerial sins and omissions in duty, in comparison with our great ministerial predecessor.—*Wherefore is it more blessed to give than to receive?* 1. Because it delivers us from ourselves; from the bonds of selfishness, the cares of superfluity, and the burden of dependence. 2. Because it unites us to the brethren, by their friendly attachment, their active gratitude, and their blessed intercession. 3. Because it brings us nearer to our God; that we are permitted to be similar to the image of the All-good, sharers in the delight of the All-loving, and expectants of the gracious reward of an eternal Rewarder.—*The saying of separating love: "Yet a little while, and ye will see me no more"* (ver. 38, compared with John xvi. 16). 1. With its bitterness: sorrow of orphanage; reproaches of conscience, if we have neglected the hour of our merciful visitation. 2. With its sweet comfort: continuing united in the Lord; reunion with the Lord.

D.

Conclusion of the Journey, amid anxious Forebodings.

Chap. xxi. 1–16.

1 And it came to pass that we set sail, after having torn ourselves away from them, and came with a quick voyage to Cos, and on the following day to Rhodes, and from thence to Patara. 2 And finding a vessel which

sailed to Phenicia, we embarked and set sail. 3 But when we got sight
of Cyprus, we passed it on the left hand, and sailed to Syria, and landed
at Tyre; for there the vessel was to deposit its cargo. 4 And when we
had found out the disciples, we remained there seven days: these said to
Paul by the Spirit, that he should not go up to Jerusalem. 5 And having
accomplished these days, we proceeded on our journey, whilst they all, with
their wives and children, accompanied us out of the city; and we kneeled
down on the shore, and prayed. 6 And having taken our leave of one
another, we embarked, and they returned home. 7 And we finished the
voyage, and came from Tyre to Ptolemais, and saluted the brethren, and
remained with them one day. 8 And the next day we departed, and came
to Cæsarea: then we went into the house of Philip the evangelist, who was
one of the seven, and abode with him. 9 This man had four daughters,
virgins, who did prophesy. 10 And as we tarried there several days, there
came down from Judea a prophet, named Agabus; 11 Who came to us,
and took Paul's girdle, and bound his own hands and feet, and said, Thus
saith the Holy Ghost, So will the Jews at Jerusalem bind the man to whom
this girdle belongeth, and will deliver him into the hands of the Gentiles.
12 But when we heard this, both we and they of that place besought him
not to go up to Jerusalem. 13 But Paul answered, What mean ye to weep
and to break my heart? For I am ready, not only to be bound, but also
to die at Jerusalem, for the name of the Lord Jesus. 14 And when he was
not to be persuaded, we ceased, saying, The will of the Lord be done.

15 And after these days, we made preparations, and went up to Jeru-
salem. 16 There went with us also certain of the disciples of Cæsarea,
conducting us to one Mnason of Cyprus, an old disciple, with whom we
should dwell as guests.

Ver. 4. *Τοὺς μαθητὰς* is fully attested, as opposed to the omission of the article.—*Ἐπιβαίνειν* is sufficiently attested, and is to be considered as genuine, instead of the more usual word *ἀναβαίνειν*.

Vers. 5, 6. The reading *προσευξάμενοι ἀπησπασάμεθα ἀλλήλους, καὶ ἐνέβ.* is decidedly attested, whilst *προσευξάμεθα, καὶ ἀσπασάμενοι ἀλλήλους ἐπέβ.* has fewer authorities for it.

Ver. 8. *Οἱ περὶ τὸν Παῦλον* after *ἐξελθόντες* is inserted as the beginning of a Church lesson, and is certainly spurious.—*Τοῦ* before *ὄντος* has not a single uncial MS. for it.

Ver. 15. *Ἐπισκευασάμενοι* is undoubtedly genuine; for of the various different readings some speak for *ἐπί*, and others for *σκευασάμενοι*, whilst a sufficient number of credible authorities support the word *ἐπισκευασάμενοι*.

EXEGETICAL EXPLANATIONS.

1. *And it came to pass.*—*Ἀποσπασθέντες* gives us to understand that this separation from his friends at Ephesus must have been very painful. Cos was the first island which they reached on their southern voyage. They then reached the famous island of Rhodes, off the south-west point of Asia Minor, and distant

about fifteen (German) miles from Cos. Patara, the next station, was a large sea-port town on the most southern projection of Lycia. From Troas they had, as it appears, hired a vessel. At Patara they allowed it to return, and embarked as passengers in a trading vessel, sailing to Phenicia. They then came in sight of Cyprus (ἀναφαίνεσθαι, a nautical expression, signifying to get sight of land), but passed it on the left hand, *i.e.*, to the north, whilst their voyage proceeded south-east to Syria. Syria is here used in the Roman sense, according to which both Phenicia and Palestine were reckoned as belonging to the province of Syria. *Γόμος, φορτίον* is the freight, the ship cargo: ἐκεῖσε, at Tyre the vessel had to deposit its cargo (ἦν ἀποφορτιζόμενον).

2. *And when we had found out the disciples.*—'Ανευρεῖν supposes a search. They knew or supposed that there were Christians at Tyre, but without knowing their name or residence. That, after the apostle had hurried away from Asia Minor, they should spend a whole week at Tyre, had its reason, without doubt, in the circumstance that they must wait until the ship had unladen, and was again ready to sail. 'Εξαρτίζειν τὰς ἡμέρας is *explere, absolvere.*

3. *And we finished the voyage.*—Τὸν πλοῦν διανύσαντες is not to be construed with ἀπὸ Τύρου, for these words refer to the complete termination of the whole voyage from Macedonia. The last part of the voyage was only from Tyre to Ptolemais or Acco (Acre), the best haven on the Syrian coast, at the mouth of the small river Belus, in sight of Carmel. From this it appears the journey proceeded by land to Cæsarea, 36 Roman miles distant from Ptolemais, and thus not more than a day's journey. Here they met with Philip, already known from chap. vi. 5, which passage Luke refers to by the words ὄντος ἐκ τῶν ἑπτά. In chap. viii. 40, we were informed that Philip journeyed from Palestine northward evangelizing, until he came to Cæsarea; and here we find him still resident, and described as an εὐαγγελιστής. This title is placed first, because Philip still laboured as a preacher of the Gospel, without being attached to any congregation, whereas his office in Jerusalem as one of the seven had, in point of fact, ceased since the death of Stephen. The connection of εὐαγγελιστοῦ with ὄντος, "who was the evangelist among the seven" (Meyer), is forced, and does not recommend itself. The observation that he had four virgin daughters who

possessed the gift of edifying discourse, occurs only incidentally, because the discourse is about Philip, and thus without any connection with the events, in particular without any prediction by them concerning the future fate of Paul. However, from this circumstance, and from the fact that Eusebius (Church History iii. 39) informs us, after Papias, that the Apostle Philip had four daughters who did prophesy, Gieseler inferred (Studien und Kritiken, 1829, p. 140) that ver. 9 is an interpolation, originating from some one confounding Philip the evangelist with Philip the apostle. But this is entirely without reason; for who will assure us that the mistake did not rather lie with Papias? It is not for the first time that we here find a notice, which does not appear to be interwoven with the course of events.

4. *A prophet, named Agabus.*—On the other hand, it is remarkable that Agabus is here introduced as if he were entirely unknown, whereas he was already mentioned in chap. xi. 28, and indeed as a prophet also. It appears that here that earlier passage was lost sight of.—Entirely in accordance with the manner of the prophets of the old covenant, Agabus represents what he has to prophesy, not only by words, but also by a symbolical action which he does to himself. He took the girdle with which Paul girded his upper garments, bound his own hands and feet in presence of the apostle and of the rest, and asserted, as a prediction of the Spirit (corresponding to נְאֻם יְהוָֹה in the Old Testament), that the Jews in Jerusalem would thus bind the possessor of this girdle, as he, Agabus, was bound, and would deliver him to the Gentiles. *Παραδώσουσιν εἰς χεῖρας ἐθνῶν* is very analogous in expression to the prophecy of Christ concerning His own sufferings, Matt. xvii. 22, xx. 19.

5. *But when we heard this.*—The prediction, partly because it was prompted by the Holy Ghost, and partly by reason of its symbolical form, affected the hearers so strongly, that the companions of the apostle, together with the Christians in Cæsarea, united in beseeching him not to venture to Jerusalem; and so urgently did they do so, that their weeping was heart-breaking. *Συνθρύπτω* is to soften, to make soft, to break the strength of the soul. The question *τί ποιεῖτε κλαίοντες*, etc., is designed to dissuade them; for Paul proceeds, (Do not this,) for I am resolved. The reply of resignation, "The will of the Lord be done," has with *κυρίου* the Redeemer in view, as Paul had

directly before this named Christ; *κυρίου* is not *Θεοῦ* (De Wette). *'Επισκευασάμενοι* refers to the necessary preparations. *Τινες* is naturally to be added to *τῶν μαθητῶν*. It is the simplest method to resolve the attractive construction, *ἄγοντες παρ' ᾧ*, etc., into *ἄγοντες παρὰ Μνάσωνα, παρ' ᾧ ξενισθῶμεν*. The object of accompanying the apostle was, therefore, chiefly to introduce him and his travelling companions to Mnason, with whom the Christians of Cæsarea were more intimately acquainted, in order that they might be his guests. *'Αρχαῖος μαθ.* is *ἀπ' ἀρχῆς μαθ.* According to his origin, he was certainly a Hellenist.

DOGMATICAL AND ETHICAL THOUGHTS.

1. The Christians at Tyre said to the apostle that he should not go up to Jerusalem. This they said *διὰ τοῦ πνεύματος*, by the inspiration of the Spirit. Here, however, it is necessary to distinguish. They knew, by the revelation of the Spirit, that Paul would have to suffer at Jerusalem. The prophecy of Agabus (ver. 11), and the declaration of the apostle (chap. xx. 23), show that nothing more than this rested on the revelation of the Spirit. The request that Paul should not go up to Jerusalem, where so much danger threatened him, was not prompted by the Holy Ghost, but proceeded only from human will and kindness. Thus the human directly attached itself to the divine, error to truth, the flesh to the Spirit. It is as with the Redeemer Himself, to whose first prophecy of His sufferings Peter attached the well-meant but ungodly dissuasion, Matt. xvi. 22. Nothing is more ensnaring and more dangerous than the *mixtela carnis et spiritus* which so easily insinuates itself in thought, feeling, and action.

2. The prophecy of Agabus is also in so far remarkable, as we are able from it, as it were, to measure how much clearer and more definite the revelations concerning the impending sufferings of Paul became, the nearer he approached Jerusalem and the period of the fulfilment advanced. This is the way, in the old and the new covenant, which all revelation, and, in particular, all prophecy takes, corresponding to the growing nature of the development in time, to which God has subjected His counsel and work.

3. What in Tyre was intricate, was clearly explained in

Cæsarea. Agabus, as the organ of the Holy Ghost, predicts the imprisonment and delivering up of the apostle in Jerusalem. And his travelling companions, together with the Christians resident in Cæsarea, importune the apostle, on this ground, not to venture to Jerusalem. But even the united request of a whole assembly of Christians, among whom were men inspired and labouring faithfully and successfully for the kingdom of God, such as Philip, Timotheus, and others, produces no decided impression on the apostle. The will of the people, even the united wish and will of an assembly of genuine Christians, is not always the will of God. The servant of the Lord does not there stand with stoical coldness; the earnest request and hot tears soften his heart, but his will is not thereby bent; his resolution to go to prison and death for Jesus is fixed; his mind is fully made up.

HOMILETICAL HINTS.

And it came to pass that we set sail, after having torn ourselves from them, and came with a quick voyage to Cos (ver. 1). True friends do not separate without sorrow; although he who cleaves to God more than to man, readily separates himself at the intimation of God.—We have to resign ourselves completely to the guidance of God, and to believe certainly that He will accomplish His design in us, whether it proceeds in a straight course or through difficulties.—Our whole life is a voyage: sometimes we have good wind and weather, and sometimes storm and tempest (Starke).—"Behold, we go up to Jerusalem:" that which the Master said (Luke xviii. 31–33), could also now be said by the disciple (Williger).

And finding a vessel which sailed to Phenicia, we embarked, and set sail (ver. 2). "The ships of the sea shall wait upon Me, to bring thy sons from far, their silver and their gold with them, unto the name of the Lord thy God," Isa. lx. 9. A merchant ship, without doubt. Little did the merchantmen in the ship suspect that the Jewish company brought on board a cargo more precious than the purple of Tyre, the spices of Arabia, and the amber of the Hyperboreans—the precious pearl of the Gospel of salvation. Compare Schiller's poem, "The Merchant."

> "Where sails the ship?—It leads the Tyrian forth
> For the rich amber of the liberal North.

Be kind, ye seas; winds, lend your gentlest wing;
May in each creek, sweet wells restoring spring!
To you, ye gods, belong the merchant!—o'er
The waves, his sails the wide world's goods explore;
And, all the while, wherever waft the gales,
The wide world's good sails with him as he sails."[1]

And came to Tyre. And finding the disciples, we abode with them seven days (vers. 3, 4). To find disciples was an important event in the journal of the travelling apostles. If the learned, the naturalists, the judges of the fine arts, in their travels, inquire after the curiosities of science, nature, and art; a servant of Jesus, on the contrary, directs his eye to the rarities in the kingdom of Jesus, and his most delightful discovery is to meet with the children of God (Apost. Past.).—That we are detained on our journeys, is often a special providence for the salvation of ourselves or of others (Starke).—Paul gained time to strengthen the disciples at Tyre, while the sailors required time for their business. Trade and commerce urged men to discover America, and God has granted to them to bring the Gospel of His Son thither (Rieger).—Why did he remain exactly seven days? Without doubt, because he rejoiced to observe a Sabbath and the Lord's Supper with the disciples. A servant of God may remain longer among the disciples of Jesus, than among the worldly (Apost. Past.).

They all, with their wives and children, accompanied us (ver. 5). Parents ought to take their children with them, where they are led to prayer and to other good works, but not where they may be corrupted.—It is observable, that here children are, for the first time, expressly mentioned in the Acts of the Apostles. Out of the mouths of little children, the Lord has ordained strength (Ps. viii. 2); and these little worshippers on the Tyrian shore may remind us of Luther's auxiliary army of "insignificant heroes" in his contest against the enemy (Besser).

And took leave of one another (ver. 6.) In this world, the best intercourse endures but for a season: it comes again to a separation. But in the blessed eternity, the children of God will delight in each other without separation, 1 Thess. iv. 17 (Starke).

And saluted the brethren (ver. 7). Christian conversation

[1] Bulwer's translation.

strengthens the faith of the pious, increases their love, confirms their hope, and raises up a heart bowed down with adversity, 1 Thess. v. 11.—It is a rare pleasure, when we meet on a journey with pious persons (Starke).

Philip the evangelist (ver. 8). In truth, an excellent surname of a faithful teacher. If we compare what is related of this Philip in chap. vi. 5, and chap. viii. 5, 26, 46, how he so impressively preached the name of Jesus, and so well explained the 53d chapter of Isaiah, we will easily perceive that his evangelistic character chiefly consisted in the gift of clearly exhibiting and representing to souls, out of the Old and New Testaments, Jesus as the marrow of the Gospel. To be such evangelists, may Jesus prepare us yet more and more (Apost. Past.).—*Who was one of the seven.* Behold, the Apostle Paul, along with the seven who, with the temporal gifts of the brethren among the Gentiles, were to minister to the poor saints at Jerusalem, now lodges with the pilgrim of the Church of Jerusalem, who formerly had fled before the persecutor Saul. Blessed conversations would take place in the house of Philip, where Paul and the seven abode,—conversations and hymns of praise, in contemplating the wonderful ways of the Lord (Besser).

This man had four daughters, virgins, who did prophesy (ver. 9). The house of Philip the evangelist (whose office as deacon terminated after the persecution), richly adorned by the fulfilment of the prophecy of Joel, is the centre of the Christian community at Cæsarea. The four daughters of the evangelist, endowed with the gift of prophecy, who represent in their pure virginity the chastity of the daughter of Zion, are a new and evident seal of the calling of all believers to the same privileges of children; as formerly the prophetesses Miriam, Deborah, etc., proved that in the kingdom of grace there is no distinction between male and female, Gal. iii. 28 (After Leonh. and Spieg.).—It is a great glory and true blessing before God, when a servant of Christ has pious daughters, as here the Spirit of the Lord says, in praise of Philip, that his daughters were not only chaste virgins, but also prophetesses of Christ. How rare are such examples in our days, when, alas! the daughters of ministers more frequently surpass others in pride, vanity, and worldliness (Apost. Past.).

Agabus took Paul's girdle, and bound his own hands and feet (vers. 10, 11). What the Spirit withheld from the daughters of Philip, He reveals through Agabus, apparently the same who, on an earlier occasion (chap. xi. 27), was obliged to announce a message of evil tidings.—*The man that owneth this girdle*, *i.e.*, who had formerly entirely resigned himself to the service of the Lord Jesus Christ and of His Gospel. The prophet purposely chooses this symbol, in order to represent the duty, by which the servants of Jesus are bound to their Lord, to crown the commencement of their course with a glorious issue. The Lord reminds us daily, that as we have girded ourselves to the service of Jesus, so we, as girded servants of the Lord, should always be found ready to fulfil all His good pleasure (Apost. Past.).—Only then, when our will is really broken, when we are bound as regards our earthly portion, are we, in truth, the free and blessed children of God, and can walk with God, although we are led whither we would not; only then is the starry band entwined in our life, which truly girdles us for eternity (Rudelbach).—*And deliver him into the hands of the Gentiles.* The nearer Paul approached the city of Jerusalem, the more pointed and the clearer became the prophecies concerning his impending sufferings; even as Jesus also, on His last journey to the city of His sufferings, spoke most plainly of His cross. It is great faithfulness in our Lord, that He does not lead us blindfold, but with open eyes and with strengthened hearts to painful contests. We are thereby perfectly assured, that all that happens to us proceeds, according to the blessed will of our Saviour, to our own real good (Apost. Past.).

Besought him not to go up to Jerusalem (ver. 12). Sometimes Christians have not only to contend with the weakness, craft, and fear of their own hearts, but also with the tenderness of their friends, Gen. xliii. 3, 4. Love intends it entirely for the good of the person beloved, but it is not always in accordance with the thoughts of God, John xx. 17 (Starke).—When Luther journeyed to Worms, friends met and warned him in every place, and when near the city, his beloved Spalatin sent and besought him not to venture into such danger. His reply is famous: "Though there were as many devils in Worms, as there are tiles on the house-tops, yet I will go thither" (Besser).

What mean ye to break my heart? (ver. 13.) The Lord,

whose eyes overflowed at the tomb of Lazarus, does not demand of His disciples the extinction of all natural feelings; only the pain, humanly justifiable, is to be glorified and overcome, by the power of childlike faith and victorious hope; and He Himself is mighty in the weak (Leonh. and Spieg.).—*I am ready not only to be bound, but also to die at Jerusalem for the name of the Lord Jesus.* The best means to help us out of all scruples and difficulties, is the pure and honest intention, to be ready for everything which Jesus will do with us (Apost. Past.).—The centre and soul of Paul's life is contained in this saying, "That I may become conformable to His death," Phil. iii. 10.—Paul strives to attain to the power of the resurrection of His Lord, only by fellowship in His sufferings: for him, there exists no other way to glory than that of the cross. Paul lives only to suffer.—It must in this point become not only better, but entirely otherwise with our Christianity. Where, now-a-days, is the striving after this resemblance to the death of Christ? Where is it known or understood?—Not the cross for the sake of the cross, but the cross for the sake of the Lord. He who desires the Crucified without the cross, snatches at his own shadow. A Christianity without the cross, is a Christianity without Christ (A. Monod).

The will of the Lord be done! (ver. 14.) The love of believers to their pastor must yield to the love of the pastor to Jesus Christ, 1 Cor. xi. 1.—As often as we are unable with our own counsel and plans to obtain what we desire, we ought to commend the whole business to God and His will, for He knows what is useful or injurious (Starke).—The chief virtue in Christianity, and the root of all the rest, is readiness, in all circumstances, to fulfil, even against our own will and inclination, the will of God, in doing and suffering (Rieger).—Happy he who gives himself up to the will of God: he can never be sad. You may do with such a man as you please. You may burn or drown him; cast him into a dungeon, or let him out: he cares not. He knows that it is all for his good (Luther).—Hereafter it will not so much please us, that our sorrow was quieted, and that great prosperity was our lot, as that the will of God was fulfilled in us and to us. Hence we daily implore, in the Lord's prayer, "Thy will be done in earth, as in heaven." O pure and serene life of the will, when nothing more of self-will remains. To be thus, is to become like to God (St Bernard).

And after those days, we discharged ourselves (ver. 15, according to Luther). It is impressive that Luke calls Paul and his companions ἀποσκευασαμένους, loosened from all pleasures, from everything earthly, from all cleaving to the creatures. This appellation, in a special manner, belongs to Paul. Thus he went up to Jerusalem, and exhibited in his example what he taught in 2 Tim. ii. 20, 21. May God engrave this word upon our hearts, so that we also may perform our ministry, as ἀποσκευασαμένοι (Apost. Past.).

Mnason, an old disciple (ver. 16). When old disciples still remain, and men who from of old possess a treasure out of the word of God, we ought to rejoice in them (Rieger).

On the whole section (vers. 1–16).—*The power of love to Jesus Christ.* 1. It brings the unacquainted near, ver. 4. 2. It forewarns of possible dangers, ver. 5. 3. It gladly cultivates fellowship, ver. 5. 4. It humbles itself before God in mutual prayer (Lisco).—The impressiveness of Paul's readiness to suffer for the cause of the Redeemer (Lisco).—*The Christian's pilgrimage to his home.* 1. Faith holds forth to him the glorious end. 2. Love helps him to accomplish the difficult journey (Lisco).—*On fidelity to the Lord.* 1. Its nature. 2. Its source. 3. Its blessing (Langbein).—*The will of the Lord be done! the Christian's watchword on his journey through life.* 1. He is the Lord. 2. His will is good and salutary. 3. It will be done, if not by us, yet in spite of us (Langbein).—*The will of the Lord be done!* 1. A vow of becoming obedience. 2. A confession of believing submission. 3. A declaration of holy courage (Leonh. and Spieg.).—*What imparts true joyfulness in suffering?* 1. Faith in the grace of God in Christ Jesus. 2. Love to Him who endured the cross for us. 3. Hope of a period of blessed refreshing from the presence of the Lord (Leonh. and Spieg.).—*Faith, Hope, and Love, the three attending angels of the Christian in his journey to the heavenly Jerusalem.* 1. Childlike faith, which on dark paths resigns itself to the will of God in doing and suffering, vers. 13–15. 2. Brotherly love, which communicates and receives comfort in cordial fellowship amid the toils of the journey, vers. 4–6, 12, 13. 3. Victorious hope, which, unmoved in joy and in suffering, looks forward to the heavenly termination, vers. 13–15.—*The sad hours of separation of the children of God here below.* 1. Solemn hours of mourning, to exhort us that here we have no continuing city. 2. Salutary hours of trial, to teach us to sacrifice everything to the Lord, in the obedience of faith. 3. Holy hours of devotion, to raise us above time and the grave to the hope of a heavenly home, where love never ceases.—*The only bonds by which a servant of God feels himself to be indissolubly bound.* 1. Not the bonds of his own flesh and blood, which he has torn asunder by the power of the Spirit. 2. Not the bonds of human force and enmity (Paul bound to Jerusalem), which cannot injure him contrary to the will of God. 3. Not the bonds of brotherly love and friendship; for whosoever loveth brethren or sisters more than the Lord, is not worthy of Him. 4. But only the bonds of love to his Lord, to whom he is bound in grateful love and childlike fidelity, even unto death.—*The girdle of Paul, an admonitory memorial for all his successors in the ministry.* 1. To remind them of the apostolic fidelity, with which he was bound to the Lord, even to death. 2. To remind them of the apostolic bonds, in which he must experience the hatred of the world. 3. To remind them of the apostolic zeal, with which he was at all times girt, to hasten to the combat appointed to him.—*What mean you to weep and break my heart?* An earnest exhortation of the Christian sufferer to those around him. 1. Murmur not against the Lord and His holy ways. 2. Aggravate not to the children of God the combat appointed to them. 3. Diminish not to yourselves the blessing of their Christian example.—*The will of the Lord be done!* the best concluding declaration to silence all our objections to the ways of God. 1. Our wisdom must be silent before the thoughts of the All-wise. 2. Our power must surrender itself, vanquished, to the omnipotence of the Almighty. 3. Our love must retire before the claims of Him, to whom we, along with all that we have and are, belong.

PART FIFTH.

THE IMPRISONMENT OF PAUL; THE EFFECT OF WHICH IS, THAT HE IS ABLE, NOT ONLY TO BEAR WITNESS OF JESUS BEFORE HIS OWN PEOPLE, THE CHIEF COUNCIL, RULERS, AND PRINCES, BUT ALSO THAT HE IS SENT TO ROME, THE CAPITAL OF THE WORLD AND THE RESIDENCE OF CÆSAR, TO TESTIFY THERE OF JESUS CHRIST BEFORE JEWS AND GENTILES (CHAP. XXI. 17–XXVIII.).

SECTION I.

OCCASION AND ATTENDING CIRCUMSTANCES OF THE IMPRISONMENT OF PAUL (CHAP. XXI. 17–40).

A.

Paul, persuaded by the Elders of Jerusalem, takes part in a vow of the Nazarite, in order to dispel the suspicion of his opposition to the law.

Chap. xxi. 17–26.

17 Now when we came to Jerusalem, the brethren received us gladly.
18 But on the day after, Paul went with us to James; and all the elders
were there present. 19 And having saluted them, he related particularly
what things God had done among the Gentiles through his ministry.
20 And when they heard that, they praised God; and said to him, Thou
seest, brother, how many thousands among the Jews there are who have
been converted, and they are all zealots for the law. 21 And they have
been informed concerning thee, that thou teachest all the Jews among the
Gentiles apostasy from Moses, and sayest that they should not circumcise
their children, nor walk according to the statutes. 22 What is it, then?
A multitude will necessarily come together; for they will hear that thou
hast come. 23 Do this, then, that we say to thee: There are with us four
men who have a vow upon them. 24 These take to thyself, and purify
thyself with them, and pay the expenses for them, that they may shave
their heads, and all may learn that those things, whereof they have been
informed concerning thee, are nothing, but that thou also walkest in the
observance of the law. 25 But in regard to the Gentiles who have believed,

we have given direction, and concluded that they need observe none of such things, except that they keep themselves from things offered to idols, and from blood, and from things strangled, and from fornication. 26 Then Paul took the men to himself, and on the next day purified himself with them, and went to the temple, and announced that he would fully keep the days of purification, until the offering should be offered for every one of them.

Ver. 17. Ἀπεδέξαντο is more strongly attested than ἐδέξαντο: Luke alone uses the compound verb ἀποδεξ., and that frequently.

Ver. 20. Θεόν is decidedly to be preferred to κύριον.—Ἐν τοῖς Ἰουδαίοις has the uncial MSS. A.B.C.E. and several versions for it; also the reading of the Cambr. MS. D., ἐν τῇ Ἰουδαίᾳ, is in favour of it; whereas τῶν Ἰουδαίων, a correction for the sake of the gen. τῶν πεπιστευκότων, has only G.H. and several versions for it.

Ver. 21. Πάντας is so strongly attested, that its omission in some MSS. is to be considered as unauthorized.

Ver. 25. Ἐπεστείλαμεν is decidedly attested, and is to be preferred to ἀπεστ., which Lachmann, on the ground of two uncial MSS., has adopted.—Lachmann, after A.B., three cursive MSS., and some versions, has erased the words μηδὲν τοιοῦτον τηρεῖν αὐτούς, εἰ μή; but they were probably only omitted, because they are not found in the parallel passage, chap. xv. 18, 19. This clause has, however, five uncial MSS. and numerous cursive MSS. for it, and is to be retained as genuine.

EXEGETICAL EXPLANATIONS.

1. *Now when we came to Jerusalem.*—Οἱ ἀδελφοί are those Christians with whom Paul and his companions came first in contact: thus Mnason and others more nearly related to Paul, or to those who accompanied him from Cæsarea; but not the apostles and the elders (Kuinoel). The elders are not mentioned until ver. 18; and probably none of the apostles were then at Jerusalem, otherwise they would have been expressly mentioned. At this time there stood at the head of the mother Church, only its elders, with James, the brother of the Lord (chap. xii. 17, xv. 13), as their chief. In the house of James, the elders met at a full and official session, which was evidently arranged expressly on account of the apostle of the Gentiles. Paul came in company with his fellow-travellers from the Gentile churches, who were the bearers, along with him, of the collection: this was here, without doubt, formally delivered over into the hands of the elders.

2. *And when he had saluted them.*—First, there was an official and cordial salutation of the elders by Paul (ἀσπασάμενος), and at the same time in the name of the Gentile Christians: then a

comprehensive and particular information by the apostle concerning his apostolic labours among the Gentiles, and concerning the success and blessing granted to him by God. The idea of the important calling of the apostle is by *διακονία* (compare chap. xx. 24) prominently brought forward.

3. *And when they heard that.*—The report, which was doubtless very ample, makes such an impression on the college of elders of the mother Church that, filled with joy and gratitude, they break forth in praise of God. Nevertheless, they are not restrained by any scruple, but frankly communicate to the apostle what a great prejudice the converted Jews, in general, entertained against him. That "many tens of thousands of converts in Judea" are mentioned, can only be surprising, when we think merely on the Church at Jerusalem. Yet the words themselves give no support to this; indeed they expressly mention Judea. And if we take into consideration the whole land of Judea, what prevents us from believing that the number of Christians in the many cities and villages of Judea, including the capital itself (where, from 20 to 25 years before, the Church numbered 5000 men, chap. iv. 4), might amount to several tens of thousands? There is then no reason from this passage, with Baur, to doubt the genuineness of *πεπιστευκότων*, or with Zeller to accuse the historian of an unhistorical exaggeration.

4. *And are all zealots for the law.*—These Christians in Judea are described as zealots of the law (*ζηλωταὶ τοῦ νόμου*), *i.e.*, men of legal strictness, zealous and passionate against all undervaluing of the law of Moses or opposition to it. It is the same expression which became the name of a faction in the Jewish war. The general opposition of the Jewish people to the Roman government and to heathenism, from which the spirit of the zealots sprung, might also exert an influence on the Jewish Christians. James himself, according to his whole disposition, was a man of legal strictness (therefore called צַדִּיק), and the elders were doubtless actuated by a similar spirit. But they were evidently not, as the mass of the Jewish Christians, prejudiced against the Apostle Paul. An opinion had been instilled into the minds of the Jewish Christians, by the designing and persevering representations of the judaizing teachers (*κατηχήθησαν*), that Paul, by means of his doctrine, made the Jews of the dispersion, apostates from the law of Moses; teaching

them, first, not to circumcise their children, by means of which circumcision would die out in the next generation; and secondly, not to observe in their conduct the Mosaic customs (ἔθεσι περιπατεῖν).

5. *What is it, then?*—This question (τί οὖν ἐστι;) is used at a deliberation, when it is inquired, What is to be done? The coming together (συνελθεῖν) of a multitude is meant, neither of an ordinary assembly of the Church (Calvin, Grotius, Bengel), nor yet specially of an onset (Kuinoel); but is to be understood of a gathering together from curiosity.

6. *Who have a vow.*—The four men who had the vow are by εἰσιν ἡμῖν evidently represented as Christians. The vow was a proper vow of the Nazarites. The elders counsel the apostle to participate with them in it, joining himself to these men (παραλαβὼν), and defraying the expenses of the sacrifices which they were obliged to offer at the termination of their vow. (This was reckoned a peculiar proof of pious zeal: Herod Agrippa did this for many Nazarites, Josephus, Ant. xix. 6.) But the apostle was also to take upon himself a certain Levitical purification with those Nazarites (ἁγνίσθητι σὺν αὐτοῖς). There exists a variety of opinion, as to whether Paul did or did not take upon himself the vow of the Nazarites. The question is, in general, answered in the affirmative, as recently by Meyer. But incorrectly: for although ἁγνίζεσθαι is certainly used of the vow of the Nazarites (the Septuagint), it also denotes every other Levitical purification. And although ἁγνίσθητι σὺν αὐτοῖς (ver. 24) may be easily understood, as if Paul was only now after the others to enter upon a ἁγνισμός, which they had already taken upon themselves; yet the expression σὺν αὐτοῖς ἁγνισθεὶς (ver. 26) does not at all admit of this interpretation; on the contrary, it can only have the meaning, that Paul with the Nazarites, and they with him, purified themselves on the same day, and in one and the same act. This purification referred only to the appearance in the temple, and to the prayers and offerings to be performed there, for which one must be specially prepared and purified by washing and bathing. Moreover, it is not elsewhere known, and is a mere supposition made from a regard to this passage, that those who bore the expenses of the Nazarites also took the vow, for some days, upon themselves (see Wieseler's Chronology of the Apostolic Age).

7. *Then Paul took the men.*—The apostle acceded to the proposal, and, in accordance with that Levitical preparation, appeared in the temple, in order to notify to the priests that each would complete the time of the Nazarite; and this then reached its full completion, when the offering (*ἡ προσφορά*, the well-known legally appointed offering) was offered for each one. This conduct of Paul was designed to produce the conviction on the legally disposed Jewish Christians that there was nothing (*ὧν—οὐδέν ἐστι*, that none of those things existed, was founded on truth) in the prejudices which they entertained against him, but that, so far from making the Jews apostates from the law, he himself (*καὶ αὐτός*) kept in his conduct the Mosaic law. The elders, in making this proposal, added the remark (ver. 25), in order to obviate a possible scruple, as if they designed to limit the freedom of the Gentile Christians, that this freedom was already secured and recognised. *Μηδὲν τοιοῦτον*, none of the Mosaic legal observances.

DOGMATICAL AND ETHICAL THOUGHTS.

1. It was a misunderstanding or a slander, when Paul was accused of teaching the Jews of the dispersion, apostasy from Moses. His doctrine was the Gospel of grace in Christ Jesus: certainly of salvation in Christ only, and not of the righteousness of the law. But it was not his business to attack the law and the Mosaic religion in themselves. He only combated the doctrine, that the observance of the law was absolutely necessary for salvation. He only opposed the tendency which recognised no other form of the Christian Church than the Jewish. But evangelical liberty, which was his vital point, enabled him both to suffer the observance of the Mosaic law in native Jews, and to contend for liberty from the law for the Gentile Christians.

2. How is the conduct of Paul to be judged morally? It has been regarded as a reprehensible dissimulation, and on that account this whole narrative has been considered as unhistorical (Zeller). But was it, in truth, a practical denial of sacred convictions, if the apostle, in order to prove by action that he neither was himself a renegade from the law, nor led others to apostasy, determined upon a Levitical transaction? And nothing more than this was the meaning and object of what he did. If he had thereby owned, that a Christian, if he

was born subject to the Mosaic law, in order to secure his salvation, and to be justified before God, must observe the Levitical law; then certainly he would have denied his holiest convictions, and would have been guilty of reprehensible dissimulation. But it was not for this purpose that he here subjected himself to the law, but only from love, in order to remove an erroneous prejudice of the Jewish Christians, by reason of which they had taken offence at him. And this entirely corresponds with what he says of himself in 1 Cor. ix. 20: "Unto the Jews I became as a Jew, that I might gain the Jews; to them that are under the law, as under the law, that I might gain them that are under the law."

HOMILETICAL HINTS.

But when we came to Jerusalem, the brethren received us gladly (ver. 17). What formerly withheld believers at Jerusalem from giving a good reception to Paul (chap. ix. 26), had long ago ceased (Rieger).

On the next day, Paul went with us to James (ver. 18). A course, in which both the moral rectitude and the unassuming humility of the apostle were manifested. For Paul, in his evangelical freedom, might feel himself repelled by the legal strictness of James; and the severely tested apostle of the Gentiles might think himself exalted above the easier and unmolested work of the president of the Church of Jerusalem. But the common evangelical ground of faith removed the first obstacle; and apostolical humility and brotherly love led him past the second rock.

All things that God had done among the Gentiles by his ministry (ver. 19). How modestly does Paul speak of his actions! God, he says, has done all things. He appropriates nothing to himself, but the joy at the exaltation of the divine name (Apost. Past.).—When we hear what God still does among the heathen, we will not be indifferent to it, but praise God for it (Starke).

And when they heard that, they praised the Lord (ver. 20). They praised not Paul, as he had not praised himself, but the Lord. But in praising the Lord for what He had done by Paul, they also recognised him as a blessed instrument of God.—*Brother, thou seest how many thousands, etc.* Though Paul and

James salute one another in a brotherly manner, and though the brethren were stirred up by what Paul had related to the praise of God, yet they are not silent about the fault which others had found in him. The most cordial brotherly love does not make them blind and dumb toward each other, but trűe-hearted and courageous (Apost. Past.).

And they are informed of thee, that thou teachest apostasy from Moses (ver. 21). What good can be said or done, which will not be blamed or perverted by the world? (Starke.)—Whoever wishes to know the innocence of Paul of this charge, let him only consult the 14th and 15th chapters of the Epistle to the Romans (Rieger).—On the other hand, such expressions as occur, for example, in Rom. ii., might certainly excite that suspicion among the zealots of thé law (Williger).

A multitude will necessarily come together (ver. 22). Sometimes it is represented as if, in the apostolic Church, there was no distinction between teachers or overseers and others. But what a careful order do we here find in the Church of Jerusalem! James appears as president, and the elders are collected to him. In this college of overseers the affair of Paul was first discussed, and only afterwards was the Church consulted. In all this there is much to learn for our times, both in opposition to an ecclesiastical democracy, and in opposition to an over-estimate of the ministerial office (Williger).

Do this now, that we say to thee (ver. 23). The refutation, which takes place in action rather than in words, is the best.—In subordinate matters, a Christian may accommodate himself to please others; but he must take heed that neither dissimulation nor fear of men is concealed under such adaptation.—We are so to use Christian liberty that we do not offend, but gain the weak.—Dissimulation is one thing; but to become, from love and for the improvement of the weak, all things to all men in indifferent matters, whose use may be sanctified by the end, is another thing (Starke).—If we would judge of this history impartially, we must say that James and the elders acted according to their knowledge of the circumstances of the times; that Paul, in order to prove that he did not act from self-will and sectarian bitterness, but from the pure power of the Gospel, stooped to the beggarly ordinances of the Jews, in order to gain some of them; and that the Lord permitted this well-meant transaction to take place, in order that Paul might be seen, even in the eyes of his bitterest enemies, to be, not a disturber of their religion, but a true friend of the Jewish Church, and consequently that their persecutions might appear the more unjust. We judge wrongly when we accuse the apostle of dissimulation, and regard the suffering which befell him as a divine chastisement. The suffering was long ago revealed to him, and was the end to which he stedfastly approached (Apost. Past.).—The counsel which the elders gave to Paul was not carnal, and designed to be an avoidance of the cross for him or for them; but spiritual, to bear with, and so to gain the weak.—It is a delicate matter, how often love must submit to be a servant, when we would be free in spirit. Christianity always gets into difficulties: one party would like it more exact and strict; another party, more free and unfettered. Truth takes the middle course (Rieger).—The Gentile Church, founded by the apostle, has just now been saluted by the Jewish Christian Church with unanimous ascription of praise to God. This was a moment which pointed onwards to the fulfilment, when the fulness of the Gentiles should come in, and Israel should recognise its God and King in the work among the Gentiles. And to this moment also corresponds the conduct of the apostle of the Gentiles, by which he gives to the law even an outward recognition, which indeed in its principles he always adhered to, although ordinarily he could only maintain it in the domain of the spirit. Thereby he brings clearly before us the final prospect of the disappearance of the exceptionable position he held as the thirteenth apostle. Under these circumstances, could Paul conceive a more beautiful employment of a part of the gifts which the Gentiles had brought, than to contribute towards the solemn sacrifices which the four poor Nazarites, from the Church of the saints, had to offer for the discharge of their vows? Must not these gifts of the Gentiles, offered by his ministry, appear as a beginning of those offerings with which the Gentiles were one day to adorn the sanctuary of Israel, and to render glorious the worship of the people of God? (Baumgarten.)

On vers. 17–26.—*On Christian forbearance.* 1. It is necessary: as such, practised by the Lord Himself; employed by His apostles; indispensable to us. 2. It is salutary: without God's forbearance, the world would be lost; by the apostles' forbearance, much weakness was gained; by Christian forbearance, we do not indeed gain all, but we promote peace, and thus the kingdom of God in general (Lisco).—*How far an advanced Christian may accommodate himself to the prejudices of the weak.* 1. He may participate in all things which, in themselves indifferent, are done from a good intention of serving God. 2. He may not do anything to favour the view that such things are necessary for salvation (Lisco).—Christian conduct with reference to the prejudices of honest but weak brethren (Lisco).—*The brotherly salutation between Paul and James at Jerusalem* (vers. 18–20). 1. A victory of love, which seeks not its own in carnal narrowness and self-will. 2. An earnest of the future union of Israel and the Gentile world under the cross of Christ. 3. A triumph of the wonderful ways of God in the spread of His kingdom, and in the realization of His plan of salvation.—*Paul among the Nazarites.* 1. Not as a slave of human ordinances, but in the might of evangelical liberty, which has power over all things that promote the kingdom of God, 1 Cor. vi. 12. 2. Not as a dissembler before the people, but in the ministry of brotherly love, which bears the infirmities of the weak, Rom. xv. 1. 3. Not as a fugitive from the cross, but in the power of apostolic obedience, which knows to deny itself from love to the Lord, Luke ix. 23.—*How may a servant of Christ become all things to all men?* 1. When in all persons, to whom he seeks to become something, he wishes not to flatter the flesh, but to minister to and aid the spirit. 2. When in all things, which he from love becomes to others, he does not yield up the one thing needful, but preaches Christ, as the word of God shows Him, and faith bears Him on the heart.—*Paul among the brethren at Jerusalem; or, what appertains to bearing the infirmities of the weak?* 1. Christian love, which is willing to bear them, while it has a tender feeling for the wants of the weak, and exercises a noble self-denial in condescending to them in word and deed. 2. Christian strength, which is able to bear them, while it possesses freedom of spirit to distinguish between form and essence, the shell and the kernel, and has strength of character not to surrender with subordinate matters the chief thing, and not to deny the Lord from love to man.

B.

The Jews from Asia Minor stir up a tumult against Paul, in consequence of which, the Roman Tribune interferes and rescues his life.

Chap. xxi. 27–40.

27 But when the seven days were almost ended, the Jews from Asia saw
him in the temple, and stirred up the whole multitude, and laid hands on him,
crying out: 28 Men of Israel, help! This is the man who teacheth all men
everywhere against the people and the law, and against this place. More-
over he has also brought Gentiles into the temple, and polluted this holy
place. 29 For they had seen before Trophimus from Ephesus with him in
the city, whom they supposed Paul had brought into the temple. 30 And
the whole city was stirred up, and there was a concourse of the people; and
they seized on Paul, and dragged him out of the temple; and immediately
the doors were shut. 31 And while they sought to kill him, information
came up to the tribune of the cohort that all Jerusalem was in an uproar;
32 Who immediately took soldiers and centurions with him, and ran down
to them. And when they saw the tribune and the soldiers, they left off
beating Paul. 33 Then the tribune came near, and took hold of him, and
commanded to bind him with two chains, and inquired who he might be, and
what he had done. 34 And some called to him one thing, and some another,
among the people. But when he could learn nothing certain on account of
the tumult, he commanded him to be led to the camp. 35 And when he
came upon the stairs, the soldiers were obliged to carry him on account of
the violence of the mob. 36 For the multitude pressed after him, crying,
Away with him. 37 And as Paul was about to be led into the camp, he
said to the tribune, May I speak to thee? And he said, Canst thou speak
Greek? 38 Art thou not then that Egyptian, who before these days raised
an insurrection, and led out four thousand banditti into the wilderness?
39 But Paul said, I am a Jew of Tarsus, a citizen of no inconsiderable city
in Cilicia. I pray thee, suffer me to speak to the people. 40 And when
he permitted him, Paul stood on the stairs, and beckoned with the hand to
the people. And when there was made a great silence, he addressed them
in the Hebrew dialect as follows:

Ver. 34. Four uncial MSS. have ἐπεφώνουν; on the other hand, ἐβόων is not so well attested.

EXEGETICAL EXPLANATIONS.

1. *But when the seven days.—Αἱ ἑπτὰ ἡμέραι* are generally and properly referred to those called in ver. 26 *ἡμέραι τοῦ ἁγνισμοῦ*. They are the days to which the Levitical purification,

for the purpose of the offering for the discharge of the vow, referred. Wieseler, in his "Apostolic Chronology," has attempted another explanation: the seven days are the preceding week, the days of consecration for Pentecost. But, first, in the context, this feast is never mentioned after chap. xx. 16; and, secondly, the idea of a week of preparation for the chief Jewish feasts rests on no certain evidence. These seven days were drawing to a close (ἔμελλον συντελεῖσθαι), they had not yet elapsed (Wieseler), when Paul was seized and arrested in the temple.

2. *This is the man.*—The Jews from Asia Minor, particularly those from Ephesus and its neighbourhood, who knew and hated him there, perceived him, looked at him for a time (θεᾶσθαι), and recognised him; and the very circumstance, that they saw in the temple the supposed despiser of the temple, so excited them, that they stirred up the multitude against him. They caught him with loud cries for help, as if he were the assailant, and as if the sanctuary must be protected against him (βοηθεῖτε). The accusation of the unconverted Jews against the apostle is to be distinguished from that which had been instilled into the minds of the Jewish Christians, in a manner which is usually overlooked. The fanatics of Asia Minor reproach him with speaking, not only against the law and the temple, but also against Israel (τοῦ λαοῦ). This had been laid to the charge neither of Paul by the Jewish Christians, nor yet at an earlier period of Stephen by the Jews. It was, doubtless, connected with his labours among the Gentiles (πάντας πανταχοῦ διδάσκων), which were suspected as exciting the Gentiles against Israel. They declared, moreover (ἔτι τε καὶ), as a second point of accusation, that Paul had brought Gentiles into the temple, and had thereby defiled the sanctuary. Ἕλληνας generalizes the individual instance from enmity, and in order the more to excite the multitude; whereas, in point of fact, only Trophimus could be intended, and who moreover did not enter the temple. It was a mere notion, a groundless suspicion, that Paul had taken him with him into the temple, *i.e.*, into the court of the Israelites. Προεωρακότες ἦσαν is, notwithstanding Meyer's objection, "they had seen him before."

3. *And the whole city was moved.*—The multitude, who quickly rushed together, drew Paul out of the court of the temple, probably because it was felt that by acts of violence the

sanctuary would be all the more polluted. The closing of the gate of the temple had not for its object to prevent Paul making use of the right of asylum, and taking refuge in the temple (Bengel, Baumgarten), for this was already provided against; but rather it was to guard against the spaces of the temple being stained by the shedding of blood (De Wette, Meyer); perhaps, also, it was done, because it was thought that the court of the temple was already polluted by the entrance of a Gentile, and it was intended to guard the sanctuary from being polluted again.

4. *And whilst they sought to kill him.*—Information, conveyed by the military sentinels placed during the festivals, reached the commander of the Roman garrison in the castle of Antonia, to the north of the temple and overlooking it (*ἀνέβη φάσις*). He was military tribune of the cohort (*σπεῖρα*). His name, Claudius Lysias, is preserved to us in chap. xxiii. 26. On the news of the tumult in the city, he repaired without delay with officers and soldiers to the temple. When he was seen from a distance, they ceased maltreating the apostle. And when he came near, he commanded Paul to be taken by his men, and to be bound with chains, on the supposition that he was a criminal, whose name and crime he thought to be able to find out by inquiry.

5. *To be led to the camp.*—*Παρεμβολή* is not the castle of Antonia itself, but only a part of it, namely, the barracks of the Roman garrison in the castle. *Ἀναβαθμοί*, vers. 35, 40 (*ἀναβάσεις*, Joseph. Jud. Bell. v. 5, 3), steps or stairs. The fortress was connected with the northern and western porches of the temple area by means of steps. See Robinson's Palestine.

6. *May I speak to thee?*—Before he went as a prisoner within the gate into the castle, and was removed from the view of the people, the apostle wishes to be permitted to address them, and on this behoof turns himself to the commander in a polite manner (*εἰ ἔξεστι*, etc.). The commander, amazed at being addressed in Greek, asks *Ἑλληνιστὶ γινώσκεις;* and then inquires whether he was not that Egyptian insurgent for whom, until then, he had evidently taken him, whereas his addressing him in Greek altered his opinion. The supposition that he was the Egyptian insurgent was the more probable to the Roman commander, as those Sicarii (named from *sica*, a dagger, hence murderers and insurgents) were accustomed at festivals, as now at Pentecost,

to mix among the multitude, and to practise their arts (Josephus, Jud. Bell. ii. 13, 3, *μάλιστα ἐν ταῖς ἑορταῖς μισγόμενοι τῷ πλήθει*, etc.). This Egyptian was, according to Josephus (Jud. Bell. ii. 13, 5), a magician, who gave himself out for a prophet, and in the reign of Nero collected a multitude of adherents, whom he led out of the wilderness to the Mount of Olives, where at his command the walls of Jerusalem were to fall down, so that they would enter the city over the ruins (Joseph. Ant. xx. 8, 6). The procurator Felix, however, made a fortunate attack upon them, slew 400, and took 200 prisoners, whilst the Egyptian himself escaped (*διαδράσας ἐκ τῆς μάχης ἀφανὴς ἐγένετο*). The Roman captain here mentions 4000 Sicarii, whom that insurgent led into the wilderness. Josephus, on the other hand (Jud. Bell. ii. 13, 5), relates that he collected about 30,000 men who were deluded by him. But this observation has evidently in view the whole followers of the man, whilst Luke speaks only of his armed followers, which Josephus in other places knows very well how to distinguish from the whole party. Accordingly these two accounts may very well agree, whilst in other points the fuller notice of Josephus strikingly confirms our passage.

7. *I pray thee, suffer me to address the people.*—The apostle introduces himself to the tribune, as distinguished from that criminal with whom he had been confounded, and requests permission to address the people. On account of this explanation, and as not the slightest information by a third party confirmed the original suspicion, the permission by the captain, who had complete authority, is not in point of fact surprising (against Baur). And as little is it incredible, that the multitude, when Paul signified that he was about to address them, became quiet and gave him audience. By the Hebrew dialect is naturally meant the living language, which at that time was the common Aramaic dialect.

DOGMATICAL AND ETHICAL THOUGHTS.

1. The counsel of God is accomplished in a marvellous manner. In order to obviate a mistake on the part of the Jewish Christians, Paul determines on a Levitical transaction in the temple. And his very presence in the sanctuary must give occasion to a danger arising from an entirely different quarter—

from the unconverted Israelites; and his very piety toward the law and the sanctuary, his love to his people, whom it is his object to gain for Christ, must accordingly contribute to the false representation.

2. It is the sign of a holy disposition, which is imparted by the Spirit of Christ, that the apostle, when he was yet in danger of his life, and after he had been most unmercifully treated by the Jews, has yet so much composure, moral courage, and love to his people, as to address them without the slightest feeling of bitterness. His heart is humbled under a sense of his own guilt, as he had formerly been as those Jews now are, and only the grace of Him, who on the cross prayed for the forgiveness of His murderers, had changed him.

HOMILETICAL HINTS.

But when the seven days were about to be ended (ver. 27). God often punishes foolish plans by an unhappy issue; but it does not always follow, that what turns out unfortunately, was commenced unrighteously, Isa. xix. 3; John i. 53, vii. 5. When a good counsel turns out ill, we must not, on that account, throw the blame on the adviser. Man proposes, but God disposes (Starke).—Now would Paul be thinking of what the Spirit of God had so often pointed out to him, as awaiting him at Jerusalem. Now also would he be frequently preparing himself, and renewing his determination, not to hold his life dear (Rieger).

This is the man (ver. 28). An upright servant of Christ makes himself so well known by the success of his ministry, that the enemies of Jesus easily distinguish him among a thousand false and unfaithful zealots, and are able to say, This is the man, seize him (Apost. Past.).—*And has polluted this holy place.* Here Paul had the honour of being treated with the same false accusations, amid as much uproar and tumult, and with similar bitterness and rigour, as formerly the Lord Jesus Christ was treated. When a servant sees himself in the image and in the footsteps of His Lord, how sweet and easy does his yoke become! (Apost. Past.)—Also Paul would remember Stephen, against whom formerly an entirely similar storm arose.

For they had seen before with him, in the city, Trophimus, an Ephesian (ver. 29). If God has appointed us to suffering, the least circumstance gives occasion to it.—How narrowly are the servants of God watched, and what great reason have they to take heed to their steps! The world gives heed to those with whom we walk, and judges preachers by their company. May the Lord make us without blame in all points (Apost. Past.).

And the whole city was moved (ver. 30). Men, who scarcely creep to do good, fly to protect the wicked, Jer. iv. 22 (Starke). —*And drew him out of the temple, and immediately the doors were shut.* They would murder him, yet they would not pollute the temple. They strain at a gnat and swallow a camel, as they had done with the Lord Himself, John xviii. 28 (Williger).

And whilst they sought to kill him, information came to the tribune (ver. 31). A servant of Jesus is not necessitated to seek patrons in his troubles, and to entreat for advocates; God sends them, at the proper time, without his asking or thinking (Apost. Past.).

And when they saw the tribune, they left off beating Paul (ver. 32). In the government of God, it is one of His wonderful providences, that even those who are not partakers of His kingdom are often divided about their dissimilar interests, views, and designs; and thus either one sword holds another in the scabbard, or the children of the kingdom enjoy protection from one party, who otherwise do not so intend it (Rieger).

And commanded him to be bound with chains (ver. 33). A servant of Christ may not rely too much on the protection of the world. Here the tribune rescues the apostle from the hands of the murderous Jews, but on the other hand he commands him, unheard, to be bound with two chains (Apost. Past.). But the prophecy of Agabus must be fulfilled.

And when he could learn nothing certain (ver. 34). Whoever seeks something certain, solid, and true, from the mouth of false teachers or from the world generally, is always deceived. "In their mouth is nothing certain; with their tongues they have used deceit" (Apost. Past.).

And when he came to the stairs, the soldiers were obliged to carry him (ver. 35). This illustrates how God uses even enemies as instruments of the exaltation of His servants: the world, with its shame and scorn, advances us to honour. Many a teacher would have remained all his life in obscurity, had not the world by its hatred and envy drawn him forth, and raised him up (Apost. Past.).

For the multitude followed after, and cried, Away with him (ver. 36). As formerly they cried against Christ, Luke xxiii. 18; John xix. 15.

Art thou not that Egyptian? (ver. 37.) A remarkable proof of the erroneous and absurd thoughts which the blind world entertains of the children and servants of God. They regard us as idiots, madmen, seducers, enemies of mankind, and under this form hate us. Thus was Christ also numbered among transgressors. "Father, forgive them, for they know not what they do" (Apost. Past.).—Paul bore the same relation to the Egyptian, as Luther did to Münzer (Besser).

And when he permitted him, Paul stood on the stairs, etc. (ver. 40). How unexpectedly must the stairs to the Roman camp serve as a pulpit, from which God made the Gospel of His Son to be proclaimed! (Rieger.)—*And beckoned with the hand to the people. And when there was a great silence, he addressed them.* What a man! Thus to beckon to an excited people! And, behold, there was a great calm, as when Jesus stilled the stormy sea. One is never more worthy to proclaim the word of God, than when he bears on his body the marks of his cross and suffering, because then only can the Spirit of God bestow both boldness to speak and words in their season (Gossner).

On vers. 27–40.—The Lord rescues His people from death. 1. Paul is unjustly accused as an enemy of the law, and a profaner of the temple. 2. His people thrust him from them: they cast him out of the temple, and wish to murder him. 3. The heathen are obliged to protect him: the tribune suppresses the tumult, and rescues the apostle. 4. The innocence of the persecuted is proved: the accusations come to nothing, and defence is permitted him (Lisco).—The advantage of a regular regiment, apparent in the narrative of the capture of the apostle at Jerusalem (Lisco).—*The capture of Paul at Jerusalem.* 1. A dark picture of human passion: foolish infatuation and wicked hatred, on the part of the Jews. 2. A bright picture of Christian courage: calm composure and long-suffering patience, on the part of the apostle. 3. A monument of the divine guidance: the power which protects His servants, and the wisdom which uses His enemies, for the accomplishment of His purposes.—*Paul in the temple of Jerusalem:* or, Man proposes and God disposes. 1. He disposes the well-meant counsels of

His servants often to another end than what they thought of. 2. But He also disposes the wicked projects of His enemies to a different result than what they intended.—*Paul in the storm at Jerusalem.* The apostle, at a later period, had to encounter a great storm on the open sea; but that was hardly more violent than what now rose against him on dry land, within the secure walls of Jerusalem, among his own people. Yet here, as there, the almighty arm of God protects and rescues him. Let us consider: 1. The outbreak of the storm. Suddenly and not to be reckoned on, as often a storm occurs in nature, this storm breaks out among the people. The tempest which Paul had seen from a distance at Miletus, and which was predicted to him on the way in a more and more threatening manner, discharges itself on a sudden, and in a place where one would have least expected it, in the holy spaces of the temple, while Paul sought to satisfy the zealots of the law. 2. The raging of the storm. The storm of the passions increases continually, the popular fury heaves and swells as a raging sea, and threatens to swallow up the servant of God. 3. The stilling of the storm. He who formerly rebuked the wind and the waves on the Lake of Gennesareth, so that there was a great calm, speaks to this raging sea: Hitherto shalt thou come, but no farther. The Roman tribune has to open the harbour of refuge to the apostle; and he himself with calm composure beckons to the people, so that they become still.—*Paul's memorable sermon at Jerusalem.* 1. The preacher; in chains. 2. The pulpit: the stairs to the Roman camp. 3. The deacons who conducted him: the soldiers. 4. The psalms which preceded the discourse: murderous outcries. 5. The congregation whom he will address: an excited people. 6. The anointing which he brings along with him: the Spirit of the Lord, as a Spirit of faith and love, of wisdom and strength.—*The defence and weapons of a man of God in perilous times.* 1. For himself, he has right and law which must protect him, as long as they have power. 2. Within himself, he carries the equanimity of a good conscience, which remains undisturbed in the storm of the passions. 3. In himself, he exhibits the power of a divinely consecrated personality, which does not fail to impress even brutal crowds. 4. Above himself, he recognises a Lord and God, to whom he belongs in suffering as well as in working, in death as well as in life.

SECTION II.

EVENTS WHICH OCCURRED DURING THE IMPRISONMENT OF PAUL AT JERUSALEM. HIS DEFENCE BEFORE THE JEWISH PEOPLE AND BEFORE THE CHIEF COUNCIL (CHAP. XXII. 1–XXIII. 11).

A.

Defence before the Jewish People.

CHAP. XXII. 1–21.

1 Brethren and fathers, hearken to my defence before you. 2 And when they heard that he addressed them in the Hebrew dialect, they became the more silent. And he said,

3 I am a Jew, born at Tarsus in Cilicia, and brought up in this city, and instructed at the feet of Gamaliel, according to the strictness of the ancestral law, and was a zealot for God, as ye all are this day. 4 And I persecuted this way to the death, putting in bonds, and delivering into prisons both men and women. 5 As also the high priest and all the eldership bear me witness, from whom also I received letters to the brethren, and went to Damascus, in order to bring even those who were there bound to Jerusalem, that they might be punished. 6 But it came to pass, as I was on my journey, and drew nigh to Damascus, that suddenly, about mid-day, a great light from heaven flashed around me. 7 And I fell to the ground, and heard a voice saying to me, Saul, Saul, why persecutest thou Me? 8 And I answered, Who art Thou, Lord? And He said to me, I am Jesus of Nazareth, whom thou persecutest. 9 But they who were with me saw indeed the light, and were afraid; but the voice of Him who spoke with me, they heard not. 10 And I said, What shall I do, Lord? And the Lord said to me, Arise, and go to Damascus, and there it will be told thee of all things that are appointed thee to do. 11 But when I could not see for the brightness of that light, I was led by the hand of them who were with me, and so came to Damascus. 12 And one Ananias, a devout man, according to the law, having a good report of all the Jews dwelling in that city, 13 Came to me, and stood, and said to me, Brother Saul, look up! And the same hour I looked up upon him. 14 And he said, The God of our fathers hath chosen thee, that thou shouldest know His will, and see that Just One, and hear the voice of His mouth. 15 For thou wilt be a witness for Him to all men of what thou hast seen and heard. 16 And now, why tarriest thou? arise, and be baptized, and wash away thy sins, calling on His name. 17 And it came to pass, when I returned to Jerusalem, and prayed in the temple, that I fell into a trance, and saw Him saying to me, 18 Hasten and depart quickly from Jerusalem, because they will not receive thy testimony concerning Me.

19 And I said, Lord, they know that I imprisoned and scourged in the synagogues those who believed on Thee: 20 And when the blood of Stephen, Thy witness, was shed, I also stood by, and had pleasure therein, and kept the garments of those who slew him. 21 And He said to me, Depart, for I will send thee far hence among the Gentiles.

Ver. 9. Καὶ ἔμφοβοι ἐγένοντο is wanting in three uncial MSS.; other three have it. The words appear to have been considered superfluous, and on that account to have been omitted; but they are to be retained as genuine, because ἔμφοβ. γιν. is a favourite expression of Luke.

Ver. 12. Εὐλαβής is wanting in the Alex. MS. (A.), and is replaced by εὐσεβής in E. Εὐλαβής, however, is most strongly attested (B.G.H.), and is a favourite epithet of Luke, chap. ii. 5, viii. 2, Luke ii. 20, and has therefore been preferred by Lachmann and Tischendorf.

Ver. 16. Αὐτοῦ is better attested than Κυρίου, which has only the two youngest uncial MSS. for it.

Ver. 20. Στεφάνου is wanting in a MS. of the first class (A.), and in one of the second class; but it is sufficiently attested to be received as genuine. —Τῇ ἀναιρέσει αὐτοῦ after συνευδοκῶν has only two uncial MSS. for it, and is interpolated from chap. viii. 1.

EXEGETICAL EXPLANATIONS.

1. *Men, brethren, and fathers.*—The address ἀδελφοί expresses his love to the people; πατέρες, his respect to their distinguished chiefs, some of whom might have been present. Also the circumstance that he addressed them in their mother-tongue, won for the apostle a more favourable hearing, inasmuch as many among the multitude did not suppose that the man, whom they did not know, understood the Aramaic dialect.

2. *I am a Jew.*—The express description of his person (vers. 3–5) was designed to refute the suspicions against him (Acts xxi. 28), by intimating his origin as an Israelite, his connection from childhood with Jerusalem, and his former disposition, strictly pharisaical and legal, and hostile to Christianity. *Γεγεννημένος ἐν Τ.—ἀνατεθραμμένος δέ*: born, it is true, abroad, yet brought up in Jerusalem. *'Ανατρέφω* is used of education in childhood. *Παρὰ τοὺς πόδας Γαμ.* agrees much better with *πεπαιδευμένος* than with *ἀνατεθρ.*, because we are here not to think of children who are brought up, but of scholars who are instructed on the floor or benches before the feet of their teachers. According to the Jewish customs, attested both by Philo and the Talmud, the Rabbins were accustomed to sit on professorial chairs, and their scholars partly on benches and partly on the floor before them. *Κατὰ ἀκρίβειαν τοῦ πατρῴου νόμου*, the in-

struction was legally strict: ἀκρίβεια is not asserted of the nature of the law itself, but of the nature of the instruction, and characterizes that as pharisaically rigid. Ἀκριβής and its derivatives designate the peculiarity of the pharisaical tendency; as, for example, ἀκριβεστάτη αἵρεσις, chap. xxvi. 5; ἐπ' ἀκριβώσει μέγα φρονοῦν τοῦ πατρῴου νόμου, Joseph. Ant. xvii. 2, 4; Φαρισαῖοι οἱ δοκοῦντες μετὰ ἀκριβείας ἐξηγεῖσθαι τὰ νόμιμα, Joseph. Jud. Bell. ii. 8, 14.

3. *And was a zealot.*—In consequence of such education and instruction, Paul was a zealot for the glory of God. He expresses this in a manner which does not appear blameable. Accordingly, the apostle says, I was once what you are: you are to-day, at this moment, what I also once was. As a proof of his former zeal, he adduces his persecution of Christianity, which he here prudently refers to only by a general name. For his deadly hatred to the Christians, he appeals to the high priest and to all the elders, who could attest it. Ἀδελφοί, as in ver. 1, brethren according to descent, brethren according to the disposition of the Sanhedrim, and to his own disposition at that time.

4. *And it came to pass.*—The apostle comes to the history of his conversion, and relates, in the first place, the appearance of Jesus to him (vers. 6–11), identical in essential points with chap. ix. 3–8. See the Exegetical Explanations to that passage. What is here peculiar in the details, has reference to the present situation of the apostle, and to his audience: for example, he adds to the name of Jesus ὁ Ναζωραῖος, which occurs neither in chap. ix. 5 nor in chap. xxvi. 15, but is here entirely in place before an assembly of unconverted Jews, to whom he mentions Jesus for the first time. Other traits are chiefly designed to cause the actual reality of the manifestation of Jesus to be recognised; thus περὶ μεσημβρίαν, ver. 6 (ἡμέρας μέσης, chap. xxvi. 13), which is wanting in chap. ix. 3. That the appearance of Jesus took place in bright day, vouches for its not being a visionary deception. The circumstance that his companions saw the light, which is expressly mentioned neither in chap. ix. 7 nor in chap. xxvi. 14, also supports the objectivity of the fact, which others experienced along with him; whilst their not understanding the words of Jesus is perhaps mentioned to show why his companions could not confirm the chief matter. The being blinded by the extraordinary light is also brought forward, as a proof of the

objectivity and of the overwhelming nature of the appearance; whilst ὧν τέτακταί σοι (ver. 10) indicates, that from this moment Paul was no more master of his own determinations, but guided by the divine will.

5. *One Ananias.*—Paul relates the completion of his conversion by Ananias (vers. 12–16), in such a manner that his conversion and his call to be a witness of Christ appears as divinely confirmed, and as harmonizing with the Old Testament. This is also inferred by his description of Ananias, as a person of legal piety, which is not alluded to in chap. ix. 10. The restoration to sight by the word of Ananias is here noticed, as a miracle which accredited his divine mission to Saul. In the address of Ananias, both God and Christ are mentioned with purely Old Testament names: ὁ Θεὸς τῶν πατέρων ἡμῶν, and ὁ δίκαιος, that Just One, in a peculiar and full sense. Further, the appearance of Christ is represented as an extended revelation of God to a prophet (ver. 14); and the ministry to the whole world (πάντας ἀνθρώπους), to which Paul was called, is represented as the testimony of an eye-witness and ear-witness, which he may not decline (ver. 15). Lastly, the exhortation to baptism and to the invocation of Jesus is a sign that Paul was not precipitate, but, on the contrary, required to be urged to take the decisive step, and that in the name of God.

6. *When I returned to Jerusalem.*—Paul (vers. 17–21) relates a revelation of Jesus, not mentioned in chap. ix. 26–28, which called him from Jerusalem to a distance among the Gentiles, in justification of his labours in heathen lands. But even here he designedly brings forward, in order to obviate the suspicion that he was an enemy of Israel, of the law, and of the temple, that this second appearance of Christ to him took place in Jerusalem and in the temple, when he was in the act of prayer. He has thus, in consequence of his conversion to Christ, not forgotten Jerusalem (Ps. cxxxix. 5), nor estranged himself from the temple as a place of prayer. And so little was he prejudiced against the people, that when the Redeemer called him hastily away from Jerusalem, because they would not receive his testimony concerning Him, he raised objections, and was unable to sever himself from the hope of finding a good footing for the word of Christ among his people. The apostle had a good design in mentioning to his hearers what, during this vision, he

replied to Jesus; namely, in order that his well-known former enmity against the Christians, and his subsequent conversion, might make an impression, and procure entrance to his word with Israel (vers. 19, 20). Only the repeated and peremptory command of Jesus to send him to the Gentiles (he intends to say) overcame his tenacity, which arose from a warm love to his people.

DOGMATICAL AND ETHICAL THOUGHTS.

1. The glory of Christ shines from this defence of the Apostle Paul. In defending himself, and apparently speaking of his own person, he bears the plainest testimony to the Redeemer, to His grace toward sinners, and to His heavenly glory and power, to His fellowship with His poor and persecuted disciples, and to His plan of salvation embracing the human race. There is a wisdom in this which only the Spirit of Christ imparts, uniting a considerately forbearing and winning love toward his hearers with the most undaunted frankness of confession.

2. Paul, in the words of Ananias, gives Jesus the name of the Just One. In this the old covenant and the new, the law and the Gospel, are united. Righteousness is the aim of the law. Saul sought the righteousness of the law in his period of zeal, and did not find it. Israel seeks the righteousness of works, and does not attain to it. Legal righteousness was the ideal of Pharisaism. But Christ is the Righteous One in a peculiar, and indeed in an exclusive sense. In Him righteousness is personally exhibited, and fulfilled in a peculiar manner. He is the Just One, and justifies all who believe on His name.

3. Baptism, a means of grace. It confers purification from sin and forgiveness of sins. The invocation of the name of Jesus essentially belongs to it, as a confession of the Redeemer, and a prayer for reconciling and justifying grace.

4. Perhaps the well-meant desire to repair, in some measure, his earlier transgression against Christ, lay at the foundation of the objection of the apostle to the command of the Redeemer: he wished in Jerusalem, in the very place where he had once persecuted the disciples of Jesus, to confess his transgression, to prove his conversion, and to minister by boldly preaching and confessing Christ. But however well intended, and however earnest this wish might have been, it was not granted. Paul

must immediately quit Jerusalem, and be sent to the Gentiles.—This fact is not only a proof how much higher God's thoughts and ways are than the thoughts and ways of men, even of the purest and the noblest; but it is especially a proof that sins are forgiven through God's free grace only, which is to be received in all humility, without there being any mention, however remote, of a reparation; and that nothing remains to the pardoned sinner but unconditional obedience.

HOMILETICAL HINTS.

Brethren and fathers (ver. 1). The spirit of meekness opened the mouth of the apostle. Although he had none but persecutors and murderers before him, yet he regarded and addressed them as brethren and fathers, on account of the covenant and promises of God. Such a disposition is not acquired by our natural powers, but must be produced entirely by the grace of Jesus, who in the hour of agony prayed to the Father for His murderers. This is a peculiar ornament of the servants of Jesus (Apost. Past.).—It is a notable proof, what security and strength Paul enjoyed from the peace of God, that in such a storm he was so composed as to make such a temperate and unruffled speech (Rieger).

When they heard that he addressed them in the Hebrew dialect, they were the more silent (ver. 2). When the people heard Paul speak in an intelligible language, they became the more attentive and quiet.—Many preachers have themselves to blame that they are not listened to with attention. They do not speak intelligibly, but affectedly, and above the comprehension of the people. A preacher, whose object is to edify, should apply himself to present the truth in the simplest and most comprehensible manner, and to address himself to the heart. The teaching of Jesus is the most complete and the most blessed example (Apost. Past.).—We cannot blame the Jews that they held so pertinaciously to that language, in which God Himself had spoken with the fathers. But their own language had become strange to them. God could no longer make Himself, in this language, intelligible to their hardened hearts.—Thanks be to God, who since Pentecost has consecrated all languages, and makes Himself more and more known by means of all languages, wherever men will but hear His voice (Williger).

I am a Jew (ver. 3). Paul, in his whole discourse, seems to speak only of himself; but in reality he proclaims the virtues of Him who called him out of darkness into His marvellous light. —*Instructed with all exactness, and a zealot toward God.* It is not enough to be well instructed in religion; we must also be zealous, for Christ will cast out the lukewarm (Starke).—From the example of Paul, it may be seen that a man may be learned, may understand the Scriptures, be a zealot toward God, and yet be an enemy and persecutor of Christ. Natural science enlightens no one; titles and offices, even in a spiritual station, are no proofs of true fellowship with Jesus (Apost. Past.).

I persecuted this way to the death (ver. 4). Paul could not speak of his former enmity against the Gospel without godly sorrow (Rieger).—A faithful witness of Jesus is not ashamed to confess his sins, when he can thereby exalt the honour of his Saviour, and awaken hope and accessibility among souls. Particularly is such a confession salutary, when it is made to men who are involved in the same sins, and who may by our example be the more easily drawn from them (Apost. Past.).—Thus might Luther, in his contest against the Romish doctrine of works, appeal that he himself was once of that way of thinking, and that if any man could have been saved by monkery, he would have been so.—*I bound them.* Without doubt, his present fetters would remind the apostle of the fetters which he once put upon the brethren. Let us penitently reflect, in all our sufferings, whether we ourselves have not tied the rods, with which the Lord chastises us (Apost. Past.).

From whom I received letters (vers. 5, 6). How orderly and exactly does Paul, after so many years, know how to relate all the circumstances of his extraordinary conversion! This is a proof, not only that all things occurred when he was in the full possession of his faculties, but also that the grace which befell him made an indelible impression upon him. Certainly he who is snatched from death to life, will never forget what the Lord has done. The recollection and the narration of these blessed paths of salvation, will constitute a pleasure in the mansions of heaven (Apost. Past.).—Great changes of mind, and of conviction in religious matters, ought to have for their foundation a true zeal for God. But how badly do many of our modern innovators in religion stand this test, who play with religion as boys with dice, and thereby betray themselves, that they do not believe anything in sincerity! 1 Tim. iii. 7 (Starke).—It must certainly be a very surprising light at mid-day, which one is constrained to observe as extraordinary (Williger).

And I fell to the ground (ver. 7). Whoever will hear the divine voice, must fall down and humble himself before the divine majesty (Starke).—*Saul, Saul, why persecutest thou Me?* God begins conversion in men by internal conviction of sin, Rom. ii. 15; 2 Tim. ii. 25 (Starke).—Now the same Lord spoke by the mouth of His servant to Jerusalem. 'Why persecutest thou Me? O my people, what have I done to thee, and wherein have I wearied thee? Testify against Me: Micah iii. 6 (Besser).

Who art Thou, Lord? I am Jesus of Nazareth (ver. 8). Before conversion we do not know Jesus, but in conversion we learn to know Him, 1 John ii. 4 (Starke).

But they who were with me saw the light, and were afraid (ver. 9). When the natural man sees a beam of the divine glory, he is afraid, and indeed with justice, for God is a consuming fire to all the workers of iniquity (Starke).—*But heard not the voice of Him who spoke with me.* According to Acts ix., the companions of Paul heard indeed a sound; but, according to this passage, they did not understand the voice. Hearing is twofold. All our hearers hear the sound of the words, but only they who hear the voice of the Son of God will live (Apost. Past.).

And I said, What shall I do? (ver. 10.) Paul kept in view that, even in his miraculous conversion, Jesus referred him to the word, which was to be spoken to him by one of His servants. He awakens him directly, yet subjects him to the instruction and pastoral care of one of the least of the brethren, and causes him to be led in the beaten track of salvation (Apost. Past.).

I was led by the hand (ver. 11). This likewise pointed to a mystery, Isa. xl. 11. On the way to heaven, we are led by leading-strings, like children (Starke).

A devout man according to the law (ver. 12). Because Ananias was not only a devout man, but also was had in estimation by the Jews, he was in this respect a useful instrument in the hand of the Lord to win one so zealous for Judaism as Paul, and to become useful to him. The Lord knows all His servants, and where He can best employ each of them (Apost.

Past.).—At these words, the Jews would become all the more quiet (Besser).

Brother Saul (ver. 13). Paul cannot forget in what a meek, kind, and brotherly manner, Ananias came to the assistance of his alarmed spirit. This may excite us to ask for grace, that we may know how to speak a word in season to those who are weary, and with brotherly tenderness to lead the troubled and sorrowful to Jesus for comfort. This is the chief business and masterpiece of the evangelical ministry (Apost. Past.).

The God of our fathers has chosen thee (ver. 14). The instruments, which are to be particularly useful to the Church, must be ordained in heaven (Starke).

To know His will, and to see that Just One, and to be His witness to all men (vers. 14, 15). Two things must precede in order that a man may be qualified for the office of teaching and witnessing: a thorough knowledge of the will of God from His word; and personal experience that he has seen Jesus in faith, and that His word has come to his soul in power (Apost. Past.).

Arise and be baptized, and wash away thy sins (ver. 16). A beautiful proof how much the holy baptism was valued in the apostolic Church. It was no external ceremony, but a means of grace for the washing away of sins, and the first entrance into the Church of Jesus (Apost. Past.).

And prayed in the temple (ver. 17). The direct illumination and grace which he experienced did not lead the apostle away from the use of the temple. And the Lord crowned his prayer in the temple with a peculiar manifestation. Thus the example of the apostle refutes all sectaries, even when they think that they have some ground to go on (Apost. Past.).

Hasten and depart quickly from Jerusalem (ver. 18). A sad condition and a heavy judgment when the divine voice says, Hasten and depart quickly, Hos. ix. 12 (Starke).

And I said, Lord, they know (ver. 19). It often appears to the true servants of God, as if they could effect more blessing in this or that place than in another. But God says, No, you err; and sends them away, when they would remain (Apost. Past.).

And when the blood of Stephen, Thy witness, was shed (ver. 20). The apostle was most anxious, as he had sinned among the Jews, to be the author of some good among them, and thus to repair by abundant conversions the offences committed. Such an earnestness prevails among true converts (Apost. Past.).

And He said unto me, Depart (ver. 21). God's counsel must stand against all human objections, even those which are well meant (Starke).

On vers. 1–21. (See also Homiletical Hints to chap. ix. 1–22.)—*How our conversion can only be genuine when we can refer it with full conviction to the unmerited grace of God in Christ.* 1. The sinful condition, which preceded our conversion, vers. 3–5. 2. The way and manner, in which the Lord brought us out of the night of sin to the light of faith, vers. 6–15. 3. The irresistible power, with which grace leads our resisting mind toward its higher destiny, vers. 19–21 (Lisco).—*Christianity is an affair of life.* 1. It proceeds from the Eternal. 2. We experience it in our own hearts. 3. We exhibit it in our conduct.—*Paul's sketch of his own life; or, how a servant of God looks back upon the course of his life.* 1. With grateful remembrance of human benefactors, ver. 3. 2. With penitent confession of his own erroneous ways, vers. 4, 5. 3. With humble praise of the divine gracious dealings, vers. 6–16. 4. With clear consciousness of the life-call allotted to him, vers. 18–21.—*Paul's confession, "By the grace of God I am what I am," proved from the course of his life.* 1. From the advantages of birth and education, which the boy received by the grace of God. 2. From the erroneous paths of folly and sin, from which the young man was rescued by the grace of God. 3. From the ministry of peace and salvation, to which the man was elected and appointed by the grace of God.—*Every self-contemplation of a servant of God, a praise of divine grace;* for in himself he finds nothing to boast; he has the Lord to thank for everything.—*The heavenly light at Damascus:* the bright light which it casts upon the paths of our life. It illuminates: 1. The dark ways of sin, which we have traversed; 2. The blessed ways of grace, by which the Lord has come to us; 3. The Christian ways of duty, in which we are to walk in the strength of the Lord.—*Paul's ordination by Ananias, an example to preachers.* From this we see: 1. What the preacher must bring along with him into the ministry: the knowledge of the divine will, and the experience of the divine grace. 2. What the preacher is to do in the ministry: to be a witness to all men by word and deed of what he has seen and heard. 3. On what the preacher may depend in his ministry: on the grace of God which has appointed him to the evangelical office, and will strengthen him in it.—*Paul, the apostle of the Gentiles, a masterpiece of divine wisdom, which says, My thoughts are not as your thoughts.* 1. According to human ideas, everything seemed adverse. His condition of life: born a Jew; educated a Pharisee, ver. 4. His disposition: before conversion, a zealot for the law, vers. 3, 4; after conversion, his adherence to his people, ver. 17. The will of men: the rage of the Jews, ver. 22; the perplexity of the brethren, chap. xxi. 20. 2. But the wisdom of God triumphed over all these obstacles: appointing Paul to be the apostle of the Gentiles from eternity, vers. 10, 14; equipping him by external and internal providences, vers. 6, 17; and accrediting him by the great fruits of his labour.—*The answer of the Lord to the "but" of His servants,* vers. 17–21. 1. Even the sincere servants of God have often a "but" against the commands of the Lord: it may arise from fear as with Jonah, or from modesty as with Moses and Jeremiah, or from conscientiousness as with Peter, or from compassion as with Abraham toward Sodom, and Paul toward the Jews. 2. Yet in spite of all these "buts," the Lord remains firm to His command, "Depart;" and at length obtains the glory, "He has done all things well."

B.

The Apostle is passionately interrupted, and nearly scourged by the military authority, from which his privilege of Roman citizenship protects him.

CHAP. XXII. 22–29.

22 And they listened to him to this word, and then raised their voices, and said, Away with such a fellow from the earth, for it was not fit that he should continue in life. 23 And as they cried out, and threw up their garments, and cast dust in the air, 24 The tribune commanded him to be brought to the camp, and said that he should be examined with scourges, that he might learn on what ground they so cried against him. 25 And as they stretched him out to the thongs, Paul said to the centurion who stood by, Is it permitted you to scourge with cords a man who is a Roman citizen, and that without trial and sentence? 26 When the centurion heard that, he went to the tribune, and informed him, saying, What art thou about to

do? That man is a Roman citizen. 27 Then went the tribune to him,
and said to him, Tell me, art thou a Roman citizen? He answered, Yes.
28 The tribune answered, I obtained this privilege of citizenship for a con-
siderable sum. But Paul said, But I was so born. 29 Therefore they im-
mediately departed from him, who were to have put him to the question;
and the tribune was afraid after he had learned that he was a Roman
citizen, because he had bound him.

Ver. 22. All the uncial MSS. without exception have the imperfect καθῆκεν; only some cursive MSS. have καθῆκον, which was a correction, the meaning of the imperfect not having been understood.

Ver. 25. The plural προέτειναν or προέτεινον is decidedly genuine; whereas the singular προέτεινεν is only found in some cursive MSS.

Ver. 26. Ὅρα before τί is not sufficiently attested, in order to be received for anything else than a gloss.

Ver. 27. Εἰ before σύ is contained only in one uncial MS., whereas the question in all the others begins with σύ.

EXEGETICAL EXPLANATIONS.

1. *And they listened to him to this word.*—The declaration of his mission by Christ to the Gentiles inflamed their fanatical zeal anew. They interrupted the speech with loud cries, in order to drown the sound of his voice. *Τὸν τοιοῦτον*, a man of that kind. Meyer refers the imperfect *καθῆκεν* to the danger of life in which the apostle already was (chap. xxi. 21), so that the meaning would be, He should not be protected, he should not be preserved in life. The meaning seems rather to be, He should already long ago have forfeited his life. *Κραυγάζειν* is an inarticulate outcry which the multitude raised. *Ῥιπτούντων τὰ ἱμάτια*: the throwing up of their garments, and the casting dust in the air, were wild signs of fury, gestures by which they gave to understand that they would gladly accomplish what they cried out, "Away with him from the earth."

2. *The tribune commanded.*—The Roman commander was convinced that now nothing more was to be made of it, and he ordered his prisoner to be taken from the stairs where he had spoken, and to be brought to the camp, *i.e.*, inside of the castle of Antonia. But also, because the fury of the people seemed certainly to suppose a crime not yet confessed, he commanded him to be scourged, as an instrument of question, in order to extort from him the confession of his crime (*ἀνετάζειν*, to inquire). In consequence of this command, the apostle was already bound to a post, in order forthwith to be subjected to

scourging. *Προέτειναν τοῖς ἱμᾶσιν* cannot be "to bind with thongs" (Luther and others), as the definite article with *ἱμᾶσιν* would then be useless; but these *ἱμάντες* must be identical with the *μάστιγες* (ver. 24), as the scourging took place by thongs; then the definite article is entirely appropriate. "He was stretched forward to the (already named) thongs," as the mark to which they were to be directed. *Προέτειναν*, namely, the soldiers enjoined to execute the order.

3. *Is it lawful for you?*—The apostle, before the order was executed, protests in the form of a question to the centurion, standing by to superintend the scourging. The question, as Chrysostom has observed, draws attention to a twofold legal wrong which was about to be committed by the scourging. 1. Inasmuch as they would punish him uncondemned (*ἀκατάκριτον—μαστίζειν*), for scourging was actually a punishment, not a mere means of examination: it is as if they would commence the trial with the execution. 2. He asserts his privilege as a *civis Romanus*, inasmuch as a Roman citizen, according to the *lex Porcia* and the *leges Semproniæ*, was not permitted to be scourged, even in the case of a proved crime; scourging being a punishment of slaves.

4. *When the centurion heard that.*—At the information of the centurion, the commander drew near, in order to learn the fact of the Roman citizenship of his prisoner. *Σὺ Ῥωμαῖος εἶ;* asked in astonishment: Art thou a Roman citizen? *Κεφάλαιον*, literally equivalent to capital. The tribune was afraid because the binding of a Roman citizen was punishable, when it took place as an act of violence, and without preceding proof of a penal offence.

DOGMATICAL AND ETHICAL THOUGHTS.

1. It was not so much his courageous confession of Jesus in and for itself, as his call to be the apostle of the Gentiles, that caused this interruption of the speech, and this outbreak of deadly fury against the apostle. He must suffer precisely on account of that which is the characteristic of his mission.

2. Roman privilege protects the apostle of Christ. This had arisen entirely in accordance with the way in which God suffered this people to walk (chap. xiv. 26): it was, in a purely heathenish and aristocratical manner, the preference of

a class. Yet it must now minister to the good of a servant of God.

HOMILETICAL HINTS.

And they heard him to this word (ver. 22). Now the envy of the Jews, who will not enter the kingdom of God themselves, and will vehemently prevent others, the Gentiles, from entering, broke out (Rieger).—Paul had delivered a powerful and spiritual speech, and yet effected nothing. Rage, hatred, fury, and wickedness, on all sides, were the consequences of it. This example should make us guarded in our judgments, that we do not always measure the value of a sermon according to its visible fruits (Apost. Past.).—*Away with such a fellow from the earth!* This was the very cry of fury which Jesus was obliged to hear from His people. It is evident that the apostle does not say too much, when he asserts of himself and of his brethren, that they were regarded as the filth of the world, and as the offscouring of all things (Apost. Past.).

And as they threw up their garments, and cast dust in the air (ver. 23). The gloomy preparatory measures for stoning. But even now a representation of men in the fury of passion. They rend their garments, cast off the last remnant of shame and modesty, and show themselves in their brutal nakedness; and they cast dust, to blacken all that is bright, to soil all that is noble, and to blind their ownselves.—"It is dangerous to awaken the lion, the teeth of the tiger are destructive; but the most terrible of all terrors is man in his rage" (Schiller).

And commanded that he should be examined with scourging, that he might know why they so cried against him (ver. 24). In a tumult, the trial usually begins with the execution. Then even able men frequently commit great mistakes. To scourge, and then to inquire afterwards what was done: thus is it with the world: it condemns what it does not understand, and passes sentence on him whom it has not convicted. But be comforted, O Christian, who art thus dealt with: there is yet another judgment-day, when God Himself will judge, and revise, and cancel all unrighteous judgments and decrees passed here; then it will sound quite otherwise (Wisdom vi. 4).—But thou, O worldly judge, consider well and use all foresight, if thou wilt not have the burden of innocent blood upon thy conscience (Starke).

Is it lawful to scourge a man that is a Roman, and uncondemned? (ver. 25.) A Christian is at liberty to appeal to law and privileges, and thus to repel unjust violence.—Christians may with a safe conscience use the Roman privileges in the Roman empire, yea, even Turkish worldly privileges, so far as these are not against God and nature, when they are obliged to live in that land, 1 Thess. v. 21 (Starke).—If a worldly privilege of citizenship is so very valuable, how much more valuable is the privilege of the children of God, who by the new birth have become citizens of heaven! Is it lawful to vex and torment, or even to neglect and slight such persons? Or, is it lawful for them to exchange their inestimable privileges for the trifles of this world? (Apost. Past.)—The emperor of the world is respected in his camp: the King of Israel is despised in His (Besser).

But Paul said, I was born a Roman citizen (ver. 28). A Christian must not despise the privileges of birth, but use them aright for the glory of God and the good of his neighbour, 1 Cor. x. 33 (Starke).

And the tribune feared (ver. 29). Before this the whole multitude cried out, Away with such a fellow; he is not worthy to live. And here the chief captain is afraid of him. Thus the Lord knows how to exalt His servants, when they seem ready to be slain. And while they carry the image of the cross in lowliness and shame, the image of Jesus, with which they are adorned, imparts such honour and respect, that even the ungodly are afraid, and retire before them (Apost. Past.).

On vers. 22–29.—*The danger, and the rescue.* 1. The apostle's danger: founded on his testimony to the truth; caused by the obstinate pride of the Jews; and threatening a fatal issue. 2. The apostle's rescue: effected by the feeling of justice in the Roman commander; by the apostle's privilege of citizenship; and by the new opportunity accorded to him for his justification (Lisco).—Righteousness exalteth a nation, but sin is the destruction of a people.—*Paul, an example of a noble sufferer.* 1. By the manner, in which he endures unavoidable sufferings: he is silent, ver. 22; he pardons, ver. 23; he submits, ver. 24. 2. By the manner, in which he averts from himself unnecessary shame: he seeks no martyrdom; he warns the authorities of the abuse of their power; he preserves the feeling of his human dignity inviolate (Lisco).—*The raging people of Jerusalem, a terrible picture of fanaticism:* 1. How it dishonours God, for whom it fancies it is zealous; 2. maltreats the innocent, whom it has chosen to sacrifice; 3. injures itself, converting men into wild beasts.—*Is it lawful to scourge a man who is a Roman, and uncondemned?* A warning from God to tyrants, to remind them of the inalienable rights of men; the sacred honour of citizens; and the inviolable dignity of Christians.—*The sacred person of a true servant of God.* 1. When he is violently attacked, he may protest in meekness and humility, ver. 25 (see John xviii. 23). 2. When he is externally maltreated, he continues internally inviolate, chap. vi. 41. 3. When he is for a time trodden in the dust, he shall be for ever crowned with honour, Matt. v. 11, 12.—*The imperishable nobleness of the children of God:* 1. obtained by regeneration; 2. pledged by the Spirit of God, who bears witness with our spirits that we are the children of God; 3. proved in trial and temptation; 4. renewed in heaven, where they shall appear with Christ in glory, Col. iii. 4.—*The noble privileges of a citizen in the kingdom of God.* 1. He does not need to be afraid of the powers of the world: Paul undaunted before the Roman commander; indeed the latter afraid of him. 2. He is uninjured by the blows of the world: a citizen of Rome must not be scourged; a citizen of Christ, it is true, has no exemption from the blows of tribulation and the scourge of persecution, but the pain and the shame thereof do not injure him. 3. He is not bound by the judgment of the world: Paul appeals from the wrongly-informed to the better-instructed commander, and at a later period to Cæsar himself. The Christian appeals from the judgment of the world to the judgment-seat of his heavenly King.—*How a Christian values, but does not overvalue, his privileges as a citizen.* 1. He does not cast away the privileges of his birth, but he knows that they are of no value without nobleness of disposition. 2. He does not sacrifice his legal rights, but he asserts them in meekness and humility. 3. He claims the protection of the authorities, but his highest confidence is in the Lord of lords and King of kings.

C.

The Apostle brought before the Chief Council, and his defence there: the comforting promise of the Lord to him.

CHAP. XXII. 30–XXIII. 11.

30 On the following day, wishing to know the certainty of what he is
accused of the Jews, he loosened him, and commanded the high priest and all
the council to assemble; and he brought down Paul, and set him before them.
Chap. xxiii. 1 And Paul looked at the council, and said, Men and
brethren, I have walked in all good conscience before God until this day.
2 But the high priest, Ananias, commanded them who stood near him to
smite him on the mouth. 3 Then Paul said to him, God shall smite thee,
thou whited wall! Sittest thou to judge me according to the law, and
commandest me to be smitten contrary to the law? 4 And the bystanders
said, Revilest thou the high priest of God? 5 And Paul said, I did not
know, brethren, that he is the high priest; for it is written, Thou shalt not
revile the ruler of thy people. 6 But when Paul knew that the one part
were Sadducees and the other Pharisees, he called aloud in the council, Men
and brethren, I am a Pharisee, and a son of Pharisees: concerning the
hope and the resurrection of the dead, I am judged. 7 And when he had
said this, there arose a dissension between the Pharisees and the Sadducees,
and the multitude was divided. 8 For the Sadducees maintain that there
is no resurrection, nor angel, nor spirit; but the Pharisees assert both.
9 And there arose a great outcry, and scribes of the part of the Pharisees
arose and strove, saying, We find nothing bad in this man; but if a spirit
or an angel has spoken to him? 10 And when there arose a great uproar,
the tribune feared lest Paul should have been torn in pieces by them, and
commanded the soldiers to go down and to seize him from the midst of them,
and to bring him to the camp. 11 And on the following night, the Lord
stood by him and said, Be of good cheer; for as thou hast testified of Me at
Jerusalem, so must thou also testify in Rome.

Chap. xxii. 30. Ἀπὸ τῶν δεσμῶν after αὐτόν is a later addition, for the four oldest uncial MSS. do not have it. The same four MSS. have συνελθεῖν, whilst the others read ἐλθεῖν: the latter is a correction, as it was thought that the Jewish rulers must have repaired to the commander.

Chap. xxiii. 6. The uncial MSS. A.B.C., seven cursive MSS., the Syriac, and the Vulgate have υἱὸς Φαρισαίων; the reading Φαρισαίου is a correction, his father only being thought of. Griesbach preferred the plural, and Lachmann and Tischendorf have with justice adopted it.

Ver. 9. The reading of the two youngest MSS., G.H., and of five cursive MSS., γραμματεῖς, without the article, appears to be genuine. Two uncial MSS. have τινες τῶν γραμματέων; two others, τινες τῶν Φαρισαίων; but these seem to be designed improvements of the original words.—Μὴ θεομαχῶμεν after ἄγγελος are wanting in the four most important MSS. of the first class, three cursive MSS., and five ancient versions, and are to be expunged as an interpolation taken from chap. v. 39, as Erasmus, Griesbach, and most of the modern critics have done.

Ver. 11. Παῦλε after θάρσει is, according to external testimonies, undoubtedly spurious.

EXEGETICAL EXPLANATIONS.

1. *On the following day.*—Τὸ ἀσφαλές, that which is certain; the tribune wished to obtain trustworthy information: τὸ τί—Ἰουδαίων is added as the apposition to it. He wished to find out the definite point of accusation against Paul; what were the complaints against him on the part of the Jews. Until this instant, he had heard nothing definite; he had only learned the passionate indignation and the excited disposition against Paul. He hoped to obtain this object infallibly by means of the Jewish hierarchy. The command to call a meeting of the Sanhedrim proves how deeply the independence of the Jews was impaired, even in the internal concerns of their religion. Συνελθεῖν supposes the usual place of meeting, while the spurious reading ἐλθεῖν proceeds upon the assembly being summoned by the Roman commander. Also καταγαγών (compare chap. xxiii. 10, καταβάν) refers to a locality in the city itself, not within the castle of Antonia, commanding the city. Ἔλυσεν: thus the tribune, notwithstanding that he was for a time afraid, because he had bound a Roman citizen, yet did not loose Paul from his bonds, until he placed him before the Sanhedrim.

2. *And Paul looked at the council.*—Paul, as the Redeemer Himself on the night before His crucifixion, and as formerly the apostles, was now placed before the council. But he regarded the assembly unmoved, with a calm and undaunted look. Also the address ἄνδρες ἀδελφοί, without πατέρες (chap. xxii. 1), shows that he feels himself on an equality with them. He commences the proceedings; for he was not cited by the assembly itself, but placed before them by the Roman tribune. Therefore they waited for what the tribune had to bring before them; and the apostle on his part expresses himself calmly. He attests his good conscience, with which hitherto he had in all points performed his duty toward God. Πάσῃ συνειδήσει ἀγαθῇ, *i.e.*, in every respect, in every instance with a good conscience. Πολιτεύομαι, "I have performed my office with a good conscience;" τῷ Θεῷ, *dat. com.* for God; to understand πολιτεύομαι

in an entirely abstract sense for *vitam instituere* or *se gerere*, is not founded on the *usus loquendi.*

3. The high priest, Ananias, is also known from Josephus, Ant. xx. 5, 2; 6, 2. He was the son of Nebedæus, and was appointed high priest by Herod, king of Chalcis, in the year 48 after Christ, and probably held this office until the year 60, when Ismael, the son of Phabi, attained to the dignity of high priest, shortly before the departure of the procurator Felix (Joseph. Ant. xx. 8, 8). Inasmuch as he had been sent to Rome by Quadratus, the governor of Syria, in the year 52, to defend himself before the emperor Claudius, because the Jews had been accused by the Samaritans of violence (Joseph. Ant. xx. 6, 2), it has formerly been supposed that he had been deposed, and at this time administered the office temporarily, or that he only bore the honorary title of an ex-high priest (Eichhorn, Kuinoel). But he came off victorious in the cause for which he went to Rome, and returned to Jerusalem, and was without doubt permitted to hold his dignity uninterrupted: so among moderns, Winer, Wieseler, Meyer, and Ewald. Thus historical information, elsewhere, confirms the fact that Ananias was at this time certainly the ruling high priest, to which the designation ὁ ἀρχιερεὺς also points.

4. *Commanded those who stood near to smite him.*—The high priest commanded those who stood near, probably the officers of justice, to smite Paul on the mouth for his first words, which appeared to him as insolence or hypocrisy. But Paul replied to him in righteous indignation, announcing the divine retributoin of that blow (τύπτειν μέλλει, not a wish, as Kuinoel thinks), pointing out his hypocrisy (τοῖχε κεκονιαμένε, where the external show of superficial paint and the internal state of filthy clay form the contrast), and bringing prominently forward the inconsistency of pretending to judge according to the rule of the Mosaic law, and yet by unlawful ill-treatment himself violating the law. *Καὶ σὺ*, Thou also, as well as the rest, while thou as judge oughtest to observe the law with double conscientiousness. This prophetical announcement was fulfilled ten years later, when Ananias, as one of the leaders of the loyal imperial party, was murdered at the commencement of the war by the insurgents (Joseph. Jud. Bell. ii. 17, 9).

5. *Revilest thou God's high priest?*—To the representation

that this invective against the high priest of God was an insult to the holy God Himself, the apostle, in justification, replies that he did not know that he was the high priest. This answer has been much twisted by commentators. Some twist the words *ὅτι ἐστὶν ἀρχιερεύς*, as if the apostle would call in question the high-priestly dignity of Ananias, because he had procured this dignity by money (Grotius), or because he was not in point of fact the high priest in office (Lightfoot). On the other hand, others twist the words *οὐκ ᾔδειν*, as if Paul intended to say, "I did not reflect on his being the high priest" (Wetstein, Olshausen, Ewald), by which the apostle would retract his words as rash; or as if *οὐκ ᾔδειν* imported, "I do not acknowledge it" (Augustin); or as if the apostle would say, "I could neither know nor think that he is the high priest, as he acts in a manner so unpriestly, so entirely unworthy of a high priest" (Calvin, Meyer, Baumgarten). These artifices were employed, because the simple meaning of the words, that the apostle did not know that he who had given that unworthy command, was the high priest in office, appeared incredible. There are not indeed wanting interpreters who take the words in their literal sense, *e.g.*, Chrysostom and Beza, appealing to this, that the apostle, by reason of his long absence from Jerusalem, did not personally know the high priest. Had Ananias been the high priest in office when Paul, invested with authority from the high priest, journeyed to Damascus to persecute the Christians, then it would be impossible that he should not have known the same man. But it has been proved, that Ananias only attained to the dignity of high priest in the year 48, whilst the conversion of Paul occurred, at the very latest, about the year 40 or 41. Moreover the high priest was not to be recognised by his robes, when not engaged in the priestly service in the temple. And indeed it is very conceivable that Ananias did not at this time preside, especially as the session was held at the desire of the Roman tribune. However, even although Ananias did preside, Paul might not have known that he was also high priest, because the Nasi (president of the Sanhedrim) did not always require to be the high priest. Paul appeals to a command of God (Ex. xxii. 28) in reference to this, that he should indeed recognise and honour the rulers of the people, but without retracting his words.

6. *I am a Pharisee.*—The apostle quickly adopts a different course. A calm defence, as he had begun in ver. 1, found no favourable hearing. Therefore, in order at least to win a party in the assembly for the cause itself, for the Christian truth, he announces himself to be personally a Pharisee, and his faith as related to the doctrine of the Pharisees. He calls himself the son of Pharisees, in reference to his fathers and ancestors, by which he intends to say that he has not only personally adopted the pharisaical view and disposition, but that he has received it as an old family tradition. To this he adds, that he was in reality judged on account of the hope and of the resurrection. *'Ελπ. καὶ ἀναστ. νεκρ.* is commonly taken as ἓν διὰ δυοῖν, the hope of the resurrection: so Bengel, Meyer, Baumgarten. But it gives a better and more complete sense to take them separately: on account of the hope, *i.e.*, the hope of redemption, the Messianic promise made to Israel; and on account of the resurrection of the dead. The latter expression can then refer directly to the resurrection of Jesus; whereas by combining them, only the future resurrection can be meant; and yet the resurrection of Jesus must have been especially before the mind of the apostle.

7. *When he had said this.*—Paul caused a division of the members of the council, who before were united in their enmity, so that the Pharisees and Sadducees strove together. This dissension grew always louder and more passionate (ver. 9, *κραυγὴ μεγάλη*; ver. 10, *πολλὴ στάσις*), so that the Roman tribune feared for the safety of his prisoner, and commanded him to be removed by military force. For the information of the reader, Luke states the difference between the views of the Sadducees and the Pharisees. The Sadducees deny both the resurrection and the existence of an angel or spirit (*μηδὲ—μήτε*, critically to be adhered to; the former word introduces another kind of ideas, the latter word places something similar beside it, inasmuch as *πνεῦμα*, an incorporeal spirit, is essentially homogeneous to *ἄγγελος*). The Pharisees confess and maintain both (*ἀμφότερα*, inasmuch as the resurrection of the body and existence of pure spirits, *e.g.*, angels or departed souls, form two principal categories). Indeed, several learned scribes of the faction of the Pharisees contended for Paul. This faction consisted partly of the learned, and partly of the unlearned: the former commenced, and declared both for Paul himself, against whom no

crime was proved, and for the possibility of a revelation being imparted to him. *Εἰ—ἄγγελος*, an abrupt speech, either as a condition without an *ἀπόδοσις*, or as a question which leaves the answer to the opponent. This undeniably refers to what Paul had related concerning the appearance of Jesus; only that the Pharisees, according to their manner, think on the appearance of an angel or the manifestation of a spirit.

8. *But when there was a great uproar*, and it was always increasing, the tribune at length became alarmed, lest Paul should be torn in pieces by the contending parties (*διασπασθῇ*, whilst the one tried to lay hold on him in order to protect him, and the other did so in rage, so that he was pulled to and fro). Therefore he ordered the soldiers to come from the castle, and to take him by force from the assembly, and to bring him again into the camp. The commander, doubtless in order not to affront the hierarchy, had not taken with him into the assembly a military detachment, but only an escort.

9. *On the following night.*—This manifestation of Jesus Christ apparently took place in a dream. Paul saw the Lord standing by him, and heard His words, full of encouragement and of promises. *Εἰς Ἱερουσαλήμ—εἰς Ῥώμην*, to both cities he must come, in both he was to bear witness: the one the religious, and the other the political capital of the world at that time.

DOGMATICAL AND ETHICAL THOUGHTS.

1. The apostle attests his good conscience, not of himself abstractly, but specially with reference to his calling as the apostle of the Gentiles. He must not, especially before the hierarchical court of Israel, be ashamed of his office: he loudly and joyfully confessed it. He appeals to God and to His gracious approval (*τῷ Θεῷ*), which is decisive, though men may greatly condemn his actions. He certainly had particularly in view his life after conversion; but he does not restrict this witness of himself to that period, but intends to affirm that he, as a Christian, serves God as uprightly and zealously as before.

2. Both in the hasty rejoinder to the violence threatened (ver. 3), and in the justification of his words, Paul places in clear light the contrast between the office and the person. The office obliges both the president and every simple member of

the court of justice to strict conscientiousness in the observance of the law; but the person injures the law in a clamant manner (ver. 3). And in consequence of such personal conduct, one may certainly refrain from recognising him as the holder of an office so holy. This is the criticism of the Holy Ghost, which places the line of right and truth on the person, however exalted he may be, and recognises in no man an infallibility, whether *in cathedra*, or in the chair of an ecclesiastical assembly.

3. The conduct of the apostle, when he avowed himself a Pharisee, is often judged as an act of human prudence, by means of which he hoped to divide the assembly, and to make the most of party interests for his own advantage. *Divide et impera*. But, assuredly, he acted thus not for himself or for his personal advantage, but for the sake of the holy cause of truth, and for the glory of Christ. He used the division between the Pharisees and Sadducees only in order by means of it to obtain a hearing for the truth, against which hitherto their minds were entirely closed. And this end he attained by the declaration that he himself was a Pharisee, and that he was tried on account of a matter which formed a chief point in the pharisaical system. He here takes hold, as he did also with reference to heathenism, of that which is related to Christianity, Israel's hope of a Messiah, and the belief in the resurrection of the dead. In point of fact, the result showed that the Pharisees were nearer the truth.

4. How far could Paul affirm, not only that he was a Pharisee, but that he continued to be so? This has been regarded as an untruth. But as opposed to the Sadducean notions (and in this contrast it is intended), he could with truth maintain that he had become nothing else, that he was a Pharisee still, and that he acted strictly and exactly in conformity with holiness and righteousness before God, and was a believer in the hope of Israel and in the resurrection. The fulfilment of that which the pious Pharisee hoped and longed for, was to him the highest blessing. He says to the Pharisees, what he formerly said to the heathen Athenians, What ye seek and know not, that I have, that I know, that I declare unto you. In this sense also the words may be applied, which Bengel in another application (to ver. 1) says of Paul, *Nunc, quum bona vetera non abjecit, sed meliora accepit, ex præsenti statu lux in pristinum sese refundebat.*

5. The manifestation of Christ (ver. 11) was consoling and also elevating. The apostle, in the midst of the greatest danger, sees the most glorious prospect. To be permitted to preach the Gospel at Rome, had long ago appeared to be the highest aim of his life. And now that was granted him. What the Redeemer intended for him, and what He had likewise at his conversion revealed to him by Ananias, now approaches its fulfilment; certainly under the sign of the cross, for he must suffer great things for the name of Jesus, chap. ix. 15, 16.

HOMILETICAL HINTS.

And Paul looked at the council (ver. 1). So Solomon formerly had observed places of judgment, where the wicked and wickedness were, Eccles. iii. 16. And also in the life of our blessed Saviour, mention is made of the effect He produced by such earnest looks, Luke xx. 17; Mark iii. 5, xi. 11. Much that was affecting must have been in Paul's heart, when he thus looked at the council—the apostasy of his brethren according to the flesh, in whose council he saw it; and also his own calling and election, by which he had been rescued from these bonds of darkness, and now never more would have to go for letters and commissions to such a council (Rieger).—*I have walked in all good conscience before God until this day.* Those whose own consciences accuse them, are usually not wont to lift up their eyes as Paul here, but to cast them down (Starke).—A good conscience toward God proceeds: 1. from true faith in Christ which obtains the forgiveness of sins; 2. from the assurance of divine grace and eternal life; 3. from the renewal of the Holy Ghost to a new life and conduct; 4. from the faithful performance of our calling (Starke).—Many appeal to their good conscience, only because no one can see it. Many also consider their sleeping conscience as a good one (Starke).

To smite him on the mouth (ver. 2). In this mode of suffering, Paul was an exact image of the suffering Jesus, who in the days of His flesh was struck on the face, because He had witnessed a good confession before the high priest (Apost. Past.).—Pious Christians do also even now receive many shameful blows, partly by revilings on all sides, and partly because men will no longer suffer them to speak the truth, and to rebuke the ungodly nature of the world (Starke).

God will smite thee, thou whited wall (ver. 3). Here was one of those whited sepulchres which the Lord Himself describes.—A striking image of an unconverted teacher. Ananias held the office of high priest, and had, perhaps, externally, in his grey hair and white priestly robes, a venerable appearance: but internally, his heart was full of rage and murder, of unrighteousness and tyranny. Our holy offices, spiritual titles, and priestly dignities, are nothing else than white lime by which the internal impurity of a carnal heart is covered. But before God no coverings can avail, and even before man the loose lime does not long hold together (Apost. Past.).—Certainly the hastiness of Paul's temper, when compared with the calm mildness and self-denial of Jesus, is not to be mistaken. But we ought not to blame the apostle too severely. In our exaggerated polite time, we recognise no greater sin in the servants of Christ than hastiness: it is said they ought to have been more circumspect. True, but this is the cause for which they have ventured their lives; they have stood as feeble men in the van. It is surely much better to be the Lord's unskilful advocate on earth, than from mere irresolution to permit others to do everything. Moreover, a Luther, for example, in Paul's circumstances would have acted still more roughly (Williger).

I did not know that he was the high priest (ver. 5). It is here to be observed, that it is possible that Paul did not actually recognise the person of the high priest in this tumult; for, at that time, it had already gone so far with that sacred office, that it could not be always known who was properly invested with it. Therefore Paul might indeed recognise Ananias for a Jewish elder and judge, and yet not know that he was at that time the presiding high priest. And even though we adopt the opinion that Paul knew him, yet his words signify nothing more than that, while he has all respect for the office, he rebukes the person who administers it so badly (Apost. Past.).—However, we must not use the conduct of Paul, either as an excuse for violent carnal passion, or for false political prudence, Tit. i. 7 (Starke).—As then Paul thus attacked the high priest who was appointed according to the law of Moses, why should I shun to attack the painted bishops and their larva, who proceed from the Pope, without any command either of God or of man? (Luther.)

I am a Pharisee (ver. 6). Here Paul stands as a sheep in the midst of wolves, and therefore he is wise as a serpent, Matt. x. 16 (Starke).—However, he did not renounce the simplicity of a dove. Paul belonged to the Pharisees, not only in consequence of his education and past life, but also by reason of his present position of faith, inasmuch as, in opposition to sadducean frivolity, he held fast the authority of the divine law and faith in the resurrection. This was the common ground on which he yet stood with them, and from which he would lead them still farther to the Gospel.—The hope of the fathers fulfilled in the advent of Christ, and the resurrection of the dead sealed by the resurrection of Christ, were in reality the two principal themes of the preaching of Paul (Apost. Past.).

And the multitude were divided (ver. 7). Here, again, we see the wisdom of God in permitting and suffering a multitude of religions. If the world were of one opinion, the truth would soon be crushed. But one sect contends with another, and thus they make room for the divine truth (Apost. Past.).

We find nothing evil in this man (ver. 9). Here the power of carnal passion raged, and yet God by His overruling wisdom effected His purpose. He rules in the midst of His enemies. "Some," says Paul, "preach Christ, even of hatred and strife; but that only Christ be preached, in all manner of ways, whether by accident or in the right way, I will rejoice" (Apost. Past.).—The behaviour of the apostle, in which human prudence becomes the handmaid of heavenly wisdom, does not belong to every one; and we do well to guard ourselves from imitating the wisdom of the serpent, when the simplicity of the dove is endangered by our doing so (Besser).

But there was a great tumult, and the tribune feared (ver. 10). When trouble is great, then God knows to stir up protecting angels, even though they should be heathen soldiers (Starke).—What kind of offence the chief captain took at this division, may be easily conceived (Rieger).—Similarly even now must it be with the heathen, when Christians in their religious hatred tear each other.

But the next day, the Lord stood by him (ver. 11). Great need, great comfort (Starke).—The encouragement of the Lord must have been particularly comforting to the apostle at this time. He might himself be little satisfied with his testimony in

Jerusalem, both as regards the result and as regards the manner of his defence. The address of the Lord raised him above such thoughts and doubts, which might cause to a servant of God, more than anything else, sleepless nights: "Be comforted, I am satisfied with thy witness, thou hast done as well as thou couldst: success lay not in thy hand. Thou hast not destroyed My way and plan: thy witness at Jerusalem is at an end, now go to Rome" (Williger).—From this place, the Acts of the Apostles is concerned with the apostolic testimony accomplished by Paul at Rome. If the defenders of Peter's supremacy had found either the whole or only the half of this ascribed to Peter, how would they urge it! (Bengel.)

On the whole section (vers. 1–11).—*The enemies of the Gospel passing sentence on themselves.* 1. In their unrighteousness. 2. In their disagreement (Lisco).—*The hope of the resurrection, the crown of Christianity.* 1. Only on this supposition does Paul's defence rest on truth. 2. But this supposition is also the truth (Lisco).—*The vehemence of the apostle before the chief council.* 1. How it was excited in him, vers. 1, 2. 2. How he mastered it, vers. 3–5 (Lisco).—*How we should unite the simplicity of the children of God with the wisdom of the children of this world.* 1. The simplicity of the children of God, by frank admission of our weakness, vers. 3–5. 2. The wisdom of the children of the world, by the use of circumstances to accomplish our end, vers. 6–10 (Lisco).—*The comfort of a good conscience.* 1. On what it rests: on justification by faith; on diligence in sanctification. 2. To what purpose it serves: to courageous working; to joyful suffering.—*Paul's defence before the chief council, or the true spirit of a witness.* A spirit of manly courage, childlike humility, collected prudence, and upright simplicity.—*Even in the vehemence of carnal zeal, a servant of God does not belie of whose spirit he is the child.* 1. The cause of his vehemence: it is the evil which excites him, the right for which he is zealous. 2. The manner in which his vehemence is expressed: even in anger, he does not forget his own dignity nor his reverence for God. 3. The victory which he obtains over his passion, whilst he ingenuously confesses it with calm composure, and manfully masters it. (Parallels from Luther's life and writings.)—*Jesus and Paul before the Sanhedrim*; or the Master and the disciple before unrighteous judges. 1. Wherein the Master and the disciple resemble each other. The same unmerited disgrace inflicted on both (ver. 2, and John xviii. 22). Both maintain their divinely bestowed dignity (ver. 3, and John xviii. 23). 2. Wherein the Master is above the disciple. The holy self-consciousness of Jesus (John xviii. 20, 21) is more than the good conscience of Paul (ver. 1). The calm answer of Jesus (John xviii. 23) is more heavenly than Paul's human vehemence (ver. 3).—*The best advocates of a servant of God before the judgment-seat of an unrighteous world.* 1. The comfort of a good conscience in his breast. 2. The curse of an evil thing in the ranks of the enemy. 3. The sympathy of the honest and unprejudiced in the world. 4. The gracious testimony of a righteous Judge in heaven.—*The call from heaven, Be of good cheer, Paul, a comfort for all Christ's faithful servants.* 1. To comfort them at the unrighteous judgment of the world. 2. To indemnify them for the reproach of their ministry. 3. To calm them under the accusations of their own conscience. 4. To strengthen them for future contests (Thou shalt bear witness also at Rome).

SECTION III.

PAUL IS SENT FROM JERUSALEM TO CÆSAREA, AND DEFENDS HIMSELF THERE, FIRST BEFORE THE ROMAN PROCURATOR FELIX, AND THEN BEFORE HIS SUCCESSOR FESTUS AND HEROD AGRIPPA II. (CHAP. XXIII. 12–XXVI. 32).

A.

A Conspiracy against the Life of Paul is discovered, and gives occasion to his being sent for the safety of his person to Cæsarea, and to his being delivered over to the Roman Procurator, Felix.

Chap. xxiii. 12-35.

12 But when it was day, the Jews combined together and bound themselves by an oath, neither to eat nor to drink until they should have killed
Paul. 13 But there were more than forty men who made this conspiracy.

14 These came to the chief priests and elders, and said: We have solemnly
bound ourselves with a curse, to taste nothing until we have killed Paul.
15 Now therefore do ye with the council give notice to the tribune, that
he bring him down to you, as if ye wished to inquire more thoroughly into
his affair: but we are ready to kill him, before he comes near.

16 But the sister's son of Paul heard of the plot, and came and entered
into the camp and informed Paul. 17 Then he called one of the centurions
unto him, and said, Bring this young man to the tribune, for he has some-
thing to inform him of. 18 And he took him with him, and brought him
to the tribune, and said, The prisoner Paul called me, and desired me to
bring this young man to thee, who has something to say to thee. 19 Then
the tribune took him by the hand, and went aside with him privately, and
asked him, What is it that thou hast to tell me? 20 He answered, The
Jews have agreed to desire thee, that thou wouldst bring down Paul to-
morrow before the chief council, as though they would institute a more
thorough examination concerning him. 21 But do not thou be persuaded;
for more than forty men of them conspire against him, who have sworn
neither to eat nor to drink till they have killed him; and now they are
ready, and expect thy promise. 22 Then the tribune dismissed the young
man, and enjoined him to tell no one that he had showed these things to
him.

23 And he called to him two centurions, and said: Make ready two
hundred soldiers to go to Cæsarea, and seventy horse, and two hundred
light-armed men, at the third hour of the night; 24 Also that they should
provide beasts to set Paul thereon, and to bring him in safety to Felix, the
governor; 25 Along with which he wrote a letter as follows: 26 Claudius
Lysias salutes the noble governor Felix. 27 I, having come with soldiers,
rescued this man, whom the Jews had taken and were in the act of killing,
when I had learned that he was a Roman citizen. 28 And when I would
learn the reason wherefore they accused him, I brought him down to their
council: 29 Then I found that he was accused only of questions of their
law, whilst nothing was laid to his charge worthy of death or imprison-
ment. 30 And when it was told me that they laid wait for the man, I sent
him immediately to thee, and commanded his accusers also that they should
speak before thee.

31 Then the soldiers fulfilled the command received by them, and took
Paul and brought him by night to Antipatris. 32 And on the morrow they
left the horsemen to go with him, and returned to the camp. 33 These,
having come to Cæsarea and delivered the letter to the governor, presented
Paul also before him. 34 And when he had read the letter, he inquired of
what province he was. And when he learned that he was of Cilicia, he
said: 35 I will hear thee, when thy accusers also are here; and he com-
manded him to be kept in the palace of Herod.

Ver. 12. The majority of uncial MSS. have *οἱ Ἰουδαῖοι*; only the two youngest, G. and H., read *τινες τῶν Ἰουδ.*, which is a correction, because it was thought that only individual Jews were concerned in it.

Ver. 15. *Αὔριον* after *ὅπως* is only attested by the two newest uncial

MSS. It is an interpolation from ver. 20, and is wanting in the best MSS.

Ver. 20. Ὡς μέλλων is undoubtedly original, and is sufficiently supported by external authorities; whereas μέλλοντα, μέλλοντες, and μελλόντων are mere corrections.

Ver. 30. Ὑπὸ τῶν Ἰουδαίων after ἔσεσθαι is wanting in the Vatican MS. and in several cursive MSS., and is undoubtedly an interpolation.—Τὰ πρὸς αὐτὸν and ἔῤῥωσο are critically suspicious, and must be considered as interpolations.

Ver. 34. Ὁ ἡγεμών after ἀναγνοὺς δέ is a spurious addition.

Ver. 35. Κελεύσας is better attested than ἐκέλευσέ τε.

EXEGETICAL EXPLANATIONS.

1. *But when it was day.—Οἱ Ἰουδαῖοι*, the Jewish faction, more exactly mentioned in ver. 13. *Συστροφή* is a seditious confederacy, a conspiracy. *Ἀνεθεμάτισαν ἑαυτοὺς*, they pronounced a curse upon themselves, an imprecation (חֵרֶם), if they ate anything until they had killed Paul. There was, however, in the Talmud, provided a loophole, namely, a mode of being freed from their vow and curse, if it were impossible to perform it; their wise masters might release them from their vow. Lightfoot has adduced a passage from Abodah Sarah to that effect. *Ἕως οὗ*, construed with the conjunctive, expresses that they thought the desired result would infallibly take place.

2. *These came to the chief priests.*—The conspirators, in order to attain their object, applied to the authorities, primarily indeed to the sadducean chief priests and members of the council. The whole Sanhedrim (*ὑμεῖς σὺν τῷ συνεδρίῳ*) were to request the commander to bring the prisoner before them, in order that the conspirators might have an opportunity to waylay and assassinate him, before he came near the assembly (*πρὸ τοῦ ἐγγίσαι*).

3. *But Paul's sister's son.*—The sister's son of the apostle, concerning whom we know nothing further, learned this murderous design. Bengel explains this, not improbably, by the supposition that they did not keep the matter very secret, because they did not consider it in the least degree possible that any one would communicate the plot to Paul or to the Roman tribune. From this it appears that Paul was not kept in such strict confinement as that a third person could not obtain admission to him; yet he was a *δέσμιος* (ver. 18), probably as at Rome (chap. xxviii. 16), in *custodia militaris*, chained to a soldier.

4. *Called one of the centurions.*—In order to keep the matter as secret as possible, Paul did not mention it to the centurion, but only requested him to bring the young man to the tribune, that he might give his information to him. The tribune came to him, and took him in a friendly and encouraging manner by the hand, to a place where he might speak with him alone (*κατ' ἰδίαν*).

5. *Prepare two hundred soldiers.*—A detachment of 470 men were appointed as an escort, in order to protect the apostle, not only against murderous plots, but also against possible violence. The company consisted of heavy-armed soldiers (*στρατιῶται* has here from the context that signification), of a small squadron of cavalry, and a division of light-armed troops. *Δεξιολάβοι* is entirely unknown in classical Greek, and occurs only in two passages of later writers, in one of them in connection with bowmen and those armed with a light shield. The explanation life-guardsmen (those who protect the right side of the commander) is to be rejected; and the meaning to be retained, "those who grasped their weapons with the right hand," whether javelins or slings, and thus they were either javelin-throwers or slingers. The supposition of Ewald is extremely probable, that these slingers were Arabian auxiliaries, because Arabia was in ancient times celebrated for its slingers. The reading *δεξιοβόλους* in the Alexandrian Codex, which Lachmann has preferred, agrees entirely with this, but is a later correction. *Ἀπὸ τρίτης ὥρας*, at the third hour of the night, *i.e.*, about nine in the evening, the detachment must be ready to march, as soon as the order was issued; thus the darkness of the night was to cover their march. Beasts of burden, that is, horses or mules, were also to be in readiness, several of them, in order to relieve one another. *Διασώζειν*, to bring in safety. The remark of Bengel, regarding the change from the direct to the indirect form of speech in ver. 24, *παραστῆσαι, ἵνα—διασώσουσι*, is extremely good and striking; namely, that this change corresponds with the affair itself, for the tribune did not at first intimate the object of their journey to be a military escort of Paul: *ἵνα διασώσ.* is thus the design of the expedition, obliged to be kept secret at first; and in order to express this, the change occurs with *παραστῆσαι*.

6. *Felix*, the then procurator of Judea, is elsewhere known to us both from Josephus, and from Tacitus and Suetonius.

His full name was Antonius Felix. He was a freeman of the Emperor Claudius, and brother of Pallas the favourite of Nero. He was appointed procurator after the deposition of Cumanus by Claudius, in the year 53 after Christ; but after having exercised his power as a prince with the spirit of a slave, as Tacitus expresses it, he was recalled by Nero, in the year 60 or 61, but yet protected against the accusations of the Jews by the imperial favour which his brother Pallas enjoyed. Grammatically *γράψας* (ver. 25) belongs to *εἶπε* (ver. 23), but, as a matter of fact, the composition of the accompanying epistle, as credentials to the procurator, probably took place at a somewhat later period. *Τύπος*, *exemplum*, is the contents in a definite form.

7. *Having learned that he was a Roman.*—*Αὐτόν* after *ἐξειλόμην* is pleonastic. *Μαθών*, from the context, gives the meaning that he learned he was a Roman citizen before this occurrence, and that it was this circumstance which induced him to interfere in order to rescue a Roman citizen. This contradicts the actual matter of fact (chap. xxi. 31, 32, compared with chap. xxii. 25–28). Therefore, in order to reconcile both, it is supposed that *μαθών* must be taken without a definite reference to time (Grotius), or that the tribune alludes to the second rescue, chap. xxiii. 10 (Du Bois). But art is here perversely directed. The tribune certainly intends to say (in order to place his official zeal in a clear light) that he rescued Paul from death, because he knew that he was a Roman citizen. He misrepresents the actual circumstances to his own advantage. And this trivial matter, as Meyer has rightly remarked, certainly speaks for the literal genuineness of the epistle. *Μηνυθείσης—μέλλειν ἔσεσθαι* is a negligent structure of sentences by the combination of two constructions.

8. *Took Paul and brought him.*—*'Αναλαβόντες* refers to their placing Paul on a beast of burden. They brought Paul by a quick night march to Antipatris, a city built by Herod the Great, and called after his father, Antipater, situated on a plain distant about 42 Roman miles, *i.e.*, 7–8 geographical (German) miles, from Jerusalem. Accordingly the company, which started about nine in the evening, could only reach Antipatris in the course of next forenoon. The foot soldiers then returned, and only the squadron of cavalry accompanied the prisoner to Cæsarea, which was 26 Roman miles farther on.

9. *After he had read the writing.*—Felix asked Paul only one question about his person, because, while his Roman citizenship was attested in the letter, nothing was said concerning his residence. *Διακούειν* is *ad finem usque audire*, to give a full hearing. *Τὸ πραιτώριον Ἡρώδου* is the palace formerly built by Herod the Great, and since inhabited by the Roman governors. The apostle was not put in a public prison, but kept in a room of the same palace, which the procurator himself inhabited.

DOGMATICAL AND ETHICAL THOUGHTS.

1. The promise of heavenly protection which is contained in *θάρσει* (ver. 11) was very speedily fulfilled. However remorseless the deadly enmity against the apostle, however great the number of the conspirators, however well-contrived their plots, yet the almighty protection of the Redeemer rules over His servant. What was concerted in secret, He causes to be revealed; and against all the designs of the wicked, He prepares a superior military power. Thus the exalted Redeemer rules in the midst of His enemies.

2. A body-guard of nearly five hundred men accompanied the apostle: he had never before journeyed with so strong an escort, and so great a following. He was certainly indebted for so much respect primarily to his Roman privileges. But still it was a matter of fact that so strong a force was demanded for the security of his person. Christ not only protects His people, but also honours them. And the honour which is often unintentionally conferred on a child of God, reflects back upon Him by whose grace a converted sinner is what he is.

3. The personal innocence of Paul is attested by the Roman tribune, who however expresses himself with an evident depreciation of the Gospel. This worldly man regards religion and what is related to it as a subordinate matter. And yet he must put in motion a considerable portion of the military force at his command to favour Paul. Thus must the world minister to the kingdom of God and exalt the honour of Christ, although it intended entirely otherwise.

HOMILETICAL HINTS.

They bound themselves with an oath, neither to eat nor to drink (ver. 12).—How much trouble do people take to hinder the kingdom of God! How much good might have been effected, if they made the same sacrifices for its promotion, and if their alliances for it were as firm!

There were more than forty men who made this confederacy (ver. 13, according to Luther).—What a fine bundle there will one day be, when the tares will be bound up together! (Rieger.)

They came to the chief priests, etc. (ver. 14). The chief priest, who, according to his office, should bear the holiness of the Lord on his forehead, and light and justice on his head, is turned into a ringleader of sworn assassins. This is the fruit of false religious zeal, and the sad consequence of an unregenerate heart. Would that it were the only example of this kind! (Apost. Past.)

As though ye would inquire more thoroughly into the affair; but we are ready to kill him before he comes near (ver. 15). These are Cain's saints, who, behind the veil of the law, conceal the club of the murderer (Starke).

But Paul's sister's son heard of the conspiracy (ver. 16). Who this young man was, whether he was already a Christian, or how he discovered the plot, we do not know: enough, that God would use him as the protecting angel of the apostle.—*There is nothing so finely spun which will not at length come to the light.* 1. For the protection of the righteous. 2. To the confusion of the wicked (Starke).—This time the Lord, to whom angels and earthquakes are at command, uses a lad for the performance of His purpose (Besser).

But Paul called to him (ver. 17). Paul had, indeed, from Christ Himself the promise of protection, but he did not therefore neglect the natural means for his rescue; on the contrary, he saw in them the stretched-out arm of the Lord.—Behold how harmoniously trust in God, and the use of ordinary means, are united in Paul!—In this, Luther resembles Paul. He reconciled himself to escape from the city of Augsburg in the night-time, by a secret gate, after his interview with Cajetan, and to ride eight (German) miles, until he reached a safe retreat (Besser).

Then the tribune took him by the hand (ver. 19). That all these great men have inclination and time to hear the young man, was a token from above; for this is not their usual manner (Williger).—Thus natural uprightness and fidelity are found even with the heathen. How rare have such qualities become among Christians! Hos. iv. 1 (Starke).

Make ready two hundred soldiers, etc. (ver. 23). Thus Paul journeyed as a great lord, with two guards and a squadron of horse. Now Paul was great in God's eyes; for whoever fears the Lord, is better than he who taketh a city. He would otherwise have to travel wearily on foot; here he proceeds on horseback. Then he would remember how all things must minister to his Lord and Saviour, even the beasts of the field (Bogatsky).—This escort of heathen soldiers is a sensible emblem of the angels of the Lord, who encamp around those who fear Him. God is a God of hosts in the kingdom of spirits and of men, and employs them when He will for the protection of His children and servants. Against forty murderers, He grants to His apostle five hundred protectors (Apost. Past.).

And to bring him in safety to Felix, the governor (ver. 24). Who will not in Paul, with his military escort, be reminded of Luther, his brother in spirit, successor in office, and companion in fortune, when he was conveyed by armed knights, and brought in safety to Wartburg?

Claudius Lysias saluteth the noble governor Felix (ver. 26). He does not think what a serious present he made to Felix in Paul. According to Felix's taste, it was certainly not so (chap. xxiv.); but there was written on Paul's countenance another letter of commendation, which said, Governor Felix, God salutes you with salvation and with peace. Would that he had understood this letter! (Williger.)

This man, the Jews had taken, and would have killed (ver. 27). When we consider this letter, we find that the Gentile writes in a much more honest, straightforward, and upright manner than the orthodox Jews, yea, even when they only open their mouth. Paul comes better off with Lysias and with Felix, than with those who wish to retain the letter without the spirit (Gossner).

I found that he was accused only of questions of their law (ver. 29). He speaks as a heathen, as if it were not worth his while to trouble his head about the religious disputes of the Jews. But God employed this disposition to rescue Paul, by means of it, out of the hand of murderers (Starke).

They took Paul and brought him to Antipatris (ver. 31).

Great men often travel incognito, and so God often brings His children through the world in very strange disguise (Rieger).

Commanded him to be kept in the palace of Herod (ver. 35). Another trace of the faithful care of God for His servant, as He granted him time and rest to pray and strengthen himself in the Lord, and to prepare for his impending testimony at Rome. He was guarded not only by the body-guard of the governor, but by the good hand of his faithful Lord and Saviour; and, after the journey was accomplished, full of faith and gratitude to God, he could think on the proofs of divine assistance, on the ever approaching nearness of his destination to Rome, and above all, on the whole blessed termination of his destiny: he could increase in the courage of his apostolic testimony, and, well prepared, go forth to meet the future. The pauses, which the Lord sometimes grants us in our labours and sufferings, should serve the same purposes (Apost. Past.).

On the whole section (vers. 12–35).—*The Lord protects His people.* 1. They require His protection against the crafty designs of enemies: these unite against the righteous, vers. 12, 13; and disguise themselves under a pious appearance, vers. 14, 15. 2. They experience such a protection from the Lord, who brings the wickedness to light, ver. 16; and directs the hearts of men for the good of the righteous, vers. 17–22 (Lisco).—*How the Lord watches over His people.* 1. He imparts to them the internal assurance of His divine assistance. 2. He brings the counsels of their enemies to nought. 3. He conducts them, by all the dispensations of their life, to the goal of their destination (Lisco).—*The murderous covenant of the enemies, and the gracious covenant of the Lord.* 1. The murderous covenant of the enemies against Paul is powerful: *a.* by their number—forty against one; *b.* by their design—sworn to kill him; *c.* by their means—craft and dissimulation. 2. But the gracious covenant of the Lord with His servant is more powerful (Be of good cheer, Paul, ver. 11): *a.* He discloses the designs of the wicked; *b.* against powerful enemies, He stirs up yet more powerful protectors; against the chief priests, the Roman chief captain; against forty conspirators, more than 400 soldiers; *c.* He brings him uninjured out of the den of murderers.—*Rejoice, ye righteous, for the Lord assists His servants.* 1. He strengthens them internally by the promise of His grace (ver. 14). 2. He reveals the designs of their enemies (ver. 16). 3. He stirs up for them active friends (Paul's sister's son) and powerful protectors (Lysias). 4. He brings them uninjured through the midst of their enemies (Paul's departure in the midst of a body-guard). 5. He gives to them an honourable testimony on the way (the letter of Lysias to Felix).—*The angel of the Lord encamps round about them that fear Him, and delivers them*, Ps. xxxiv. 7. The guardian angel was in a threefold form near the apostle. 1. The comforting vision in prison, ver. 11. 2. The careful friend in the person of Paul's sister's son, ver. 16. 3. The powerful body-guard in the form of the Roman soldiers, ver. 23 (compare 2 Kings vi. 17, "And, behold, the mountain was full of horses and chariots of fire round about Elisha").—*Many are the afflictions of the righteous, but the Lord delivereth him out of them all*, Ps. xxxiv. 19. 1. The afflictions of the righteous. 2. The assistance of the Lord.—*Fear not: for they that be with us are more than they that be with them*, 2 Kings vi. 16. 1. With them are wicked intentions of murder (ver. 12), numerous confederates (ver. 13), and powerful helpers (vers. 14, 15). 2. With us are the divine promises of peace (ver. 11), supplicating friendly spirits (ver. 16), and the protecting hosts of the Lord (ver. 22).—*How the Lord turns the hearts of men like the rivers of water for the good of His people.* 1. He smites the crafty enemies with blindness, so that their murderous design is divulged. 2. He arms the modest youth, Paul's sister's son, with stedfast resolution, so that he presses through to the chief captain. 3. He touches the conscience of the Roman commander, so that he provides for the safety of the apostle, as if he were a crowned head.—*Paul's last departure from Jerusalem.* 1. The mournful departure of a witness of the truth, whose message of salvation his blinded people have rejected. 2. The glorious triumphant march of an anointed servant of God, whom the Lord leads victoriously through the midst of enemies 3. The solemn homeward journey of a warrior of Christ, who goes to meet his last fight, his last victory, and his last reward.

B.

Judicial proceedings before Felix: Paul defends himself against the accusations brought forward; nevertheless the judgment is deferred.

Chap. xxiv. 1–23.

1 But after five days, the high priest Ananias, with the elders, and a certain orator, Tertullus, came down and informed the governor against Paul. 2 And when he was called, Tertullus began to accuse him, and said: That we partake of great peace through thee, and that excellent regulations result in good to this people by thy care, 3 We accept it always and everywhere, most noble Felix, with all thankfulness. 4 But in order not to detain thee long, I pray thee to hear us briefly of thy clemency. 5 For we have found this man a pest, and who excites sedition among all the Jews throughout the world, and is a ringleader of the sect of the Nazarenes; 6 Who also attempted to profane the temple: whom we also seized. 7, 8 And thou mayest, when thou appointest a hearing, learn of himself all those things, whereof we accuse him. 9 And the Jews likewise assailed him, saying that these things were so.

10 Then Paul, the governor having beckoned on him to speak, answered: As I know that thou hast been for many years a judge of this people, I can with joyfulness defend myself. 11 For thou mayest understand that it is no more than twelve days since I came up to Jerusalem to worship. 12 And they neither found me in the temple disputing with any one, or raising up a popular tumult, neither in the synagogues nor in the city. 13 Nor can they prove the things of which they now accuse me. 14 But this I confess to thee, that after the way which they call a sect, so I serve the God of my fathers, believing all things which are written in the law and in the prophets. 15 And I have hope toward God, which they themselves also expect, that there is to be a resurrection, both of the just and unjust. 16 Herein also do I exercise myself, to have always an unviolated conscience toward God and man. 17 And after the lapse of several years, I came in order to bring alms to my nation, and offerings. 18 While doing this, they found me, after I had purified myself, in the temple, without noise or tumult: 19 But certain Jews from Asia (found me), who ought to have appeared before thee and to have accused me, if they had anything against me. 20 Or let these same say, if they found any crime in me, when I stood before the chief council, 21 Except it be this one word, which I called aloud standing among them, On account of the resurrection of the dead I am judged by you this day.

22 But Felix adjourned their cause, because he was more exactly instructed regarding that way, and said, When the tribune Lysias is come down, I shall examine into your matter. 23 Also he commanded a centurion to keep him, and to grant him indulgence, and to prevent none of his friends from ministering to him.

Ver. 1. Τῶν πρεσβυτέρων is only attested by G. and H., together with most of the cursive MSS.; but is from internal evidence to be preferred to πρεσβ. τινῶν, as the latter has decidedly the appearance of an attempted correction.

Ver. 5. Στάσιν is to be preferred to the plural στάσεις, a correction for the sake of οἰκουμένην.

Vers. 6–8. Here the textus receptus has a long insertion, which has only one uncial MS. in its favour, and all the rest, and among them the Sinaitic Codex, against it, while it betrays its spuriousness by many variations of reading. The words are καὶ κατὰ τὸν ἡμέτερον νόμον ἠθελήσαμεν κρίνειν· παρελθὼν δὲ Λυσίας ὁ χιλίαρχος μετὰ πολλῆς βίας ἐκ τῶν χειρῶν ἡμῶν ἀπήγαγε καὶ πρός σε ἀπέστειλε, κελεύσας τοὺς κατηγόρους αὐτοῦ ἔρχεσθαι ἐπί σε. Had these words been genuine, their omission would have been inexplicable; whilst their insertion may easily be explained from chap. xxi. 32, xxiv. 27, 30. Mill, Bengel, and Griesbach regarded the sentence as an interpolation; and Tischendorf and Lachmann have erased it from the text.

Ver. 10. The preponderance of authorities is in favour of εὐθύμως. The comparative εὐθυμότερον, which is in only two uncial MSS., appears to be a well-meant correction, because it was thought that the apostle from the above-mentioned circumstance might have become the more joyful, but must have been joyful before.

Ver. 15. Νεκρῶν is wanting in several of the oldest MSS.; but as external authorities seemed here equal, we would have decided against νεκρῶν from internal evidence, as it would not have been omitted, if originally there, but might easily have been inserted, if originally wanting. Recently, however, the testimony of the Sinaitic Codex, which omits νεκρῶν, is to be added, so that the preponderance of external authorities is against it.

Ver. 16. Καὶ αὐτός is decidedly better attested than δὲ αὐτός.

Ver. 18. Ἐν οἷς is to be preferred to ἐν αἷς, which is certainly a correction.

Ver. 19. Ἔδει, though authorities are somewhat equal, is to be regarded as genuine, instead of δεῖ.

Ver. 22. Five uncial MSS. have ἀνεβάλετο δὲ αὐτοὺς ὁ Φῆλιξ; whereas the reading of the textus receptus, ἀκούσας δὲ ταῦτα ὁ Φῆλιξ, ἀνεβάλετο αὐτούς, has only one uncial MS. for it, and is certainly an insertion. The Sinaitic Codex also wants the addition.

Ver. 23. Αὐτόν is undoubtedly genuine: τὸν Παῦλον is spurious.—Ἢ προσέρχεσθαι is also a later addition; it is wanting in four uncial MSS.

EXEGETICAL EXPLANATIONS.

1. *And after five days.*—At the order of the tribune (chap. xxiii. 30), the opposite party came quickly. Five days after the arrival of Paul at Cæsarea, the high priest, with a deputation of the elders (οἱ πρεσβ. representing the whole of the elders), came down. They took with them the orator Tertullus, in order that as an advocate he might bring forward, in their name, the

charges against Paul. The name Tertullus, a diminutive of Tertius, as again Tertullianus is derived from Tertullus, frequently occurs among the Romans, and indicates his Italian descent. Ῥήτωρ was at that time the frequent title of barristers, who represented their clients before courts of justice. Ἐμφανίζω must here, as in chap. xxiii. 15, 22, and according to the constant usage of the language, be taken transitively,—"declared," "informed;" not intransitively (Vulgate, Luther, Bengel), "appeared," in which case it would have been in the middle voice.

2. *That by thee we partake of great peace.*—The orator begins with gross flattery, in order to secure the favour of the judge for his party. 1. He praises the great peace which they owed to Felix. The first duty and the chief praise of a procurator was indeed to give peace to his province. Ulpian: *De officio præsidis: Congruit bono et gravi præsidi, ut pacata sit provincia.* Felix had, it is true, partially suppressed the disturbances which arose, partly from political discontent, and partly from base love of rapine. But, on the other hand, he did not shrink from employing Sicarii to assassinate the high priest Jonathan; and, in general, he conducted himself so passionately and tyrannically, that he rather fanned than allayed the spirit of sedition. So far the first expression of Tertullus was a falsehood. 2. He mentions the good arrangements and fortunate results (*κατορθώματα*) which, by the careful government of Felix, were imparted to the Jewish nation. This also, in face of the arbitrary rule of Felix, a man of a servile disposition (*servile ingenium, libido*, Tac. His. v. 9), was an audacious falsehood. 3. That the Jewish nation was always and everywhere thankful, soon turned out completely untrue, as the Jews accused Felix at Rome after he was recalled (Joseph. Ant. xx. 8, 10). Ἐγκόπτω (ver. 4) is to hinder, to interrupt, to detain. Also ἐπιείκεια, to which the orator appeals as a well-known quality of the procurator (τῇ σῇ ἐπιεικείᾳ), did certainly not belong to him.

3. *For we have found this man a pest.*—Εὑρόντες does not stand, as Bengel and others think, for εὕρομεν, but is an anacoluthon. Λοιμός is used by the later Greeks, as *pestis* is in the Roman classics, for exciters of mischief. The ground of the heavy charge contained in these words is comprised in three accusations. 1. That Paul excited disturbances in the Roman empire

among the Jews. 2. That he was a head of the Christian sect. 3. That he had attempted to pollute the temple. Here the name Nazarene occurs for the first time, as a sectarian name of the followers of Jesus of Nazareth from the Jewish stand-point. *Πρωτοστάτης*, originally a military expression; a front-man or file-leader. *Ἐπείρασε βεβηλῶσαι*, cleverly chosen, accuses Paul only of the attempt, not of the actual deed, as in chap. xxi. 28, and might, should the accused also deny any real attempt, be referred to mere *animus*. *Παρ' οὗ—ἐπιγνῶναι*, *i.e.*, Paul himself will not be able to deny these matters of fact. *Συνεπιτίθεσθαι* is to join in the attack: the Jews, at the conclusion of the speech of their advocate, united in the same accusations.

4. *Forasmuch as I know.*—Paul opens his speech, not with flatteries, as his opponents, but states in the introduction only the simple matter of fact, that Felix had for a long time possessed the highest authority in the country; and that therefore, because its circumstances were known to him by experience, he could with good courage defend himself before him. *Πολλὰ ἔτη* elapsed, as Felix was appointed at the close of the year 52 or beginning of the year 53 after Christ, and it was then the year 58,—nearly six years, which, in the frequent changes of governors, which was the rule at that time, was comparatively a long period. And, at all events, Felix had sufficiently learned to know the character of the Jews and their chiefs; and Luke informs us, in ver. 22, that he had also, in point of fact, received some knowledge of Christianity.

5. *Because thou mayest understand, that it is not more than twelve days.*—Paul further touches on a circumstance which facilitated his defence, namely, the fact that he had only lately come to Jerusalem, so that his conduct there might be the more surely ascertained. The twelve days, which the apostle mentions since his arrival at Jerusalem, may be reckoned as follows:—

I. Day after his arrival: visit to James, chap. xxi. 18.

II. Levitical purification, and first visit to the temple, chap. xxi. 26.

III.–VII. Days of the Nazarite-offering: onset against Paul and his capture, chap. xxi. 27.

VIII. The apostle before the chief council, chap. xxii. 30, xxiii. 1.

IX. The conspiracy and its discovery; in the evening, Paul is removed from Jerusalem, chap. xxiii. 12, 31.

X. Arrival at Antipatris, chap. xxiii. 31.

XI. Arrival at Cæsarea, chap. xxiii. 32, 33.

XII.

XIII. Trial before Felix, chap. xxiv. 1.

The trial before Felix accordingly took place on the fifth day (*μετὰ πέντε ἡμέρας*, chap. xxiv. 1) after Paul's departure from Jerusalem, if the day of the departure be included. On the other hand, the fifth day had not yet elapsed, and therefore is to be excluded from the twelve days, as also is the day of the apostle's arrival at Jerusalem (Anger).

6. *And they neither found me in the temple.*—Paul, in reply to the accusations, urges the fact that he came to Jerusalem to worship (*προσκυνήσων*, ver. 11), thus not to set himself in opposition to the legal worship in the sanctuary, but, on the contrary, to practise it; his journey, according to its design, was a pilgrimage to the place of worship. He thus also directly combats the accusations, that he could have been in any manner guilty of desecrating the temple and of stirring up disturbance. *Παραστῆσαι* occurs here, as occasionally in the classics, in the sense of *ostendere, persuadere, probare.*

7. *But this I confess to thee.*—Paul further replies (vers. 14–16) to the assertion of Tertullus, designed to excite suspicion against him, that he was a ringleader of the sect of the Nazarenes. He boldly and joyfully confesses his Christianity (*ὁμολογῶ*), only he gently shifts off the expression *αἵρεσις*, used in a bad sense as a schismatic sect (*λέγουσι*, my opponents call it so; in point of fact, he intends to say, it is not). The description, which in this confession he gives of Christianity, brings designedly forward the unity of the new covenant with the old. *Λατρεύω τῷ πατρῴῳ Θεῷ, i.e.*, his religion is not apostasy from, but fidelity to, the God of his fathers. *Πιστεύων πᾶσι, i.e.*, his religion does not consist in doubt and unbelief in the Jewish Scriptures, but in complete faith in them. Passing over to the object of his faith, he describes it as a pious hope of the resurrection; in this also emphatically stating his agreement with the Jews. *Καὶ αὐτοὶ οὗτοι*, my opponents also share in this expectation: only *προσδέχεσθαι* and *ἐλπίδα ἔχειν* are subjectively to be distinguished; the first expression is a mere cold and external

position toward the truth; the second, on the other hand, reckons that hope as a personal and precious possession. In ver. 16, his confession passes over to the practical and moral side of his Christianity. *'Εν τούτῳ* is not to be limited to the hope mentioned before (Bengel), but to be referred to the whole ground of faith, so far as the apostle has here indicated it. *Καὶ αὐτός*, I also, as well as the rest of my companions in the faith.

8. *And after the lapse of several years.*—In vers. 17–21, the apostle returns to the accusation that he had defiled the temple, and, with the refutation of that, combines the refutation of the accusation that he had stirred up tumult. His object on his return to Jerusalem was partly to bring aid for his nation—the collections from the Gentile churches for the Jewish Christians—as a proof of his love to his country, and partly to offer sacrifices in the temple (compare ver. 11, *προσκυνήσων*). The latter (the offerings) also corresponds to *ἀπρόσκοπον συνείδησιν ἔχειν πρὸς τὸν Θεὸν*, and the former (the alms) to *πρὸς τοὺς ἀνθρώπους*, ver. 16. *'Εν οἷς*, in this occupation; *ἡγνισμένον*, thus according to the requisite purification, and not in a profane manner, I entered the temple; I desecrated it neither with multitude nor with tumult: thus contradicting also the accusation that he had stirred up tumult. *Τινες δὲ* belongs to *εὗρον*: certain found me (not these, as they seem to say, ver. 5), but certain Jews from Asia, whom I miss here in court. In conclusion, the apostle appeals to the testimony of his opponents then present, that the whole Sanhedrim was unable to convict him of any crime. *Ἢ περὶ*, *i.e.*, it must consist only in this, that I made this exclamation in the midst of the assembly.

9. *But Felix adjourned.*—*'Αναβάλλεσθαι* is the usual expression for "to adjourn;" usually indeed it is the sentence or decision that is adjourned, but it occurs also, as here with *αὐτούς*, of an assembly which is adjourned. *'Ακριβέστερον εἰδώς*, etc. (ver. 22), according to the construction, can only be a reason for *ἀνεβάλετο*: he adjourned it, because he was more accurately instructed concerning Christianity. (So Chrysostom, Luther, Wetstein, Meyer, and others.) The reference which Beza, Grotius, and Ewald give to these words is incorrect, as if they belonged to the final sentence itself: "when I have been more accurately informed concerning this way, and when Lysias is come down:" *εἰπών* would not then follow at such a distance.

The procurator, because he possessed some exact knowledge of Christianity (which is very comprehensible after a government of Judea for at least six years), did not condemn Paul, but out of respect to the Jews did not acquit him; but deferred the matter, on the pretext of wishing first to hear the tribune Lysias. Paul thus remained in military custody (*ἑκατοντάρχῃ τηρεῖσθαι*), yet with some alleviation of his imprisonment (*ἄνεσις*), particularly inasmuch as he was permitted to receive visits of his own people (*οἱ ἴδιοι*), *i.e.*, probably of friendly Christians and relations, as his nephew, and to receive small services from them: perhaps also the mode of his custody was relaxed (Wieseler).

DOGMATICAL AND ETHICAL THOUGHTS.

1. The speech of Tertullus, the only man to whom the title orator (rhetorician) is given in Scripture, is a model of eloquence as it should not be: untrue and insincere, in its contents; artfully combined and patched, in its form. The speech of the apostle is as the words of Jesus, and all the words and writings of the other apostles: the contents, truth and a disposition without falsehood; the form, simplicity and plainness.

2. This is a sign of a godly disposition, that the apostle in his answer is not satisfied with contradicting the false accusations and with personally defending himself, but he passes over as soon as possible to bear his testimony and to defend Christianity. It is not so much his own honour, as the honour of God and of the way of salvation, that appears to him to be at stake.

3. What the apostle asserts in his confession, are the ground-lines of an apology for Christianity against Judaism, namely, that Christianity is not an apostasy from the old covenant, but its fulfilment. The chief thought is in fact nothing else than that which is contained in the words of Jesus: "Think not that I am come to destroy the law and the prophets: I am not come to destroy, but to fulfil," Matt. v. 17. In entire conformity with the words of the Master, the disciple confesses that he believes all things that are written in the law and in the prophets; that he holds fast, as a precious treasure, the hope which Israel also cherishes; and that he serves none other than Jehovah, the God of his fathers. It is the same stand-point as the Reformers in the Augsburg Confession have taken, in opposition to the

Catholic Church; the chief aim of which is to refute the reproach of sectarianism and of apostasy on the part of the Evangelicals, and to establish their unity with the old and true apostolic and Catholic Church.

4. The declaration of the apostle, that in his attitude of faith and hope he exercised himself to preserve a conscience void of offence toward God and man, is very essential. This was not only, in face of the accusations of temple-profanation and of exciting sedition, of practical importance for his personal vindication, but as a confession to the honour of Christianity is of the highest value. Christianity is "the conscience of the conscience." The word of Christ has not been truly apprehended by a man until it penetrates his conscience. And a man has only truly apprehended and appropriated Christianity, when he applies it as a divine power to moral practice, to preserve the conscience void of offence. Otherwise, Christianity is only colour, form, chaff, not being, power, essence, and life.

HOMILETICAL HINTS.

The high priest, with the elders and a certain orator, Tertullus, came down (ver. 1). Only in this passage of Scripture, does an orator and the name orator occur (Bengel).—God's preachers are not orators of acquired words, but witnesses of revealed facts (Besser).—No cause is so bad, but it will find an advocate (Starke).—Eloquence is a gift of God; but eloquence in a bad man is poison in a golden cup (Augustin).—Wickedness has always new colours with which to paint itself, and new weapons to use. When craft, assassination, and conspiracy will not avail, then men take refuge in the colouring of oratory, and seek to conquer by the weapons of flattery. But faith and truth remain in their simplicity and integrity. When the high priest appears with his orator Tertullus, then Paul places himself in opposition to them with his good conscience and believing heart (Apost. Past.).

Tertullus began to accuse him (ver. 2). How cunning and crafty are the children of darkness, how full of malice and subtlety, as the cage full of decoy birds (Jer. v. 27), to crush the poor and the innocent! But are not the courts of princes and the halls of justice full of such decoy birds? (Starke.)

That by thee we partake of great peace, etc. (ver. 3). To

such an extent is the compliment carried, with which Tertullus flattered, in order by it to gain his point (Starke).—The ungodly never use the name of peace with more vaunting, than when they would destroy peace and create disturbance, Ps. lv. 22 (Starke).—Tertullus, by gross flattery, paves the way to his accusations. Felix was a vicious man, and hated by the people, who at a later period accused him to the emperor. But in order to gain his favour, this flatterer deifies him, and ascribes to him good deeds which were due only to God. This proneness to flattery ever adheres to all false and unfaithful teachers (Apost. Past.).—How much is carried on and effected in the world by flattering words! It is a wonderful exchange-business, by which the great abuse the weaknesses of the little for their own designs; and also, conversely, the little know the weak side of the great, and seek to make an impression on them (Rieger).

But in order not to detain thee longer (ver. 4). This pleased Felix best; a long flattering introduction, and when it comes to the matter as short as possible, that, in accordance with his distaste for business, he need not trouble himself with it (Williger).

We have found this man a pest (ver. 5). As it is said of God Himself, "With the perverse Thou art perverse," so it fares no better with His servant. The world beholds the beautiful image of a witness of Jesus with perverse eyes. The message of salvation is called a "pest;" zeal to arouse dead sinners is "stirring up sedition;" to preach Jesus is "sectarianism;" to build the kingdom of God is "to desecrate the temple."—If it thus happened to Christ and His apostles, why not also to us? But it is a great comfort, when the Spirit of truth gives us the testimony, "As deceivers, and yet true" (Apost. Past.).

Whom we also caught (ver. 6). Tertullus does not hint at the designed assassination. Over all the abominations of wickedness, he draws an ingenious covering (Apost. Past.).

The Jews also assented to it (ver. 9). Their amen to the edifying discourse of Tertullus! (Williger.)—Falsehood quickly finds an assenter; not so the truth. But although thousands confirm a falsehood, it remains a falsehood still (Starke).

Paul answered, Because I know that thou hast been for many years a judge of this people (ver. 10). Be sparing in titles, as Paul here. Shouldst thou call an enemy of God, an unrighteous judge, a proud Haman, an Ahab sold to wickedness,—an excellent, incomparable, and highly esteemed man? Shouldst thou talk about his great merits? "Blessed is he, in whose eyes a vile person is contemned," Ps. xv. 4 (Starke).—Well does Paul honour the office of a judge, even in a Felix; the dignity of which does not depend on the personal worthiness of the person who occupies it, but on the ordinance of God. But by addressing Felix as judge, he also reminds him of law and justice. Thus Paul himself practises what he teaches in Rom. xiii. (Leonh. and Spieg.).

I came up to Jerusalem to worship (ver. 11). These were not mere words of course. He actually wished, if it were possible, to be at Jerusalem on the day of Pentecost (chap. xx. 16), (Williger).

And they neither found me in the temple, disputing with any one (vers. 12, 13). Observe how Paul first discreetly honours the office of a judge, plainly and briefly relates the matter, temperately denies the accusation, calmly maintains the contrary, undauntedly challenges examination and proof, and clearly discovers the true reason of the complaint. Act in a similar manner before the court of justice (Starke).

But this I confess unto thee (ver. 14). Paul here uses his liberty of speech, not only to repel the accusations, but still more to witness a good confession (Rieger).—*That after the way which they call a sect, so worship I the God of my fathers.* Paul is not ashamed of being a Nazarene, but he denies that Christianity is a newly-formed heresy, and that the Church of God is a sect recreant from the faith of the fathers; as, on the contrary, the Gospel of Christ is the essence and the aim of the whole old covenant (Leonh. and Spieg.).—The true Church of God has always employed the same proof, when it is called a sect. Thus could the Evangelical Church in opposition to the Catholic, by which it was called a faction, confidently maintain that it is precisely the old apostolic Church (Williger).—Thus also may living Christians, when they are reproached as sectaries, pietists, and the like, prove, on the ground of Scripture, that their sectarianism and pietism are nothing else than the simple imitation of Jesus, and an earnest walking on the way of salvation which Christ has traced out by His word, His conduct, and His blood.

And I have hope toward God, which they also expect (ver. 15).

The hope of the resurrection is not a doctrine whose glory arose for the first time in the New Testament; the same golden thread of eternal life is interwoven throughout the whole of the Old Testament. The Creator who animated the dust by His breath, the covenant God who made an eternal covenant with Abraham, Isaac, and Jacob, is not the God of the dead, but of the living. Job comforted himself in the resurrection (Job xix. 25–27); Isaiah prophesied concerning it (Isa. xxvi. 19); and Daniel testified of it (Dan. xii. 2). Certainly in Paul this hope became firm, living, and fruitful by the resurrection of Jesus Christ from the dead (Leonh. and Spieg.).—The foundation of our Christianity is the resurrection; if this falls, Christianity must fall along with it (Starke).—*I have hope toward God.* Hast thou this hope? If the Spirit has not yet imparted it to thee, rest not until thou art certain of thy blessed resurrection; rest not, for there is nothing more terrible than to be forced to die, without hope of the resurrection (Kapff).

Herein do I exercise myself, to have a conscience void of offence toward God and man (ver. 16). The apostle here shows to what he applied his religion. This is the true end. To this all religion must lead men. So long as our confession of faith remains an affair of the brain, or an hereditary custom, or an apple of discord, or a source of heresy, it is the shell without the kernel, a shadow without life. It deserves the name of a true faith and of a living hope, only when in it and by it the daily exercise is carried on to be righteous, and godly, and pious (Apost. Past.).—How will he love God with all his heart, who believes in God and is assured that He wishes us well, seeing He has given His Son for us, and with Him the hope of eternal life! How will he fear and honour Him! How will he diligently apply himself to show his gratitude for such great gifts and benefits! How will he exhibit patience and obedience in misfortune! Thus faith brings with it a multitude of other glorious and fair virtues, and is never alone (Luther).—As strictly as Paul deals with his conscience that he will preserve it always void of offence both toward God and man, so humbly does he speak on this point. He does not say that he has and possesses such a conscience; but, considerately, that he exercises himself to have it. It is most beneficial to deal strictly with the conscience, and never to connive at it (Apost. Past.).

Brought alms to my nation (ver. 17), *and purified myself in the temple* (ver. 18). If he who does so much good to his neighbour is called a pest, what then must he be, who does evil? And if he who pays his vows in the temple is called a profaner of the temple, what shall he be called who breaks in the temple his baptismal vow? (Starke.)

Or let these same say, if they have found any crime in me (ver. 20). The apostle, in his defence, challenges all those who knew him, saw him, associated with him, and were witnesses of his conduct, whether they could lay anything to his charge. This was the impulse of a good conscience, unstained before God and man. It would be a great disgrace for many a teacher, if his acquaintances, his intimate friends, his comrades, those who knew his secret actions, were to stand up and testify against him. From this arise the feeble courage and despondency which make the exercise of the ministry so lukewarm (Apost. Past.).—The whole speech of the apostle shows the composure of a heart which is strengthened by the Lord. Observe: 1. The temperateness, with which he listens to the accusations of Tertullus, and does not open his mouth until Felix beckons on him to speak. 2. The uprightness, with which he avoids all flattery toward Felix, although he honours his office. 3. The fearlessness, with which he wards off unrighteous accusations. 4. The simplicity, with which he gives an unvarnished statement of the circumstances of the case. 5. The boldness, with which he makes a joyful confession of his faith, hope, and love toward God and man, in short of his true and living religion (Apost. Past.).

But Felix adjourned the matter (ver. 22). In Felix many forms of the natural heart are developed, which a teacher in his treatment of souls must thoroughly know. He represents the image of a man of the world, and shows how the Gospel is treated by such men. They know about this way, but their knowledge is without influence on their heart. They interest themselves indeed with the things of the kingdom of God, but only from curiosity. They wish to seem impartial, in order to profit by one party or the other. This is the character of the men of the world; so that a teacher has to show great wisdom and godly simplicity, in order to be, in reference to them, neither too credulous nor too timid (Apost. Past.).—Felix here shows himself to be another Pilate (Besser).

To grant him alleviation (to let him have rest, Luther, ver. 23). To be long in the world, and to have to do with the bustle and confusion of carnal passions, makes a servant of Jesus weary. It is good for him when his Saviour grants him rest, and indeed such a rest as he, with the other members of Jesus, may be strengthened and refreshed in faith and in grace (Apost. Past.).

On the whole section (vers. 1–23).—*The sect which is everywhere spoken against.* 1. It believes what is written in the word of God (ver. 14). 2. It confesses what by the grace of God is given it to hope (ver. 15). 3. It practises what by the commands of God has become its duty (Florey).—*By what does a Christian refute the groundless accusations of his enemies?* 1. By genuine faith (ver. 14). 2. By joyful hope (ver. 15). 3. By a godly life (ver. 16), (Leonh. and Spieg.).—*The power of the hope of the resurrection of the dead.* It imparts courage and wisdom in action, patience and comfort in suffering, and pleasure and readiness in dying (Leonh. and Spieg.).—*How will a Christian defend himself against the accusations, which are so often made against him in the world?* 1. He will keep himself pure from all reproach, in order that the Gospel be not blasphemed on his account. 2. He will, by the joyful confession of his faith, put to shame the groundless enmity of the world. 3. He will point to his life, that it may bear witness to the truth of his faith (Lisco).—*The Christian's defence against the accusations of the world.* 1. When should he defend himself? *a.* If the Lord is reviled, and not himself. *b.* If he may hope to conciliate men's minds, and not to increase their bitterness. 2. How should he defend himself? *a.* Without fear of men. *b.* Convincingly, by a good conscience.—*The orator Tertullus and the preacher Paul, or false eloquence and the true.* 1. False eloquence is flattering: it speaks to please the hearers, ver. 3. True eloquence does not flatter: it addresses the heart and conscience. 2. False eloquence is hypocritical: it dwells only on the lips; it is honey in the mouth, and gall in the heart, vers. 5, 6. True eloquence does not dissimulate: it proceeds from the heart, and speaks as it feels, vers. 10, 14–16. 3. False eloquence is deceitful: it makes black white, and white black, vers. 5, 6. True eloquence does not lie: it denies only what is false (ver. 13), but confesses what is true (vers. 14, 15), and makes the matter speak instead of the words (vers. 16–20). — *Are true*

Christians sectarians, as the world upbraids them? No, for, 1. The Chief whom they follow is not the head of a sect, but Jesus Christ the Head of the Church. 2. The communion which they renounce is not the Church of the Lord, but only the ungodly world inside and outside of the Church. 3. The way which they take is not self-chosen worship, but the old way of salvation, as the word of God points it out. 4. The praise, which they follow after, is not empty honour, but to have a conscience void of offence toward God and men.—*The noble praise of a Christian, or what it is to have a blameless conscience.* 1. What is included in it? *a.* Thou must have a conscience void of offence, not only toward men, who see what is before their eyes, but also before God, who looks at the heart. *b.* But, on the other hand, thou must have it not only before God, whose judgment eternity only discloses, but also thou must be able to maintain it before men, who will know thee by thy fruits. 2. How is it to be obtained? *a.* Thou must learn believingly to know the way of salvation from the word of God. *b.* Thou must learn diligently to walk in that way by the practice of godliness. — *The Christian's best defence against the poisoned shafts of calumny.* 1. A joyful confession in the mouth, ver. 14. 2. An unviolated conscience in the heart, ver. 16. 3. A blameless life in the past, vers. 17–20. 4. A righteous judgment of God in view, ver. 15.

C.

A second hearing of Paul before the Procurator is also without result; and Felix leaves Paul as a prisoner to his successor.

Chap. xxiv. 24–27.

24 But after some days, Felix came with his wife Drusilla, who was a Jewess, and sent for Paul, and heard him concerning the faith in Christ.
25 And as he discoursed concerning righteousness, and soberness, and the future judgment, Felix trembled, and answered, Go for the present; when I obtain a convenient time, I will call for thee. 26 At the same time also he hoped that money would be given him of Paul; therefore he sent for him the oftener, and communed with him. 27 But after two years had elapsed, Felix received a successor in Porcius Festus; and as Felix wished to bind the Jews to gratitude, he left Paul bound.

Ver. 24. Ἰησοῦν after Χριστόν is indeed in three uncial MSS.; but as it is wanting in three others, it is to be regarded as spurious.

Ver. 25. Tischendorf has received ἔσεσθαι after μέλλοντος as genuine; but only the two youngest uncial MSS. have it, and it is wanting in the four oldest: it is therefore to be rejected as an addition.

Ver. 26. Ὅπως λύσῃ αὐτόν is without doubt an explanatory insertion; it is wanting in the majority of uncial MSS.

Ver. 27. Χάριτας, plural, is indeed only in one uncial MS. (H.), but also in the great majority of cursive MSS. Of the other uncial MSS., three have χάριτα and two χάριν; but the singular is an evident correction, because the plural was considered not suitable.

EXEGETICAL EXPLANATIONS.

1. *Felix came, i.e.,* into the place, where he wished to hear Paul; or perhaps he returned to Cæsarea, after being absent for a time elsewhere in the province.

2. *With his wife Drusilla.*—Drusilla, a daughter of Herod Agrippa I.,—the same who slew James, and died at Cæsarea, chap. xii.,—was a noted beauty. She had been the wife of Azizus, king of Emesa. Felix became acquainted with her, and by means of a Jewish sorcerer, Simon of Cyprus, made her faithless to her husband, and married her (Joseph. Ant. xx. 7, 1). The summons to Paul doubtless occurred at the wish of Drusilla, who, as a Jewess of the Herodian family, had heard much of Christianity, and might be curious personally to see and to hear one of the chief leaders of the Church. This is manifestly implied, as on this occasion Paul was not heard specially upon the accusations brought against him.

3. *And as he discoursed.*—When Paul was permitted to speak, he discoursed not only of those things which Felix or his wife wished to hear, but also of things which Felix did not wish to hear; but on which he himself felt the more bound in conscience to discourse. He discoursed of righteousness to the judge; of soberness to a prefect, notorious for his licentiousness and sensuality; and of the future judgment to him, who required to be warned of his future account. Διαλεγομένος is here used, because Paul spoke not in a formal and public discourse, but in a private interview with the procurator and his wife.

4. *Felix trembled.*—He trembled, because such a discourse he had not in the least expected, nor indeed heard for a long time, particularly from the mouth of a prisoner whom he had completely in his power. But he quickly broke off the inter-

view, and sent Paul back again to his imprisonment. *Τὸ νῦν ἔχον*, for the present, frequently used, in the later classics, by Lucian, Diodorus, and others. The participle *ἐλπίζων* is still joined with *ἀπεκρίθη*. Without doubt, Felix knew that the Christians took a great interest in the fate of Paul, and that they would be willing to make great sacrifices for him. He would, therefore, willingly have allowed himself to be bribed by Paul, although it was expressly forbidden by the *Lex Julia, De repetundis*, to receive anything for a person's imprisonment or liberation.

5. *But after two years had elapsed.*—These two years are naturally to be reckoned from the commencement of Paul's imprisonment, and not from the entrance of Felix into office, which was here of no importance. Felix was probably recalled by Nero in the summer of the year 60. He left Paul as a prisoner and in chains, in order to induce the Jews to gratitude and forbearance toward himself. *Χάριτα κατατίθεσθαι* is a classical expression for *beneficium conferre*, properly, "to dispose them to gratitude." The object was not attained; for scarcely had Felix departed, when the Jews sent a deputation after him to accuse him to the emperor. Porcius Festus was invested with the procuratorship, which he executed in an upright manner for two years at the longest, when he died suddenly; and Albinus was his successor in the autumn of 62.

DOGMATICAL AND ETHICAL THOUGHTS.

1. It is to the glory of Christ, that the apostle cannot speak of Him without alarming the conscience of Felix. Frequently, men, of whom we would not expect it, are willing to hear the Gospel of Jesus Christ, as Herod Antipas had a great desire to see Jesus. But it is only the flesh that is inclined to this, and they wish to form such an idea of Christianity as might be agreeable to them. But the word of Christ is essentially of that nature, that it must seize on the conscience.

2. Felix is terrified. Thus the one edge of the word of God has struck him. But he has not experienced the other edge, which by the power of God again heals through reconciliation, forgiveness, and renewing grace, because he has withdrawn himself from the penetrating operation of the word, and has preferred evasive conduct to earnest knowledge of sin and

change of disposition. A single sin, which a man wilfully cherishes, places him under a secret ban which renders conversion and salvation impossible.

HOMILETICAL HINTS.

And after certain days, Felix came and sent for Paul (ver. 24). Because men are in love with variety, so a wish to hear the Gospel may occasionally occur, either to seek by it entertainment for the natural sense, for which reason Herod had for a long time a great desire to see Jesus, or often to take something out of the Gospel, and to make a cooling salve of it, for the wounded conscience. Thus now-a-days many hear one witness of the truth after another, but properly they listen to none; but would snatch something from each, which, joined together, would constitute an idea of religion, endurable to the flesh (Rieger).—We here find Paul again before Felix; but no longer in the court of justice, but in a private interview. Therefore he has not now to defend himself, but to gain the heart of his judge for Christ through faith and repentance. This time he does not stand before Felix as one accused, but as a preacher of the Gospel (Leonh. and Spiegel.).

But Paul discoursed concerning righteousness, chastity (Luther), *and the future judgment* (ver. 25). Paul turned his conversation concerning the faith of Christ in such a manner, that he at last came to the truths of righteousness, chastity, and a future judgment, which are so deeply rooted in the conscience. This was certainly offensive to a judge, and to such a couple as Paul had before him. But it could not, and should not, be otherwise. When divine things are rightly treated, the thoughts of the heart must be judged by them (Rieger).—Paul here preaches to a man of rank, to his judge, on whose favour, according to human opinion, he was dependent; and, nevertheless, he preaches to him the whole counsel of God, without any abbreviation. He does not make the way to heaven broader for him, nor does he tickle his ears and flatter his lusts. He preaches the Gospel to him, but is not silent concerning the law. He even attacks the favourite sins with which Felix was enslaved, and does not heed giving offence with his preaching. A noble example of a faithful witness of the truth (Apost. Past.).—The text and the subject are appropriately chosen for these hearers. He preaches of righteousness to the venal judge; of chastity to the adulterous pair; and of a judgnent to come to the unrighteous judge, on whom the imperial judgment of Rome was impending.—However, Paul did not speak directly of the sins of the governor, but he discoursed of these solemn matters in general. The express application was unnecessary; the Holy Ghost applied them to the heart of Felix. Reproving sermons should not give the impression, as if they were personal; but they are, when of the right kind, heart-penetrating expositions of the call, Repent ye, by which those touched feel that, not the preacher, but the Lord has touched them (Williger).—Felix trembled. Behold the power and the majesty of the word of God! Here the judge trembles before the accused; the governor before a tent-maker; a great man, who has many servants under him, before his prisoner. This is not to be ascribed to the powerful discourse of Paul, but to the word of God, Ps. cxix. 120; Heb. iv. 12, 13 (Starke).—Felix trembled,—a proof that he was not wholly bad and corrupt: there must have been something good in him, that felt itself drawn by the good: he could yet be ashamed: he could yet be moved. Happy had it been for Felix, if he had availed himself of this wholesome trembling, suffered himself to be entirely penetrated by the sharp word of God, entirely enlightened by its light, and purified by its fire (Menken).—*Go for this time; when I have a convenient season I will send for thee.* Great lords, great sinners, and to whom it is not good to preach; for if their conscience is touched, they soon dismiss the preachers in disgrace, or send them home without their heads, Matt. xiv. 10 (Starke).—He will wait for a convenient season, and yet the present was for him the accepted time, and the day of salvation. How often is this saying used by us! As a diversion for an idle imagination, as a stimulant to draw forth carnal tears, we are pleased with the Gospel, we love to hear sermons on the paternal love of God; descriptions of reunion in the other world, painted in striking colours, delight the ear: but when the word 'Repent' is emphatically uttered; when the discourse concerns the strait gate of self-denial, and the narrow path of holiness, and the terrors of the judgment; when the sharpness of the word strikes at our favourite sins, and demands a complete regeneration of the whole man, then it is said, "This is a hard saying, who can hear it?" Such reproving preaching is not convenient to me. When I am old, when I have enjoyed the pleasures of life, when I come to die, then will I crucify the flesh, convert, and prepare myself for eternity. But alas! if then it be too late; if then God should reply to our wanton "Depart" with His rejecting "Depart from Me!" "When I have a more convenient season!" When, do we think, will that be? In the bottom of our hearts do we think, never! and yet, in truth, it is always! O had we only eyes to recognise it, and courage to apprehend it! But herein are we wanting; herein art thou wanting, O Felix! Now has the hour of thy salvation struck; but thou delayest, and expectest a more convenient season. Did it ever come to thee? After two years thou wert called to Rome, accused by the people, to answer before Cæsar. It happened, according to the wonderful counsel of God, that Paul was once more in the same city with thee. Didst thou then make use of the convenient season? Or didst thou again delay? And did death at length come to thee at an inconvenient season? Let this example of Felix terrify us, and let our answer never be the same as his. Let us not say, "Go thy way for this time," lest it should happen to us as to Capernaum, Chorazin, and Bethsaida! Let us never wait for a convenient season, lest our end be that of Pharaoh and of Saul! Let us never, like Felix, request to hear the word of God from impure motives, lest we experience what Simon the sorcerer experienced! When the word of God comes to us, we will answer with Abraham, "Here am I;" or with Samuel, "Speak, Lord, for Thy servant heareth;" or with Cornelius, "Now we are all here present before God, to hear all things which are commanded thee of God" (Fr. Strauss).

Also he hoped that money would be given him of Paul (ver. 26). When covetousness takes root among official persons, then justice is sold for money, and the innocent are not helped, for they pay money; as also the guilty are not punished, for they have corrupted their judge, Deut. xvi. 19; Sirach xx. 30 (Starke).—*Therefore he sent for him the oftener.* Paul was certainly caressed by Felix. His liberation was at hand, if he would purchase it by money. But he would rather wait on the will of God than rescue himself from sufferings by such carnal means (Apost. Past.).

But after two years were elapsed (ver. 27). God's children are not only often afflicted by God with the cross, but also with a long and tedious cross, Gen. xxxix. 20, xli. 1, 14; Ps. xiii. 1, 2 (Starke).—The leisure years of the man, who had laboured more than all others, were for the watering of his own soul in quietness, and have produced their fruit to the Church. But it is terrible, after two years of visiting grace, to be as the stony ground on which it has rained. Unhappy Felix! (Besser.)

On vers. 24–27.—*The reasons of the fact, that many are willing to hear the Gospel, but not the law.* The reasons may be, 1. An error of the understanding, that the Gospel renders the preaching of the law superfluous. 2. An error of the conscience, that our spiritual state no longer requires the law. 3. An error of the feeling, which is hurt by every earnest exhortation. 4. The dominion of the flesh, which holds the will strictly enthralled (Langbein).—*Wherefore do so many never apply themselves with earnestness to Christianity?* 1. Because they are unable entirely to break with the past. 2. Because they do not seize on the present, but wait for a more convenient season. 3. Because they give no room in their thoughts to the future judgment (Langbein).—*When I have a convenient season.* This is the saying, 1. Of all those who know indeed the vanity of the world, but are too indolent to tear themselves from its pleasures; 2. of those who feel indeed the disgrace of the slavery of sin, but are too weak earnestly to repent; 3. of those who have experienced indeed, in a measure, the power of the word of God, but are too frivolous to resign themselves entirely to it (Leonh. and Spieg.).—*Felix, a sad representation of many hearers.* 1. He trembled, vers. 24. 25. 2. And yet he remained as he was, vers. 25–27 (Lisco).—*The power of the word of God.* 1. It awakens bold preachers: the undaunted Paul. 2. It awakens sleeping consciences: the trembling Felix. 3. It decides and separates: Paul is dismissed, "Go thy way;" Felix remains unconverted (Lisco).—*Two usual expressions, by which men evade the severity of repentance.* 1. Everything, except one thing. Felix was willing to hear all things from Paul's mouth, except the one thing which concerned him, touching righteousness, chastity, and judgment. Felix was willing to do all things, except the one thing needful, to renounce his bosom sins. 2. To-morrow, but not to-day. Felix tells Paul to go away for this time, and when he has a convenient season he will call for him; he defers repentance, and he never attains to it.—*When is it the convenient time to repent?* 1. Always, for him who is willing: *a.* God calls us always and by every means to repentance, by internal emotions and external providences, by the law and the Gospel, by joy and suffering; *b.* always, and in every condition of life, man can find time to hear the word of God. 2. Never, for him who is unwilling: *a.* When God calls, it is never convenient for him; *b.* when he will one day call on God in the last extremity with his dying spirit, or beyond in the eternal judgment, then it is no more God's time, then it is too late, then it will be said, Ye shall seek Me, and shall die in your sins, John viii. 21.—*Paul's penitential text before Felix, a text also for our times.* It treats of the fruits of a true repentance: 1. Of righteousness in relation to our neighbour. And is not this text suitable for a time, when unrighteousness gains ground in all stations, when ancient fidelity and honesty become always rarer among high and low? 2. Of chastity in curbing our passions. And is not this text suitable for a time of prevailing carnal lust and corruption of manners, when the ancient modesty and chastity become more and more antiquated in the country as well as in the town, when so many couples come to the church, step before the matrimonial altar, united by sinful bonds, as Felix and Drusilla? 3. Of a judgment to come before an eternal God. And is not this text suitable for a time of shameless unbelief, which mocks at God and eternity, at judgment and retribution, at heaven and hell, and deceives itself with the sadducean motto, "Let us eat and drink, for to-morrow we die"?—*Paul before Felix; or, the judicial power of the word of God.* 1. Paul stands before Felix as an insignificant man before the mighty, one bound before the free, an accused before his judge; and yet, in virtue of the divine word, whose minister Paul is, everything is reversed. 2. Felix rather stands before Paul: as the accused by the word of God and his own conscience before the incorruptible judge; as bound by the cords of unrighteousness and sensuality before the freeman of Jesus Christ; as insignificant, terrified, and irresolute before the mighty hero of God, who even in bonds shows, "I can do all things through Christ, who strengtheneth me."—*The two years' imprisonment of Paul at Cæsarea, or the painful and yet blessed resting and waiting times of the servants of God.* (Compare Joseph in prison, Moses in the wilderness, David in the mountains, Elijah at the brook Cherith, John the Baptist in prison, John the Evangelist in Patmos, Luther at Wartburg, faithful preachers on sick-beds.) 1. Painful for the servant of God, whose hands are bound; and for the congregations of the Lord, who are deprived of their pastors. 2. But yet blessed for the servant of God to quiet consideration and to deeper purification; and for the Church of the Lord to the increase of its strength, to its grateful estimation of the grace bestowed by God by means of faithful teachers, and to earnest continuance in prayer for pastors and flocks.

D.

The new Procurator, Porcius Festus, at the urgent solicitations of the Jews, takes up the accusation against Paul; but as Paul appeals to Cæsar, he assents to the appeal.

Chap. xxv. 1–12.

1 Now, when Festus was entered upon the province, after three days he
went up from Cæsarea to Jerusalem. 2 Then the chief priests, and the
first men among the Jews, informed him against Paul, and besought him,
3 Desiring favour of him, that he should send for him to Jerusalem, intend-
ing to lie in wait for him, in order to kill him by the way. 4 But Festus
answered, that Paul should be kept in Cæsarea, and that he himself would
in a short time journey thither. 5 Therefore let those in power among you
go down together with me, and bring forward accusations against this man,
if there be anything in him. 6 And he remained among them not more
than eight or ten days, and then went down to Cæsarea. And the next day he
sat on the judgment-seat, and commanded Paul to be brought. 7 And when
he appeared, the Jews who came down from Jerusalem stood around him,
and brought forth many grievous accusations against Paul, which they were
not able to prove. 8 While Paul defended himself: I have neither against
the law of the Jews, nor against the temple, nor against Cæsar, offended in
anything at all. 9 But Festus, willing to show the Jews a favour, answered
Paul, and said, Wilt thou go up to Jerusalem, and there be judged before
me concerning this complaint? 10 But Paul said, I stand before Cæsar's
judgment-seat, where I ought to be judged: against the Jews I have done
no wrong, as thou also knowest better. 11 If I then be in the wrong, and
have done anything worthy of death, I refuse not to die; but if there be
nothing in those things whereof these accuse me, no man can give me up to
gratify them. I appeal to Cæsar. 12 Then Festus conferred with his coun-
cil, and answered, To Cæsar hast thou appealed, to Cæsar thou shalt go.

Ver. 2. Ὁ ἀρχιερεύς is not so well attested as the plural οἱ ἀρχιερ.

Ver. 4. Εἰς Καισάρειαν has the four oldest uncial MSS. for it, and is to be preferred to ἐν Καισ.

Ver. 5. Ἄτοπον instead of τούτῳ is, indeed, attested by four important MSS., but nevertheless it is to be erased as spurious, because it might easily have been inserted for the sake of explanation, whilst its omission would be improbable. So Tischendorf.

Ver. 6. The majority of MSS. have οὐ πλείους ὀκτὼ ἢ δέκα, and this reading is to be considered genuine. Two MSS. G.H., read πλείους ἢ δέκα; and in one cursive MS. and some versions οὐ πλείους is omitted.

Ver. 7. Καταφέροντες has the preponderance of evidence for it; whereas ἐπιφέροντες and the simple verb φέροντες have each only one uncial MS.

Ver. 11. Οὖν is decidedly attested; γάρ is an evident correction.

EXEGETICAL EXPLANATIONS.

1. *Now when Festus was entered upon the province.*—Ἐπιβὰς is understood by some, "to come into the province:" but many passages, adduced by Wetstein, attest the meaning, "to enter upon office," "to undertake the government." Ἐπαρχία, taken strictly, is used only of proconsular provinces, but it may also denote a procuratorship, for which ἐπιτροπή is the official name. Festus arrived in the summer or autumn of the year 60 after Christ (Wieseler, Ap. Chronol. p. 91; Anger). The procurator hastened, after he had come to his residence in Cæsarea, to visit Jerusalem, the proper capital of the nation.

2. *Then the chief priests.*—The high priest in office at this time was Ishmael, the son of Phabi, whom Felix had appointed in the room of Ananias (Joseph. Ant. xx. 8, 8 and 11). The chief priests and first men of the people appeared before the new procurator, who gave them an audience. Οἱ πρῶτοι is not identical with "elders" (Grotius, De Wette), but denotes, apart from official position, the chief men, the most distinguished of the nation. Without doubt, they made use of their first attendance upon Festus to bring before him their wishes, as an affair of the whole nation. The proposal which they made, and the granting of which they requested as a first favour from the new governor, was that he should cause the prisoner to be brought up to Jerusalem, in order to place him there before the judgment-seat, because Festus himself was then present in the capital. The participle ἐνέδραν ποιοῦντες attached to παρεκάλουν, imports that while they made this request, they were already occupied with malicious designs and preparations for lying in wait.

3. *That Paul should be kept in Cæsarea; i.e.*, that he should

remain there, and that he himself would not stay long here, so that it was not worth the while to bring the prisoner up to Jerusalem. "Those in power among you," *i.e.*, those who are empowered by office to act; for many among the Jews then present may have been prominent only by birth, riches, and the like, while the Roman governor, for judicial proceedings, recognised only those in office as competent. *Δυνατοί* can only arbitrarily be understood as meaning those who are able to perform the journey (Bengel), or who are in a condition to accuse Paul.

4. *They stood around him.*—In a threatening manner, and in order to intimidate him, they placed themselves on all sides around the apostle. The first points of accusation, regarding the violation of the law and of the temple, were the same as before; but the Jews added, as is evident from ver. 8, a third and purely political accusation, according to which Paul was calumniated as a traitor, as if he had committed an offence against the Roman government or Cæsar himself, perhaps similar to the accusation at Thessalonica, chap. xvii. 6, 7.

5. *Before me* is an ambiguous expression, probably chosen designedly; inasmuch as ἐπ' ἐμοῦ might be understood as *me judice* (as this is apparently the meaning in chap. xxiii. 30, xxvi. 2); but also, and as it might eventually turn out, *coram me*, so that the Jewish Sanhedrim might be the judicial court, and the procurator be only present watching the trial. Besides, the journey to Jerusalem and the removal of the trial to it would have been superfluous, if a change of the court itself had not been intended. Only in the latter case, this arrangement was an actual and special favour to the Jews.

6. *I stand before Cæsar's judgment-seat.*—Paul evidently understood the question, that he should be placed before the Sanhedrim as the judicial court. And this he refuses: 1. Because he already stands before Cæsar's tribunal, and has to expect his sentence from it (βῆμα Καίσαρος, inasmuch as the procurator was the representative of Cæsar, and spoke in the name of the imperial government). 2. Because he was guilty of no offence against the Jews, as Festus well knew, and knew better than he will say. *Κάλλιον*, better in comparison with the ostensible expression of the procurator. This explanation was sufficiently definite and deliberate. In ver. 11, the apostle

draws an inference: If I have merited it, I submit to the punishment which the law appoints; but if the accusation is groundless, I bespeak the protection of the law (Meyer). With *χαρίσασθαι*, the apostle speaks without reserve; that, as it is a question of justice, an act of favour, by which he should be delivered up to the Jews, durst not take place. In conclusion, Paul resorts to the right of appeal to Cæsar, and he does so in the shortest form. The observation that Festus was not entirely firm with reference to the Jews, and also the fear that he might not in the end be perfectly secure against the intrigues of his deadly enemies, evidently induced the apostle to take this step. Moreover the promise which he received (chap. xxiii. 11), that he was appointed to bear witness of Jesus at Rome, encouraged him to do so. These circumstances taken together convinced him that now the way of appeal must be taken, by which neither his person nor his ministry might be at stake. The right to appeal to Cæsar belonged to him as a Roman citizen; it was strictly forbidden by the *Lex Julia* to put any impediment in the way of a Roman citizen, when he had appealed. The appeal might be made in writing, but also, when it took place at a judicial trial, by word of mouth. See quotations from the Roman laws by Wetstein.

7. *Then Festus conferred with his council.*—This council consisted of certain officers, who are called by Suetonius *consiliarii* and *assessores* (the former in Tiberius 33, the latter in Galba 19). What they consulted about was, whether the appeal was to be received and confirmed.

DOGMATICAL AND ETHICAL THOUGHTS.

1. The apostle presses his duty and justice upon the conscience also of the new judge, before whose tribunal he was placed, with perfect boldness as concerns the matter, and with considerate respect as regards the person of the judge. Here also must Roman law and government minister to the ends in view of the kingdom of God.

2. The course of the apostle, according to the counsel of God, proceeds from Jerusalem to Rome; indeed, the course of the Church of Christ in that age proceeded from Jerusalem to Rome. But it is remarkable, as tokens of God's ways in general, how this counsel was fulfilled. The falsehood and deceit of

the one party, and the weakness of the other, at length left the imprisoned apostle no other choice than the appeal to the emperor himself. Not calculation, nor cowardice, nor inclination brought him to this resolution, but he found himself constrained to take the step. The instant that the procurator formally declared that the appeal was accepted, and Paul's journey to Cæsar was determined upon, is a decisive turning-point in the life of the apostle. Henceforth the signal is "to Rome." To this he had looked forward for years; and now what was appointed to him by revelation from the Lord, was in near prospect. What man intended for evil, God intended for good, Gen. l. 20.

HOMILETICAL HINTS.

Now when Festus had entered upon the province (ver. 1). With the change in the government Paul had indeed to do with another man, but yet with one who acted toward him from the same worldly disposition, and according to similar temporizing motives. Who then will promise himself much good in the government of the world from such changes, when there is only a change of persons, but always the same earthly disposition? Faith, which has overcome the world in all its forms, is a richer source of comfort. Yet God employs such changes, in order by them to touch the conscience of worldly men with this goad, How vain and how fugitive are earthly rulers! Especially it is here remarkable, that in a land where God Himself was once the Ruler, one heathen governor succeeds another. From this the Jews should have observed how much they had deteriorated (Rieger).—Kings may die and governors be changed; but Jesus Christ is the same yesterday, to-day, and for ever (Apost. Past.).

And desired favour against him (ver. 3, according to Luther). Thus are the bodies and lives of Christians for sale, so that they are requested as a favour, and given away, Matt. xiv. 6–11; Mark xv. 15 (Starke).

But Festus answered, that Paul should be kept at Cæsarea (ver. 4). God here in a wonderful manner protected Paul. Not only this speech, but also ver. 9 proves how difficult it was for Festus directly to refuse this petition of the Jews, by granting which he might at the beginning of his government have obtained a good name among them. But his dispassionate disposition suffered him to be led by God to righteousness.—And

Paul knew nothing of all this great danger, from which his life was once more rescued. Only before the throne of God, will we be made aware how many such deliverances and protections have remained unknown to us (Williger).

Commanded Paul to be brought forth (ver. 6). In the whole trial of the apostle, we never find that he forced himself before the tribunal of the authorities. He suffered himself always to be called and brought; and when he was requested to speak, he remained within the limits of his defence, without in the least degree meditating revenge upon his bloodthirsty accusers. A beautiful example, how a servant of God is able to forget the injuries done to his person, to leave vengeance to God, to deny himself in his sufferings for Christ's sake, and to overcome his enemies through meekness and patience (Apost. Past.).

And brought forward grievous accusations against Paul, which they were not able to prove (ver. 7). Here also it is with the servant, as with the Master. As before Pilate, false witnesses arose against Christ, who were not able to establish their calumnies, so here the Jews acted before Festus against Paul. The nature of these false accusations are the same here, as there: transgression of the law, violation of the temple, and rebellion against Cæsar (Leonh. and Spieg.).

Neither against the law of the Jews, neither against the temple, nor yet against Cæsar, have I offended anything at all (ver. 8). The simpler and the more unadorned a defence is, the nearer does it approach to the disposition and conduct of Christ, John xviii. 20, 21 (Starke).

But Festus, willing to show the Jews a favour (ver. 9). Although men, who live without the fear of God, may for a time be on the right path in a matter, yet they veer round again from worldly motives, before one is aware of it, and act deceitfully. Therefore we should not trust in man, but in God, Ps. cxviii. 8, 9 (Starke).

But Paul said, I stand before Cæsar's judgment-seat. I appeal unto Cæsar (vers. 10, 11). Therefore we have imperial and temporal privileges, letters of safety and protection, and civil rights, that the righteous may be comforted, and the bad thwarted. On this account, God has ordained government with law and documents, with wax and seal, with the gallows and the wheel, to curb the wickedness of the wicked, and to protect the defenceless and the righteous, Rom. xiii. 3, 4 (Starke).—With the three land plagues, war, famine, and pestilence, is a fourth, long law-suits, in which advocates often represent an endless eternity. Paul's trial did not yet come to an end, 1 Cor. vi. 7 (Starke).—The apostle would not have appealed to Cæsar, had not the will of the Lord been made known to him, that he should bear witness at Rome. The Lord opens up a path to His servant by this appeal, in order to fill the capital of the world with the testimony of Jesus (Apost. Past.).—He appeals to Cæsar, not in order to obtain deliverance from a Nero, but by this door to reach Rome. But this appeal is also a striking proof against a false spirituality, which considers it unchristian to appeal to civil law and worldly authority, for the maintenance of our rights (Leonh. and Spieg.).

To Cæsar hast thou appealed, to Cæsar shalt thou go (ver. 12). Yes, Festus, thou art right: Paul shall to Rome, but not because thou and thy council will it, but because it was thus determined in the counsel of God. Therefore the ordinance of the Roman empire, the real nature of which is hostility to the kingdom of heaven, must, up to its highest authorities, minister to the ways and aims of the kingdom of Jesus.—The wheels of Divine Providence move everything, and men are obliged to assist without knowing it. They think that they themselves do everything (Gossner).

On vers. 1–12.—*The noble firmness of the Christian in the maintenance of his rights.* 1. It is different from the effrontery of the hypocrite; for he only makes use of a defence founded on fact, vers. 7, 8. 2. It is different from the defiance of the wicked; for he refuses no judicial examination, vers. 9, 10. 3. It is different from the obstinacy of the litigious; for he submits to every just decision (Bobe).—*I appeal to Cæsar.* This is a proof: 1. of a conscience void of offence toward God and man; 2. of a humble submission to divinely ordained authority; 3. of an evangelical and sober avoidance of an unnecessary martyrdom; 4. of an unwearied zeal for the extension of the kingdom of God.—*Law and justice, the highest ornament of magistrates.* 1. Festus does not refuse to receive the accusations against Paul, vers. 1–5. 2. He hears the accusers and the accused, vers. 6–8. 3. He grants to the accused the appeal to Cæsar, vers. 9–12 (Lisco).—*How a Christian pre-*

serves his rights. 1. Without arrogance, vers. 6–8. 2. Without fear, vers. 9–12 (Lisco).—*The Christian in reference to the changes of human governors.* 1. In looking back on departed governors: *a.* without harsh judgment, for he knows that they now stand before the highest Judge; *b.* without immoderate praise, for he sees that all the glory of the world is vanity. 2. In looking to the new government: *a.* without extravagant hope, for he knows that there is nothing new under the sun, Eccles. i. 9; *b.* without anxious fear, for he believes that Christ is the same yesterday, to-day, and for ever.—*Paul before Festus, an instructive example how both the children of the world and the children of the light remain the same.* 1. The children of the world. *a.* Paul's accusers. They have learned nothing and forgotten nothing; they bring forward the old lies and employ the old artifices which they had devised under Felix, indeed the same which they had brought before Pilate against Christ. *b.* Paul's judges. Instead of the licentious Felix, a proud Festus, who at first showed a noble bearing, vers. 4, 5, but soon, like his predecessor, surrendered righteousness from a desire to please men, ver. 9,—in short, under another name, the same man of the world. 2. The children of God. *a.* Paul is the same in undaunted courage. The two years imprisonment had neither broken his courage nor paralyzed his presence of mind: his defence is as clear and as firm as ever. *b.* In his meekness and patience, he is also the old man. No desire of revenge against his wicked enemies, no conspiracy against his unrighteous judges, no impatience at so long a trial; but calm submission to human law, and confident trust on the divine protection.—*From the appeal of Paul to Cæsar, we inquire, Where may a Christian seek his denied rights?* He may appeal: 1. from the sentence of the wicked to the judgment of the righteous; 2. from the passions of the moment to the justice of the future; 3. from the opinions of the world to the testimony of his own conscience; 4. from the tribunal of man to the judgment-seat of God.—*To Cæsar thou hast appealed, to Cæsar thou shalt go.* From whom did this decisive sentence concerning the life and death of Paul proceed? 1. It came from without: Festus pronounced it, as the possessor of power. 2. It came from within: Paul willed it, as the apostle of the Gentiles. 3. It came from above: the Lord ratified it, as the King of kings. (Application to the decisions in the life-course of the Christian.)

E.

At the request of Herod Agrippa the Younger, Festus brings the Apostle before him, whereby Paul receives an opportunity of publicly defending himself before the King, and of bearing a testimony, which is not without effect.

Chap. xxv. 13–xxvi. 32.

1. *Festus informs King Agrippa concerning Paul, and at the King's desire brings him forth for examination in the presence of a distinguished assembly.* (Chap. xxv. 13–27.)

13 And after the lapse of some days, king Agrippa and Bernice came
to Cæsarea to salute Festus. 14 And when they had tarried there several
days, Festus brought the matter of Paul before the king, saying, There
is a man left behind by Felix in imprisonment, 15 About whom, when
I came to Jerusalem, the chief priests and elders of the Jews informed me,
and desired judgment against him. 16 To whom I answered, that it is
not a custom among the Romans to surrender any man, before the accused
has seen his accusers before him, and has received an opportunity to defend
himself in regard to the charge. 17 When then they came here together, I
delayed not the matter, but on the next day sat on the judgment-seat, and
commanded the man to be brought forth. 18 But when his accusers stood up,
they brought no charges of such things as I supposed; 19 But they had only
certain questions regarding their own religion, and concerning one Jesus
who was dead, whom Paul affirmed to be alive. 20 But as I was without
advice regarding this question, I asked him whether he would go to Jerusalem, and there be judged of these things. 21 But when Paul appealed to
be kept for the judgment of Cæsar, I commanded him to be kept until I
might send him to Cæsar. 22 Then said Agrippa to Festus, I would also
wish to hear the man. And he said, To-morrow thou shalt hear him.

23 On the next day, therefore, Agrippa and Bernice came with great
pomp, and went into the place of audience, with the chief captains and
principal men of the city; and at the command of Festus, Paul was brought
forth. 24 And Festus said, King Agrippa, and all men who are present with
us, ye see here the man, about whom the whole multitude of the Jews, both
in Jerusalem and here, pleaded with me, and cried out that he ought not
any longer to live. 25 But I perceived that he had done nothing worthy
of death; and as he himself appealed to Cæsar, I resolved to send him.
26 However I know nothing certain to write about him to my lord, and
therefore I have brought him before you, and especially before thee, O king

Agrippa, that, after having heard him, I may know what I ought to write.
27 For it appears to be unreasonable to send a prisoner, without stating
the charges against him.

Ver. 16. After ἄνθρωπον, some MSS. and versions add εἰς ἀπώλειαν, which was evidently an explanatory addition.

Ver. 25. Καταλαβόμενος is indeed not so strongly attested by external evidence as κατελαβόμην; but the internal evidence is in its favour, as it would certainly not have been changed into the participle, if κατελαβόμην had been the original reading.

EXEGETICAL EXPLANATIONS.

1. *King Agrippa and Bernice came to Cæsarea.*—The visit of Herod, as it was the first salutation of the new governor, would doubtless follow not long after the event last related, so that the expression "after some days" is to be understood literally. Herod Agrippa II., the last of the Herods, was the son of Herod Agrippa I., and had in the year 48 after Christ received the principality of Chalcis, and four years later exchanged it for the former tetrarchy of Philip, on the north-east beyond Jordan, with the title of king. He also possessed authority over the temple, and the right of electing the high priest. Bernice, his full sister, was married at an earlier period to her uncle, Herod the prince of Chalcis; and after his death (48 after Christ), she lived with her brother, and, as it was believed, in incestuous intercourse with him.

2. *And when they had tarried there several days.*—The information concerning Paul appeared to the procurator not so pressing, as that he should make it immediately; but only after Agrippa had remained some time at Cæsarea, did Festus take the opportunity to talk the matter over with him. Probably he hoped, as he was a stranger to the country, to receive information concerning Paul and his cause from Agrippa's experience and knowledge of the Jewish people, whose religion was also his own.

3. *There is a man left by Felix.*—It is striking, how studiously Festus proceeds to place in the clearest light, first his personal rectitude and conscientious official zeal in this matter, and then the excellence of Roman law in general, before the king, who was in reality a vassal under him, but yet in rank above him. So also in the answer he gave to the Jews (ver. 16); which, however, he relates entirely differently from what he actually

gave (vers. 4, 5). *Χαρίζεσθαι* has, from the context, the meaning, "to condemn a man in order to please one." *Τόπον ἀπολογίας λάβοι*, latinized, is *locum respondendi accipere*.

4. *They brought no charges of such things as I supposed.*—Festus had, on account of the bitterness with which the Jews were filled toward Paul, thought that they would bring some heavy accusation against him: but it concerned only a religious question. Festus here designedly chooses the word *δεισιδαιμονία*, which Agrippa might understand in a good or in a bad sense (see chap. xvii. 22); and in saying *τῆς ἰδίας δεισιδ.* he takes the prince himself for a Gentile, or at least as by far too enlightened to share earnestly in the Jewish superstition. What Festus says of Jesus, proves that in the above transactions much occurred which Luke has not related. On the other hand, the tone in which the Roman speaks is evidently the conversational tone of the man of the world, touching in a careless manner on the most important and the holiest matters; especially when he comes to speak of the person of Jesus, and disparages the testimony of Paul, that Jesus lives, as if it were a mere assertion (*φάσκειν*).

5. *But because I doubted of this question.*—The procurator designedly places in an entirely inoffensive light the proposal which he made to Paul to be judged at Jerusalem, and explains it only as a wish to bring the examination, to which he felt himself incompetent, before a proper court. *Ὁ Σεβαστός*, Augustus.

6. *And on the morrow.*—*Φαντασία*, with the later Greeks, as Plutarch, Diodorus, and others, means: pomp, splendour, procession. *Fantasia* denotes even now, in all the western maritime lands of Turkey, lustre or splendour. It was a numerous and splendid assembly, before which the apostle was placed. Festus solemnly brings forth Paul, and designedly makes the matter important, representing, in an exaggerated manner, that the whole Jewish community applied to him concerning this man.

7. *To my lord.*—*Κύριος* (*Dominus*) was a title which not only Augustus, but also Tiberius had resolutely declined, because it belonged only to the gods; *e.g.*, Tacitus, Anal. ii. 87; Suetonius, Aug. 53. But the emperors after them were flattered with this honourable title, and it was at this time much in fashion. *Ἀσφαλές τι*, an exact and definite charge.

DOGMATICAL AND ETHICAL THOUGHTS.

1. The heathen governor, although there was in him no earnest disposition to the apprehension of religious truth, has rightly observed, that the chief difference between Paul and his Jewish opponents referred to the person of Jesus, and especially to the question whether He was risen or not. That Jesus expired on the cross, both parties were agreed. But Paul maintained that Jesus lives, that He has risen again: this the Jews contested with all their might. In point of fact, the change, by which Paul became another man, was originally and in its chief features founded on its being made undoubtedly certain to him, by the appearance of Jesus, that the Crucified One lives. Therefore his announcement, that of an eye-witness, was thus a proper testimony; while Festus considered it as a mere assertion founded on fancy. The resurrection of Jesus is, and continues to be, the central fact of redemption through Christ: historically, inasmuch as without it the Church of Christ would have attained to no historical existence or duration; doctrinally, both as regards the person and the work of Christ; vitally, inasmuch as every one who is united to Him by faith, lives and receives divine strength through Him as the Risen One; and as regards the future, because all Christian hope, for time and eternity, of the individual and of the race, is conditioned and guaranteed by the resurrection-life of the Redeemer.

2. The feeling of incompetency was certainly not the actual motive, on account of which Festus wished to refer the trial of Paul to Jerusalem. However, there is in his statement, as he gives it, a sound discernment. Instead of relying on his own judgment in all controversies, on account of his high worldly position, he finds it not inconsistent with his official dignity candidly to acknowledge his helplessness in this question. And, very far from dictatorially and peremptorily deciding a question of faith by right of his authority, he would rather place the judgment concerning it into proper hands. An honourable restriction of the magistracy, which gives to Cæsar the things that are Cæsar's, and to God the things that are God's: an example for the imitation of all Christian magistrates in the territory of matters of faith and of the Church.

HOMILETICAL HINTS.

And when they had tarried several days (ver. 14). The first days were spent in those amusements, by which men are accustomed to honour distinguished strangers. But after many days, when all other matters were exhausted, they came to the business of Paul (Rieger).

To whom I answered, that it was not a custom among the Romans (ver. 16). It were to be wished that this just rule and custom of the Romans were everywhere inscribed in great letters, in stone and brass, in the palaces of great men and in council chambers; or rather, that they were written on the heart of all judges and magistrates, Job xix. 23, 24. Those are hangmen, and no judges, who begin with the execution, and condemn the accused, be they guilty or innocent, without a hearing and an ordinary trial. The Gentiles were more reasonable and just, and will be judges of such men (Starke).—Festus, in his speech to Agrippa, makes a great parade about his own rectitude, and extols his impartial conduct. But if we consider the whole matter, it is as clear as day that his heart did not correspond with this. "He would do the Jews a pleasure," it is said (ver. 9). He wished, in an underhand manner, to deliver Paul into their hands at Jerusalem, and was only restrained from doing so by the apostle's appeal to Cæsar. Festus was a man of the world, who wished to please all men, and to spread his sails to the wind. This evil disposition adheres to all of us by nature. We are much inclined to magnify our own works, and to justify all that we do, although our conscience convicts us of many human frailties (Apost. Past.).

They had only certain questions regarding their own religion (Luther: of their own superstition, ver. 19). Festus does not here speak of the Jewish religion with that respect which we would expect, seeing he had before him a Jew in the person of Agrippa. But because it is easily believed that great men do not internally and at heart put much stress on the religion which externally they profess; so other insolent tongues easily venture to speak disparagingly of it to their face (Rieger).—*And concerning one Jesus, who was dead, whom Paul affirmed to be alive.* From this statement of Festus, it is evident that Paul, in his speech before the chief council at Jerusalem, and in his defence before Festus, not only dwelt on the resurrection in general, but taught and maintained this doctrine in connection with the resurrection of Jesus. For it was a chief point of his dispute with the Jews, that he testified that Jesus whom they slew was risen and lives. Festus regards this matter of dispute as a superstition and a trifle. But it was (and is) the great central truth of the whole Christian faith, and the important boundary line at which Jewish (and modern) infidelity separate from the faith of the whole Christian Church (Apost. Past.).

But as I was in doubt concerning this question. (But as I did not understand this question; Luther, ver. 20.) Although we abhor the disregard with which Festus, as a Gentile and a man of the world, from ignorance looks on the disputed question of the truth of the resurrection of Jesus, yet we must, on the other hand, praise his equity and moderation; that he would not deal with such questions of religion and faith in a dictatorial manner, and even would not bring the dispute before his tribunal. This heathen has in this better principles than many Christian magistrates, who do not scruple to treat religious controversies as civil matters, to forbid doctrines and truths with excommunication, fire, and the sword, and set themselves up as judges of the conscience (Apost. Past.).

And Agrippa said to Festus, I would also wish to hear the man (ver. 22). It was perhaps something more than mere curiosity. Festus had not taken particular trouble to awaken that. A flash of lightning had struck Agrippa's soul, a foreboding that here a heavenly matter was to be treated of (Williger).

Agrippa and Bernice came with great pomp (ver. 23). How would this splendour soon fade before the simple words of the man of God! (Williger.)—Here again God prepares for His servant a numerous audience of the great and the noble, to whom he should preach the Gospel, according to His own declaration, "He is a chosen vessel unto Me, to bear My name before the Gentiles, and kings, and the children of Israel." Shortly before this, Paul received rest and liberty to hold familiar intercourse with his friends. Soon after, he was involved by Festus in the trial with the hostile Jews, and testified that Jesus, the Crucified One, lives. Now he must bear witness before kings and princes, and address a great assembly.—We adore in this the faithfulness of God, who always takes care to bring forward His servants anew, and to employ them when they are most despised by the world; He makes for them an open door, when the world thinks to confine them with bonds and prisons. But we honour also the representation of such a servant of Jesus, whom Christ could employ in every capacity: now as a witness of His sufferings, now as an exhorter of the people, now as a preacher of His resurrection, now as the herald of His grace before emperors and kings. The Lord grant to us also grace to be useful, and to be very faithful in everything in which He employs us (Apost. Past.).

Ye see here the man (ver. 24). Behold what a man! John xix. 5 (Williger).

Therefore have I brought him before thee, O king Agrippa (ver. 26). As Pilate sends Jesus to Herod, Luke xxiii. 7 (Williger).

For it appears to be unreasonable to send a prisoner, without stating the points of complaint against him (ver. 27). Statesmen well understand that it is an improper thing to imprison and punish men for the sake of their religion; but their conduct does not always correspond with their opinion, for the supposed interest of the State has always the mastery over reason, Matt. xxiii. 3 (Starke).—That such evil decisions in legal matters proceed from courts and the highest judicatories, when appealed to, may perhaps happen, because the information has not reached them correctly in all particulars. Would that princes and great men saw with their own eyes and heard with their own ears the miserable and the oppressed, and did not let everything depend on their councils and officers! (Starke.)

On the whole section (vers. 13–27).—*The judgment of worldly men concerning matters of faith.* 1. Their highest stand-point is that of civil law, as here with Festus (vers. 13–18). 2. Their judgment concerning matters of faith is depreciatory; they reckon them as belonging to the domain of superstition, and pride themselves on not understanding such questions (vers. 19–21). 3. Their sympathy in such matters is, as with Agrippa, an affair of curiosity and of fashion, ver. 22 (Lisco).—*Why are those to be accounted blessed who are persecuted for righteousness' sake?* 1. Because persecution puts the innocence of their cause in the fairest light, ver. 18. 2. Because persecution gives them an opportunity to bear witness of the truth, ver. 22 (Lisco).—*The principles of a sound administration of justice from the mouth of Festus*, vers. 14–27. 1. It should do everything which belongs to its office. *a.* In respect of the accusers: to receive and listen to them patiently, vers. 15, 17, 18. *b.* In respect of the accused: to hear their defence impartially, and to protect their persons against the craft and violence of their enemies, vers. 16, 18, 21. 2. It should omit everything which does not belong to its office. *a.* It should assume no judgment in matters of faith, vers. 19, 20, 26. *b.* It should not arbitrarily anticipate the higher judge (ver. 25), but conscientiously prepare the way, vers. 26, 27.—*The blindness of mere worldly education in matters of Christian truth.* 1. The precious articles of the Christian faith are to it the offspring of superstition, not worth the trouble of being more accurately instructed therein, vers. 19, 20. 2. The living Head of the Church is to it one Jesus who is dead, of whose living power and presence there is no trace, ver. 19. 3. The chosen servants of God are to it incomprehensible and whimsical men, of whom nothing can be made, vers. 24–27.—*Festus and Paul, or the plain man of God in his superiority to the showy man of the world.* 1. He is superior to him by the internal nobleness of his divine sonship, before which all external splendour of station fades; 2. by the wide view of faith, before which all worldly culture must confess its ignorance; 3. by the stedfast maintenance of an unblameable conduct before God, compared with which the lax morality of the world wavers uncertainly between right and wrong, truth and falsehood.—*The saying of Agrippa concerning Paul, "I would wish to hear the man," in its different applications and meanings.* 1. As the wish of a supercilious curiosity, which seeks nothing more than a passing entertainment. 2. As the wish of a worldly desire of knowledge, which is only concerned about interesting information. 3. As the wish of a pious desire of salvation, which feels the need of spiritual instruction. (Application to church-going, hearing sermons, reading books, etc.)—*Paul, the servant of God, before princes and rulers at Cæsarea*, a noble picture, from which we recognise: 1. The glory of the Lord, who sets open doors before His servants, even in fetters and in bonds, and knocks with His word at palaces as well as at huts. 2. The fidelity of His servant, who bears his testimony to the Lord everywhere, undazzled by the splendour of human greatness, and unclogged by the fetters of his own trouble.—*The audience-chamber of the governor at Cæsarea.* 1. A drawing-room of worldly glory, by the splendour of the assembled nobility, ver. 23. 2. A lecture-room of holy doctrine, by the testimony of the apostle, chap. xxvi. 1–23. 3. And lastly, a judgment-hall of divine majesty, by the impression of the apostolic discourse, which discloses the bottom of the hearts, chap. xxvi. 24–32.

2. *Paul publicly defends himself before Festus and Agrippa, so that his speech makes a considerable impression, and excites the general conviction of his innocence.* (CHAP. XXVI. 1–32.)

1 And Agrippa said to Paul, It is permitted thee to speak concerning thyself. Then Paul, stretching forth his hand, defended himself. 2 I esteem myself happy, king Agrippa, that I may defend myself this day before thee, on all things of which I am accused by the Jews. 3 Especially, because thou art acquainted with all the customs and questions of the Jews. Wherefore I pray thee to hear me patiently. 4 My manner of life, then, from my youth, as I lived from the beginning among mine own nation at Jerusalem, know all the Jews; 5 Knowing me from the beginning, if they would testify, that after the strictest sect of our religion, I lived a Pharisee. 6 And now I stand on trial concerning the hope of the promise made by God to our fathers, 7 To which the twelve tribes of our nation, serving God continually day and night, hope to attain. On account of this hope, king Agrippa, I am accused by the Jews. 8 Why is it considered incredible with you, whether God raises the dead? 9 I indeed thought that I ought to do many things contrary to the name of Jesus of Nazareth. 10 Which I also did at Jerusalem, when I shut up many of the saints in prison, having received authority from the chief priests; and when they were put to death, I assented to it. 11 And I punished them often in all the synagogues, and compelled them to blaspheme; and full of immoderate rage, I persecuted them even to foreign cities: 12 Whereupon I also journeyed to Damascus with authority and commission from the chief priests; 13 And on the way, O king, I saw at mid-day a light from heaven, brighter than the sun, which shone around me and my companions. 14 And when we were all fallen to the ground, I heard a voice speaking to me, and saying in the Hebrew dialect, Saul, Saul, why persecutest thou Me? It is hard for thee to kick against the goads. 15 And I said, Who art Thou, Lord? And the Lord said, I am Jesus whom thou persecutest. 16 But arise, and stand upon thy feet; for to this end have I appeared to thee, to appoint thee a minister and a witness of those things which thou hast seen, and in which I will yet appear to thee. 17 And I will rescue thee from the people and the Gentiles, among whom now I send thee, 18 To open their eyes, and to turn them from darkness to light, and from the power of Satan unto God, that they

may receive forgiveness of sins, and an inheritance among them who are sanctified by faith in Me. 19 Wherefore, O king Agrippa, I was not disobedient to the heavenly vision; 20 But proclaimed first to them at Damascus, and in Jerusalem, and in all Judea, as also to the Gentiles, that they should change their disposition, and turn to God, and do works worthy of repentance. 21 On this account, the Jews caught me in the temple, and attempted to kill me. 22 But I received help from God, and stand even to this day, and witness before great and small, saying none other things than what the prophets and Moses have said should happen, 23 Whether the Messiah will suffer, and whether He, as the first of the resurrection of the dead, will proclaim a light to the people and to the Gentiles.

24 But as he thus spoke in his defence, Festus called out with a loud voice, Thou art mad, Paul! Much learning makes thee mad. 25 But he said, I am not mad, most noble Festus, but I speak the words of truth and soberness. 26 For the king knows well of such things, to whom I address myself joyfully; for I am convinced that none of these things are hidden from him, for this thing did not happen in a corner. 27 King Agrippa, believest thou the prophets? I know that thou believest. 28 But Agrippa said to Paul, With a little persuadest thou me to become a Christian! 29 And Paul said, I would to God that with little or with great, not only thou, but all who hear me this day, were such as I am, with the exception of these bonds. 30 Then the king arose, and the governor, and Bernice, and those who sat with them. 31 And when they had retired, they communed together, and said, This man does nothing which merits death or bonds. 32 And Agrippa said to Festus, This man could have been set at liberty, if he had not appealed to Cæsar.

Ver. 1. Περί is more strongly attested than ὑπέρ.

Ver. 6. Εἰς τοὺς πατέρας without ἡμῶν is to be preferred to προς τ. π. ἡμ. 'Ημῶν has indeed the majority of uncial MSS. in its favour; but it would hardly have been omitted, whereas it might easily have been added.

Ver. 7. 'Υπὸ 'Ιουδαίων without the article, which is wanting in all the uncial MSS., is the original reading.

Ver. 10. 'Εν φυλακαῖς is attested by all the uncial MSS., except one which omits the preposition.

Ver. 12. Καί after ἐν οἷς is decidedly attested.

Ver. 14. Φωνὴν λαλοῦσαν πρός με καὶ λέγουσαν appears to be the original reading; whilst the shorter reading, which leaves out λαλ.—καί, was formed from the parallel passages, chap. ix. 4, xxii. 7.

Ver. 15. Κύριος after ὁ δέ has all the uncial MSS. for it, with the exception of one.

Ver. 22. Μαρτυρόμενος is in four uncial MSS.; the reading of the textus receptus, μαρτυρούμενος, passive, has only one MS. of the first rank for it. Griesbach, Lachmann, and Tischendorf have adopted μαρτυρόμενος; Meyer has recently defended the passive reading, but without sufficient evidence. The recently discovered Sinaitic Codex is in favour of μαρτυρόμενος.

Ver. 25. Παῦλος after ὁ δέ is wanting in several MSS., and is not original.

Ver. 28. Ἔφη after πρὸς τὸν Παῦλον is wanting in a number of MSS., and was wrongly inserted in the textus receptus.

Ver. 29. Also εἶπεν after ὁ δὲ Παῦλος is spurious.—Μεγάλῳ and πολλῷ have until lately been equally attested; only from internal evidence, Lachmann and Tischendorf have preferred the former reading. This opinion has been established by the Sinaitic Codex, and now the preponderance of external authorities is in favour of μεγάλῳ.

Ver. 30. Καὶ ταῦτα εἰπόντος αὐτοῦ before ἀνέστη is omitted in the Alexandrine and Vatican MSS.: it is certainly an insertion.

EXEGETICAL EXPLANATIONS.

1. *It is permitted thee.*—Agrippa calls upon Paul for his defence. As king, he occupied the highest rank in the assembly; and as the guest of the procurator, he enjoyed the honour of president. Accordingly he opens the proceedings, and also, though he does not formally close the meeting, yet he breaks it up (ver. 30). However, he says designedly, not ἐπιτρέπω σοι, but ἐπιτρέπεται, in order not to derogate from the honour of the governor. Paul immediately commences his address, stretching forth his arm (to which a chain was attached, ver. 29), thus making the formal action usual in public speeches before courts of justice.

2. *I esteem myself happy.*—The conciliating address to Agrippa rests chiefly on the fact that Agrippa was conversant with Jewish customs and questions. In fact, some anecdotes are related of him in the Talmud, which testify to his knowledge of the Jewish law. See Schöttgen, Horæ Hebr. to chap. xxv. *Μάλιστα* is not to be referred to γνώστην, "in the highest degree acquainted with" (Meyer), but to the principal sentence, ἥγημαι ἐμαυτὸν μακάριον, as the reason why Paul esteemed himself happy to be permitted to defend himself before Agrippa. Another reason of his gratification was, that he was permitted to bear witness before a king (see chap. ix. 15). Therefore he gives him his title, and repeats it as an indication that he puts peculiar stress upon it, vers. 7, 19, 26, 27. The participial sentence in the accusative, γνώστην ὄντα σε, rests on a loose construction, while strictly the genitive after σοῦ (ver. 2) should have been continued.

3. *My manner of life, then.*—*Οὖν* deduces the immediate opening of the defence itself, both from the satisfaction occasioned by Agrippa's knowledge of the matter, and from the favour and patience in listening to him which Paul had requested. *From*

the beginning is a stronger expression than from youth. Paul mentions: 1. how long the Jews knew him; 2. where they learned to know him; 3. how they knew him, namely, as a Pharisee, ver. 5. The words ἀπ' ἀρχῆς γεν.—ἐν Ἱερ. suppose, in conformity with ἀνατεθραμμένος ἐν τῇ πόλει ταύτῃ, chap. xxii. 3, that Saul was brought to Jerusalem in early childhood, and educated there. Therefore, they knew me before, *i.e.*, before I myself mention it, namely, that I lived a Pharisee according to the rule of the strictest sect (compare chap. xxii. 3). *If they will testify*, which perhaps they would not be sufficiently upright and honourable to do, because they might fear by this admission to advance the honour of Paul.

4. *And now I stand and am accused.*—In vers. 6–8, Paul passes rapidly from the first period of his life to the present, and testifies, that however much his present condition and disposition appear a contrast from his former, yet he is accused and tried, not on account of apostasy from the Jewish religion, but, on the contrary, on account of the common purely Jewish hope. And this hope rests on the express promise and revelation of God to the fathers, and is ardently shared in by the whole people. Paul names the twelve tribes, without reference as to where individual members of the nation might at this time be: thus he may have alluded to the descendants of the ten tribes, perhaps still in the districts of their exile. By this hope, nothing else can be understood than the Messianic; so that Paul intends to say, All pious Israelites hope for the Messiah promised by God, and he himself also believes in the fulfilment of this promise by the appearance and resurrection of Jesus of Nazareth. This last thought leads him to the question which attacks the doubts themselves (ver. 8). He directs this question to the whole assembly (ὑμῖν), including Agrippa and Festus, supposing them to be unbelievers on this point. The expression εἰ ὁ Θεὸς νεκροὺς ἐγείρει (ver. 8) marks the object interrogatively, inasmuch as he who considers it incredible, calls the truth in question. Εἰ, "whether," as in ver. 23: the meaning "that" is ungrammatical; not so the construction "if" (Meyer, after the Vulgate and Erasmus), which however does not properly suit either the mind of Paul or that of the doubters. Ἐγείρει is significant: not past, referring to the resurrection of Christ; nor future, referring to the general resurrection; but

present, indicating that it refers not to a single historical fact, but to a universal idea, in other words, to a permanent attribute or power of God.

5. *I indeed believed.*—With this Paul again takes up the thread of the narrative of his own life, dropped for an instant, without οὖν being specially united as a consequence to the above-mentioned unbelief (Meyer). *I ought to do, i.e.,* I considered it my duty to labour against the name of Jesus—the confession of Him. Paul here calls Christians "the saints," which he avoided doing in his speech before the people at Jerusalem; but here, before an unbiassed audience, he designedly so expresses himself, in order to bear witness for Christ and His Church, and to confess his own guilt. *When they were put to death, I assented to it.* Ψῆφον καταφέρειν, properly to lay down the voting stone, is, as little as the German word "beistimmen," originally signifying the same thing, to be understood literally of a vote given by a judge and lawful assessor of the court, but expresses only moral assent and approval.

6. *With authority and commission: i.e.,* as the authorized agent and representative of the chief priests. In the account which follows of the appearance of Jesus in the neighbourhood of Damascus, there are several things peculiar. 1. Some traits which mark out the overwhelming nature of the appearance; as, for example, that the light which shone round about surpassed the brightness of the sun, ver. 13; whereas chap. ix. 3 has only φῶς ἀπὸ τοῦ οὐρανοῦ, and chap. xxii. 6 has φῶς ἱκανόν. Also that the whole company fell to the ground, ver. 14, of which chap. xxii. 7 says nothing, and chap. ix. 7 apparently asserts the contrary. See Exegetical Explanations to the latter passage. 2. The observation that the voice spoke in the Hebrew, that is, in the Aramaic dialect, which is not hinted at in the two parallel passages, and in chap. xxii. 7 was so far unnecessary, as Paul himself then spoke in the Aramaic. 3. The addition in ver. 14, σκληρόν σοι πρὸς κέντρα λακτίζειν, which in chap. ix. 5 is critically to be rejected, and in chap. xxii. 7 is only found in one uncial MS. and in some versions. This figurative expression (borrowed from the mode of ploughing with draught oxen, which the Eastern farmer, walking behind and managing the plough with his left hand, goads on with a rod six or eight feet long, and furnished with a sharp point, and, if they are obsti-

nate and kick, punishes them the more severely) is to declare how his resisting will must be broken by the decided command of the Redeemer, appearing in overwhelming majesty. 4. The circumstance that the communication of the Lord, concerning the call of Paul to be the apostle of the Gentiles, as well as concerning his protection in the dangers which threatened him (a communication which, according to chapters ix. and xxii., was first imparted in Damascus by Ananias), is here directly represented with the appearance of Jesus by the way, as an integral part of the first direct revelation of the Redeemer. This representation has not only the negative reason, that the mediation by a legally-pious Jewish Christian, on which, when addressing a Jewish audience, Paul had a special reason to lay stress, was of no importance for Agrippa and his present audience (to which Baumgarten with justice directs attention); but Paul also had a positive reason for selecting this form, because it was his purpose to bring prominently forward the circumstance that this revelation, indirectly imparted to him, proceeded from Christ Himself. Paul here, with regard to the form, claims a liberty of representation which is not slavishly bound to the letter and to single circumstances. And it is by no means necessary to suppose, for the sake of reconciliation, that Jesus at His first appearance to Paul gave him a survey of his later ministry, as Baumgarten thinks possible, without, however, positively adopting that hypothesis. And as little has Stier reason "to despond over the presumption of learned theologians," and to grow so very hot, as he has done, in his protest against this view of ours (Words of the Apostles, vol. ii. p. 301, 2d edition). For the supposition that "Paul here put his own thoughts in the mouth of the Lord" is not ours; on the contrary, we maintain that Paul here quotes the actual words of the Redeemer which He spoke to him, through means of Ananias. The Acts of the Apostles is our guarantee that the exalted Lord revealed these ideas to Ananias (chap. ix. 15, 16). And the only question can be, whether Ananias repeated immediately to Paul all that was said to him by the Lord. This, so probable in itself, may certainly appear doubtful from chap. ix. 17, but the apostle's own testimony (chap. xxii. 15) speaks decidedly for it; although he there refers to the speech of Ananias in a very summary manner merely. We therefore hold the view not to be disproved, that the apostle in chap. xxvi. 16–18 combines the words of Christ, which He spoke to him by the mouth of Ananias, with those which at His appearance before Damascus He spoke directly to himself. And in this we think that we are chargeable with no "learned presumption;" as little as Stier himself can be charged with the same fault when, in commenting on Matt. xix. 5, he asserts, in entire accordance with truth, that the words which there (not an apostle of the Lord, but) the Redeemer Himself quotes as the words of God, were not spoken directly by God, but by God "through Adam" (Stier's Words of Jesus according to Matthew).

7. *I am Jesus whom thou persecutest.*—Jesus declares the purpose of His appearance to Paul to consist in this, that he should be His minister and witness, especially for the conversion of the Gentiles, on which mission the protection of the Redeemer is assured to him. *Προχειρίσασθαι* is primarily "to determine," "to choose," but this cannot be its meaning here; only the signification suits in which the word occurs in Polybius, "to take in hand," "to employ in something." Paul was to be a witness of what he already saw, and of what he will yet see. But the latter is with *ὧν ὀφθήσομαι* so expressed, that Jesus Himself in person is the only chief object of future visions, as He also (according to *ὤφθην σοι*) was in what Paul had seen (*ὧν εἶδες*). The participle *ἐξαιρούμενος* belongs grammatically to *ὀφθήσομαι*, but in point of fact to *προχειρίσασθαι*. The meaning of *ἐξαιρεῖσθαι* cannot here be "to choose" (Kuinoel), because Saul was not chosen from the Gentiles, but from Israel; and because, according to the construction, the participle must indicate something coming after, not preceding, the mission among the Gentiles. Therefore *ἐξαιρεῖσθαι* here can only signify "to rescue from danger." The mission of Paul refers primarily to Israel (*ὁ λαός*), and the Gentiles are named only in the second place, entirely as Paul himself expresses it in his epistles.

8. But the object of his mission is so described that we can only think on the Gentiles. It is to open their eyes, *i.e.*, to open and awaken the mind for the truth, and this in order to convert them (*τοῦ ἐπιστρέψαι* intransitive, the aim or design of *ἀνοῖξαι*). The change is denoted by a twofold contrast,—by that between darkness and light, and by that between the ruling power of Satan and the liberating fellowship of God. Finally, the last

gracious design of God in their conversion (τοῦ λαβεῖν) consists in the forgiveness of sins and the bestowal of an inheritance, *i.e.*, of a share in the glory among the sanctified. Both forgiveness and blessedness, however, can only be obtained by faith in Jesus (πίστει τῇ εἰς ἐμέ).

9. *Therefore I was not disobedient.*—Paul now relates his resolution to comply with the divine call and his labours from that time forward, vers. 19, 20. Because the vision was heavenly and powerfully convincing, he did not refuse obedience to it, as the Jews thought he should have done. *Οὐκ ἐγενόμην ἀπειθὴς* gives us to understand, that in fact the matter in question was obedience or resistance to the will of God. *Ὅθεν*, however, is not to be restricted to the immediately preceding promise of employment, but to be referred to the whole circumstances of the appearance as it is represented in vers. 13-15. Paul sums up his past labours, since his conversion to the present day, as an announcement which insisted on change of disposition (among the Jews) and conversion to God (on the part of the Gentiles), united with proofs of sincerity by the actions of a changed heart. And he describes the circle of his labours as fourfold, embracing first the cities of Damascus and Jerusalem, then the whole land of Judea, and lastly the Gentile world.

10. In conclusion, the apostle passes quickly to the present moment. *Unto this day*, I stand unharmed (ἕστηκα), being rescued by divine aid from murderous hands, and I prosecute my ministry. *Μαρτυρόμενος* (not μαρτυρούμενος) refers to μάρτυς, ver. 16: I bear witness before great and small, that is, before high and low. The explanation of μαρτυρούμενος in the passive (Meyer), "well-reported of by small and great," does not suit the context, for the circumstance that he is engaged in a defence proves that he has opponents and accusers. Thus, then, the connection shows that μαρτυρόμενος as well as λέγων is intended to describe his personal labours. The participial sentence declares that the testimony which he bore before every one, was nothing else than the announcement of the actual fulfilment of what the prophets and Moses had promised should happen. Paul puts the object of the biblical promise in an interrogative form (ver. 23), because it was disputed by the Jews. There were these three questions: 1. Whether the Messiah is παθητός, *i.e.*, not only capable of suffering, but subjected to

suffering, *necessitati patiendi obnoxius*,—so throughout in the classical *usus loquendi*. 2.. Whether the Messiah will rise again, and be the first in the domain of the resurrection. 3. Whether the Messiah will announce light (salvation) not only to the people of Israel, but also to the Gentiles. The two last thoughts are grammatically fused into one question, but, according to the nature of the subject, are to be regarded as separate.

11. *Thou art mad, Paul.*—With this call, Festus interrupts Paul in his address. This referred not exclusively to the last words, but to the whole speech, and in particular to the narrative of the appearance of Jesus. This appeared to the Roman as folly. He certainly intended it in full earnest, and not as a light jest, "Thou art a visionary;" otherwise, he would not have cried out with a loud voice, which indicates emotion. *Γράμματα*, according to the usual explanation, "learning;" not "books," as Kuinoel and others understand it.

12. *I am not mad, most noble Festus.*—With perfect calmness and due respect, but with all firmness, the apostle disclaims the reproach, and declares that his speech was (objectively) truth and (subjectively) sober. *Σωφροσύνη*, presence of mind, a sound understanding which is master of itself, in opposition to mental disorder. In proof of the objective rectitude of his assertion (*γάρ*), Paul appeals to Agrippa (ver. 26), who must have been acquainted with the facts. *Such things* refer chiefly to the incidents in the life of Jesus, and in the history of the Christian Church, which had been touched upon in the speech of Paul. With these the king must have been acquainted, because they occurred with the greatest publicity. Yet he seeks to draw Agrippa to the side of truth, not only by means of his knowledge through hearsay, but also by means of his conscience and heart (ver. 27); and he fastens on him so strongly with his belief in the prophets, that he can scarcely evade it.

13. The king might indeed be struck for an instant, but he immediately replies in mockery. *With a little*, with slight means, *persuadest thou me to be a Christian!* *'Εν ὀλίγῳ*, not "in a short time" (Calvin, Wetstein, De Wette), nor "almost" (Chrysostom, Luther, Grotius): the first cannot be the meaning, on account of the contrast *ἐν μεγάλῳ*, the reading critically to be preferred; and the second would have been expressed with the genitive *ὀλίγου*, or with *παρ' ὀλίγου*. The correct meaning is given by Œcumenius,

δι' ὀλίγων ῥημάτων—χωρὶς πολλοῦ πόνου: see Meyer. This is the second place (see chap. xi. 26) where the Christian name occurs, and that in the mouth of one who was not a Christian, and in a disparaging sense. Paul, however, answers with great earnestness and pious fervour. *Εὐξαίμην ἂν τῷ Θεῷ*, literally: "I would pray to God," namely, if I did comply with the impulse of my heart. *Καὶ ἐν ὀλίγῳ καὶ ἐν μεγάλῳ*, with little or great means. *Except these bonds*, says Paul, pointing to the chains, with which at other times he was bound to the soldiers who kept him, but which now hung on his arm.

14. *Then rose up the king.*—Agrippa dissolved the session, whilst he arose first, and after him the procurator, and the rest in order. After they had retired to another room (*ἀναχωρήσαντες*, not aside, in the same place), they conferred together about Paul, giving their judgment that the man certainly designs nothing criminal (*πράσσει*, not in the signification of the past, as Kuinoel thought, but reviewing his whole life and also his present character). The declaration of Agrippa was, that Paul could have been properly set at liberty (*ἀπολελύσθαι*), namely, at an earlier stage of the process, if he had not appealed to Cæsar, by which his cause was already taken from the inferior court.

15. The speech before Agrippa is one of the most detailed of Paul's speeches which Luke communicates. It is, as the speech delivered on the stairs of the castle of Antonia in Jerusalem, a defence. But it is not delivered before the excited Jewish people, but before the highest persons of the land—before king Agrippa and the imperial procurator, and various officers. Therefore Paul is not here necessitated to prove his personal innocence, but he passes over to vindicate his mission and labour as an apostle, and, along with that, to defend Christianity itself. The present speech is distinguished from beginning to end by a peculiar joyfulness and confidence, by a lofty tone and a courage certain of victory. Although, according to form, a defence, this speech is yet aggressive in the noblest sense; whereas the speech in chap. xxii. is peculiarly defensive. Da Costa strikingly characterizes this speech before Agrippa, as a truly kingly speech of the apostle before his kingly hearers in the opinion of the world; whereas his defence at Jerusalem was a speech of the love—humble, and exhorting to humility—of a sinner and of a

former zealot to fellow-sinners and blinded zealots.—In both speeches, the apostle apprehends Christianity in its unity with the old covenant; in both, his peculiar conversion to Christ and the appearance of Jesus on the way to Damascus, the cause of that conversion, form the centre-point of the discussion. Only, in his speech to the Jews, he lays peculiar stress on the communication of the legally pious Ananias at Damascus; but in his speech before Agrippa, he passes him over in silence, and relates as a revelation of Christ what the Lord had spoken to him through Ananias. This was the last public testimony which the apostle delivered in Palestine; and this was the most splendid worldly assembly which he ever had before him, for it embraced the then king over a part of Canaan, the governor under the Roman emperor, and a number of military and civil hearers—the principal people of the community.

DOGMATICAL AND ETHICAL THOUGHTS.

1. The apostle assumes the offensive against doubt (ver. 8). Instead of restricting himself to his defence, or, as his well-founded custom was, of testifying positively to the truth, and of directing his address to the conscience, he here quickly turns to attack the understanding along with all its doubts. He removes the war into the enemy's country, and questions doubt as to its reasons. He does not certainly enter minutely into the matter, but satisfies himself with a question which remains without an answer. But in this he shows to the apologists of Christianity a way which, according to circumstances, may be taken with success. For doubt and denial not unfrequently rest on mere prejudices, or on pretended axioms which, as soon as they are thoroughly examined into, will be found to have no ground to stand on.

2. The description of the operations of grace which Paul gives (ver. 18), is excellent. The design of the mission imparted to him was: 1. Enlightenment or communication of knowledge, both as regards sin and salvation. 2. Conversion; that is, the turning of the will from misery to divine aid, from darkness to light, from the power of Satan to God. The consequences of conversion are: 1. Forgiveness of sins, or justification; 2. the grant of an inheritance in glory. The means to receive forgiveness and the inheritance, the ὄργανον ληπτικὸν

(τοῦ λαβεῖν αὐτοὺς), is faith in Christ. Nothing more, but also nothing less. If we chiefly direct our attention to forgiveness, the proposition of justification by faith is here directly expressed. Yet it is to be observed, that only enlightenment is ascribed to the apostle as an act (ἀποστέλλω ἀνοῖξαι ὀφθαλμοὺς αὐτῶν), whereas conversion appears as an act of the hearers (ἐπιστρέψαι, intransitive). But there is thus something great which is referred to the human labour of a teacher: he is the organ of the redeeming grace of God.

3. The apostle in his speech, indirectly indeed, but yet clearly and impressively, bears testimony to the freedom of the will; in other words, to the resistibility of divine grace. This thought is contained in the passage just now discussed (ver. 18, compare ver. 20), inasmuch as conversion is represented chiefly as a personal act, as the act of the free will of individuals. But this truth is still more clearly seen in what Paul says of his own conversion. In asserting that he was not disobedient to the heavenly vision (οὐκ ἀπειθής), he indirectly indicates that it might have been possible not to comply with the divine will, but to resist it. This possibility of resistance is even included in the apparently contrary words, which the Redeemer speaks to him: "It is hard for thee to kick against the goads." For this proverbial expression by no means imports that it was absolutely impossible for Saul to resist the divine will, but only that he would be obliged to repent from bitter experience, if he did resist it. The brighter the light of the divine glory, the more humbling the exalted majesty, and the more powerful the fulness of might in which the exalted Redeemer appeared to Saul; so much the more gloriously shines the grace of God, which wooes a human soul with all respect for its personal freedom, and without any trace of force and violence, as it concerns only free love, willing obedience, and joyful surrender of spirit.

4. The threefold question respecting the Christology of the Old Testament is interesting. It is asked, first, whether or not the Messianic prophecy knows a suffering Messiah; *i.e.*, whether, according to the prophecies of the Old Testament, the Messiah is not only capable of suffering, but also subjected to suffering in the course of His work, or not. The latter was the usual Jewish idea. The first occurs, from the very outset, in the predictions of Jesus concerning His sufferings (Matt. xvi. 24, and other

places), and in His words after His resurrection (*e.g.*, Luke xxiv. 26, ἔδει παθεῖν τὸν Χριστόν, comp. ver. 46). Secondly, whether the Messiah will be the first of the resurrection from the dead. Here πρῶτος is not to be overlooked; for this word has only its full meaning when the idea is presupposed, as Paul himself has more fully developed it (1 Cor. xv. 20–23, 45–49; Rom. v. 17, 18), namely, that Christ is the second Adam, the beginning of a series of development of life and resurrection for mankind. This is a trait which is of importance for the Pauline authenticity of the apostle's speeches in the Acts. Thirdly, whether the Messiah, as the suffering and the risen One, was to announce salvation both to Israel and to the Gentiles. This idea strongly reminds us of the words of the risen Saviour in Luke xxiv. 47. At all events, the idea of the universality of Christianity is contained in it, and is founded, without doubt, as regards the Messianic prophecy, on a multitude of prophetical passages.

5. Paul protests against the reproach of madness and extravagance, by the assurance that he spoke the words of truth and soberness. The truth of divine revelation is authenticated by the correct measure and soberness of the form in which it is clothed; not truth without soberness, but also not soberness without truth. If we would make soberness and rationality the only and absolute measure of the truth, we would soon arbitrarily curtail and dilute the truth itself.

HOMILETICAL HINTS.

It is permitted thee to speak concerning thyself (ver. 1). It was permitted to the apostle to speak for himself. But he does not speak for himself, but for the glory of Jesus Christ. This is an important mark, by which the servants of Christ may be distinguished from false teachers. False teachers, in their public discourses, have no other object in view than to speak for themselves, to show their art, to make themselves popular. But a true John thinks: Christ must increase, but I must decrease, John iii. 30 (Apost. Past.).—*Then Paul, stretching forth his hand, defended himself.* Paul, in chains, raising up his hand for a joyful testimony of grace received by him, as a pattern to all (1 Tim. i. 16), opens the mouth of all preachers, and the ears of all hearers (Williger).—Paul, stretching forth his hand, approached the king, and aimed at his heart (Besser).

I esteem myself happy, king Agrippa (it greatly pleases me, Luther, ver. 2). Paul was delighted with this opportunity, and threw not away the confidence that something would be effected. A Christian does not depend on the result alone, but is content to do what God puts in his way (Rieger).—The apostle greatly rejoiced at the liberty granted to speak before king Agrippa. But in what consisted the reason of his joy? Not on account of the honour of speaking before a king; not in order to wreak his revenge, and to raise himself above his enemies; but because he had an opportunity publicly to testify, and solemnly to confirm, the truth of Jesus before Agrippa, to whom the circumstances of the Jewish nation, the promises made to the fathers, and the history of Christ were not unknown. It is seen from this, that it was not only Paul's chief refreshment to preach Christ on every opportunity, and that by this he sweetened his present imprisonment, but that he also availed himself gladly of all circumstances which might aid the diffusion and exaltation of the name of Jesus, and laboured to direct them to their proper end (Apost. Past.).

Therefore I pray thee to hear me patiently (ver. 3). The introduction as well as the whole speech: humble without servility, fearless without pride, powerful without passion and rancour, mild without laxity, prudent without art, simple yet not unskilful.

My manner of life, from my youth upwards, know all the Jews. After the strictest sect of our religion, I lived a Pharisee (vers. 4, 5). It has been observed above (chap. xxii. 3), that with a legally righteous life, and a fancied zeal for God, a man may continue an enemy of Jesus. But, on the other hand, we would oppose an observation to those who fancy that dissolute students may become the best ministers. Paul's example does not confirm this. Though he was, in his unbelief, an enemy of Christ; yet he was, according to his then knowledge, a friend of virtue, attached to the strictest sect, according to the law blameless. He had not sacrificed his youthful years and strength in carnal lusts to Satan. It cannot be believed that men of that description are so soon converted. Ordination does not change the heart, and a black coat does not convert (Apost. Past.).

And now I stand, and am judged concerning the hope of the promise (vers. 7, 8). The apostle so contemplates his former manner of serving God as a Pharisee, that he does not indeed conceal the evil zeal with which he was hurried along, but he also shows what good he was able to receive from it, namely, faith and the hope of the resurrection. On the other hand, the present rage of the Jews against the Gospel of Christ destroyed their ancestral religion, and they in reality rejected all the better additions received from the God of their fathers (Rieger).

Why should it be thought a thing incredible with you that God should raise the dead? (ver. 8.) A question of conscience addressed to all deniers of the resurrection, to lead them to consider the reason, or rather the want of reason, of their unbelief.

I indeed thought with myself that I ought to do many things contrary to the name of Jesus of Nazareth (ver. 9). Paul must have found a special blessing, when he represented his example as that of a great sinner pardoned by God, of a bloodthirsty persecutor, but now a joyful confessor of his Saviour. He has already done it in chap. xxii. Here again he refers to it a second time before Agrippa, and in 1 Tim. i. it occurs a third time. Little as he was accustomed to speak of and for himself, yet his discourse, when he comes to this matter, is copious. The blessed change which Jesus effected in his soul remained to him a constant miracle. He could never forget the grace which happened to him. He tells Jews and Gentiles, kings and princes, what God has wrought in him. And in 1 Tim. i. 16, he adds the reason why he so speaks: "for a pattern to them who should believe on Jesus to life everlasting." Happy is the teacher who not only with words, but also with his example, teaches and preaches, builds up and edifies (Apost. Past.).

At mid-day, I saw a light from heaven brighter than the sun (ver. 13). The first gleam of the light, the commencement of our conversion, is worthy of eternal remembrance and consideration, 2 Cor. iv. 6 (Starke).—If Christ's countenance shone as the sun when He was on earth, in a state of humiliation, how much brighter must it shine, now that He has entered upon His government in heaven! Rev. i. 16 (Starke).

But arise and stand on thy feet (ver. 15). The Lord kills and makes alive; the Lord bringeth down and raiseth up those who are bowed down (1 Sam. ii. 6; Ps. cxlvi. 8).—The three disciples heard this same evangelical exhortation from the Lord, when they were with Him on the holy mount, after the voice out of the cloud had cast them down upon their faces (Matt. xvii. 7). Saul arose, and continued standing in the strength of Jesus Christ until this day (Besser).

That I may ordain thee to be a minister and a witness, etc. (vers. 16–18). A glorious representation of a truly divine ordination to the ministry. Observe herein: 1. True ordination is a divine work. Prayer and the imposition of hands do not suffice to make of an unconverted worldly man a faithful witness of Jesus. The Lord must first internally heal, anoint, ordain; Jesus must impart strength to stand, to witness, and to minister. 2. Jesus does not ordain Paul to be an eminent bishop, and to a high spiritual station; but when He imparted to him the highest spiritual dignity of the apostleship, He ordained him to be a witness and a servant. He does not promise him comforts, honourable titles, and riches; but that he should bear witness, and be His servant amid labour, sweat, sufferings, martyrdom, and troubles: this is the apostleship, the highest dignity of the disciples of Jesus. How unlike the clergy of the present day to this ordained witness of Jesus! 3. Christ ordains Paul to be a witness not only of what he has seen, but of that also wherein He will appear to him. Thus a faithful witness of Jesus must always progress. The old experiences of the grace of Jesus must be renewed and enlivened by new and daily communications of His salvation, and by this our testimony must continue always fresh. 4. The Lord Jesus attaches to His ordination a safe-conduct, that He will protect and deliver Paul in his testimony and ministry. A faithful witness of Jesus may be assured, that where the Lord uses him, there He will and can protect him (Apost. Past.).—The Lord kept faithfully His word to His apostle. What He promised him at the outset and to what He ordained him, twenty-four years have now richly displayed, before many thousand persons saved, and before still more numerous enemies overcome (Besser).

To open their eyes, and to turn them from darkness to light; that they may receive forgiveness of sins, etc. (ver. 18). See here a complete plan and draught of the New Testament ministry. It aims at, in souls: 1. Enlightenment—"to open their eyes;" 2. Conversion—"that they may be converted;" 3. Pardon—"to receive forgiveness of sins;" 4. Glory—"and the inheritance among them who are sanctified;" 5. And the means to all this is faith—"by faith that is in Me."

Therefore, O king Agrippa, I was not disobedient (ver. 19). Not even Paul's conversion was irresistible (Bengel).—The apostle ascribes his obedience to the divinity of the appearance which happened to him; but especially, if we consider the proximate words, to the precious contents of the ministry conferred upon him. It is because there is conferred upon him, with such divine authority, a ministry so very precious, by which so many darkened souls were to be enlightened, and were to attain to the inheritance of the saints in light, that he has not been able to resist this heavenly call. Certainly, if all teachers diligently considered what honour and joy they might prepare for God in eternity, and what salvation for their own and others' souls, they would be more diligent, more faithful, and more obedient (Apost. Past.).

But showed first to them at Damascus, and at Jerusalem, etc. (ver. 20). Where we have given the greatest offence, there we must seek first of all to remove it (Starke).—The apostle brought forth such abundant fruits, because he applied himself to the work immediately after he had received the call. By delaying, strength is evaporated (Apost. Past.).—*That they should repent and turn to God.* Without repentance, Christ avails us nothing. But without Christ, true repentance is impossible. Only an evangelical sermon on repentance is of any real use (Apost. Past.).

On this account, the Jews caught me in the temple (ver. 21). If a teacher will have in his conscience the testimony to his fidelity before God, he must always be prepared to become a martyr for all Christian truths, but especially for the doctrines of repentance and conversion, and of works meet for repentance; on these points, he must suppress nothing in order to please men (Starke).

But through the help of God (Luther's version, ver. 22). This was the triumph of faith of a witness of Jesus, who shuns no work and no sufferings to be obedient to the call of his Lord. This was his glory amid the shame of his bonds. Who can imitate him in this? (Apost. Past.)—*I continue to this day witnessing, etc.* Paul rejoices that he continues to this day; but he adds the reason, namely, to witness. We justly thank God for every prolongation of our life, that it is yet continued to us in so many dangers and hardships. But the continuation of our life would be to us no blessing and no joy, if it were to be converted to anything else than to the active service of our Jesus (Apost. Past.).—*Saying none other things than what the prophets and Moses have said.* He showed to small and great, to high and low, the same plan of salvation. He taught nothing but what was revealed in the word of God. He preached Christ in His humiliation and exaltation. He had respect to Jews and Gentiles. A description of a faithful teacher, worthy of imitation in its entire compass (Apost. Past.).

That Christ should suffer, and that He should be the first of the resurrection, and should proclaim light to the Gentiles (ver. 23). These are the three chief points in the writings of the prophets: Christ's sufferings, and resurrection, and the publication of them among all nations. And it was precisely these three points that the Jews were most against: they were offended at the first, denied the second, and grudged the third (Starke).

Paul, thou ravest! (ver. 24, according to Luther.) The world esteems men to be prudent when they rave, and to be raving when they cease to rave and become prudent. So long as Paul raved and raged, he passed for a prudent and clever man; but when he recognised his madness and became a Christian, people esteemed him a fool. But one day the tables will be turned, so that the worldly will say of the righteous, "We fools counted his life madness; how is he now numbered among the children of God!" Wisdom v. 4, 5 (Lindhammer).—Thus the whole success which Paul attained was to be accounted mad. For that any one in his sound senses could believe such things, and venture his life on such a faith, this a worldly man does not comprehend. If he cannot accuse a disciple of Christ of hypocrisy, because he sees and feels that he is in earnest, he can only explain it on the supposition of a disordered mind. Yet Festus explains it still more exactly, "Much learning makes thee mad." Thus is it even in the present day. If it is granted to a preacher to wield the sword of the word, the world is not disinclined to recognise in him some talent; but then it thinks, He preaches the Gospel only in order to display his talents. And yet we are in truth no actors; and as little is it madness, when, in the name of the living God, we discourse of an eternity, of a Saviour, of a resurrection. These are words of truth and soberness, resting on the eternal truth of God, and proving their truth by the resistance of the human heart (Palmer).—How often does one in the present day hear this wisdom of Festus, to which the preaching of the Cross is foolishness! Childlike and simple faith in the whole revealed truth of Scripture is esteemed as old-fashioned stupidity; justification by faith in the merits of Christ is called the sanguinary theology of the heathens, etc. When one is in earnest with his Christianity and breaks with the world, he is pitied as an extravagant melancholic man, whose understanding overmuch reading of the Bible has deranged. They even blasphemed the gracious movement of the pentecostal Spirit as an intoxication of sweet wine; yea, they even said of Christ, "He is mad, and has a devil," John x. 20 (Leonh. and Spieg.).

I am not mad, most noble Festus (ver. 25). Paul did not abuse and revile Festus, but modestly represented to him the unreasonableness of his reproach, and referred him, partly to the publicity of the whole history of Jesus, which did not take place in a corner, and partly to the testimony and conscience of Agrippa. He opposed Festus with his rational joyfulness of faith, and taught, from the fulness of his divinely convinced and pardoned heart, that Christianity was no fable, and faith no madness. Such an example must faithful teachers present, both when they have to do with mockers of religion in society, and when they are called upon in their writings to testify against mockers and free-thinkers (Apost. Past.).—*I speak the words of truth and soberness* (I speak true and rational words, Luther). What he spoke was true: the manner, in which he spoke, was rational (Besser).

King Agrippa, believest thou the prophets? (ver. 27.) Paul, who studied psychology in the school of the Holy Ghost, immediately recognises the secret spark of a believing inclination to the word which begins to glimmer in the heart of Agrippa, and incited by his hope and love for the king of the Jews, he seizes on his heart and conscience with the bold inquiry, whether he might lead him by the prophecies of the prophets to Christ, the true King of Israel. Those are the true court preachers, who are not deterred by the star on the breast to inquire, whether the heavenly morning star also shines in the breast (Leonh. and Spieg.).

With a little, persuadest thou me! (Not much is wanting to persuade me, Luther, ver. 28.) With a little, persuadest thou me to be a Christian! As if he had said: Thou makest a short process with my conversion. Something more is necessary, methinks, to persuade a king of the Jews to become a Christian (Besser).—This indeed sounds as if spoken in mockery; but it was a jest showing that Agrippa was not easy at heart. He was touched, but yet as a statesman he wished to suppress his feelings. There are still plenty of such "almost Christians" in the present day. The world would fain be saved, were it not for Luke xiii. 24 (Starke).—How often have we also been near the kingdom of heaven! Almost we had pressed from darkness to light, from unbelief to faith, from sin to repentance, from anxiety to peace, from the world to God. The heart was touched, the mind enlightened, the will moved, the hour favourable, that hour of grace which might have decided our blessed eternity; not much was wanting. But the little that was wanting, we would not add: from one possession we would not tear ourselves, one sin we would not give up; a temptation presented itself, and the hour of grace was past; and the crown which we had already almost in our possession was again lost, and we were again at a distance from the Lord.

And Paul said, I would to God that not only thou, but all who hear me this day, were such as I am, with the exception of these bonds (ver. 29). To the light jest of Agrippa, Paul replies with deep and holy earnestness.—What painful sorrow and what zeal for the glory of God shine forth from these bold words! The spark of faith which flew out from Agrippa's answer, stirred up into a bright flame the fire of love which would fain see all saved. Paul assures even those standing at a distance, Felix and the other courtiers, on whom he may perhaps have cast a penetrating glance, of his intercessory love; and in a friendly and earnest manner he beseeches them not to allow the hour of grace to pass away (Leonh. and Spieg.).—What a variety of dispositions toward the Gospel of Christ did this assembly contain! Paul living wholly in the faith of the Son of God, Agrippa touched, Bernice indifferent, and Festus at a still greater distance. How gladly would Paul have brought them altogether to an enjoyment of the salvation which flowed in upon him from his faith! (Rieger.)—To Felix much was wanting, to Agrippa only a little. But Paul teaches that the grace of God can remove the much as well as the little that yet stands in the way of faith, and he testifies his ardent desire that both Festus and Agrippa, and all who hear him, might be led over all obstacles to grace, and be placed in fellowship with Christ. Thus a witness of Jesus is not perplexed in his courage to hope for conversion and grace, even among the most wicked mockers and the worst of men (Apost. Past.).

And when he said this, the king arose (ver. 30). The king was no longer able to hear Paul, always speaking the more boldly, the smile died on his lips, and he quickly put an end to the proceedings (Besser).—Faithful servants of Jesus are grieved, if they see no other use of their discourses than that the hearers say, The preacher is a good man, or he is a pious man, or he has preached well. But here it did not fare better with the apostle. When he had in such an earnest, joyful, and impressive manner witnessed of Jesus, and his heart was opened with such confidence in eager desire for the salvation of all his hearers, then the assembly arose, conversed together, and finally said: "This man is a good man." Should they not have learned much more, and much more important things, from his discourse? Thus is it with the world (Apost. Past.).

On the whole chapter.—The wonderful providential dispensations in the life of the Apostle Paul, vers. 1–18. 1. His conduct in Judaism, vers. 4, 5. 2. And now the enmity of the Jews against him, vers. 6–8. 3. His resistance to Jesus, vers. 9–12. 4. And now his miraculous conversion, vers. 13–18 (Lisco).—*The call of Paul.* 1. The Lord violently agitates the hardened disposition of His adversary, vers. 5–15. 2. He converts a broken adversary into a blessed servant, vers. 15–18 (Lisco).—*The faith of the converted must always be active, in a similar manner as with the Apostle Paul.* 1. By awakening the unconverted to repentance, vers. 19, 20. 2. By a stedfast testimony to Christ, vers. 21–23 (Lisco).—*The impressions of a Christian, when he surveys his life in the light of greater knowledge.* 1. The retrospect of the past period of sin. 2. The look to the grace which took away his sins. 3. The glance forward to the glorious termination, to which the renewed life tends (Lisco).—*How does the power of divine truth manifest itself in those who are lost?* 1. It draws them. The word acts upon them. *a.* A higher world, hitherto unsuspected, rises up before the worldly spirit, on which it looks with astonishment: Festus, "Paul, thou ravest," ver. 24. *b.* When the word of God meets with traces of the divine life, it fastens itself to them, and awakens recollections of a time when one still believed: "King Agrippa, believest thou? I know that thou believest," ver. 27. It stirs up the earlier love, in order to establish anew with its aid the shaken faith, vers. 26–28. It fills them with internal respect toward all true believers, vers. 29–32. 2. It repels them. They oppose themselves to the operations of the word. *a.* The earthly disposition is soon persuaded that inspiration for everything that is higher, is pious enthusiasm: Festus, ver. 24. *b.* The better motion and impulse are again suppressed in frivolity and indifference: Agrippa, vers. 28–32 (Lisco).—*Paul and Agrippa.* 1. Paul's holy zeal, and Agrippa's frivolous mockery. 2. Paul's joyful assurance of faith, and Agrippa's lamentable indecision. 2. Paul's apostolic fulness of love, and Agrippa's supercilious indifference (Leonh. and Spieg.).—*Paul's stretched-out arm in the princely hall at Cæsarea.* 1. A warning-signal for all the great of the earth: Attend to the things which belong to your peace, ver. 3. 2. A way-mark for all the erring: Jesus receiveth sinners, vers. 9–18. 3. A banner for all the preachers of the Gospel: Endure hardship, as good soldiers of Christ, vers. 21–27. 4. A rope of hope for all the lost: Be ye reconciled unto God, ver. 29.—*The value of an unblameable conduct from youth upward.* 1. Not to be overvalued, for therein the unconverted may walk on erroneous paths, vers. 9–11. 2. But also not to be undervalued, for thereby the converted may testify and labour so much the more powerfully, vers. 4, 5.—*Why is it incredible that God should raise the dead?* a question of conscience to all deniers of the resurrection. 1. Is it the pride of a limited understanding, which rejects what it cannot understand? 2. Is it the despondency of a faint heart, which will not credit the wonderful power of the Creator? 3. Is it the anguish of an evil conscience, which is afraid of eternity and of the judgment? —*Paul's conversion recorded the third time; or, the never-to-be-forgotten hours of grace of the children of God,* recorded: 1. For the eternal praise of the Lord: His wonderful power and love. 2. For wholesome remembrance for themselves: sins committed and grace received. 3. For a permanent memorial for the world: to rebuke them in their sins, and to call them to the way of salvation.—*The blessed work of the ministry to sinners,* ver. 18. 1. To open their eyes to the light of truth. 2. To turn their hearts from the works of darkness. 3. To comfort their conscience by the forgiveness of sins. 4. To sanctify their conduct for the inheritance of the saints in light.—*Paul, a model of a noble witness of God.* 1. Through whom, does he bear witness? Through the Lord, whose strength is perfected in his weakness: "through the help of the Lord I continue unto this day." 2. Before whom, does he bear witness? Before all who have ears to hear: "witnessing both to small and great;" "a light to the people and to the Gentiles." 3. Of whom, does he bear witness? Of Christ, who was promised and has appeared, who was crucified and is risen: "saying none other things than those which the prophets have said, that Christ should suffer, and that He should be the first that should rise from the dead." —*Paul, thou art mad! Much learning hath made thee mad:* an exhortation to self-examination for all preachers of the Gospel. 1. Whether no unbiblical extravagance mingles with their doctrine. 2. Whether no carnal passion mingles with their zeal. 3. Whether no unspiritual art mingles with their eloquence.—*Paul, thou art mad! the usual judgment of the worldly man on the men of God.* 1. By it he intends to bring them to naught, interpreting their childlike Christian faith as narrowness of spirit, their pious Christian life as melancholy, and their blessed Christian hope as enthusiasm. 2. But in reality the worldly man condemns himself, discovering by this his own poverty of spirit, which understands nothing of divine things; his hardness of heart, which puts no value on the admonitions of the Holy Spirit; and his spiritual misery, which feels nothing of the blessedness of the children of God.—*Who is mad? Paul or Festus? the Christian, or he who is not a Christian?* 1. Whether the Christian is mad, who founds his faith on the sure revelations of God in the word of Scripture, and in the experience of the heart; or he who is not a Christian, who blindly derides what he cannot handle with his hands and comprehend with his senses? 2. Whether the Christian is mad, who regulates his life according to the commands of God, and makes sure steps on the narrow path of holiness; or he who is not a Christian, who, the sport of his passions, staggers helplessly along the broad path which leads to destruction? 3. Whether the Christian is mad, who places his hope on an eternity which, amid all the changes of time, is ever before his eyes; or he who is not a Christian, who seeks his happiness in the present, which vanishes like a dream, and leaves nothing behind but a terrible awakening?—*Paul was right when he said, I speak true and rational words*, ver. 25. 1. Proved from the past history of the Church; for the words of Paul remain to this day, whereas the wit of Festus has long since died away. 2. Confirmed even now by the approbation of honest hearts, who have found in these words their clearest light, their best strength, and their sweetest comfort. 3. Placed in the light at the great day of eternity; for heaven and earth will pass away, but the word of God endureth for ever.—*King Agrippa, believest thou? an earnest question for all princely courts.* 1. To admonish princes and great men of their soul's salvation. 2. To admonish court preachers of their ministerial duty.—*Paul before the nobility of Cæsarea, a model of a genuine court preacher.* 1. Full of bold courage, and yet full of modest respect. 2. Full of fiery zeal, and yet full of delicate wisdom. 3. Full of holy earnestness, and yet full of tender love.—*Paul and his princely hearers; or the different attitudes of men toward the Christian truth.* 1. Festus, who turns entirely aside from it: "Paul, thou ravest." 2. Agrippa, who is half turned toward it: "Almost thou persuadest me." 3. Paul, who entirely lives in it: "I would to God that all who hear me were such as I am."—*When has the sermon actually produced fruit among us?* 1. When it has convinced, and not merely persuaded. 2. When it has actually won us, and not merely "almost." 3. When it has acted on all, and not merely on one.—*The dangerous word, "almost."* Dangerous: 1. Because it leads to the notion that it is easy to enter the kingdom of heaven; 2. Because it makes our account so much the heavier, if, not being far from the kingdom of God, we have not entered it.—*The curse of spiritual lukewarmness.* The lukewarm are: 1. An abomination to the Lord, for He will have a whole heart: "Because thou art lukewarm, I will spue thee out of My mouth;" 2. The contempt of the world, who make sport of them; 3. A torment to themselves, without support and comfort.—*The breaking up of the high nobility after the sermon of Paul.* 1. According to appearance, a gracious dismissal for the honest servant of the Lord. 2. But in reality, an orderly flight before the word of divine truth.

SECTION IV.

VOYAGE OF PAUL FROM CÆSAREA TO ROME (CHAP. XXVII. 1–XXVIII. 15).

A.

Voyage to Italy, with its dangers, but also with the care of the Lord over Paul and his companions. The shipwreck and the rescue at the island of Malta.

Chap. xxvii. 1–44.

1 And when it was determined that we should sail for Italy, they delivered Paul and certain other prisoners to a centurion named Julius, of the Augustan band. 2 We then embarked in a ship of Adramyttium, which was about to sail to the places in Asia, and set sail; Aristarchus, a Macedonian of Thessalonica, being with us. 3 And the next day, we landed at Sidon. And Julius behaved toward Paul courteously, and permitted him to go to the friends and to enjoy himself. 4 From that, we set sail, and sailed under Cyprus, because the winds were contrary. 5 Then we sailed over the sea along Cilicia and Pamphylia, and came to Myra in Lycia.

6 There the centurion found a ship of Alexandria sailing to Italy, and he embarked us in it. 7 But we sailed slowly many days, and came with difficulty to the neighbourhood of Cnidus; but as the wind did not suffer us to land, we sailed under Crete, over against Salmone. 8 And we passed it with difficulty, and came to a place which is called Fair Havens, not far from which was the city of Lasea.

9 Now when much time had elapsed, and the voyage was already dangerous, because the fast was now past, Paul admonished them, and said to them, 10 Sirs, I perceive that the voyage will turn out with hardship and great damage, not only of the lading and the ship, but also of our lives. 11 But the centurion believed the steersman and the shipowner more than the things which were spoken by Paul. 12 And because the haven was inconvenient to winter in, the majority resolved to sail from thence also, if they might perhaps reach Phenice, in order to winter there, a haven of Crete, lying toward the south-west and north-west.

13 And when the south wind blew softly, they thought to have attained their purpose; and they sailed from thence, and coasted close along Crete. 14 But not long after, there arose against the ship a tempestuous wind, called the north-east. 15 As now the ship was hurried on by it, and could not resist the wind, we gave it up, and were driven along. 16 And coming into the neighbourhood of a small island, called Clauda, we had much work to secure the boat. 17 And having taken it up, they used helps and under-

girded the ship. And fearing to fall on the sand-banks, they let down the
tackling, and thus were driven. 18 And as we suffered much from the
storm, the next day they cast the merchandise overboard. 19 And on the
third day, we cast out with our own hands the furniture of the ship.
20 And when for many days neither sun nor stars appeared, and no small
tempest was against us, all hope of the safety of our lives was taken away.
21 And when we had not eaten for a long time, Paul stood in the midst of
them and said, Sirs, ye should have yielded to me and not have sailed from
Crete, and so have saved yourselves this hardship and damage. 22 But
now I exhort you to be of good courage; for there will result no loss of any
life among you, but only of the ship. 23 For there stood by me this night
an angel of God, to whom I belong, and whom I serve, 24 Saying, Fear not,
Paul! Thou must stand before Cæsar; and, behold, God has given thee
all those who sail with thee. 25 Therefore, sirs, be of good courage, for I
believe God that it shall happen, as it was told me. 26 Yet we must be
stranded on an island.

27 And when the fourteenth night came, and we were driven up and
down in Adria, at midnight the sailors thought that land came near to
them. 28 And they cast the sounding lead, and found it twenty fathoms
deep; and after a little distance, they sounded again, and found it fifteen
fathoms. 29 Then fearing to be stranded on rocks, they cast out four
anchors at the stern of the ship, and wished for day. 30 But when the
sailors sought to escape from the ship, and had let down the boat into the
sea, on the pretext as though they would let down anchors from the bow;
31 Paul said to the centurion and to the soldiers, If these do not remain in
the ship, ye cannot be saved. 32 Then the soldiers cut away the ropes from
the boat, and let it fall down. 33 But as the day began to dawn, Paul
exhorted them all to take nourishment, saying, It is now the fourteenth
day that ye have waited and continued fasting, and have taken nothing.
34 Therefore I exhort you to take food; for it is necessary for your preser-
vation; for there will not a hair perish from the head of any one of you.
35 When he had said this, he took bread, and thanked God in the pre-
sence of them all; and broke it, and began to eat. 36 Then were they all
of good courage, and likewise took food. 37 And we were in the ship
altogether two hundred and seventy-six souls. 38 And after they had
eaten enough, they lightened the ship, and cast the corn into the sea. 39 But
when it was day, they knew not the land; but they discovered a creek with
a beach, into which they resolved, if it were possible, to drive the ship.
40 So they cut away the anchors and let them fall into the sea: also they
loosened the rudder-bands, and drew up the foresail to the wind, and made
for the beach. 41 But falling into a place which had the sea on both sides,
they ran the ship aground, and the fore part remained fixed, but the hinder
part was broken with violence. 42 But the soldiers formed the resolution
to kill the prisoners, that none might escape by swimming. 43 But the
centurion wished to save Paul, and kept them from their purpose, and com-
manded those who could swim to cast themselves first into the water and
get to land; 44 And the rest, partly on boards, and partly on pieces of the
ship. And thus it came to pass, that they all came safe to land.

Ver. 2. The dative singular μέλλοντι, which the Alexandrian and Vatican MSS., 20 cursive MSS., and several versions have, is to be preferred to the plural μέλλοντες (a correction to suit ἐπιβάντες), which is only found in the two youngest uncial MSS.

Ver. 12. Κἀκεῖθεν is, indeed, only attested by one uncial MS., while three uncial MSS. have ἐκεῖθεν. But the καί in composition was probably omitted, because its reference was not perceived.

Ver. 19. Tischendorf has with justice preferred ἐῤῥίψαμεν in the textus receptus, which is attested by two uncial MSS., to the reading ἐῤῥιψαν, approved by Lachmann, which is found in three uncial MSS., as αὐτόχειρες is in favour of the former reading.

Ver. 34. Μεταλαβεῖν is more strongly attested than προσλαβεῖν.—Ὑμετέρας according to external authorities is to be preferred to ἡμετέρας, a correction, because, as all were to be rescued, it was thought that the inclusive form of speech would be used.—Ἀπολεῖται has the three first uncial MSS. for it, A.B.C.; whilst πεσεῖται has only the two youngest MSS. G.H.

Ver. 41. Τῶν κυμάτων is wanting in the Alexandrine and Vatican MSS., and seems to have been added as an explanation of τῇ βίᾳ.

EXEGETICAL EXPLANATIONS.

1. *But when it was resolved.*—The resolution, which was now adopted, referred not to the purpose, but to the manner and time, of the journey to Italy, namely, that it should be made by sea, and immediately. It was now late in the harvest of the year 60 after Christ. By ἡμᾶς the historian indicates, along with Paul, himself and the Macedonian Christian, Aristarchus of Thessalonica (see chap. xix. 29, xx. 4), who voluntarily accompanied the apostle. Here, for the first time since the arrival at Jerusalem (chap. xxi. 15–18), the inclusive form of narrative occurs, which is continued until the arrival at Rome. *Τοῦ ἀποπλεῖν* is grammatically remarkable, the subject of the resolution being treated as the design. In carrying out this resolution, Paul and his voluntary companions, along with other prisoners to be transported (τινας ἑτέρους, certain of another sort), were officially delivered up to a centurion named Julius, so that he might become responsible for their transport. The *cohors Augusta*, of which Julius was a centurion, has been explained in various ways. Kuinoel, after Schwarz, *De cohorte Ital. et Aug.* 1720, supposes that a cohort of soldiers from Sebaste (Samaria) was meant; but this supposition has many reasons against it. Wieseler (Apos. Chron. p. 389) conjectures that Julius belonged to the imperial body-guard of Nero (*cohors*

Augustanorum), and that about this time he was sent on some occasion to the East, and that Festus made use of his return in order to transport the prisoners under his care. But, according to this passage, we are obliged to suppose that the centurion as well as the cohort were stationed at Cæsarea, and subject to Festus. There remains an obscurity about this name, which cannot be cleared up by arbitrary conjectures.

2. *We embarked in a vessel.*—The prisoners, with a guard of Roman soldiers to keep them, were embarked at Cæsarea in an Asiatic trading vessel which was from Adramyttium, a sea-port not far from Troas and Assos, in the country of Mysia, opposite the island of Lesbos. The ship was homeward bound, and was yet to visit several sea-ports along the coast of proconsular Asia. The object in view was to change the ship in one of the ports of Asia Minor, and to get an opportunity of sailing to Italy, which might be calculated upon with certainty. The nautical and topographical incidents of this voyage have been illustrated, in a manner worthy of all praise, by a learned Englishman, James Smith of Jordanhill, in his work entitled, "The Voyage and Shipwreck of St Paul," London 1848, 2d edition, 1856. This gentleman employed a winter's residence in Malta for the purpose of examining accurately the localities, consulted with skilful and educated seamen concerning the navigation of the Levant, ransacked modern nautical books and descriptions of sea voyages, and especially studied the ship-building and nautical knowledge of the ancients by means of all the documents and aids at his command, in order to cast as much light as possible on the narrative of the Acts of the Apostles. The result was, that he has in fact cleared up much that was formerly obscure, and has also in a remarkable manner established the historical truth and credibility of the Acts. In particular, he has in many places shown in the clearest manner, that the author of the narrative of the voyage could not be himself a sailor, as his language on nautical matters is not that of a professional man; and also still more certainly, both from the narrative of the proceedings in the ship itself and from the geographical details interwoven with it, that he must have been an eye-witness, inasmuch as a man, who was professionally unacquainted with nautical knowledge, could not possibly have composed a description of a sea voyage so consistent in all its

parts, unless he described it from his own experience and actual observation.

3. *And the next day we landed at Sidon.*—If they reached Sidon the day after they sailed from Cæsarea, the wind must have been favourable, as the distance amounts to about fifteen geographical (German) miles. In that part of the Mediterranean west winds generally blow, and such a wind was favourable for this direction. The kind treatment on the part of the centurion might arise in the first instance from an order of the procurator, while, however, the person of Paul certainly made a favourable impression on every unprejudiced and educated man. The putting in of the ship at Sidon was doubtless for the purposes of trade; and thus in the interval Paul was permitted to visit the Christians in that city,—in company, of course, with a guard.

4. *Sailed under Cyprus.*—On account of the contrary winds, they sailed from Sidon under Cyprus; that is to say, instead of sailing in the open sea, they sailed to leeward. Expositors, however, have hitherto been at variance as to what side of the island of Cyprus they sailed by. Some, as, for example, Falconer and Meyer, think that they left Cyprus on their right, and sailed along the south side of the island; but Erasmus, Wetstein, and Bengel suppose that they left Cyprus on their left. The latter opinion is undoubtedly correct; for ver. 5 imports that they sailed through the sea of Cilicia and Pamphylia; and thus they must have taken the course at first between Syria and the east coast of Cyprus, and then between the coasts of Cilicia and Pamphylia on the one side, and the north coast of Cyprus on the other (Smith, 2d edition, pp. 64–68). Myra, where they landed, was at that time a flourishing port of Lycia, distant, according to Strabo, 20 stadia from the sea, but on a river navigable to the city.

5. *There the centurion found a ship.*—At Myra the centurion Julius and his military company embarked along with the prisoners in a merchant ship, which came from Alexandria, and was on a voyage to Italy. According to ver. 38, the freight consisted of wheat; and Egypt was at that time the granary of Italy. Corn was then usually shipped from Egypt to Italy in vessels of great size: according to a passage in Lucian, they could not have been inferior in size to the largest merchant ships

of modern times. By this is explained that no less than 276 persons were on board, ver. 37.

6. The first part of the voyage was from Cæsarea to Myra, vers. 1–5; the second part was from Myra to Crete, vers. 6–8. Here the voyage proceeded slowly by reason of contrary winds: that it was not a mere calm which occasioned the delay, Smith infers from *μόλις*, which supposes a struggle with the wind. Moreover *μὴ—ἀνέμου* appears to be the explanation of *μόλις γενόμενοι κατὰ τὴν Κνίδον*. The distance between Myra and Cnidus, a peninsula between Cos and Rhodes, was not too far, but that it might have been accomplished with a fair wind in one day. From Cnidus to Italy the voyage should properly have taken a south-western direction, so that they would pass by the northern side of Crete. But, on account of the continuing contrary wind, they chose another course, namely, to the south-south-west, to the eastern coast of Crete, where Cape Salmone forms the eastern extremity. From this the voyage proceeded along the south coast of the island, in a constant struggle with wind and waves (*μόλις*), to a place called "Fair Havens," not far from the city Lasea. On the south coast of Crete, as Smith (pp. 80–82) has pointed out, there is a bay which now bears the name *λιμένες καλοί*, in which a ship is sheltered from the north-west wind.

7. *Paul admonished them.*—Here a crisis took place. The favourable time for the voyage was over, for the fast—namely, the festival of the atonement (*νηστεία*)—was already past, so that it was after the autumnal equinox. Paul therefore warned them not to continue the voyage, but to winter here, in view of the danger pressing upon them, if they did not. The construction is loose, *ὅτι—μέλλειν ἔσεσθαι*. Meyer and Ewald take *ὕβρις* in a moral sense, "presumption;" but then the word must also be so taken in ver. 21, where it is likewise united with *ζημία*, which would be inappropriate in that connection. Accordingly, it must be taken, in accordance with the usual explanation, in a natural sense: "the violence of the tempest," "hardship." Paul here speaks from intelligent observation and reflection; it is only at a later period that he speaks in consequence of divine revelation. The event justified his fears, only all their lives were saved. The centurion, however, put more stress on the opinion of the steersman and shipowner than on the advice of Paul, and naturally, because they were professional

men. Also the reason, which they gave against wintering in that place, was not to be rejected: the bay was inconvenient to winter in; for ἀνευθέτου—παραχειμασίαν, ver. 12, evidently contains the reason of the opinion opposed to Paul's advice. They agreed with Paul so far that they should not sail to Italy; only the majority of those who had a voice in the matter (*οἱ πλείους*) were for choosing a more favourable place for wintering, namely, Phenice, a haven situated on the south-west of Crete, provided they could reach it. Luke describes this haven as directed towards *Λίψ* and *Χῶρος*. This is generally understood of the two coasts of the haven, that the one ran toward the south-west and the other toward the north-west. Smith (2d Ed. pp. 84–89), on the contrary, in order to identify the haven with the modern Lutro, supposes that *κατὰ Λίβα καὶ κατὰ Χῶρον* denotes the direction toward which these winds blew; thus the north-east and the south-east. But this does violence to the usage of the Greek, and that to suit a mere hypothesis.—See Hackett's Commentary.

8. *And when the south wind blew softly.*—Vers. 13–44 describe the voyage from Crete to Malta, which closed with the shipwreck. A soft south wind began to blow (*ὑποπνεύ.*, used for a gentle breeze). This was supposed to be favourable for their purpose, because not far from the Fair Havens the coast of Crete at Cape Matala turns to the north-west, and for a voyage in that direction the south wind was a fair wind. Wherefore they took up the anchors (*αἴρειν*, used nautically without *τὰς ἀγκύρας*). *Ἆσσον* was formerly regarded as a city of Crete, and, united to *ἄραντες*, was considered as the place from which they sailed, or as the direction in which they moved. But it is the comparative of *ἐγγύς*, "nearer," *scilicet* than usual: thus very near to the coast.

9. *But not long after.*—*Ἔβαλε*, cast itself. Luther referred *κατ' αὐτῆς* to *προθέσεως*, ver. 13; Meyer referred it to *Κρήτην*; but it is most suitable to the connection to take *ναῦς* as the subject, although the word is not here expressly named. *Τυφωνικός*, from *τυφών*, a whirlwind, a hurricane. *Εὐρακύλων*, compounded of Eurus and Aquilo, is the north-east. This reading is to be preferred to *εὐροκλύδων*. *Τυφωνικός* marks the wind according to its strength; *εὐρακύλων* according to its direction; for only a north-east wind could produce the effects which follow. The

wind veered round against them. Ἀντοφθαλμεῖν is to look a person in the face, to make head against, to strive against. Ἐπιδόντες scil. τὸ πλοῖον.

10. *But we came to an island.*—Ὑποτρέχειν is, as Smith remarks (2d Ed. p. 100, Note), a striking nautical term, which is here entirely appropriate. It expresses, first, that the ship had the wind behind it; and secondly, that it had the wind between itself and the island, hence that it passed to the south-east of the island. Clauda or Claudos (Ptolemy) is the modern Gozzo. At this place they attempted to bring on board the life-boat, with which the ship was provided, in order to save themselves in an extremity, because otherwise it might be torn away, and be lost by the violence of the wind and waves. Having with difficulty accomplished this (Luke does not explain wherein the difficulty consisted), they considered it indispensably necessary to undergird the ship, in order to prevent it from being broken up. This took place by means of βοήθειαι, such helps as cables, chains, and the like, by which they undergirded the keel of the ship, in order to hold it together as firmly as possible. In mechanics, the ancients understood by βοήθειαι "supports."

11. *And fearing to fall on the sand-banks.*—They feared to be driven (ἐκπέσωσι, out from the open sea against the land or rocks) on the Syrtis, *i.e.*, the *Syrtis Major*, a dangerous shallow with rocks on the African coast, between Tripoli and Barca. They feared this, because the north-east wind blew directly toward that quarter. The lesser Syrtis lay farther to the west, and cannot be here thought on; but the danger was imminent of being driven upon the greater Syrtis. There is therefore no reason to understand Σύρτιν as designating a sand-bank generally, especially as it has the definite article. In order to avoid this danger, they let down the tackling. Τὸ σκεῦος (ver. 17) here, according to the context, is intended to denote the sails which were furled up, in order not to allow too much power to the storm. Accordingly οὕτως ἐφέροντο means that the ship was allowed to be driven without sails. But the expression here is exactly of that kind that an historian with a knowledge of the sea would have certainly made more specific, if he had mentioned the circumstance at all. Smith understands the words, certainly more from an *a priori* consideration as to what was requisite to be done in the circumstances than from

the sense of the words themselves, of "lowering the gear," hoisting up the storm-sail, and tacking (2d. Ed. pp. 108, 109). These were (vers. 13-17) the incidents of the first day after their departure from the Fair Havens.

12. *And as we suffered much from the storm.*—On the following day, much was cast overboard, probably the heaviest and the most superfluous articles of the cargo. On the third day, they were obliged to proceed further, and to cast out the furniture of the ship, as tables, presses, etc. Now the passengers themselves must also give a hand (*αὐτόχειρες*).

13. *And when for many days neither sun nor stars appeared.*—Now followed the most terrible period. For eleven days the voyagers were in imminent danger of their lives; indeed, from the continuance of the storm, they gave up all hope of being saved, as for many days and nights no light appeared, and especially as the ship had already suffered much damage. The *πολλὴ ἀσιτία* (ver. 21), *i.e.*, the long-continued and strict abstinence from regular meals, could not be occasioned from actual want of provisions, as the ship's cargo consisted of wheat, and as this was still undamaged. But partly the impossibility of properly cooking food, and partly the constant exertions and the mental distress arising from fear and despair, prevented them from coming to meals.

14. *And when we had not eaten for a long time.*—During this most dismal period (how long before the catastrophe itself is not indicated), Paul encouraged the whole company, and promised all of them deliverance on the authority of a divine revelation, vers. 21–26. When, however, he commences with the statement that they ought to have followed his advice, he does this not from positiveness; but he only wishes to found his claim to the faith and confidence which they ought to bestow on him, by reminding them how much the result had as yet confirmed the advice which he then gave to them. He uses *κερδαίνειν*, as it frequently occurs from Aristotle to the later classics, which does not positively consist in obtaining an advantage, but negatively in the avoidance of an injury and of a loss which is spared; and for this reason *ὕβρις* is not to be understood, as Meyer and Ewald understand it, in a moral sense (presumption). In ver. 22 the construction is, For there will be no loss of life to any of you, except of the ship. *Πλήν* inaccurately used for

πλὴν μόνου. This night, *i.e.*, the preceding night, for Paul made this speech to the company in the day-time. *Οὗ εἰμί*, whose property I am; *ᾧ λατρεύω*, to whom I offer my worship: this referred to acts of prayer, of which the people in the ship may now and then have been witnesses. The appearance is not to be considered as a vision in a dream (Ewald), but as a vision when awake. Though the promise (chap. xxiii. 11) is dwelt on, which referred more especially to the person of Cæsar, yet the assurance of the safety of Paul's own life is contained therein. *Κεχάρισται*, etc., promises not only generally the safety of all his fellow-travellers, but specially their safety for Paul's sake, God having promised it as a favour to the apostle. Without doubt, Paul in his prayers (λατρεύω) had prayed not only for himself, but for all; and now God has heard his petitions. *Δέ*, ver. 26; they were indeed to escape with their lives, but they were to suffer much. That they were to be cast on an island, appears to have been a part of the vision; but when and where, Paul did not know.

15. *But when the fourteenth night came.*—The reckoning proceeds from the bay in Crete. Adria was certainly understood in ancient times in the narrow sense, what is now called the Adriatic Sea, namely, the gulf north of the Straits of Otranto; but frequently, and so here, the Adriatic Sea including the Ionic Sea; so that the sea east of Lower Italy and Sicily, in which Malta is, belonged to it. The supposition of the sailors, that land was in the neighbourhood, is expressed by *ὑπενόουν*, *suspiciebant*, because they justly apprehended danger from this. *Προσάγειν—χώραν*, according to the optical delusion; as, conversely, *terræque urbesque recedunt.* Luke does not give the reason on which the supposition was founded; but it doubtless consisted in the increased sound of the breakers. Smith (pp. 118, 119) refers to a remarkably similar instance, in which the British frigate "Lively" foundered, on 10th August 1810, in the same region of Malta as the ship here, not far from the point of Koura. He has from the Acts of the Admiralty related the remarkably analogous incidents in the English frigate, as given in evidence at the court-martial held on its officers.—In order to convince themselves of the reason or want of reason of their fears, they sounded, and found at first a depth of 20 fathoms = 120 feet, and a little distance farther on only 15 fathoms = 90

feet. Such a rapid decrease of depth caused them to fear lest they should fall upon rocks (τραχεῖς τόπους).

16. *They cast out four anchors.*—The design of anchoring was twofold: first, to keep the ship from foundering on a reef; and secondly, to wait for day, in order to cause the ship to strand on as favourable a spot as possible. They let down no less than four anchors, for the ancient ships had no such colossal anchors as modern vessels have. The reason why they cast the anchors out at the stern, was because the ship, if the anchors had been cast out at the bow, would have been an easier prey to the north-east wind which still blew, and would have been more badly wrecked. An English writer, Howson, mentions that Nelson anchored astern before Copenhagen in April 1801, greatly to the advantage of the fleet, and that he had that morning read the 27th chapter of the Acts, which had suggested to him that measure.

17. *Sought to escape out of the ship.*—The sailors doubtless considered the ship to be in such a woful plight, that they feared it would not last the night. They also feared that the coast might be of such a nature, that the ship might not be able to strand with any fortunate result. Therefore they endeavoured to escape in the life-boat, and would have left the ship and its company to their fate. The boat had been brought on board (vers. 16, 17); and now they let it down, on pretext of casting anchors also from the bow.

18. *If these do not remain in the ship.*—Paul frustrated this faithless and treacherous design by communicating it to the Roman commander. The soldiers were naturally ignorant of the management of the ship, and if all the sailors were away, would not have known how to assist. They therefore cut the rope by which the boat was yet attached, and resigned it to the waves.

19. *But when the day began to dawn.*—Ἄχρι, *i.e.*, before it was day; thus before they could go to work, and set about their rescue. And now, in order that every one might collect his strength, and be strengthened for the endurance of the exertions to be expected in order to reach the shore, Paul exhorted them all, by word and deed, to take a full meal. He himself showed the example, after he had, in the presence of them all, given thanks.

20. *And after they had eaten enough.*—Now they set about to

adopt measures for rescue. First, the corn was cast overboard, in order to lighten the ship (ver. 38). Meyer thinks that only the ship's provisions are here intended; but these did not consist wholly of corn, but of biscuits and other articles of food, and were doubtless already so diminished, that their weight would be too inconsiderable to be of any consequence for the design in question. They wished to put the ship in a position to get as near the shore as possible before it struck. The corn then must have formed the chief cargo; and this is the more probable, as the ship sailed from Alexandria to Italy, and the chief export from Egypt consisted of corn. This view, that ὁ σῖτος was the cargo of the ship, has been held by Erasmus, Luther, Beza, and recently by James Smith, Hackett, and Baumgarten. In particular, the American commentator, Hackett mentions an ingenious observation of Blunt, that many notices occurring incidentally in various parts of the chapter, when brought together, illustrate this circumstance. In ver. 6, we are informed that the ship was from Alexandria, and sailed to Italy; from ver. 10, we learn that it was a merchant vessel, and had a freight (τὸ φορτίον), without being told in what the freight consisted; and, finally, from ver. 38, it appears that the cargo consisted of corn. They naturally tried to save the freight as long as possible.

21. *But when it was day.*—The sailors did not recognise the land when it became visible, although Malta might be well known to Egyptian sailors; because they were at a part of the island which was distant from the best known havens. Smith has proved, beyond all doubt, that this shipwreck must have occurred on that spot which the tradition of the Maltese denotes as St Paul's Bay. It lies in the north-east corner of the island, and forms a tolerably deep indentation into the land, between two beaches, of which that to the south-east ends with the point of Koura, and that to the north-east terminates in the little island of Salmonetta. The bay, we are informed, had an αἰγιαλός, *i.e.*, a flat beach; ἀκτή, on the other hand, is a coast considerably elevated above the sea-margin. Thus Luke here uses a hydrographical term perfectly correct (Smith, p. 136, Note). The shores of this bay consist of a series of rocks; only two flat places lie between them. The sailors chose one of these two, in order, if possible, to push the ship upon it (ἐξωθεῖν, *ejicere navem*).

22. *So they cut away the anchors.*—In order to set the ship in motion, they let the anchors fall into the sea, for they had not time to draw them up. They also loosed the rudder-bands. Ancient ships had in general two helms, one on each side of the stern, which they called the right and the left helm. While the ship lay still, they drew up the helms from the water, and fastened them to the ship; but now they loosened them, to use them in driving the ship ashore. Moreover, they stretched out a sail τῇ πνεούσῃ, scil. αὔρᾳ, to the wind. Ὁ ἀρτέμων (ver. 40) is not known as a Greek expression, but occurs in the Latin as *artemo*, and is here very differently explained. According to Smith, it is the foresail, *i.e.*, the sail nearest the prow. After these preparations were made, they steered the ship to the flat beach (κατεῖχον εἰς τὸν αἰγιαλόν).

23. *But falling into a place which had the sea on both sides.*—Τόπος διθάλασσος was a place where the sea flowed on both sides. Smith supposes a place in the neighbourhood of the island of Salmonetta, which is separated from Malta by a small channel 100 yards broad, so that there would be a flowing of the sea inside and outside of St Paul's Bay. Here the ship suddenly struck, so that the fore part was held fast in the sand or mud, while the hinder part was broken by the violence of the breakers.

24. *The soldiers formed the resolution to kill the prisoners.*—This proposal arose from the guards being answerable, under the severest penalties, to suffer none to escape (compare chap. xii. 19). The centurion, however, frustrated this cruel design. He commanded that those who could swim should first swim ashore, in order possibly to come to the assistance of the rest. These last made use partly of σανίδας, deals and boards, which were in the ship, and partly of pieces of the ship itself, as planks and the like, which could be loosened or torn away, that they might climb up upon them, and let themselves be washed ashore by the waves.

DOGMATICAL AND ETHICAL THOUGHTS.

1. Paul in this voyage appears in every respect so venerable, that in his person the glory of Christ, by whose grace he was what he was, shines forth before us. The divine-human person of the Redeemer manifests itself in His apostle. As the

eternal Son of God through His incarnation appropriated to Himself everything that is human, with the single exception of sin, in order that He *nihil humani a se alienum putaret*, and as He descended into the lowest depths of human sorrow; so the apostle here faithfully follows His footsteps. He not only shares in all the dangers, necessities, and hardships of the voyage, which he could not avoid; but he does so with his whole soul. The welfare of his fellow-voyagers, the safety of the ship, yea, even the freight which it carries, lie as anxiously on his heart, as if he had nothing higher to care for. He observes all that goes on so carefully (and with him his friend Luke, who was thus qualified to give such an exact and faithful account), and deliberates so soberly and rationally, that he can impart the most rational advice; and, even before the last catastrophe, by prudent warning and opportune encouragement, along with his own example, he contributes to the rescue. Thus his sympathy, presence of mind, deliberation, and resolution are not only in themselves worthy of all acknowledgment, but especially in a child of God are a proof of genuine human virtue and excellence.—But, on the other hand, Paul, in this position, is also evidently more than a mere model of human ability: he is a redeemed servant of the God-man. He acknowledges himself unreservedly to be the property of God, when he is enabled by the angelic appearance to prophesy safety in the most desperate circumstances. And this promise (on account of which he will not be put to shame) he repeats, whenever an occasion presents itself. But the chief matter is, that God promises the safety of all that are in the ship for the sake of the apostle, and fulfils the promise (*κεχάρισταί σοι*, ver. 24). They have to thank Paul for their lives, or rather the grace of God in Christ which was directed to him.

2. The concluding remark of the historian (ver. 44) reads simply and without pretension, but is nevertheless of vast significance. Not only does it pictorially round off the history of the voyage from Cæsarea to Malta, as an inclusive whole; but it also points back to vers. 21–24, especially vers. 22, 24. Luke unites the fortunate issue to the preceding hope, expressed by Paul in the midst of extreme danger, on the authority of divine revelation. The concluding clause is thus that member in the chain which unites the fulfilment with the promise itself, and

points to that promise as actually fulfilled and completely verified. The simple concluding sentence causes us to recognise the invisible in the visible, the eternal counsel of God in the final result, the secret in what is manifested, grace in nature.

HOMILETICAL HINTS.

But when it was determined that we should sail to Italy (ver. 1). The path of believers certainly appears often abandoned to the fluctuating course of the world, and to be subject to the caprice and determinations of others; but it is yet purely the fulfilment of the promises of God (Rieger).—Why has God caused these external circumstances of this voyage to be inserted in revelation? 1. To teach us that even the strangest and roughest paths of believers are under the most exact direction and providence of God; and to show how times, seasons, places, company, the weather, and all the elements, prosperity and adversity, are adjusted by God, and directed to the good of believers. 2. To warn us that when things at first appear somewhat confused, we are not to despond, but to believe in spite of all difficulties. 3. The Holy Ghost, in this section, displays to us the godly character of a servant of Christ, who even in the greatest dangers, among the wildest and roughest people, and in the most perplexing circumstances, remains true to himself and to his Lord: "as chastened, yet not killed; as sorrowful, yet alway rejoicing; as poor, yet making many rich; as having nothing, and yet possessing all things," 2 Cor. vi. 9, 10 (Apost. Past.).—Earth and water are full of the Spirit of the Lord; why should He not also have moved on these waters and on this voyage? Thus the wonderful works in nature form one system with the wonders in the kingdom of grace. The compass in this voyage points to the work of God (Starke).

And there was with us Aristarchus (ver. 2). God knows to alleviate our cross, as He did Paul's imprisonment, by yet another good companion, besides the faithful Luke (Starke).—Aristarchus gave himself voluntarily, as a companion of the suffering apostle. This brotherly taking up of the cross was in the eyes of the Spirit of God so precious, that He causes it to be recorded for our example (Apost. Past.).

And Julius behaved toward Paul courteously, and permitted him to go to his friends (ver. 3). God, who comforts the lowly, not only furnished to His servant a precious help in a believing companion (Aristarchus), but also by inclining a man of the world (Julius) to friendly behaviour (Rieger).

And they sailed under Cyprus (ver. 4). How strangely must Paul, now at the close of his missionary course, have contemplated this island, in which he had gathered the first-fruits of his harvest! chap. xiii. 4 (Williger).

And they sailed through the sea, along Cilicia and Pamphylia (ver. 5). Thus God conducts His people by devious paths, and brings them to the port by contrary winds.

But we sailed slowly many days (ver. 7). As on board ship, one has not always a favourable wind, and does not always proceed quickly forward, so the Christian in his journey through life is often required to wait.

Nigh whereunto was the city of Lasea (ver. 8). On this voyage, every place otherwise forgotten is important, because Paul, the elect of the Lord, was on board. There were brought before him many known and unknown lands, places, and cities; and how may he not have visited in spirit every place, however insignificant, and greeted it with the salutation, "In the name of the Lord!" (Williger.)

Now when much time had elapsed, and the voyage was already dangerous, Paul admonished them (ver. 9). God often imparts to His people enlightened views and good counsels in temporal matters, so that, if complied with, all would go well (Starke).—Say not that the servants of God are useless in the world. That is certainly not their chief business, but "godliness is profitable unto all things." The pious Joseph was employed by God to preserve by his wise counsel all Egypt and Canaan in the time of famine. But a servant of the Lord, if his counsel is not taken, does not obstinately persevere, but lets God rule (Apost. Past.).—Paul, in his Christian disposition, showed himself watchful and solicitous about warding off bodily danger and temporal damage; and in this he teaches us, that a Christian is not rash, and does not squander even temporal things, for he considers well: "My body and soul, and whatever I possess in this poor life, are Thy gift, O Lord" (Rieger).

But the centurion believed the steersman and the shipowner more than Paul (ver. 11). How the sailors might have boasted and bragged after the manner of seamen, and have laughed at the gloomy Paul and his fears! (Williger.)—In the matter of advice, we are not to regard the appearance of the adviser, but whether or not his advice is well founded. How often in this, has a plain, simple man surpassed the wisest! 2 Kings v. 3 (Starke).

Because the haven was inconvenient to winter in, the majority resolved (ver. 12). It is a bad rule, that we must not weigh voices, but count them. For often the majority are the worst, 1 Kings xxii. 12, 13 (Starke).—To men, something is often not sufficiently convenient: they seek something more convenient, but in doing so, they fall into yet greater inconvenience—from the drop into the shower (Starke).

And when the south wind blew softly, they thought to have attained their purpose (ver. 13). Then would the sailors exultingly exclaim, How gloriously it goes! What do the devout know about sailing? They should not meddle with such matters (Starke).

But not long after, there arose a tempestuous wind (Luther: a hurricane, ver. 14). Boast not thyself of the morrow: think not, because thou hast a fair wind, it will be always so; for thou knowest not what a day may bring forth; whether a hurricane may not follow a fair south wind, Prov. xxvii. 1 (Starke).

And when the ship was hurried on by it (ver. 15). How often does it happen to a believing soul, as to this ship, that it cannot withstand the wind of opposition! It must indeed succumb to it, if Jesus comes not to its assistance, Isa. xxxii. 2 (Starke).—Paul, in this memorable voyage to Rome, became a sailor to the sailors from love which accommodates itself at all times, and to all. The centurion Julius could inform the governor Festus, that much learning had not made Paul mad (Besser).

They cast the wares overboard (ver. 18). How vain and fleeting are human treasures! A conflagration or a flood may arise, by which, before we are aware, all things may go to ruin (Starke).—For the preservation of his temporal life, a man must often cast from him what otherwise he holds dear; but who would listen to us, if we commanded similar sacrifices for the preservation of his eternal life? (Rieger.)

But when for many days neither sun nor stars appeared (ver. 20). As here in the external world, so it often happens in the internal world with temptations, that men pass many days without the light of divine grace, Isa. li. 10, lxiii. 17 (Starke).—Yet to Paul there shone a star which no storm could extinguish—the promise of his Lord: "Be of good cheer, Paul; for as thou hast testified of Me in Jerusalem, so must thou bear witness also at Rome" (Besser).

Sirs, ye should have yielded to me, and not have sailed from Crete (ver. 21). Wise and pious men, when their counsel has been rejected, and misfortune ensues therefrom, do not lose time with reproaches and pettishness; but advise, where yet they can advise; and assist, where yet they can assist.

And now I exhort you to be of good courage; for there will result no loss of any man's life among you, but of the ship (ver. 22). The servants of God have no privilege to remain free from the external troubles which God inflicts upon the world—they have their share of them; but they have the privilege that under all the troubles of earth they remain safely housed, and are not in the least injured by them. And though the sea raged and foamed, and though the mountains fell into it from its violence; though all men should lose courage, and every one should regard himself as lost; yet they can lift up their heads with joy, because they know that they have an almighty and faithful Lord, who will not leave them in any strait (Apost. Past.).—Although Paul was an apostle and endowed with miraculous powers, yet we do not find that he here used the gift of prophecy, until he received a direct command from God for that purpose. Hitherto he had reflected on the danger of the voyage, and had employed all the ordinary means of safety in company with the sailors, and might have experienced fear and anxiety as others, ver. 24. He affected nothing peculiar, but waited on the help of the Lord. But when the Lord had appeared to him, and had assured him of the safety of himself and his fellow-voyagers, then he prophesied from divine authority, and the result confirmed his prophecy. A servant of Jesus follows this example, and abstains from all prophesyings which proceed from the human will or an excited imagination. We are directed to the Gospel, and our work ought to be to exhort and to beseech in Christ's stead. But if God calls us to announce something, He will know how to accredit us (Apost. Past.).

An angel of God, whose I am, and whom I serve (ver. 23). Blessed is every one who can coincide in the confession of Paul,

"It is God, whose I am, and whom I serve;" and who, amid all that may occur in the stormy ocean of this world, can use the petition, "O God, whose I am, and whom I serve, preserve me" (Rieger).

Fear not, Paul; thou must be brought before Cæsar (ver. 24). Thus the apostle was not particularly anxious about his life, but about the design of his life. This is the chief anxiety of a faithful servant of God, that God's purposes be not injured in him.—*Behold, God has given thee all those who sail with thee.* Paul must thus have cared and prayed for his fellow-voyagers. The ungodly are benefited by the righteous. For the sake of one righteous man, a hundred or a thousand are preserved. For the sake of Lot, Sodom could not be destroyed, so long as he dwelt in it. Know this, ye ungodly and proud children of the world. Ye have to thank the insignificant lights, simple Christians despised by you, a scorned and imprisoned Paul, that ye are permitted to cover your table, to breathe the air, and to look at the sun (Starke).—We and the souls entrusted to us are also, as it were, in a ship, on the restless and dangerous ocean of this world. Let us, then, so long as we are with them, wrestle unceasingly in prayer, and so labour that we may convey them with ourselves as a precious gift to God; that we may secure them and ourselves from shipwreck in faith and from eternal destruction; and that, at length, when the vessel of life is broken in pieces, we may land with them in the secure haven of eternal life (Apost. Past.).

Yet we must be stranded on an island (ver. 26). O Lord, reveal to us the island of safety, in which we, according to Thy will, may repose for a while in the restless ocean of this world, until our last voyage is over, and we can call, with a look to an approaching eternity, Land! Land! "The haven is in all the world, when we lie at Thy feet; and it is left to Thee in what manner we greet it: if only Thine eternal kingdom remains to us, all else is to us the same"[1] (Williger).

And when the fourteenth night came (ver. 27). O how many sad nights have there been in the meantime, not only to those who sail on the sea, but also to those who call to the Lord from the depths, and wait for His aid from one morning watch to another! (Rieger.)—*We were driven up and down in Adria.* It

[1] From a German hymn.

was on the same stormy Adriatic that once the great Cæsar called to the terrified sailors, "Steer bravely, you carry Cæsar and his destinies." Paul could say more: he could address the pilot, "Be not dismayed, you carry Christ and His salvation."

They cast out four anchors, and waited for day (ver. 29). The spiritual anchor of the Christian—faith with living hope—goes not downwards, but upwards, Heb. vi. 19 (Starke).—In the night we wish for the day, though we have already slighted many a day, Eccles. xi. 7 (Starke).

But the sailors sought to escape out of the ship (ver. 30). See how faithfully the world stands the test in the time of need. Those preachers are to be compared to those timid and fugitive sailors, who in the time of need fall away, and desert the bark of the Church committed to them, John xix. 13 (Starke).

But Paul said, If these do not remain in the ship, ye cannot be saved (ver. 31). Paul had a heart full of faith and love to man. By these two main-springs, all his actions were regulated. He had himself imbibed the strength of the divine promises; therefore he was undismayed and of good courage, and could support and comfort all his companions. God had given him all the souls in the ship; therefore his zeal was watchful not to suffer any one of them to perish, and he urgently warned them not to go out of the ship; afterwards, he exhorted them to take food, and urged them to save themselves by swimming. In short, he cared for their safety in all manner of ways. We learn from this, how a teacher may become a blessing to others by faith, experience, and true love, especially in times of need and danger (Apost. Past.).

Then the soldiers cut away the ropes from the boat (ver. 32). It was a strong faith which did that, by which the last bridge was broken down between the ship, helplessly lost, and the neighbouring land. The centurion, in cutting away the ropes of the life-boat and allowing it to fall into the sea, embarked with his people in the life-boat of Paul's words, and this was attached with strong ropes to the faithfulness of the Almighty. Cut away the ropes from every bark on which, besides God, thou placest thy confidence; for the morning light will break in upon thy night, so that thou mayest behold the glorious help of God (Besser).

There shall not a hair fall from the head of any of you (ver.

34). How wonderful is God! A prisoner in chains can be a prophet and a saviour to those who have bound him, Gen. xli. 12–14 (Starke).—In great danger, we should remember the omnipresence and the gracious providence of God, that the hairs of our head are all numbered, Luke xii. 7, xxi. 18 (Starke).

And when he had thus spoken, he took bread and gave thanks (ver. 35). With this grace, Paul became as a good savour among them all (Rieger).—This early meal on the billow-tossed ship is by Paul's thanksgiving the true counterpart of the gentle sleep of the Lord Jesus, on a pillow in the ship, when the waves covered it, Mark iv. 38 (Besser).—The whole of the 46th Psalm is here appropriate. This was in very deed a heroic meal (Lindhammer).

They were all of good courage (ver. 36). The word of God imparts true courage, and a word spoken in season is as apples of gold in dishes of silver, Prov. xxv. 10. "Therefore let your light shine before men, that they may see your good works, and glorify your Father which is in heaven," Matt. v. 16 (Starke).

They cast out the corn into the sea (ver. 38). Behold, O Christian, these men cast their temporal necessaries from them to preserve the remnant of their temporal life, and wilt thou not let thine earthly goods go to preserve thine eternal life?—"What is a man profited though he should gain the whole world, and lose his own soul?" (Starke.)

And when it was day (ver. 39). The light breaks in after the darkness, the sun arises after the night; and our troubles will one day change, and come to an end. When need is greatest, God is nearest (Starke).—*They knew not the land.* In striking contrast to this is the pilgrim-hymn of Chytræus: "The land is near, well known to us, thither we turn the bark" (Besser).

But the soldiers' counsel was to kill the prisoners (ver. 42). The soldiers were anxious on account of their responsibility if one of their prisoners escaped, and hence this cruel thought occurred to them. Thus many a one may allow himself to be misled by mistaken zeal, so that he considers one side of a matter only, and entirely forgets what he owes to others (Rieger).

But the centurion, willing to save Paul (ver. 43). Still, at the last moment, it might have been over with Paul, had not

God inclined the heart of this heathen centurion to friendliness and gratitude toward the man, who had become dear to him and respected by him (Besser).

On the whole chapter.—The good counsel of a man of God is not to be despised even in worldly matters. 1. Paul's counsel, ver. 10. 2. The objections to it, ver. 11. 3. The consequences of slighting it, vers. 13–43.—*When trouble is greatest, God is nearest.* 1. Trouble must first become very great, in order that we may despair of ourselves, vers. 16–23. 2. God then helps those who believe on Him, vers. 23–26, 31–44 (Lisco).—*The dangerous voyage of Paul to Rome, a type of many a voyage of the bark of Christ.* 1. The conflict of the ship with the elements: wind and waves, vers. 14, 15. 2. The exertions of the sailors: they undergird the ship, and cast the furniture into the sea, vers. 16–19. 3. The apparent hopelessness of safety, ver. 20. 4. The wonderful rescue: Paul's exhortation and God's aid, vers. 33–43 (Lisco).—*Paul, an example of Christian self-possession in a dangerous situation.* 1. He frustrates faint-hearted and pernicious projects, vers. 27–32. 2. He encourages desponding minds, vers. 33–38 (Lisco).—*The voyage of life.* 1. The setting out. The various changes of surrounding objects, vers. 1, 2, 4–8. The friendships, ver. 3. The first clouds in the heavens, vers. 9–15. 2. Fear and hope. The fear of unbelief, vers. 16–20. The confidence of faith, vers. 21–26. 3. The contest with adversities. Trouble discloses hearts, vers. 27–32. Trouble leads to God, vers. 33–38. 4. The haven of rest. The shipwreck and the billows of death, vers. 39–43. The rescue and the landing on the unknown land of rest (Lisco).—*Paul in the storm, a noble picture:* 1. Of manly courage: his prudent counsel, ver. 10; his presence of mind, ver. 31. 2. Of Christian peace of mind: his friendly address, ver. 21; his confident trust in God, ver. 25. 3. Of apostolic unction: his prophetic exhortation, ver. 24; his priestly love-feast, ver. 35. —*Paul as the chosen instrument of God, tested in storm and tempest.* 1. In his firm believing confidence in his God and Saviour. 2. In his apostolic pastoral fidelity to the souls entrusted to him. 3. In his undaunted heroic courage amid the storms of trial.—*Paul in Adria, and Christ on the Lake of Gennesareth; or the great servant of the greater Lord.* 1. The critical calm before the storm: the sleeping Christ and the imprisoned

Paul. 2. The majestic sublimity in the storm: Christ reproves His weak disciples, and Paul encourages the dismayed sailors. 3. The wonderful rescue from the storm: Christ rebukes the winds and the waves, and Paul brings his shipwrecked companions safely to land.—*Paul in the storm, a proof how the glory of the Lord is reflected in His servant,* 2 Cor. iii. 15. We see reflected in the apostle: 1. Christ's prophetical office: Paul's warning, ver. 10; and his promise, ver. 25. 2. Christ's priestly office: Paul's pastoral care, ver. 21; his love-feast, vers. 34, 35: compare Christ at the last supper. 3. Christ's kingly office: Paul's greatness of mind, ver. 35; the souls given to him, and rescued for his sake, vers. 24, 31.—*Paul, the apostle, on the stormy ocean; or a greater than Jonas is here.* 1. Jonas flees from the presence of the Lord; Paul journeys in the service of his Lord toward the great city of the Gentiles. 2. Jonas brings the wrath of God upon his fellow-voyagers; Paul becomes the comfort and safety of his companions. 3. Jonas is rescued from the jaws of death; Paul brings 276 souls safe to land. 4. Jonas goes to Nineveh to preach repentance; Paul goes to Rome to proclaim the Gospel with the sacrifice of his own life.—*Paul on his journey to Rome, a noble example how the Lord is mighty in the weakness of His servant.* 1. As a prisoner, the apostle journeys, and yet as a free man in Christ, free from fear, living in the Spirit; while his companions, paralyzed with fear, tremble in deadly anguish. 2. As one ignorant of the sea, he stands among sailors; and yet gives them the most rational advice in external matters. 3. As one despised, he is pushed aside by the men of the world; and yet in the time of need, he is the comfort and the support of all. 4. As one shipwrecked, he is cast ashore; and yet he brings that Gospel ashore, to which Rome and the whole world shall be subject.—*Paul in the storm; or, if God be for us, who can be against us?* 1. Not wind and waves, with their violence; for wind and waves must be obedient to the Almighty. 2. Not men, with their designs and plans; for the Lord says, Resolve, and it will come to nothing. 3. Not our own heart, with its doubts and anxieties; for comfort comes from above, Fear not.—*The Christian's comfort and means of safety on the stormy voyage of life.* 1. Prudent foresight in the uncertainty of earthly things, vers. 9, 10. 2. Brotherly union in the time of need, vers. 21, 24, 30. 3. Prompt renunciation of the possessions of this world, vers. 18, 19, 38. 4. Courageous trust in God in the storms of temptation, vers. 22–25. 5. Grateful use of the divine means of grace, vers. 34–36. 6. Hopeful regard toward the heavenly land of rest, ver. 44.—*The bark of the Church of Christ on the stormy ocean of this world.* 1. Its dangers: contrary winds, vers. 4, 14; foolish guides, vers. 11, 12; superfluous possessions, vers. 18, 19; disunited associates, vers. 30, 42; concealed rocks, vers. 39, 41. 2. Its means of help: the testimony of pious teachers, vers. 9, 21; the prophecies of the divine word, vers. 23, 24; the comforts of the holy sacraments, ver. 35; the blessing of believing prayer, ver. 35; the rescuing hand of Almighty God, vers. 24, 34, 44.—"*Though mast and sail be broken, yet God does not desert His own:*" the blessed experience of the children of God, vers. 39–44. 1. In the billows of external life. 2. In the storms of inward temptations. 3. In the contests of the Christian Church.—*The comforting exhortation of the Lord to His servant in deadly danger.* 1. He imparts to him the testimony of faithful obedience: "It is God, whose I am, and whom I serve." 2. He renews to him the promise of divine guidance: "Fear not, Paul; thou must be brought before Cæsar." 3. He bestows on him the souls, whom he bears in love upon his heart: "God hath given thee all them that sail with thee."—*In storms and dangers, hearts are disclosed.* 1. The man of the world in his nakedness: his want of counsel, want of courage, and want of love, vers. 22, 30, 33, 42. 2. The Christian in his greatness: trust in God, presence of mind, and love, vers. 21–25, 31–35. 3. The Lord in His glory: His fearful majesty, righteous judgments, and compassionate grace, vers. 20, 24, 25, 35, 44.—*The sea, a sublime theatre of the holy acts of God from of old.* 1. Of His creative power, from the days of creation, when the Spirit of God moved upon the waters. 2. Of His retributive justice, from the days of the flood. 3. Of His saving grace, from the days of Noah's rescue and Israel's passage through the Red Sea.

B.

Experiences and Actions of the Apostle at Malta.

CHAP. XXVIII. 1–10.

1 And when we were escaped ashore, we learned that the island is called
Malta. 2 And the strangers showed to us no small philanthropy; for they
kindled a fire and took us all in, because of the rain which had set in, and
of the cold. 3 But when Paul had collected together a bundle of sticks
and laid them on the pile of wood, there came out a viper from the heat,
and fastened on his hand. 4 But when the strangers saw the beast hanging
on his hand, they said among themselves, Certainly this man is a murderer,
whom, after his rescue from the sea, retribution suffers not to live. 5 But
he shook off the beast into the fire, and suffered no harm. 6 But they ex-
pected that he should have swollen or fallen down dead suddenly. When,
however, they waited long and saw that no harm befell him, they changed
their minds, and said, He is a god.

7 In the neighbourhood of that place, the first man of the island, named
Publius, had an estate; who received us and lodged us three days cour-
teously. 8 And it happened that the father of Publius was sick of a fever
and dysentery; to whom Paul went and prayed, and laid his hands on him
and healed him. 9 Now when this was done, the rest also in the island who
had diseases came, and were healed. 10 They also showed us many honours;
and when we went to sea, provided us with what was necessary.

Ver. 1. Ἐπέγνωμεν is better attested than ἐπέγνωσαν.

Ver. 2. Ἀνάψαντες is indeed only in two uncial MSS., whereas the majority have the simple verb ἅψαντες; but the ἀνα was probably omitted.

Ver. 3. Ἐκ is only in cursive MSS.: all the uncial MSS. have ἀπό.

EXEGETICAL EXPLANATIONS.

1. *And when we were escaped ashore.*—Ἐπέγνωμεν, apparently by inquiry at the inhabitants, many of whom were doubtless drawn to the coast by the wreck of a ship. The island was called Melita. Formerly, this island was not universally believed to be Malta, but sometimes an island in that part of the Adriatic off the coast of Dalmatia, now called Meleda. At first Giorgi, a Venetian, after the example of Constantine Porphyrogenites, a Byzantine, then De Rhoer, a Dutchman, several Englishmen, as for example Bryant, and also D. Paulus, have advocated the opinion, that the island was the Illyrian Meleda, off the coast of Ragusa. The chief reason for this opinion was a mistake of

the name Adria, chap. xxvii. 27. But that Malta near Sicily must be meant is no longer doubted, especially when we consider: 1. That Malta lay in the direction of a ship, driven by a north-east wind from Crete; 2. that the Alexandrian ship, on board which Paul again embarked, would naturally winter at Malta, and not at Meleda; 3. that the voyage to Puteoli does not suit a ship sailing from Meleda, but one sailing from Malta. The island of Malta, eight square (German) miles in superficial area, lies about fifteen geographical (German) miles from Cape Passaro, the southern point of Sicily, and about fifty (German) miles from the African coast.

2. *And the strangers.*—Luke calls the islanders βάρβαροι, in reference to their language, because they spoke neither Greek nor Latin. That the expression is not designed to denote moral barbarism and want of culture is evident from ver. 2, particularly from οὐ τὴν τυχοῦσαν φιλανθρωπίαν. On the other hand, as the islanders were of Phœnician descent, their mother-tongue was without doubt a Punic dialect.

3. *There came a viper out of the heat.*—The serpent (ἔχιδνα denotes the female, while ἔχις denotes the male) was without doubt a species of adder or viper. These reptiles, whenever the temperature falls sensibly below the mean temperature of the district, become torpid. This serpent was apparently in such a state, but was roused and irritated by the heat, and thus fastened on Paul's hand. Certainly Luke does not expressly say that it had bitten him: and on this account, certain interpreters suppose that this was not the case, but that it only twined itself round his hand. However, the narrative—taking into consideration καθῆψε τῆς χειρός, ver. 3 (it attached itself, fastened on his hand), κρεμάμενον ἐκ τῆς χειρὸς αὐτοῦ, ver. 4, and the expectation of the islanders that he would swell and fall down dead—evidently supposes an actual bite; just as the last circumstance rests on experience, that the bite of this viper was deadly. If notwithstanding the apostle did not suffer the least harm, we must suppose a divine preservation, in accordance with the promise of Jesus, Mark xvi. 18.—There are now no poisonous adders in Malta; and the modern Maltese believe that since Paul shook the viper which bit him into the fire, the whole race have lost their poison. However, it is well known that in other districts, in proportion as the woods are cleared and the cultivation

of the soil is increased, poisonous reptiles disappear. Thus, for example, in the island of Arran, on the west coast of Scotland, vipers have gradually disappeared, as the island became more frequented (Smith, 2d Ed. p. 146). And there is perhaps nowhere a surface of equal extent which is so completely cultivated, and in so artificial a state, as Malta in the present day.

4. *The first man of the island.*—The Roman Publius is called *ὁ πρῶτος τῆς νήσου*. This cannot refer to his rank on account of family and riches; for if so, not Publius, but his father, who was then alive, would be the first man of the island. But this designation must necessarily rest on official dignity and authority. He was doubtless the Roman governor, that is, the legate of the prætor of Sicily, to whose province Malta belonged. There is no passage in any ancient writer, where this designation for the governor of Malta occurs, and from which Luke might have taken it. But, on the other hand, two inscriptions have been discovered in Malta, the one in Greek and the other in Latin (the latter discovered in the year 1747, at the foot of a pillar in Citta Vecchia), which contained the same honorary title, *πρῶτος Μελιταίων, princeps.* These inscriptions thus confirm the otherwise unusual title which Luke gives to this man.—It does not clearly appear whom Publius received as guests. Certainly *ἡμεῖς*, which occurs here (ver. 7), is usually employed in this narrative to denote the whole company; and chiefly on this ground, and also from the shortness of the time (only three days, whereas the abode in the island extended to three months), Baumgarten infers that Publius received all the 276 persons. But in ver. 10, *ἡμεῖς* is evidently to be restricted to Paul and his intimate friends, for it can only be understood of them, and not of the whole 276, that they were so greatly honoured by the islanders: and so also *ἡμεῖς* in ver. 7 may well be referred only to them (Meyer). Moreover, in ver. 2, where the whole company are meant, it is expressly said *πάντες ἡμεῖς*, and this also might have been expected in ver. 7, especially as the reception and lodging of 276 persons on one property was much more astonishing than the assemblage of the same number at a fire in the open air. It is then much more probable that Publius received for a few days, as guests, Paul, Aristarchus, and Luke, and perhaps also the centurion Julius.—As regards the sickness of the father of Publius, it has been remarked that no writer of

the New Testament uses such exact technical expressions for diseases as Luke, who was trained as a physician. Formerly, it was maintained that a dry climate such as Malta did not generate dysentery and inflammation of the lower bowels; but recently physicians, resident in the island, have shown that these diseases are by no means uncommon there at the present day (Hackett).

DOGMATICAL AND ETHICAL THOUGHTS.

1. It was a double testimony of God in favour of His servant Paul, that he was not only himself protected from injury arising from the bite of the venomous serpent, but was also enabled to heal and to help others. The honour which was conferred on him and his companions by this, pointed in fact to the Lord.

2. How much moral and religious truth is in every man! That there is a *Δίκη* or Nemesis, *i.e.*, a moral law of nature which the transgressor cannot escape, is indelibly engraven on the conscience. But how great is the distortion of the truth in the natural man! At one time, they regard Paul as a murderer, because one evil befell him after another; and at another time, they deify him, because he received no injury from the bite of the serpent. The further man departs from the truth, the more does he go into extremes.

HOMILETICAL HINTS.

And when we were escaped ashore (ver. 1). The ship was lost, but Paul and his companions were saved. Kingdoms and principalities sink, but the Christian Church floats ashore and is miraculously preserved (Starke).

And the strangers showed to us no small kindness (ver. 2). We often receive the greatest kindness from those, from whom we least expect it (Starke).—Pity, compassion, and kindness are such precious virtues that the Spirit of God notices and praises them even when found among heathens and barbarians; particularly as thanks were due to the gracious government of the Lord, who knew by means of them to procure for His weary children and servants, an alleviation in their distress. If God will not allow a cup of cold water to be unrewarded, should not we Christians, to whom the loving-kindness and mercy of God have appeared, excel all the heathen in these virtues? (Apost.

Past.)—Christian dwellers at the coast may learn a Samaritan love from these strangers (Besser).

There came out a viper and fastened on his hand (ver. 3). When the Lord will accredit His apostle among these strangers, He first of all sends to him an evil, which by faith he overcomes, and thereby makes an impression upon the hearts of men. Our cross is thus to be as a bell to draw the eyes and thoughts of men toward us; and the faith which we manifest thereby, or the victory which we gain by the grace of Christ, is to stir up imitators (Apost. Past.).—The serpent hanging on the hand of Paul was a beautiful bracelet to him (Lindhammer).—How many serpent-bites wound the benevolent hands of Christians, but only in order that the glory of God may be manifest in them; for Christians cannot be poisoned (Besser).

This man must be a murderer, whom retribution suffers not to live (ver. 4). Thus the heathen recognised from the light of nature, that God is unchangeable in His righteousness (Starke). —That which is still written on the conscience of men concerning retribution, they do not know one time out of ten how to apply properly (Rieger).

But he shook off the beast into the fire (ver. 5). God often makes known to His servants that Christ has restored to us the lost dominion over the lower animals, Gen. i. 26, 28, ix. 2; 1 Sam. xvii. 34, 35 (Starke).—Then was fulfilled the promise of the Lord, They shall tread on serpents, Mark xvi. 18; Luke x. 19. There are now no venomous serpents in Malta, and, according to the tradition of the knights of Malta, vipers and adders which are brought to the island lose their poison. We expect at the end of our voyage an island where no serpent or viper will injure, Isa. xi. 18. Until then, let us use our Christian power, and cast off the venomous beast, sin, into the fire, to which it belongs.—Paul knew that he must come to Rome as a witness of Him who treads on serpents, and therefore through faith he deprived the bite of the serpent of its venom, Heb. xi. 33 (Besser).

They changed their minds, and said, He is a god (ver. 6). The multitude know no moderation; it either exalts one to heaven, or thrusts him down to hell, Acts xiv. 12, 13 (Starke).—Here the apostle went very impressively through honour and dishonour. At one moment, he was a murderer; in the next, he is called a god. But it is remarkable that the passage does not suggest the slightest emotion which the one or the other produced on Paul. Thus must it be with us, through the grace of God. We must not be easily affected either by the world's smiles, or by the world's frowns (Apost. Past.).

But it came to pass that the father of Publius was sick: to whom Paul went (ver. 7). God does not let the good deeds shown to His children and servants go unrewarded, bodily or spiritually, Matt. x. 42 (Starke).

Now when this was done, there came others also who had diseases, and were healed (ver. 9). It is to be taken into serious consideration, that no real blessing of the Gospel, or more distinct offer of salvation in Christ, is mentioned as a consequence of Paul's residence; nothing is noticed but a concourse of people on account of bodily health; at which, however, an opportunity for inquiry after further salvation both might and would have been afforded (Rieger).—Men take much trouble to obtain a bodily cure, but they are too lazy to give themselves trouble for the cure of their souls (Starke).—A willing servant of the Lord is ready not only to speak, but also, if needs be, to be silent. Thus the Gospel has its season (Williger).

On vers. 1–10.—*How foolishly the world judges.* 1. In its uncharitable judgments, ver. 4. 2. In its favourable judgments, ver. 6. 3. Therefore, undisturbed by the judgments of the world, do thy duty, and be not weary in well-doing, vers. 7–10 (Lisco).—*The virtue of hospitality.* 1. Esteemed and practised even by the heathen. 2. Much more suitable and blessed among Christians (Lisco).—*The perniciousness of superstition.* 1. How it is united with all manner of uncharitableness, vers. 1–4. 2. How it leads to all manner of idolatrous worship, vers. 5, 6 (Lisco).—*How the Christian finds his home everywhere.* 1. Everywhere he experiences the love of God. 2. Everywhere he finds loving hearts. 3. Everywhere he has the opportunity of showing love (Lisco).—*The people of Malta, an expressive supersentation of the heathen world.* 1. In their need of redemption: their dark superstition, vers. 4–6; their manifold misery, vers. 8, 9. 2. In their capability of redemption: their friendly hospitality, ver. 2; their dim knowledge of God, ver. 4; their lively susceptibility for the impressions of the divine, ver. 6; their earnest desire of assistance, ver. 9; their childlike gratitude for kindnesses received, ver. 10.—*Paul and the viper; or the servant of God as the conqueror of serpents.* In the power of his Lord (Mark xvi. 18) he casts from him: 1. The venomous serpent of slander, vers. 3, 4; 2. The shining adder of flattery, ver. 6; 3. The dangerous reptile of worldly anxieties and cares, vers. 8, 9. 4. The old serpent of sin (with application to ver. 4, "a murderer").—*Paul's arrival at Malta;* a fulfilment of the promise, "He shall give His angels charge over thee, to keep thee in all thy ways," Ps. xci. 11. The angel of the Lord draws him out of the waves of the sea; protects him from the poison of serpents; turns the hearts of barbarians towards him; and blesses the curative works of his hands.—*Paul at Malta; a memorable picture in travel:* wherein we recognise: 1. The lights and shadows of the heathen world; 2. The sufferings and joys of the apostolic office; 3. The wonderful and gracious ways of the Lord.—*Evil report and good report,* 2 Cor. vi. 8. This is the manner of the world, the calling of the Christian, and the will of the Lord.

C.

Conclusion of the Journey from Malta to Rome.

CHAP. XXVIII. 11–15.

11 But after three months, we set sail in a ship of Alexandria, which
had wintered in the island, with the sign of the Dioscuri. 12 And landing
at Syracuse, we remained there three days. 13 From thence we came
round and arrived at Rhegium: and after one day, the south wind having
arisen, we came on the second day to Puteoli. 14 There we found brethren,
and were requested to remain with them seven days. And thus we came
to Rome. 15 From thence the brethren, having heard of us, came to meet
us as far as Appii Forum and Tres Tabernæ. And when Paul saw them, he
thanked God and obtained confidence.

EXEGETICAL EXPLANATIONS.

1. *After three months.*—If the commencement of the voyage (chap. xxvii. 9) took place after the autumnal equinox (A.D. 61), and, accordingly, the residence at Malta embraced November, December, and January, the journey would be continued in February of the year 62. The ship in which they now embarked was also an Alexandrian vessel, and bore, painted or

engraven on its prow, the sign of the Dioscuri, that is, of Castor and Pollux, the tutelar deities of voyagers among the Greek and Roman sailors. The sign of a ship is called *τὸ παράσημον*; here, however, *παρασήμῳ* appears to be an adjective: *Dioscurorum effigiebus insignita.* Meyer's objection to its being considered an adjective, that *παράσημος* adj. is always used in a bad sense, is unfounded; for in the later classics, as for example Plutarch, *παράσημος* often occurs in a good sense: signifying *insignis, conspicuus.*

2. The voyage went by Syracuse, on the south-east coast of Sicily, distant about 18 geographical (German) miles north-east of Malta; then by Rhegium in Lower Italy, opposite the north-west corner of Sicily, to Puteoli, the modern Puzzuoli, about a (German) mile west from Naples. The three days' residence at Syracuse was doubtless for the sake of commerce. The meaning of *περιελθεῖν* is doubtful: in no case can it be intended to mean that they sailed round Sicily (De Wette), but rather that the ship was obliged to tack about on account of the wind. The voyage from Rhegium to Puteoli, about 50 geographical (German) miles, in less than two days, was very quick; but is explained by the favourable south wind. The port of Puteoli was, in the century before and in the century after Christ, the most famous in the western coast of Lower Italy, particularly for eastern commerce. Here the Egyptian corn-ships were accustomed to unload. It was the custom also to land here from Syria, and to proceed to Rome by land.—See Josephus, Ant. xvii. 12, 1, xviii. 7, 2; only he uses the Greek name Dicearchia.

3. *And thus we came to Rome*, namely, without tarrying anywhere after leaving Puteoli. This is said proleptically; afterwards, ver. 15 informs us that Paul was greeted and joined by Christians from Rome. This occurred both at Appii Forum and at Tres Tabernæ. Appii Forum was a small town, situated on the northern edge of the Pontine Marshes, about 43 Roman miles distant from the city, on the Appian Way, which led from Rome to Capua, and was named after Appius Claudius Cæcus, its builder. Tres Tabernæ was an inn for travellers, ten Roman miles nearer the capital. As Paul tarried seven days at Puteoli, the news of his arrival might soon reach Rome by the Christians there, so that the Christians could come from Rome to meet him, some thirty, and others forty, Roman miles.

DOGMATICAL AND ETHICAL THOUGHTS.

It is unity and relationship in Jesus Christ, by which men, though unacquainted with each other, are yet so known to each other and internally near, that meeting is a joyful discovery (ver. 14), a refreshment of the spirits, and an increase of courage and joyfulness (ver. 15). See Rom. i. 12.

HOMILETICAL HINTS.

With the sign of the Dioscuri (Luther: the banner of the twins, ver. 11). The Dioscuri were esteemed the guardians of seafaring men; but the true banner, under which Paul sailed, was the banner of the cross of Christ, on which was written, "By this sign, thou wilt conquer."—Castor and Pollux are nothing (1 Cor. viii. 4); but all the ships belong to the Lord, and no idolatrous banner can injure those who sail with thankfulness on that account. A consolation to the followers of the apostle of the Gentiles, who go forth with the banner of the cross, and sail in ships which have the golden calf of "Mammon" for their banner (Besser).

From thence to Rhegium (ver. 13). According to this narrative, the apostle journeyed through many places; but it is not mentioned that anywhere a special blessing resulted. Paul was one bound, he could not do as he would, he was quiet in the Lord, and waited on His intimation. However that was fulfilled which the Lord promised in Ezek. xxxiii. 33: "And when this cometh to pass, lo, it will come, then shall they know that a prophet hath been among them." Thus at Malta. Also the other places here mentioned were afterwards filled with the Gospel. We ought not then to despond, if a perceptible blessing does not immediately appear in all places, where the Lord employs us. We ought to commit ourselves and our work to the Lord. The seed lies for a time, but at a proper season the fruit comes. Many a servant of Jesus goes to his grave, and the Lord causes the seed of his sermons, tears, and sufferings to flourish only after his departure (Apost. Past.).

There we found brethren (ver. 14). God has His hidden ones everywhere. Let no one think, "I am left alone," 1 Kings xix. 14, 18 (Starke).—Christians are spiritual brethren, begotten by one Father, of one seed of the living word; they have one brother, even Christ; and they expect one inheritance, Rom. viii. 16. Therefore we should all bear brotherly hearts toward each other, Jas. i. 18 (Starke).—The hearts of Luke and Paul became very lively when they found brethren at Puteoli. They pass unnoticed the honour at Malta, but to meet with the children of God was a true treasure found. To love the brethren, to desire their fellowship, and to refresh ourselves in their faith, is still a sure sign of a heart firm in the true faith. Paul took courage, when, after a long fellowship with rough sailors, he again found brethren; and remained with them seven days, without doubt to observe a Sabbath with them, to proclaim to them the word of God, and to celebrate the Lord's Supper. May God, through His Holy Spirit, preserve in us this true love to the brethren (Apost. Past.).—*And so we came to Rome.* How would the heart of the apostle and his companions beat, in anxious expectation, when the heathen imperial city, with its cupolas and battlements, lay before their eyes! But also, how would the heart of the Roman Cæsar, in his palace, have beat, had he a presentiment that at this hour, in the form of a Jewish prisoner, a power entered by the gates, before which the Roman empire and the whole heathen world was to sink into the dust! This was even a more decisive moment than when, formerly, it was said, *Hannibal ante portas.*

From thence the brethren came to meet us (ver. 15). It was a considerate love of the brethren at Rome, a fruit of the epistle written before this to them, that they, by coming to meet Paul, refreshed his spirit. So there are many things which cost nothing, by which we might refresh one another, in the course of this weary life (Rieger).—*Then Paul thanked God, and took courage.* The Spirit of God will hereby indicate that Paul, in all these trials of faith hitherto mentioned, remained a poor man; and as he now approached Rome, perhaps it was with him as with a delinquent when he approaches the place of execution. How many things may have presented themselves to his mind, and what traces of weak faith may he have experienced! Therefore God bestowed upon him new strength and encouragement, by means of the believers at Rome (Apost. Past.).—With this solemn entrance of Paul, as accused before the imperial tribunal, but yet joined by his friends, we are reminded of Luther's entrance into Worms, when he was to stand his trial before the emperor (Williger).

On the whole section (vers. 11–15).—*The blessing of Christian fellowship*, vers. 14, 15 (Lisco).—*Christianity forms mankind into one divine family.* 1. This was already intended by creation. 2. Enmity has come into the world through sin. 3. Peace shall again visit the earth through Christianity (Lisco). —Here we have no continuing city, but we seek one to come.—*Paul before the gates of Rome.* 1. As a homeless stranger, and yet welcomed by loving brethren. 2. As an evil-doer in bonds, and yet with the gracious testimony of God in his heart. 3. As an offering appointed unto death (for sooner or later he was to lose his life within these walls), and yet a victorious conqueror who plants the standard of the cross in the citadel of heathenism.—*The arrival of Paul at Rome in its decisive importance.* 1. For the apostle: the aim of his life is fulfilled, and the end of his life is determined. 2. For the Gentile world: it becomes serious with its gracious invitation, but serious also with the setting of its glory. 3. For Judaism: in Rome the apostle turns himself for the last time to his people; the kingdom now comes to the Gentiles, and Rome supplants Jerusalem. 4. For Christianity: in Rome bloody contests await it, but also most glorious victories.—*Paul's entrance into Rome, and Christ's entrance into Jerusalem.* 1. The servile form of those who enter. 2. The jubilee of the reception. 3. The bloody tribunal in the background.—*The brotherly reception of Paul, a lively image of the communion of saints;* as it unites the children of God, overcomes the kingdoms of the world, and proclaims the glory of the Lord.

SECTION V.

RESIDENCE AND ACTIVITY OF PAUL AT ROME (CHAP. XXVIII. 16–31).

A.

The Discussions of Paul with the Jews at Rome end with the Rejection of the Gospel by them.

CHAP. XXVIII. 16–29.

16 But when we came to Rome, it was permitted to Paul to dwell by himself with a soldier who guarded him. 17 And it came to pass, after three days, that he called together the chief among the Jews: and when they were come together, he said to them, Men and brethren, though I have done nothing against our people or the customs of the fathers, I have been delivered a prisoner from Jerusalem into the hands of the Romans; 18 Who, having examined me, wished to release me, because there was no guilt worthy of death in me. 19 But as the Jews opposed it, I saw myself compelled to appeal to Cæsar'; not as if I had an accusation to prefer against my nation. 20 For this reason have I called for you, to see and to speak with you; because for the hope of Israel I bear on me this chain.

21 But they said to him, We have neither received letters from Judea concerning thee, nor has any one of the brethren come who has showed or spoken any evil of thee. 22 Yet we desire to hear of thee what thou thinkest; for concerning this sect, it is known to us that it is everywhere spoken against. 23 And they appointed him a day, and more came to him to his lodging; to whom he expounded and testified the kingdom of God, and sought to convince concerning Jesus, out of the law of Moses and the prophets, from morning till evening. 24 And some were convinced by what was spoken, but others believed not. 25 But when they were discordant among themselves, they went away, after Paul had spoken one word: Well has the Holy Ghost spoken by the prophet Isaiah to our fathers, saying, 26 Go ye unto this people, and say, With hearing ye shall hear, and not understand; and with seeing ye shall see, and not perceive: 27 For the heart of this people has become fat, and they hear heavily with their ears, and their eyes have they closed; lest they should see with their eyes, and hear with their ears, and understand with their heart, and be converted, and I should heal them. 28, 29 Be it known therefore unto you, that this salvation of God has been sent to the Gentiles, and they will also hear it.

Ver. 16. The words *ὁ ἑκατόνταρχος παρέδωκε τοὺς δεσμίους τῷ στρατοπεδάρχῳ* are probably spurious. They are wanting in the oldest authorities, and were on that account considered spurious by Mill, Bengel, and Griesbach, and have been erased by Lachmann and Tischendorf. No reason can be assigned for their omission, whereas they might easily have been inserted. Meyer has defended the genuineness of these words, yet without convincing reasons. Also here the Sinaitic MS. is in favour of the criticism.

Ver. 17. Αὐτόν is decidedly better attested than τὸν Παῦλον.

Ver. 23. Ἧκον is not externally better attested than ἦλθον, but is to be preferred from internal evidence, because ἥκω is an unusual word in the New Testament.

Ver. 25. The external authorities for ἡμῶν (textus receptus) and for ὑμῶν are equal. Lachmann and Tischendorf have preferred ὑμῶν, which is contained in the Alexandrian, Vatican, and Sinaitic MSS.; however, it is very possible that transcribers, because the speech is a severe reproof, thought that the second person ought to be put in place of the original first person.

Ver. 28. The three oldest MSS., including the Sinaitic, have τοῦτο τὸ σωτήριον, which is to be considered, with Tischendorf and Lachmann, as the genuine reading; for the omission of τοῦτο is more easily explained than its insertion.

Ver. 29. Καὶ ταῦτα αὐτοῦ εἰπόντος, ἀπῆλθον οἱ Ἰουδαῖοι, πολλὴν ἔχοντες ἐν ἑαυτοῖς συζήτησιν is spurious: it is wanting in A.B.E., the Sinaitic MS., several cursive MSS. and versions; it is found in G.H., which have the interpolation in ver. 16.

EXEGETICAL EXPLANATIONS.

1. *But when we came to Rome.*—Paul entered Rome by the Via Appia, through the Porta Capena, from which the Castrum Prætorium, built by Sejanus the favourite of Tiberius, lay not far distant to the east. The words ὁ ἑκατόνταρχος—στρατοπεδάρχῳ are indeed spurious, but correct in point of fact; for the *Præfecti prætorio* had, along with the supreme command of the imperial guard, the custody of prisoners sent from the provinces to be tried before the emperor. The reason, however, why Luke speaks only of one commander (whereas in general there were two, and only under the emperor Claudius, Burrus Afranius was appointed sole prefect), is, on the supposition that the words in question (ver. 16) are interpolated, of very little consequence. Also the reckoning of the apostolic chronology (Anger and Wieseler), resting on the fact that Burrus Afranius died in the beginning of the year 62, or in the month of March of that year, after which the command was again shared by two generals, loses its force, inasmuch as the statement of Luke, which was combined with that date, is wanting.

2. *It was permitted Paul.*—Paul was permitted to dwell καθ' ἑαυτόν, *i.e.*, not only apart from other prisoners, but also, as is

evident from vers. 17 and 30, in a private dwelling, doubtless in the immediate neighbourhood of the prætorium. This favour he most probably owed to the accompanying information of the procurator Festus, and to the personal intercession of the centurion Julius. There was certainly always with him a prætorian soldier who guarded him, and was, according to the Roman custom, fastened to his arm by a chain, ver. 20. Seneca, Ep. 5: *Eadem catena et custodiam et militem copulat.*

3. *And it came to pass, after three days.*—Three days after his arrival, Paul invited those at the head of the Jewish community. Until then he required rest after his journey, and would devote himself to the Christians at Rome, part of whom had come to meet him, and to whose society he had for years looked forward with joy, Rom. i. 11. But his first step, beyond the narrow circle of those already converted, was, according to his principle and custom, directed to Israel. And as Paul was not in a condition to go to the Jews of his own accord, to visit their synagogues as he did in other places in Asia and Europe, so nothing remained to him but to invite the leaders of the Jewish Church to his dwelling. The chief of the Jews were without doubt the rulers of the synagogues, and those who were socially exalted. And these accordingly came to him.

4. *Men and brethren.*—The address to the assembled Jews (vers. 17-20) was essentially of a personal nature, and was designed to oppose the prejudices which the Roman Jews might have entertained against Paul, partly from his imprisonment generally, partly from the circumstance that he had appealed to Cæsar, and partly from the slanders which might have been brought from Judea. In order to justify himself before them, he assures them, first, that his imprisonment and deliverance into the hands of the Romans was not occasioned by any offence against the people of Israel or against the law of Moses, ver. 17. And this he mentions with perfect justice; for that he offended against his nation, no one believes. And that he, by his doctrine of Christ as the end of the law, attacked the law, can only be maintained under a mistaken notion of Paul's position toward the law. Paul acted with all piety to the law, as an actual revelation of God; and he attacked not the Mosaic religion in itself, but only its sufficiency for justification and salvation.

Accordingly what Paul here asserts, is in perfect accordance with truth.

5. *Who having examined me.*—Paul declares, secondly (vers. 18, 19), that his appeal to Cæsar was rendered unavoidable, because a protest had been entered on the part of the Jews against his liberation, whereas the Roman authorities judged his liberation to be just in itself; but that his object was not to make any accusation against his countrymen to Cæsar. Paul here calls Israel, not ὁ λαός as in ver. 17, but τὸ ἔθνος μου; because he had them in view not as the people of God, but as the people to whom he belonged, and toward whom he had behaved in a patriotic manner before the Roman government.—In conclusion, Paul says, thirdly, ver. 20, that his faithful and upright disposition toward his people, united with the circumstance that only for the Messianic hope of Israel he was bound with this chain, had induced him to invite them, in order that he might see and speak with them. Περίκειμαι, inasmuch as his arm was embraced by the chain.

6. *But they said to him.*—The reply of the Jews, that they had neither by writing nor by word of mouth heard anything unfavourable of the apostle, has been much impugned as historically incredible. For it is thought that we must suppose that the Jewish community at Rome must have, at all events, received communications from the Sanhedrim concerning Paul. But, on the other hand, it has with justice been observed, that before Paul's appeal, the heads of the Sanhedrim had no reason to write to the Roman Jewish Church about him, because this turn of events was completely unexpected by them; and that, after the appeal, there was not sufficient time to inform the Roman Jews before the personal arrival of Paul (Bengel, Meyer), as his departure probably took place soon after his appeal. It is certainly more surprising, that the Roman Jews had not privately and incidentally heard something about Paul from Jews coming from Palestine. However, they do not say that they heard nothing whatever of Paul. They acknowledge (ver. 22) that they were well aware that Christianity was everywhere spoken against. Thus they heard of Christianity and of the disputes to which it gave rise; and assuredly also must have heard of the preachers of the Gospel, and of Paul in particular. But what they affirm is only that they had heard nothing evil,

nothing morally bad, of him. And this declaration might proceed partly from caution toward the imperial court and power, from which the Roman Jews had already suffered much, and partly from a wish to encourage Paul to an unreserved communication. If the speakers are silent about the Christian Church in the capital, this, considering the circumstances of such a capital as Rome, may the less surprise us, as here also there appears to be intentional reserve. If a contradiction between this ignorance and the existence of a Christian Church at Rome was here actually obvious, the author must have been extremely short-sighted to forget here, in ver. 22, that he had only seven verses before spoken of the Christian Church in that place.

7. *And more came to his lodging.*—On the second occasion, there were not only the chief of the Jews, but many others with them. This time Paul delivered a comprehensive discourse which lasted all day. His exposition (ἐξετίθετο) was twofold: first a testimony to the kingdom of God (διαμαρτύρεσθαι), *i.e.*, an announcement of the facts of redemption and of the establishment of the kingdom of God through Jesus Christ; and secondly, an argument drawn from the Old Testament concerning Jesus, aiming at their conviction (πείθειν). The former was purely a testimony to the historical Jesus of Nazareth: the latter was a declaration, that He is the Messiah promised in the Old Covenant; and on this the strength of the proof was founded.

8. *And some were convinced.*—One portion of the hearers were convinced (ἐπείθοντο), but others continued in unbelief. They doubtless expressed themselves loudly on the opposite side (ἀσύμφωνοι). To the expressions of unbelief on the part of those present, the concluding words of the apostle referred. Ῥῆμα ἕν, after so many words, one more, but that a most weighty word. This consisted simply in the quotation of a prophetical expression concerning the hardness of Israel, which the apostle evidently applies to the present, and to the unbelievers among those assembled. This is evident from the context, especially from ver. 28, and from καλῶς, which indicates the perfect suitableness and appropriateness of the prophecy. The word of God to the prophet (Isa. vi. 9, 10) was to be announced to the people; and in so far ἐλάλησε—πρὸς τοὺς πατέρας is entirely correct. The words from ἀκοῇ to the close are

given verbatim from the Septuagint. Paul referred the divine direction πορεύθητι, etc., to himself and his mission. Compare xxvi. 17.

9. *Be it known unto you.*—The consequence of this obduracy of Israel at Rome is, that this salvation of God (τοῦτο τὸ σωτήριον, the salvation which was this day announced) has been sent to the Gentiles. Ἀπεστάλη refers, as formerly πορεύθητι, to the apostolic mission of Paul. "Also" with "hear" (καὶ ἀκούσονται) places God's offer of salvation, along with the corresponding reception of it on the part of the Gentiles, in contrast with the οὐ συνιέναι, βαρέως ἀκούειν, etc., of Israel: the Gospel will not only be sent to them, but they will also hear it.

DOGMATICAL AND ETHICAL THOUGHTS.

1. The apostle of the Gentiles, at the close of his course, turns himself at first to the Israelites at Rome, before he proclaims the kingdom of God to all without distinction, in particular to the Gentiles. Instead of finding this a stumblingblock, and historically unimaginable in the "legally free, and genuinely evangelical and universal Paul," we ought rather to honour in it both the consistency of preaching Ἰουδαίῳ τε πρῶτον καὶ Ἕλληνι, Rom. i. 16, and also the tender love and faithfulness toward his people, flowing from the Spirit of Christ (compare Rom. ix. 4, 5). It is not from mere natural patriotism, but in truth from a love for Christ's sake, indeed a true love of enemies, that Paul, after he had suffered so much from his people, is nevertheless far removed from wishing to appear in any way against them (ver. 19); on the contrary, he is mindful to turn the salvation of Christ in the first instance toward his countrymen.

2. Paul, first of all, justifies himself before he announces the Gospel to the Jews. And with good reason, because he cannot expect to receive a favourable hearing to his words, if they are prejudiced against his personal character. It was not only prudent, first of all, to clear his personal character before them, but it entirely corresponds with the moral character of Christ and of Christianity; for a corrupt tree cannot bring forth good fruit, Matt. vii. 18.

3. In Rome, Paul at last experiences that the opposition to the Gospel is too strong in Israel. Here also he turns himself

from the unbelieving Jews to the Gentiles, who receive the Gospel in a better spirit.

HOMILETICAL HINTS.

When we came to Rome, it was permitted to Paul to dwell by himself (ver. 16). We are everywhere happy, if we possess the grace of God (Starke).—When a man's ways please the Lord, He makes even his enemies to be at peace with him (Starke).—The hand of God, which, according to His counsel, had guided the apostle to Jerusalem and on his difficult journeys, was also in Rome ruling over him (Apost. Past.).

And it came to pass, after three days, that he called together the chief among the Jews (ver. 17). It costs no small struggle to retain affection for our people and our mother-church, even although evilly treated by the powerful in it (Rieger).—He who once penned the incomparable hymn in praise of that love which endureth all things and hopeth all things, has not only praised that love, but also exhibited it in his life, by ever anew, and even after the saddest experience in body and soul, meeting again, with patience and hope, the most deadly enmity of his own brethren (Baumgarten).—Never indeed did a teacher, who came to a strange place, make a more wretched appearance in external things, than the Apostle Paul when he came to Rome. And yet no one has effected so much as this witness of Jesus in chains. For inwardly a fire burned within him to testify of Jesus,—an earnest desire to save the souls even of his bitterest enemies; and the divine call directed all his steps, made ways for him, opened doors, and caused his paths drop fatness. Thus it does not matter to a teacher what kind of external show he makes, and with what parade he is received in a new place. It matters only whether he is a witness of Jesus, whether he carries the cross after the Saviour, whether his heart burns with the love of Jesus, and with a desire for the salvation of souls (Apost. Past.).

Not as if I had an accusation to prefer against my nation (ver. 19). All the wickedness of his enemies could not produce revenge in him, or even an aversion of mind. He did not wish to accuse, but to convert them. This was an actual proof how grace mastered nature, and how the love of Jesus conquered in him all pettishness, selfishness, and self-exaltation (Apost. Past.).

For the hope of Israel, I am bound with this chain (ver. 20).

If this hope flourishes in the heart, we can bear our chains so much the more easily and joyfully. Also the thorn in the flesh, the messenger of Satan with his buffetings, can be overcome thereby (Apost. Past.).—The iron chains, which were borne for the hope of Israel by a righteous Israelite, are in the sight of the God of Israel a greater ornament than all gold chains are in the eyes of the world (Lindhammer).

Concerning this sect, it is known to us that it is everywhere spoken against (ver. 22). It had come to this with the Jews, after thirty years' gracious visitation, that they spoke everywhere against the Gospel, and that the sign of Christ predicted by Simeon ("a sign which shall be spoken against," Luke ii. 24), was set up, wherever the Jews dwelt from Jerusalem, even to the ends of the earth (Besser).—The poor Jews at Rome knew nothing more about the matter of which Paul treated, than that the doctrine of Christ, which they called a sect, was everywhere spoken against. This is the danger which exists when men rely too much on the judgment of others, and either believe loosely in implicit faith what others believe, or reject in blind zeal what the multitude reject (Apost. Past.).—The aged Simeon had already recognised that Christ should be set up for a sign which shall be spoken against. This is the characteristic sign of genuine Christians; they are everywhere spoken against by the whole world (Gossner).—And yet the doctrine of that little sect has become the religion of the world, and has vanquished the enmity of Israel and Rome, without sword or bow, but by the David-sling of the divine word (Leonh. and Spieg.).

And persuaded concerning Jesus out of the law of Moses and the prophets (ver. 23). There is no better means to convince the Jews that Jesus is the true Messiah, than to lead them to their law and to the prophets (Starke).—*From morning until evening.* Should not this faithful and unwearied labour of the apostle shame the lukewarmness of those teachers who restrict their whole ministry to the pulpit, and think it a sin to open their houses to the awakened for instruction? (Apost. Past.)—If we wish to know Jesus rightly, and to come into the kingdom of God through Him, we must thoroughly search the word and persevere therein, and not desist; not reading the word hastily, but with all diligence, as Paul here preaches from it until evening (Bogatsky).

Some were convinced by him (ver. 24). The seed of the word with some falls by the wayside, with others on stony ground, and with others among thorns, but here and there on good ground. —To the one, the Gospel is the savour of life unto life; and to the others, the savour of death unto death (Starke).

But when they were discordant among themselves (ver. 25). The wickedness and malice of unbelievers are the cause why Christ, who is our peace and the only bond of holy union, becomes an occasion of dissension, and creates strife among those who were friends before. When the Jews come together to hear Paul, they are of one mind; but when they have heard the doctrine of reconciliation, they split up into two hostile camps. Yet we must not think that this discord first commenced with the preaching of the Gospel. No; the discordance, which before was concealed in the heart, does then appear, as the brightness of the sun does not bring forth new colours, but only reveals their variety, which was not to be perceived in the darkness (Calvin).

With hearing ye shall hear and not understand (ver. 26). In a similar manner John also makes a general conclusion of the discourses of Jesus, John xii. 37–39 (Williger).

For the heart of this people is hardened (ver. 27). When the apostles of Jesus speak of the judgment of hardening, they do so with such a view, and in such a manner, that it must be evident how God is not to be blamed in the destruction of such souls. The hardening is not only a natural consequence of long-continued despite of divine grace, but also a divine judgment which befalls those who hold the truth in unrighteousness. We must thus preach the doctrine of hardening, but be on our guard that we do not speak harshly against God, or repel thereby darkened minds (Apost. Past.).

Be it known unto you that this salvation of God has been sent unto the Gentiles (ver. 28). Even behind the dark night-piece of the rejection of Israel, the heaven of grace again reddens for a sign that the Lord will not be angry for ever, but will remember His covenant and the sure mercies of David (Leonh. and Spieg.).—Although the hearers should become angry, yet we must not smooth the word of God to them (Ezek. xiii. 8). If the Jews will not come to the great supper of God, the Gentiles will fill His house, Luke xiv. 8 (Starke).—*They will also hear it.* Thus we are included. Blessed be God! (Besser.)

On vers. 16–29.—*Paul's farewell discourse to the Jews at Rome.* 1. A last testimony to his innocence (vers. 17–20). 2. A last confession of Jesus Christ, as the Messiah (ver. 23). 3. A last effusion of love toward his people (vers. 17, 19, 20). 4. A last stroke of the hammer on hardened hearts (vers. 1, 25–28).—*The chains of Paul* (ver. 20). 1. A disgraceful monument for his blinded people. 2. An honourable sign for the faithful servant of God. 3. A precious comfort for all who suffer on account of the truth.—*The sect which is everywhere spoken against, proved by this very contradiction of the world to be the chosen people of God.* 1. The accusations, coming from all sides against Christianity, have mutually refuted each other: a proof of its undeniable truth. 2. In the midst of so many enemies on the right hand and on the left, the little company of confessors have grown up to be the world-ruling Church: a proof of its indestructible power of life.—*The twofold fate of the word of God wherever it is preached, even to the end of time.* To some, it is a savour of life unto life; to others, a savour of death unto death.—*The terrible judgment of obduracy.* 1. Inflicted, not by an unmerciful Creator, but by a righteous Judge. 2. Merited, not by an aggravated sin, but by a continued resistance to saving grace. 3. Announced, not to cause comfortless despondency, but wholesome fear.—*Be it known therefore unto you, that this salvation of God is sent to the Gentiles, and they will hear it;* a warning to modern Christianity. 1. To rebuke it for its coldness and ingratitude. 2. To put it to shame by the desire of salvation among the heathen. 3. To warn it of the impending judgments of God, Rev. ii. 5.

B.

Paul preaches the kingdom of God for the space of two years at Rome, without restraint, although a prisoner.

CHAP. XXVIII. 30, 31.

30 But Paul dwelt for two whole years in his own hired house, and received all who came in unto him, 31 Preaching the kingdom of God, and teaching concerning the Lord Jesus Christ with all boldness, without molestation.

EXEGETICAL EXPLANATIONS.

1. Without doubt, the Christians at Rome paid the rent for the house of the apostle, as he himself, being a prisoner, could earn nothing with his own hands; while also other churches, as the church of Philippi, supported him in his imprisonment.

2. The book did not certainly, as Schleiermacher has supposed, remain unfinished by an accidental hindrance on the part of Luke; and as little is the conclusion of it lost, as Schott has imagined. For the observation, which Meyer has made, is appropriate and correct, that the two last verses are linguistically sonorous and rounded, and form a suitable conclusion. Precisely as at the close of the Gospel (Luke xxiv. 52, 53) the employment of the apostles, during a certain space of time, is mentioned in a participial sentence; so here, the description of the activity of the apostle, during a longer period, closes with a twofold participial clause.

DOGMATICAL AND ETHICAL THOUGHTS.

We are certainly grieved to miss the information concerning the final determination of the fate of Paul. But however great and faithful Paul was in his apostolic office, yet he was only the herald, and not the Lord and King Himself. Jesus Christ rules as King; this is the conclusion of the book. On account of the chief matter—that the kingdom of God and the Gospel of Jesus Christ were for so considerable a time preached by the apostle of the Gentiles in Rome, the capital of the world, without hindrance—the person of Paul himself steps imperceptibly and completely into the background.

HOMILETICAL HINTS.

But Paul dwelt two whole years in his own hired house, and received all who came unto him (ver. 30). His own hired house, and liberty to dwell there, was a fortunate consequence of the thorough information of Festus concerning him, and thus also a happy result of his testimony to the truth borne at Cæsarea. But it was a state which required money, to which in particular the Philippians willingly contributed, Phil. iv. 10–14 (Rieger).—Nothing so hard and difficult shall occur that should be allowed to turn us aside from our calling, Matt. xi. 2; 1 Cor. vii. 20

(Starke).—*Paul received all who came to him.* What a glorious character of a servant of Christ, to become all things to all men, to afford free access to every one who seeks counsel and comfort for his soul, to open his house and heart to all who wish to be saved! It is not good, when it is said of a minister that he is difficult of access. Our Lord Jesus had often to do with hypocrites and deceivers, but He always knew how to meet them beneficially, and His language was, "Him who cometh unto Me, I will in no wise cast out" (Apost. Past.).

Preaching the kingdom of God (ver. 31). God opens the door to His word in a wonderful and unlooked-for manner, chap. xiv. 27; Col. iv. 3. When the Church has good weather and peace, we must extend the truth, and prepare ourselves for the future, chap. ix. 31. Christ, after sending the Holy Ghost, extended His Gospel over the whole world not with arms and weapons, but by preaching, and has hitherto powerfully protected it against all obstacles. May He continue doing so, and permit His word to be everywhere proclaimed "unforbidden," to the salvation of many thousand souls, and to the glory of His great name (Starke).—*Preaching concerning the Lord Jesus with all joyfulness* (Luther's translation). His Epistles to the Colossians, Ephesians, Philippians, and to Philemon, written at Rome, all of which exhale the oil of joy, attest this joyfulness of the apostle, with which Jesus anointed him (Besser).—*Unforbidden.* At this period, this was a rare blessing: teachers then rejoiced over it as over a great possession, and carefully redeemed the time in which they could enjoy it. We, on the other hand, have with our established liberty almost forgotten the greatness of this blessing. While we have time, let us labour and do good (Apost. Past.).—Beautiful termination of the Acts of the Apostles! The course of the Gospel from Jerusalem to Rome! When will it return to Jerusalem? Thus God employed His most gifted servants to minister to His will in their day and in their task. To survey the whole was granted to none, but is reserved to the Lord. O God, may Thy kingdom come! (Rieger.)—In spite of every persecution, the Gospel proceeded so systematically, that Luke can conclude his apostolic history with such a word as an Amen to all the divine promises. Thus the end of the book is most fitly united with the beginning, chap. i. 3 (Williger).—In the rich and great capital of the world, Paul proclaims the power and glory of the kingdom of God as a spiritual kingdom, whose nature and fruits are, peace, joy, patience, kindness, goodness, meekness, chastity. The message of Christ, the King of peace, around whom all things, great and small, individually and collectively, move in the kingdom of God, penetrates even into Cæsar's palace (Phil. i. 13). Thus Paul employs the time of his captivity in founding the important church at Rome, which henceforth was to become the maternal and missionary church of all the congregations among the Gentiles (Leonh. and Spieg.).—Concerning further events, Luke is silent, for he did not intend to write a biography of Paul. He has exhibited the riches of the grace and power of the Lord Jesus, in the course of the Church from the Mount of Olives to the City of the Seven Hills: he can relate nothing greater, and Theophilus has read sufficient in order to close with a Hallelujah (Besser).—Let us then emulate Paul, and take his strong adamantine soul for our pattern, in order that we may follow his course through the stormy ocean of this life, and put into the waveless haven of peace, and obtain the blessedness which God has prepared for those who love Him, through the grace and kindness of our Lord Jesus Christ, who with the Father and the Holy Ghost lives and reigns in like majesty and glory, to whom be glory for ever (Chrysostom).

On vers. 30, 31.—*Paul preaching the kingdom of God at Rome.* 1. A glorious fulfilment of what God had promised to His servant at the beginning, chap. ix. 15. 2. A grand prophecy of the future victory of the kingdom of God on earth.—*Paul at Rome.* 1. A living monument of divine mercy. 2. A shining example of apostolic fidelity. 3. A joyful herald of the universal kingdom of Christ. 4. A warning messenger of judgment for dead heathenism.—*Paul's two years' ministry at Rome, the crown of his apostolic course.* 1. In the centre of the heathen world, he erects the cross of Christ, before which all heathen temples shall sink into the dust. 2. Bound in body, he cares in true pastoral love for his distant churches (the Epistles). 3. Waiting on the call of the Lord, he is ready to seal the labour of his life with his blood.—*From Jerusalem to Rome.* This is the course of the Gospel in the Acts of the Apostles. 1. A painful course, full of shame and persecution. 2. A heroic course, full of the power of faith and the glow of love. 3. A victorious course, full of mighty acts and divine wonders. 4. A blessed course, full of salvation and grace for the present and the future.—*Paul the preacher in chains; or, the word of God is not bound.* It is bound: 1. To no place in the world: thrust out of Jerusalem, the old city of God, the apostle erects his pulpit in the Gentile capital of the world. 2. By no power of the world: the power of Rome was as little able as the hatred of the Jews to close the mouth of the apostle. 3. To no man in the world: after Paul had finished his course and sealed his testimony with his blood, the preaching of the cross proceeded victoriously over the earth.—*Paul, a prisoner at Rome, to-day, as he was* 1800 *years ago.* Though it be a gentle and becoming imprisonment as formerly under the Roman empire, still he is also now bound under the spiritual ruler of Rome. 1. Paul, the herald of evangelical liberty, bound by the fetters of human ordinances. 2. Paul, the preacher of justification by faith, bound under the law of external righteousness of works. 3. Paul, the man of apostolic poverty and humility, bound beside the splendour and pomp of the Popish dominion.—"*Unforbidden,*" *the significant concluding word of the whole apostolic history.* 1. A word of victory over ancient Rome, announcing the victory of the Gospel over all the opposition of Judaism and heathenism. 2. A word of warning for modern Rome, warning it of the vain and wicked attempt to repress the word of God. 3. A word of exhortation to the evangelical Church, exhorting it to the grateful use of the unforbidden word of God. 4. A word of promise for the Church of the future, pointing to the fulness of time when the Gospel will have conquered the world.—*The Acts of the Apostles, no fragment.* The conclusion indeed comes to us too early: there are many things which we would wish to ask and to know, but still we have enough. We have, 1. The laying of the foundation-stone of the Church, against which the gates of hell shall not prevail. 2. The mighty acts of the Saviour, who is with His people always, even to the end of the world. 3. A mine of wholesome doctrine, secure comfort, and impressive example for the Church of all ages.—*The transition of the apostolic history to Church history.* 1. A retrogression indeed from the pentecostal time of the first miracles of the Spirit, from the flourishing period of the first faith, from the youthful period of the first love. 2. But, according to the ordinance of God, a progress from patriarchal narrowness to the length and breadth of the earth, from festive inspiration to the toil and labour of common life, and through the struggle of ages to the final victory, when, in the triumphant Church, the first pentecostal Church, glorified, extended, and perfected, will be restored.—*The quiet disappearance of the Apostle Paul at the close of the apostolic history.* 1. It points to the exalted Lord of the Church, who abides, although His servants disappear: Jesus Christ the same yesterday, to-day, and for ever. 2. It points to the blessed rest, into which the faithful servants of God are permitted to enter, after the well-concluded day of work. 3. It points to the work of faith and labour of love, which is left behind to us from these first chosen witnesses. 4. It points to the great day of eternity, which will bring to light all that is now dark in the providential dispensations toward the children of God, and in the history of His kingdom.

END OF VOL. II.

ERRATA.

Page 63, line 5, *for* "into chief parts," *read* "into two chief parts."
Page 171, line 9, delete the words, "a term."

CPSIA information can be obtained
at www.ICGtesting.com
Printed in the USA
LVHW040412200422
716646LV00005B/171

9 783752 591842